MY TRUTH
LIES IN THE RUINS

By
DEBORAH RICHMOND FOULKES

© 2004 by DEBORAH RICHMOND FOULKES. All rights reserved.

No part of this book may be reproduced, stored in a retrieval system, or transmitted by any means, electronic, mechanical, photocopying, recording, or otherwise, without written permission from the author.

First published by AuthorHouse 04/05/04

ISBN: 1-4184-1289-9 (e-book)
ISBN: 1-4184-1288-0 (Paperback)
ISBN: 1-4184-1287-2 (Dust Jacket)

Library of Congress Control Number: 2004090079

This book is printed on acid-free paper.

Printed in the United States of America
Bloomington, IN

ACKNOWLEDGMENTS

When I first decided to embark on a trip to Scotland in search of my family history, I could not possibly have imagined the outcome: a published book about the lives of these redoubtable, courageous, real life Scottish Patriots, the Douglases.

Writing their story became a passion, a Spiritual journey as I felt led to discover the truth about these inspiring human beings. At every turn I was being helped; someone would enter my life that would assist me with the next step. During the times of doubt it was the encouragement of my husband Ed that came first to my aid. As the chapters filled the pages, the friendships I made in Scotland kept the fire kindled within me. I can not thank Jim and Jeanette Fleming of Douglas enough for the personal encouragement and true Scottish hospitality they shared with me; a friendship that will long endure. Jim also provided the foundation for my research through his records at the Douglas Heritage Museum in Douglasdale. When I needed to see medieval sword fights, Hugh Robertson of Fire and Sword came to my assistance. He generously shared his knowledge of medieval Scotland through his own reenactments. His hero: James Douglas; I knew again, this was not by chance. Hugh went a step further; giving me honest commentary to my first drafts. Each of these wonderful people helped to instill a confidence that has carried me through the many challenging steps to final publication.

Many others too numerous to mention gave selflessly to the completion of My Truth. Dennis and Evalie; Cinzia; Peggy; Susan and Anne; you all have been invaluable in your words of support and encouragement. And in Scotland: the Laird of Balgonie, and the rest of the Morris entourage including the wee Deerhounds; Sue Brash of Fa'side; and in England, Sharon Hutton-Mayson of Woodham Ferrers and Brian Harrison, former Yeoman Warder and Honorary Archivist of the Tower, who has a book coming soon on the prisoners f the Tower of London; I can not thank you all enough for your openness, generosity of information and kind sentiments that helped me steer the course.

And one final round of thanks: to the ISF, Robert Brown, Suzane Northrop, John Goldingham, Arja Helkiō, Mia Johnson, Rita Berkowitz, John Holland, Muriel Tenant and Maureen Harrison Skinner for their honest messages and validations. Your work is inspiring and valuable to us all.

Dedication

Willelmi, dominus de Duglas
1250 to 1298

Larry
1982 to 1999

Antiquities may be looked upon as the planks of a shipwreck which industrious and wise men gather and preserve from the deluge of time. Francis Bacon

This humble knight knows only to follow his truth; God's own truth within him, held here in his heart. William le Hardi, Lord Douglas

Contents

Acknowledgments iii

Part I 1286 to 1288 1
Douglasdale, the Good Sir James born 2
Ayrshire, Chance Meeting near Girvan Parish 29
Fawside Castle, Travernent Raid of the Heart 65
Kelso, Abbey Wedding 73
Isle of Mann, Muriel Douglas born 112
Douglasdale, Lanarkshire, Willelmi, dominus de Duglas 115

Part II 1289 - 1296 117
Fife Murder, Baronial Court, Passing the Doom in Douglas ... 145
Douglasdale, Martha Douglas born 151
Douglasdale, John Douglas born 183
New Castle, Edward I grants Marriage License for Eleanora ... 191
Avoch, The Highlands and de Morays 200
Douglasdale Amy Douglas born 215
Woodham Ferrers Drowning 240
Ware, Hertfordshire, Hugh Douglas born in England 243
Berwick on Tweed, Edward I Genocide of the Scots 258

Part III 1296 - 1298 271
Hertford and Berwick, Hugh, William freed from Edward's prisons 272
Douglas Castle, Douglasdale, Archibald Douglas born 284
Douglas Castle, William Lord Douglas joins William Wallace 296
Douglas Castle, Fire and Sword; Brus Kidnaps Douglas family 311
Irvine, Capitulation at Knadgerhill and de Percy's Ignoble Ruse 323
London, William Douglas held prisoner in the White Tower 358
London, Noble Knight, Crusader falsely changed, executed 386
Little Dunmow Priory, Martyred Patriot buried 389

Part IV 1299 – 1302; Epilogue 393
Woodham Ferrers, Lady Douglas dower restored 396
Stebbinge Park, Muriel Betrothed 410
Fawdon, Berwickshire, Fife, Kirkcudbright, Wigton collecting rents ... 422
Stebbinge Park, Visions of Willelmi, Lord Douglas, Poet Knight 447
Glossary 449
Who's Who, Historical Figures in My Truth 451
Author's Notes 453

The House of Douglas

From the annals and peerages of the Great House of Douglas come the tales of one Sholto Du-glash, the swarthy skinned man who in 770 came to the aid of Solvathius, King of the Scots. This brave warrior soon claimed great victory over the fierce invader one Donald Bane. For this service he was royally rewarded by his King with lands given to him in the county of Lanark, called Douglas. This follows the story of one of his noble descendants, William Le Hardi, seventh Lord Douglas, fifth of his name, redoubtable in his courage and word, a man of core values; My Truth.

Part I
1286 Douglas, Lanarkshire, Scotland

The year began with good tidings of a son for William and his wife, Elizabeth. His older brother Hugh was Lord Douglas and Chief of the Douglas Clan. Without heirs himself, he depended upon his younger brother William to produce offspring, the future of Douglasdale and their family heritage was in his hands. Hugh was a distinguished warrior. He served King Alexander during the Norwegian invasion into the Firth of Clyde in 1263 that ended October 2nd with the skirmish at Largs on the Ayrshire coast. The summer next brought Sir Hugh to Scotland's western isles in the king's service of Earl William of Mar seeking the peace of Alexander and death of the traitors who encouraged the Norwegian invasion. Injuries from this warrior's good service to his king yet affected him, and his wife Marjory was now gone, so this news of a young son to insure an heir to Douglasdale was welcome news indeed. The Chief would send news to his younger sister, Willelma, who lived in nearby Dalserf with her husband William de Galbrathe, rounding out the political and social prominence of this Scottish Lowland family.

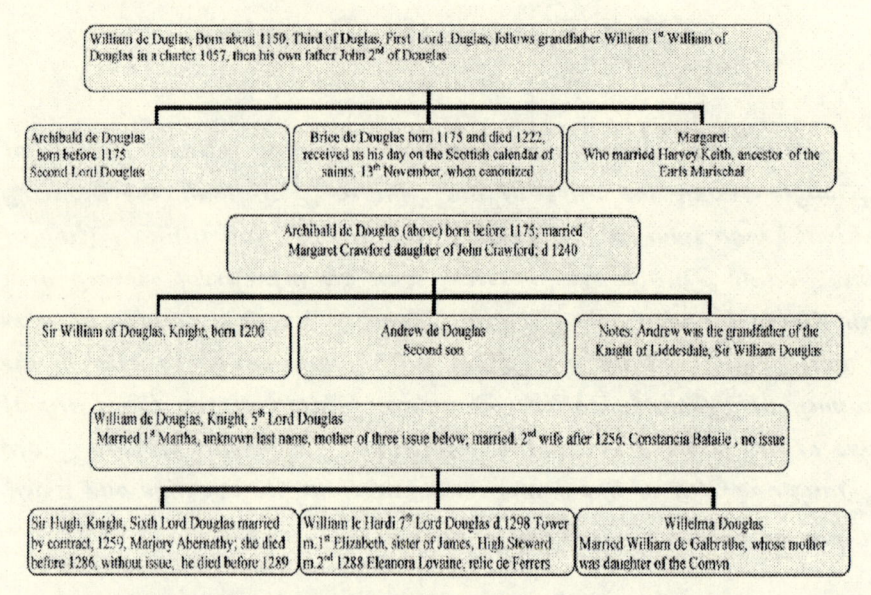

Figure I Part One; the Pedigree of the House of Douglas

- William de Duglas, Born about 1150, Third of Duglas, First Lord Duglas, follows grandfather William 1st William of Douglas in a charter 1057, then his own father John 2nd of Douglas
  - Archibald de Douglas born before 1175 Second Lord Douglas
  - Brice de Douglas born 1175 and died 1222, received as his day on the Scottish calendar of saints, 13th November, when canonized
  - Margaret Who married Harvey Keith, ancestor of the Earls Marischal

- Archibald de Douglas (above) born before 1175; married Margaret Crawford daughter of John Crawford; d 1240
  - Sir William of Douglas, Knight, born 1200
  - Andrew de Douglas Second son
  - Notes: Andrew was the grandfather of the Knight of Liddesdale, Sir William Douglas

- William de Douglas, Knight, 5th Lord Douglas Married 1st Martha, unknown last name, mother of three issue below; married, 2nd wife after 1256, Constancia Bataile, no issue
  - Sir Hugh, Knight, Sixth Lord Douglas married by contract, 1259, Marjory Abernathy; she died before 1286, without issue, he died before 1289
  - William le Hardi 7th Lord Douglas d.1298 Tower m.1st Elizabeth, sister of James, High Steward m.2nd 1288 Eleanora Lovaine, relic de Ferrers
  - Willelma Douglas Married William de Galbrathe, whose mother was daughter of the Comyn

The little boy was strong, and William was now making plans with purpose again. Though he and Elizabeth had been chosen for each other in their marriage, for the political alliance of these two powerful families, Elizabeth came to love William and he her, though she was wary of his bold ways, mirroring his surname of le Hardi. The couple had been married some three years, but the frail woman was unable to carry her babies to term and none survived, until James. Elizabeth insisted on naming him James after her brother the High Steward; an unusual name even for the Stewarts, derived from St. James, a patron saint of the family. All the other male births had been given Douglas names; none survived. A new name would change their luck she thought. But young James' birth was not mere luck, rather the result of early skills and more recently, unusual training given to her husband by an old woman in the village of Douglas. The skills of healing and herb medicine William studied diligently, day and night.

William sought a remedy from the other children who died in the womb or shortly after birth. He determined to learn more about the Celtic healers and requested the help of an old Celtic woman with second sight, a speywife, in the village of Douglas named Helisant. The ordinary midwives had not been able to help his wife, or his infant children, so it was up to him, William concluded, to learn the mysteries of healing and child-birthing. He began to collect herbs with Helisant and secrete them in a small room in the vaulted cellars. The mysterious room remained the domain of the knight; residing beneath one of the donjon towers that aligned the portcullis at the front gate of Douglas castle. This secluded room was next to the large kitchen fireplace used for smoking game and fish; locked at all times it became the talk of servants in the house of Douglas, curious that a fierce knight would be so consumed by the art of healing, and so interested in collecting the herbs and roots with the speywife.

Poor Elizabeth the midwives moaned, to have her husband present in the lying-in chamber and actually deliver the young child. And the way he forced her to deliver the baby: lying down. All babies were supposed to be delivered while the mother sat crouching on a birthing stool; never lying down. William told Elizabeth to be calm, and breathe in, taking more breaths to keep calm. He told her that Helisant had said to him he must watch how the animals delivered their young, seemingly tranquilized in a position of comfort for the circumstances, conserving their strength for the final push. Child birthing was dangerous enough for both mother and child and hampering delivery with discomfort and fear only complicated things further, he explained to her. She patiently complied with William's guidance, though still unsure of his knowledge.

Figure II-Part One; Dundonald Castle, Ayrshire; birthplace of Elizabeth Stewart

As soon as the baby was born, off William went with his son, but a minute old, and still covered with the fluids of birth, first to the small chapel next to the laird's chamber, to christen the little boy himself. "I christen thee in the name of the Father, the Son, and the Holy Ghost, he said out loud in Latin, then in Lallans, the language of lowland Scotland, just to be sure. He was holding the wee lad's left hand, the "unblessed hand," as William noted; his own sword hand was the left hand as well, the unblessed hand that would do the deeds of the warrior, the Celtic way. He then took the boy down to his locked cellar room, where he cleansed the baby and rubbed him with oils and tonics as Helisant directed. It was at this moment that William took time to really look at the little boy, what a miracle from God, he mused. "There, now, young James, you are going to live a long and prosperous life, you will be a leader of men, a true Douglas, a tribute to your race", said William. And it was then that William noticed the raven hair, all wildly tufted upon his small head, and then, all the hair on the little lad's body. A curious little boy, so long and thin, and all that black hair! "What a little beast you are" said William, "a black knight as sure can be, aye!"

When William returned to the lying-in chamber, Elizabeth was just falling off to sleep, but upon seeing her husband and baby, leaned up slightly to receive her son James to her breast. "Oh, William, I did not feel the pain of those other births this time, you have worked wonders and magic," she smiled as she spoke, so lightly, you could barely hear, but so happy. "Here, please drink this for me," he said, handing her a tasine from herbs and water that he made in the cellar, "you will need your strength to feed this hungry laddie," barely concealing his elation, "He is doing his best to make us happy Elizabeth, and he is a fighter."

Figure III-Part One; Douglas Castle mid 19th century; note the partial digging out of the motte under the ruined tower

William took his leave quickly, excitedly on his way to speak with his brother Hugh and set up the feasts for a fitting celebration, and a christening at the Douglas Kirk. His cousin Archibald, the son of his Uncle Andrew of Douglas, was the priest at the family kirk; he would arrange for the ceremonies for William's new son. Willelma his sister and her husband William de Galbrathe had been chosen for James' God parents. Soon they would notify the Douglases when they would be coming for the christening. "It is fine news my little brother that you have brought this day. I will make the plans for festivities of this joyous occasion!" roared a jubilant Hugh. William was himself quietly humble, thanking his brother for his help in the preparations. "I must take myself some time to reflect on this day's fine events. Please excuse me dear brother," he replied as he left the great hall. William climbed the turnpike stairs to the parapet of the battlemented keep; his private place where he would do his thinking of importance. He first gave thanks to St. Bride for the knowledge of healing ways. He then thanked his God for the time he spent in the Levant that furthered his study of alchemy healing. All these experiences came to prepare him for this glorious day; so strange the fate of life and what it brings he mused. He thought now of how he first learned of Celtic healing; skills he learned as a youth, during his convalescence at Fawdon.

William was a young squire at Fawdon in 1267, living at his father's manor there, when on the evening of St. Margaret, July 19th, de Umfraville with 100 men of Redesdale attacked their household. His father, William, 5th Lord Douglas, was captured and taken to Harbottle castle, and held for eleven days. The attackers set three fires, burning the houses and breaking in windows and doors; stealing swords, money, gold jewelry and other goods from not only Lord Douglas and his second wife Constancia but also their servants, valued at over £100.

But the worst of it fell on young William. Hearing the commotion of armed horse descending upon the manor; the clash of swords from armed foot attacking Douglas men at arms; and the screams of hostility from women and warriors, the young squire made haste to reach the great hall. This quick response would prove him grave hardship; he allowed no time for putting on his gambeson, the quilted surcote used for a warrior's protection. With the surprise attack William grabbed not his mail or other armor, but his father's old standard, a one handed sword capable of thrusting and cutting. As he was leaving the laird's chamber, he spied his father's prized tournament shield hanging on the wall; he took that too. He cautiously entered the great hall, becoming aware of a strange quiet; the two small tallow torches burned evening low, creating shadows that danced about the chamber. On the far wall the large fireplace only glowed now in the amber hues of spent peat; flickering now and then with a soft golden light.

Suddenly an armed marauder burst into the hall; the first of three that would come one by one to attack the young squire. One was to carry sword and shield; another to come with a knife and the third an axe would wield.

The man with the axe reached him first, was the first to die. William made a cutting stroke vertically with his left hand, holding his father's shield in the other he cut the neck through; near severing head from cord. The man fell dead before him. The second man entered the hall wielding a knife; he too was no match, as young William made a diagonal left to left upward cut, striking the attacker in the groin. During the foray with the Redesdale invaders, William sustained a deep cut on his left shoulder and a lang gash on his arm. Two of de Umfraville's men were now dead or nearly so he reflected with satisfaction; while his own injuries were not life threatening. But there was little time to bask in his glory.

The Douglas squire righted himself and found that he was face to face with a third man. Both men moved, studying the other. William feigned an attack from the high guard position, watching the reaction of his opponent he suddenly made his cut. The opponent countered with his shield, only to leave it out, not returning to its guard position. A fatal flaw in his training William noted. Warding off the opponent's thrust, parrying with his shield, sparks flew as metal hit metal in the dim glow of the great hall. William made his counterattack, cutting deeply into the man's right hand, crushing bone beneath. The hand was left to hang strangely off its wrist; of no further use to his opponent. William stumbled over the body of the second man as this third man pulled out his knife held behind his targe. Summoning all his strength, using his remaining left hand he cut William from the cheek bone across the ear lobe, down his neck. It was his last living action. William righted himself, paused, and with a steady, slow attack made his strike, blending his body's momentum with his weapon, he made a precise, clean, killing cut.

William looked around for more of these Redesdale attackers, only now noticing the warmth of his own blood soaking his right shoulder through the silk cote he wore. He knew the shoulder was a deep wound, and would have been prevented had he made time to put on his gambeson. The throbbing of his neck was becoming a dull headache; something was really wrong there he felt. He pulled himself forward to the stairs leading down to the kitchen area, a bloody sight and wobbly at best; exhausted from the battles and the injuries he sustained, William summoned all his might not to collapse down the spiral stairs.

In the kitchen sat his brother Hugh, receiving treatment for his wounds. William's cheek bone was covered with blood and dirt, and the neck wound was soaking his cote on one side, the shoulder gash on the other. Hugh's face when he saw William betrayed his fears. "William, you must seal and cleanse the wound on your face," said Hugh, trying to minimize the injuries with a controlled response. The cook grabbed a poker used for cooking game on the spit and placed it directly in the kitchen fire. His plan was to

MY TRUTH LIES IN THE RUINS

use the heated metal like a cautery iron: to seal and cleanse the wound on the open cheekbone. From the kitchen stores the cook returned with a poultice of herbs to deaden the intense pain before applying the iron now aglow in red and white hues. The lad would have a nasty scar there, if he lived, the cook mused. Though the pain was intense even after the special herbs were applied, William barely allowed himself to wince as the cook delivered the cleansing seal to the cheekbone. Then Hugh applied maggots to the wounds; a treatment that would assist in preventing putrefaction.

The other injuries, the large wound on his shoulder and cut on his arm were painful and deep; both required stitching. The wounds to the neck were gashes, and did not appear to be life threatening, just ugly marks that ran around his neck; but this injury proved later to be lingering. There was interior neck damage; revealed by William's continuing headaches, head pains that would increase in frequency and severity over time. These ugly scars and nagging neck pains were the enduring memories of Fawdon that would be with him sporadically, for the remainder of this life. William sat in silence; weakened not only by his wounds but also by the cook's surgical remedies. At least there would be no blood letting, there was none left, he mused as he faded into unconsciousness.

Figure IV-Part One; Fawdon on the River Breamish near Ingram, Northumbria; some of these buildings were once part of the mains of Fawdon Manor

William's injuries healed slowly and required him to lay motionless for weeks, treating the wounds with herbs and salves. But they were not infected; his wearing of a silk cote was his advantage; other such garments of linen would have caused infection if some of the fibers remained in the injured areas of flesh. His often maligned vanity of attire aided him this day, he reflected during one of his longer days of required inactivity. William's remarkable recovery was directed by the Celtic woman named Bridie; a speywife, who had been in the Douglas household since his mother died when he was six. The speywife had her hands full; this was an impatient young man before his convalescence. The recuperation was taxing on the entire household, only Bridie was reprieved from his anger, as her patient caring began his career in healing.

As William's health improved from the Fawdon attack he learned much about Celtic herb healing. And from his determined fight for survival from the life threatening wounds, he earned his sobriquet. "Le Hardi," his father pressed upon his youngest offspring, "a name that will warn all others of your strength and courage from this day; to be most wary of the heart that beats within you. A father's true hero and brave son." he praised the youth. The healing skills learned from Bridie's good care were broadened further when William sought adventure, leaving for the Crusades in 1270 at the age of twenty; searching the mysteries of the Levant. As a squire he served under the banner of Earl Adam of Carrick and fought for the Holy Sepulchre; part of the Scottish contingency sent by King Alexander to assist Lord Edward, who would arrive later. While in Acre he found himself working with herbs and healing; treating Crusaders, warriors stricken on the battlefields of the strange land of the sun.

His Celtic herb knowledge plunged him further into the curious study of Alchemy Healing and his work did not go unnoticed. One evening after a battle with the Mamlukes, he was tending to the wounds of a Scottish knight. Others had said the wounds in the abdomen would prove fatal to the young man. But William worked well into the night and over the next several days. Surprisingly the knight recovered, under the watchful eye of one Edward Plantagenet, who inquired as to the identity of the healer. He is a Scot they said, one from Northumbria, and the lowlands of Scotland, in Lanarkshire. Lord Edward would make note of this strange Scot, for William was a fierce warrior on the battlefield attending his knight, yet a gentle giant of a man when tending to his fellow warriors. Well over 6 ft., 4inches tall, with a large, menacing frame and huge hands, he made quite a stir among the other healers attached to these knights. How could such a man exist, wildly and boldly cutting his way through the barriers of human flesh in battle, laying waste anyone and anything in his path. While at night this chaotic warrior transformed to the calming, disciplined healer as he treated the injured with a gentle touch, a healing touch. Now his Alchemy Healing skills delivered him a son and heir.

MY TRUTH LIES IN THE RUINS

    Standing now, William peered through the old crenelles of the tower looking downward towards the moorlands and the jutting shoreline of Loch Douglas. He marveled at the beauty of his family's lands as if seeing the moors for the first time. He watched with the curiosity of a child the beguiling glow of the mist forming on the valley of the Clyde; a blanket of soft grey brume covering the countryside, gliding over the wee braes of Douglasdale. The new father sighed at the beauty of his homeland as he watched contentedly from his favorite viewing place. He stood patiently, following the darkness drawing shadows over the spring growth of the meadows; the peaceful approach of the gloaming drawing near as the daylight retired. The still of the evening was abruptly disturbed by the wee sounds of a mavis, a song thrush not often heard this late in the day William reflected, perhaps a sign from God, heralding the birth of our James, he chuckled. He made a mental note to always think of the peace of this day when he heard a moor bird sing her song.

Figure V-Part One; Ruins of tower are all that remain of the once mighty fortress of Douglas Castle; the Douglas Water is visible below

    A brief look to the south revealed a light rain beginning to fall over the Douglas Water in the distance. Deciding to take his leave of the parapet walk while still dry, the Crusader turned father happily made his way to the turnpike stairs and down towards the great hall two floors below. My path, God's own truth for me; what miracles have been provided that I might deliver my own son this day, he sighed. A son, I have a son, he proclaimed to himself over and over, what a wonderful day this is! "Praise be to God and the good St.Bride, the patron saint of healers and fair Douglases as well," he said aloud as he descended further the turnpike stairs. It was then that he recalled the words of his father: with a death, comes a birth, it is the Celtic way. These words so true to me now he mused. It was only some weeks before that good King Alexander, upon returning from the Castle of Maidens, was killed in a storm trying to make it back to Dumfermline and his young bride. The Golden Age of Scotland was about to mirror the fate of its king, and bow to a new master.

Figure VI-Part One; Elizabeth Stewart as she might have appeared in 1286; first wife of William le Hardi, mother of James

October 1286, Essex, England

Five years had gone by since that dreadful day of her marriage to Lord de Ferrers. Now Eleanora was becoming a woman, turning eighteen in just three days. Would there be a party she wondered allowed, as Ana came in with her tray of food to break her fast. "M' lady, don't you worry yourself, your Ana would never let them forget your special day!" "Oh Ana, I feel like I am rotting away here in Woodham Ferrers," said Eleanora. "And my husband, what news do you have of him, is he coming back from Groby anytime soon?"

"There is no news my love of the lord returning to the manor; you are safe to celebrate your birthday with those who know how to treat one so nice as you." Eleanora got up and began to fix her hair; the long chestnut hair curled halfway down her back, as Ana grabbed the long comb, "Let me help you now to plaite your hair. And we have a beautiful green surcote that

MY TRUTH LIES IN THE RUINS

your mother has sent from Little Easton, on the occasion of your birthday. I had to take it in some when it arrived, so I kept it a secret from you." "Oh Ana, its so beautiful," squealed Eleanora, as she opened the package on her bed. "At least you and mother remember me with love."

Figure VII-Part One; Groby Village today; photo courtesy of Mike Pratt, Groby Directory on line

Eleanora set out for a ride that afternoon on her mare Winter Rose, a beautiful horse of commanding size and grace, and the noble palfrey gait. She used a man's saddle for comfort fashioned with a custom side foot rest to ride side saddle as ladies were now doing more frequently, though she only rode that way with Lord de Ferrers. Eleanora was an excellent horsewoman, a necessity for any lady her grandmother Muriel would often say. Now Muriel was with God, and there was only her mother and Ana to love. Ana had joined her as her maid in wait when Eleanora was first married to Lord Ferrers, and living at Stebbinge Park. She was just a young girl of only thirteen then, when her father Lord Lovaine arranged for her marriage to Sir William de Ferrers, or "sold her to de Ferrers" as Eleanora would say, a man twenty eight years her senior; a man her father's age, with a daughter almost her own age. Her fondest memories these days were of riding up the short distance from Stebbing, to her mother's manor in Little Easton.

Her father Lord Lovaine was the Steward of Eye, spending most of his days in Eye and in Bildeston. A stern man, with little time for a daughter, it was better when he stayed in Bildeston, so Eleanora and her mother could spend some happy times together. They both would take large mounts from the stables and plan long rides together with some beautiful spot to stop and enjoy some meat pies and wine. These moments were the only times she felt safe. Riding horses on her manor at Stebbing was always without incident she mused. As she rode, Eleanora was surrounded by de Ferrers tenants, for there were some twenty messuages and ten tofts, both with dwelling houses and other buildings, making up the over 1200 acres of arable lands, pastures and woodlands.

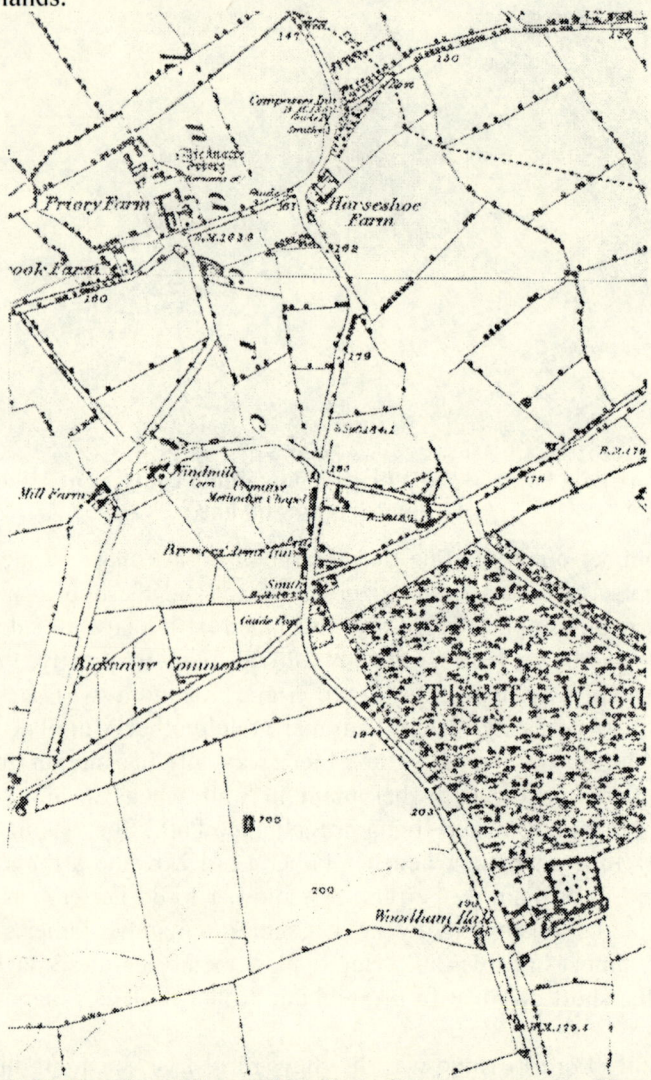

Figure VIII-Part One; Map of Woodham Ferrers courtesy of Landmark Information Group; main manor house near Thrift Wood was Woodham Ferrers Hall now Woodham Hall; Woodham Ferrers Priory called Bicknacre Priory today is shown at the top of the map

The early years of marriage were terrifying to Eleanora; she was so unlike the first wife of Lord de Ferrers that he all but despised her. William de Ferrers married Anne Despenser around the time his second wife was born. Lady Anne was then a widow closer to his age; she bore him a male heir and a daughter. She also was the granddaughter of Hawise Lovaine, Lord Matthew Lovaine's sister, and Eleanora's cousin. When this first wife died in child bed, Lord de Ferrers sought to find a younger lady to provide him more heirs. At the suggestion of Matthew Lovaine, the great uncle of Anne Despenser, William de Ferrers married the thirteen year old cousin of his late wife, Eleanora of Lovaine. He quickly found this marriage to the younger girl unsettling. She was strong willed, and independent beyond her years. Well educated, she spoke and wrote Norman French and Latin as well as Inglis and understood the monetary affairs of the Manor. Certainly she was not the little girl he could dominate and control, as he had hoped when he wed her in 1281. His failing health and tendencies to over imbibe made his attempts to consummate the marriage less than successful. And his anger at his inability to perfect this union made him lash out at Eleanora in rages and fits of pique that erupted during the middle of the night and frightened the household servants for her very life

One terrorizing night Ana found Eleanora crouched in a corner of her room sobbing, in a pool of blood from a cut under her right eye. "Oh my lamb, don't worry yourself, that beast of a husband of yours is gone back to Groby," Ana told her as she comforted her girl and rocked her in her broad arms. "Why does he hate me so Ana?" she cried. "I would try to like him, but he only beats me. He is so unkind to me; what did I do to make him so quarrelsome? Oh, dear sweet God, please save me from this life." Finally as the years passed, he stopped coming home. He would send for her to come to Woodham Ferrers, and she would go reluctantly. On some occasions, there would be a huge party planned and they would be entertaining some of his friends and kin from London, Groby, or Derbyshire and Stafford. She was always a wonderful hostess, and he seemed to accept this as her role. Within a few days Ana would come to her room and announce that he had left for Groby. And they both would pack up for Stebbing again.

Today she stayed close to the manor. She never felt as comfortable in Woodham Ferrers as she did in Stebbing. She didn't like the moat that more than half surrounded the manor house, and felt uneasy with the strange hidden staircase and secret passage that reportedly led from the house to the Woodham Ferrers Priory. This passage way dated to early Norman times when it may have been used as an escape to safety if the occupants found themselves under siege from the frequent band of marauders that blanketed the countryside from the days just after the conquest. But later, rumors had it that the old lord of the manor had a consort living in the priory confines that he would visit in secret by means of the passage. Everything about the place made her uneasy, except the church in the village. The priest at St. Mary's church was young and made her feel welcome. Father John always made it a point to call on her when she arrived back at Woodham Ferrers Hall. She was faithful to the church, and found his presence a real comfort in her life, like Ana, someone she could trust. Eleanora was making her own family of support around her.

Weeks passed since her eighteenth birthday. Ana had given her a little party with some of the household servants and her friend Alice from Hertford, who had come down to Woodham Ferrers as a surprise. Alice was a cousin of the de Ferrers, but completely the opposite in demeanor from that of her husband. She was sweet, and kind, and gentle and the best friend Eleanora had in the world now that her mother was spending more time with her father in Bildeston. These two young noble ladies would ride their horses all over the wood farm and make up fantasy adventures of knights rescuing them from their dreary lives. Riding with Alice made the days pleasant for Eleanora. She was glad for her friends. Few as they were, friends helped her forget the cold chill of her marriage bed.

Figure IX-Part One; Cherubs on 13th century pillars are still visible in St. Mary's Church Woodham Ferrers

MY TRUTH LIES IN THE RUINS

Another year passed into the next, nothing much had changed. It was 1287 and Eleanora had enjoyed another birthday much as the last. She was feeling her age she told Ana, "nineteen years Ana, and nothing to show for it, I feel so old!" "Oh child, you are barely a girl, now, so don't go fretting away. Where would you like to be for Christmas?" Ana asked her, to change the subject. "I would like to be in Stebbinge Park. Do you know where Lord de Ferrers will be?" Ana shook her head no, and looked away. It pained her so to see this child so neglected by that man, a woman with so much love in her heart, sure she would make some younger lord a loving wife, if only.....

This afternoon Eleanora and Alice were happily returning to Woodham Ferrers Hall from their brisk ride. Alice was a constant figure at Woodham Ferrers now, keeping her friend company and sharing the gossip of courtly love. The days were getting shorter; the daylight fading in the afternoons as the fall rolled into winter. Riding up the cart path from the old priory the ladies entered the gates of the hall; they were surprised to see a group of men on horseback already dismounting near the drawbridge of the moat. One of the riders Eleanora recognized immediately as her priest from St. Mary's church in the village. Ana ran out as she saw her girls ride up and told Eleanora the news: Lord de Ferrers was gravely ill. They wanted to bring her to the Priory of Ware. He was staying in the old Alien or French Benedictine priory as it was situated within his Hertfordshire manor, left him by his mother. Lady Eleanora accepted the request to attend her husband as was her duty and she was grateful for their offer of escort she told them; bidding Ana to prepare for their journey immediately. Alice lived close by in Hertford just over the Ware Bridge and would journey with the de Ferrers' party, departing the next day as well.

It was more than a day's travel in good weather, but it poured and the winds howled. Eleanora insisted on stopping near Chelmsford, just north of Writtle, for the night; then at her mother's manor in Little Easton they stayed the second night. When they reached Hertfordshire early the third day, de Ferrers was dead. Eleanora and Ana sat in her room and just looked at each other. "I can't cry for him Ana," said Eleanora, "I only feel relief, and for the first time since I married, I can sleep in my bed without fear of his coming in during the middle of the night to hurt me." Ana went over and hugged her, knowing now that a new adventure for them would begin. Where they would go did not matter. At least there would be changes and opportunities for her girl now, and perhaps she could meet a wonderful man that would love and cherish her, a nobleman and knight she so deserved. Eleanora sighed; she too was hopeful for the changes about to come. If only those silly, girlish fantasies that she shared with Alice not so long ago could come true: that she would be rescued by some handsome, chivalric knight on a beautiful destrier, she mused wistfully.

DEBORAH RICHMOND FOULKES

Douglasdale, Scotland

It was more than a year since William's wife Elizabeth had died. William had barely left her side for the months following the birth of James. With their walks and rides through Douglasdale, the couple enjoyed the spring and summer days together, while their young son thrived. But a pressing matter at Fawdon, the estate left him by his father for his sustenance, called him away for weeks in mid July over the diversion of water from his lands by one Richard de Brus in Northumbria. When he returned to Douglasdale, he happily found his bride again with child; taking to her bed as a precaution she told him. But in few short weeks the chilling winter of 1286 began; bringing howling winds and an early winter to the Scottish lowlands. Elizabeth felt her lungs fill with fluids more each day; then she began to sink in the fits of fever. She fought for her life and that of her baby, just five months growing within her. But Elizabeth would carry her child with her, to the heavens of her God, and William became a widower, a father alone with his infant son. "Even Helisant and this knight's good healing could not save my dear bride and wee son," said the grieving husband out loud; wondering in silent despair why God sought to take his wife and child from him in this way.

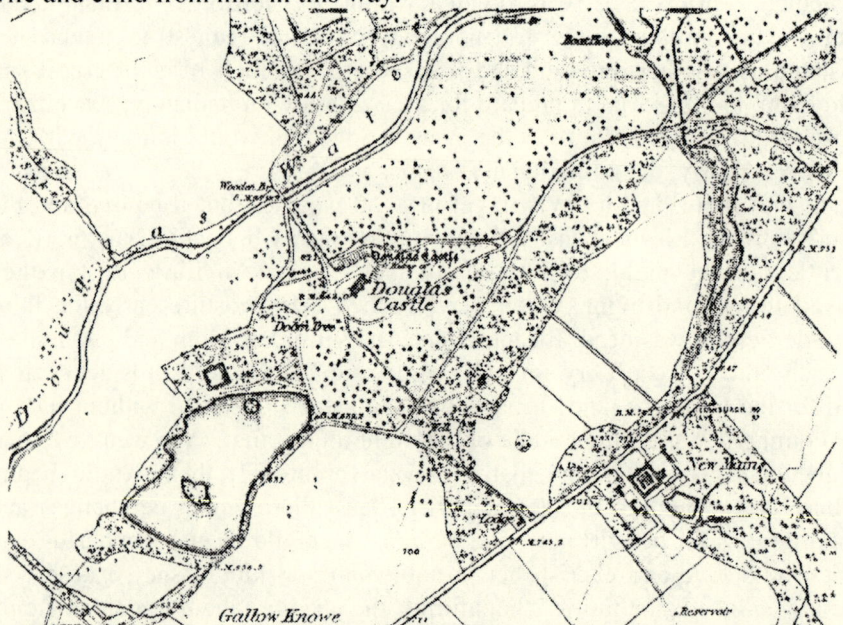

Figure X-Part One; Map of Douglasdale courtesy of Landmark Information Group; note the Doom Tree beside the ruins, proudly claimed to hold seven Englishmen for hanging

The next twelve months were a blur of activity for William, trying to know what to do. He felt the loneliness for the first time since his mother had died so many years ago. Would God provide him with another wife? The ugly facial scars from his battles at Fawdon made him shy with women. And he really couldn't marry just anyone, unless he could find someone who would love James as her own. William looked in on the little boy sleeping in the nursery. "Oh James, we can not stay alone now; we need the sound of a woman's sweet voice and the gentleness of her touch to welcome the new day. I have my work to do my son, to find us a wife and mother to brighten our lives again."

After the thaw in January of 1288, William decided that a special hunting trip with some of the knights of the Douglas parish was in order. He invited his brother in law, James' God father, to join them, bringing his de Galbrathe men at arms from Dalserf as well. This adventure would solve my winter moodiness le Hardi vowed. While hunting for game was part of the daily activities of the castle, this trip would have more flourish, and hopefully more variety of sport. He informed Hugh that morning that he would ride to some of his lands in Ayrshire near the parish of Girvan with some of their men at arms and set up temporary lodgings for his hunting party. He happily told his brother he would be leaving in a few days. "Fresh game and maybe a wild boar would brighten our nightly feasts would it not dear Hugh," said William. "I can think of nothing else at present that would cheer me more than a full belly of meat and good wine." Hugh was glad his brother was going away for a few weeks. The strain of his moods was taking its toll on the household, but he could sympathize. When his Marjory passed, he would go for days without leaving his chamber. A good woman brings laughter and love to a castle. If only William could find himself a bride for his bed. Hugh knew that he was too old now with the scars of battle nagging at his every breath. Some days he could barely rise to make it down the lang stairs to the great hall. He didn't share this recent bout of fatigue and ill health with his brother. William would come to know soon enough he mused. A few weeks with his brother away would improve both their demeanors thought Hugh. "This is a wonderful idea William, take what you need. We will be happy to see you back in a few weeks."

Essex December 1287

Eleanora and John le Parker were meeting in Hertford with her late husbands' solicitors. She was given some coinage, mostly silver, for expenses of travel and an inventory of the estates of Margaret de Quincy, William de Ferrers' mother, who had left him lands in Scotland as well as manors in Stebbing and Woodham Ferrers in Essex that would eventually be her dower. The king was in Gascony and would order the English manors to her held in tenancy until he assigned dower to her; an official procedure that was required but awkward with the king out of the country. The official order for temporary tenancy was issued on 20 January 1288 to Henry de Bray, escheator 'this side of the Trent' to complete the action. Eleanora was also required to sign an oath to her liege lord Edward to not remarry without his consent and license; this she did today as witnessed by two knights of the shire with her solicitors.

The Countess de Ferrers left other properties to her late son, in addition to these two Essex manors. Groby and Ware and other messuages and lands would be held in ward for the de Ferrers children by Eleanora's kin, Nicholas de Segrave. Eleanora questioned the odd situation of the manor of Ware. The manor was held by her husband though Lord de Ferrers gave the manor to his uncle Robert de Quincy while he remained the overlord. Now the manor would be held in ward by Queen Eleanor for John Wake, grandson of Robert yet a minor. "Thusly, these lands will not be part of your dower or those estates of the children," the solicitors informed the widow. The remaining lands were vast, but mainly resided in Scotland and were the same holdings that caused so many lawsuits, tying up the English courts for years following the death of Roger de Quincy, Constable of Scotland, the father of Margaret and her two sisters. Eleanora would have to go before Scotland's Guardians to request an assignment of dower before these lands could be delivered to her. She was confident about that task as two of the Guardians were her kin: Earl Duncan of Fife and the Comyn. I am going to Scotland, she kept saying to herself, I am leaving Essex behind, this is my new life. And I will take this gift from God of my new freedom to have an exciting venture in the wilds of the kingdome in the north!

Ana was waiting in the anteroom of the solicitors' offices, and the others in their party were still back at the manor in nearby Ware waiting her return. Eleanora handed John the coinage to add to her coffer and the estate documents they would need. He had managed the manors in Essex for William de Ferrers for the last five years as his seneschal, and Eleanora trusted his word; his family was Scottish in origin residing in nearby Bennington. They were all going to Scotland, along with various maids in waiting, and an escort of de Ferrers men at arms she chose from Stebbinge Park and Woodham Ferrers. And she was not waiting for spring to leave England. She was going now, a week before Christmas. "Come on Ana, we are off for Scotland, a land of savages and adventure!"

Making their way up north, winding through Cambridge, to Leicester, then up further to Leeds, they rode with nearly thirty riders among them, leading eleven extra horses, pack horses and palfreys, while drawing two small carts behind the mounted travelers; truly an entourage worthy of note.

MY TRUTH LIES IN THE RUINS

Departing from Leeds, the de Ferrers' household moved stoutly north again; continuing their journey despite the colder weather and brief encounters with snow as they passed through Yorkshire, arriving at Newcastle upon Tyne where they stayed but one night at Eleanora's insistence. They were ultimately going to Fawside Castle in the barony of Tranent where the widow also held lands. The owner of Fawside was Elena de la Zouche sister of Margaret de Quincy, her late mother in law. Eleanora would take up temporary residence there while sorting out her fees and rents; waiting for her dower to be directed to her by the magnates of Scotland in absence of a king.

The trip was taking at least three weeks when at long last they were approaching the marches or borders of Scotland. Riding the final miles of frozen ruts that formed their cart paths, the joyous travelers made light of their hardships of travel as they neared Berwick on Tweed, the premier Royal Burgh of Scotland. Here Eleanora insisted on staying an extra day, then another night as well that she might do some shopping and take a proper bath she told Ana. Berwick was the kingdome's busiest port for commerce and most thriving community. Lady de Ferrers planned to order some surcotes of fine silk and velvet, in colors suiting her youthful figure from these Scottish merchants. Soon enough she could wear these lovely garments, she sighed; she would not be a widow in mourning forever. Lord de Ferrers had not denied her fine clothes. But he selected everything himself. Now she could pick and choose as she only dreamt of doing before; be her own conscience on what she wore. This shopping spree was a defining stamp on her new found freedom. Her next stop would be more for manorial business she mused, so this excursion was for pleasure! Rushing from shop to shop she eagerly filled her carts with goods: yards of velvet and silk, trinkets of every size and color, Eleanora spared herself nothing in the quest for finery.

Scotland's major port was in deed a place of adventure; a strange blend of refined culture that could be found in major English cities, yet distinctly different with a mysterious barbarism lurking about, a romantic intoxication of a wilder sense filled the air. The burgh was crisscrossed with unpaved cart paths, worn by deep gullies; the consequence of the frequent rains. The atmosphere was exciting and chaotic. Games of chance were being played on every corner by rough looking men; unkempt ruffians with long, thick hair tied back or hanging over their faces; grizzly beards of reddish curls covering all but the eyes. These barbarians were wearing unrefined leather boots or shoes from deer hides; bristling with hair not yet removed from the skins, glistening in a ghoulish way. The wearers of these crude adornments bent over the game boards hand-drawn in the dirt and sand of Berwick streets, the object of their play for coinage. Eleanora felt an excited tingling in her being as she passed by these strange and wild men of Berwick, making her way to the higher, more expensive area of the burgh where the merchants' shops resided.

The few paths spouting cobblestones were on the merchants' row. The clip clop of horses' hooves bringing well dressed ladies in their horse drawn carts or on their own escorted palfreys to the busy market place seemed oddly out of character, somehow signaling a more civilized community than Berwick on Tweed could yet command. The shopkeepers had sophisticated displays of a desirable and cosmopolitan style in their show cases. Yet the infancy and plainer aspects of the rest of the port stood by in stark comparison to these often garish shops, exemplifying the growing pains of a Scottish burgh becoming an international city of prominence.

Eleanora busied herself, flying in and out of shopkeepers' doorways, buying gifts for the others, including all her escorts, ladies in wait, John le Parker, and Ana, and something she would send back to her mother; all in a day's shopping she chuckled. She went into currier shops and purchased leather goods and furs for trimming her new surcotes. Stopping in Berwick was uplifting to the very spirit of the young widow; she had never before been her own lady to purchase goods herself; to satisfy her own needs and wants. "Oh Ana," Eleanora squealed out loud, "look at these fine treasures; the lace work most fine, as any in Brugges!" she exclaimed, comparing the Scottish burgh with a port city in her ancestral home of Flanders. Eleanora was very impressed by the woven goods as well as intricate handwork, not often seen outside of Brabant, she would explain. Her Lovaine ancestors were of Flemish extraction; many coming to England with the Conqueror in 1066 and marrying into noble Norman families in England. But Brabant was their home; their heritage.

Before she was Lady de Ferrers Eleanora traveled often to Brugges and Lovaine in Flanders with her father and mother, Lord and Lady Lovaine. Searching for expensive and well made goods became a passion for this lady, a product of her training from her mother and the Lovaine ladies of the duchy as they shopped the major merchants' establishments in Brabant. An exhausted but happy girl returned to the inn where the de Ferrers' household stayed for the night. Eleanora held a manor just outside of the royal burgh but was yet unsure of the location; deciding to stay in the burgh and within the protective embankments interspersed with a partial enclosure of wooden palisade and King David's stone walls that guarded Berwick from intruders. "What excitement for one small day!" she exclaimed. Ana told her that she had never seen her girl look so happy. "These days in the wilds of Scotland are becoming on my dear one," she chuckled. "So many cities we have seen my Ana," she began, "but none so strange as this Berwick! One rue is most the likes of Lovaine or Brugges; yet the strangeness of the next turn most

MY TRUTH LIES IN THE RUINS

perplexes this lady," she said shaking her head at the disparity; the cosmopolitan atmosphere that was sprinkled with the odd gruffness of the outreaches of the hinterlands. "This Scotland is most wild in her true nature," she sighed "romantic in the very thrill of danger that seems to hide among the dark places."

Figure XI-Part One; Harbor of Berwick on Tweed; today the burgh resides in England

Before leaving Berwick Lady de Ferrers had some important decisions to make. While England maintained its roads, many dating back to Roman times, Scotland was a poorer country and few if any cart paths were passable with even the smallest of carts these days. The widow reviewed her options and concluded that it was wiser to use beasts of burden such as pack horses to carry her trunks and other belongings. "That my father can so send these carts back home," she instructed her men at arms. Eleanora intended to discharge the carts back to the Yorkshire estates of her father; from there de Ferrers servants would retrieve them to the Essex manors. It was now mid January 1288 when this small band of riders with their assorted boxes, pack animals, horses descended upon the barony of Tranent, which was up in the East Lothianes; wherever that was, thought Eleanora.

They arrived at mid day and were greeted by Elena. Lady de la Zouche just returned from her daily ride and pleasantly greeted them all. It was not long before the widow de Ferrers was making herself comfortable in the castle of her kin, near some of her own manor lands of that same estate. "The views of the sea are magnificent," she cooed. "There is nothing like it where we live in Essex Ana; Fawside is even better than my father's prized manor of Sezincote in Gloucestershire." Le Parker was busying himself with the records of the barony, and accessing the income. He would also arrange to meet with the de Ferrers solicitor in Ayrshire, and the de Ferrers stewards of the manors in Wigtonshire, Dumfrieshire, Berwickshire, and Fife, where she held the other dower rights.

The peaceful appearance of tranquility in the countryside in Tranent was glorious to behold. As the sea mist evaporated with the morning sun, the brightened landscape revealed braes of withered green sprinkled with pathways struck by a glistening snowfall. There was a light drifting of white snow softly cuddling the craigs, glancing off the rocky cliffs, moving downward towards the shoreline. On the barren fields of winter's farmland there was a crystallizing frost forming; the brisk winds of the clear, crisp day scampered happily down the glens as the sea mist seemed to escape back into the skies above. Riding through the lands of Travernent and the barony was exciting and made Eleanora feel alive again. This Scotland is a place of my dreams, I feel so alive and truly happy she sighed. When she returned from her ride this new morning, Ana came out and scolded her, "you can't ride off alone like this M' Lady, this is Scotland; there are brigands about that would do you harm." "Oh Ana, I will take an escort with me tomorrow, I was just so thrilled to wake up in Scotland with no worries, no husband to scold me, or…." her voice trailed off, as Lady Elena came to greet her. "My dear, where did you wander to? You must stay near our Fawside and only ride with escort. Scotland is a place of savages." Eleanora began to laugh, and said "Between you and Ana I won't need a grouchy old husband to chide me!"

But Elena continued her admonishing words. "Since the death of Alexander, there have been more such outbreaks of unrest. This rough and barbarous kingdome has most been a place of discontent where lords of manors fight amongst themselves, taking law into their own hands; clannish ways of Fife, just across the firth; most strange to our civilized constraints of English law," she explained, haughtily defending English ways as she contrasted the uncouth ways of the Highlands and the kingdome of Fife visible just across the Firth of Forth. "But the lands beguile me so with their serenity, the very wilderness is romance to my heart," said the young widow de Ferrers.

Ana interrupted Eleanora's words and carefully explained that while the appearances bespeak of serenity there is truly a danger about. "These poorer lands of Scotland yield much less to their villeins, many forced to steal for life of their families. The barons of the realm are most impulsive; taking what they want, a lawless nation is this Scotland now. Without a king to rule these nobles, a most unsettled nature has prevailed; so this lady has been told," Ana said ominously; with far more emotion than Elena exuded. She then added that such times of danger should be warning enough to not go riding without escort. "This lady would be most saddened if de mischief so befell my sweet girl," Ana said with quiet concern. Eleanora shook her head, "This girl will be most careful in her venturing about in the future," she assured both ladies. Changing the subject, Lady de la Zouche boasted of her plans for the day. "We will share in fun this afternoon my dear Lady Eleanora. We have invited a speywife from Winton village to come and tell our future." Eleanora's face lit up into a broad smile. "Oh, perhaps there is a handsome laird or knight in my future," squealed the young widow. Ana threw her a quick glance, as if to remind her that she was but a wife without her husband, just two months a widow and should show some respect for the late lord who had left her with some fine estates for her sustenance.

Figure XII-Part One; View of the Firth of Forth from Fawside Castle

As they entered the great hall, a servant brought in a package from the tailor in Berwick. "It's my new blue velvet surcote Ana, look," said Eleanora as she began to unwrap the package. Ana shook her head as if to say no, it was not yet time to wear such garments. They brought the package up to her room, and Ana spoke softly, "my love, you must bear in mind others do not know what a beast that man was. You need to keep up the image of a widow in mourning for her husband of six years. Please dear, remember who you are, you are Lady Eleanora of Lovaine, relic of Lord de Ferrers." "Yes Ana, perhaps I have been a bit too jovial for my own good lately. I will be more circumspect in my behaviour. After all, we would not be here without the dower lands he provided for me." agreed Eleanora, a little ashamed of her seeming disrespect of the dead.

Several friends of Elena de la Zouche were seated around the withdrawing room off the great hall at Fawside. Everyone was all excited about the speywife from Winton. What would their futures be, the theme of all of their hushed giggles and sighs. Eleanora made her entrance and was true to her promise to Ana, demure and quiet in her tone, but underneath she was tingling. What would my life be like by and by, what love might come to this lonely life that would fill my days with sunshine and my nights with passion, ah the dreams of all in this room she mused as she looked about her. The old woman joined them now and sat at the games table near the fireplace at the end of the chamber. Eleanora would be first Elena decided, as her newly arrived guest from England.

The speywife began to tell her of her life, her strained marriage, her husband's death. Eleanora was told that she could have many children, but to do so she would risk her husband's life. "What do you mean by that dear woman?" she asked, "I am confused." "You must be careful to never marry, or if you do, choose carefully, a timid man is less likely to be at odds with the King, for your husband will find himself in the King's wrath, to die at his hand if he is not careful." the woman said in low tones of foreboding truths. "What name has this King?" asked Eleanora. "Edward that is what I hear." Edward Plantagenet, whispered Eleanora under her breath. The others took their turns then, but she never heard a word after that, only saying over and over to herself, I must never marry, never take a husband? Oh why should this be my fate?

Figure XIII-Part One; Village of Winton

The next day le Parker announced that he should leave for Ayrshire on the morrow next. Some of the receipts were confusing and he wanted to evaluate the extent of the losses from a fall storm that hit the west coast of Scotland some months before. Eleanora was still depressed from her reading with the old Winton woman. A trip might take her mind off her trouble fate. "We will go with you," she said. Ana was pleased at the opportunity to

MY TRUTH LIES IN THE RUINS

leave Travernent and the barony of Tranent, because it might improve her girl's disposition. No matter what Ana said, Eleanora could not get those words out of her mind: you must be careful to never marry, or if you do, choose a timid man.

Ana packed Eleanora's new surcotes and a lovely brocade and velvet cloak the tailor just sent from Berwick, hoping that the new garments of bright colors might cheer her. The trip to Ayrshire would take a week with all the travelers, sundry baggage and pack horses. Eleanora rode her own horse the entire trip, or walked her mare when the nonexistent Scottish cart paths proved too treacherous for riding. But she would never ride double with one of her men at arms as some ladies did; she was too independent. "This country is very primitive" she said aloud to Ana, "and I haven't seen a man near my age of any noble stature since we arrived, except that one in Berwick at the tailor shop." Ana was no longer warning her to speak with caution, as the travelers going to Ayrshire were all de Ferrers household members and knew the difficulty of her late husband's troubled ways. "My girl, here is your Ana's prediction of second sight: you will meet a handsome knight who will sweep you off your feet, and you will marry him and have many beautiful children." "Oh Ana, would that I could believe you, but you have not second sight, you are a Norman," chided the young widow. "Normans have second sight too M' lady," said Ana, "And they don't fill young girl's heads with bitter nonsense of the likes of that woman...." Her voice trailed off as she realized that Eleanora was no longer listening.

Along the journey west to Ayrshire, there were few choices of places to stay overnight; inns were seldom found and the few small abbeys and priories held but sparing room for their large household. This day the de Ferrers party was finally able to settle down for the night in Selkirk. The abbey there was long abandoned for another in nearby Kelso they were told; but there was plenty of room at a small inn on the cart path towards the Whitmuir manor. The mains of the former abbey's old motte and bailey castle could afford safe stabling for their horses and belongings they soon discovered. The days now were shortened by the lack of winter sun, so they were all happy to have found the rooms early. Eleanora had not taken a bath in two days of long, cold, damp riding and she was pouting and grumbling in her disposition; nagging at her attendants. But even more unsettling than her physical discomfort, this day's traveling brought a mindful fear to her very being.

Their peaceful day was ominously interrupted by a harrowing experience; one that could have had more dire consequences. The landscape of their journey allowed for many hiding places along the way. In a jagged glen where they decided to rest and water their horses by a scant burn, taking sustenance themselves, three armed men approached the English travelers. The menacing marauders were in search of a thief so they told her knight and men at arms that formed her escort. There was no battle or threat of altercation; it was just the thought of one that never came to be that scared Eleanora to her very core, making her most wary of the journey they were undertaking now. Perhaps they should have waited for spring she reflected more than once; it's my folly to be so impetuous. The daily travel seemed endless, the meals less than filling, the accommodations shabby and the weather an uncooperative damp and rainy by mid week.

Figure XIV-Part One; Maybole Castle in Ayrshire; a manor of the de Ferrers-de Quincy estates resided nearby

But Eleanora would not relent; she would continue on to Ayrshire she boasted to her household. The last day of the journey finally arrived; the weary travelers grew giddy with anticipation as they entered Maybole at last, a village not far from the de Ferrers' manor nearby. Their long journey was down to hours when finally they came upon her small manor house near Pennyglen, warm and cozy; ready to accept the new Lady of the manor, Lady Eleanora de Ferrers. As they rode up the shortened drawbridge across the small moat surrounding the earth and timber tower house, Eleanora realized her mare was troubled by a loosened shoe that had taken on some small stones. The young boy from the stables said her horse needed a few days rest, and he would have the farrier tend to a new shoe if necessary. "We have had few problems for such a long trip, coming all that way from Essex," Eleanora said out loud, "we are very lucky Ana to have made these travels without incident. Just a new shoe for my mare, that is very fortunate indeed." Ana beamed, "You know my love, since we left Essex; we seem to be following a course, finding our way to where we are supposed to be." "Oh Ana, you are so optimistic! Let us give thanks to God tonight at evening prayer, for bringing us to a new home and a new life. Maybe that old woman from Winton village was wrong after all."

The sun gleamed through the small window of oiled parchment, brightly lighting up her chamber as Eleanora awoke the next morning. A light rap of the door signaled Ana's arrival with some food to break her fast. "Oh Ana, I am going riding this morning, on MY land." "Remember dear, to take some of our men at arms with you as escort, you are in a strange place, with strange customs," cautioned Ana, "And don't go riding bare back or like a man. You ride side saddle like a proper English lady when riding for pleasure." "Yes Ana, I won't go far, I won't ride bare back, and I won't let any man catch up to me! I can out ride most men, so don't worry about me, I won't get abducted...."then she giggled, "unless of course, he is tall, dark and handsome, in which case I will let him catch me!" "Stop with that nonsense Eleanora, have some dignity!" But her lady was not listening to Ana once again. The young widow was in her own world of deep sighs, and dreamy gazes as she peered through the tiny window, out on her courtyard.

Douglasdale

William was humming away, happy to have an adventure in his midst. He was in the vaulted cellars, checking off provisions for his hunting party. As he unlocked the door to his small room, he realized he had not been in here in months. He found some dried herbs he wanted and packed them in his healing box. While he made this final check of his list, the squires were loading the pack horses with tents, bedding, bows, knives, and a good stack of arrows. And, he noted, I need to pack a small tub for bathing; it might get colder again, so bathing in the tent may be the only alternative. Oh yes, I must tell the cook to prepare some extra breads, sweet cakes and biscuits, and some meat pies; the first day of hunting could be scarce prey. William then decided to travel south through Crawfordjohn; Douglas lands from his great grandmother's dowry. For nearly twenty years there was always some quarrel with the Crawford heirs and de Lindsay clan over the Douglas' rights and the marches of these lands. Then in 1283 Lord Hugh resolved the issue, uniting the de Lindsays and the Douglases in marriages, both to sisters of the Steward. With the castle and mains of Crawfordjohn now peacefully held, these pheasant woodlands became a favorite for good hunting; a perfect stop for the first day's travel William decided.

Finished with the final list of food and drink provisions, he went out to the court yard to watch the daily archery practice. He would later stop by the falconer and tell him to bring the kitchen hawks, goshawks, for the hunt, and perhaps some of the falcons. I can make plans for some excitement, he mused in grateful anticipation for this distraction to the winter doldrums. William would bring Shamus his Deerhound too. The two had become inseparable daily companions on his long walks around the lands at Douglasdale. He was glad Hugh had given him a dog for Hogmanay, right after Elizabeth passed. At least he had someone to listen to him, someone he could confide in, who always agreed with him, aye, Shamus is special, he reflected, very special.

Figure XV-Part One; Charles of Invercarron, Charlie to his friends, a Deerhound of distinction at Balgonie Castle, Fife; the laird of Balgonie and his family have been part of Deerhound Rescue in Scotland for over thirty years

    The next morning William rose early, and went in to check on his son. He spoke with the lad's nurse and she said that James was sleeping well, and she would keep him so busy that he has no time to miss his father. There were sixteen others of the household waiting in the court yard of Douglas Castle, just outside the large keep that held the family lodging and the great hall. Shamus ran and jumped about; galloping at times as he surrounded the litter the falconer fashioned to bring the hunting birds in their cages. The other hounds and harriers were leashed and walked behind the falconer, in jovial procession, with the Master of the Hounds and his squires and pages that handled the kennels. Everyone was in good spirits. His brother in law William de Galbrathe was joining them with two of his knights, some squires and other men at arms, and pages from Dalserf. It would be a good group William thought. The horses were saddled and ready, and before long they would be in Ayrshire and some of the best forest woods in the Lowlands.

MY TRUTH LIES IN THE RUINS

Half way into the second day, they had arrived near Girvan parish where William held some acres of prime hunting for small game. Though all forests were under the king's control for hunting, William was granted rights to hunt on his own lands. The underbrush was perfect for hare to hide and Deerhounds to flush them out he mused. He was barking orders, happily supervising as the rest of the hunting party was setting up camp. The late morning sun was beaming down and the fresh air seemed to revitalize him. Shamus came running out of the low brush all covered in mud. "Where have you been, you silly wee dog?" asked William, as if expecting Shamus to respond, "I have been searching all over for you." Kneeling down to wipe the mud from the dog's face and ears, William began to laugh, "You will be the undoing of me yet! You get yourself lost on the king's lands and I will disavow you, silly beast." "Carry on your work," he said to the squires, "I will forage about with the hound for some signs of game, and here, I will take my bow as well, just in case."

So off they went, the two of them, William on his old palfrey, Nightly Manners, and Shamus, the silly, playful Deerhound running up and back, doubling the distance, as if impatient for his master to get to some destination. They were traveling on foot now, William leading his horse silently, for about a half hour when Shamus ran way up ahead of him, into a small clearing, only he did not return as he had been doing. When William finally caught up with the hound, he realized they were not alone. Quietly moving through the dense brush, as if stalking some prey, he realized that Shamus had come across another rider.

"Oh you awful hound you," chided Eleanora in Norman French, "you have spooked my horse!" She was dusting herself off from a spill off this older ambler, the only one who would take to her mare's saddle. "Shoo, get along now, leave us, this is my land and I won't have you disturbing this beast and causing me another fall." She began to mount the horse again, and thump, down she dropped. Again she got up and brushed the dirt from her surcote. "I have never fallen from a horse the likes of you in my whole life, what is the trouble in you now? Are you afraid of this beastly dog?" Eleanora had ridden ahead of her escorts and maids in wait, and gotten lost. She was sure she could find her way back; she never had a problem before. Losing male escorts was easy, even on this horse, and the maids no match to her riding skills. No one expected a lady could ride like the wind, but she did. Riding her horse was her escape, her travels into the fantasies of her youth.

As she tried to remount the horse bucked again, down she went the third time. Now Eleanora was angry, furious, with the fire of complete rage in her eyes, she let out a swear word in Latin. Spluttering under her breath, she suddenly looked up, but all she could see was this tall, muscular figure of a man; a nobleman she guessed from the clothing. He was peering down at her, with the most beautiful deep dark eyes she had ever seen. He looked upon her with such silent compassion, and a shy, curious smile, as he offered his hand to help her up; she was locked in his gaze. "Oh to be so loved," she sighed in a hushed voice, "and who must you be, do I dream this?" "No my lady, I am real, but you are one stubborn woman," replied William, also in Norman French; then in Lallans, "I am sorry my wee dog has frightened your

Figure XVI-Part One; Gandolph is a Deerhound reminiscent of Shamus; residing happily in his retirement at Balgonie Castle in Fife; the Morris family supports Deerhound Rescue and St. Hubert's Hound Sanctuary in Scotland

horse." Afraid that he had heard and understood her every word, she took the offensive with quick retort, "Wee dog, there is nothing wee about this shameless hound." Her Inglis words were betrayed by her actions as she then knelt next to Shamus, petting his ears while he licked her hand and lapped her face, "You are some strange creature, a real vixen you are. Did you train him so then?" she asked William, "to go preying on ladies riding in the woods alone?" "Aye, that I did, it's the only way I could find to speak with one so fair as your fine self," said William with a bemused look. He was totally enthralled with this headstrong lass, and by the looks of her fine saddle and expensive surcote, she was well taken care of by some wealthy laird.

"I am Guillame, Sir Guillame, of Duglas, at your service my lady, and this noble beast is my Shamus," he said softly as he bowed. "I am Lady Eleanora, late the widow of William de Ferrers, who's lands you are now on sir knight." William grimaced. "Oh, you are wrong my lady, these are lands adjoining my mother's dowry of Girvan parish given me on the occasion of my marriage some five years ago, to my late departed wife." The two young people both reflected on their words, the sparring took a standstill, as they looked shyly at one another, then glancing away, in their silence they each quietly rejoiced upon a discovery: they held in common the recent loss of their spouse. William broke the silence first, "where are you staying Lady Eleanora, may I escort you home? This forest is not safe for riding unescorted." "Oh, I had an escort, but they couldn't keep my pace, until now," as she motioned to two men at arms, riding into the clearing. "Ah, Lady de Ferrers you have given us all a fright," the older man said, "we felt sure you had come upon some band of thieves by now." "Only this wee hound who was set upon me to spook my horse," she teased. William helped her up on her mount and took her hand, "I will be out riding tomorrow, will I see you then?" She smiled brightly as she said her words. "I would say you will, for I must make closer acquaintance of that raucous hound, and tame his manners some!" she replied. Her face beamed fully as she looked down at him, her eyes enveloped him in way that he had never experienced before. "Tomorrow then," he said as she rode off, her heart beating so fast, her face tingling with a warm glow. Was such odd sensation what love must feel like, she wondered?

"Oh Ana, I met a beautiful knight, the most handsome of knights I have ever to set my eyes upon, oh Ana," Eleanora was flying into Ana's arms, barely one step off her mount, "we met in the forest, his dog spooked my horse, and those eyes, the most compassionate eyes I have ever seen, and he is a nobleman" she rattled in excited tones to Ana. Her escorts were shaking their heads, "M' lady rode off fast and lost us, we were frightened by her boldness, and she is very lucky to have come upon a knight of good character." The other ladies in the party were giggling and laughing, "We couldn't understand why she rode so wildly, in no apparent direction, and off she was, to find a clearing and a fine Scottish knight to her rescue he was." "What will I do with you child?" asked Ana, "These fine men are only trying to protect you." "Oh, I am sorry," she pouted, "I forget we are not in Essex anymore. But Ana, he is so handsome," forgetting her apologetic demeanor, "oh to be so loved, I would give my love to such a man without another thought of it." "You will calm yourself down now, and come inside for some sensible talk. You are spinning my head with your words!"

William returned to camp, as the others were preparing for the afternoon meal. His brother in law William spoke to him; then realized that something was very different about the knight's demeanor. "What is it that you found out there; you have a strange manner about you?" William le Hardi chuckled. "Aye, it was odd enough, as Shamus came upon a fair lass out riding in the forest, an English lady, recent a widow. And as she smiled upon me I felt like the tears of an angel had touched my cheek." De Galbrathe suppressed a chortle. "What is her name William?" he asked him. "Eleanora, the relic of de Ferrers I think her knight escort said." Willelma's husband thought for a moment. "Aye, de Ferrers is it? Recall you now the lang court battles of the de Quincy family heirs for almost eight years, and the lands half here in Scotland?" "I do, I guess. That it so caused our king, the noble Alexander many sleepless nights. But the lands would be of her husband; dower lands, not her lands except for current use and income while she lives as he had heirs," replied William, "I am not looking first for someone's dower lands. I am seeking of a woman to fill my lonely nights; be a mother to my son. This lass could do that, and with a little fire to make it interesting, aye!" His squire Patric de Duglas turned around and saw a look on his knight's face that he had never before seen, "you have been bewitched by fair visage on your face Sir William." Le Hardi shook his head wistfully. "If she has bewitched me, than I am blessed, for this is a lady, a sweet lass, with fire in her soul and passion in her breast. And she even likes our Shamus; he was the one who found her for me! Now how can you improve on that for a hunting dog?" He gave the reins of Nightly Manners to Patric as he entered his tent. I cannot believe that God has sent me a gift of love; this fair lassie is true answer to my prayers and dreams, sure aye!

William went out early the next morning with the huntsman and his apprentices; they were followed shortly by the Douglas and de Galbrathe knights, squires, and pages that formed the rest of the party. The dew was heavy in the cold, clear air of this late winter day, giving a good scent for the greyhounds. As the master of the hunt William had many responsibilities including giving the orders at the mort for the huntsman to kill the quarry. The knight-Crusader usually thrilled to the chase; enjoyed working with the huntsmen and the kennel dogs. He truly admired the work of the falconers as well as they flew the goshawks, sparrow-hawks and falcons in concert with the huntsmen as they slipped the spaniels to flush out the feathered game. Barking and galloping these sturdy, boisterous bird-dogs ran through the fields and underbrush to find the cover of pheasants and quail. William even enjoyed the more classic, simpler pursuit of game; with bow at the ready, chasing his quarry on horse. But today he returned with barely his share of game. His thoughts were on the English lass and their ride later that afternoon. Would she meet him he wondered, he prayed she would.

"Come on Shamus" he bellowed, "you have to go meet your new lady friend." Patric brought out his palfrey and asked him "Are you bringing the lass back to camp Sir William?" Shaking his head in the affirmative William responded, "Aye, if they will come I am to do just that. Be sure to tell the other squires to mind their manners and keep their attention on their work. Leave the entertaining of our guests to me," he said, with a shortened clip to his speech that indicated a marked seriousness from his usual style. "Or leave it to Shamus, for he has done well so far," quipped Patric, hoping some humor could break the tension in the air, for had known William le

Hardi many years; his serious side could come to rage quickly if not broken by laughter. The knight's face cracked a wry smile. "Yes Shamus, you have done well so far, let's go round up your unsuspecting prey, come along."

Figure XVII-Part One; William le Hardi as he may have looked just returning from the Crusades 1272

Eleanora was preparing to leave for her appointed rendezvous; to at last go and meet her knight, when Ana came out with some provisions. "Here you are my love, some cakes, meat pies, and wine to enjoy when you stop to rest." Eleanora gave her a look of surprise. "Rest Ana," she asked with mock confusion, "why ever would we stop to rest?" "Get on with you, and don't think you're fooling me with those tones of indifference. I know you didn't sleep all night thinking on him. Your circles have circles this morning my child." Eleanora was listening this time. She wheeled her horse quickly around, and asked in earnest, dreading the true answer, "Do I look so awful that I should not go Ana?" Ana smiled, "One look from the young man and you'll have glow enough in your cheeks that he won't notice the circles under those eyes. Enough of this now; enjoy yourself and be weary of your surroundings."

Riding only with her men at arms as escorts Eleanora arrived at the clearing to find William already there, biding his time, throwing sticks for

Shamus to fetch. Ana was right she thought, her cheeks barely burned when he came towards her, those beautiful, intense eyes never leaving her gaze for a moment. "Would you like to follow to my camp, and then your men at arms might rest, while we take a short ride marking the bounds of my lands?" Eleanora looked down at her hand; he was holding it in his hand, caressing it so lightly with his other hand. How gentle this man is with his touch she thought, while his hands are so large and powerful they could crush mine instantly. "Oh, I would like to do just that," she smiled as she answered him quietly, wanting to hide her anxiousness.

The camp was a grand site to Eleanora; she had never seen a fine Scottish hunting party. Perhaps she might get invited to go out on a hunt someday, she mused. As they entered the temporary hunting village, Lady de Ferrers marveled at the elegance and primitive beauty. Brightly colored tents in hues of reds, blues and greens, of many shapes and sizes, formed the boundaries of the camp. The center yard opened to long tables of trestles and boards for cooking and eating upon, covered with brightly covered cloths of linen. There were huge fires of wood and peat burning brilliantly in the center of the camp; waffling in grey smoke, curling upward in pungent aromas of the mixed woods and sweet dried herbs with peat. The dressed game cooked slowly on the portable spits. Here the riders were greeted by another nobleman and laird. "This is my sister's husband, Sir William de Galbrathe, Lady Eleanora, Sir William." Greetings were pleasantly exchanged. "So you have met the fine Deerhound Shamus, he is truly the one with the best manners in our group Lady Eleanora," said de Galbrathe. "Have you been in such a camp before?" asked William, "we could take some time to look around if you like." Eleanora was beaming, and barely able to hide her enthusiasm, "Oh, that would indeed be my wish."

William took her hand and helped her down off her mount. They walked arm in arm through the colorful paths of the tented village; taking in the lingering scents of the smoked game as they neared the cook's tent. The open fires sparked in pert sounds as the fat from deer meat and roasting game birds cooking on the spit dripped down onto the flames. Ellie smiled at everyone as William glided her through the camp; introducing her to his entire party. She made a striking figure of graceful beauty. Her long chestnut hair curled down her back flowing beneath her veil; her elegant surcote of bright blue velvet and silk brocade made a stark contrast to the bare, frozen earth as she swept her way through the paths of this temporary hunting lodge. He walked her by the quarters contrived for the Deerhounds and spaniels; their grooms were busy carefully checking paws and legs for inflammations, making sure their animals' eyes, ears and limbs were free of injury from the last hunt. The knight and his lady moved further towards the far side of the camp where the birds were being tended to by the falconer and his apprentices. Hunting with hawks and falcons was common on English manors, but William's falconer was a different breed from the others Eleanora had met. He was very informative, answering her many questions with patience and kind respect as he showed her the makeshift mews he fashioned to keep the birds safe, dry and warm.

This day was like the one she had fantasized so long ago, at the arm of her handsome knight, sighing and smiling, enthralled by his fine manners and shy, charming demeanor. Ah, but he is too perfect for me she thought, too handsome to find me the lady of his dreams; I would be a fool to love such a man. Yet as they were walking the path back to where the horses were stabled, he on her right, Eleanora looked up at him and noticed oddly that he was still wearing his hood, even in the warmth of the afternoon sun. As if reading her mind, he stopped and pulled her around in front of him. He drew down his hood, revealing long raven tresses streaked with deep red hues; she reflected upon the most gorgeous mane of hair she had ever seen. Then as her eyes moved to his face she saw what he was so intent on showing her: a horrible disfiguring scar that seem to run from his right cheek all the way down to his neck. An anguishing pain ran through her as she thought of the courage it took to reveal this mark on his beauty so early in their friendship. Did he fear that she would run from him once she knew? He started to pull away from her, but Eleanora held him fast, taking her left hand and pushing back his long thick hair, to allow her touch to caress the old wound with love and compassion. So that is what has caused your shyness with me she said to herself; knowing now that she could indeed love this kind knight now.

"Shall we take in a ride then Lady Eleanora?" he asked, beginning to smile again, as Patric brought their horses to them. "Too bad I don't have my own horse or I would challenge you to a race," she flirted. "You would be better to ride *with* me until you know the land, little one," William said in a half paternal tone, but followed by a knowing smirk that said he realized she was head strong, and would show him no heed if she wished. Surprised by her own response, she replied, "Oh, I would follow your good counsel then Sir Guillame, but once I learn the countryside, I will again lay down the challenge." "Accepted," he nodded. "Come on Shamus, we don't ride without the escort of our wee hound." "Oh Shamus my sweet Deerhound, better you come with us than surprise us and spook my horse again. I have spent more time off my horse in your company, beast, than ever in my past!" Eleanora chided good naturedly. They rode off, Shamus running in front, and all traveling at a comfortable pace. After a short time, he led her to a clearing by a stream, where they stopped.

He helped her down from her horse and took out a quilt from behind his saddle, which he laid upon the ground. "Ana has packed us some wine and meat pies and small cakes," she said, hardly believing she was sitting in the company of such a caring man. They sat quietly for awhile, and then he spoke first, "I have never met with a woman like you Lady Eleanora. You have such strong will about you that I was afraid that you would not come today." Suddenly Shamus ran between the two of them, grabbed a meat pie from the basket and made off with it. "Get back here thief," cried William, as he started up to find his hound. "Oh, never mind of the meat pie, there are more. He is like a member of our little party here anyway, for it is he who brought us to this day." "Right enough Lady…I would like to call you Ellie, it suits you far better than the other, would you permit me such familiarity?" Eleanora blushed; she felt the heat rise up her face and knew she was glowing red, "Only if you permit me the same, that I might call you Gilley, sir knight." "It is done," he said. And the two started to laugh and smile shyly as new lovers do when they first come to know the other.

William spoke of the hunt tomorrow and looked up at her, "Ellie, would you like to join our party, you would bring others and your maids in wait if you like. We would feel graced by your acceptance." No longer hiding her enthusiasm she responded happily. "My heart leaps for joy at your words, of course I would come." And they went on to spend an hour at their small feast and speak of many subjects. Ellie broke the barrier of subjects when she spoke of the nature of courtly love, "Do you believe Gilley that love is passio, do you embrace the concepts of spiritual love of Andreas the chaplain?" referencing the treatise on the Art of Loving Honestly.

William looked into the eyes of his young lass, "Ellie, I am thirty-seven. I have fought in the eighth crusade as a squire in 1270, and I have fought as a knight for King Alexander in battles since. I have married a lady chosen for me, and have a young son, her gift before she died some seven months later. I have never embraced the ideas of Andreas. I have my own core values, my truth, and I will share these with you tomorrow, when we ride out by ourselves after the hunt. As now I know that you read Latin, it is fitting that I can share this writing with you, for I wrote it for my only love, that I had yet not met. It is time we must return," he said quietly.

"Oh no, here comes Shamus, and he is covered with burrs," Ellie cried, looking at the Deerhound with a coat matted with the large sticky pods. Gilley just shook his head, "My two year old son gets in fewer tangles than you silly hound. You will lose most of that hair of yours when Patric is done grooming you, and shiver you will," he admonished the Deerhound. "Gilley, you can't take off his hair, he'll freeze in the cold of night." He chuckled in his response. "Don't trouble yourself lass, he sleeps in my bed, he will be warm enough!"

When Ellie and Gilley returned to camp they found her escorts drinking fine wine and feasting on game with Sir William. "We are enjoying your kind hospitality Sir Guillame," spoke Sir David, the elder of the two knights from Stebbinge Park. "There will be more of the same tomorrow good knight, as Lady Eleanora has agreed to join us for the hunt. Now it is turning colder, I fear, and it is time you must return M' lady to her manor." Patric was coming from where the horses were stabled; leading the de Ferrers squires and horses as the party prepared to leave. Ellie got on her horse with Gilley's help, more a courteous gesture than requirement, but a nice sentiment she would never refuse. He held her hand fast, covering it with the other.

He whispered to her quietly as he drew her nearer to him. "Tomorrow we will enjoy the hunt and then enjoy the walking. Tell your Ana that I will supply the repast this day, and I will read to you My Truth, that you would come to know the man who courts you better." Ellie barely heard his words, but smiled as she replied in wondrous tones, "I wish now would be the morrow, good day my dear Gilley." He bowed, kissed her on the hand, as she turned to leave. Ellie was deep in thought the entire ride home. Did he say the man who *courts* you, she felt her heart leap, oh no, pray he won't ask to marry me; but what do I want from him, this lovely knight? She must speak with Ana for this man is so different, so kind. How can she not continue to see him she wondered? But what about those words from the Winton speywife?

The pre-dawn departure came especially early for Ellie; she had to hurry to reach the hunting party on time. Although she had intended to speak with Ana about Gilley the night before, she had no time. Her seneschal was there at the manor when she arrived; laying out his findings from his work so far. He was riding to Ayr the morrow next and "returning in three days hence" le Parker informed her. "Some records I require are in Ayr. I will not review the lands in Dumfrieshire this time as the manor's descriptions are lacking some; the Grange of Senwick does not bear location of a barony in my findings. And Wigton is too far to travel for this journey." They should then commence their return trip to Tranent, so he could go on into Fife and Berwickshire for the remainder of his review. The time schedule contrived of le Parker will solve my problems, she said to herself: I will not have to make any decisions, because I will be leaving soon enough.

The morning hunt was like none she could have imagined. Gilley had the falconer put on quite a show with his prized falcons and hawks. Ellie even tried her hand at archery in the early going. She had used a ladies' bow before when she watched the morning practice with the men at arms at Little Easton. But she had never had the tutelage of a fine knight and bowman such as Gilley to show her the proper handling of the weapon. The wooden frame of the smaller bow was most the height that she was. Ellie giggled nervously at first as she held the long curved band of yew, grabbing it in the middle with her right hand. Gilley reflected that her normal instincts were for using the weapon in a left handed manner. It was rare that a warrior would use his weapons with that hand, though Gilley did just that. He was left handed and so was his lady he chuckled to himself. Ellie found the well waxed silk string difficult to fasten to the catch of the lock until Gilley gave her some insights. Then she joyously lifted the arrow, holding it between her first two fingers of her left hand she let it go with a whooshing sound that ended with melodious thud, hitting the target on her first attempt.

Ellie was in her glory. Her friend Alice had hit the target regularly and that knowledge cheered her to try her hand at archery this day. There is nothing this girl would shy from she vowed, and now she was successful the very first time! So began her day at the hunt. Her father was a knight and warrior, fighting in service of his king, now Edward Plantagenet. He had forbidden her to go on a hunt until she was older; then she was of age to go but he married her off to de Ferrers, and she shared no entertainment of a hunt after all. The Douglas hunt was a pageant; it began with the shrill sounds of trumpets and the mournful cries of hunting horns as the nobles with their hunters and apprentices galloped gallantly forward, paced only by the yelping greyhounds, scampering ahead, though still leashed and held fast by their grooms. Ellie thrilled to it all and Gilley was a real showman. Everyone seemed to play for his attention, even the other hunting dogs pranced for his words of praise and excitement. I wonder why he is so important to these men at arms from Douglas Castle, for he is not their lord, she questioned in her mind? Well, he is highly skilled on a horse and with a bow; but then a knight is supposed to be so.

Gilley told her that earlier that morning before her arrival he had met with the huntsmen to review their findings, and determine the directions for the hunt. The droppings from the animals and the tracks they left were clues to their identity and their location he explained. "Only the deer is so elusive to circle in their travels, to throw us off their destination so," he said. Ellie was amazed by how much information the apprentices and huntsmen could obtain from their outing with the sleuth hounds. They could determine the weight and sometimes even the gender by a track or dropping of an animal she was informed. Gilley told her that such training he would give to James his son, "and my sons to come, not yet born," he said with a funny smirk as he looked knowingly into her eyes. Ellie looked away and blushed only to turn back to her knight to find his deep, passionate gaze was still intently focused upon her.

After the hunt and the feasting they shared at his private table in his tent, the couple went off with Shamus for a short ride and a longer walking. It was colder today and they huddled together as they sat inside the quilt to keep warm. He read from a small scroll of parchment, where he had written in Latin prose:

My Truth, the Core Values of Sir Guillame de Duglas, Knight:

1. One must always be faithful in the vows of marriage.
2. One must be honest in the relationship, tell the truth in all ways and in your actions.
3. One must be respectful of the other person, do not hurt them emotionally, physically, or Spiritually.
4. One must have a purpose together, that will make a common bond between the two people.
5. One must always be a partner in the relationship, take care of the other person, but not so as to control their life experience.
6. One must be careful to be less demanding than instincts would dictate, but demanding enough to maintain a balance, harmony and personal level of expectations, keeping your standard of conduct high.
7. One must never commit acts that would violate conduct in the laws, such as thievery, adultery, murder, or other crimes against the laws of the kingdome and God, except in the climate of war, that would jeopardize the state of well being of the partnership and family.
8. One must maintain an identity within the relationship.
9. One must act respectfully at all times in the public eye, but behind closed doors of the bed chamber one can act privately in a playful, provocative manner of fun, frivolity.
10. One must celebrate dates and events all the time to keep the relationship in the forefront of existence.
11. One can maintain harmony by always being on time and being positive in mind, and always in the bed chamber, as it is not a place to argue and be sullen.
12. One must be in the moment always, keep the relationship in view, if something in the future or past takes prominence, one loses a little on life.
13. One must be kind, thoughtful and take interest in what is important in the other ones life; be a partner at all times, ever weary of being a partner at all times.
14. One must be a source of strength for your partner's weaknesses or worries, and concerns, provide advice when solicited but not unmitigated criticism; provide help when asked, never owning control of another's life.

DEBORAH RICHMOND FOULKES

15. One must be prepared to intervene with your partner with others if the partner breaks with core values due to over-indulgence and other detracting behavior.

He had made a seal at the bottom of the scroll in wax with his seal ring, a raised image of little letters and armorial achievements that represented his name; then he signed it by his own hand again, a rare but personal touch he determined necessary for this occasion:

To my dearest Ellie, these truths are mine and I would pledge to you these words with all my love, Gilley.

He gave her the scroll, tied up in a small ribbon. Then he looked in her eyes and held her hand, softly caressing it, and he drew nearer to her, "Ellie, I feel at last that I have found the woman to be a match to me. A woman who could love and spar with equal passion, who could return fire to my soul and divine love to my being. Your heart is pure and I would want to cherish you always with the love you deserve, and the love I know you desire. Would you consider this humble knight, a Crusader and warrior proven, for your husband, for I am asking to marry you? I can well provide for you, and I would want many children to fill our home and lives." Ellie's eyes dropped and she moved her gaze away from his. "Oh Gilley, I am not free to marry of my choice. My liege lord is in England, King Edward. I can not marry without his license. But far worse, I have had a woman of second sight, a speywife of Winton tell me of my future, that I should never marry, or my husband would die at the hands of the king, Edward Plantagenet."

At first Gilley was unsettled, she was refusing him, and he was feeling an old anger well inside him. But as she continued, as he heard more of her earnest words, he realized that her main reasoning was to be faulted. "Be serious now Ellie, there is no King Edward to rule of Scotland." She looked up at him, pouting now with a serious tone, "Gilley! You mock my words, you toy with my seriousness? I can not bear the burden that old woman has given to my heart; what if my husband were to die at the hands of the king, the guilt would kill me sure, if the grief had not done well its job." Gilley put his hands on her face, and reached her mouth with his lips, to silence her fears. "We will talk more on this tomorrow, will you come for a ride and walking again, then?" Ellie smiled in relief of the postponement of any decision. "Of course I will Gilley. There is nothing to please me more." Shamus came up to them and dropped a stick in front of her. "Not now my wee hound, our lass has to return to her home."

MY TRUTH LIES IN THE RUINS

When they met up with her men at arms at the camp, the knight repeated his ritual goodbye, holding her hand, and touching it with his, ever so gently; then he quite quickly pulled her down towards him, and he kissed her again on the lips. Ellie was surprised by his assertiveness in camp, but realized he was making a statement with his boldness: we *will* continue our discussion tomorrow! Her ride home was in the silence of deep thought. She must speak with Ana; she needed to understand what she should do. When Ellie arrived at the manor, she was told that Ana was resting in her room and she did not reappear until after the evening prayers.

"Are you all right Ana?" Ellie asked. "I am just tired my love, I did some embroidery on one of your other surcotes so that you might wear it when you are with your knight on the morrow." The work was lovely and certainly brightened up her outfit. "I must speak to you about my knight; I am in a quandary as to what I must do." Ana knew at once that Sir Gilley had courting on his mind, for the look of concern on her lamb's face was one of wonder and confusion that could only be from the bitter words of the old Lothianes speywife. Ellie went on to say, "I really love him, at least I think I do. I am so upset, for here he is asking for my hand that I am not free to give. I have this passion within me now too, that wants to be soothed; that fire growing in my womanhood for the man of my choosing. I want to share my love with him; that very deed I just may do before we leave for Tranent. Would I be too daring to share myself with him and though not in a bridal bed?" Ana was stunned, and caught herself before admonishing Ellie, in fear she might alienate her girl, so she joked, "so would you have to have your constable fine you for such an activity, assess leirwite for your bold ways, as Lady of the manor?" Ellie's eyes began to well. "You do not take my troubles seriously, I am consumed by this problem, and I have no help in the solving of it!" she cried, holding back her tears as best she could.

"Hush now, Ana will listen to you. I was only teasing, to get you to calm yourself. Now, you love this handsome knight. He has asked to marry you and you refused, for sundry reasons I assume?" Ellie nodded yes. "What was his response?" "Well, he said we would take up the discussion again tomorrow and he dismissed as folly my warning about a doomed marriage." A good sign, thought Ana, he must be as strong willed as she, perhaps the very match she needs. "My words would be to sleep upon your troubles and go out to meet him tomorrow. We have some more days here and then, Tranent is not so far from Ayrshire, or where did you say he is from?" "Douglasdale, but then a day's ride or more from here he said, so I am not sure," replied Ellie, a little less distraught than before.

The next day it poured, raining hard from the moment she rose for the day. Ellie was in the great hall of the manor house with Ana when her some of her men at arms came in to ask if she was riding out to the camp today.

Sir David began to ask, but he already knew the answer, "Are we riding today M' lady?" "Yes, Sir David, we are going to the hunting camp, if we don't drown on the way." Ana waved goodbye to them, with a feeling of uncertainty for the day. When the little group arrived, Ellie was soaked through her cloak and veil, sleeved surcote, and right down to her cote. William knew enough to now to realize that she would be there, down pour or no down pour; he was ready with a dry cloak, a blue velvet cloak with fur trim, and one his elaborate neck finishes when she arrived in camp.

Gilley prided himself in his appearance, especially in elaborate garments in velvets and silks, when appropriate. This day he would allow her to see his penchant for elegance, his knowledge of fine manners, as a true nobleman of station. As he led her into his tent, he motioned for her to take his cloak and go behind the dressing drape he fashioned near the far side. She came out from behind it several minutes later, draped in his garmet that covered her body twice with some to spare. "What shall I do with these?" she asked, holding her dripping wet clothes. "My squire will see to them. Patric," he called out the opening flap of the tent. "I want you to take M' Lady's clothing to the cook's tent and dry them by the smoking fires; take of these fragrant herbs to spread over the wood," removing some lavender flowers and stems from his healing box. "Caution them to not scorch my garments," she winced, as Patric left with all her garments. Everything was well organized, she thought. He had a table of warm food and fine wine in great quantity awaiting her arrival. "Perhaps this was a poor thought to come out in such weather as this." Gilley dismissed her words. "Come sit here Ellie, you must warm yourself with some food and wine. I am very pleased you came today."

"I was thinking I should meet you at your manor but realized I was not sure where it might be. You are just beyond Maybole, a former de Quincy place, is it not?" She nodded as she sipped the hearty red wine. The conversation was chatty and they laughed and sparred with each other. "Would you like to play a game of Merels?" he asked after they finished eating. A young lad named John, a page to Sir William, came in to remove the platters of left over food and pour more wine for the couple. "The meal was just what I needed," she smiled, "and a game of Merels would be perfect to pass the time of such a cold and rainy afternoon." The small fire in the tent waffled smoke through the top, and it became more warm and cozy with each glass of wine. Ellie enjoyed her wine, and could drink with him, but soon the board game was over and the rain had not stopped, so he offered more wine. She accepted as he took her hand and led her to sit on the old war chest near his bed, covered in the familiar quilt from their first afternoon, those few days ago. "This chest was of Sir Archibald, my grandfather," he told her as they sat together.

"I wish to continue our conversation from yesterday," he said in his muted tones, "and I want no more to hear of words from a speywife who does not wish a beautiful lady to be happy." Ellie interrupted him. "Gilley, I can not think of accepting an offer of marriage at this time, even though I have never felt love as this before. My late husband was the age of my father, twenty eight years my elder; we were not well suited. He was cruel and I grew to dislike him so. We never shared a bridal bed," Ellie's words trailed off, as Gilley looked at her, surprised by her last words. "If you never shared a bridal bed, you should keep that to yourself, for there would be challenges to your dower rights, sure aye," he told her like a big brother scolds his wee sister. "But if you are true that all those years, six was it you said?" she nodded her head yes, "That he was much the fool to ignore the love of a fair young wife as you can only be; that now I might be the humble benefactor of his grave folly?" He continued to speak quietly. "That from his blindness to your beauty then, that I could be your first and only love?" Gilley kissed her and drew her closer to him still.

Hours later there was a sound of digging and scratching at the tent side, then a pounding of four muddy paws and a thud, as Shamus made his way upon their bed. Gilley had instinctively reached below the bed for his dagger, when his sleep was first interrupted by the unknown intruder. Ellie squealed as Shamus landed right on top of her. "It's his side of the bed Ellie," he said with a smirk. They were both laughing by then, and Gilley admonished the hound. "We almost beheaded you my silly friend. Next time, would you please have the courtesy to announce yourself before you leap upon us?" Then they both looked up to find Gilley's brother in law standing at the doorway of the tent. "Come along now you two, the rain has stopped and it will be nightfall before long. Here are your clothes, all dry and ready for the ride home Lady Eleanora."

Slightly embarrassed, and a little groggy from the wine and warmth of the moment, Ellie got up and dressed in silence. The night's air would revive me she thought, before I meet up with my Ana. Gilley came and helped her with donning her long cote with its sewn-in arms, lang laces and tiny buttons that were proving difficult for her to put on and fasten. Then he grabbed the brooch neck closure and clipped it on her surcote. When they were both in their surcotes, she reached for her cloak and veil. Gilley came and kissed her on the top of the head. "I will see you tomorrow. And we can ride till your heart's content," he said light heartedly to her, no longer a question in his mind that she would come. Then more seriously, he brought her closer to his body and just stood and looked deeply into her eyes. "I love you with all my soul for eternity," he whispered. She replied softly, "I have known no other love than you Gilley, and find it the sweetest love that I could thus imagine."

DEBORAH RICHMOND FOULKES

Outside the tent, Patric was bringing her saddled horse, readied for the ride home to her manor. "Off with you then my Ellie or your Ana will think I have abducted you!" She turned to wave goodbye, but he was already running back to her side, "I have forgotten to give you this, a little something that I wrote for your last night, a few words from your poet knight." He handed her a little folded piece of parchment, which she put inside her cloak, safely in her drawstring purse until she could read it under the light of a good candle. He continued with his ritual, kissing her hand, then drawing her down, he kissed her on the lips.

When Ellie arrived home, Ana was sitting in the great hall at the large trestle table. One look from her girl and she knew that the rain had done for Ellie what no marriage bed had accomplished for her. The glow of her eyes, the fire in her cheeks, and the happy calmness in her voice, something Ana had not seen or heard before in this Lady Eleanora: confidence as a woman, exuded from her very being. "What have you there my child?" asked Ana, as Ellie untied the tiny scroll. "Something from my poet knight as Gilley calls himself."

My love is for the ages
My love is of the seas

Bountiful and Hardy
But light enduring breeze

I caress your face with kisses soft
And hands that strongly hold

The love for you eternity
That only time unfolds

"Oh Ana, I feel like I am in a dream, and I never want to wake from it. He is so kind and gentle. He makes me feel so special, so important." Ana knew now that this is the husband for her lady; this man was the answer to her nightly prayers, ever since those days that seem so long ago, in Essex. "When is it then that I might meet this knight of yours?" she asked. "Tomorrow, I will ask him and some of his party to share our evening meal with us, and escort me home with Sir David and the others. He will most likely come with his brother in law Sir William, as well as their squires and a few others in their party." "I will tell cook so that he can prepare. We shall have a fine feast our last day here." Ellie looked up and realized it was time to return to Fawside as le Parker was coming home that very night. She would have to tell Gilley tomorrow that she was leaving mid day the next.

Gilley was in his tent when Sir William appeared. "Oh, it is you again," he smiled, then Sir William began to speak with mild concern, "My dear brother, I see a need to talk with you of the lady. You seem to have grown fond of her and she holds the same for you I see. Her knights have been subtle but curious about you, but we have offered little." Gilley was surveying his brother in law, and replied "I have asked for her hand and she has refused me now twice. Edward Plantagenet is her liege lord and she can only marry by his license. She thinks I am a simple knight of no means, in the house of Douglas, and that is the way I want it for now. But she loves me, and I am confessed, all consumed by her wit, her beauty, her innocence," his words trailed off as de Galbrathe gave him a knowing glance. "Some of that innocence seems to have been lost today I surmise, or was I tricked by the dim light of this tent and that ruffian hound that seemed bent on sleeping in his bed?" said Sir William with some amusement. Gilley was smiling to himself, "No, you were not mistaken." As he continued to speak he was careful not to reveal the entirety of Ellie's confessions to him. "Imagine, being married six years to a laird almost thrice her age and he not taking much the interest in this wife, a beauty such as this girl? She is truly a unique lass aye," he sighed happily, gazing off in his personal reverie. Then he seemed to catch himself in his day dream; turning now to Sir William Gilley added with a more serious overtone, "When I do ask her the third time, she will say yes to my request for marriage and her hand; it is done!"

Still lingering, with something yet on his mind, Sir William asked, "Did you know they are returning to the Lothianes two days hence?" Gilley looked up, startled, "No, she has said none of that, but then I have not given her much time for speech this day. Did they say where?" The older knight smiled broadly, "That we should so find out!" he chuckled. "Fawside Castle in the old Tranent barony of de Quincy the destination for your lassie; is it yet near your Uncle Andrew's tower house in Herdmanston?" A twinkle reached Gilley's eyes, "Yes, the manors are few hours ride apart; the same short distance from my brother's wee tower house in Glencorse. Well, that is good news, excellent work my dear brother. My sister Willelma had great fortune to marry one as you!" he exclaimed heartily. Gilley continued to share his plans with Sir William with the gleeful words of a poet knight when first in love. "To be most happy as I return to Douglasdale, sharing this great adventure with my brother Hugh; then to take my leave; heading for the Douglas stronghold on the river Tyne for fairer game, this sweet lass, my bride to be! The Lothianes, aye, it is God speaking to me, I know it now." Sir William rose to leave, "We are breaking camp in three days ourselves, are we then?" Gilley nodded and said as he gestured a rounder frame on himself from the recent feasting, "Our pack animals are weighed down with prized game, our bellies full that we can eat no more of it, and my mind is on a lass that I will take for my wife. Yes, it is time for us to return to Douglasdale; to reflect on the bounty of our good fortune. That means you too my Shamus, you have done yourself proud this hunt."

When Ellie arrived at the camp with her men at arms she announced the small feast Ana was planning with cook, and invited Gilley and William and those they would travel with as well, for an evening at her manor. "A good suggestion then," said Gilley, "we will be most pleased to eat under a thatched roof, with the good food of your manor on our platters to enjoy." Ellie smiled graciously, pleased with his response. "And there is much fine wine as well, so nothing needs to be carried to meet our needs this evening," she replied. Gilley mounted his horse and the couple now rode off in a new direction. When they stopped to do their walking about, Ellie noticed the strange plants growing yet in the winter cold. "What are those spike-like green plants, hardy they must be to endure the cold and damp of these long winter nights?" "Aye, those are the thistle, they sprout beautiful purple flowers in summer, but they are deadly to pick if you know not the secret how. The thistle has defended our lands against the invaders for centuries of our Celtic history. One foot upon those spikes and the invader is doomed to cry out in pain of his folly to attack us; and we are quick to put him down." "I have seen such odd plants in the woodlands of our Essex; but not so large as these and so bountiful in number," Ellie said. "How strange to have such flowers in the forest, that they defend your people." Gilley went on to tell her more of the ways of his forbearers. "There is an old Celtic tradition about the great warriors who fell in battle; only to return as flowers in the forest. So I would say those returning as the thistle must surely be the fiercest fighters of them all!"

Shamus was running with a large stick, more like a limb from a tree. He brought it to Gilley who began throwing it back and forth, the hound retrieving it; the game they loved to play. The lovers were walking slowly, arm in arm, through the grey green of the winter forest, frozen in beauty by frost of the clear night gone by. Then Gilley abruptly stopped and turned her to face him. Before he began speaking, Ellie had raised her hand pushing back the hood he wore; pulled far forward to cover his facial scars. "When you wear your hood as this," she chided him quietly, "that handsome profile, the very one this lass finds so agreeable to gaze upon; it is most hidden from me Gilley," she whispered to him. Ellie gently touched the scars, running her long fingers down the side of his face to his neck. "I would like to have seen the man who did this to you when your countered his attack." Gilley's face took on a sobering countenance. "There were three men, of almost a hundred that raided our manor at Fawdon, in Northumbria when I was but sixteen. I rushed to fend off the attack and foolishly so. For in my haste I did not wear my gambeson or other armaments that would have protected me;

some further reminders of that encounter you felt on my arms and back most yesterday," he said apologetically. "Those three men died that night, and I was left with their marks to remember the treachery of one named de Umfraville and his *homines ad armas*, men at arms. But it is a lesson to me that I will teach my son James, and our sons some day too: always take time to protect yourself, to put on your gambeson, and your hauberk; to be properly armed, for the battle will wait on the warrior."

Ignoring his words "our sons", Ellie asked if he had ever been in tournaments. "Every knight enjoys tournament. But it is not so easy as you might believe. The weapons are rebated, blunted on each side, rounded on the ends in stead of honing them to a point. But if a knight picks up the wrong weapon, and there are many about, this could prove to be the death of the opponent. It could also be of trickery that lays a knight to his death in tournament, but it is quite often an error that turns one to fatal harm." "I remember stories of my father's family, of one knight, Godfrey Lovaine, at tournament one hundred years before I was born. He was killed by feud when his rival Baldwin turned the affair into a battle." Gilley told her that feuds were no longer at issue, as most tournaments were now run by more formal rules and tournament societies. He explained that once the feuds started to become more frequent, resulting in the deaths of participants, the church interceded, and tournaments were prohibited for a number of years.

As the couple began to retrace their steps Gilley reflected on the varied knowledge of this young lass, her many interests seemed to surprise him. He could speak sensibly to her about any subject, and interject several languages for the emphasis; she knew them all, except the Gaelic. She would learn that in due time, he said to himself. The sheer fun of conversation was exciting to him, for he had never known a woman to share such talk so comfortably. And he could speak of love, the deep thoughts that came from his heart he shared so freely with her. This Essex lady was truly a gift to his every need; a most astounding discovery to this humble knight, he mused. In all his years no lass had come to know him as he truly was, a man with deep thoughts and honest compassion; until he met his lady: Eleanora Lovaine, relic of de Ferrers.

"Gilley, we are leaving mid day on the morrow," she started speaking slowly, "I may not see you again. I want you to know this, that I have never known a man as good and as kind to me as you. You listen to my words, you engage me in thought, and you delight me by your consumed attention in my presence. Were I free to accept the hand of any man, it would be yours that I would accept. For now, my sweet knight, I must say I could love no other as I do you, but I can not give you the answer you desire...." Her words were interrupted, as he turned round to her, to pull her close, to cover her mouth with his own in a deep, passionate kiss. "I will not be asking for you to marry me a third time now, for when I do, your answer will be yes. Let us mount our horses and return to camp so we can make your manor in the day's light."

Everyone was waiting on them when they returned. Gilley put a rope around Shamus's neck and gave him to Patric, "Here you go silly hound, be good to my squire and mind your manners." The ride to Pennyglen passed quickly, and the gloaming was fast approaching as the party arrived at the small manor once used for hunting by the de Quincy family. The young stable boy was out walking Ellie's mare. He had just groomed her as well; the pure white coat barely glistened, still quite visible in the fading light of day. The lad was trying out the new shoe. "Is that your horse?" asked Gilley. "My Winter Rose, yes she is my mare. Oh how well she is doing, thank you dear boy. You will be well rewarded for your good work with my horse," she told the lad. Her generosity and good words for the boy did not get by Gilley, who seemed impressed with her kindness, "You are forever thinking of another my sweet lass. A generous deed is repaid thrice over the stories of Celtic ancestors tell us. Did you hear of that one afore?" he asked as he helped her down from her mount. She smiled as he took her hand and kissed it, "No, but I think I would like to learn more of these Celtic ways, for they seem very comforting to my soul."

Ana came out to greet them, "This is my Ana, Sir Guillame, Ana, my knight." Gilley bowed to her, a gesture that was surprising to some as she was not a lady of station, but not to Ellie. And he meant to show this woman the respect he had for her, for what she has done for his girl, his dear lass; the woman he would marry. Ana curtsied and led the party to main hall where the table gleamed with festive decorations as the cook and kitchen maids began the procession of platters. There were large gilded chickens, eel with Ellie's favorite, a dark sticky sauce, and a wonderful curried capon dish. There were also platters full of baked rabbit, pheasant and roasted pigeon. Out too came large croc bowls of beans, fried with garlic and onions, and spiced with ginger, cinnamon and nutmeg. And there were wines in great quantities, followed by breads and cakes of many fashions and flavors and a lovely egg custard served with honey. To say that Gilley was impressed would be an understatement: he was thrilled. She knows the fine art of entertaining her guests well, he noted.

As her servants were bringing in the platters, Gilley's squires and page were bringing in some gifts of game from the morning's hunt. Ellie knew he would be generous, even after she told him not to bring anything. The cook was thrilled to have some fine meat to replenish the larder from the night's feast. Gilley sat next to her at the large laird's table, and proposed a toast for a safe journey for her party's return to the East Lothianes. And he ended with, "and safe passage to us all, until we feast together in such bounty and comfort, soon to be again." One of her maids in wait performed on a small Celtic harp for one of the entremets, between courses; another sang an old lovely ballad of young lovers separated by war. Fine food, good wine and sweet entertainment, it was a merry night for everyone, and came too soon to an end.

When her guests rose to leave, Gilley pulled her aside and told her that he would call in the morning before she left for Fawside Castle. Again he continued his now famous ritual, first kissing her hand, but when it came time for the embrace she was expecting, he instead kissed her on the top of her head. Amusement swept over her face and she whispered in his ear, "You fear the words of my Ana, should you kiss me on my lips?" Challenged by her ploy, he pulled her close and kissed her solidly, squarely on the mouth and said with carefully monitored tones of a man in charge, "Good night, Lady Eleanora, on the morrow then will I see you." And he was gone, out the gates of the manor, and away on his palfrey, leaving Ellie to watch him through the doorway. Feeling Ana move close behind her she whispered aloud, "I told you he was special, my Gilley." Ana sighed as she spoke her words of quiet counsel, "He is decidedly that my love, you found a unique man when you met Sir Gilley. She then added, "And if you're smart, you'll not lose him!" Too tired for objections, Ellie announced she would retire.

She rose early, eager to review some of the business of the estates with le Parker. He would be waiting for her in the great hall, having his porridge and ale. The income would be steady he said, and he authorized some repairs on the stables and on the mews where the roof was damaged by the last storms. The information at Ayr was helpful and he felt that if all the other estates were in the same shape, she should be in good stead with an excellent income, able to do some travel and make some expenditures of extravagance here and there. Good news in deed, she said to herself. One of the servants announced some riders approaching, and of course one was Gilley on Nightly Manners.

Ellie went out to greet him and forgot entirely about finishing the estate review. She quickly introduced John le Parker to Gilley; then off they went to do their walking. "You did not bring Shamus?" she questioned, as if the hound meant more or equal to her than her knight. "Of course I brought him, see there he is, frolicking by the stables. Come hound, meet your lady friend, for she is traveling this day, and will not see you for some short time." She looked up at his face now, his hood was down, and his eyes shown with the deep, dark intensity of the passion she loved so well. "I will miss our walking and..." again he interrupted her. He was so impatient; when he was intent on doing something he would not wait she laughed to herself. But then Guillame is Guillame she reflected; that was just his way.

DEBORAH RICHMOND FOULKES

"I have this for you, and I will read it to you now," he said, as he sat her down on a large boulder in the clearing. He knelt before her as he took her hand.

> My love for you has
> Grown and grown
>
> It crosses o'er the seas
> And it spans the
>
> Moors and mountains high
> While it grows inside of me
>
> I find it hard
> To collect the words
>
> That tell you why I kneel
>
> For my love of you has
> Grown and grown
>
> Beyond the words
> I feel

He took both her hands and held them inside his large, warm palms; wrapping her long fingers with his in a gesture of prayer, as he said quietly, "You must pray for divine guidance in your struggles on this, your life's most important decision, for in four months hence, in June after the solstice, I will be at your castle in the East Lothianes to demand an answer to my words I give you today: I have loved no other Ellie, until you there has been no passion in this knight's heart. You have brought to me the sense of life eternal, for which I am ever grateful. Now I want you to share my dreams, to bear me many sons and daughters, to bring warmth to my bed and songs to my heart. It is only you who can end my life long search for love. Say nothing now, keep your thoughts till then, but when I come for you, the answer will be yes, I know, as long as God is in his heaven."

He gave her the little scroll to add to her collection, and he took a small gold adorned rope of velvet from around his neck and tied the scroll to it. "This is for you, to keep close to your heart, to know that I will be back for you, to marry you. And when ever you have doubts, take it out and read it, for you will know my words are true, my one and only love is you." As he helped her to her feet, he noticed tears welling in her eyes, but she was not saying no, she could not; something in her was changing and they both knew it. Some force stronger than any king or mortal man was transforming them, influencing them; all Ellie could do was to accept the path God gave her, she knew that now. They held each other close; their thoughts secured inside their very souls. The enormity of the moment diminished any words they might have said; their silence spoke their truth.

They returned to the manor, and he said farewell to Ana, le Parker, Sir David and the others. Shamus was kissing Ellie as she knelt down to pet him, "You are the one who started all this, it is you who have brought this hard decision to my heart to bear," she whispered to the silly Deerhound as if he understood her words. "Take care of my dear friend here," she said to Gilley. They embraced, only he was the one leaving on his horse this time. "I will see you four months hence, after the solstice, look for me and have the answer I am waiting to hear." He turned and rode off, only looking back once to see her waving good bye. Ana came to her, "He asked you again?" "Yes Ana, he said he would not allow me to respond now and he gave me this," showing her the gold and velvet rope with the tiny scroll of poetry. "Good that he knows you so well, to give you time with your thoughts. He is strong willed and honest, with good character, and he expects the same from others."

Ellie nodded and looked back at her, "I came here to find adventure, never dreamed I would find a knight to love me so. One never knows what fate has in store for us, but something has changed within me Ana; for I will never again be Eleanora of Lovaine, the relic of de Ferrers, a girl in search of love." She stared down the cart path from her manor for some time; then turned back to the moment at hand, "Are we ready to begin our journey back to Fawside?" The party was packed, the horses ready, and the little wooden chest she packed was full with gifts for her sister in law, and others in Tranent. "What stories I will have of my adventures in Ayrshire. That they would chance believe me for the stories of my knight and that silly hound, and of the great hunt! I know it so, as I hardly believe it myself." She went to the stables to look after the saddling of her mare. She went looking too for the groom, the young lad who took care of Rose and gave him a coin for his work, praising him again, "You will make a good farrier some day dear lad." I am starting to use his words now, she reflected, lad, lass, aye, again there I go....time to leave, time given to me to discover what I should do.

The week long travel was complicated by snow they encountered outside of Edinburgh. February was finally providing the winter weather they hoped to avoid and had successfully until now. They stopped in this royal burgh to do some more shopping and sleep in good lodging, waiting out the storm. In the shops of the Royal Burgh Ellie spotted the perfect gift; a present for Gilley. Should I buy him that, she wondered, and then she saw a small leather strap with a little buckle, suitable for a collar for the Deerhound, "I will take those two large silver buttons," she said, "No, the two large, decorated ones there, suitable for a man's ceremonial mantel or cloak closure. Yes, those, and I'll take the small leather strap with the buckle there as well." A few trinkets for herself and Ana, and that would do it, she thought. That night they could enjoy a good meal and a fine, comfortable room, for this was a city, not like London, but a city none the less. And there was a huge castle that sat upon the hill, guarding the burgh, "Someday I should like to be invited to a party at that castle Ana," Ellie said. "Oh and you were the lass that refused parties," she replied. "Lass, Ana, you said *lass*, you see, he has gotten to you as well, using those words." Then they giggled, surprised that this man had permeated their lives, in only a week of time, how much influence he had with them even though he was not there. "He is probably home right now in Douglasdale, and has forgotten all about us, quipped Ellie, knowing in her heart, there was little chance of that.

Ayrshire

Gilley returned to find the rest of the hunting party beginning the preparations to leave the next morning. Surveying the cook's pack horses he realized they had really done well on their trip, as there were barrels full of cured boar and deer, salted meats, and smoked game. "Hugh will be pleased that we have so much for his table," he said to Sir William. "Your brother will be equally pleased when he hears of Sir Shamus' enterprises." Gilley was laughing now. "You have knighted my hound?" asked Gilley, amused by the prospect. "I would think you would do it yourself for the prize he has brought you. She is a wonderful lass, and knows well how to throw a good feast." He realized Sir William was looking to know the result of their morning of walking and talking; if she had accepted his proposal of marriage. Gilley said, "I have told her I will call upon her at Fawside in four months, after the solstice. She will say yes to me then, and a wedding we will plan," he said, one way or the other, he thought, *it is done*.

The journey homeward to Lanarkshire was relatively uneventful, save the light snow they encountered near Crawfordjohn. But the flurries soon subsided and they were riding through the gates of Douglas Castle. Gilley could not contain his excitement: the news he so wanted to share with his brother Hugh. He made an entry worthy of a great prince returning home to his castle, sweeping into the great hall past the squires of Sir Hugh that announced his arrival. With great presence and bravado he doffed the velvet hat that he wore now; threw his sword belt to his squire and gallantly swirled off his flowing supertunic. Gilley spoke excitedly; his words joyously reverberated in the great hall. "Dear brother, we have brought you great tidings and a larder full of game for your belly." Sir William added, "And Sir Shamus has brought us other game to our good measure, surely you would get to that Gilley," using Ellie's name for her knight, his brother in law. Hugh looked up from his ledger-rolls he was reviewing with his steward, "Gilley, who is this Gilley? And Sir Shamus is it? You have gone and knighted the hound?" he bellowed, reminiscent of his father, William, 5th Lord of Douglas.

Figure XVIII-Part One; Crawfordjohn lands on Duneaton Water given as a dowry by John Crawford for his daughter Margaret in her marriage to Archibald Douglas, grandfather of William le Hardi

"Gilley is your youngest brother, tamed by an English widow, with the dower of a princess," announced de Galbrathe. The widower was oddly circumspect as he told Hugh of how he met his English lady. "Our Shamus found my sweet lass in the woodlands of Ayrshire. She is indeed an heiress from Essex, but the lands are in her dower from her late husband. You might recall de Ferrers who married the widow of Earl Colban of Fife?" Hugh nodded, recalling well who he was. The Douglas Chief beckoned his brother to continue. Gilley's face lit up as he spoke of his chance encounter with the lady. Then his tone changed, becoming more somber as he related her circumstances and position. "Ellie, Lady Eleanora, is his second or last wife, now his widow, relic of de Ferrers. She is in Scotland to retain her lands of dower, and plans to stay here, returning to Essex only for holiday. Her lands she holds in dower are most the children's lands in tenement, as is the custom and she must have Edward's license to wed," Gilley said, barely taking a breath to tell his tale. Hugh interrupted his soliloquy at last. "The income from these lands would be welcome for you my brother, and worth the responsibility to so manage," said Hugh, always the practical one. "But the license of Edward Plantagenet is another matter."

Changing to a more festive mood, Hugh happily proclaimed, "We will discuss this on the morrow, younger brother. For now, a great feast and some fine entertainment to have this night. You are staying, good brother; dear husband of our sister, are you not?" Willelma's husband was quick to accept the invitation. "Of course, and I will leave when the sun rises on the day next; eager to return to Dalserf and my dear wife waiting patiently my return. I hope to be there one day early to surprise her," said Sir William. Shamus came in with one of the squires, and went over to give greetings to Lord Hugh. "A great hunter you turned out to be, good hound. I got my money's worth when I bought you!" Just then, a screaming, happy two year old boy came running into the great hall, "Fad' er, Fad' er." His nurse was close behind, apologizing for the exuberance of his youthful, uncontrolled entrance. "My son, I am so glad to see you dear James, you have grown so. He has grown some nurse, in these few weeks?" asked Gilley as he danced him around the room in his arms, a silly Shamus barking at his heels. Hugh began to roar a big barrel of a laugh, "It is good to have you home my brother, or should I say, Sir Gilley?" "You will like her Hugh, when I bring her home as my bride, after the solstice; that is my plan. And my son, she will be your mother, a new mother you will have."

Fawside

Ellie woke to a beautiful spring morning, but when she stood up from her bed, she became overwhelmed with nausea, and felt as if she would purge the contents of her stomach at any moment. It was the second morning she felt like this, so it could no longer be blamed on something she ate. Ana came in humming a Scottish tune, "What's the matter with my girl?" "I don't know, I should have recovered if I am sick from foul meat by now, or be in peril for my life, I suspect. But I am still with nausea. What can this be?" She looked up, and saw a look of some concern come across that loving face, as this kind woman, who cared for her so quietly asked her, "My love, when did you last have cycle?" A wild look of disbelief crossed Ellie's face; there was almost horror in her eyes, "No, on no Ana, it can not be, it was only the once I was with him." Ana drew her near, and held her fast as Ellie began to sob, "I would not know what I should do, I can not accept his proposal now. He would forever think I would do it for the child I carry; not that I loved him, risking all my holdings to marry without the King's consent." She sobbed and sobbed, the tears stuffing her nose, she could hardly breathe, "Why, Ana, it was only once; why is God so angry with me?" "There now, my lass, perhaps it is only the excitement from the

MY TRUTH LIES IN THE RUINS

last two months that has brought change to your body. We will wait for two more weeks and I am sure you will feel better by then, and all will be well."

But Ana knew her words were hollow. She had been noticing a change in Ellie since February. Her face was taking on a new look, and her demeanor, aside from the recent nausea, was oddly calm. "We will keep this to ourselves, all right? Just like we forbade speaking of de Ferrers and never consummating your marriage to him; it will be our secret." A light rapping was heard at the door, and in walked her late husband's Aunt Elena. "I was passing by your room and heard your crying, are you all right my dear?" Ellie wiped her face, "Oh yes, I was just reflecting on my fate with that kind knight; too bad that he is not an English land owner and baron, so dear Edward would consent to my marriage with him." Elena smiled, "Poor dear, the weight of the world is upon your shoulders. Should we have a party and invite some friends to brighten your demeanor?" Ana began to joke with Ellie, "Oh a good party is just what you need about now!" Ellie looked away from them; suppressing her tears. "I believe I would like to take my mare Rose out for a ride and think on all this. Have your party Elena, I will stop in and visit with your guests."

Another two weeks of nausea, and still she was without her cycle. Ellie began to accept what she had known all along, she was with child, Gilley's child. She was working on her fine handwork for another new surcote that finally arrived from Edinburgh. It was made from beautiful gold brocade and she was appointing fine embroidery in silver and white around the collar, where the neck tie would be held by a lovely brooch. Ana knocked on her door, and came in to see her. "I am still with nausea and nothing has come to convince me I am not with child. I will have to make plans to secure myself to a convent and have my baby without notice. Will you help me write my Gilley and let him have the choice to take his child, for I can not in my station, without a husband?" Ana was filled with sorrow that she could not convince Ellie that her knight was worthy to marry her, that he would welcome her, child and all. "Of course I will my love, I will be most glad to so assist you." "Others now in the household are suspecting of my condition I fear; not being able to eat has revealed my fate. Would you have cook prepare me some more herb water with some oregano, or perhaps a tasine with ginger and lavender to ease my stomach?" Ana told her that a tasine was already on its way; the lavender and ginger would soothe her sickness with child.

She began with heavy heart to write her knight:

Sir Guillame de Duglas, Knight
Douglas Castle, Douglasdale, Lanarkshire

Dearest Gilley

I have found to my great sorrow and extreme shame of an embarrassed heart, that I am with child, your child Sir Guillame. I am seeking shelter of a convent to conceal my foolish deeds in Ayrshire's forests, lo those many weeks ago. I am revealing these words to you as my lover and friend, that you may seek your child for I have no husband to give name. My knight, Sir David, will arrive with this letter, he knows not the contents, but will await a letter of reply. I choose not to trust such news to an ordinary messenger. Please do not dally with your response, I am faint of heart to do this and will worry all the more if I do not receive word from you most quickly.

Lady Eleanora of Lovaine, relic of de Ferrers
Fawside Castle, Tranent, East Lothianes

And she then wrote: *My love for all eternity, to you always, Ellie*

4th of April, 9 days afore the Ides, Douglasdale

Hugh and Baron John Wishart were in the great hall, sharing a breakfast of porridge, cakes, and some fragrant Mounchelet, lamb stew. Sir John had just returned that morning from Northumbria, with a report on the manor of Fawdon and Gilley's other lands in Warndon, near Hexam and his own manor of Monilawes. Wishart and Gilley made the travels on each other's behalf on an annual basis as their land adjoined the other's nearby. It was not that their seneschals were untrustworthy, but a personal visit from the laird was always prudent and required in feudal business. Gilley was just rising for the day, his valet Thomas Dickson was bringing his clothes for the morning ride he planned. He did not go on the early hunt with the others this day, because he did not sleep well the night before. His neck was giving pain from the change in weather, as it had so every spring since the injury at Fawdon, doing battle with sword in the great hall.

Shamus was scratching on the door to come in, but Gilley was ready to leave now, so they both made their way down the carved wooden staircase: the unusual center stairs that connected the second floor of the great hall to the third floor of the laird's private chamber and other smaller chambers sectioned off for family members. "Oh Wishart, my friend, it is your boastful voice that I heard all the way up to my chamber. How are you and how are my tenants and rents from Northumbria?" Wishart rose to greet his old friend, laughing and smiling, knowing tonight would be a feast and celebration with some entertainment; it always was when one came to visit Douglasdale. Suddenly they all turned their attention to the main doors of the great hall. Shamus was barking loudly, when a squire came in with news of three riders coming up to the drawbridge that secured the castle from unknown visitors; one was a knight, the squire indicated. "Let him in, if we can't handle a single knight and his two riders, we should be of no further use to ourselves or this castle," barked Hugh.

Gilley rose at once with a look of surprise, then a wide smile spread across his face as he recognized the knight who just arrived, "Sir David, what brings you here to Douglas Castle?" "I have come with a letter for you Sir Gilley, from Lady Eleanora." Wishart gave a quizzical look to Hugh, as if to say, who is Sir Gilley, and who is this lady? Gilley grabbed the letter abruptly, and opened it, letting out a warrior's yell, which started Shamus to barking all the more. Hugh said to Wishart, "What my brother is trying to say is that our Shamus here scouted out a young English widow while on hunt some two months ago, and ever since, **Sir Gilley**, as he is now called, has been making plans of matrimony, yet without her consent I might add." Remembering his manners, Gilley began to introduce Sir David, first to Sir Hugh, "my brother, Clan Chief, and Lord of Douglas, and my friend of many years, Sir John Wishart of the Mearns and Northumbria." Then Gilley went to the visitor and asked directly, "Are you aware of the contents Sir David? You must know it is important to send a knight such as you to insure delivery, rather than a messenger servant." "I am not informed officially of its content, but there has been some talk at Fawside," he replied, giving Gilley a knowing smile that was returned. "She can not refuse me the third time, didn't I tell you! She is with child, another heir for Douglasdale, and a new bride for me! Shamus, you were dubbed a knight by your uncle Sir William, and you are ever bit the chivalric knight, a great hunter of the higher game."

With that, he sat down to pen a response to his lady, his bride to be now, he was sure. "Sir David, I will need your help in this endeavor, and you too Wishart, are you ready for an abduction of a beautiful English lady, and a wedding at the Abbey at Kelso, performed by my dear grandfather's friend, Father Josh?" Sir David hesitated as he sat down, "I can not be party to such an action, but I might help by saying the guarding of the castle is that designed by ladies unsuspecting and inexperienced of any foul play in that region." Gilley looked up, and smiling said, "Sir David, you have only to take as many of the men at arms as you can without suspect; to join you on the morning hunt three days hence. Sir John and I will arrive with a stately number of horsemen, arms and men at arms to convince the lady the prudence of accepting my proposal of marriage; giving our child the benefit of the Douglas name, and inheritance due. I have my uncles's tower house at nearby Hermanston, and Sir John, you can go ahead to meet me there." Then turning to his brother, "Your manor of Glencorse is too small I fear for our large entourage," he allowed, "and should we need reinforcements, dear Andrew could provide us with Douglas men so garrisoned at that good manor."

Hugh interrupted, "It is Andrew's son our cousin William Douglas, laird there now; for just this week have I received word from him, leaving his Linlithgow for the Lothianes' spring weather. He will be happy to have a visit from you. I will send some gifts for his generosity of lodging for you both and your men at arms." Gilley was now looking at Wishart who was enjoying the exuberance of the moment and the intrigue being planned, "Will you join me in this rescue? I know you like a good adventure, sure aye!" The baron nodded in amusement, "I came here to tell you of the bountiful, enthralling numbers of pigs and sheep, adding then only the great harvest of corn, barley, beans and wood, and you want to know if an adventure is on my mind to do? With such excitement of Northumbria just at hand? Aye, count Wishart in on this raid of matrimonial bliss. You will need the help of a steady influence in that endeavor. Where is this lady now staying, in all her mystery?"

"At Fawside Castle, the barony of Tranent," said Gilley. "She is a widow, though barely nineteen, and the relic of one de Ferrers, who married the widow of Earl Colban, do you recall the man?" Wishart knew immediately of de Ferrers, "More than a little forceful, making some enemies in Fife. He held the barony of Leuchars and Castle Knowes, an old de Quincy manor. So, he is dead, and she holds the dower?" Motioning to Sir David, "This good knight here has been in service to the family for nearly a decade and now with others in their party from Essex, they have been traveling across our Scotland, reviewing the lands, estates of her dower for her sustenance in life. These estates remain his children's from his marriage to Anne, the relic of Colban." Then more seriously, "There is one catch, her liege lord is Edward Plantagenet. I will have some explaining to do about the marriage without permission, even with a child involved. He has a vengeful temperament and might take this strongly. With your other lands and your manor of Monilawes both in Northumbria under English rule, you should know the risks." Without hesitation Wishart said, "I would not shy from such a tangled web of intrigue and adventure, so I will lead the charge for you. When do we begin?"

MY TRUTH LIES IN THE RUINS

Gilley finished his letter to Ellie, and passed it to Hugh, "Here my brother, these words should hold her there while we make our arrangements for the wedding. I will go to Kelso and bring the news, making preparations with our grandfather Archibald's friend, Father Josh, as he called him." Then turning to Ellie's knight, "Many thanks for your kind part Sir David, in this venture of the heart; for I truly love your Lady Eleanora. I had not admitted my station to her as I courted those many days in Ayrshire; wary of the many that have sought to wed a Douglas knight, yet could not bear to look upon this face so scarred in battles past. I have a young son, who comes here now, that needs a loving mother to raise him and mentor him in the finer ways." Young James was making his appearance with his nurse, squealing his name for his father, "Fad' er!" "Come here lad, your father is glad to see you."

Hugh was reading Gilley's letter to Lady Eleanora:

My dearest Ellie-

I am grieving for your unrest at such an inconvenience of our time together. I assure you that the Holy Mother Kirk will welcome you and our child yet growing in your fair self and that I, Sir Guillame of Duglas, Miles, will provide for this fortunate child of our creation as any noble father would. In the time of two Sundays, you will have word of my plans and provisions for your painful conveyance to a haven of safety and anonymity for the quiet counsel of your stay. Your words do not reveal a mind of one who would choose marriage to a rogue of a knight such as I, so I will not yet inquire in that manner. Should you reconsider your heart, please send me notice for I will rush to your side for a ceremony of grace and promise in the most holy of kirks of your discretion and preference. I remain humble and faithful aye, to your service.

My love for you has not waned, it is stronger still. I yearn to touch and comfort you, and in two Sundays, will. Gilley

"My brother, your words are well chosen. Take whatever you need for provisions; horses and men at arms. Will you and your riders honor us with your company this night Sir David? For we were putting on a good feast for Wishart, and now have a betrothal to celebrate," said Hugh, uncharacteristically exuberant. "It is my pleasure to be a guest in this fine house of Douglas, Lord Hugh. And I believe our Lady Eleanora could do no better than to marry your redoubtable brother Sir Guillame." Gilley sealed the letter with his ring as it sank firmly into the blue paraffin and beeswax, then he gave it to Ellie's knight to take with him when he returned to Travernent. "My birthday comes on the Ides, and I will be thirty eight, with a young son, another child on the way, and a lovely bride to share my bed. I am truly a fortunate man this day," he said, giving James to his nurse. "I must find Thomas to help me choose some fine mantel and surcote for this special day. And dear brother, where are the wedding clothes of our own sweet mother? And you know I mean not the Lady Constancia. I will pack Martha's lovely surcote of gold velvet and white brocade and the shimmering silk veil that so graced her lovely face." He looked away, saying quietly, "I miss our mother, though thirty years she has been gone from us." Then Gilley abruptly stood up; he was already on his way to find Thomas and begin packing clothing and gifts for the wedding at Kelso Abbey. Hugh called out to him, "You will find our sister has stored the wedding clothes of our mother in the old war chest of our father, in the laird's chamber. Our good father's mantels and cloaks you will find as well. Take what you need."

Gilley was up early the next morning, writing a letter to his cousin William at Hermanston that Wishart would deliver. He then visited the vaulted cellars and his locked room there where he kept his healer's box and dried herbs. He quickly perused the chamber, grabbed his wee box and locked the door behind him. As he made his way through the dark corridors, he quickened his step when he saw the light of the turnpike stairs ahead. Gilley deftly bolted the steps to the kitchen; he was on a mission to find the cook and supply himself with fresh herbs that he might need for Ellie, now that she was with child. I am to have another wife and heir; how quickly my life has changed so, he mused. It was then that he reflected on the wedding he planned. He hoped that Josh would agree to perform the ceremony at the small chapel at Kelso Abbey.

The traditions and history of the abbey were closely tied to the Douglas family over many decades. Kelso Abbey was a special place ever since William's uncle, Brice of Douglas, posthumously the good St. Brice, first served Kelso Abbey, where he was the Prior of Lesmahagow. He was later to become the Bishop of Moray; returning to their Flemish roots, residing near Moraydale. In that ancient shire in the Highlands, Bishop Brice built

MY TRUTH LIES IN THE RUINS

Spynie Palace. He was canonized after his death at Spynie, and buried near the family seat there. The proud descendent of Freskin the Fleming was the first of many Douglas sons who entered service in the House of God. Four more Douglas men, Alexander, Henry, Hugh and Freskin, were canons at Spynie; Freskin becoming dean of Moray while Hugh was archdeacon of that see. For the Douglas's continued support of these houses of God, they received many gifts. Some forty years later in 1270, Gilley's own father William received lands and the messuage of Polnele from the Kelso abbot's holdings in Lesmahagow for his faithful counsel and service to the abbey. The Douglas family in turn entrusted the abbey to hold the Douglas family charters for safe keeping at the priory. Being married at Kelso Abbey was a special choice, for a special situation he thought.

Figure XIX-Part One; ruins of Kelso Abbey; small chapels framed by wooden screens were once in stone alcoves near the left of the image

As Gilley reflected on his plans he said out loud, "On the first year anniversary of our marriage, we can hold a fine ceremony to celebrate our vows, at our family kirk in Douglasdale." "Or perhaps her family might enjoy the pleasure of a ceremony at their manor kirk," groused an amused Hugh. Gilley just sighed at his brother's words; he was very pleased with his work. Planning these events was a labor of love for him. He thrived in such matters. Gilley barely heard Hugh as he continued to speak; his mind was on the wedding and his plans. He would wear the mantel of his father, an exquisite red velvet cape, trimmed in ermine and gold brocade. A matching hat in red with ermine too, he added, would remind his lady that he was not some ordinary knight, but a Douglas, someday to become Lord Douglas, as his brother often reminded him; his health deteriorating so formidably this year.

Figure XX-Part One; Pittarrow Mains; the only remains of the once great estate of the Baron of the Mearns, Sir John Wishart

Looking over at Hugh, reflecting on his lonely life without his Marjory, Gilley decided he should be more respectful of the man and laird who looked after him since their father passed. "Yes my brother; you are most correct. We will address such matters with her family when we return," Gilley told him. He was overcome with sadness as he got up to take his leave of Hugh. His brother's health was on his mind; but there was nothing Hugh would allow Gilley to do. Hugh was so much like their father in his demeanor he thought; even the gruffness of his voice and the choice of his words were similar to Sir William's. The younger son often felt that his brother had actually become the father that he barely knew. Now the grave pallor on Hugh's face and his slow steps revealed the agony of a body deteriorating faster than his forty-six years. Hugh had always been there for him. Even at his birth, it was Hugh who helped his mother to the laying-in room for the midwives to take over. His father had left in 1249 to visit his kin and the house of Moravia at the family seat of Kinloss in Morayshire.

There he witnessed charters at Kinloss Abbey. William, fifth Lord Douglas, did not return to Douglasdale until the summer of 1250, two months after Gilley was born.

The sun peeked out over Douglasdale that next morning; the moorish, grouse heather lands glistened in the silver of morning dew. In just four months the Tinto would be awash in a sea of purple heather, reflected Gilley as he perused the Clyde valley that was Douglasdale, his paradise. But there was little time to waste he told himself! Out he ran to round up his men at arms, along with extra horses for themselves and for the ladies for the long ride; some pack horses too, laden with gifts for his cousin were commanded to the courtyard. These horses and provisions would soon set out with Wishart and his men for their journey of the heart, as he called it. The baron of the Mearns with his Pittarrow men at arms, and some good men of Douglasdale, took the pack animals heading north towards Edinburgh and then east to Hermanston. Gilley with a smaller contingency of Douglas men at arms went south through Peebles; then continued on to Kelso.

It was just outside of Peebles near Traquair that they planned to stop overnight at a Douglas stronghold, one of several estates owned by the family in the area. Because they were making good time, riding hard all the day, Gilley chose to stay in Craig Douglas, the more accessible earth and timber tower keep north of the Yarrow Water. By the second day they had arrived at Kelso Abbey, where Gilley met with Josh. Always glad to see his old friend's grandson or any others from the noble house of Douglas, Josh was flattered that he had chosen him and Kelso Abbey's chapels for their sacraments of marriage. Gilley explained their meeting in Ayrshire, that they were both widow and widower, both exuberant at finding love to celebrate their lives. And in that festivity they were brought to an embarrassed circumstance, requiring a quickened pace for their courting and marriage, as the Lady was with child. Josh told him that the Abbot would not return until the end of May, so his time was free to perform the happy ceremony. "It would be a celebration for me as well as you young people," he said, as he called Gilley and Ellie now.

Gilley thanked the old priest, and told him they would be back before the end of three days, giving himself an extra day in case the Scottish spring weather made travel too strenuous for his bride. And before this second day was over, the small group was heading west to Dryburgh for the night. When they rose the next morning, the longer hours of the spring day beckoned them with clear skies and bright sun for their journey. Riding north, through the wilds of Tweedale, Gilley and his men at arms spurred their horsed forward to their destination; arriving at Hermanston in the late evening by a setting sun. His cousin was excited by the knight's arrival, greeting him with a feast in his honor. "We are sorry to have started without you dear cousin. Old Wishart here said you would come this night certain, so we set the feast and so began, hoping the sounds of our merriment would entice you to come all the faster."

"Dear Will, I am so glad to look upon your fine face, and now I hear, the laird of his manor, this is a fine night indeed." The younger cousin smiled at Gilley, pointing now in mocked tones, "It is true then, that you are going to abduct yourself a bride from the barony of Tranent?" Gilley was laughing in his festive mood, "Yes it is true, but she is an angel, a Flemish lass from Essex; she would consent most freely were she to know of our plans. So the abduction is to hide her true circumstance, and allow her to marry without consent of her liege lord, Edward Plantagenet." Will gave his cousin a curious look. "The baron Wishart here did not tell me of this subterfuge, what is this mystery, and consent of Edward? Are you that bold le Hardi, to defy the King of England with your manors at risk in Northumbria?" Gilley lowered his voice, and quietly told his younger cousin, "She is with child, our child, from our courting in Ayrshire, a hunting trip and much rain causing the embarrassment of our situation." Young Will beckoned the Douglas knight to come and sit at the large table in the great hall, "The rains in Scotland's forests, the curse or the blessing, upon us, who is to decide that one?" The laughter of many men at arms drowned out any response that might have come, for the jesters and other players were about the gallery.

Figure XXI-Part One; Hermanston was one of two manors given in charter by the Earl of Fife to Sir Archibald of Douglas, 4th Lord Douglas; the manor later settled on his younger son Andrew Douglas of Linlithgow; ruins above are of a later tower owned by the St. Clairs.

Gilley excused himself early, adjourning to a third floor chamber reserved for Douglas family members. He was grateful for his friend Wishart's support in the Tranent endeavor and for his cousin's generous hospitality in lodging this night. Tonight as well Gilley gave thanks to his God; praying for His grace for the deeds so planned. The Crusader then asked of St. Bride, the Douglas patron saint, that she protect them on the morrow most as well; that his deeds of the heart meet with success. As he lay awake in his chamber he reflected on is good fortune: in just four days he would bring Ellie home to Douglasdale as his bride, Lady Eleanora Douglas. Sleeping was not easy for Gilley this night, he was too happy.

Fawside Castle, the same night

Ellie was reading the letter from Gilley that her knight Sir David delivered just before evening prayer. "Ana, he is going to send me word in two weeks on a haven that I might seek to hide my sorry self." Ana looked up from her work. "Is that all he says dear lass?" she asked surprised with the absence sentiment. "He did not mention his proposal?" Ellie looked up from her bed, still with nausea, sipping her ginger and lavender tasine, trying valiantly to improve her condition. "I can not think on this, I am too wanting to pout this evening, too miserable in my nausea and self pity to understand his meaning." She tossed the letter aside with a dismissive defiance. Ana put away her surcote while asking her about her plans for the next day. "Are you going riding on the morrow?" Ellie pouted even more, "No! I can not, my knights and squires are all going on the morning hunt and I am left to wait on *them*!" Sensing an outburst of temper coming, Ana decided to make light of the situation. "Well at least you will have time for your beauty sleep," she quipped jovially. With a fit of pique on her tongue and an aching pain in her heart, Ellie looked up at Ana with a pitifully grimace. She about to speak when she broke down into tears instead. "Why can't Gilley just come and take me off to Douglasdale?" she sobbed. "We could be wed and I could be happy for once in my sorry life." Ana went to her girl and held her, rubbing her back and drying her tears. "There love, your knight will come, just give him time."

Ellie was barely off to sleep when loud disturbing noises followed by chilling screams from Lady de la Zouche came from outside her door. Entering Ellie's bedchamber, the elderly woman shouted her concerns. "Quick Eleanora, we are under siege and all our men at arms save the ancient one who works with the kennel hounds, are out on the hunt. Get up at once I beseech you child; here is your Ana to help with your dressing." Lady Elena was already on her way to the great hall as Ellie barely rose from her sleepy, grouchy state. She looked up from her bed, "Is it always so

DEBORAH RICHMOND FOULKES

light here so early in the morning, and what of all this commotion? Is what I hear those dreadful Fawside winds that prey upon us; those loud, unsettling noises of unrest? I despise so those gales of discontent," she moaned, consumed by her own petulant state and physical discomfort. Ana quickly brought Ellie her clothes. "It is not the winds my child. We are being attacked by a band of armed marauders. They are riding horses up the hill to the castle; looks to be twenty or thirty men at arms. They are brandishing armor and arms, carrying standards, the likes of which I do not recall."

Figure XXII-Part One; the raid of the heart may have begun from this vantage point, Fawside Castle

The frightened cries and shrieks of maid servants in the lower floors were heard; the portcullis rumbled open, the command of a foreign male voice was plainly heard. Horses' hooves were pounding on the wooden drawbridge in an ominous and foreboding rhythm; a raw fear swept over the castle like the chilling wind, creaking and moaning through the shuttered arrow slits. Suddenly these armed horse dismounted. They became armed foot invading the castle, penetrating the walls within; overcoming Fawside's meager defenses, as they brandished swords and shields, carried battle axes; hiding daggers discretely behind their targes. In confident control now of the fortress, their commander threw open the large oak door of the keep. Perceiving no resistance, he led his men up the tight, dark quarters of the turnpike stairs to the great hall, dimly lit by tallow torches mounted on the far wall by the huge fireplace, barely aglow from the prior evening's feasting. Seated at the head of the trestled table of the great hall was the wrathful, defiant Lady Elena de la Zouche. Without words the Scottish knight motioned his squires to carefully assist this indignant lady to the stone steps that lead to the family quarters of the keep.

Figure XXIII-Part One; Fawside or Fa'side as it is called today sits perched upon this hill near the village of Tranent; on a clear day one can see as far as Ben Lomond

Mounting the turnpike stairs once again, brushing aside the few servants he encountered the Scottish knight beckoned his men at arms with their captive lady to the upper levels of the dunjon tower. These thirty armed marauders engulfed Fawside castle, overwhelmed the household, spreading fear and panic wherever they went. Pandemonium raced through the upper chambers as younger servants fled the invaders; running in hopes of finding safety in the other parts of the tower. Ellie was barely adjusting her surcote and veil, when Lady Elena was forcibly escorted into her presence by six men at arms. Ellie looked upon their commander; he appeared to be a knight or baron, wearing mail with full armaments and a tabard with armorial achievements that she did not recognize.

This flamboyant warrior bowed to the ladies with a bemused look and began to read from a scroll of parchment: "By the orders of Hubicus, Dominus de Duglas, these men at arms have been sent to secure one Lady Eleanora, late the relic of de Ferrers, to his castle in Douglasdale for the purpose of marrying his brother, Sir Guillame of Duglas, miles." Ellie felt light headed, the words she repeated, questioning her own hearing, "His brother?" she said in disbelief, "Gilley is his brother?" "Yes, he is the brother of Lord Hugh, Chief of the Douglas Clan," said a deep voice from behind her. Ellie recognized at once, her heart leaping with joy, the words of her knight now walking up behind her. Gilley had slipped through the side door to her chamber. "Sir Guillame is here to claim his betrothed!" he said with the bravado and mocked gestures of a great laird making his entrance to court. Then in more modest tones he said, "My Ellie, I told you, your answer would be yes the third time," as Ellie rushed to his arms.

He was in full armor for the times, wearing a metal helm over his mail coif, his eye plate opened so she could see his face. Ermine adorned his helmet in a flamboyant display of his prowess and station. A white and azure silk tabard with armorials of three mullets on a chief was worn over his mail hauberk and gambeson. What a glorious figure he is, she thought as her eyes ran up and down his manly frame. Her knight in armor was in deed coming to her rescue, just like the dreams she shared with Alice on those rides at Woodham Ferrers. Elena de la Zouche released her grip on her captors, realizing this raid was an affair of the heart not a robbery with fire and sword as she had feared. She begged her leave to her chamber and was escorted there without resistance.

"Oh Gilley, I am so sorry..." Ellie started to say, only to be interrupted, as was his dismissive fashion when he was set upon an action. "Ana, please see to her packing; we will send for the others of her belongings to be delivered later when we are settled. You will have to pack for yourself too Ana; we could not leave without you," Gilley motioned to the men at arms to depart his lady's chamber, instructing some to watch the rest of the household; holding off any chance of mischief. Sir John began barking orders; speaking quickly and with authority. "A look around outside; then a patrol to set, I will secure it le Hardi," Wishart said to Gilley as he turned to leave the chamber. He was the perfect man for the day; he gave orders and directed the men at arms without mishap. "Now, my dear wife to be, you will do me the honor of a kiss for all my trouble here," and he leaned down and took her in his arms, and kissed her strongly on the mouth. Pleased with himself and his raid of the heart, Gilley began to take a breath, to take in everything, to take good look of her. Then as if he just realized the magnitude of his deeds this early morning, he said, "I am truly blessed to have such a beautiful lass."

"Oh Gilley, I did not want it to be like this," she moaned, then looking very ill, she moved away from him quickly, motioning to Ana to help her to the latrine. "Are you quite all right, my sweet lass, what is the trouble here?" "She is with the sickness of being with child, it should subside in a week or two," said Ana. Gilley knew what to do at once, and was grateful that he had brought his healing box of herbs and oils, and that he had replenished his fresh herbs before he left Douglasdale. "Please, concentrate on the packing Ana, I will take care of Ellie. I have something outside in my healer's box that will ease your nausea; to give it you shortly. We must make fast on our leaving here, before the riders of the morning hunt return." He turned to his

MY TRUTH LIES IN THE RUINS

squire Patric, "Please go to my horse and get the box for remedies I carry; be quick about it."

When Patric returned, Gilley got out some ginger and added lemon, honey, and a little thyme with lavender, in a thickness he gave to her on a spoon. "Take some of this while sipping the tasine Ana has sent for, but taking care to swallow as much of this as you can keep down. There are more remedies we can use, but some like hyssop can not be taken when one is with child." Ellie looked up at him thinking to herself, where have you been hiding all these years, that some fortunate lady, prettier than I would not have caught your eye? Then she said to him quietly, "You amaze me so with your knowledge; a healer too, my sweet knight?" A broad smile crossed his face for a moment, "Wonders you have not yet seen, do I perform for you my sweet lass. Now, pull yourself together, we have a long ride ahead of us if we are to be wed on the morrow night." The words suddenly registered, he is here to marry me, and tomorrow night!

Gilley left the room, in his usual abrupt manner with something pressing on his mind. When he at last returned he was pacing; growing impatient with Ellie and Ana, as his bride was taking more items out of the traveling chests than she was putting back in them! "We must leave immediately. Ana, you finish as best you can, we will send for the rest." "Oh no Gilley, I need these things, please don't be so quick with your words." He turned to her, as he would in the years to come; he would be kind, yet firm with his words: "Ellie, we have not the time to dally with whims of a lady and her maid in wait. Men at arms must now depart, to avoid the confrontation of warriors and their weapons. You would feel great pain of guilt should one of my men run afoul of a sword, unnecessarily detained by your decisions of attire. I know you would, so we are departing fair lady, and now!" With that, he picked her up carefully in his very large, strong arms. He motioned to Ana to finish packing what she had set out and went through the door of the chamber, down the curved stone steps of the turnpike stairs to the small drawbridge at the front of the tower entrance.

Ellie was not surprised. He had his ways; she knew that the first day. "So it's le Hardi that your friends know you by; now I know why. You have bold ways my knight, I should not be frightened though, I warn you. I am of the same temperament that you so gallantly display. I tell you that now, so you may change your mind before it is too late!" Gilley set her down and patiently, quietly said to her, "I have not ridden all these days to change my mind. We are to be married, aye; *it is done*." With one fluid motion he got up on his horse and instructed Patric to hand her up to him. "You don't trust me to ride on my own horse?" He simply looked at her with those deep dark eyes, and then a broad smile crossed his face, "Not one bit M' lady; not for one moment until Fawside Castle is far behind us and your fears of Lord Edward have become lost in your memory."

Elena's groom was coming from the stables with Ellie's mare; saddled and ready from a quick walk and warm up. Ana was coming out from the castle with Patric and another squire not far behind, carrying two chests and a small cloth bag. Ellie recognized the bag at once, containing the gifts she purchased for Gilley and Shamus in Edinburgh. "Oh Ana, thank you for remembering," she said as she gave the small package to him. "Here, a wedding gift for you and one too for your, ah, *our* silly hound now, as I bought them on our journey back from Ayrshire; stopping at the royal burgh we did some shopping." Ana took Ellie's horse Rose with the special custom saddle of side footings; she would be riding the mare side saddle this day she chuckled at herself.

Le Parker was now making his way out through the fray. "M' Lady, will you advise me of your plans in some few days. I need to know if my services should be retained." Before she could respond Gilley said clearly, "Your services are most required and appreciated as well. An honest seneschal is worth his weight. Lord Hugh will contact you directly; continuing your employment by an agreement to your liking. You may write us through that laird, Hugh de Douglas, if there is great hurry for reply." And Ellie added, "But please do not inform my family of what has transpired, unless you have no choice. Please tell them I am going willingly, but tell Edward nothing. We will contend with him at a later time." Then turning to her late husband's aunt, "And my dear Lady Elena, please do not send the men at arms after my person when they shall return. I am quite in concert with this good knight's intentions." Lady de la Zouche smiled, "I should say that abduction by a handsome, noble knight is the highest compliment can be given any lady! I will not interfere. Let us know where to send the rest of your things when all is safe to do so."

Wishart was returning from his patrol of the manor with his men. "It looks to be safe for us to depart, but we should do so quickly, the morning passes fast." Gilley nodded to him and said, "Let's go." And suddenly the Douglas entourage was riding fast, spurring their destriers and palfreys forward; leaving Travernent far behind them, they arrived at Dalkeith before they would finally stop. Gilley dismounted and went over to his friend, "Wishart, I am forever in your debt. I shall name our first son John, after the great baron of the Mearns who made this wedding possible. You and your men are set to go, as we shall ride on to Kelso Abbey." The old knight removed his round battle helmet, in polite gesture to Ellie, "My dear lass, I hope you can improve on the angry disposition and the lack of good manners from this rogue of a knight le Hardi. Good luck there, aye. And the best of health to you and the young Douglas you carry in your sweet self."

He turned to Gilley with a silly grimace. Then Baron Wishart mounted his horse with stylish bravado; he was eager to depart the Lothianes for the kingdome of Fife then northward towards the Mearns and his Pittarrow. As he turned to leave he smiled triumphantly. "I will want to be at the christening of my God son, so keep old Wishart informed!"

Ana suggested to Gilley that they make time to rest and eat, "for my girl has not yet broken her fast from the night." Gilley took Ellie down from his horse, and motioned to Patric and the other squire Henry, "Set up the cakes and stew that the cook from Hermanston has packed for us." Looking over to his bride to be he said, "Do you think you could eat a little now, my girl?" Ellie surprised herself, she was feeling better, and accepted some of the stew, realizing she had not held food for almost two days. "This feels good going down. I think it might stay there too," she smiled. Nothing feels better than this day, this moment she thought. I am marrying a man who loves me, who risks everything to be with me, even his lands in Northumbria. No man has ever risked his lands or his life for me. Ah, but nothing is safe from King Edward's wrath should he put a mind to it she sighed. I do pray that old woman from Winton is of a foolish mind, and her words will be unfounded. I do pray it is so.

They made Galashiels late that evening, having stopped for meals and short rest earlier in the day. By nightfall they were all exhausted and hungry. Even Ellie's appetite was improved and she was gaining her strength. Once they reached Stow, Gilley allowed her to ride her own mare. She looked over at him as they rode down the old cart trail, "I can not believe this day for us has come, I am sure this is a dream. Only please don't wake me from it Gilley, never wake me from this wonderful dream!" The knight sighed and gave her his now famous smirk. "This dream of yours is your new life with your loving husband, my dear sweet girl. We will have twenty children and acquire many lands for them all to inherit. And I will teach my sons to be gallant knights, true warriors with core values to guide them in their lives. They will be trained in the arms of our great country, Scotland, aye. And tested true by their redoubtable father, a Knight of the Kingdome of Scotland, for I will see to their training myself," Gilley told her proudly; but he was not finished. He cheerfully continued, filling her head with his vision for their lifetime together. "And their dear sweet mother will school them in the finer arts of song, and dance, poetry, and fine wine and the language of the court. This was my dream that has come true now with your consent to marry me."

Ellie's eyes were wide with astonishment, "Twenty children? Who is it that you plan to marry then, me or a brood mare? I will be with child from June to May the year next. Twenty Children! You seem to have planned much in my absence since we left Ayrshire," she teased him. And the next words from her warrior knight, took her breath away all the more. Gilley peered shyly at her as he spoke softly. "With child is how I love to see a woman, for it is then that she holds two spirits within her, one God's gift of love that she nurtures growing within her; the other one her own sweet self," he said. The poet knight drew a loving portrait of a wee one not yet born, inside the mother; creating the perfect roundness of a woman with child. "It is this lass, my sweet wife yet with child I crave so to hold in my arms," he told Ellie; sharing his most private thoughts with her. She shook her head in mock disbelief of his words, tilting back her head with a teasing sigh, "You are a strange warrior le Hardi, one with deep thoughts and passionate ideas that surprise me more each day," Gilley was unmoved by her response. He looked at her with a bemused countenance; my plans are made and will betide, he resolved. *It is done*.

The lodging at Galashiels was comfortable, but awkward as they were unable to secure enough rooms. Gilley slept in a small bed in the same chamber where Ellie shared a bed with Ana. "I feel silly that you should sleep on the little bed Sir Gilley," she said. "Ellie and I have not shared a bed since she was thirteen, and it was just before her wedding night to Lord de Ferrers. On this occasion, I would say that the lady to be your wife is happier this day," she chuckled. "Do not fret Ana; you will not be sleeping with my Ellie on the morrow for I will be seeking my rights as her husband and laird. Good night you two, and don't keep this laird awake this night with your giggling or I will have to take strong measure to silence the two of you!" he said laughing all the while in mocked indignation at their cramped accommodations. It was a wonderful night, even if he had to sleep on the floor it was a perfect night in deed.

Father Josh was pleased to see his guests arrive, and happy that the abduction of the lady evolved as planned into a rescue, for the lovers appeared inseparable. They were shown rooms they would use to dress for the ceremony, the sacraments of their marriage. "Here Ana, I have brought these from Douglasdale," as he handed her a bundle that held Lady Martha's wedding clothes. "They are my dear mother's Ellie; she would want you to wear them in her honor." Ellie was taken aback, clearly moved by these words and deeds. "How could you think of so many things; how could one man be so thoughtful of my needs?" Gilley just nodded and went towards his room, "I will call for you when we are ready to begin." Ana closed the door behind them, "You are one fortunate lady, here let me help you with that," she said, undressing her girl as she spoke.

A light wrap on the door announced Patric's arrival with another package from their laird. "Sir Guillame has sent you these," he said, giving her a ribboned strand of rosemary to adorn Lady Martha's lovely fillet. "And one for you as well," he smiled, giving the second one to Ana. "Are you both yet ready?" he asked. They nodded yes, so he led them to the chapel. Gilley looked upon her, marveling at his good fortune; she looked so young and innocent, and beautiful beyond words. Ellie was overwhelmed when she saw her handsome knight in the red velvet cloak of his father; trimmed with the ermine and a grand hat to match. Then her eyes caught the familiar silver buttons, her gift to him that he used as the fasteners on his exquisite mantel of lush purple silk brocade. He took her hand and kissed it. Then patting it gently he said, "You have made radiant the lovely surcote of Lady Martha, my mother. Were she here to see you, she would be so happy and proud, this our wedding day." Gilley took her arm and they entered the small side chapel, one of several at Kelso Abbey. The twenty guests were their escorts, squires, Ana, and some others of the Douglas household traveling with them. The ceremony was simple; their vows were taken in the archway of the wooden screen, then the sacraments were ceremoniously given at the altar. Some weddings take so long Ellie reflected; but this one seemed to rush before her own eyes. Suddenly the ritual was coming to a close; she looked down at her hands, a little woven gold band was on her left hand ring finger, as she watched herself put a gold ring on his left hand. Gilley wrapped a two foot long piece of black and grey woven cloth around the grasp of both their hands, as the priest completed his words. The wedding was over; the mass having been said Gilley pushed aside her veil and kissed her gently. "There will be time for more of this later," he whispered in her ear triumphantly.

"Thank you Father Josh. We are both indebted to you for the inconvenience of our matters." The priest spoke jovially as they walked out from the chapel, "My dear Guillame, if all my ceremonies would unite two such lovers as you and Lady Douglas, I would be a happy priest in deed. It was my pleasure, for you both. Now, a light repast has been planned by some in the monastery to honor you both, will you come this way?" Ellie was barely feeling the floor beneath her feet as she walked; Lady Douglas, I am Lady Eleanora Douglas. Oh what changes have come in my life in these four short months.

Their escorts and small traveling party brought them to Moss Tower, four miles from Kelso, where they would stay the night. "This tower house is the home of my cousin, William de Moray, who has his family seat at Bothwell, to the north and east of Douglasdale," said Gilley. "I made arrangements for our stay, but as you can see, only the steward of the manor is here now, along with the rest of the household servants. We will visit Bothwell after we leave Douglasdale, for some private travels of our own. It is a glorious place on the Clyde, yet not completed." Ellie asked about the relationship between the two families. "These de Morays, they seem to be very close to the Douglas clan, is that so?" Gilley explained, "My great grandmother was a de Moray; we keep close in our ways with them as well as with our lands; my Flemish heritage of the Highlands ways," he told her. Then Ellie looked quizzically at him, realizing they never spoke of their true heritage. "That my kin are from Flanders most as well," she said excitedly. Gilley smiled, "I know." He then explained how close the de Morays were to his family. "My father signed for surety for Walter de Moray, father of William, for the barony of Bothwell, for his heirs and lands forever. By this agreement alone would we be kin, closer than kin, where a Scotsman's land surety was pledged, aye. We will enjoy our stay with the de Morays too I think," he told her happily.

The accommodations were perfect, and Ana had her own small room, a nurse's room nearby, while the squires took turns outside their door, watchful of any mischief that might transpire. "We must still be alert Ellie," Gilley told her, "We can never be too careful until we have settled this matter with Lord Edward. But we are safe this night I feel. No one knows we might come here to the de Moray stronghold." He then came to her as she was sitting on a small bench, watching him, listening to his every word. She had placed herself on this bench since Ana had helped her with a scented bath and attire for her bridal night; waiting for Gilley, feeling a little awkward. "I want you always to feel safe my Ellie, for I would never hurt you, and would kill instantly the man who did." He picked her up and set her on his lap. As he reached for the brooch on her neck fastenings he asked in his charming shyness, "May I?"

Figure XXIV-Part One; little remains of Moss Tower today; a small sign, a wee mound of rubble and stone that once was the proud fortress of the de Morays, before them the Olifards

MY TRUTH LIES IN THE RUINS

They stayed overnight in the Douglas stronghold in Traquair that next evening. The larger estate was more luxurious than their manors in Craig Douglas he told her. And more difficult to access; for security alone it was Gilley's first choice. This last night of their journey was quiet and comfortable: secured by Douglas men at arms; served by Douglas family servants. When they rose the next day, the excitement began to build with each passing hour for their arrival in Douglasdale. They stopped briefly at Broughton for sustenance and quick rest. The newly weds were chattering away. Gilley had explained that he lived with his brother as Hugh had no other family now; leaving the seclusion of Park Castle for the family seat at Douglas Castle where the laird maintained his residence. It would be a good welcome when they arrived. The travelers covered many miles this day, riding long hours, deciding not to stop again until they reached home.

Figure XXV-Part One; the beautiful Borders region of Scotland; a scenic view near Traquair, once a stronghold for the Douglases

As the sun began its slow descent Gilley became more animated anticipating their arrival at Douglasdale. "We have been fortunate to miss the rains this journey; to so arrive before the hour now at Douglas Castle," he said with a broad smile. "It is only an hour's ride?" Ellie gasped, letting out a squeal of excitement. "And tell me more of what this castle looks like." He began to describe with the detail of an architect the newer angle towers, two of which protruded from the rubble and stone walls built around the front entrance. "My father commissioned the building of three donjons; protruding towers, battlemented to add to our defenses. He did so in his life time, but never saw of their completion sadly. Sir William's intentions were to emulate the castle of his cousin; that he planned to rival competition with Bishop Gilbert's Kildrummy," he chuckled. "Our de Moray kin hearing of his plans built of more himself. That Aberdeen fortress is immense!"

Ellie wanted to hear more about the family's living space. Gilley responded happily, as he described their four story battlemented keep; the third floor reserved for family's lodging and the laird's chamber. The fortress itself was constructed of stone and rubble, a tower built on a motte. This tower used for the family's living areas came decades before the three outer donjon towers his father designed. Ellie listened intently; learning quickly that Gilley had a penchant for telling the complete story, to the very last detail. His bride was not feigning her interest however; she shared in his enthusiasm; enjoying the thoughtful replies to her inquiries. He explained the need for defensive measures in the lowlands to her; elaborating on the vulnerability of Scots living in the marches. "My father said the family took their lessons from the past, the knowledge of our Highland kin he applied to Douglasdale. He often told us of the men of Moray so easily defeated; their rebellion ruthlessly thwarted by King David; their fortresses laid to waste and quickly. Well before he was Lord Douglas his father had decided on a motte and bailey structure for defensive measures to provide enough security for our Douglas stronghold," Gilley said as he told her how thoroughly pleased he was with her interest in such things.

Figure XXVI-Part One; artist's concept of Douglas Castle 1289; three protruding towers and a keep or donjon surrounded by a moat, accessible by only a wooden drawbridge

Ellie smiled shyly and begged him to continue. Life with her Gilley was certainly different from any other lord she had known in England. He took her request cheerfully, continuing the stories of his family's history. "My father revered his great, great grandfather Freskin the Fleming and envied his massive fortress at Duffus in Morayshire, the family seat. But before our

MY TRUTH LIES IN THE RUINS

Freskin moved north to Moray, he built himself a tower house near our lands in Livingston with a motte and other defenses in place." Ellie wondered if the family always lived in such splendor. "Did your Douglases command forever such a tower house and fortress my Gilley?" she asked. "No Ellie. The family's first residence in Douglasdale was a two story earth and timber hall with vaulted cellars, yet standing behind the keep, filing in the courtyard. We use the old hall for baronial business and court." Ellie and Gilley chattered away as she gave him question after question. "Where will we sleep? How many men at arms do you need to defend such a stronghold? Are servants made to sleep in the great hall or do they have their own quarters?" On and on she went with the enthusiasm of a young wife so happy with her new home. And Gilley was her equal, ready to share the minutia of detail. "The keep has vaulted stone cellars, far grander than the others. We use these for kitchens, storage vaults of vast quantity, my healing herb room, as well as the baronial prison and a pit."

Ellie was intrigued by the special herb room and wanted to hear more. "What is this private chamber or vault that you speak of?" Ellie asked. "You will see in good fashion, when your time comes to bring our child into the world; for with my work you will experience no pain with the delivery." Taken aback by his answer, she realized he meant to be a major part of that activity as well! What else must he intend to do, she mused. He took her pause as opportunity to continue all the more. "The most unusual feature is the scale-and-platt stair of carved heavy oak that leads from the second floor off the great hall to the third of the family residences. There is a lovely chapel there too, next to the laird's chamber, where we shall have morning prayers. Above this floor is the parapet entered by means of a turnpike stair." With true passion for details of his family home, he continued to speak of the wall walk and the small timber buildings there that housed some of the men at arms.

In knowing words he shared the privacy of his special place, "The parapet walk makes for a wonderful vantage point to enjoy the night air in safety, surveying our lands. In my father's day we only had the keep; that after he returned from the Isle of Mann in 1266, completing there his work for King Alexander, he began the construction of the two donjons near the drawbridge." Gilley went on to explain that the third tower was financed from the Abbot of Kelso's largesse; a gift of much appreciation for his father's fine work on the abbey's finances. "My father spent much time securing the Abbey's rents and other income, once in great confusion," said Gilley, "These towers took almost eleven years to construct; but my father saw not their completion as I have said." his words trailing off as he reflected on the great laird who held the peace in Douglasdale for thirty-two years as Lord Duglas.

"Would he be here now my father, he would be happy to welcome you into our clan," said Gilley. He still used the Highland expression of clan to designate the family and tenants of their lands even though in the Scottish Lowlands these relationships were more like the feudal arrangements of Norman England. That was his way; reverence for the past. Ellie seemed to hang on his every word; there was much she had to learn of the ways of Scotland. But for now she was content to ride at his side, listen to his kind words; welcoming words that pleased her greatly. Gilley seemed so proud that she was his wife. No one had ever loved her so, she sighed wistfully to herself.

"You do not feign enthusiasm about our Douglasdale; I can see your face light with each word I speak. How is it so that such a fair lass like yourself has such interests?" "Oh Gilley, I enjoy seeing you so happy; and I am intrigued by the building of great castles that seem to defend your Scotland so well." He thought for a few moments and added, "The castles are not so much to defend our Scotland, but the families inside." He went on to explain that the protruding towers were built for better vantage point should the castle be attacked. "It sounds so perfect, there must be little left to do but enjoy the living there," sighed Ellie. He shook his head with a strong no, "There is much left to do. We have only a small stone curtain wall. It is not yet half extended around the castle inside; only running the length between the two front towers. The rest of the defense is of timber extraction. And there are many timber buildings in the courtyard behind the keep....I should like to change that and the timber palisade someday."

He looked over at his bride, and smiled sheepishly, realizing that he had monopolized their conversation, allowing her barely a word between his speeches. "I am sorry to go on so, my little one. But second to you and my son, there is only Douglasdale in my heart. Are you feeling better now?" he asked, trying to change the focus. Ellie nodded yes and began to tell him how happy she was, "The ride these last few days and your mixture of herbs seems to have ended my sickness with child." Then she added, "Perhaps too, I am finally happy in my life," and her eyes met his, and he seemed to ride taller on his horse as he told her, "We can have a good second start in our lives, we are truly blessed Ellie to have found each other at last in this life." As the riders approached the road leading into the barony, a familiar barking noise was heard; they were being greeted by "our wee Shamus" as Gilley called him, "Sir Shamus, look who I brought to stay with you, and mother you my fine furry friend. Its your girl here to see you, my silly hound!" They got down from their horses and greeted their friend. "Oh Shamus, I do love you so," said Ellie and he lapped her face heartily. Gilley took her by the hand now and gave their horses to Patric to take to the stables.

"We will walk the lands and tour the castle and court yard tomorrow. For now it's the feel of a warm scented bath, good food and plenty of wine to celebrate our return." They were almost over the drawbridge as he picked her up and carried her under the portcullis, into the small courtyard. Before setting her down, they proceeded through more iron gates, into the keep, passing through the heavy wooden doors carved from Douglas oaks. "There really are a great many defenses here," she said as he carried into their home. "Not enough, not yet," he told her. Hugh was seated at the lang trestle table in front of the fireplace, in his heavy carved chair that had been his father's seat, the laird's chair they called it. He looked up at the commotion of people entering the hall, with a barking Deerhound running round them. When Hugh spied Ellie, he began to smile a broad, caring smile that Gilley had not seen in years. Then to his true surprise, Hugh rose and came to greet his bride. "So you are the lass that was found by our Shamus? I do hope my brother's plans for marriage were of your own satisfaction as well my dear." Gilley made the introductions. "Ellie, my brother, she is Lady Eleanora de Duglas now," smiling broadly as he looked at Hugh. "We were wed in the chapel at Kelso as I planned; the visit to Fawside Castle was without incident and Wishart is now back in the Mearns," he declared heartily.

Ellie spoke quietly now, "Lord Hugh, I am most happy to be here and to be wed to your brother, I love him so..." As he barged into her words Hugh said, "Good. We will have a feast with entertainment in your honor tomorrow evening then; I have some invited guests who will arrive within the hour. And I have made many special preparations for your arrival, dear Ellie; we have long waited the sound of a woman's good voice to grace this old castle. Do come and sit with me and have some food and drink," he continued, offering his arm to escort her to the table. "Sir Gilley, you are welcome too," he smiled, then laughing good naturedly at his own joke, "I am most pleased you are here my dear girl and you too my little brother; you have chosen wisely in your search for a wife."

Wine was being poured by a young page, a de Lindsay lad from Craigie Castle in Ayrshire and Douglas kin. Platters of food were streaming up from the cellar stairs. The sound of running feet of a small boy led by his nurse, followed by shrill screams of a happy two year old lad, announced the entrance of young James. "Fad' er, James happy you here!" Gilley picked up his little boy and said gesturing towards Ellie, "I have a surprise for you son, this is your new mother." The wee laddie peered over at Ellie with wide eyes, silently checking her every move, looking over at her face, then suddenly turning away, feigning shyness. "Come," said Ellie holding out her hand. Gilley released a hesitant James. His nurse brought out some carved wooden blocks, some smoothed small stones, and a stuffed rag dog; his eyes lit up as he grabbed the toy dog. "Baby Shamus, where you go?" Ellie seated herself on the small woven carpet near the hearth next to him, and began to arrange the blocks and stones; the laddie just watched her, studying her.

At his young age James has excelled other two year olds in his speech. He understood the Lallans words of the Borders; similar to the language of Inglis spoken in Anglia where Ellie grew up. He also knew some Gaelic as it was spoken by the Douglas household. The two began to play and laugh, as Gilley looked on, smiling broadly. Ellie stared at the little boy. My own son to raise and school in languages and music, dance and social graces; so many to love and so much to do now, she thought. For a moment she reflected on her early days at Groby Manor and the other de Ferrers estates. She recalled living with Lord de Ferrers and his two children by his first wife Anne; the children almost Ellie's age. How different her life was now. And she would thrill to raise James as her own son. In most medieval households the second wife was never required to raise the offspring of the previous spouse; but taking James as her own son was Ellie's dream come true; Gilley's most as well.

James stopped giggling and talking; he looked up to Ellie and gestured to her in that silly way small children do as they pretend shyness, cupping his left hand at his face; motioning for her to move closer to him. She leaned down thinking he would whisper something to her, but he surprised her by placing a calculated wet kiss right on her mouth. "James dov you. You stay here," the little boy said with his slight lisp. "Oh James, don't you worry, I am here to stay with all of you. I wouldn't leave you for the world," said Ellie, just as she looked up to see Ana standing near her, radiating a beautiful smile as she watched her girl with her new son. "Shamus!" screamed James, as the Deerhound bolted across the hall, knocking the blocks everywhere. Hugh had been quiet throughout, now broke his silence, "Well le Hardi, my little brother, you have certainly brought much commotion with you this day. I was worried that we would have silence of words not knowing what to say to your new wife. But your family now entertains this old laird reminiscent of when our mother was alive with us children about. This is a grand day for us all."

He looked around at some of the new faces, and Ellie introduced Ana and the others. Hugh began to speak in unvaried tones, "I have brought in a laundress, a tailor, and three others to work with your Ana, all at your wait Lady Eleanora. And I have prepared the chamber of my late wife, Lady Marjory, for you. My vassal will escort you up to M' Lady's chamber Ana; give you a tour of the castle, some food and drink, and show you to your room in the outer tower as well." Hugh was very matter of fact, but clearly had everything well thought out; a well known Douglas trait reflected Ellie. Gilley looked up suddenly, realizing what his brother had said about the bed chambers, "Lady Eleanora shares my chamber and my bed, it is our way." Hugh looked at his brother with a bemused smile, "Suit yourself, Sir Gilley. The accommodations are offered."

And turning to Ellie, "If there is anything you need, you have only to ask me my dear. I am very pleased you have come to our home." Ellie nodded as Gilley began to speak, "We will stay for some days, enough time that I show my wife about the castle and our lands. Then off we will be to Bothwell, as guests of our cousin William de Moray." Hugh looked more serious now and spoke quietly to his brother, "You have reminded me of what I have to say now of importance regards to Edward, the lady's liege lord. Our own kin, Sir Andrew de Moray was want to request the Guardians of the kingdom to remove the grievance of Andrew and his wife Euphemia, the widow of William Comyn, who married without King Edward's license; in accordance with the custom concerning women with lands in both countries. This request but two years ago met with good success, the Guardians being the Steward and the Comyn, both brothers in law to you. What say you to making such a request now?"

Gilley looked over at Ellie and then to Hugh he said, "We have matters of a child to address first dear brother. Then we can speak of solicitors and escheators for resolving the grievances of our marriage with Edward Plantagenet." Looking to his wife, "Shall I show you our living quarters, Lady El?" And the two rose to go to Gilley's chamber; young James went happily with his nurse and Shamus up the stairs to bed for the night, turning briefly to wave goodbye to his father and new mother. "What a happy child our boy is," said Ellie. "I gave a start when he kissed me, I must say." "It is his way, even at this young age to study and plan his moves; what an amazing child he is," answered his father, "And he does not feign affection; a true judge of character, aye."

With that Gilley grabbed his wife up in his arms, with intentions of carrying her to their room. Ellie shouted at him in mocked protest "Let me down this instant my husband or I shall kick and scream till you do." Up the carved wooden staircase he continued carrying her; first six stairs to a small landing, then five more to a second landing, and seven more to the third floor of the family chambers he strutted boldly, carrying his bride to their chamber. All the while he was ignoring her words of indignation and threats of retaliation; laughing heartily as she teased him all the more, "I was warned that Scotland was a country of savages; I will not be handled like chattel. Let me down now I tell you, or you will pay for your sorry ways!"

Gilley opened the ornately carved door of his room. The creak of the iron hinges in the arched doorway opened to a cheerful paneled chamber draped with lovely tapestries of reds and blues. The burning torches glowed in hues of yellow and bronze on the far wall curling upward in finely drawn swirls of lattice like smoke. The flames gently melted the tallow, causing the wax to drip in intricate patterns woven like rococo lace down the length of the paneling. The comforting intimacy beckoned the lovers inside. Gilley set his bride down in front of the small fireplace; as she stood there in the shadows her eyes widened to behold an extraordinarily large tub, the largest bathing vessel she had ever seen, placed strategically in front of the warm fire. The aromas of scented oils reached her and she inhaled their fragrance. "When did you have time to arrange this?" she asked with startled amazement. "I did so last night with my squire. Your husband thinks of everything Lady El, and most of all, he thinks of you." He brought her forward to him, closer so he could whisper his words to her. "I will call Ana to come and help you; I shall return when you are ready to join me." Gilley smiled down at her and kissed her gently, "I hope you don't mind a husband who is anxious to share a scented bath and then his bed with his new wife."

The relaxing sensations of the soothing scented water and the gentle, loving ways of their first love making in their own room followed with a deep slumber. The lovers entwined in embrace were fast asleep in Gilley's large bed. Suddenly they were rudely awakened; all too soon there was a brisk knocking at their door. Ellie woke first and whispered to her sleepy husband, "Gilley, someone begs entrance to our chamber." A groggy husband responded half asleep. "Come in," he shouted, much to Ellie's chagrin. It was Patric, bringing the hound with him as well. It was then that Ellie began to experience a strange sensation, "Gilley, this bed is crawling on its own. I am red with itching everywhere about myself. Are there fleas about or others of the like?" "Fleas there can not be, but there is mischief afoot in this bed" Gilley said finding his own body experiencing the same profound itching. "Shamus, come here." He rolled the hound over on the bed and said, "Here's the source, I will swear to it," pointing to the belly of the Deerhound, covered with hopping, happy fleas. "Patric, take this wee hound and dip him in the lemon, geranium oil, and rosemary bath now; don't wait till the end of the week as we do. He is infested, and so is this bed I fear. Well my brother did to set up the other chamber, for we shall be sleeping there tonight!"

Ellie was in hysterical laughter, and they all were laughing in unison now. The squire knew his job. "I will have the room made safe as well; washing the bed clothes in lemon and herbs, burning the herbs of rosemary and oregano in the chamber, maybe the cinnamon too; then salting the carpet and tapestry to rid the rest. That should send the wee critters on their way," said Patric, reciting his training from Gilley on vanquishing the fleas. "Come with me Sir Shamus. And the reason for my interruption, the laird has asked for your presence as some guests have just arrived this late."

MY TRUTH LIES IN THE RUINS

"I thought you were being silly when you said the hound slept with you," chided Ellie. Gilley was shaking his head, "I have him washed so every week, and he has never had the fleas." How ever the pests could get to the hound this short week now, he asked himself. "I will call for you at our new chamber shortly." Gilley was really unnerved by the fleas she thought as she made her way to the Lady Marjory's former chamber. Ana looked up as she came in, "What ever is the matter, are you crying?" "No these are tears of laughter. The Deerhound has infested our wedding bed with fleas. It seems it was alright for us to marry, but he wants the bed!" Ana just smiled and then began to really laugh, "What a happy life this is for us now. Our biggest problems are Deerhounds with fleas!"

Gilley escorted his wife down the exquisite wooden staircase to the great hall. Both the bride and her husband were dressed in velvet surcotes with fur trimming on the hems, and rich brocade insets on the sleeves and sides of their garments. Gilley wore a cote of green silk under his blue velvet while Ellie glowed in her red and gold silk brocade that was complimented by her demure cream velvet surcote; a stunning pair radiating a glow of true happiness. The gallery musicians announced the couple's arrival with trumpets and smaller horns resounding with the ceremonial music given the laird of the manor, a dignified chorus of entrance that made all the guests riveted to the handsome couple as they seemed to magically glide down the stairs. Hugh rose to make a toast as they took their seats. There was quite a contingency of guests, and Gilley was surprised that he did not notice their arrival at castle. "I wish to give a wonderful welcome to our newest member of the family, Lady Eleanora Douglas," said Hugh, then turning to Gilley, "and take a few seconds to wish my little brother a most pleasant celebration of his thirty-eight years, as it is his birthday this day too." Ellie gasped, realizing that this first special day at Douglas Castle was also his special day; and as his wife she had missed his birthday! She frowned at him, "How could you not inform me of your day?" Gilley turned to her and whispered, "You are my greatest gift for this blessed day. *Tu es perfecta*," you are perfect he said to her in Latin.

Then to break the solemnity of the evening he turned to Hugh, "Sir Shamus has decided to present us with a wedding gift too my brother. He has infested my room and our wedding bed with fleas. Good that you have made us an extra chamber." The noise from the gallery entertainers was drowning his words, so Hugh had to inquire, "What do you mean, you have already fallen out and she is taken to the other chamber?" Gilley was laughing very hard now, "No! Shamus has infested my chamber with fleas, we must seek another chamber. I can not imagine what has happened to have caused this inconvenience; you know how careful I am with the constant bathing of the beast." Hugh looked sheepishly over at Ellie and then Gilley, "The wedding gift would be then from me; that on your absence the hound went howling at your chamber door. I put him in the kennels with the other of the hunting dogs but he made fast his escape. The cook allowed him in the keep, so back he came to your chamber door howling."

Hugh, caught in the celebratory moment, raised his head like the Deerhound, imitating the howling sounds so well that Shamus came running up the lang stairs that led from the kitchen. "Then losing all patience, and wanting for a night of peaceful sleep, the laird made a baronial decision: Sir Shamus, in the absence of Sir Gilley, you shall be assigned his chamber and bed. Isn't that right, wee hound?" he asked Shamus as he came to him. "I told Ana he wanted us to marry, but did not want to give up his side of the bed," laughed Ellie. "I should say he is a determined beast, a true Douglas, is he not?" Her husband took her hand and held it in his, smiling at her teasing words; happier than he could ever recall. Then he remembered the third event, "We have another toast, to our son, who will late celebrate his second birthday," Ellie looked on in startled confusion as he continued. "Just one day before we wed was the anniversary of his birth. Three glorious events in one month to celebrate all at once; a grand day this!"

Figure XXVII-Part One; farm near the location of Crawfordjohn castle and manor; nothing remains of the castle as surviving stone was likely used to build nearby Boghouse

After some wine and much feasting, some of the guests came to be introduced. Ellie looked up to see Sir William, "I am so happy to see you again after the grand hunting party in Ayrshire. And this lass, must she be Willelma?" inquired Ellie. Gilley was about with another couple he beckoned over to meet his bride, "Yes, this is my lovely sister; you will recall Sir William?" And I want you to also meet Sir Alex de Lindsay and his wife, the lovely Alice, sister of my late wife." Alice said sweetly, "I know my sister Elizabeth would be pleased knowing her dear son was now in such capable hands. Welcome my dear." Sir Alex interjected, "We hope you two will honor us with a visit to our Luffness, our lovely manor in the Lothianes." Gilley interrupted his brother in law, "Once the matter of Ellie's liege lord is thus resolved, would we enjoy your good company in the East Lothianes; for now we must avoid such journey near Travernent and Fawside Castle."

It was then Sir Alex and Lady Alice recalled that the two married without the king's license. Alice said most seriously, "Perhaps my brother James can assist you two in that endeavor as a Guardian of Scotland." And then more happily, "If Luffness is not now your choice, you would to come to Crawford then, still surrounded by the protection of nearby Douglas lands in Crawfordjohn. We are not at Barnweill in Ayrshire as much work of building is going on there. But in Crawford, I would love for the company!" Gilley injected his enthusiasm. "Crawford, aye, would be a good choice that."

Figure XXVIII-Part One; remains of Crawford Castle, a de Lindsay stronghold built on a motte

Ellie just radiated with happiness; so many people were ready to assist them. Then Sir Alex interrupted her private thoughts with his . "Are you not related then in Suffolk to one Matthew Lovaine?" he asked. Ellie shook her head with some sadness, "I am most the daughter of that lord of Bildeston, and how would you come to know of him?" Sir Alex explained that his father owned the manor of Petteshoe in Pettaugh,"Just some few miles north of your fair Bildeston." Turning to Gilley, "I was sure I had known of that name before. Yes, the Steward of Eye; one father most annoyed by Scots who marry their daughters and heirs, aye!" chided Sir Alex. "As one who was dubbed by an English king, our dear Edward, you would have much knowledge of such English lords," retorted Gilley with a smirk. "Fortunate was this Scot to be raised in ward in Northumbria by my good uncle John de Lindsey; to have met the Douglases there at Fawdon," chuckled Alex, happy to oblige William his teasing ways, "and to have married well this Scottish lass to raise many children, good Scots all!" Alice was blushing at his words, "Lady Eleanora, do join us in Crawford; your good company is most welcome there."

Willelma cheerfully extended her hospitality and home to the couple as well; yet in the Douglas tradition, it was more a command than an invitation. "We will expect you two to stay with us in Dalserf within the month!" And Sir William said in reassurance, "My grandmother is a Comyn, kin to another of the Guardians, like the Steward; we will request assistance on your behalf with Edward as well. Do not fear my child; and a hearty welcome to our family." The entertainment was beginning in the gallery. There were jesters and much music. Someone motioned to Gilley, and called him up to join in the playing. "Excuse me dear lass. I have been asked to play the small pipes. Do not leave without your husband at your side!" Ellie watched and listened as Gilley played two tunes on his lowland pipes. What can he not do she asked herself? When he returned, the couple excused themselves to take at walk along the parapet, enjoying the night air and the quiet of their own company. "I always hated those dreadful parties at the de Ferrers and Lovaines," she sighed, "But I have enjoyed myself this evening so…" Then she added, "Thank you for suggesting this walk. It has been a long day of much excitement." "Just look below us my dear Ellie," said Gilley, "I have always wanted for my love to walk with me here and sit in the silence of the night's stars." He held her fast and told her "I shall remember this night with you, looking down through these old crenelles to the Douglas Water below us, for all eternity my dear lass. It has always been my favorite place for solitary thought. How much better it is to see it with you in my arms Lady El."

She reached for him as he turned her around, "I have never felt more loved in all my memory of creation. And I have never loved another such as I have come to love you, Gilley. Tui semper sum, I am yours forever," she told him using her Latin skills. He met her gaze and whispered, "I wish tonight that I had danced with you my dearest love. And you do know what I mean by that?" He drew her up to him and they kissed for a very long time. "It has been a long day, time for us three to retire. Let us go." "You mean the two of us and the hound?" she teased him, knowing he meant the child she had growing inside her. He picked her up like a little girl; carried her down the steps to the next floor and the Lady's chamber. "I will return most quickly" and turning to Ana who was waiting in her chamber, "And I will see you on the morrow!" Ellie shook her head, "Guillame is Guillame.

He is so intense, so direct I suppose. Some may find that abrupt manner too abrasive, but I find it uniquely him."

The next morning the sunlight brightened their chamber and she rolled into his waiting arms. "Have you been awake long?" she asked. "Only a little while, but I amused myself watching you breathe so peacefully," he replied, "and I am amazed by my own deep sleep this night." She looked quizzically at him now, wondering what he meant. "Do you have trouble with your sleep my dear husband?" He sighed, "Another of the lasting effects of Fawdon and the faithful servant of your Lord Edward, Gilbert de Umfraville. I have bouts with headaches from this hardness in my neck." She looked deep into his eyes and saw the pain that lingered there for so long. She quietly realized that he could have become a bitter, hateful man; but he chose not to be; and how grateful she was now for that man. "You have only to tell me when that pain returns, for my hands can give you healing. I have been told this so, for I have cured the pain in my mare's leg from years gone by now." "You compare me to a horse, a mare no less, do you now, my wife? I will retaliate on that," and he began to tickle her, forcing tears of laughter as he would not stop." "You are a beast Guillame, stop right now or I shall run from the castle and never return!" With her words he stopped, smiling down at her, running his large fingers through her hair. "You will never leave me, nor will I ever take leave of you. Only God can separate us now."

Before breaking their fast they both visited the chapel next to the laird's chamber and said their morning prayers together. It was a beautiful spring morning as they walked the grounds of Douglas Castle. The sun was breaking through the mist that clung to the grouse heather, the moorish lands that surrounded the castle. Gilley pointed out the trees, the beautiful ash trees that graced the rolling braes and woodlands of Douglasdale. He showed her the orchards and the two small gardens, one used exclusively for his herbs. "I thought only the priests would grow such healing herbs," she said. Gilley looked at her and replied, "I do many things that others do not understand. I make my own rules according to God's own laws, and my truth."

Then he went on about showing her the other buildings; the original family earth and timber house was just as she had imagined. The Douglas servants and those working within the castle grounds were scurrying about with their morning chores. If they were curious about the newest Lady Douglas, they did not display it openly. Gilley led his bride to other of the manor out buildings. She was really impressed by the mews and the number of falcons that were in residence; though none of these were Peregrines as those birds were held only of the king. The number of bee hives the Douglases kept was astounding to Ellie; but then she rationalize that there was great need of tallow for all those torches just lighting the keep. "Beeswax too is required in great quantity; used for lining the silk strings of bows and other uses." he reminded her when they discussed the need for beehives. As they strolled through the courtyard, the kitchen workers were milling about, waiting to retrieve their buckets of water. "You have the castle water well within this court yard too?" she asked him as they passed near the cellarers filling their vessels. "We do so to maintain our independence if there is ever a siege," he replied, always explaining every reason for the indigenous architecture. The couple was now making their way up the lang stairs of the third tower that overlooked Douglas Water in the rear of the court yard; adjacent to the postern, the rear gateway to the castle. "What is that small lodging by the water Gilley?" she asked pointing down past the far wooden palisade. "That secures the end of a tunnel that leads from the vaulted cellars under this tower, going out to the waters. We have a hidden room to store armaments and other supplies there too. He whisked her up in his arms again. "I will not have you falling down the lang

Figure XXIX-Part One; remains of cellars and possibly a kitchen underneath the ruined tower of Castle Dangerous, Douglas Castle, Lanarkshire

stairs my Lady Douglas." And she giggled with his protectiveness as he again carried her down to the courtyard below. A lot of men at arms were surrounding the archery butt for morning practice. "Hurry now, let us watch the competition," Gilley said, grabbing her hand and guiding her quickly to join the onlookers.

One of the Douglas knights hit two center targets in a row. This performance tweaked Gilley's competitive spirit so that he grabbed a bow and split one of the knight's arrows in the bull's eye. "Showing off your husband is he now, dear Ellie?" questioned Hugh in his gruff voice, coming up from behind her. Gilley reached for a second arrow and split the two again. "Quit now dear brother, there would be no further practice here if you choose not," barked Hugh. Gilley was pleased, but not surprised by his ability. He was a perfectionist about everything he did. Archery was one thing he did well. "Dear brother, I am only grateful that you no longer practice or compete, as it narrowed the field to my prominence without you." "Flattery, so early in the day, what is it that you want from your Lord of Douglas?" Hugh chuckled at his quick retort. Gilley and Ellie followed him into the withdrawing room next to the great hall; Gilley was happy to see the smile broaden on his brother's face.

"So tell me, what are your plans for the immediate days ahead you two?" asked Hugh. "We plan to go to Bothwell for some few days, without our son, or hound too for that matter." Gilley said, though his words came as

Figure XXX-Part One; well within the curtain walls of Tantallon Castle, similar to the well within the wooden palisade of Douglas Castle; Tantallon was built by Ellie and Gilley's grandson William, the first Earl of Douglas

a surprise to Ellie; he had not consulted his wife and she was looking a little startled. "We will all then travel, including our son and the hound, from Ayrshire by sea to Ireland and then to the Isle of Mann, with a fare contingency; staying near the former family stronghold there at Douglas until our child is born." "Good that you have told me," she chided him. Gilley chuckled; "That this humble knight does so forget, he has another to consider in his plans; forgive me my impetuous nature. In the future, this husband will of course consult with his wife," he said apologetically. Then he admonished himself for his carelessness: sensitivity training must I now consider, he chuckled silently.

Hugh sighed impatiently. "Your plans do not include an appearance with Lord Edward?" Gilley shook his head, "Ellie has expressed a desire to have our child, then return and inform her mother and Lord Lovaine, the faithful Steward of Plantagenet in Eye. She will write too of the happenings in her absence from Essex." Hugh was visibly concerned. "My fear is that the longer you wait, upon discovery dear Lord Edward will throw a fit of ill humor; not accepting of apologies or intercepts of the Guardians of Scotland." Gilley looked at his wife, whose face was contorting in fear, "We will go to Mann, stay in Douglas there, and return with our child before Edward is informed. It is done. This I have promised to my wife." "Well you may face the loss of the dower rights not to mention the possibility of confinement or a doubling of fine to repledge her lands. Are you prepared for that loss of income?" Ellie spoke now, "I would prefer the loss of dower to the rage of Edward's wrath and my father's disdain that I am with child and newly wed, without the license of one and the blessing of the other. Please understand, I am so fearful..." Gilley said, "It is done, the decision is made."

"And what about your family Ellie; your mother must worry for her child and more if she knew of a grandchild on the way?" continued Hugh, not content with their decision. She sighed with a long, deeply audible breath. "I am my father's only living child, since three years my sister left us. To be true, my father would be more the angry than Edward. I would write my mother after the birth of our child and our return to Douglasdale." Gilley looked at her now and interrupted, "I did not know your father had no other heirs. He will be sure to press the abduction and have us called to Lord Edward's court, in breach of license. A letter is in order to your mother who can inform Lord Lovaine when a wife knows best." Ellie looked over at her husband and realized his words were true. "Will you help me compose such a missive?" Gilley nodded. "We will do this now and one to le Parker as well."

Hugh seemed somewhat relieved that a letter would be written. The newly weds worked the rest of the morning on their letters; the first to her mother. Ellie described their last months in grand detail of a young wife blushing with new felt love. She said she had met Guillame in Ayrshire's lush forests, falling from her horse no less. Then she elaborated how the Scottish rains induced such a closeness that fostered a love affair for the ages. A license from Lord Edward would have been respectfully submitted and requested for the service given of one Sir William Douglas his loyal and precious Sir William of Fawdon, Northumbria; had there been more time. A child on the way, the name and inheritance at stake, she had consented to his

MY TRUTH LIES IN THE RUINS

proposal to take her hand in all immediacy. And she added: "Pray do not take the word of others that I was abducted for it was a ruse of noble doing to hide the shame of your daughter for this untimely incident of being with child. I went with the courage and consent of all my heart's love and adoration for this dear knight. Do not try to find me for we are leaving the country for another, and I am under heavy guard of person for protection, until your dear grand child is born to us. Then only can I face Edward in the court of his allegiance to answer for the sins of love without license of my liege lord. Tell my father, your dear husband when the moment is right."

And she closed, *All my love to you my dear mother, Eleanora*

The letter to le Parker was straight forward. Gilley instructed him to bring any matters of importance to his brother Lord Hugh. And they thanked him for his circumspect handing of her affairs. She assured him that a meeting with Lord Edward would occur once the child was born and that she had written her family, so secrecy was not longer at issue. "Le Parker can as one manage the business of both the Essex manors. But he will need to find good help for himself when rents and other payments are to collect for your dower lands of Scotland," said Gilley. "We will tend to some clerks to aid him and any others he may require when we return from Bothwell." Hugh returned to join them now in the withdrawing room, having adjourned to the great hall before to allow them to do their business alone. He happily said, "I have committed some messengers for the urgency of your letters." Adding, "It is wise to take the offensive in this matters my dear brother. The writing has cheered my foul humor this day; I thank you both." As messengers departed Douglas Castle for Essex and the Lothianes, another writ was being issued to Master Henry de Bray, escheator: to deliver the manor of Stebbing extended, £54 6sh. 9 ½ d and the manor of Woodham extended, £23 1sh. 5 ½ d both in Essex to Eleanora late the wife of William de Ferrers as the king has assigned the manors to her dower.

The evening was to herald another great feast, and the arrival of another kinsman, James the High Steward, uncle of young James and brother of Alice de Lindsay. As a Guardian of the realm, he would first be notified of Edward's wrath when it should come. After being introduced to Ellie, he offered his assistance of station for what ever he could to remedy the trespass on her liege lord. "Lord Edward is not our king here in Scotland. But I speak as one not troubled with land holdings in his England. All my lands reside in Scotland. What ever I may do to make your stay and ease of marriage, please allow me to do for you Lady Eleanora," said James. "Ah, my dear namesake, here come to your uncle," he motioned to the two year old who was making his rounds of farewell for the night with his nurse.

DEBORAH RICHMOND FOULKES

"Big James, hug for you!" said the little lad, laughing and giving his uncle an embrace. And spying Ellie, he let out a squeal of delight, "Shamus bring me mother." Gilley started to laugh, "It was the Shamus who found Ellie for me, on our lands in Ayrshire." And then Alice came to her brother's side, "My William knighted the hound for his brilliant deeds. What a story for the ages, this love affair!" The music started in the gallery and processions of platters filled the room with joyous aromas; another night of excited conversation, feasting, and much wine. There would be dancing too, only this time Gilley did not run for the gallery. He danced with his girl.

Another surprise guest arrived later in the evening; the Bishop of Glasgow Robert Wishart was announced with flourish as he and his large entourage entered the great hall. "Good evening dear Robert, what brings you to Douglasdale?" beckoned Hugh. "Come join out feast and merrymaking in the celebration of my brother's marriage with our lovely Eleanora." Willelma interrupted the Bishop in his answer, "Whilst making our journey from Dalserf, we met up with the good Bishop, yet on his way to his castle at Carstairs." Quickly adding, "In the excitement I forgot to tell you my dear brother that we extended the hospitality of Douglasdale." It was Ellie's turn to interject her words. "Another of these Wisharts, but a Bishop you say?" asked Ellie. Gilley began the introductions, adding "Your nephew the Baron of the Mearns was my accomplice in my abduction of Lady Douglas from Fawside Castle, held of her kin. It was a daring rescue, an affair of the heart I should amend, a willing abduction." Gilley smiled to his bride, continuing to describe the chivalric endeavor, "Sir John Wishart the valuable commander of horsemen and armaments; a site to see, sure aye!"

The Bishop looked at Ellie and asked her pointedly, "You agreed willingly to remove your dear self with this band of rogues, and then to yet accept to marry one of them?" he inquired; amused by the tales of valor and intrigue. Ellie replied to the Bishop, "The baron's ruse truly did frighten me at first, arriving in full armaments with men at arms, entering my chamber so, that early morning. I was convinced they were marauders of grave mischief!" By now they are all laughing; the Bishop chuckled as he visualized the absurdity of the feigned raid and abduction. And then with the manner of a patronizing parent he added, "Know you too that I am a Guardian of this fair kingdome and should you require the interference with one Lord Edward on your behalf, may I offer my own self to your service and assistance fair lady." Ellie nodded a grateful thank you to this strange churchman; the uniquely charming and intriguing Robert Wishart.

Retiring early with the excuse of much excitement and long days of traveling, the newly weds adjourned to their chamber. The rains that came so often to Scotland in the spring prevented them from taking in the night's air on the parapet walk, but it did not detract from their evening. All the night they sat up talking and laughing; sparring over who would make the plans for their travels. "I should like to visit Crawford and Dalserf, but I would want to stay some time with you alone my husband. Let us plan for this concern as well Gilley." "Allow my choice for travel, lass. You know not the country and the strongholds that secure fine hiding, only to be found by Douglas men." "I want to choose more, to have more say in where we journey," she pouted. He just looked at her with amusement, his eyes dancing and smiling at her as she grimaced with displeasure.

Not able to persuade him otherwise on their travels, Ellie changed the subject. "I should say to you as one who does not inquire of my own family, that I too am kin to the Comyn. It was my late husband's mother, the Countess of Derby, who resigned as Constable of Scotland in favor of her sister, wife of the Comyn. Elena de la Zouche of Fawside is the third heiress and daughter of de Quincy." Gilley seemed surprised, not at his wife's relations but at his own disinterest until now of his wife's family. "I have filled your head with talk of Douglas pride of ancestry; the men of Moray, Theobold the Fleming, and our Sholto, the fearless warrior; giving little time for your own sweet words. Do tell me more my girl." Ellie began to talk in greater detail of her Flemish heritage; of Brabant, her father's family in the duchy of Lovaine. She spoke of others of her ancestors and knights that fought in the Crusades. "Earl Duncan of Fife the Guardian is my cousin; my mother Helisant kin of Henry III," she concluded, with a silly, feigned smugness. "I will remember to bow in your presence M' lady," he chided her, "But for now, it is time for us to seek our rest." He picked her up, carried her across the chamber, and dropped her playfully in their bed. "We can't have the kin of Henry III touching her fair feet to this cold floor, now can we." Ellie looked at him, choosing carefully her next words as he joined her in their bed, "This chamber floor is not sufficient cold for you to sleep upon should you to continue your sparring words, Sir William." "Pax?" asked Gilley. "Pax," replied Ellie.

Bothwell, Early May 1288

The couple had the vast estate of Bothwell all to themselves for most of their stay as the de Morays left for Moss Tower alleging feudal business in Liddesdale. Before the de Morays left, William, son of Walter the rich, showed them around Bothwell, all the while expressing his exasperation with obtaining the quarried stone and timber and the subsequent delays to his vast building plans. His own woodlands were somewhat depleted, he sighed, but he would not quit until the entirety of his castle was complete. De Moray went on to show Gilley and Ellie his latest point of pride: the new foundations for the two grand towers to be built for family and quest chambers on the opposite side of the court yard. These towers when built would face the enormous laird's donjon. "You both are staying in the small tower that will house prisoners of nobility when these other finer towers are complete," chuckled Sir William. But the most impressive of all was the laird's chamber with its magnificent window seat, enormous as the donjon keep itself; a majestic architectural accomplishment. The spectacular view of the Clyde and the surrounding lands brought gasps from Ellie, "I have never seen such splendor! I could pass my days here quite content by this glorious window."

Figure XXXI-Part One; Bothwell Castle ruins, fortress and family seat of William de Moray

Gilley and Ellie spent their days at Bothwell in contented bliss, a lover's paradise that gently embraced the couple in their solitude. They shared daily rides along the banks of the firth, passing the small Augustinian house, the Blantyre Priory, on the far shore as they continued to one of the falls that flowed into the waterway. These rides together they enjoyed on end, challenging each other to races, or just riding and talking, taking their time in the day's sun that warmed their way. It was Scottish lowlands; the wee hills of brilliant green nurtured by the frequent rainfall, sprinkled with the brilliant hues of gold: the yellow gorse that grew in abundance in the spring: this was their playground. They rode their palfreys over undulating cart paths through the moors dotted by patches of bluebells that followed the river banks to then turn up through the wee braes, beckoning the lovers with majesty of color and the serenity of nature.

In the evening they retired to their private chamber in the small tower adjacent to the laird's donjon. Gilley would feed the fire in the tiny fireplace, adding peat and wood kindling, then dried lavender to enhance the aroma. He would do this himself to relieve Ana or Patric from entering the chamber during the night. It was the usual occurrence in some households for squires or maid servants to sleep on mats outside the door of the sleeping chambers of their laird or lady. But the Douglases were more generous to their household; allowing for others who slept the days to stand guard at night while their personal servants got their rest in the privacy of their own bed. As he stoked the fire, he enjoyed the pleasant fragrance and the feeling that he was taking care of his lass. "You are my own sweet bride you know it true now," he said. "Bride?" she questioned. "Aye, bride is what we say, in honor of the good St.Bride; the patron saint of many who rode to the Crusades and the Levant, land of the sun and the Douglas patron saint as well," he told her, chuckling some as he realized he had never called her his bride afore; merely thought of it without the word so spoken.

Then more quietly he added, "I wish always to take care of you and provide for your needs." As Ellie looked up into his eyes she asked, "And will you love me tomorrow as you love me today?" He answered as he would in similar fashion for the many years to come, "Oh no my sweet lass, for I will love you all the more. And you, will you love your William tomorrow as you love me today?" Her response too was always the same sentiment, "Yes dear Gilley, but all the more shall I love you then." He began to speak his words to her again, "On the morrow next we must return to Douglasdale for I have the duties to my brother as his Seneschal. I must spend the Whitsunday collecting his rents and other obligations. You can assist me this day as we would serve a fair feast for our guests: fine food and generous quantities of wine." "You share food and wine with those who come to pay their rents?" she asked. "Aye, it has been our way to honor the men of Douglasdale who come with their financial offerings to their patron laird." He told her too that it meant much needed coinage for the two of them as he received a portion for his labor. "And we require haste and funding to complete our plan for the voyage from Irvine to Dublin and then Mann."

"Would you feel comfortable as the guest of the Steward at Dundonald, the birth place of my late wife Elizabeth and the home of her brother James?" Gilley asked. "Certainly my husband, as James was most generous to us on the occasion of our wedding; and that of course our young James does love him so." she answered him. And in his characteristic demeanor he responded forthrightly. "Aye, it is done then, and would you not know there is a passage way from Dundonald to Seagate Castle in Irvine should there be a trouble with the weather as we make way to the sea vessel for our passage

DEBORAH RICHMOND FOULKES

on our journey. Though," he continued, seeing her uneasy face of concern, "we will not sail if the weather is impending." In mocked seriousness Ellie said, "It is done then." She was imitating his expression in both visage and words; noting the decision that was done indeed! He laughed heartily with her, "I chose right when I made you my bride."

Figure XXXII-Part One; postern or rear gate of Bothwell

They arrived home to pandemonium in the great hall. Some of the kennel dogs were racing about and James was not happy they had spoiled the wood block structure he was building. "Out hounds. James says go. The noo!" said the young lad, gesturing his commands with his left hand. The boy's nurse was seeing to the removal of the hounds to the court yard as Shamus came running down from the top landing of the stairs to greet the return of Ellie and Gilley. "Have you been watching James order about the kennel dogs good Shamus?" asked Gilley while greeting his Deerhound. Ellie was already holding James in her arms and trying to reconstruct his creation. "A good temper you have wee one," said Ellie. "And so impatient at this young age, but I know the source of your impatience," throwing a knowing glance at Gilley. Hugh bellowed up the turnpike stairs leading from the cellar kitchen, "William, come down to tell cook what to prepare for Whitsun feasting! And Ellie, good to hear you chose to return to Douglasdale. I worried the weeks alone with my little brother might have dampened your spirit. But no! Courage you must have lass. Good. Come

MY TRUTH LIES IN THE RUINS

William, the now!" "Fad' er, Fad' er, James dov you!" "Come here laddie," beckoned Gilley. "You can cool the temper of our testy laird," he continued, picking up his son and carrying him down the stairs to the kitchen. Ellie and Ana took Shamus up with them to Gilley and Ellie's chamber. As she rolled the hound over on the bed, she checked for fleas. "I'll not leave it to chance again," she chuckled to Ana, "I suspect he has slept here every night since we left for Bothwell."

Whitsunday 1288

It was May 15th, Whitsun or Whitsunday, one of the two times yearly the estate designated for the collection of rents and other financial obligations of the tenants of their estates. One by one the men of Douglasdale came to settle their fees due with the laird's brother. Gilley had set up his collecting and feasting in the small earth and timber hall that was the first Douglasdale abode, now used for such activities as Whitsun in May and Martinmas in November. A large crowd gathered in front of the trestled tables covered with platters of game, fish, beans and other such treats. Ellie beamed as she acted hostess to Gilley's Whitsun food and wine celebration. She instructed the pages on the proper way to pour the wine, turning the carafes as they poured, to spare every drop. At first some of the farmers and other tenants seemed ill at ease with the English lass they were told had come to Douglasdale. But her persistent good humor and pleasant graces won them over by the end of the event. Besides she boasted, she was Flemish lass, most like their laird's own kin in the Highlands.

Gilley and Ellie made their way back to the great hall in the keep with coffers full. The Douglas cellar stores were overflowing with crops harvested and counted; crops growing noted. "A good day's collection dear brother," said Gilley, "Only four yet not paid, six more only the half paid with promises for the final by Lammass, next August sure. One being the widow of young Alex from Glespin who met with mischief on the Ayr Road," Gilley told him. Hugh shook his head sadly; he remembered how he himself was once attacked on the lonely and often dangerous cart paths that crisscrossed the shire. Though a proven warrior, he was nearly taken in that unprovoked assault were it not for good men of Douglasdale who came to his defense that day. This poor villein was traveling in the early evening and met with marauders of despicable ways. Sadly he was slain; his only horse the object of the theft and murder. These times in the wilds of Scotland's borders were unruly. The lairds left to administer justice among the lower classes that lived on their lands. Such crimes would not go unpunished. The Douglas laird sent about his men at arms who caught up with the brazen felons and hanged them on the spot.

"I will adjust the widow's rents this quarter day and next as well; sending her word on the morrow. Mark your records Gilley," said Hugh. The laird's actions were typical of all the Lords of Douglas gone before him; the just and sympathetic Chief of Douglas personified in deeds the Douglas ways. A laird was supposed to take care of his people; he was to protect them and look after their needs. In turn the tenants would serve him; some worked his lands while others served in his retinue when called upon to do battle for their chief. "Well done my brother, take another portion for your voyage as my gift for your marriage and hard work this Whitsun." Gilley's face lit up with surprise, "Another portion, that offer is well received; appreciated all the more, by us both dear brother." Ellie found Hugh's gruff temperament amusing; but the size of his heart, the generosity of another portion from the coffers was overwhelming. "Dear Hugh, you have been so good to us already," she told him. "We are finding few words to express our thanks to you." Hugh snorted a gruff response, feigning his displeasure with their words of praise. "And I want to hear you spent some of the coinage on some silver trinkets and bundles of fine cloth from Ireland's fair shops," ordered Hugh, now with a mild tone of amusement. "Now don't go encouraging the lass to spend all my money!" chided Gilley.

"That brings my thoughts to this," said Hugh, taking out the coffer Ellie recognized at once as the one given her nearly six months ago in Hertford. "Your le Parker was here with some of your men at arms and maids in wait. I have retained Sir David and his squires and your maids. This does meet with your approval Eleanora?" he questioned. Before she could answer William said "You have done well Hugh. Sir David is a fine addition to our household and for the voyage now coming to Mann. Ellie will require her maids, more when yet the child arrives. As for le Parker, this seneschal is worth his weight. Where is he now?" Hugh told them that he authorized the services of le Parker's brother in law, a man called Foster, to handle the Essex manors and their feudal business as was allowed. Le Parker would remain in Scotland until the dower and the matter of Edward's license to marry was resolved. "He was this day onto Dumfries and Kirkcudbrightshire; then west again to Wigtonshire where there seems to be a seaside manor in her late husband's estates," Hugh elaborated. "I was not aware of a seaside manor, this is a wonderful surprise," exclaimed Ellie, "And I am happy Sir David and my maids will accompany us on the sea voyage, staying with us in Mann. You have done splendidly Lord Hugh." The old warrior grimaced, wrinkled his brow. "Please lass, Hugh, call me Hugh," he bellowed, "I am becoming my father too well without such title from your lips to remind me all the more!"

William looked up from counting the coins in Ellie's coffer. "My dear bride it seems as though you have brought more than beauty and grace to my humble life. There is great wealth here." Then Hugh interjected with a wry smile, "You wish to return my Whitsun portion of gift this day?" and all the more merrily he continued, "In my haste I did not count the contents, ha, ha, ha," laughed Hugh enjoying his own joke. "It is this haste that cost me with my generosity!" Gilley was laughing too at Hugh's folly, then turning to Ellie he said, "You continue to amaze me so, for you know to the very "d." how much is here, now don't you dear girl?" Gilley beamed at his wife, and at her quiet humility, realizing her wee dower coffer held more than his own collections this Whitsunday. Ellie smiled up sweetly at him and began explaining her good fortune, "I was indeed of good chance to have solicitors who were fair in managing the dower rights, taking little of the coinage then for their fees; preferring to wait the tenant payments to collect." Ah, a woman of beauty with a steward's mind; I can use her wisdom to manage our own Fawdon, Gilley mused.

"We will leave for Dalserf dear brother three days hence. I will send word to Willelma of our arrival," said Gilley. "And from there we will go to Dundonald to await the ship to take our household to Ireland's green shores." Hugh looked down dejectedly; quietly it seemed with a sad sense that surprised his younger brother. "You leave so soon then?" he asked. Gilley looked briefly at Ellie. And knowing his look she replied, "We could stay the now three more weeks, should you approve of our long lingering. But not to ire the laird of the castle staying too far on the welcome he has offered us so graciously." A relieved smile crossed the old laird's face, "Good, you will stay till June first week." Gilley realize the extra time would help him organize the journey and make the arrangements for James and Shamus more easily as both would make the voyage. But he was troubled by Hugh's uncharacteristic soft appeal that they linger with him until June. The sadness was like none he had seen before he reflected. Perhaps Ellie had realized that in her quick response, agreeing to stay longer in Douglasdale.

Ana quietly closed the door of their chamber as Gilley was turning the final step on the stair way. "Good night Ana," he nodded, as he entered the door of his dressing room off the sleeping chamber they shared. Patric was quietly sighing as he took his knight's surcote and cote, handing him the velvet chamber cloak and shorter silk sleeping cote. "What troubles you my squire this night?" he asked Patric. Another long sigh followed, another deep breath taken; the young lad began to speak carefully, in low tones, "There is much talk of Lord Hugh. He has missed several evenings in the great hall." His knight nodded in agreement, "I have seen his sadness. We will wait three weeks more the least before we yet depart for Dalserf, then Dundonald. Oh yes too, we might make stay at Crawford for some few days. Tell the others of the household about our delays." Then to himself, just let him last dear St. Bride till our return to Douglasdale for Martinmas. Then per chance he might allow this humble healer to treat his ailments, I do pray so.

As he joined Ellie in their chamber he began to discuss Hugh's disposition with her "The winds of Largs blow through him still my wife. It was not the skirmish fought there, aye that troubles Lord Hugh," Gilley said as he began to tell her the story of Hugh, his poor health and heavy heart. "It was our brother, his young squire who joined him for this his first time to armaments; to learn the art of war. Archibald was his name but fourteen. Hugh felt himself responsible that our dear brother met with poisoning of unknown origin sometime during that incursions; to meet his God on St.Brice's Day six weeks hence. That tragic loss hangs heavy on his heart as that of his Marjory. I pray he fights on like the brave warrior he is for our return on Martinmas, but fear," his words trailed off. And Ellie barely heard him, her eyes welling with tears, "He has been so kind to me, I feel he is my own sweet brother." She agreed with Gilley that the old laird was failing in health, "Would you not change our plans to stay on in Douglasdale then my husband for the birthing then?" "No Ellie, he would see through our deeds. Hiding his sickness as he does is his way. The warrior never leaves the field of battle without a good fight. I would want greatly to stay, if he but let us." Ellie looked at him, sighing deeply, "His body betrays his years so plus ten, my Gilley." Staying in Douglasdale until the Ides of June at the least is now my plan Gilley resolved to himself, knowing his wife shared his concerns as well.

The month passed quickly and Hugh's bright spirits improved all their moods. Ellie reflected on her dear grand mother, those last months before she passed. Muriel had seemed so recuperated that everyone thought her well to live for many more such years. But the improvement seemed to fade, like the Spirit when it knows the end of life is nearing. She wondered if Hugh would retain his recovered health; she hoped so, for the thought of her husband becoming Lord Douglas put a fear into her like no other she had ever felt. A fear of losing the one man she loved beyond her wildest dreams kept running through her head. Dear Hugh, please stay with us, she prayed.

While Hugh sustained his happy demeanor, Ellie and Gilley took their days together at Douglasdale riding often, taking wine and smoked fish with them as they took the cart paths north towards Lanark and the Falls of the Clyde; their men at arms followed closely behind. It was still not safe to ride about unescorted, even in the woodlands and moors of Douglasdale there could be treachery about or even an English sheriff lurking. Gilley thought up adventures they would go on; on this one occasion he showed his bride ancient settlements of Celts in old stone circles just south of Douglas Castle. They also enjoyed the hunt together in the wee hours of some mornings.

MY TRUTH LIES IN THE RUINS

And they took James on regular walks through the castle park taking in the warmth of the day with the afternoon sun. Hugh came one such day and found the hand of the two year laddie to grab his own; to fill his heart with joy. "You have a fine family Sir Gilley," as Hugh called his brother when ever he could tease him; which was often enough for Gilley. "I miss Marjory's kind ways some now." When they returned to the castle a messenger brought Gilley word of a cog, a large ship that would sail on the solstice. "The date I was promised to come for you at Fawside, aye. This is the vessel to take our household to Mann. It is done."

The packing and organizing were underway for their journey and yet their excitement was muted. Concerns for Hugh overshadowed their jovial moods and Hugh himself was sensing it. That morning as they broke their fast Hugh began in his familiar gruffness, "Are you not off from Douglasdale yet this day or shall I make the preparations for your leave myself?" Ellie feigned some giddiness and chided him, "You ask me to stay now you want I should go. You Douglas men are strange ones in deed!" "We shall go on the morrow my brother," said Gilley showing enthusiasm for the journey at hand. And yet in his mind he said dear St. Bride do heal him; keep him well till our return and more.

They arrived at Dalserf to much fanfare. Willelma had a two year old daughter who kept James busy the entire three days of their stay. Then the seventeen travelers of their household made their way to Ayrshire. The visit to Dundonald was cheerful and pleasant. The Stewarts fawned over James and made Ellie feel like family. Their stay was very brief, and soon the travelers rode off to Irvine; beasts of burden, Deerhound, horses and James all in succession with their men at arms, maids in wait, Ana, Gilley and Ellie. It was a colorful procession with banners flowing and pennants waving and other such demonstrations of station. The Douglas entourage was not without panache. The flamboyant style was a Douglas trait; becoming the expected manner of their travel to all that marveled at this prominent family; all wanted to live up to the Douglases. Gilley's choice of Irvine for their port of departure was for the convenience of Dundonald; that they might store their litter and pack animals; keep their palfreys there until they returned from Mann. Irvine was a smaller port than nearby Ayr, the busiest port in western Scotland; but the frequency of vessels available to passengers was sufficient here to offer a good choice of ships and dates for their departure and return.

Gilley went to Irvine to meet with the ship's captain and inspect the vessel that would sail their chosen route. Shipbuilding and designs had not changed dramatically since 1270 when he sailed for Tunis, then Acre with Earl Adam. He would have some knowledge to guide his choice of transport for their journey. The captain took an instant liking to Gilley and the greeting was returned in kind. Captain Gregg was an experienced Scottish sea captain with a crew of many extractions, including French and Flemish sailors. He was jovial but serious about his work; cautious in his tone as he discussed the dangers of a sea voyage. "We will travel at a speed made good of three to six knots," Gregg said. Gilley wanted to know about the navigation system, and Gregg's knowledge of the contours of the sea-bed.

Gregg showed him how the crew took soundings; the significance of being "in soundings" meant that the water depths were lower, approaching shore. He also showed Gilley his sea charts, explaining the use of rhumb or direction lines with the seaman's horizon divided into the thirty-two parts of the compass-points. The compass was the skippers pride and joy as he explained a recently developed dry compass that he was using. "The compass needle is mounted with this bowl," Gregg said to Gilley, "and has a pivot on each end." "A good choice I know now I made in selecting your sea worthy vessel Captain Gregg," said Gilley with a confident tone, "Your vast sea knowledge, and competent crew give me no cause to worry. We will see you on the morrow three days hence." The lieutenant now came in to join in the discussion. He was a Scot as well who came from North Berwick, and had many years sailing with Gregg. "We think alike, a good partnership on the sea to protect vessel and crew alike," the lieutenant said. Gregg went on to say that he would make arrangements for the Douglas household to spend two days in Dublin with suitable lodging in a small manor of his brother in law outside the city, near the Priory of St. Catherine. "It is done," said Gilley. "All that is left is the sailing then."

Gilley returned to Dundonald with a joyous demeanor that was apparent to everyone immediately. He was explaining the use of the dry compass and how it aided the captain in determining his direction when the pole star was not visible, when the Steward came into the great hall. "Well have you done then in your choice of captain and cog, a good crew too is it?" he asked. "Oh yes," said Gilley, "and the lieutenant a Scot as well from North Berwick. And there will be no shortage of good wine on board as that is their major cargo besides our wee group of travelers." Ellie was thrilled and eager to travel now. "And we will go from Dublin to Mann, arriving in the week with good speed."

Departing for Irvine with the same flourish as when they arrived in Dundonald, the travelers said their goodbyes with much excitement and ceremony. Now they were really going to Dublin, then Mann sighed Ellie; a voyage that would take them all for new adventures and the birth of Muriel or John. As they rode out Ellie asked her husband, "Are you quite happy with our choice of names for our dear child yet unborn, my husband?" Gilley looked over at his bride realizing that she was beyond the half of her term to carry. Smiling warmly he said "Ellie it pleases me to name our daughter Muriel after your grandmother; or our son John as we promised Wishart months ago when we were yet in Dalkeith. And by God and St. Bride, I will be happy with either child to grace our family and our humble lives."

The Douglas entourage was growing. It now included some of the de Ferrers men at arms: Sir David, his squires and page; joining with the Douglas men at arms, and Sir Gilley with his vassal Thomas Dickson, the knight's own squires, and his de Lindsay page, Ellie with Ana and three maids in wait, James with his nurse and Shamus with a young groom from Douglasdale named Gillerothe. "Sir Gilley, you do not wish to take the horses with us then?" asked Sir David. He answered by describing the travels made to the Levant with the horses in 1270. "Many of the horses we took to the Crusades perished from the sea voyage with swollen bellies and other ailments. To risk our own palfreys or Ellie's mare for even such short voyage was not of my liking. I have made arrangements for horses in Dublin and Mann. It will give us an opportunity to take a look at the Irish Hobini, the fast ponies of the isle. Have you heard of them?" Gilley asked. Sir David responded that he had never been to Ireland, but tales of these agile, strong ponies were the talk among the knights returning from the isles serving de Hereford, "Since the beginning of the Crede mihi, our thirteenth century, de Hereford's men at arms have spoken much about these ponies. I would pleasure to see them and ride one for my own good mount if the opportunity be given." Gilley enjoyed Sir David's easy ways and affable demeanor. "Sir David, it is done, you will take of the ride of the Hobini. And Lady El, you too will enjoy such fun!"

Dublin

The busy port of the Dublin was coming into view as the sun broke through the morning sea mist onto the deck of Captain Gregg's cog. Everyone was bustling about getting ready for the embarking at the docks. Ellie and Ana had never been to Ireland and were very eager to reach the shores and begin their shopping. "As you leave the dock areas you will see le Tholsey or the Tholsel, where the merchants meet yet on the second floor; you will know it then. That guildhall will lead to the town wall gates," said Gregg. Gilley asked him curiously, "What has happened to old Skynners Row; I recall it just there, but not the noo from what I see." Gregg explained that the row was destroyed just four years before in 1284 and was replaced by the new guildhall built of hewn stone." Gilley laughed to himself; on this marshy land, the new tholsel may not long last, he mused.

The pack horses from the manor where they would stay arrived at the docks perfectly as planned. Horses for the travelers were also provided; but for the shopping they would travel on foot. "We will break our fast, then lay way to Dublin's merchants to take of our coinage," said Gilley. The horses remained waiting at the guildhall until the party later made their way out of the city, past St. Catherine's Priory to the manor that would be their home for the next two days. "What a busy city, and it is walled. Is there peril to be met here?" Ellie asked him. He responded in reassuring tones, "Not of recent times. Last I was here, there were promises of trouble but none came." The shops were bustling with trade. It was an exciting day and Ellie and Ana found Gilley equally proficient with the merchants; he filled several traveling chests with his many bundles while topping off their baskets with his smaller purchases and just as quickly as the ladies. Ellie peaked into one basket only to hear a booming, deep voice chiding her from behind. "Take haste to leave of that package that has not your name upon it my Lady Douglas!" Gilley bellowed as he gave her a mocked look of severe admonishment that broke into a wide smile.

"We lost sight of you at Curriers Row," said Ellie, "And now I see you were quite able to shop on your own. Did you purchase leather there as well Gilley?" He nodded yes, pulling out a new elaborate sword belt that drew the attention of Sir David. "I have not seen the likes of such a belt; Curriers Row is it that you found this fine workmanship?" "You will have to wait for Hogmanay good knight as I have bought the good merchant his full house of such finery." Sir David looked at Gilley with a questioning look. "Hogmanay, it is our celebration and feast of the new year where we share gifts and much feasting; your English ways of the Christmas day and feast of Stephen." "Where to now my Gilley?" asked Ellie. He told them they would take the northern bank of the Liffey river, "We must find the road leading west from Dublin, to Bleach Green I think. But here now come our escorts from Captain Gregg," pointing to the men at arms bringing their palfreys, "who will lead us to our lodging."

The next days passed quickly and the small band of travelers wearily returned to the vessel at Dublin's docks. Captain Gregg joked that he was pleased to have sold so much of his wine tunage that he might have room for the Douglas's purchases adding to the weighted cargo below. Gilley was in silly form when he said "Look here dear Captain, my bride has spent all m' money now. You see for your own eyes the baskets and clothed parcels that fill the hold complete of tunage that replaces your wine!" Ellie looked at him with eyes wide in an admonishing stare of indignation, "You mock your own good work at such purchasing; leaving this lass to take the brunt of your teasing, I say not!" They were laughing and giggling at their own extravagance, sparring and teasing each other. Their attention then went to James and Shamus running about wildly on the deck chasing each other, under the disparaging cries of his nurse.

MY TRUTH LIES IN THE RUINS

One word from Gilley and the pandemonium desisted: "James!" The little lad stopped fast in his step and Sir Shamus moved obediently to James' side. Ellie looked at them; is that all it takes she asks herself? The merriment of the moment, the excitement of the day was felt by everyone. But as the second part of their journey was about to begin Gilley determined that all must be more circumspect for the voyage. "It is time that we should leave Dublin my wee son, you too my good hound. Come, we will go into the cog's castle and make ready for the voyage to Mann." Gilley took the lad's hand and put the lead on Shamus; and they proceeded to the quarters provided by Captain Gregg. Ellie and Ana and the rest of the household followed Gilley as the crew began to pull up the stone anchor, and row out of the channel.

Figure XXXIII-Part One; Douglas Bay Isle of Mann; once held by the King of Scots, the island became an English possession, annexed by Edward I in 1291

Landing on the eastern side of Mann at Douglas Bay, the Douglas household made their way to St. Bridgett's nunnery. They would stay in the manor near the nunnery, as William 5th Lord Douglas did in 1266 when he came to Mann briefly in the service of King Alexander III. Sir William was there to assist in reviewing the escheator's records and set up methods to augment collections of taxes and rents on royal manors, as he was doing for Kelso Abbey and Lesmahagow Priory back home. Now his youngest son also William was here to entrench his family in an old Douglas stronghold of his great uncle, far from the view of his wife's liege lord, far from the ire of one Edward. "Douglas Bay is so beautiful, I would never have dreamed this isle, this Mann would be so beguiling, though it is not our Scotland" cooed Ellie. As Gilley stood behind her at the window, "It is for you my bride that we come here so you might gain more strength for your lay-in at the end of your term." He turned her to him, "I pray to dear St. Bride each day that we will have a child like our James, to thrive and grow; and to return safely home in Douglasdale, for this Mann is yet Scotland, our own dear kingdome and home." Ellie expressed surprise, and told him she had not known that Mann was part of Scotland, so far south at sea. "The Isle of Mann came under the Prince of Scotland, dear Alexander, Lord of Mann in 1266 through the Treaty of Perth. Would that our good king have lived, it would be thriving all the more, sure aye."

"What happened to King Alexander, why did he go about the night in such peril to end in his passing?" she asked him. Gilley explained that he and many others suspected mischief of the most treacherous kind from an ambitious vassal that may have caused Alexander's death; "more murder than accident of weather or much wine," he said quietly. "I fear that ambition and scurrilous intrigue is at the bottom of that ravine; the craigy brae-hag, the rough cliff overhanging the turbulent waters below hides the evidence of true crime." Gilley paused to catch his breath and compose his anger that rose within him every time he reflected on the king's strange end. "The wild crag holding of many secrets that perhaps in time will give up your Edward; revealing the truth of his own devices. Behind this treachery is murder true enough." Ellie's eyes widened in horror, "You don't suspect Edward," her words trailed abruptly stopped as she saw Gilley's face, his nod yes, affirming his suspicions of Plantagenet's involvement. "He is a man of odd instincts and bearing; a mad man of greed and ambition for his own legacy the man I saw in Acre. One king I fear for his cunningness for he has not core values to temper his soul. Remember, to kill a king takes a king." Ellie was too stunned to respond. To kill a king, takes a king; what horror would that be if true she thought.

Ellie and Gilley toured the coast of Mann, traveling toward the southern part of the island the next day. With their escorts and men at arms they rode south nearing Castletown, or Balla Cashtal, as it was called in Manx. "One week we will travel once to see Rushen Tower, more south yet still, and on the other side of Mann," said Gilley, "You will see a harbor there so fortified with its imposing tower keep; not like the beauty of Douglas harbor, but more severe and menacing." Gilley told stories of the Manx warriors and the hostilities of the Isles from early times when the Vikings came to Mann. "The Manxman is an implacable enemy to anyone he thinks has injured him or his own. Like a true Celt he wished to live in peace I think; not at heart the fighter." Ellie looked into her husband's eyes; as they dismounted she asked, "And you dear Gilley, are you a Celt at heart desiring only to live at peace?" Helping her down he responded, "I am a poet knight my sweet lass, and a healer of special training. I desire only to live in my

Douglasdale and raise my family, doing the king's business of war reluctantly, but go I would as is the custom. I am a warrior trained to fight."

Figure XXXIV-Part One; Rushen Castle contains a 13th century tower in Castletown, Isle of Mann, using the ancient spelling

 He held her close and pointed to the surrounding hills. "In September come the hills to be a purple glow of heather; the seasons coming late in Mann. Then you would see the harvesting of corn as villiens pull their sleds to cart the yield. Their customs stranger still; the soil for crops they use of seaweed that we would use manure." Now they did some walking to a clearing where they rested and enjoyed some food and wine before returning to Douglas. In the nearby pasture grazed a small horse or so it seemed to Ellie. "Is that a Hobini or some other kind of horse?" she asked him. "That would be a Manx pony," he replied. "Come let us return and find young James to do more walking; it is good that you move more about. The walking will help you gain more strength." And the small group turned around and made their way back to their manor. Ellie looked back over her shoulder at the pony; what wonders she discovered traveling with her knight, and what more would come her way to expand her life with knowledge of the ways of other lands.

 Ellie was with Ana later that evening, changing into her bed clothes. "Your husband spares himself nothing when he shops as well, my love," joked Ana. "Were you two in competition in Dublin for the win my sweet one?" Ellie chuckled, "He bought himself as many robes as he bought hats with ermine and mantels of velvet, all that match in color and design. Why I have never seen such a man enthralled with dress that he must buy so." "Aye, your husband enjoys the finery that is sure," said Gilley, his booming voice reverberating from the chamber doorway. He was wearing one of his new hats as was young James, followed by the hound. Ana and Ellie let out peels of laughter, spying Sir Shamus. "You didn't have enough heads that you gave one hat to the wee hound too?" Ellie chided. Ana just kept shaking her head, "You three silly men, all parading about in your ermine trimmed hats like peacocks at court!" By now everyone was laughing and enjoying themselves at the expense of Gilley and his extravagances.

Even Ana was given coinage by Gilley to spend as she had mind to do in Dublin. Never having much, she spent half and put away the rest for another time. She reached now in her drawstring purse under her surcote for two large matching decorated silver buttons, fasteners for a nobleman's mantel that she purchased with Ellie's help for Gilley. Proudly, she took them out and presented them to him. "For all you have done for my girl, for us all Sir William," she smiled, thanking him all the more. "You were to spend the coinage on yourself dear Ana," then realizing her kind intent he continued, "I will treasure your fine gift for all my years dear Ana. Thank you."

James was by now running back into the chamber through the open door. His nurse and Shamus were close behind. "Fad' er, James waiting, the now!" said the little boy. Gilley looked down at his son, taken aback by his tone, "What is it that you are waiting for my son?" asked Gilley. "James' sister; yes, James is wanting his sister noo!" His nurse said that he has been chattering the entire day and the one afore since they arrived in Mann about getting his sister now and a brother the later. Patiently and carefully Gilley kneeled down to his young son and held him close so he could be at his eye level as he explained that only God and the Good St. Bride knew if he was getting a sister or a brother and when that day would come. It was Gilley's way never to talk down to his son, but to answer him with true words and to look him in the eye so when the words were important. James wrinkled his brow, reminiscent of his father Ellie noted, when he was struggling with thoughts not of his liking. "Not now, a sister?" asked the little boy.

No, Gilley nodded. "We are not always able to have things as we want them to be. And this sister or brother will arrive in God's time, a lesson of patience for you laddie. And your father too!" he said. Ellie added, "James, if I could I would give you your sister or brother the noo! My back aches so this day," she moaned. James waved good night as his nurse led him off to the nursery. "I will tend to your back Lady El, just allow me time to work some herbs into a salve for you." He left the chamber to return about an hour later and rubbed her back. "You are to be my midwife too Sir William?" she teased. "That is to come later my bride, for now I will take my rights with you as your husband. May I?" he asked quietly. Ellie giggled at his shy demeanor and just held him tightly to her, when he felt a kick

MY TRUTH LIES IN THE RUINS

from her belly against his. "That is life I feel inside you Lady El, I have never felt such before," he said with the complete innocence and surprise of a young lad. Ellie's face just glowed in the warm light of the small candle on the chamber table, as she brought his hand to her belly to feel the child move again.

The summer days were spent riding to different parts of the island. One day they traveled north to Ramsa, or Ramsey as some called the wee port now. "This is where our King Alexander had us land in 1275. On the next day, 8th October, this humble knight was engaged in battle with the Manxmen; 537 perished against few Scots" said Gilley of his service under the king's banners some thirteen years earlier. He also explained that the village was devoid of many fine buildings as it was the first point of attack by other invaders who would lay waste the settlement on their way to battle. Ramsa was a beautiful little village. "In the ancient times, thousands of years before us the old story tellers speak of a land bridge to Scotland from this side of the island just a wee journey north of here," he told his bride, in that voice he used when he was teaching his girl about the past ways of his Celtic people.

Figure XXXV-Part One; Ramsey, Isle of Mann

The couple with their escorts took their time in their travels. Ellie was still comfortable riding on these slow paced mounts; these sturdy horses were certainly not noted for speed she mused. On their return journey south to Douglas Bay the little party of travelers stopped at Kirk Maughold; named in honor of St. Maughold who is said to have been cast ashore near Maughold Head. In the kirk yard Ellie found a tiny chapel. "This is a keeill; constructed in the ancient days of sod, but you can see this one is newer and made of stone," Gilley told her excitedly. "You will find here as well some fine crosses of Celtic design that the old ones tell us were here to greet the arrival of the Norsemen." Ellie was very impressed by the lovely Celtic high cross. "The likes of this fine art work I have never seen," she gushed with enthusiasm.

As the Douglas party continued their journey home to Douglas Bay the lovers talked animatedly about the intriguing history of Mann. Gilley told her that being out in the waters away from the protection that land and neighbors provide the Manx people were constantly invaded by other cultures and peoples. Many forts from other times rose up from the landscape. "Vikings added to the island their own ways; some buried their dead, their lost warriors with their ships. You can see the remains of such burials yet undisturbed; the Manx people hold their history much entwined with the Vikings that settled and raised families marrying Manx women," he continued to tell his wife. "How is it that you have come to know so much of these people," Ellie asked him. Gilley paused, realizing that he had spoken the entire afternoon of the ways of the ancient ones gone before them. "My dear lass, you spoil me with your thoughtful questions; I have only teaching words for you this day Lady El, and you so patient with your husband," he smiled shyly. She asked him again how he came to know the old ways and stories. "Very well little one; your husband has come to Mann in service to his king as you know in 1275; it is my passion to learn of these old ways, their history. And our dear Hugh brought back many stories that he shared in the great hall during Douglasdale winter nights as well from his journeys here," he smiled broadly. The poet knight felt so happy that Ellie shared his appreciation for the past ways; that she respected his Douglas heritage and the ancient peoples that went before him. He loved too that both he and his wife were of Flemish extraction, respecting that ancient culture; as they held for his Celtic ancestors as well.

The next few days the Douglases made plans for a journey to the western side of the island: to an islet called Patrick's Island where Peel Castle stood as if pointing to the heavens, protecting the old Manx church. This church was called St. Germans Cathedral and was built by Bishop Simon who was the prelate until 1249. William was surprised to learn that the cathedral was only closed some few times due to the wars and its proximity to Peel Castle, a fortified site for this part of Mann. Ellie marveled at the lovely chancel of the church, "And the views of the waters surrounding us on this side with the village to the east are so lovely," she gushed. By now Gilley was carrying her up the wee hills; he was concerned for her stamina, but he also enjoyed her dependence on him, doting on her every need.

Their last journey was set for a date several weeks before Ellie's lay-in. Gilley was very cautious; he knew that very soon she would be too large for safe travel and only at her insistence did they take this last trip. They traveled to Castle Rushen in Castletown, the island's center for fortification

MY TRUTH LIES IN THE RUINS

and government. They also visited St. Mary's Abbey that was situated not far from the castle. Ellie loved the chapels at the abbey; the monks were the

Figure XXXVI-Part One; ruins of the ancient Manx church at Peel Castle, Isle of Mann

"white monks" who shaved their heads and wore only the white robes. "You will see the same monks from Melrose Abbey travel through Douglasdale, stopping at the Douglas Kirk on their way to Mauchline and Ayrshire," he told her. "Do these monks really sleep in their white robes at night too?" she asked. Gilley nodded his head. "The life of a monk is prayer and work on their lands," he said, studying her face, staring at her eyes wide with sympathy for the young men who left the ways of the outside world to give their life to God. When they stopped at Castle Rushen Ellie was relieved to learn that the governor was not there; the visit would be short and they could return to Douglas Bay. Ellie was growing weary; she tired more quickly now as her time for lay-in drew closer. Gilley sensed her fatigue and made their excuses for a hasty departure home.

Fall came to Mann in a gradual way; with a cooling breeze and the smell of heather filling their senses. Ellie's twentieth birthday arrived and she could barely get up from her bed to celebrate at evening meal. "I am so large and carry this child so high, but by night the young one is so low," winced Ellie as she felt the baby move again. The hard kicking had since ceased, but the child yet moved often within her. "The lad or lass does move around, high and low; a ruse to keep us guessing as to lad or lassie, my girl," joked Ana. "Come, I will help you get to the hall for the celebration of your birthday; an important one for you and your knight." William made a toast to his wife and presented her with a lovely compact mirror of gold backing, over a bilbous glass with mercury. On the back were these letters in a design with pearls.

She had never seen such a mirror and the beautiful details of gold and pearls on the back were of precious design. "Oh Gilley, you embarrass me so with your extravagance; and I the one who gave no gift on your last celebration of your birth." Gilley just smiled, proud that he could buy her gifts that impressed and delighted her; protested or not. "You are my one and only love. I want you to have things that express the depth of my love for you dear girl," he said quietly to her. Ellie sighed with her thoughts as she turned the mirror over in her hand, "What is the meaning of these letters so, my husband?" Gilley showed her: the "L" and the "E" are for Ellie, and the "E" up to "ov" to "L" is for Eleanora of Lovaine; L O V E, when the letters run together, a design of secret words for his special girl.

November 1st 1288

The birthing pains began for Ellie as she was breaking her fast, just a little over two weeks from the celebration of her own birthday. Gilley was out on the early morning hunt; not due to return for another two hours. "Ana, oh Ana, call the midwives, I shall not know what to do. My timing is so poor that my husband is not home," cried Ellie. "Shhh, now my lamb, you are in good hands. Your husband has left us all with instructions as to what we shall do." Ana brought in some salve that Gilley had prepared to be applied to Ellie's lower back. Then too he left them strict orders of each next step to follow; of most importance, keep Ellie comfortable. He said to wipe her lips with cool moist linen and help her count breaths, taking her mind off her pains, counting one, two, three, then again, one, two and three. "There my girl you are only just started with this child. Your husband will return before you are much further along," Ana said confidently. The midwives from Douglas on Mann arrived. The were already instructed on their duties as well, and quite amused by the prospect of a husband present. A hogs head half full of wine arrived, but Ellie was not to consume any until her husband allowed. A tasine of pear and ginger was brought for Ellie to drink now. Her pains became more frequent so Ana applied more salve to her back.

Though the contractions increased, the pain began to subside. The door of the laying-in room abruptly burst open as Gilley arrived. He dismissed all but Ana for the time being. "Tell me, how often does she feel the discomfort

MY TRUTH LIES IN THE RUINS

cycles?" he asked. "They are as you said much closer now," Ana responded. "Good. Give me my healing box." Ana was his perfect assistant, doing as he directed with few words. Ellie watched in grave uneasiness, her pressing becoming more rapid. "Oh Gilley, I am so scared. Blessed Virgin, I pray to you for help. I know not what to do." "There now my girl, dear lass, you are fairing well. Trust my words and push when I say to do so, breathe when I say breathe, hold my hand here when ever you fear the pressure," said Gilley. "Ana, come hold her other hand. I will check her course." He uncovered her bare legs, and began to feel with his hands the progress of the birth. "I feel a head, this is good news," he said joyfully.

Then he gave Ellie some herbs to keep under her tongue. She began to relax and feel little more than the pressure of his hands working on her. She felt him apply a cold compress where the baby would come, and then saw a frightening sight; she watched in frozen terror as Gilley removed his dagger from it's sheathe. He cleaned off the goose fat in the flame of the candle on the nearby table. And then wiped it clean again with wine, then a linen cloth. "What must you do with that my husband?" she uttered in staggered words, barely able to speak. Ana wiped her brow, and said "He is preparing the way so you do not open yourself too harshly as the babe's head protrudes in the birthing." Ellie was pushing harder, breathing more rapidly, and with a final push of force she never knew, "It's a girl we have Ellie, our Muriel is born!" shouted Gilley. He called in the midwives now to remove the birthing fluids from the infant, as he sought the holy water from the manor chapel. "I baptize these in the name of the Father, Son, and Holy Ghost," he said in Latin, then in Lallans; as he had done for James almost three years ago.

Ellie's face glowed with pride as Gilley brought Muriel to lie on her mother's breast. "Hold her Ellie, she has the beauty of her sweet mother, and the raven hair of a true Douglas. Ellie gasped in amazement. "Gilley, she has a full head of hair, and look, her tiny fingers and toes, those sweet nails so perfect..." The proud healer smiled. "Aye, they are all there for I have counted twice," he said happily. After the midwives cleaned Ellie, and changed the bed linens, Gilley returned with his healing box, applying salve to the cuts he made to ease the deliver. Then he stitched them closed, the salve cleansing and preventing any sensation of discomfort during his work. "You will be able to begin our travel home in less than one week hence. A brave girl you were my Ellie. I will leave you now to get some rest for your sweet self." Mother and daughter slept soundly under the careful watch of Ana. My child she sighed quietly; what wonders have become you in this last year's time she thought to herself. And what will come these next years wondered Ana; more of the same good tidings I must believe now.

Muriel thrived and enjoyed both her mother's milk and the breast milk of the wet nurse from Mann. She cooed on cue it seemed whenever Gilley came to peer in on the young lass. James and Shamus were permitted a visit when Ellie allowed, which was often. The hound would lie by the bed protecting the newborn and James just stared not sure what to make of Muriel just yet; studying her every move. They were all packed and ready to depart Mann on November 7th. Their ship, the seaworthy cog of Captain Gregg would bring them to Irvine just two days later on the 9th. When their shipped docked the travelers were greeted by many familiar faces: men at arms from Douglasdale bringing their pack animals and other horses they had stored at Dundonald. These happy greeters had been checking the ship arrivals daily after they received the word from Gilley on Muriel's joyous birth. But even on her familiar, gentle mare Winter Rose, the going home from Irvine for Ellie was slow, and Gilley insisted they take their time traveling only half the miles daily as before. They stopped in Auchinleck for one night at the old Douglas earth and timber tower there, one of three manors the family held in Ayrshire. Ellie had wanted to continue on to Douglasdale, but her face betrayed her exhaustion.

The tower house was small but had many excited Douglas servants eager to assist with Sir William's young family; and honored that they were called upon to welcome them home first. "We will reach Douglas Castle within few hours, even at our slowed pace, on the morrow," said Gilley, reassuring Ellie that her need to stop more frequently worked well with his intentions of arrival date. He was glad the wet nurse from Mann agreed to join them on the journey home to Douglasdale. Ellie required her rest at night as the day's travel was trying on her strength. The new mother barely noticed the beautiful hues of the foliage, the leaves yet remaining on the trees had turned wondrous colors in their absence from Scotland. Ellie always took such joy in noticing the landscape; but barley looked up to see it this day. And she did not put up a word of protest when Gilley suggested she should allow a Douglas man at arms to lead her horse slowly while she rode side saddle, barely able to stay mounted. Yet her husband noticed the trees in their unique and colorful array. "My dear lass, do you have such colors in you Essex?" he asked her, referring to the foliage. Getting no response he went on to explain that they must have had a dry fall for so many leaves to remain on the trees crisscrossing the glens in spectacular arrays of orange, red and yellow. But Ellie merely smiled; she was too worn out to do otherwise.

They arrived home at last with James, Shamus, and baby Muriel; with barely time to set up the Douglasdale Martinmas feast and Scottish quarter payments day. The notices for payments due and collections scheduled had been delivered to Douglas tenants some weeks before, set up with Douglas squires and men at arms in advance of the family's departure for Ireland and Mann.

MY TRUTH LIES IN THE RUINS

Gilley was soon fast at work in the great hall making the final plans for the feast and computing the fees and other payments due Lord Douglas, that would short time commence. Hugh rose from his bed this afternoon in expectation of his brother's arrival as Gilley sent word ahead. He was quiet but smiling as the entourage invaded the great hall. And when Gilley brought him baby Muriel to hold, the gruff old laird looked up with tears streaming down his cheeks, "I have never held so beautiful a lass, so young and happy she is and so small," then catching himself, he growled "Not at all like your large self, Sir Gilley, for I held you that fateful day, thirty-eight years ago, on the event of your birth." James bolted over to his uncle, "James have sister," the laddie said beaming as he touched her tiny hand. "Mur-a sleep now," he told his sister, and then he ran off to play with Shamus and his nurse.

Ellie was the epitome of exhaustion. Gilley picked her up and without a word from her, he took her up to their chamber. She didn't bother to count the steps: six, landing, five, landing, seven, home as was her habit when he carried her off. Ellie was asleep in his arms when he and Ana laid her down on the bed. "She is in your good hands, Ana, as he kissed his bride's cheek and left, closing the door quietly behind him. The nurse from Mann had taken Muriel from Hugh as one of Ellie's maids in wait showed the young girl the nursery in readiness adjacent to young James' room.

Hugh barked at Gilley as he returned, "We will be outnumbered by women in our own castle William if you continue this pace!" "Don't worry dear brother, next will be a happy lad to increase our numbers, sure aye!" said Gilley. While he had grown stout filling out his broad form, Hugh had become drawn and thin he observed. "My brother would you allow this humble healer to see to your discomforts? Perhaps I can ease some of those pains I see, cutting across that homely face of yours." Hugh looked down considering his words to his brother. "William, Gilley, I have been happier to stay long hours in my chamber now. I find the days too long to endure alone. I seek soon the company of my wife Marjory to comfort my angry self." Again Gilley pressed the matter, "Would you refuse me my healing ways that might make your remaining days less anxious?" Hugh shook his head, "You may come to me tomorrow with your herbs and salves. For today I am too weary." Hugh looked at his platter of food, and asked his squires to assist him back upstairs. "I will take my meal in my chamber," he sighed.

The Martinmas activities commenced on time; fees and rents were collected with few excuses for delay. And the feasting met with much success. Ellie insisted on greeting the men of Douglasdale and bringing with her baby Muriel for everyone to see; but it was Ana who ran the feast sending her girl often back to rest in her bed; carried up by Sir David at

DEBORAH RICHMOND FOULKES

Ana's behest. The next weeks saw Gilley go from chamber to chamber; where Ellie thrived and grew strong, Hugh sank deeper in depression and overwhelming pain. The salves and herbs gave short relief to Hugh. His fight continued through Christmas Day; but by the feast of St. Stephen he was with God and Marjory.

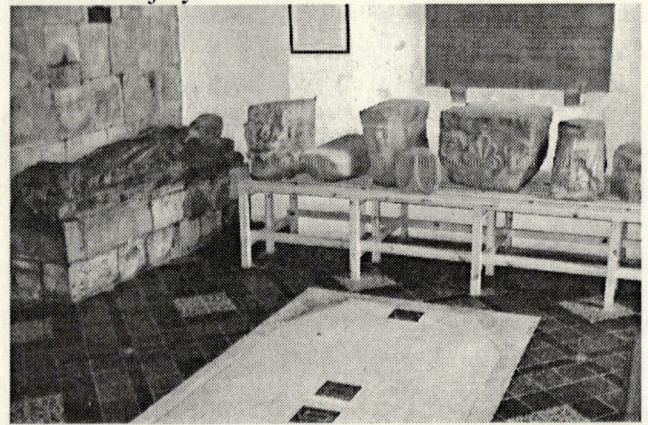

Figure XXXVII-Part One; effigy of Marjory Abernathy wife of Hugh, 6th Lord Douglas at St. Bride's Kirk in Douglas, adjacent to the Douglas Heritage Museum

Gilley sat at his brother's side that morning, holding Hugh's lifeless hand in his. Ellie came in to the laird's chamber to see her husband's eyes well with tears. "He wouldn't let me stay with him Ellie." Ellie sat beside Gilley and moved Hugh's hands together, holding them up in the prayer position. "See my husband, his eyes were closed, his smile so peaceful; he died in his sleep as we all pray to do. He wanted to go alone, his privacy sustained, his way." Gilley looked at her now, and nodded his appreciation for her caring words. She was right, it was Hugh's way to meet his God alone. And again he noted his father's own words, "With a birth comes a death; with a death comes a birth. It is the Celtic way."

The baptism of Muriel just past, there was another ceremony of the sacraments to fill the Douglas Kirk. Gilley ordered funeral hatchments, carefully prepared to properly include the armorial bearings of Marjory Abernathy as well.

Part II

Hogmanay, New Years 1289
Guillame de Douglas, Lord Douglas

The usual festivities for Hogmanay began on December 31st 1288, but were tempered by the recent loss of Lord Hugh. William knew his responsibilities: he had to extend the family's gratitude to the men of Douglasdale and their families for another year of service to their laird with feasting and gifts for each villein, every tenant. He barely knew where to begin these days; there was so much to do; for he was now Lord Douglas and his own seneschal. As Hogmanay was coming to a quiet close William withdrew to the great hall of the keep to review his days' accounts. He was reflecting out loud when his squire came to join him. "Lady Douglas is a great asset to her laird; she would make the perfect seneschal as good as any man could be, sure aye." Patric agreed, "Lady Eleanora has earned her right to your good praise Sir William." Smiling at Patric's pleasant words, "A good judge of others you are my squire," then more seriously "A seneschal is what I need; perhaps the Fleming in Glenbuck would be such choice. What word have you on this knight?" Patric said that such a man is well respected for his honesty; and well liked. "Good," William responded enthusiastically. "I will speak to him before St. Hilary's term, near the Ides."

"Is that the day's end then?" asked Patric. His laird nodded that he could take his leave and rose himself to return to the old hall where Ellie was supervising the conclusion of the feasting. Somehow the celebration of Hogmanay went on successfully. As he smiled at Ellie he realized he had forgotten to give her his gifts. "My dear lass, you have been so patient with your husband this day. For you I have this wee gift, and a parchment from your poet knight." As was his manner, he untied the little scroll and began to read his words for her:

<u>Hogmanay... for our new year of 1289</u>

A year gone by
For more to come

My angel's eyes
Reflect my own

DEBORAH RICHMOND FOULKES

    For now we are
    With years to spend

    Handsome fit and
    Neatly finnis

    With words that laud
    From laughter in us

Ellie's eyes welled with tears, thinking of their first year; so much that happened with so many deep emotions. She smiled up at him, "Dear Lord Will, I am so sorry that our Hugh could not yet celebrate with us; we have so much to thank him for you know."

She began to remove the bright cloth covering the gift he had for her. "Oh William," she gasped as she found a delicate leather coffin with fine iron fastenings, mottled with five small cloisonné medallions of gilded birds. "The little birds are lovely, I am so pleased," she smiled as she spoke in whispered awe of the exquisite craftsmanship. "Look inside my bride, here is the key." More, she questioned with her grimace? When she opened the tiny box she gasped aloud, "Lord Will, however did you find this?" she asked holding up a carved comb in ivory with her initial *E* on the silver handle. "I must hurry to plaite my hair with this fair instrument, too delicate to use I fear, but use it I shall! Now, for you I have this one gift only, and you must come this way," she said to him, almost ordering him about. They entered the keep, passing through the great hall to the withdrawing room. There by the fireplace was a new war-chest nearly nine feet long, of solid oak that had been 'dug out' from one large tree. "I struggled fast to paint the Arms of the Chief, and our family crests of Douglas and Lovaine, with the rampant lion azure. The cherubs are not now complete," she said apologetically. William's eyes reflected his surprise, "Lady El! How managed you this secret from your laird?" He was kneeling as he opened the lid of the huge chest. He marveled aloud at the exquisite details of her art work.

Ellie beamed at his praise; proud of her successful ruse she told him how she kept the gift a surprise. "It was not an easy task when one finds her husband coming about so often. Remember you now the many days you found me in the stables with my mare?" she quizzed him. William nodded, saying "I wondered so that I would look about and not see you; only to catch a glimpse of my lass scurrying back from the stables. I thought you were angered by my moods of late for the loss of our Hugh." What mystery you wield, unnoticed by my somber self, he sighed. "Come here my girl and receive the gratitude of your embarrassed knight and grateful husband."

Figure XXXVIII-Part Two; this old wooden chest at Fairstead Church is similar to a war-chest in size and design

Ellie came over gleefully to sit in his lap; giggling as she told him how the farrier hid her secret task. "Dear Ana was to watch your leave and send Patric out to warn us. Once so informed, we would each take our assigned tasks: one to hide the pigment, one to disguise the presence of a chest, and one to divert the laird should he come too quickly that he might chance discovery our covert activity." William was laughing and smiling, pleased with her fine work; impressed by her scheme of intrigue. "Oh more than just my Ana and your Patric were in liege but we were the main deceivers Lord Will!" she said smugly, "I am so relieved you are happy with my choice of gift."

Two weeks later on January 14th, 1289, Gilley signed a receipt for the Douglas family charters that were just delivered by messenger from Lesmahagow Priory, where the Abbot of Kelso had retained them for safe keeping. This practice of storing valuable documents with a trusted Abbey was not uncommon, but Gilley wanted to have the deeds in his own charter-chest so he might review them as necessary. The family had acquired many lands in over six counties; some lands so obscure even Gilley only knew them from the location of the lands themselves. I must teach Ellie and our James some day as well where every carucate of land is located and every messuage can be found, he reflected. He began to read through the many charters some dating to the late eleventh century when the first William of Douglas received his lands. How interesting the documents seemed to the new laird as he read through the Latin descriptions and noted the seals of the witnesses. Douglas family history was preserved for many generations in these records; invaluable to the laird and chief he mused.

DEBORAH RICHMOND FOULKES

Ellie joined him in the withdrawing room to compose a letter to Lady Helisant Lovaine and Lord Mathew Lovaine, Estaines Manor. The Estaines Manor was in Little Easton or Estaines Parva east of Stane Street and had been the Lovaine manor in Essex, England since the days of Godfrey Lovaine, Ellie's great grandfather. The letter would take some days to arrive. She addressed the missive to both her parents hoping her father's anger might be tempered by the arrival of his granddaughter and heir for the Lovaine estates. She wrote cheerfully of Muriel's birth and of their travels in Ireland and Mann. Then she added with heavy heart, Hugh was now with God. Ellie told them that her husband William became Lord Douglas, Clan Chief with the sad passing of his brother; and once feudal obligations for Douglasdale and Scotland were behind them, they would seek Edward's license for her marriage in England, making the suitable financial offering to the King as was required to gain seising to her dower lands. Then she announced happily: we will come join you both for a reunion with our dear daughter, named for my precious grandmother Muriel Lovaine. Certainly my father will not refuse his grandchild she said confidently to herself.

Figure XXXIX-Part Two; Lesmahagow Priory ruins; the Douglas family kept their charters here until January 1289 when a new Lord Douglas, William le Hardi requested their return to Douglas Castle

Ellie began a second letter to her dear friend Alice in Hertford when Gilley noticed the slight frown, an unhappy face for a lass writing of her happy marriage; so he chanced to read her words. "You are displeased with the events of our lives now Lady El?" he asked her. She sadly shook her head, "Lord Will, I am fearful I will no longer share your life." With a voice of true concern she told him that as a baron he would be often away from

MY TRUTH LIES IN THE RUINS

Douglasdale on the king's business or on campaign, or in Parliament; the same long absences of Lord Lovaine that her mother dreaded so. "Our past year together was heaven in its paradise. I know in my heart I will lose you now. It is my life," she moaned softly. William pulled her to him now, looking deeply in her eyes he said, "I want you with me always Eleanora. You are my wife and partner to all that I am. When we are in king's council, I will have you lodge with me nearby. Only God can separate us, for I have told you so."

"Lord Will, I do not see you most these days; I miss you so, the walking and the riding too," she said. William wrapped his arms about her, hugging her all the more. In his reassuring way he told her that a choice for seneschal was made; once familiar with the Douglas ways and the family charters, the seneschal would relieve his laird to spend more time with his family. "Sir Andrew de Fleming, our Douglas knight from Glenbuck is my choice. Know you too his fair wife Amy of Kirk Mychael." Ellie did indeed know Amy de Fleming for this sweet lady had come to Douglas Castle with her husband on Martinmas last, bringing gifts of fine embroidery to the new bride of Sir William. "A kind lady who does beautiful hand work too I must say. Where will they live once he is our seneschal?" she asked. He explained that he would have them live at Parkhall. "As for Park Castle nearby, this laird will build more defenses and a better entrance. Our James and other sons when they are knights shall live there one day as Hugh and I enjoyed our time so spent in that keep when our father was Lord Douglas. As for Constancia, she may remain at Totheral until her last days."

Figure XL-Part Two; ruins of Thorril Castle, a tower unearthed during the building of the M74 according to Martin Coventry's invaluable work, The Castles of Scotland; a different tower built near Park Castle may have been called Totheral

DEBORAH RICHMOND FOULKES

Then Gilley realized that he had never mentioned his step mother to Ellie before. "I suppose I should explain that not a lover do I keep at Totheral," he said with a slight smile, "but my father's second wife. She is someone I can not bear to see." And speaking more gravely he added, "When my father took to his bed so ill both Hugh and I tried to see him. Fair Constancia refused us both and kept us out of Douglas Castle with her men at arms till funeral hatchments hung over our castle doors." Ellie's face clouded over, "Such awful treachery from one your father loved?" He told her that his father chose to marry when Gilley's older brother Archibald died after the battles with invading men from Norway. "King Alexander requested horsemen, knights and men at arms to follow the king's banner; to expel the Norwegians in the Firth of Clyde. My father sent Sir Hugh and our brother Archibald then fourteen as squire to learn of armaments and calls to serve one's King." Sir William, 5th Lord Douglas, sent two Douglas sons, but not all his sons were allowed to join in the king's retinue; William the youngest at thirteen remained reluctantly behind at Douglasdale.

Gilley continued the story: Hugh distinguished himself in the king's service but young Archibald suffered a poisoning of unheard origins that was to suffer him to God some weeks hence. This part Ellie heard before, so William digressed to tell her more about the source of Hugh's other ailments. "Hugh's suffering from that sad passing of our brother was more punishing than the wounds of limb he received years later at the hands of men named Purdy. One ride he took without company of Douglas men, an attack of violence as Purdy men lay waiting; a younger Hugh turned such mischief to his victory. Spurring his palfrey on, riding for them he gained the support of Douglas tenants coming to his aid yet with great cost to his dear heath I fear," said Gilley. It was after that death of his brother Archibald in 1263 that his father sought more heirs to his estates, deciding to marry Constancia Batayle of Northumbria and Carrick he explained.

"From her dower of one husband past my father had carucates in Fawdon; adding the purchase of one messuage in its entirety to commit the manor to his own freehold for Lord Douglas and his heirs forever, held in freehold from de Umfraville." He shook his head sadly, "Would that she had let me see my father…" his words left him. "Now she demands increase of dower rights; more rents of our lands. Hugh would send her little more. I will not break with his way." Gilley rose to leave the room. "Join me now as we take our feasting. We have earned our celebrating this fair day dear bride," as he extended his arm to escort her to the great hall where food and wine awaited them.

MY TRUTH LIES IN THE RUINS

Little Easton Manor, Essex

The letter from her daughter announcing the arrival of granddaughter Muriel sent thrills of joy through Helisant's very being. Her Eleanora sounded so happy at last; recalling with satisfaction the end of that dreadful marriage to Lord de Ferrers. She found what she felt was a perfect time to share the glad tidings with her husband and lord, only his response was frightening. "I will not allow this marriage any merit from King Edward. She is my one and only heir and my estates will not come to the hands of that greedy savage! What kind of man, this Duglas, can he be but seeking her inheritance?" spouted Lord Lovaine. The fifty year old lord was pacing furiously, flailing his arms wildly, and the veins in his neck protruding a purplish glow. "My lord, she is your daughter and he loves her, she in love with him; they have a child named for your own sweet mother. What evil rages in you to speak such words my husband?" Lord Lovaine, King Edward's trusted Steward of Eye; the noble knight in service to his king was in no mood for his wife's nonsense. The man from Duglas sought only the Lovaine estates he was sure. He made plans to speak with Edward's Chamberlain in private and apprise him of the Scot's desperate deed; then to seek council of the King himself for revenge of this treachery.

Figure XLI-Part Two; Little Easton churchyard, the Lovaine Manor of Estaines is in the background; a secret passage that ran from the church to fortified dwelling is now closed off

Within days the king's cousin and keeper of England was filled with stories from Sir Matthew Lovaine. Edward's trusted Steward of Eye demanded immediate action from his king! The counselor and cousin

Edmund of Cornwall was at Westminster to hear the complaint and he notified Edward firsthand. The king was still abroad in France and took the matter lightly in the beginning. But the relentless pursuit of an outraged father finally prevailed and Cornwall was forced to respond. Lovaine painted himself a grieving father with his beloved daughter the victim of grave peril to her person. His only daughter and heir to Bildeston, Sezincote and Little Easton manors, plus his lands and messuages in Yorkshire was savagely abducted with atrocities placed upon her by this cruel abductor and his accomplices. Sir Matthew described in details he thus imagined. He told of a terrorizing raid in the early morning at the castle in Travernent, the manor of Lady Elena de la Zouche where his precious daughter had been staying. With many men at arms, armaments and armed horse, this terrifying, destructive creature, this Duglas, set upon kidnapping and raping his daughter, taking the fair Eleanora against her will and desire, the king's own ward, for his personal gain. The barbarian made way into the inner lands of Scotland with his beloved Eleanora held under heavy guard; unspeakable deeds hence forced upon her as she now bears the Scotsman's child. Could it be that one Edward Plantagenet would allow such a man to defy the king's will, to remain at large, and with his lands in the king's own bailiwick, Lord Lovaine begged to know. Rage filled his heart the grieving father stammered; justice cries out he pressed with Edward's cousin, the keeper of England!

The king's counselor Edmund of Cornwall believed the Steward of Eye. On January 27th he requested to the Guardians of Scotland to arrest William de Douglas and Eleanora de Ferrers wherever they are found and send them before the king and his Council to answer for contempt. He followed with a second order on the 28th. Then Edmund wrote the sheriff of Northumbria on the king's behalf to seize the possessions of Douglas until further notice, for the violent abduction of Dame Eleanora from her manor of Tranent, to arrest and imprison him as well. Each royal mandate issued by the king's cousin from Westminster included some of the details of the abduction, adding the assuring phrase 'from words of one who would know' or the justifying sentiment, 'the faithful relation by worthy men'. The outraged words of Lord Lovaine were accepted as truth by the counselor in the grave matter surrounding Douglas and de Ferrers.

Lord Edward though still in France sensed a different truth existed from the one he was being told; he was not convinced of the lady's lack of consent in the matter. The king had an exceptional memory for faces and names of those he chance encountered. He recalled this William Duglas from the days of the Levant; the strange healer who made his impression on a young Prince. During Edward's stay in Acre with his own Lady Eleanor and beloved bride, one of the Saracens serving his household attacked him, near fatally. Healers were consulted from all around, and a decision was made to have slaves suck out the poison from the tainted dagger's wound in Edward's hip. William was not consulted on the treatment as the first healing was successful; Prince Edward recovered. But healers were always of paramount interest to Edward from that day forward. Healers can give life, so therefore they must have such skills to take life after all; he pondered this theory often.

Continued inquiries from Lovaine through the king's counselor and a deafening silence from Scotland's Guardians roused Edward to fury; angrily embarrassed by the wrathful indignation of a father scorned he must act and harshly he determined. His agitated state overshadowed any doubts of Lady Eleanora's compliance in the abduction, so he responded in concert with a father's contempt. Again Lord Lovaine pressed the king's cousin for Edward's council, restating the same unanswered complaint. Edmund of Cornwall responded quickly and issued another order on March 28th; this time he addressed it to a proven ally of the past when the king was yet Prince Edward: to the Bishop of St. Andrews, William Fraser. An outraged Edward through the keeper of England in his absence formally acknowledged all associates in the Regency of Scotland with this one correspondence to the bishop. He blatantly ordered the Scottish magnates to produce William de Douglas and Eleanora de Ferrers in a week from Easter! Feeling powerless was never an option; this brash Scot became the cause of his discredit and Edward through his cousin now would not relent.

The broken vows of one Eleanora relic of de Ferrers must be appraised as well; hopefully she was detained without consent yet in fear for her own well being Edward mused as he again reviewed the correspondence from his counselor. His anger and impatience grew in tandem as his requests reflected this increased frustration. Order after order, mandate after mandate, were seemingly ignored. Perceiving a demeaning tone in Edward's writs issued by his cousin, Scotland's Guardians took umbrage. Little would be done to address his demands these magnates vowed in concert. Edward in turn promised to bring the culprits to their knees if necessary; why would they not respond appropriately he demanded to know. Back in Scotland the foreboding words of the Winton speywife reverberated in Ellie's mind. 'Eleanora you must never marry. But if you do marry make it a timid man you take for husband; a bold man will die at the hands of the king. Edward is the name I hear.' Ellie prayed faithfully in the chapel by their bed chamber; daily she begged the intervention of St. Bride: protect us from the English king that we might live in peace in our Douglasdale, she asked humbly.

In April Edward commanded orders to be sent to the sheriff of Northumbria. The keeper of England obediently responded with a letter to

DEBORAH RICHMOND FOULKES

Richard Knut, sheriff: to seize all of the lands of William Douglas and those lands of his accomplice John Wishart as well. Royal mandates on the matter of Douglas and de Ferrers were being addressed every other week; Douglas and Wishart were forever on the king's mind, causing him grave concern in Gascony. Another mandate followed; issued to the sheriff of Tyndale Thomas de Normanville to seize lands of the barons there as well; the last writ of April was finally served. Weeks turned into months and still no response came from Scotland's magnates. In July Edward signed yet another royal command, to the escheator ultra Trent to take the land and chattels of Douglas and Wishart. However long it takes, I vow to have it done; at least Lovaine shows some patience now in this endeavor, he sighed.

Early March 1289 Douglasdale

William was reviewing his wardrobe with his valet Thomas for their first appearance as Lord and Lady Douglas with their family in Edinburgh. They would be joining with some of the magnates of the realm and their ladies who accompanied their husbands to the royal burgh for festivities on the occasion of their gathering. Some of these noblemen would be chosen for the delegation to go to Salisbury; to draw up an agreement of marriage between young Margaret of Scotland and the oldest son of England's king, Edward Prince of Wales. Ellie was going through her surcotes and embroidered silk cotes and cloaks with Ana at the same time. Clothes were

Figure XLII-Part Two; view from Fawdon Manor on the River Breamish, near Ingram, Northumbria; many nobles holding lands in both countries felt torn in their allegiances to two kings, one in England and the other in Scotland.

everywhere; nothing was in its place. The couple had recently moved into the spacious laird's chamber with their separate dressing rooms for the laird and his lady. But now it seemed neither could find their clothes; or at least the right clothes to mark this special occasion. "Ana, I fear I will not feel much like travel with my sickness of child," she whispered. Ana asked her quietly, "Have you told your husband yet M' lady?" Ellie shook her head, "I am afraid he would say I must remain in Douglasdale." Then as if her body was betraying her secret, she grabbed Ana and made a fast path to the latrine closet. Gilley took notice immediately, dropping his mantels and cloaks on the great bed in their chamber. "Ellie, what is the trouble my girl?" he asked peering into the small chamber that was their garderobe. Ana glanced to him and said, "Better get some of that ginger and lavender with honey. You will need it for the trip."

Figure XLIII-Part Two; a latrine closet or garderobe similar to the one above would have been situated off the laird's chamber at Douglas Castle; set apart for privacy by heavy draping or a wooden screen and usually lighted by a small opening in the wall, it could be cold in the winter

Ellie just looked up at him with a hopeless grimace. Gilley's eyes were gleaming, "You were not going to tell me, were you silly lass; no, you feared I would forbid your travel did you not?" he asked her. She just shook her head yes and pouted. "Patric, get me my healing box, the now!" he said giving Patric the key to his special room in the vaulted cellars of the castle.

DEBORAH RICHMOND FOULKES

He spoke more softly as he turned to Ellie, "I would show you off all the more, adding to our clan another fair Douglas that you carry; a dream come true to me now, aye!"

Gilley wanted to know everything: how long had she known, when she last had cycle; every detail he would question. "Why had I not noticed, that is my question," he said aloud, chiding himself for this oversight. Ellie told him she felt she would lay-in after the Ides September but certainly by her birthday there would be a new member of their family. Just then young James arrived with the hound. In one fast second most of their garments met the floor as Shamus jumped onto *his side of the bed.* "You naughty Deerhound; look what you have done with your muddy feet!" chastised Ellie, knowing it would bring little change to the situation. "Ana, would you help me remove Sir Shamus's paw marks from my cote?" James and his father were busy now trying hats on the little lad. "James likes this one with fur." His father smiled broadly, "You have fine taste my son that is your laird's finest hat for Parliament." There was much choosing and packing left to do, but William was preoccupied; another heir for Douglasdale. A fine day, aye!

Figure XLIV-Part Two; looking into the vaulted cellars of Dirleton Castle ruins; similar chambers were built beneath Douglas Castle and held Gilley's healing room

The household traveled first to Livingston then onto Edinburgh, a familiar route to Ellie, from her first journey's ride from Ayrshire the year before. During the unofficial gathering of some of Scotland's magnates, many of whom would be at the Parliament in Birgham the year next, the

Douglases took up residence in the abbey with other nobles they knew. James and Muriel rode in a litter with their nurses followed closely by the wee hound while everyone else rode or walked their own horse depending on the terrain as men at arms and servants led the extra palfreys and pack animals.

Figure XLV-Part Two; Edinburgh Castle today taken during the Military Tattoo

When they first arrived at the abbey James was ready to go to Edinburgh to see the castle with his father, and let William know in clear terms; "James go now." William contained his laughter, remembering fondly his own impatience at a young age. When Gilley was just a wee laddie of five he demanded to accompany his father to Roxburgh, to see the king and watch the selection of new councilors who would meet King Henry of England in Sprouston later that month. His father challenged him that if he could ride the war horse Patrick, he could come along. Try as he would, he could not stay on the large beast nineteen hh, hands high, even after contriving a way to mount the animal. His mother Martha attempted to soothe his temper, assuring the lad that he would grow to large height, enough to ride such a horse one day. But he just stormed off, angry with his small frame; impatient with his youthful age. Now he was of huge stature at six feet four, and faced with his own stubborn son.

"You will come to the royal burgh and meet the great barons of our kingdome soon enough young James; but not this time. Will you offer your kind self to our Thomas here whilst he assists your father in preparations of the finery such appearance at such noble gatherings demands?" James calmly shook his head yes, then added with the seriousness of a lad three times his age "James will speak with his mother; a fine surcote and fur hat to have!" He helped Thomas unfold some finery from the trunk; then the little lad went with Shamus to explore the courtyard of the manor. "Only three years old our son, and already he must have the mantels of office. He will have them by the year next for Parliament or will send me to an early grave I fear," said Ellie with a knowing smile to her husband. Gilley chided, "And don't forget the fur hat! Where does he get these ideas at so young an age?" Ellie rolled her eyes, "I do wonder."

Figure XLVI-Part Two; site near Sprouston Manor, where Sprouston Tower once stood a few miles outside of Kelso on the Tweed; the site of a meeting with the visiting English king and the magnates of Scotland in 1255

The week of festivities was exciting; barons met here and there discussing their plans as the business of the kingdome electrified the city with a special, intoxicating energy. Each evening brought gatherings and great feasting, excellent wine and exciting entertainment including minstrel and magic acts and dancing. Ellie and Gilley found themselves surrounded by many of their friends and kin. The de Lindsays were there with the Stewards; Bishop Wishart arrived as well, followed by many Comyns. Earlier that day the Guardians had made their choice for the Scottish barons selected to go to Salisbury; sending a greeting to Lord Edward, beginning the long formal process that would end the year next with an agreement of marriage with Margaret daughter of Eric, King of Norway, the rightful heir to the Scottish throne and Edward's son and heir. Gilley fashioned himself as **Guillame de Duglas,** using his old seal "SGILL. GUILLAME DE DVGLAS" on some documents; he witnessed charters for some of his kin and friends, his first official act as Lord Douglas, a baron in the Kingdome of Scotland. As the guests came around on the last night of the festivities, introductions were made and Ellie remarked at just how many Comyns there were of station. "At the time of my birth it was said there were thirty knights named Comyn," said Gilley.

Bishop Wishart approached the couple, greeting them with his normal bravado, "It cheers me so to see you both yet so happy, married now a year." he teased the couple. "You must have had good news from England then?" Ellie gave her husband a perplexed look as he began to tell her that Edward through his cousin Edmund of Cornwall had sent mandates to the Guardians, but they were being ignored. "We will address such matters when we are free to travel, after the birth of our child the Ides September next," said Gilley. The bishop was laughing now, "The way you Douglases have young ones, that travel may not happen during Edward's reign." Ellie looked at both of them, a little shaken from the news, "Many months with child is preferable to any in the presence of King Edward, I fear him so." This good bishop reminded her in reassuring tones of a protective parent "You are in the Kingdome of Scotland there is no King Edward here my dear lass. The Guardians are a solid barrier in your defense; fear not his power nor arrogance of same."

Glencorse

One of the smaller manors held by the Douglas laird was Glencorse; located in the Mid Lothianes, just six miles outside of Edinburgh. The pretty village near the River Esk that comprised the manor boasted a lovely kirk that resided near the mains and the nearby manor house, a small keep of earth and timber extraction built on a motte. The intimate surroundings of the wee manor were a comforting departure from the bustle of busy markets and the fast pace of the royal burgh just some short hours' ride away. Here in the shadows of the picturesque Pentland Hills, the beautiful braes and glens of the Mid Lothianes, the Douglases would stay two nights so the laird of manor could learn more of his lands and tenants. As they rode the few miles south to Glencorse Gilley reminded his bride of the raid of the heart from Fawside. "That we can stay here in great security these nights; though just some one year past, to remain here at Glencorse would have been most dangerous I do know it," he sighed, smiling as he recalled the many adventures that filled the year since their first meeting in Ayrshire.

Now when they arrived at Glencorse, they were but just twelve miles from the Hermanston manor held by his cousin, William Douglas where Gilley and John Wishart stayed the night before they led their men at arms on that early morning raid in Tranent to rescue Ellie. These manor lands had belonged to Hugh; given to him in 1259 on the event of his marriage to Lady Marjory. Hugh was but seventeen when his father proposed the unique and rarely executed marriage contract with Sir Hugh de Abernathy that would unite these two politically powerful families. Acting on behalf of his younger sister Marjory, de Abernathy gave charters for lands, including one for twenty merks worth of land in Glencorse for the use of the newly weds. As the charter allowed, these lands were to remain in Hugh Douglas's possession and passed in freehold to his heirs forever unless the marriage was annulled. Gilley had never stayed at the manor and he knew few of the tenants. His intentions were quite specific: learn the lands and meet the villeins.

Figure XLVII-Part Two; the gates of Glencorse Manor; once a stronghold of the Douglases

Taking the Abernathy charter in hand, he rode the marches or boundaries of Glencorse, leading his family through rough woodlands and down through the moorish glen. He began to speak proudly of the Mid Lothianes estate, "Perhaps these lands are the most fertile for crops growing in all of Scotland," he noted. Pointing to an area he called Turnhouse Hill he told them the story of his first visit to Glencorse. "Some weeks past the Lammas, when yet a squire, I accompanied dear Hugh to find of the dowry land from his marriage to Lady Marjory. The day's sky was never clearer as it was that day, the blue shown brightly; the very color of Douglas azure on our pennons as if to signal us of something special yet to see. As we rode up the craigy paths more for sheep than knights on horseback, we came upon a view, aye; the Turnhouse was in breathless wonderment. Never had this lad so seen the heather as it was that late summer's day; her majesty most prevalent in yet so small a glen as this, to paint the hills a solid glow of the deepest purple hues," Gilley told them passionately; sighing the poet's refrain of Scotland's beauty. Ellie brought her mare beside his palfrey, sharing a prescient thought with her eyes as they met his. He smiled shyly at his wife; realizing his words were allowing little time for other's thoughts to be articulated this day. "My husband's only fault to be that he loves his Scotland most ardently," she teased him with a twinkle in her eyes.

The Douglases continued on their wee ride around the manor, stopping only to observe of Castle Law, one of the landmarks noted on the charter. Gilley recalled an ancient fort upon that conical shaped hill; just then his thoughts were interrupted by James, spouting of "a question of importance." James was riding with Gilley on his palfrey; he turned back to his father and with his most serious tone the wee lad inquired, "Are these to be the lands of James?" Gilley told him soon enough he would be Lord Douglas, "Allow this humble knight your father his due time as chief and laird," he chuckled. As they arrived at the modest tower house the laddie told his father that he would desire a better castle, "Most without delay!" he said. Ellie giggled as she teased her husband, "A headstrong lad; yet with plans to expand his lordship!" Gilley shook his head; the willful James was ever a surprise to him with his determined ways. He turned quietly to his bride as James ran off with Shamus, now exuded his well known smirk, "Perhaps my Lady Douglas, that you should so keep reasonable watch of that ambitious laddie; a usurper to be of our kingdome," he said while taking her arm, escorting her into the small keep. "Or this lass might find herself yet without a castle to call her own," she retorted with mocked disdain.

Douglasdale April 10

A celebration of James' third birthday was underway in the great hall. In many medieval homes birthdays or similar events were rarely celebrated. But William was adamant: we will honor these family days as we do those saints' days in the calendar of the Book of Hours, the prayerbook commonly found in every Scottish household of similar standing. The next several days were nothing but parties and feasting; on the morrow they would celebrate their first anniversary, followed by a grand commemoration in honor of Gilley's 39th birthday on the Ides of April, the 13th. James received two gifts from his parents. One was a young foal that he would learn to groom and later ride. The foal was in the great hall when the young lad came down with his nurse that morning. "Fad' er, James dov his horse!" cried the little boy as he saw the young animal barely his own height. "What is his name?" asked the wee lad. "That is for you to choose my son," said Gilley. He thought hard, looking the foal over in great detail. "He must be very brave to be in this big castle without his mother," said James. "We can call him Fortis if you like; that means brave," said Ellie. He wrinkled his brow as if in deep contemplation, then said to the wee foal, "I name thee For'is."

Suppressing her amusement of James' serious tone, Ellie took out her gift for him; his Parliamentary robes as she called the green velvet surcote, trimmed by her own hand embroidery. "James and For'is can go with Fad'er to Pa'ment," he said enthusiastically putting on his new surcote. The foal must be returned to his mother now Gilley told the lad; travels to Parliament would wait. James said his goodbyes reluctantly to his foal and followed his nurse into the courtyard to play. "Come Shamus," he called to the Deerhound bounding down the stairs. Ellie gave Gilley a knowing look. "I held my breath that he did not ask for his fur hat!" Chuckling as he spoke, "The palfrey he envisions from this wee foal filled his mind, for this day and more we do pray!"

For their first anniversary Gilley had a surprise for his bride; they would celebrate their vows of marriage at the Douglas Kirk later that afternoon. Ana brought her lady a beautiful new surcote that Gilley had ordered from the tailor in Edinburgh; purchasing the fabric months ago in Dublin just for this special day. "He always plans these events in advance, yet to surprise me so," giggled Ellie as she spoke. Ana reflected on he lady's loving knight; holding a deep admiration for him that had grown profusely over these last months. "He is most amusing that he does these deeds; and yet so tender to my girl, I hold him dear myself," she said, holding her hand to her heart. Ellie sighed at Ana's kind thoughts, "You my dear Ana, with your Norman ways of second sight. Remember now that you would say I might meet this handsome knight and have many children. Most right you have been, most precious to me you are." The ladies embraced each other, soon chuckling at the times they shared. "We have seen so much joy since meeting my sweet Scottish knight; a rare man he is that, there are no more!" said Ellie.

Ellie and Gilley with Ana, Thomas, Sir David, the new steward and his wife, and many others of the Douglas household, and James with Sir Shamus following in joyous procession on foot, crossed the draw bridge over the moat; then the wedding party and their witnesses walked gaily down through the glen from Douglas castle the short mile to the Douglas Kirk for the quiet ceremony renewing the vows of their marriage. It was truly a blessed day thought Ellie. The sunlight streamed through the trees that lined the cart path leading from the castle to the kirk. Villiens from the wee cottages that stood outside the main gates of the enclosed estate peered out their doorways, entire families crowding the small apertures to get a glimpse of the elegantly attired celebrants as they passed by; the Douglas

MY TRUTH LIES IN THE RUINS

tenants waved and cheered happily for their laird and his bride. Ellie smiled, beamed as she nodded in gratitude for their recognition of her day.

Figure XLVIII-Part Two; stained glass window from the chapel at Douglas Castle, on display at the Douglas Heritage Museum, Douglas, Lanarkshire

James was proudly wearing his new green surcote; shaking his head at the wee hound racing up and back, doubling his travels as was his habit. "No running for James; he has his work to do. No wee hound," as he motioned him not to jump up. A wee lass from the last tenant's cottage, a farmer's simple hut, bolted free from her mother's grasp and ran right to the Douglas laddie. She determinedly walked beside the laird's son the last steps up the brae to the kirk. The pretty child was about his age and he grinned shyly at her in a friendly, caring manner as was his way. She was dressed in a dark, coarse woolen surcote with a plain flax cote underneath, worn and frayed on the edges; a stark contrast to the delicate and colorful embroidered, new green velvet surcote worn by James. Her bare feet were calloused and darkened by weeks of running and playing in the nearby bogs and gills that formed the wild lands of the Douglas parish. Shoes for nobleman's children were of simple leather but the lesser born frequently did without, at least in warmer weather. While James was tended to by nurses, kept clean despite his normal boyish ways, bathing and grooming were infrequent luxuries for tenants and villiens and their offspring. The odd young couple finally arrived at the Douglas Kirk. James bowed politely to the villein's daughter; grinning as he beckoned Sir Shamus to his side. The wee lass made her curtsy then quickly took her leave; satisfied with her exploits, she ran back to her anxious mother, coming up the hill from the farmer's hut.

Figure XLIX-Part Two; Douglas Kirk, later called St. Brides was rebuilt by Archibald the Grim, the last surviving son of James, and maintained today by Historic Scotland

Archibald of Douglas, William's cousin, was still the priest in the family kirk. He greeted them at the door and beckoned them to come inside. At the entrance to the nave was a small group of pipers. Ellie was thrilled to hear the sound of the wee pipes at their ceremony renewing their vows of sacrament. She made her way into the nave, looking into the cozy chapel she beheld the beauty of the kirk, dimly lit by tallow torches in the nave and candles suspended from the ceiling on iron rings, chandeliers of dancing flames. The chapel was truly a Douglas shrine. The armorial bearings of the family were proudly displayed on the walls of the kirk; brightly colored silks edged with golden braid bespoke of noble accomplishments; pennons of Douglas knights, small ensigns with colorful fringe and pointed tongues decorated with the family badge were draped from ropes of velvet in lush hues of red and purple; ancestral stories, the exploits of Douglas chiefs were drawn upon the walls, then painted in brilliant colors as they filled the area above the chancel arch; just below these praiseful depictions, hovering over the ornately carved screen was a beautiful, yet primitive portrayal of the passion of Christ.

Figure L-Part Two; examples of Medieval paintings at the Little Easton church; English churches are ardently preserved by their parishioners

As Ellie waited for the ceremony of the sacraments to begin she looked around her; studied the details of the walls and ceilings. Many churches in Essex were equally lovely; but none bore a family's noble heritage as gracefully yet respectfully as the Douglas Kirk. Beautifully painted funeral hatchments, the double coat of arms of the previous lairds and their ladies, lined the walls of the holy shrine near the nave. Behind the font, the christening bowl where Gilley had been anointed with the holy water when first born, were hung the funeral hatchments of Gilley's father and Lord Hugh; posted at either side of the current laird's own grand escutcheon. This massive shield held the armorial bearings of Willelmi, dominus de Duglas and was surrounded by a dozen smaller shields of brilliant colorings; the arms of the Chiefs of Douglas that went before him. As much a kirk as a sanctuary celebrating the lordship of Douglas and the barons that held of Douglasdale, this glorious chapel now heralded this noble couple; welcoming Ellie and Gilley to take their rightful place in history this day.

As everyone was now seated on the benches in the chapel, except for James, his nurse and the laird with his bride, William looked down at Ellie and pulled her gently to him. "Will you love me tomorrow as you love me today?" he asked her quietly. She shook her head no, "But I will love you all the more. And you my husband, will you love me tomorrow as you love me today?" He replied as was their way, "I too will love you even more my sweet lass." Then it was time. Shamus was sitting beside Ana, though Father Archibald seemed not so pleased; it was only right she mused. As the couple made their way down the aisle to kneel before the priest, Ellie whispered to Gilley, "And I with child just as the first we did these vows of sacrament." He beamed, smiled as broadly as ever she had seen him grin. Their happiness was glowing from within and seemed to fill the kirk with a joyous spirit that only lovers know. Then on silent word from Ana, James walked tall, on tiptoe at times, down the aisle bringing with him a new ring of gold that William had fashioned for his bride. The wee lad proudly, carefully carried this ring on a small cushion fashioned with blue embroidery on white silk the family name, DUGLAS. The same small, worn piece of woven cloth of black and grey from their first ceremony crossed the wee cushion and was delivered safely by young James. This special ceremony ended as the one at Kelso Abbey did the year before; a bride and her husband exchanging the vows of their true love.

The third day of festivities began as the sun rose on the morning of the 13th. Ellie quietly slipped out of their bed and brought back the gift she had ordered; crafted specially for his birthday: a silver medallion with the arms of the Chief. She also had several braided silk sashes of many colors and styles made to hold the silver medallion. This day she tied it on a golden braid to gently place it on his neck. Just as she was slipping it over his head, Gilley opened his eyes and let out a great war-cry "A Douglas, Douglas!" and grabbed her fast. She was furious with him until her anger broke into laughter. "I wondered that you sleep so lightly I might do this task. You scared me so with that frightful yell! You are a savage beast Lord Douglas. I will take back my gift."

He brought her closer still on top of him, and no amount of struggle could set her free. "Fortunate for you that I was awake, for I might have pulled out my dagger safely hidden here; not without some serious consequences for your eminent self." Then answering her question, "The words; it is our Douglas sound to arms, our war-cry to unite our men in battle." Ellie started to cry, tears ran down her cheek. "You scared me; I am sorry to have thought this surprise might please you. I meant no harm; but can see now it was a silly, a folly to do more harm than jest." Gilley wiped her face with his large fingers and gently moved her to his side. Stroking her hair he said gently, "It is I who must apologize this day for you meant only sweet surprise and mirth was your kind thoughts. Let us start the day anew."

MY TRUTH LIES IN THE RUINS

And he kissed her lightly on the nose and looked deeply into her eyes, "I love you more than I love myself these days. A knight and warrior might fear these sentiments, but not your William." She smiled and cuddled into him, "I love you the same Lord Will."

Whitsunday

The good men of Douglasdale came to greet their new laird, William Lord Douglas; and were greeted too by one knight of Glenbuck, the laird's new steward Andrew de Fleming. "Our sincere best wishes to you Sir Andrew, we are most pleased to see you make your mark with our new laird." These happy sentiments were proclaimed throughout the day. Lady Amy the wife of the steward and Ellie served the wine and supervised the feasting table. Sir Andrew was surprised by the ease with which the payments came, with few sad stories to postpone to Lammas or the further now. The total rents and fees twice paid annually at 435 marks, added with another 200 marks annually from the Douglas Kirk, the income totaled a staggering 970 marks. "We have obligations to the escheator from these rents, good steward; you will see when the tally comes much less. But then too we have yet to add our rents from good Selkirk, the Lothianes and the rest."

Figure LI-Part Two; ruins of Douglas Castle on the recently refurbished Loch Douglas, a pond near the old stables

Gilley instructed Andrew next on the income from Ellie's seneschals in Essex and in Scotland; they would bring their tallies to him as well. "Though some delay will come from Essex and Northumbria this year I fear as Lord Edward waits on our appearance in his Council to seek license for our marriage. "With your second child now on the way, would that be such a question?" asked Andrew. Ellie replied for her husband, "With one Edward Plantagenet, no amount of reason is accepted; the longer he must wait the more he does hold fast to his convictions. We will meet with him too soon for this reluctant ward." Gilley continued, "As for the rents from Northumbria, they will come from Baron Wishart, Sir John, or from me when it is my charge to venture south to collect and complete the feudal business as the laird there. Then too some rents arrive in corn or other grain, but I will show you then."

Andrew was making notes for there were many questions and details not yet answered. William had written out the key to his abbreviations; "P" for partial payment, "D" for debt now owed, "T" for payment on a prior debt, and so forth. "I am pleased with your progress Sir Andrew. This day has been a good start to your new charge and station. Thank you for your fine work; a bonus for you now," Gilley said as he handed him another amount of coinage that was not expected. "Your generosity speaks well of your Sir William; my pleasure is to serve you faithfully and honestly. Come dear Amy, it is ours to part now for our new home." Amy came to William and spoke softly, "Lord Douglas, I mean Sir William, I am most grateful for the graciousness of Parkhall you have bestowed upon us. A long and prosperous relationship between us; thanks be to God and St. Bride for our good fortune in serving one as you."

Dumfrieshire Late May

Ellie had received word from Sir John concerning her dower lands and manors in Dumfrieshire and Wigtonshire; rents were not forthcoming as he desired. Le Parker also requested that Lord Douglas consider coming there in person to determine if the steward's assessments were of his liking. Some immediate repairs at Senwick Grange were required; he also wrote that the several years of bad weather without refurbishment had not only caused the damage to buildings but also to crops growing, thereby effecting tenants and the fees. After reviewing le Parker's letter Gilley decided that a journey to Scotland's southern coast was in order. The family would first go to Senwick, then travel west and north, following the beautiful coastline through Newton Stewart; then they would turn south again towards Wigton. They left Douglasdale: a caravan of nannies and children, men at arms, nurses, maids in wait, Ana, one silly Deerhound, and the laird and his lady, was readied for adventure in just one day by the fastidious work of Ana and Gilley's squires and valets.

MY TRUTH LIES IN THE RUINS

Figure LII-Part Two; Douglas Castle coffer on display at the Douglas Heritage Museum, Douglas

Very late on the third day of their travels they arrived at Senwick Grange, near the de la Zouches' lands and tower at Balmangan. Ellie's dower lands in Scotland were all held of William de Ferrers, heir to his mother's de Quincy lands; these were no exception. Douglas pack horses were led into the courtyard of the manor; Lord Douglas and his bride with Sir David and men at arms from Douglasdale entered the gates at Senwick where Gilley was to meet with John le Parker.

The storm damage to the mews and the detached kitchen were manageable Gilley told them. Two months of work from his good men at Douglas Castle would put the manor in fair condition for the winter next to come. Ellie was thrilled with the views of the sea at Ross Bay as it flowed into the larger Kirkcudbright Bay. And the lovely Senwick Kirk nearby impressed her as well. William told le Parker to call out the tenants of the manor; the villeins finding it too difficult to pay their rents to their laird. Perhaps by Lammas next he would thus extend them, the baron told his steward, showing his generosity of favor to his new tenants.

The next day these farmers came to speak with Lord Douglas about their fees and rents, some paid him in full at that first meeting. Hardships of weather and some crops not grown caused them to fall in disfavor was the excuse given by the non payers. Lord Douglas made suggestions; extended deadlines; arranged some loans; approved water rights and granted other dispensations to his villeins. Prosperity returned to Senwick Grange by the generosity and knowledge of a laird who understood his people and their needs.

DEBORAH RICHMOND FOULKES

Figure LIII-Part Two; Senwick Upper Grange near Balmangan Tower; a manor held of the de Quincy estates by three daughters; one daughter was Margaret de Quincy, mother in law to Eleanora Douglas who now held a share of the manor in her dower

Gilley was pleased with their progress this day. Scottish lairds for Scottish tenants; success to practice this fair rule in collecting rents in this fair shire he so reflected. "These wild men of Dumfries follow their own lead Ellie," said Lord Will. "They are an independent breed; living on the far borders of our Scotland they hold little respect for others coming to their hamlets that are not of this shire. The name of Douglas they have heard and know; my word to them is bound by Douglas honor. These rents will now come freely for our coffers." Sir John was relieved; he was concerned with these strange tenants, their attitude of indifference was not known to Essex gentlemen. But Gilley knew the men of this shire from his crusader days with Earl Adam. Many armed horse and foot from Ayrshire and Lanarkshire joined with those men of Dumfrieshire, riding together under banners of that laird; William included, as they traveled to the Levant in 1270.

Ellie and Gilley found time to walk about and ride their palfreys by the sea. They would ride each day to nearby Ross and look out into the sea to Little Ross and the Solway Firth. "It is here that the old Celts told us of that land passage to the Isle of Mann," said Gilley as he pointed south and west, "there at Burrow Head. One day when we so have more time to spend in Wigtonshire; that you dear Lady El are not with child, the lay-in so soon to come, we will ride to Whithorn," he told her. "This lass would love to come again to Scotland's southern shores and seas," she sighed as he stood behind her, wrapping his long arms around his bride as he did so often. "Will you love me tomorrow as you love me today," he began, whispering in her ear as he turned her now to face him. Ellie came round, giggling as he brought her now to sit upon his lap. "This is a happy place; most pleased is the laird that you have this lovely manor for us now to so enjoy!" Then he reached for the brooch closure on her surcote, "May I?" he asked softly. Here, she questioned with her eyes, bright with fascination for her knight and his romantic ways. He nodded yes, with that well known smirk; they cuddled into each other oblivious to the beautiful scenery before them.

The Douglas household traveled onto Wigtonshire; fording the Cree before turning south towards the village. Wigton was a smaller manor and the Douglases were very cramped with many servants sleeping in the great hall and in the passageways to the family chambers. But the views of Wigton Bay and Baldoon Sands were breathtaking. This day they took the wee Muriel and her nurse, with James riding with his father, followed by Sir Shamus as they traveled some few miles east of their manor. They rode to see some standing stones and Gilley explained the Celtic ways to his wee son and Essex wife. He spoke of the ceremonies and use of a special wand that would empower the priest of the tribe with God's own power and just words. "That to our north are some stone circles, once dwellings; reminding us of the ancient ones who have gone before us. Dear son, this father will often speak of these sage people for they are the wise ones who knew the lands so well they felled many an invader to their lands," Gilley told James proudly. Lord Douglas valued the ways of the Celts and imparted that knowledge often to his son and family. Such journeys with his children he enjoyed; Ellie took much solace in his teaching. She eagerly learned of the ancient ones that left their unwritten words in stone circles and standing stones all over Scotland; she marveled at their foresightedness of these creative people, to leave clues that others might learn from their ways.

The Douglas' stay at Wigton with Sir John was short; promising to return in the spring or summer the year next. The tenants there were current in their fees; only a few owed of any of their rents after their meeting with Lord Douglas. Those villiens who were partial paid agreed to meet their obligations by Lammas. "Gilley, are there many repairs to be made here as well," Ellie asked her husband. "That we can do for future, we shall do this year. Sir John, when the half of rents most due again, spare some to shore up the stables and enlarge this side as well," said the laird. He explained to the seneschal that the Douglases needed more room for their household as well as for their horses and pack animals as their larger family was yet growing, he chuckled proudly. "The good tenants here can serve you most as well in the building of that new wall," he also instructed. Le Parker appreciated the intelligent plans of his laird; telling Ellie and her husband that he knew of one fair carpenter and mason to assist the work they requested. "We will begin just after Lammas for this work," said the steward.

Figure LIV-Part Two; Ross Bay near the manor of Senwick Grange

Ana came into the great hall and told them all that the cook was most pleased with the larder so full, "The hunt this morning of Sir David and Sir William brought so many rabbit and several deer, he is overjoyed! And the pheasant and the grouse he would use this time as well," smiled Ana. Gilley started laughing and announced the feasting to commence at once, "This day to end for word and work of seneschals, all; time to enjoy platters full of game and much wine to pass around, sure aye!" Ellie turned to le Parker, "You have done well for us Sir John; my husband and this lady wish that you would take an extra portion now for your own service here in Wigtonshire." Then loudly with his well known bravado, Lord Douglas said in a toast to his steward, "Sir John, to you!" as he poured le Parker some wine as well. The laird was enjoying the company and fair times at this good manor; making his plans for their return in a year, when they could stay longer.

Yet the fate of Scotland flowed unknowingly from the ambitions of one greedy lord in England. Gilley's plans would change; he never again enjoyed the peaceful serenity of that shire. Ellie and her children were left to fulfill his promise to return to these lovely seaside manors alone, without him. And when she came back to Wigton with her family the days of tranquility, of lives carefree with children laughing, running with their silly Deerhound all about were but cherished memories. These barons in the lowlands and their families, these wardens of the marches were a hearty lot; they had to be. The lives and safety of these border folk were pawns in the hands of greater lords seeking control of their shire. But for today it was celebration and much laughter for this Douglas family: William le Hardi and his lady were content, enjoying the bounty of their hard work and generosity to their villeins.

MY TRUTH LIES IN THE RUINS

Figure LV-Part Two; Wigton Priory ruins

Douglasdale September 10, 1289

Ellie knew her time was coming soon, perhaps the next few weeks as she was barely able to rise from bed without the help of Ana or William. "That the air is cool and dry with a day of bright sun that I should venture out this day Ana. Have you seen my husband?" Ana told her that some riders came early that morning with an urgent message from Lord Petty as Justiciar of Scotia north of the Forth. "Lord Petty, that is his kin Andrew de Moray I feel. What brings him so far south on business of the court?" Ellie questioned aloud. "I pray this business will not take my husband far." Ana told her that Gilley had taken some twenty men at arms including Sir David and another knight to Colbanistown in Covington. "It seems indeed quite serious from the manner of your knight my sweet lamb. But do not frighten yourself with worries now, he is able and of good courage in these matters."

Ellie was finally dressed and making her way down the stairs to the great hall when one of the squires announced a large band of riders with Douglas standards and banners was approaching. James was playing in front of the fireplace with his blocks; Muriel was nearby with her nurse, as Shamus was taking his afternoon nap quietly beside them. Lord Douglas

145

came in the great hall quickly. "Eleanora, take the children with their nurses into the withdrawing room. Ana help her quickly, the now!" Ellie had never seen William so riveted, so alarmed but under control. Afraid to take time to ask why, the ladies moved the children and Shamus into the side room waiting William's word when it was safe to return. "Please have the cook send my sustenance to the withdrawing room; James, Muriel, the noo!" barked Ellie as she gestured them into safety of the side chamber.

From the great hall they heard a din of frightening noises; the clanking of swords, the dragging of iron chains against the wooden floor, men at arms rumbling, running through the hall shouting in pandemonium, the loud slamming of doors, furniture crashing about, violently pushed aside as prisoners tried to escape their captors. There were fearful shouts of defiance from the prisoners in fetters; commands in unseemly words and unusually harsh tones came from the Douglas men at arms. The cacophony, the hysteria of disruption began to subside as Lord Douglas informed the prisoners that a court session would be held that day within three hours hence. A court session thought Ellie, what must they have done?

Three dangerous prisoners held fast in iron chains were being led away; taken to the donjon prison as William entered the withdrawing room. "Ellie, please pardon so frightening an entrance to our home, but Sir Andrew here has been on a tragic chase to avenge the death of someone you know. Young Duncan of Fife, your cousin and the Guardian of our Kingdome was brutally murdered just three short days ago. This good and true justiciar with the brave men of Moraydale and Petty, have tracked them to our baronial ward." Gilley explained that they would hold court in the old residence hall this day. Ellie sat down quietly; shaking her head in despair, the young earl was dead. He was the son of her cousin Anne de Ferrers, the first wife of her late husband and the half brother of her step children. "What tragedy has come to Scotland with young Duncan dead; he yet alive to speak with young de Ferrers in Fife this Lammas past," she said. She wanted to know more of the details, but Gilley was reticent to tell her; her lay-in was due and this could upset her he advised. "William, I demand to know the names of these men held in the prison of our home and more of the details of this terrible crime," she said emphatically. "I am not some silly child to hide from the truth, but Lady of this castle and your wife. Continue, the now."

"Quiet now Ellie, the children are here, I will give of you the details, but first you must calm your sweet self and let us have the children take leave with their nurses." Gilley started to explain the last three days of frantic chase, when he turned to his kin Sir Andrew, "Your words are better here than mine, for I must hold baronial court, passing on the doom as you defend." Sir Andrew told Ellie that Sir Patrick de Abernathy and Sir Walter de Percy with counsel and consent of Sir Patrick's own father, Sir Hugh de

MY TRUTH LIES IN THE RUINS

Abernathy, did brutally attack and slay the young earl in Pitteloch. Sir Hugh waited in secret with a large party of men at arms on another road so that young Duncan would not escape. Ellie's eyes watered now. "It is well Lord Hugh is with God that he not hear of this treachery and dishonor on the house of Abernathy. And my kin, Sir Walter, what discord he brings to me his cousin so?" William looks at her quizzically, "Your kin is the de Percy knight?" he asked. She nodded, "Our grandfathers, half brothers, both Lovaines." Harder still will this now be he mused. "There is more." The justiciar told her that the crimes took place in Pitteloch, where two squires were put to their deaths at once by his men. "Lady Eleanora, this vicious crime will call for swift justice, but only one of true courage could imprison such a man of station as Sir Hugh de Abernathy; should the court's doom come to that end."

William's steward Sir Andrew de Fleming was chosen to serve as Officer of the Court. Father Archibald from the Douglas Kirk was asked to be the Clerk of Court, recording the proceedings in writing. Before the official opening of the session William brought in young James to show him how a baronial court functioned. The wee lad was very solemn as he father led him into the great hall of the old residence; standing at times again on his tip-toes to appear taller with noble bearing, his father noted, but only because he did the same so long ago to impress his own father. Ellie, Ana, the Douglas servants of rank joined James and Gilley to hear their laird speak. "The Steward of Douglasdale acts as Court Officer and calls the Court to order." He continued to describe the rituals of tradition; the marking of the bounds of the courtroom with a white wand of Scots Ell in length, the scepter of the officer of the court. "This simple wand is of our Celtic ways of Druid origins where the white wand was the symbol of the divine, able to lay boundaries for Celtic worship anywhere required. Remember now the standing stones near Wigton and our manor there?" he asked the lad. James said that he certainly remembered the ancient ones and their sacred place. "The Druids would most use such an instrument in their sacred ceremony at that place," said Gilley.

In adult terms the father told his son and the others now in attendance that the wand symbolically marked a power emanating from God. "This power of temporary nature would allow the court and Baron Judge, the Chief Magistrate, the autonomy of decision under God's influence and grace." Taking the lad to the front of the hall Gilley showed him a horn that would be used to summon the court in session. "It is not permissible for you to stay this day for such proceedings are of grievous nature. Do you understand my son?" he asked, kneeling and looking young James in the eyes, man to man. James very serious in his words, "Yes thank you Sir William." Gilley gave the boy to his nurse, and she escorted him out. "What will he say next, the words yet still amaze me so!" said Gilley to his wife. She smiled up at her husband, "Sir William, time to change to the robes so befitting your office." He took her arm and escorted her to the withdrawing room where she waited his return. "I fear I wobble so that I might fall; thank you for the escort my husband."

The prisoners were brought to the courtroom with many men at arms with full armaments. Swords and armor clanked, chains and fetters rattled as the solemn, rigid procession made its way from the donjon prison to the hall of the old residence. Gilley was coming down the stairs. Ellie peered through the doorway; letting out a small gasp; how wonderful he looked, so prestigious and dignified. The baron wore a black velvet robe lined in striking blue silk. It was trimmed around the neck and down the open front on both sides, than along the hem as well, all in ermine. Gold braid feathered with white fur formed the three bands around the billowy long sleeves of this magnificent robe. Underneath the robe was a blue and black silk surcote that fell to his knees over another black brocade cote with long sleeves. William wore a silk braided rope of red brocade around his neck that held the silver medallion with the Arms of the Chief Ellie had given him for his birthday. His long tresses of thick raven hair flowed beneath a striking red velvet hat trimmed with gold and black braid also lined with ermine.

He was very solemn now, his attire bringing a distinct bearing of responsibility and dignity to his demeanor as he took her arm and escorted her to the hall that was now the Baronial Court. Sir Andrew de Fleming blew the horn commencing the court to session; all in attendance were asked to rise as the Chief Magistrate entered the court room. Sir Andrew de Moray read the names of each defendant and the charges against them. One of the de Moray knights was asked to give testimony. He described his discovery of the young earl's body in grave detail and gave words of the pursuit that took Lord Petty's men into Clydesdale three days later. When the others had testified, William allowed the prisoners to speak on their own behalf. Sir Hugh de Abernathy requested to come before the court as did Sir Walter de Percy. Both knights requested surety of rank and free release, being the custom in some baronial courts to allow others to serve the nobleman's sentence in his place. "Denied," said the magistrate. Then one by one he called them forward and pronounced the doom. Sir Walter de Percy's doom was death by beheading; his squires already dead; hanged by order of the justiciar earlier that day. Sir Patrick, the son of Sir Hugh was to be hanged by the neck until dead.

An outburst followed the Chief Magistrate's words; Sir Walter further disgraced his knight's rank. "I would falsify the doom; you have not right in this jurisdiction. I demand appeal of the doom." William looked at the arrogant knight and spoke these few words: "You have forfeited your rights by such unspeakable acts; perjure yourself further will revise a more cruel doom to your fate." The kin of Eleanora would not rest. "A curse upon you Douglas; the gallant men of Percy will not relent in your pursuit, till you serve the same doom for your arrogance and folly! And a curse upon the house of Moray too I vow this very day!" William spoke sternly above the din of the prisoners' discontent. "Good men of Moray remove this prisoner to meet his doom by the executioner's axe," ordered a solemn William.

Turning now to the third prisoner, Sir Hugh de Abernathy, Lord Douglas issued words as the baronial judge: "You have discredited the fine and noble house of the family of Abernathy with your tempestuous act of lawlessness and greed. To your own son you have given a legacy of dishonor and a sentence of death by hanging; when a father's own truth and love should be his greatest gifts to his son. As the magistrate your sentence shall be no less than were you not kin to the noble house of Douglas by the marriage of your sweet sister Marjory to my dear brother Hugh, both now with God. These words to come, your fate determined: lang will you have to reflect on your callous mischief and ill chosen path of no restraint. No more shall you see the light of Scotland's fair days for you shall remain a prisoner in Lord Douglas' donjon prison till God calls home his wayward servant. It is done."

The judge rose and left the court room, followed by Ellie and the others of the Douglas household in attendance. The two remaining prisoners were removed to their respective prisons. Lord Petty joined Lord Douglas in the great hall of the keep. "It will take true courage to remain constant when others of greater station will come to lay plea to Sir Hugh's release." William told him that Sir Hugh's wife Mary, a Comyn, was kin to his sister Willelma and the de Galbrathes. "Many families will feel the gravity of their crimes and suffer the sorrow of their fates." Then he shook his head in pained remorse, "This baron Sir Hugh, to hold so much authority that he sought to corrupt his actions of greed for more power. This laird holds a history of such brazen behavior, do you recall? My father told me Sir Hugh with other magnates seized young Alexander, the young King yet in ward; a usurping of the government in realm; he tried upon our Scotland," Lord Petty nodded sadly yes, he did recall. "A tragic path with no core values led him to his sorry end, aye," said Sir Andrew.

Ellie interrupted them, "Why would the Justiciar not pass the doom my good husband, but to turn the court over to baronial authority?" William explained to his wife that the Justiciar of Galloway might have some more authority; but he was a Comyn who sister was the wife of Abernathy. "Good Andrew here had asked of me to thus respond so quickly; to pronounce the doom and avoid the mischief of those of higher station that might free the prisoners before a court could thus convene," Gilley said, adding, "Were there a King in Scotland living, for such felony would he have thus presided. In that absence, we have made this choice." Ellie spoke with more than worry on her mind, "My own concern would that the good men of Percy, my own kin, not hearing the truth of Sir Walter's grave deeds might take it on themselves; thus unleash a vengeful terror for our work here." William looked at his cousin, then his wife; and replied to them both with calm demeanor, "I have always held to my truth, my own core values. Even with the closeness of kin would I not be tempted to break with what is now done. I fear only God's displeasure in this life; to release the distasteful criminal and grievous murderer, Sir Hugh, would offend my God. To not enforce the rightful doom of the slayer of Earl Duncan would be betrayal to God's own words. This I know for my truth."

Sir Andrew joined the Douglases this next morning to break his fast, sitting around the table in the great hall. Ellie recalled this laird's own ordeal with Edward Plantagenet and licensing for his marriage in 1284. "That this humble knight did not receive one shilling from my dear Euphemia's dower," he scoffed. "The lands of my sweet bride's inheritance in England were yet held by Edward's cousin for the king. My lass worried so for those fees; that she left me too soon for the Otherworld but not before delivering me a son, dear Andrew; for she is now with God since Hogmany this year," he shook his head sadly. William and Ellie offered their condolences on the great loss of his wife, for they had not known about Euphemia. "Dear Andrew, to lose a wife in child-bed is most tragic an event," she said poignantly.

Lord Petty, Justiciar north of the Forth was about to depart Douglasdale when a nervous Douglas squire came running into the great hall. "Sir Patrick has escaped Lord Douglas!" he said cautiously, fearing the wrath of his laird. "I have checked his father, but he was held in fetters the night long and has yet remained in our good prison. His son was held in the small rear tower; sadly in a chamber with one wee window yet wide enough for such a man to slide through to his freedom. A rope of some bed linens his method of escape I fear." William looked up calmly, but seriously, "have Sir David bring about some other horsemen and search the Douglas lands as far south as Crawfordjohn. I fear though that he has made fast his escape to England then to France. Is his horse still about?" The squire told his laird that one horse was missing and believed to be Sir Patrick's. "Our good men of Douglasdale are not so experienced in these baronial matters dear Andrew," said an apologetic William. "I am not so concerned about Sir Patrick. It is his father and de Percy the villain in this brutal slaying. Perhaps your men will find the knight; would you like the assistance of my men at arms?" he asked. "No, we will set about a search for we know the lands and the people residing. If he is still about, he will be found. I will send you word." Lord Petty thanked his cousin again and set about his return homeward, north to Avoch.

Weeks passed since the baronial court handed down the doom. Word came from Lord Petty that Sir Patrick arrived safely in France where he thus remains, unless full pardon for his deeds is sent to him, wrote Gilley's kin. It was the morning of October 2nd Ellie made her way down the stairs and then suddenly she was calling Gilley and Ana. "My time has come." Gilley came to her side and swept her up in his arms, barking orders as he climbed the stairs to the laird's chamber then through to the lay-in room beside it. Ana knew her work to do, making her girl comfortable. Three hours passed when Gilley made his first check and he was again so pleased, "I feel the wee one's head!" The Douglasdale midwives recalled the birth of young James, chuckling now as Lord Douglas prepared to deliver his third child. "Push Ellie, we are almost done," he said calmly, gleefully. "Praise be to our good St.Bride another girl for our glorious Douglasdale!" This time he christened the child and then handed her to the midwives to remove the fluids of birth. "A fine wee lass she is too Ellie, you will see. Are you all right my dear girl, you seem so quiet now?"

She smiled sweetly but her pallor betrayed her fatigue, "I am so tired this time, I feel I would sleep some now. Perhaps I am more comfortable with the birthing, so scared was I in Mann." She spied Ana now bringing little Martha named for William's mother. "My dear daughter, we are gaining control in number of this castle; soon the dames of Douglasdale will rule their lands in their own right!" Gilley shook his head at her, feigning his disdain for her taunting words "There will be no talk of mutiny, no more wine for courage; bold talk of insurrection against your laird and husband! These two sweet daughters soon to be outnumbered by our many sons. It is done, aye." But Ellie didn't hear his words; she was fast asleep.

Just three weeks later on November 6th that the Treaty of Salisbury was agreed to and a Parliament was called for March 1290. William's name, Guillame de Duglas, was appended to the letter from the guardians, forty-four ecclesiastics, twelve earls, and forty-seven barons to the King of England agreeing to a marriage of the Queen of Scots and Prince Edward of England. "Ellie, I fear this strange alliance with your Lord Edward's son. But it is done; agreed to now," he sighed. "The path of Edward's plans seems open to his gain," replied his wife. "Strange now the outcome; an Edward to be King of Scotland from this marriage." Gilley looked at her quietly, "You can not allow the words of the old woman to cloud our hearts with fear dear Ellie. Only God knows our future; only we control our destiny I pray so."

DEBORAH RICHMOND FOULKES

January 1290

Sheriff Richard Knut of Northumbria was arrested and taken to the castle prison at Roxburgh as he crossed the borders into the kingdome of Scotland. He was here on important business of his king; to find and arrest William de Douglas and Eleanora de Ferrers. But the Guardians of Scotland were un-amused and seemingly unconcerned by Edward's mandates. Knut would be held there under arrest until the end of the Parliament of Birgham so as not to inconvenience any of the participants from the proceedings. Once Parliament convened and the signing of the Treaty of Salisbury was completed, Knut would be released. Guillame de Duglas, Lord Douglas, would be one of the signers. Sheriff Knut wrote in his letter to his wife Eva that he would most return by the English quarter day; should there be more delay, requesting her to record the day. Eva Bolteby was a good match for Richard Knut; she was a bright woman with unusual skills, most able to record the financial year in his absence, with a clear escheator's hand.

The Douglas household traveled east to Roxburghshire that Lord Douglas could attend Parliament through the 14th of March. Then the family would begin their journey to England; to make their peace with Edward Plantagenet. James was walking hand in hand with his father, peering into the chamber, before the session began. The Steward was making his way into the hall when he spied his namesake and William. "Young James good nephew, Parliamentary robes I see," remarking on the lad's new green velvet surcote in with gold braid embroidery of his mother's hand. "Are you ready to join our council dear nephew?" he asked, nodding hello to Sir William. "Sir James, my uncle, I am four and ready." Four, questioned the Steward, has it been that long? "Recall James your birthday is not for four more weeks, then you will be four my son. Do not hurry the days of your youth; you will need them to comfort on reflection as I do now in my later years."

"A word with you William," said the Steward. They moved aside out of hearing of any who might be about. "I fear this treaty, but have no other to yet substitute. What say you on this my trusted kin and council?" William nodded in agreement. "Any treaty with Lord Edward is suspect now; I fear his ambition. Only I offer no recourse at this time as well; the deed is done." "Aye, the deed is done," agreed the Steward. "Oh, one more thought for you. Lord Edward has sent his Sheriff Knut to find and bring you back to England. We hold him now in the prison at Roxburgh Castle and will until the Parliament is called to close then to free his sorry self."

MY TRUTH LIES IN THE RUINS

Figure LVI-Part Two; William le Hardi's first recorded act as a baron of the realm was to sign the Treaty in Birgham in 1290: Guillame de Duglas

William thanked Sir James for the information and assured him that the couple was on their way the England to meet with Edward's council. "We leave from Parliament's last session for Little Easton Manor, home of my wife's father the Steward of Lord Edward at Eye in Suffolk. Then to make our peace and ask for license of our marriage." Sir James was relieved, "Good! I shall pass the news to the other three guardians. Our number dwindles all the more with Alexander Comyn gone. What tragic death that of young Duncan; and righteously held you baronial court for our justiciar Lord Petty passing doom on Sir Hugh thus correctly. Courage and truth; your reputation is redoubtable Lord Douglas." James waved good-bye to his uncle as the Steward went to greet another guardian of the realm Bishop Wishart; to share the word that Edward's mandate of Douglas and de Ferrers was soon to be resolved.

Fawdon, 22nd March 1290

Sheriff Knut was released form the prison at Roxburgh Castle on March 20th and was advised that Douglas and de Ferrers were on their way to England; perhaps to stop at their manor in Fawdon, he thought. The Douglas procession of travelers arrived at Fawdon nearly a week before Knut's return to Northumbria. They were only staying one more night, when riders approached under the standard of Sheriff Richard Knut of Northumbria in the early morning hours. Patric came hastily into the great hall of the manor, "Sir William, the sheriff approaches." William had the nurses remove the children to their nursery. "Ellie, we will not resist the efforts of the good sheriff, he is one known to our family. When first I was given land of my father in Northumbria I was ward of John de Haulton kin to this knight; a former sheriff yet himself of this good shire."

William went out to meet the riders, two Douglas men at arms following close behind him. "We will offer no resistance to your words and required deeds good Knut. What is the manner we must respond?" he asked. The sheriff held back his own horsemen as he dismounted. "I must remove you to the prison at Knaresburgh Castle; the King's mandate too I have for the arrest of Lady de Ferrers who's presence I conjecture by your good civility." William took the three documents from Knut and began to study them carefully. "As we make our way to good Edward's ward in Knaresburgh, allow your good will to not arrest the lady finding only Lady Douglas, a mother yet with child, who will but follow in procession?" Knut studied William carefully before he spoke. "Two months have I been guest in Scotland's prison; that our Northumbria allows such generosity were you alone I might consider more. Knut will grant you travel with your family; your wife with child, as our good escort here demands." He told William that they would depart within four hours. Another quarter day that will be missed but with fair excuse on this the king's own business; good that my Eva will hold the day mused Richard Knut.

"Come now with me as I inform the household of our hasty departure to Knaresburgh's good hospitality." William led the sheriff and two of his men at arms into the manor. "Lady Eleanora, good Knut has extended the escort of the Sheriff of Northumbria to our travels south towards Leeds. In Knaresburgh Castle, one day's march from Leeds, we will stay as guests of the king until we arrange surety for our appearance with our dear Lord Edward." Ellie was frozen in her place where she was sitting now at the large table; unable to move; barely able to speak, "Good sheriff, would you and your men grace our table here in fine repast as we extend to you?" Knut smiled and spoke quietly to her, "Lady Douglas, your good husband has agreed that we should in four hours leave. My men at arms and I would much indeed accept your kind offer; giving apologies for the inconvenience of this matter." William did not know Knut before this day, but regarded his good manner with respect. He began to give out orders to the household to make ready for their departure. He took Ellie aside and told her that all would be well; surety and bail could be arranged he had been told. He did not explain the full mandates that held her arrest and ward restrictions. By the time they reached Knaresburgh he hoped to have her charges yet redressed in deference to her three children and condition now with child.

MY TRUTH LIES IN THE RUINS

Figure LVII-Part Two; Fawdon Farm today; the Douglas manor of Fawdon was held for half a knight's fee from Gilbert de Umfraville

Ellie made her way into the laird's chamber with Ana and finished the packing that was nearly readied for their departure planned on the morrow. She was shaking but refused to cry. "Ana, I have dreaded this day with all my being. And now we are in England but five days and under the arrest and ward of Edward's sheriff. I will free my husband and then to Essex we will begin again our journey. It is done!" she spoke those words that Gilley used with his resolve, now her determined will. Ana continued the packing and then turned to her girl, "You are so brave my lamb; your husband needs the woman of strength I see before me now. All will finish with our Sir William free and our household on its way to Stebbinge Park." They held each other now in strong embrace, "I would be weak and scared today without your help my Ana. Thank you." Ana reminded her the more her condition of child requires strong faith in her God, "You must think of the child you yet carry; allow no one to cause worry. God and your husband will the worry solve."

At the appointed hour the Douglas household departed Fawdon in the guarded escort of the Sheriff of Northumbria as they headed south for Knaresburgh Castle. They arrived in good time for the days of their travels; the weather giving some leave of their difficulties. The stronghold stood towering on a cliff, high above the River Nidd in Yorkshire; a fortress that Edward was currently renovating in some anticipation for his future needs in

DEBORAH RICHMOND FOULKES

the Marches of England. The king desired that the overall structure of Knaresburgh Castle would remain the same, just better. The ancient citadel was divided into two wards and surrounded by a moat that went to the edge of the cliff; a very functional design. As the Douglases entered through the east gates of the outer ward they could see massive rubble and stone work being moved away from the damaged walls near the cliff while masons were busy creating the footings in preparations for the king's new tower to be constructed within the inner ward.

The family with their personal servants was directed to a smaller corner tower where they would remain as Edward's guest until the court could set bail and relieve them from confinement. From their temporary residence they could see down to the outer ward and the smaller structures that supported the daily functions of the castle. These earth and timber buildings were of lower height and occupied almost half the enclosed area; yet the tower for the king's administration and the business of the court dominated the landscape in height and eloquence. The entire massive stronghold of Knaresburgh Castle was enclosed by a large rubble and stone curtain wall. Here William would remain in ward officially for almost six weeks, with most of the Douglas household staying with him at Knaresburgh for the extent of his involuntary visit. As was the custom of the times however, he was permitted to come and go as he desired leaving surety and value to his pledge of return until the final bail hearing.

After they settled in at Knaresburgh, Ellie immediately began her work to free her husband. She sent messengers to her kin in Yorkshire, Essex, Kent, Sussex and Monmouthshire requesting their advice and assistance. She also set up meetings with her de Ferrers solicitors for herself and William. Eleanora then made the preliminary arrangements for the bail and required pledges for surety of mainperson from her kin. On advice of her attorneys she contacted her cousin Johannis de Hastings by messenger; he would initiate the mainperson release. Upon receiving the Douglas vassal, the Lord of Abergavenny replied immediately to Ellie's requests, offering his assistance and pledge of surety. Soon Lady Douglas received word from another of her kin; the guardian of her stepson and cousin William de Ferrers. This lord was Nicholas de Segrave, an English knight with lands in several shires; he too was pleased to offer Eleanora of Lovaine his lands and person for the surety in William's release.

Sir Nicholas, Nicky as Ellie called him, arrived within the week to make his pledge. He then suggested that Ellie, William and the rest of the Douglas household join him at Groby Manor, the family seat of Ellie's late husband. "You step son William extended his kind invitation; and as his guardian I do affirm it," said Nicky. It was agreed with the constable of Knaresburgh that one Walter de Douglas a Douglas man at arms and William's squire Patric de Douglas would stand surety for Gilley's return; he now in the company of Sir Nicholas de Segrave the younger to report to his parole in three weeks hence. "These weeks to spend at Groby will assist your time in ward to pass more quickly. And Eleanora, you will be pleased to see young William; he has grown taller in your absence."

Figure LVIII-Part Two; Knaresburgh Castle ruins from a nineteenth century engraving in the author's collection

    The peel of children's laughter rang through Groby Manor as Muriel and James with Sir Shamus were wild in their excitement to leave the somber tower at Knaresburgh that was their temporary home. Young William de Ferrers, only two years younger than Ellie greeted her in a teasing manner, "Good mother it is with happiness I welcome you now." James halted himself abruptly. "Mother?" he questioned, "My mother is your mother too; you one so grown as this?" asked the young lad in earnest. Gilley pulled his wee son to his side and began to explain that in the ways of families, his mother married the young laddie's father after the passing of his brave mother; identical to his own occurrence. Ellie flashed a look of feigned scorn at young de Ferrers, "See what you do with your teasing ways, dear cousin?" referring to the fact that his birth mother was also a Lovaine, a member of her family. She then spoke more seriously and offered her condolences on his loss. "Much sadness do I have for the death of young Duncan, your stepbrother, son of your dear mother Anne, my own cousin most as well."

    De Ferrers motioned Lord Douglas and Eleanora into the great hall of Groby, as nurses and Douglas servants were shown about by Ana, quite familiar with Groby Manor House. Young William offered wine and feasting to his guests and guardian as he began to talk of the sad tidings to come five months ago on the Earl of Fife. "I was overcome with grief when I heard of his tragic end, some three months when last I saw young Duncan at his home in Fife. That he was murdered so was grave discomfort to me."

DEBORAH RICHMOND FOULKES

Turning to Gilley he asked, "And you were the Baron-Judge to pass the doom on these men of great treachery?" Gilley nodded yes and told de Ferrers that it was his own brother in law he now held in the donjon prison of Douglas Castle.

Figure LIX-Part Two; Groby Old Hall today at the site of the de Ferrers manor there, courtesy of Mike Pratt, Groby Directory.

Surprised by Lord Douglas' action of imprisoning his own family, young de Ferrers asked further, "You would not spare those of your kin for such doom of death or donjon confinement?" Gilley said to him in his quiet tones that Ellie knew so well, "I fear only God's wrath in this world; freeing one named Abernathy or one named Percy for the closeness of our families would be against God's own laws and my core values; my truth. There can be no other fate for men the likes of these; sadness fills our hearts, many more affected by their violence and crime." Silence filled the great hall at Groby. Nicky looked at Ellie's husband now with different eyes; respect for his courage, fear for his convictions that one day might become the grief of his own family.

Nicky started teasing Eleanora, to change the words and feelings of the moment to more folly and fun. "Dear cousin, you are again with child?" he asked, "And but married two short years with two girls I see already. Good William here must keep you locked in chamber!" Ellie flushed knowing Nicholas well for his taunts. "So confidant you speak to me and freely that I were your wife, dear Nicky," she admonished him for his intimate talk. "And your own dear Alice now with child, just married to your sweet self my Nicky; you must know from your own good work of hasty fashion. As for my William here, my own dear husband; he fears his own majority outnumbered by fair ladies in the castle of his ancestors, these brave men of Douglasdale." Gilley was laughing heartily and joined in the fun. "Perhaps the good wine of England will cause us luck to have a son," as he poured his wife a glass. "Another lass for our noble Douglas clan is welcome as a wee lad too would be; but of no fear to Lord Douglas as twenty children do we plan, aye!" Ellie feigned her look of dark brooding and disdained pout, "Lord Douglas does think a brood mare he has captured from the barony of Tranent! Think twice Lord Douglas now; a fair Essex lady have you married to bring fine family; all dames of the noble house of Lovaine to rule your Douglas lands!"

Nicky was enjoying his teasing of Ellie and joyously challenged her all the more, "My dear kin and friend, our own sweet precious Eleanora, have you tamed the Scotsman so; such talk forbidden for an English wife, her lord's dear chattel, before noble company?" "Chattel!" she flashed her dark eyes at him in anger less pretended now, "Noble company! You knights and your fair chivalry; chattel indeed!" Gilley realized his wife's last response was more serious than others knew. "We will have the children God has intended; lass or laddie, a whim of the Divine," he said. Then to the others, "Happy we are to join your good company in this fine manor. The largesse of Lord Edward at Knaresburgh Castle was too confining for our fair household, growing now in number yet before us!" he chuckled.

De Ferrers asked Gilley now, "Are you not baron of English lands in Northumbria as well Lord Douglas?" He nodded yes, adding, "But for that arbitral decision of the papal legate Cardinal Otho, my plough gates near Hexam and my manor of Fawdon would be of Scottish freehold; now residing in your England." Sensing that de Ferrers was referring to his mild disdain for the king he added, "But that was long ago, 1242. I have served your King Edward, as a squire in Acre first following Earl Adam's banner; sent by our King Alexander. But Scotland is my home, my Douglasdale my own paradise." Nicky added, "Now you will have feudal responsibilities in Essex once Edward grants you license of your marriage to my good cousin here."

"And as a Knight might you serve with Edward in his campaigns?" asked de Ferrers. "Such feudal obligations of the Essex Manors are for you dear William, heir to Lord de Ferrers. How long now will it be till you are dubbed?" asked Gilley. Nicky interrupted them now, "In just fifteen short months will he have reached his age; and I his guardian will be thus relieved of ward. As for his training, young William is almost now complete." Then in quieter tones Nicky said, "But for the dubbing, I say now in confidence, more than few English men of station are thus resisting to become a Knight. With many campaigns of the king to wage as Knight and Lord their expenses mortgaged against their lands, they are reluctant."

"For families of Crusaders or their sponsors such forfeit of land by sale or mortgage was most common; that practice plagues me still," said Gilley.

"Many noblemen would mortgage lands to raise silver and gold in proxy, to help a brother or son to perform his journey to the Holy Land. Then once the Crusader was thus sent forgot the reason for the mortgage and would not honor it. Such is the way with one named de Lucy; his lands mortgaged sometimes twice and sold; that I now hold in freehold a charter in Northumbria." Nicky nodded, "My mother is a de Lucy; recalling now messuages and carucates of her family held by king and council until title proven; from those dealings of dishonesty of that kin. Our families to share these same lands again Lord Douglas!" Ellie added her words, "Many lands of the Lovaines were tangled webs of mortgages for one Jocelin of Lovaine to meet with his expenses; rents of many years pledged for his Crusader's journey of his de Percy lands. A knight's campaign for his king caused many to loose their lands for debts I fear."

Nicky turned to Gilley, "You can save yourself expenses of a seneschal with our Lady Eleanora as your wife," he boasted, "She has a man's mind for one so fair." Ellie flushed, "Nicky that is the first compliment from your sweet self in all my years. I thank you." Then from Gilley, not to be outdone, "And a clear escheator's hand she has with her abbreviated Latin." Nicky chided his cousin that she should thank the teaching of her father the good steward of Lord Edward; "How is your proud father in this acceptance of his new kin," he asked. Ellie looked at Nicky then young William as she answered, "He seems to be of mournful counsel these days. I pray the sight of his two granddaughters will heal his foul humor." Then Gilley spoke in wry tones, "Lord Lovaine has lost his sight of eyes should he not see the love that grows between us. And for Lovaine as steward of the king this knight would say: better to be a great warrior, great thinker, and great lover than an accountant!" he chuckled.

Nicky was laughing too. "Lord Lovaine is half the steward of his daughter and not nearly as pretty!" said young de Ferrers entering the game of praise for Ellie. "Enough kind words, her head to swell I fear," said Nicky turning to toy with her the more, "Your strategy with Edward is cleverly devised; your three children to convince our dear king to grant quick license; clearly now I see!" Ellie was laughing heartily, "Edward Plantagenet is one of Norman stubbornness, like you dear Nicky, difficult to change his course once on it. I must try the harder still that he allows us benefit of marriage!" she said holding her belly where her child now grew. Everyone was laughing at her impish ways; never one to be without words of retort. "Perhaps you are right; that I should have four, perhaps more children to attest the right of marriage to my husband. I would gladly wait the longer before I see dear Edward."

Gilley told them now that he will be relieved to have the business of license for their marriage behind them and thanked Nicky for his pledge of surety as well. "I will be most pleased to enjoy your Essex as I do now your Leichestershire," referring to the county where Groby Manor resided. "And you both most welcome guests to come to Douglasdale. Your good hospitality has cheered me so today!" "Your household too is most welcome here Lord Douglas, Lady Eleanora," said de Ferrers, adding with a wink, "I mean dear mother. And then to you Lord Douglas I thank you for your courage in your truth; the kind support post mortem of my dear friend and stepbrother Earl Duncan. That his murder is revenged by doom of grave punishment is my only solace now in my great sorrow of his passing."

Young William and his guardian Nicky left later in the week for a hunting trip to last some several days. The Douglases had Groby Manor House all to themselves. "This time in Groby is most strange to me," said Ellie to her husband. "I feel not the same person I was here then; to see your loving face when the morning comes is the odder still." William put his arm around her in his reassuring way, "The memories you have are but thoughts now Eleanora; they can only do you harm should you let them. A new life with happy faces of your children and a husband so devoted..." his words were interrupted by the bounding leaps of a silly Deerhound as Shamus ran through their chamber trying unsuccessfully to hide himself under their bed. James comes running in not long after, "Where is Shamus, I search him now." Gilley motioned to the lad, "Shhh..." he said, pointing to a Deerhound half hiding, his head and only half his body so secreted under their bed. "There is no Shamus here about; I wonder where he is. Could dear Shamus be hiding from his James?" asked Gilley in mocked seriousness. Shamus' tail was wagging fiercely as Ellie and Gilley doubled over in laughter at the wee hound's silly game. "Come out Sir Shamus, dear James' surrenders to your successful ploy," said Gilley.

"Do you know what tomorrow brings wee lad?" asked Ellie. James shook his head yes, "James is four; he can say four years now." Gilley spoke to him, "Yes, James is four and Fortis is one. When we return to Douglasdale we will start to train him on a bit; and soon to train with saddle. Then James can learn to ride him," as he pulled out his gift, a new blue velvet surcote and leather shoes, "wearing these new garments for your birthday." James took the package and smiled a big smile as he unwrapped his gifts. "Thank you Father; I love you," he said giving his father a hug. He was losing the slight lisp of a young child in his speech. "Is there yet a hat to match?" he asked. Gilley was about to say no when Ellie surprised them both, "Here James; this Ana made with her own hands and I did the embroidery." His eyes grew wide as he slowly took the hat from her, examining it ever so slowly and deliberately. Then with his charming way he beckoned Ellie closer. "James loves his mother too," he said and kissed her on the cheek. He went off with Shamus to show his nurse his new surcote, shoes and hat, "For Parliament with Lord Douglas," he told her in the hall.

Their second anniversary was a quiet day. The couple rode to nearby Ratby to attend church; giving thanks for their two years now married. "You had to travel yet so far from Groby to your kirk?" asked William. Ellie told him that the small chapel in the rear of Groby Manor was only for the family's use. The Church of Syston some ten miles north providing value to the family like our Douglas Kirk; too far for weekly worship. The de Ferrers family thus travels weekly to the Ratby Church two miles only now, that serves both villages of the parish. They rode up the hill to the church, the highest point in Ratby Ellie told him. "And see this yew tree growing still; it was here before this lovely church now built of stone and rubble; then of wood and smaller too, so Lord de Ferrers had told me." Gilley was impressed by the large, well built tower. "And the yew tree yet fair symbol for immortality of this fine kirk. I do like it so," he said. They went into the church and said their prayers; then were interrupted by a priest that Ellie did not recognize. He was quite jovial and offered them a blessing for their marriage, once she told them who they were. The Douglases thanked him for the performance of the sacrament and rode back to Groby Manor. "A fine day to share and ride with you my lovely bride. An apple day it is for your humble knight and husband." When they arrived at Groby he gave their horses to the groom. Gilley took out a little parchment from the small pouch he carried on his belt; taking her hand in his they began the walking through the orchards of the manor. "I wrote this for you yesterday as I looked out at the pear trees and gardens," he said. Then quietly he began to read his poem to her.

Smiling now I come to you
With visions of an apple day

Where we would sit beneath the trees
Entwined in lovers' strong embrace

We speak together of times we knew
And sigh forever of deeds so true

For now we reach through veil of time
To capture rhythm energy

That once endeared to us a place
Of good times replete with thee

She moved closer to him, "I am most surprised to be here at Groby Manor with my husband yet so happy; more pleased still that it is you I love and love only. Will you love me tomorrow as you love me today?" she asked him. And he responded with their ritual response; then asking her the same. "Oh Lord Will, I do love you all the more and more will I tomorrow."

The Ides of April would be Gilley's fortieth birthday. Ellie had planned to shop in Hertford a very special gift. With six weeks delay for obligations of Knaresburgh's good prison I would to purchase his gift by now, she mused. "William, I must have time in Hertford's shops to find your gift to celebrate this day. Your year a milestone; I again with no gift but this," she held out a dagger that looked strangely familiar to him, yet different. "When last you were at Douglasdale; the younger squires then so shown by your using sword and shield; broke your father's sword. Do you recall it?" she asked. He nodded then told her yes, of course he remembered. "I took the handle and sword remaining to our blacksmith for new fashion of a dagger; this long knife." Gilley took the newly formed blade and familiar handle seeing now a small inscription, "40 years & 40 more * Willelmi * dni * de Duglas." "Only this you do have for me," he said with words touched with deep emotion, "This knife forever will I treasure; forty more, sure aye!" Reading the words over and over, 40 years and 40 more, William Lord Douglas.

When the Douglas household returned to Knaresburgh to surrender at William's parole, they were informed that the final bail hearing was set for May 14th. "My dear Ellie, in these two weeks, we will thus be finished with this folly," he assured her. The next day Ellie and Gilley met with her procurators. A bail of some consequence was prepared by her solicitors Henry de Porter and Walter Giffard. Then to her surprise, these two gentlemen of the court addressed another of her grave concerns. Her own personal appearance before king and council would not be required. Acting on her behalf to answer for her charge of marrying without license, her solicitors completed the arrangements for her financial offering to the king in Northumbria without her. "This is great relief to my good countenance," she told the de Ferrers' family attorneys.

Johannis de Hastings or Josh as Ellie called her cousin appeared two days prior to the final hearing. A knight and baron of England with proven virtue to his king Josh was more cautious then Nicky or William de Ferrers when he first met Lord Douglas. "Dear Eleanora, how pleased I am to see you once again, and this must be Sir William," said Josh. The small compartment used by the Douglas family while in ward at Knaresburgh meant that the children were about. Young James curious about the new visitor came forward with his sister at his side, holding her by the hand as he led her to the English knight. "This is our son James, my cousin," said Ellie,

DEBORAH RICHMOND FOULKES

"and our Muriel." Josh smiled broadly, the children thrilled him all the more, "Sweet Muriel, you have our de Hastings' eyes and coy demeanor," Josh said proudly as he picked her up in his arms. Then looking at her brother, "And James, it is good sign of chivalry and a future knight thus you lead dear Muriel in kind escort." James bowed and told Josh he met others of Ellie's family and her other son, young William. Josh looked up quizzically at Ellie, "More of Nicky's influence on young de Ferrers, he greets me *as dear mother*," said Ellie chuckling. Gilley interjected, "At the good haste of Sir Nicholas and kind offer of young William, we were thus allowed departure to Groby Manor, leaving some for surety two weeks with Leed's good constable. With our growing family, thus it made for more convenience." Josh was feeling more comfortable with Ellie's family. "Were I to have my leave of one lord named Edward where I must rightly serve this day, then too would I invite your good household as my guests."

"Oh Josh, that you are here brings happiness enough to your dear cousin," sighed Ellie. Josh moved closer to her, putting young Muriel in the arms of her nurse. He teased her some, and eyed her up and down in silly fashion, "And you yet not with license for this marriage, good Edward must make haste he does so grant before these children are having children of their own." Then quietly looking at the child growing yet within her, "Dear Eleanora, how joyous you must be with family of your own; and the glow on your sweet face bespeaks of happiness I have never seen on your good countenance." To Gilley he added with a wry smile, "The life in Scotland fares well with this little Essex lady; Sir William, welcome to our family. Though sorry would I say that some named Lovaine may not share our words and sentiments."

Gilley told Josh that he was hopeful that Lady Helisant and Lord Lovaine would come to understand their reasoning for the delay of license. "We fell in love so deeply, as if touched by Cupid's arrow, the rains of Scotland's good forests giving cover to our eagerness; a child came more quickly than words to Lord Edward," said Gilley, explaining that it was their circumstance and Ellie's fear that kept them from complying with the required license to her liege lord. "We will make it right; to pay the fine as would so be required; and lay to rest this inconvenience to friends and family. Thank you for your surety of lands and person Sir Johannis." Josh told him that Lady Helisant was elated by the marriage. "But for Lord Lovaine a man of much ambition with his daughter his only heir," his words trailed off as Ellie threw Josh as look of disdain. "My father should he but come to forgive this daughter; that more should I forgive of him with one named de Ferrers as his choice for husband."

Josh had not forgotten the terror he witnessed staying at Groby Manor House some eight years ago. The screams from his young cousin in the middle of the night now flooded his memory with those awful thoughts of de Ferrers' ritual beatings of his young wife. Gilley went to his bride and held her close, "Those memories are only thoughts that can no longer hurt your sweet self my lass. Let us speak of happiness you now can share with your dear cousin Josh." Turning to the English knight he added, "A good name Josh to have; for our own dear Josh our family priest and long time friend from Kelso Abbey, gave us the sacraments of marriage in the chapel there; without fear of some reprisal, brave in his kindness to us." Ellie smiled and began to tell her cousin about the raid of the heart at Fawside, the men at arms with horses and full armaments, banners and standards in furl, coming up the hill that morning, to rescue her from her sorry state. Josh was riveted by the tale. "I had heard of such abduction that much differs from your words here; pray your father did not know what actually had happened?" he asked them. Gilley spoke, "He was well informed in letters Ellie sent him; his words that you describe were false and slyly crafted I do fear."

"Come, let us depart," Josh said, motioning the Douglases to take leave of Knaresburgh Castle. He took them all including the children to a manor of his friends yet now in Stafford for the week; near to the castle they would only leave the day. They feasted on two types of fish and capons, enjoying good wine and conversation as the children played in the courtyard of the manor house. "Have you plans to spend more time in Essex, or are your days thus diminished by Knaresburgh's good hospitality as Edward's guest?" Gilley told them that he had not been in Essex before but was eager to enjoy the good fishing and hunting described by Nicky. "But with more time yet to spend next year when we return," he added. "Eleanora can tell you better, but there is no finer place in all of England for yield of milk, butter and cheese in great abundance than Woodham Ferrers; and the oyster layings providing fine additions to fare of table, with the many creeks extending the farthest stretches of the sea in all of Essex," Josh told Gilley. Ellie spoke up now, "Even though its marshland with salt the main production, our woodlands are of the belt of Essex's Great Forest, giving bounty to its income. But of all the goods produced upon the manor my favorite is the milch of kine and ewes; to produce fine cheese and butter from these good animals; I could live on that!" Their visit together was comfortable and enjoyable; coming to an end too soon they all lamented. Leaving the family again in ward at Knaresburgh Josh told them he would return the following day for their relief; then to appear on their behalf at the bail hearing on the morrow next.

The bail was accepted on May 14th as promised; posted by "Eleanora late of de Ferrers on behalf of one William de Douglas" read the receipt of court. Johannis de Hastings made his pledge for surety of person and lands for Sir William of Duglas. Nicholas de Segrave came as promised; his appearance was accepted on behalf of the Duglas knight, his surety and bond that William would come before the king on a date to be determined was recorded and approved. Within the hour two others of Ellie's kin arrived in person, bringing the total to four noblemen as was required for surety of mainperson for William's release. These last two Englishmen came from Staffordshire and East Sussex; Robert Bardulf and William de Rye. The pledges and bail payments were now complete; William's manucaptor accepted, his appearance was set for St. Hilary's feast, January 1291 nearly three years after their first meeting in Ayrshire. The next day William was officially discharged from ward; released May 15th on the mainperson of Johannis de Hastings and others, it was written. The household of Douglas was free to travel now to Stebbinge Park in Essex; English sheriffs could no longer bring fear to Ellie's countenance.

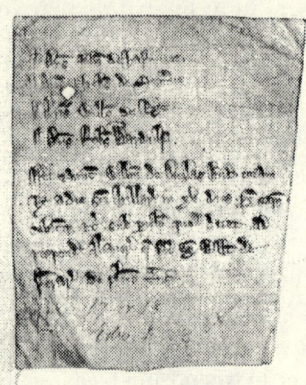

Figure LX-Part Two; bail receipt of Eleanora Lovaine relic of de Ferrers, posted for William le Hardi Douglas in May1290; used with permission of the National Archives, Kew, Surrey, England

"Ellie, you have made this humble knight your husband proud of your good spirit and true endeavors. And you with child, traveling so, on my behalf; a true warrior as no man can challenge." Ellie looked over at her husband, "I was determined; relentless in my pursuit that we would make our way to Essex. Now we will travel in peace; and your wife feeling more the happy having that behind us now I know." Ellie was experiencing the fatigue of her condition with child and the riding was uncomfortable; the more she rode the more the child kicked her from inside. They traveled shorter days staying one night in Derby with Earl de Ferrers, another at Ashby de la Zouche; then again at Groby Manor and on to Ware in Hertfordshire. When they finally arrived at Stebbinge Park they were all weary of the traveling; two months and more since leaving Douglasdale; but with much accomplished. Within another week, on 24th May Edward Plantagenet signed a writ to Sheriff Knut of Northumbria to repledge the lands and goods of William Douglas and his men, that were seized for his abduction of Eleanora, relic of de Ferrers. And a similar writ was issued to the escheator ultra Trent on behalf of Johannis Wycharde his accomplice it was written; for the same.

Stebbinge Park manor house sat on a motte overlooking the broad farm lands of the village, tofts and messuages that comprised the estate. The earth and timber house was surrounded by a spring fed moat that was stocked with fish and attracted the nesting of many birds and other fowl. The elegant cart path that led up to the gates then over the small drawbridge was fashioned on each side by deciduous trees that had grown tall over the years forming lovely arches of shade over the pathway. The building itself provided three floors of living space over a cellar for cooking and storage. The two family levels included a great hall on the lower floor with a huge lord's chamber on the second; a third floor attic with low ceilings under the roof of thatch housed servants and children's nurseries. Because the house had been added onto so many times it was a maze of small stairways. These many small flights of stairs would lead from one level to another in haphazard ways; perfect for young children to run about, amusing themselves at play, but trouble for Lord Douglas. Ellie would long remember how often Gilley would hit his head on the overhanging beams of these wee hallways and shortened steps; it was hard for her not to giggle at his expense. Gilley had plans for changes of his own should they decide to visit more often. Besides eliminating the confusing labyrinth of hallways and steps to small rooms and tiny closets or chambers, there were other problems: the manor had no latrines. Garderobes were common in Scottish tower houses and castles. But chamber pots ruled the day in English manor houses; sometimes even in their castles. Lord Douglas bristled at the practice and would make that his first priority.

James had come into their chamber with his nurse to say goodnight. "On the morrow we will visit with Lady Helisant my mother," she told James. "You may wear your fine blue surcote." She went on to tell him that she was born in Little Easton Manor where her mother now resided, and then christened in the same font still used in the baptistery of the church adjoining the estate. "I will take you and Muriel to see the church and monuments of our proud and noble family Lovaine, in the Chancel near the Altar." Muriel was coming in now with her nurse; she beamed when she saw her brother. He took her hand and guided her to Ellie's side, carefully insuring she did not fall. "And a lovely new cote do I have for you too wee lass; with these hair ribbons to match!"

DEBORAH RICHMOND FOULKES

Muriel was a beautiful little girl with thick dark hair and a dark olive skin; the Douglas family trait. She was talking and learning to say "no" and walking some now too; as was the way with wee ones but nineteen months. She laughed and cooed when she saw the bright colored ribbons for her hair. "Muriel's?" she asked her mother. Ellie told her yes, the ribbons are for her. Then their nurses came to get them as Lord Douglas entered the lord's chamber. "Goodnight Lord Douglas," said James. Muriel smiled and waved good night. Martha was then brought in by her nurse; she cooed and smiled for her father when he held her. Gilley shook his head, "Our girls just smile and laugh contentedly; our James" his words trail off..." Gilley was shaking his head, "Sometimes I am sure what next he will say; and then he will surprise me so." Ellie looked at him, "If you are cross with his words your must correct him." Realizing now that his own fatigue was making him less patient he added, "That I will do. Calling his father Lord Douglas; that surprised me yet this night. But I am not cross. We will discuss this on the morrow when I am less weary."

Figure LXI-Part Two; Stebbing church steeple proudly greats the traveler to this picturesque medieval village

Ana was combing out Ellie's hair from the plaiting she wore during the day. "I am feeling strange in Stebbinge Park; to sleep with no fear of the night," she whispered. Ana was quiet in her response. "All of the de Ferrers servants here are pleased to have Sir William as their lord. And seeing you so peaceful has made them happier still; there, you are complete for your readiness of sleep. I will leave the now!" Goodnight Ana, they both called back to her. William put his arms around Ellie's shoulders, turning him to her gently. "You must know that your husband holds you dear and true. I could think of no other place to be than at your side my dear lass." Ellie held him closer to her. "And I Lord Will, I could never be with another in your place were you to leave me; for I could not replace a man of quiet grace and strong love as you my kind knight, my dear husband. Will you love me tomorrow as you love me today?" she asked. He responded with their ritual, "No, for I will love you all the more. And you Lady El?"

Mid morning the next day the little group mounted their palfreys for Little Easton Manor. James rode proudly with his father. Muriel and Martha were carried, riding with their nurses; close behind the children came Ana riding next to Sir David, followed by their other men at arms. The household always traveled now with escorts and flourish. "I have not forgotten the way from Stebbing as I feared I might," said Ellie to her husband. "Mother, James is riding his father's horse. Now he must have a fur hat." Unable to respond to her young son without a burst of laughter at his words, she nodded a knowing look at Gilley. He was wearing his own fair cloak of green velvet with a fur hat trimmed in a red and blue silk. "My wee lad wherever do you get these thoughts to have such things?" he asked. Before Ellie could interject her words their son said "James wants to be like his father; Lord Douglas. And he wants a fur hat," pointing to the one on Gilley's head. William just looked at Ellie realizing that he just allowed his son to best him in their sparring. I will be more wary of your questions in the future young James, he sighed to himself. "You must wait to have a fur hat. When your Fortis grows tall as my palfrey here and James is able to ride without help; a fur hat you shall have. For now your new hat with embroidery shall sit on your wee head; no more words of fur hats till then will I hear! It is done."

The Douglases arrived at the Manor of Estaines, Little Easton, without difficulty. Ellie's mother Helisant was not yet ready to receive her visitors but would have Ellie come alone to her chamber. When she entered the room of her mother a chill spread over her very being and she ran to her mother's side. "What has happened to make you so thin my mother?" she asked with grave concern. "I was foolish to take the younger palfrey and not my old mare when I was about a ride in the park of our manor. I took a fierce fall; hitting my head and bending my leg in such ways that I broke some bones. The leg is mending well but my head aches most daily." Ellie took her hands and placed them in a healing way to relieve her mother's pain. "My sweet husband is a healer of great talents; he will cease the pain

DEBORAH RICHMOND FOULKES

of your headaches that I can only ease some now." Helisant looked at her daughter, "With child again?" she asked smiling. "You must truly love this Lord Douglas, three children you will have in fewer years of marriage!" she teased. "He makes me feel happiness that I have not felt before," she sighed. Her mother's quick wit was returning, "I can see from the shape of your sweet self, a child now growing; testament to that strong feeling. Allow your mother now the time to pretty herself for this knight of your affection," she said calling for her maids at wait she motioned her daughter to leave her. "I will be down to see all soon; Father Paul is visiting our church this week and asked of you. Do take your family to visit him; now would be a good time, do you think?" Ellie told her mother to take her time to dress; they would indeed visit Father Paul this day.

The children and Shamus were playing in the withdrawing room off the great hall of the manor; a small thick carpet was in the center of the small room near the fireplace. Muriel was crawling and walking some as James rolled about with the Deerhound. "James, your good surcote; you must remove it to play so with the hound." Then to Gilley she said, "My mother is not well, but desires to come down and see us soon. She told me to take the children to see an old friend of mine, Father Paul who does visit at our church this day." Gilley asked the children's nurses to bring James and Muriel as they headed for the village church next door. The short walk from the manor to the church yard was filled with children's laughter and a hound's happy barking; the day reminded Ellie of her childhood when she would follow her mother and grandmother to the church for daily prayer.

Figure LXII-Part Two; the ancient font, upper right in image, of Little Easton Church is reputed to be 13th century and may have been the one used to christen Eleanora Lovaine Douglas in 1268

MY TRUTH LIES IN THE RUINS

As they entered the nave of the church, Ellie pointed out the font used in her christening with its carved wooden canopy. As she made her way to the chancel, she peered into the open door of the vestry and inquired of Father Paul; he would return shortly she was told. Ellie showed the children the escutcheons; the banners, standards and arms of the Lovaines. "The ruling house's emblem is the blue lion; field ore, a lion rampant azure, the very one we placed upon our castle walls at Douglasdale," she explained. Then Ellie led them all through the chancel arch to view the tomb of one of her noble forebears, a Crusader knight from the last century. "You see here a Lovaine knight in effigy," she told the children. James took Muriel's hand and led her to the large arched tomb near the Altar. There an exquisitely detailed carved effigy of a warrior lying prone in death drew the young lad's attention; but it was so tiny, yet two feet long full length, dwarfed in size by the vaulted tomb recessed in the wall of the chancel. The carved stone figure was one of great rarity in Essex, something of true pride for the Lovaine family.

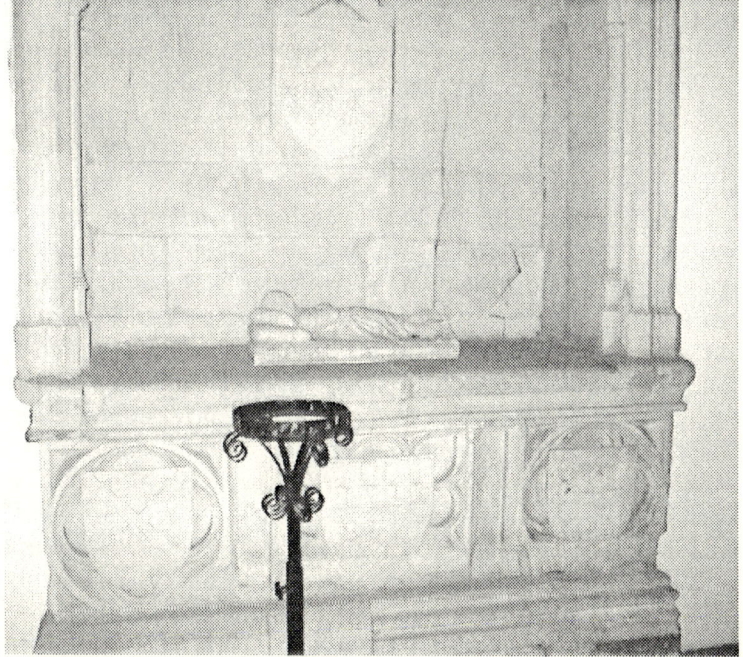

Figure LXIII-Part Two; a rare effigy of a Lovaine Crusader Knight is only two feet long and rests on the tomb of Eleanora Douglas' great niece and name sake, Eleanor de Lovaine; Little Easton Church

Ellie continued with the history of the family manor and church, "the Manor of Estaines was first held by the family de Windsor, who by female descent passed these lands to Godfrey de Lovaine. He was my great grandfather, brother of the bearded Duke of Brabant, possessing many great estates; the main of these Brabant estates were in Lovaine." All the while she spoke of her proud heritage young James was studying the small effigy of the Crusader knight. With wrinkled brow he turned to his mother and asked "Are all the Lovaine knights so small mother?" Ellie's eyes narrowed, first throwing William an impatient look and imploring his support, to admonish the lad; she paused to respond. William was gasping, suppressing his laughter with little success as James continued, "How does he ride his horse?" "You men of Douglasdale, take leave of us now! Muriel and I not to listen to the words of envy from the descendants of the savage Sholto; making jest of our proud knights of the Crusades! Go, the noo." William was laughing so hard that tears were streaming down his cheek, "Yes pray dear wife, how does he ride his horse?" Ellie was ready to throw a fit of pique when she saw Father Paul come round the corner.

"Dear Father, you have caught me having cross words with my dear husband. He and our wee son here boldly making jest of the Lovaine Crusader lying there in effigy." Father Paul, finding humor in the small size of the effigy himself, extended his greeting to Lord Douglas, as introductions were exchanged. Father Paul spoke happily, "I asked your mother dear Lady Helisant to beckon you here. For your good years so often at this church when I was pastor, would you enjoy sweet ceremony; a renewal of your vows of marriage? Your dear mother would feign to ask herself, but no." Before Ellie could answer the priest William spoke, "That was just our purpose in coming to see you. Such a ceremony of the sacraments would be most satisfying to us Father Paul that her dear mother and perhaps Lord Lovaine, were he about, might attend." Father Paul realized that the couple was unaware that Lord Lovaine left two days ago for Bildeston; not wanting to meet the man who stole his daughter from his plans of future marriages, alliances for his own gain. Turning to Ellie he said, "Your father has just recently departed; called to Bildeston on feudal business he did say. But the morrow next we can have your ceremony should that be your wish." "It is done," smiled William. "It is done," said Ellie in a slight tone of resignation, realizing it was hopeless to argue with so many. "My mother will be most pleased Father Paul; your kind offer does fulfill my pledge some years ago that I would exchange the vows of marriage with my husband in this our family church. I Thank you."

Ellie was shaking her head wearily as they strolled across the open meadow to the gates of her mother's manor. "What troubles you my bride?" asked Gilley. She looked up with that silly pouting look he loved so much, "Another kirk, more vows to say; and I again with child!" She laughed loudly at her own circumstance, realizing the irony of her life. "Someday I hope to say our vows in ceremony, without a child yet growing in me; and too when I can see my feet!" As they were walking through the manor gates Ellie noticed a new horse being brought around to the stables. "Alice, that is the palfrey of my dear friend," she squealed. "Oh that I could move fast to see her." Inside the great hall there was a tearful reunion of Ellie and her closest friend and kin of the de Ferrers, Alice of Hertford. Alice looked first at her friend, and then at the handsome knight, so tall and yet so gentle as he put his arms around his wife. "Oh Alice, I am so happy you are here." Then she grabbed Gilley's hand and brought him round her. "This is my knight, my husband of the dreams we shared so long ago in Woodham Ferrers." "Even more handsome than you described in your letters," Alice said. "Lord Douglas, Sir William, I am most pleased to meet you at long last. You have kept my dear friend so happy now I see by the smallness of her sweet self."

Ellie was laughing as she spoke. "You like Nicky and young William, and Josh the same; all of you do tease me for my condition of child." "No Eleanora, we tease for your third event of child in just two short years!" the words and voice of Helisant were now heard as she made her gracious entrance into the great hall of her manor. "Lord Douglas, Sir William, I am proud to call you son, husband of my daughter, welcome." William was surprised to see a woman once of true beauty so ill as she now approached them. Taking her arm gently he escorted her to the lord's chair at the trestle table in the hall. "This knight is much obliged to your kind words and generosity of spirit. Our wee ones, your grandchildren do come here now." The children, their nurses and the wee hound were entering the hall. Helisant's eyes welled immediately as she saw them coming to see her. James held Muriel's hand, as he escorted her proudly while Martha's nurse brought her to Helisant's arms.

"Grandmother, I am James, this is my sister Muriel," said the young lad. Ellie sighed happily that he remembered the words she taught him to say. Helisant was moved by the boy's good manners and his reference to her as his grandmother happily surprised her. "Did you know that your mother is my little girl?" asked Helisant. James nodded, trying to comprehend her meaning. Muriel spoke first. "You pretty grandma," she giggled, holding on to the lady's surcote of fine velvet with brocade trim and closures. James bowed and told Helisant that was happy to be at Little Easton. "My mother has many children," said the wee lad. "Do you?" he asked. Martha cooed to her grandmother and smiled. "No, your mother is all I have now. She is my special girl," looking to Ellie she said, "My dreams fulfilled seeing your fine family here; and your husband a good man that brings cheer to this good grandmother; **grandmother,** how long I have waited to hear those words. Thank you both for your kindness of visit."

She began addressing James who was chattering away with his sister Muriel, "Your name my grandson, it is most unusual. Is it from a Douglas ancestor?" she asked him, waiting with curiosity for his reply. "For James the Great" he said, "and I have a day." Ellie interjected that her son was named for St. James the Great, a patron saint of the Stewart family and the abbey at Paisley in Scotland they endow; the name given his uncle, brother of his mother. "His day is July 25, the feast of St. James," Ellie added shielding her amusement from the wee lad. Helisant invited Ellie and Gilley to join her in some wine. The children's nurses took Shamus, James, Muriel and Martha with them to the nursery; chambers once part of Ellie's rooms when she was growing up at Little Easton. Platters of food were coming in from the kitchen wafting scents that elated Ellie, recognizing the preparations as some of her treasured repasts. "My favorite sweet wine and eels in sticky sauce, mother you are so kind. Oh, and oysters too!" she squealed in delight.

"I am glad to please you daughter. Now sadly I am to speak more seriously; I must tell you of ill intended words so given by Lord Lovaine. At one time he was my lover and dear husband, now grievously only the vows of sacrament before my God and the child I bore for him are the tie between us," spoke Helisant in even tones. She told Gilley and Ellie that he left abruptly after receiving word from Ellie's messenger that they were at Groby on their way to Ware, then Stebbinge Park. "Your troubles with Edward were much advanced by your own father I fear. When first I told him of your marriage to good William here he flailed his arms and cursed his God like a man possessed by the devil." Ellie looked down as tears welled in her eyes, not knowing if she could speak. "Mother, Lord Lovaine has no love in his heart for his daughter; were it not your presence here I would feel an orphan."

Gilley's words interrupted her recriminations. "The morrow next we will celebrate a blessing of our vows, the sacrament of our marriage. Would you do us honor and attend?" he asked of Helisant. Alice was entering the great hall of the manor as Gilley spoke his words; refreshed and eager to join the conversation and feasting. "A wedding in our midst and I was not told?" she quizzed Ellie in mock indignation. Ellie was chuckling as she responded to her friend. "My dear husband has me celebrate the blessings of our marriage at every kirk we pass I should say. And each time I walk the aisle I am with child." Helisant told them it was her very wish to see her daughter repeat her vows with William in the church of her christening. "Lord Lovaine would prefer at Bildeston for marriage vows exchanged, at St. Mary's church or kirk is what you say?" Ellie told her that kirk was indeed the word Scots used, the same word they used in Brabant for God's house. Then she replied angrily about her father, "He will not again see me at Bildeston for the sacrament of marriage!" Gilley took her hand and held it in his own and then he rubbed her shoulders with the other. "We shall not spoil the day we have thus planned with anger toward another; one who loves is loved Ellie. We have much love to share with family and friends here I know and feel."

With much enthusiasm Gilley suggested a trip to Hertford for shopping. "Your own manor just nearby the village is it not Lady Alice?" he asked Ellie's friend. Alice shook her heard yes adding, "It is most close to the royal castle there as well, used often by dear Edward and his consort." Ellie feigned a frown, "That they are now in London brings me cheer, for Hertford is a blight of space when once they come to stay." Alice chided her friend, "Fear of Edward now such foolish thoughts;" then turning her attentions to Gilley, "There are many fine shops and merchants there Sir William to empty out your coffers! Let us plan the day to go and most happy will I show you." Helisant suggested that they stay the night as well, leaving the grandchildren with their nurses in Little Easton for her to entertain. "You are most welcome at my manor; are you going on to Woodham Ferrers before returning home?" asked Alice, happy with Helisant's suggestion. Ellie told her that Gilley wanted to meet with Sir Mathew Foster, le Parker's brother in law and new seneschal in Essex for their estates. Foster was presently at Woodham Ferrers Hall he told them. "After feudal business, shopping in Hertford would I most enjoy," said Ellie. "It is done," said Gilley. Ellie was thrilled; a day in Hertford was just what she needed to take her mind from the absence of her father from this celebration of her new life with friends and family in Essex.

Helisant was growing tired and Ellie could sense her pain from the grimace on her face. Gilley excused himself to return in minutes with his healing box. "Would you permit this humble healer to offer some herbs and salves to soothe your headache Lady Helisant?" he asked her. "How did you know of my headaches," she asked him. Gilley told her of his incidents at Fawdon, the injury to his neck causing many such attacks. "From that lang time for regaining of my health did I learn the Celtic healing; and then in the Holy Lands to find of alchemy healing." Ellie added, "Gilley delivered as midwife young James and our two sweet lasses." Helisant was stunned. "Your own husband in the lay-in chamber and brought your children into life?" Ellie told her how she had no pain and that with Ana he would tell her to remain calm and breathe. "Only once when he did take a dagger to prepare the way did I become alarmed; but then from Ana would I hear the reason and stayed calm." Ana was coming in the great hall and Ellie beckoned her over to her side. "Here the assistant of my good husband for the lay-in now," said Ellie proudly. "Ana, we are preparing to depart. Would you inform the children's nurses?" "Come here first my Ana," said Helisant. "Tell me true dear one, this knight and husband of my daughter was the midwife for the lay-in?"

DEBORAH RICHMOND FOULKES

Figure LXIV-Part Two; village of Bildeston, Suffolk; originally part of the manor the same name, held in chief by Matthew de Lovaine

Ana chuckled, "There is not much Sir Gilley does not do for us Lady Helisant. And my lamb with no pain, I was most pleased to assist him so. Excusing herself, "I will bring the children," she said to Ellie as she left the hall. Gilley was speaking to his squires to bring about the horses as Alice took Ellie aside. "More than a handsome knight on a beautiful destrier have you found in Scotland my dear friend," she said. "Is there a brother of this Scottish chevalier for your old friend and confidant?" "I have never been happier, felt more loved in all my days Alice," Ellie said plainly. Alice told her what Helisant had said about her father. "He demanded council with King Edward; thus he said your were abducted much against your will, unspeakable acts put upon your person that your were now with child." Ellie's eyes welled with tears. "He does not want me happy. He wanted only for his profit in another marriage to some lord three times my age and many manors for his boasting," she sighed.

The Douglases were making their way back to Stebbinge Park when Ellie broke her silence. "Lord Will, my own father I do fear had put King Edward thus upon us with his false words of a father scorned." Gilley nodded and told her that the three documents from Sheriff Knut contained sad reference to her father: "from one who knows," he said, "these words were thus so written; deceptive words of imagined treachery put upon his daughter; accepted as truth." She sighed deeply and looked up into his eyes as they rode next to each other. "I could love no man but you Lord Will. And Scotland is my home."

Woodham Ferrers, Woodham Ferrers Hall

John Le Parker and Sir Matthew Foster greeted Sir William and Lady Eleanora as they arrived at the small manor of Woodham Ferrers. Stebbinge Park had a full moat around the manor house and was larger than the few messuages that were part of Woodham Ferrers Hall. The half moat and the strange passageway that led from the great hall to the Woodham Ferrers Priory were the features that first impressed young James. He and Muriel were wide eyed with the secret door and chamber leading to the passage. Ellie said she would take them through the passage but they must never go alone; a fateful turn would bring one to an outlet of the spring fed moat and certain danger if they fell. Shamus came up behind her, covered with the sludge of the moat. "No need to ask where you have been wee hound; the site and smell most telling. Patric!" she called to William's squire. "Sir Shamus here has taken quite a swim; a bath he will need, the now." Patric was shaking his head, "Are we sparring you attention that you would have the more?" he asked. Gilley looked up from the records of the seneschal and said, "James, it is now your charge to mind the hound and know his whereabouts. Alert us should he try another bit of mischief as this; but thus tell us only, do not try to stop him. Thank you James for your service to your father." James nodded. "Yes Lord Douglas; Sir Shamus, follow James, the noo! A fine bath you will have."

Their stay at Woodham Ferrers was brief. The six weeks lost at Knaresburgh compromised their plans as Ellie's time for lay-in drew closer now three months with some few weeks. "We will leave for Little Easton on the morrow. Sir Matthew is competent and true. Sir John has thus explained our needs and more. I am satisfied with their good work." Ellie was reading over the ledgers, "You see the leaseholds here not mine, my husband; tenements of young William and his sister Anne. One part of the manor for my sustenance with nine more parts for fees from lands to others, have I but £16 annually to keep, the children earn the rest £140, a tidy sum." She then continued her review, "The stock and yields are good, see the rise in corn we have produced?" Gilley chuckled now, "Your cousin's words so true; a good steward would you make my wife!

As for the leaving, what say you lass?" Ellie looked over to him. "I am most pleased my husband; our journey so long to stay such little time. But for my first return with you as lord, the time is good to leave here." Gilley realized they were finally alone and started to tease her; pretending that he would take her at his will, then and now. She responded by trying to escape; feigning fear should she be captured. "Lord Will, have you no shame?" she flirted all the more, "You are a beast, descended from the savage Sholto. You will not catch this fine Essex lady; kin of Henry III." Giddy now the two were sparring and then he grabbed her and picked her up, high over his shoulders. "Put me down this instant Scotsman; we are in England now; the men at arms under my command!" she toyed the more with him. Gilley was laughing heartily as he carried her to the lord's chamber. Ellie playfully pounded his back with her fists, "Unhand me now; I am not your chattel to be bandied about so!" Ana looked up as they entered the chamber, and gave a knowing nod, "The morrow will I see you then," she chuckled, leaving for her own chamber. More laughter have I heard this one day than all the times before at Woodham Ferrers Hall, Ana sighed happily to herself.

Little Easton Manor

Traveling to Hertford for a day of shopping was perfect Ellie thought. Her mother seemed improved too this morning; the children making her smile the more. Now for some time to bargain with merchants and laugh with her husband and Alice. "Lord Will, the travel now is slow I fear as I am getting large with child." Gilley was deep in thought. "My wife, your words have been lost upon me; my apologies to you." Ellie told him that she was concerned that her growing child would slow their journey. Then she asked him what was troubling him. "Your dear mother's recovery is not what it should be now from her fall so long ago. The herbs I have given her...Ellie, I do not want to spoil this day and your mother so cheerful when we departed so leaving her to enjoy her grandchildren," he said. "But I fear for her continued health and good humor." Ellie nodded at him. "Lord Will, my mother has grown thin and drawn; her strength is waning more. My fears are yours but she will not share her true self with me. It is her way; all we can do is pray for her recovery." Gilley was relieved that Ellie sensed her mother's time was drawing near. But he knew the loss of Helisant would weigh heavy on his wife; hoping such sad events would wait, surely for the birth of their third child.

The day in Hertford was as Alice promised; the shops and merchants happy for the Douglases to visit them and cheerfully part with their coinage. Ellie found the gift she wanted for Gilley. She, Ana and Alice were shopping together as Sir David and Patric accompanied Gilley. "What a beautiful mantel of ermine," Ellie exclaimed. "I knew that I would find one here!" Ana was admiring it closely, "Sir William will be most pleased M' Lady." Alice was stunned that she would purchase such an extravagant mantel. "You would buy your husband such a gift me dear friend?" Ellie's

MY TRUTH LIES IN THE RUINS

eyes were gleaming, "It is the one I hoped to find sure aye!" Giggling as she looked at Alice, "My William has a deference for finery as do I my dear Alice. And it is a purchase thrice the fun for I love to buy it, he loves to wear it and I enjoy to see him in it!" "And nothing for yourself then dear Eleanora?" asked Alice. Ellie pointed to the three boxes just packed by the tailor next door, "Those are mine," she chuckled. "Gilley and I compete on filling up carts and loading down our pack animals on each shopping trip."

Figure LXV-Part Two; St. Mary's church in Woodham Ferrers

    The three ladies caught up with Lord Douglas and his entourage. The extra pack horses they brought were laden down with Gilley's purchases. "Oh Lord Will, you have put my valiant work to shame in these fair shops!" she teased him. Alice was impressed by the number of boxes and bundles from Hertford's merchants and shops of distinction. Gilley was smiling broadly, "Look fair Essex ladies, for I have found a gift that will entice you all the more," he said as he brought our some small packages of a strange black substance. "This is black delight; to feed the soul," he said playfully.

DEBORAH RICHMOND FOULKES

The ladies looked at the licorice he handed them and one by one they all ooh'd and ahh'd about the candy. Ana said she had never had anything remotely like this black delight, "Wait till young James and Muriel see this treat!" she exclaimed. "I should bring some to my mother; black delight would cheer her so" added Ellie. Gilley was pleased and told them that he had bought out the merchant's entire supply. "Then some for me as well Sir Gilley," said Alice. "Your knight has a cheerful way about him my dear friend. You are most blessed with your Scottish laird."

Figure LXVI-Part Two; the ruins of Hertford Castle

When the Douglases returned to Little Easton they were greeted by a happy grandmother. "Your sweet children so wonderful to fill the chambers of this old manor house; they please me so. They are much the family I dreamed to have so long ago," she told her daughter wistfully. "And Sir Shamus too, the hound was well behaved." Ellie brought out the bags of

MY TRUTH LIES IN THE RUINS

black delight and gave some to Lady Helisant. "Oh Eleanora, you know how to please your mother so!" she said. "You can thank my William, he is the one who found such strange confection in Hertford's good shops," said Ellie gleefully. Helisant called for the children and James led his sister Muriel by the hand, the nurse brought in little Martha and the hound followed in procession. "Look what your father has brought from Hertford," she told them. James took his little package of the licorice and studied it for some time. Ellie finally said, "James, this is black delight and can be eaten." The wee lad smiled and put some in his mouth. "Here Muriel, this you can have with James," he told her, sharing some of his confection with her.

Ellie gave two more pieces to Muriel. Shyly Muriel started to offer one to James, then just as he was taking it, she grabbed it back and giggled. "No James. Muriel's," and she began to give him the other piece; then to pull it back. "What a tease you are Muriel to your dear brother." Ellie said, starting to correct her daughter. Just then the Deerhound ran through the hall and grabbed Muriel's remaining piece from her hand to run off with it. The little girl's face pinched in grimace and she began to cry. Ellie went down on her knees, "Here is one more for you. And for the time again when you receive it, do not tease your brother. Sharing is giving love; and James shared lovingly with you." Muriel looked over at James and then at her mother with her big brown eyes open so wide, knowing she was wrong. Slowly she went to James, feigning to look at him; she put her arms around him, to apologize in her own way. "Mura, here is more for you," he said, giving the little girl another piece. She kissed her brother and sat down on the floor to eat her licorice. Ellie was laughing now, "William, please come to your wife; unable is she to rise to her feet wherever they may be!" Gilley came and helped her up. "Your time approaches sooner than your months I fear. Tomorrow next we will depart for our journey home to Douglasdale."

Leaving Stebbinge Park, the Douglas household made their way to Estaines Manor. Helisant was waiting for them in the great hall. "Come here my daughter," she called to Ellie. "I have this for you." Helisant gave Ellie a beautiful brooch of gold with pearls and rubies. "Oh mother, this is the fair brooch of my great grandmother, a de Hastings family piece; I can not take this now," she said in protest. "It is mine to give, and to my only daughter shall it go. I will of course insist," said Helisant adamantly. Ellie kissed her and gave her a hug. "Mother, your kind support for me has been my only hope. The times we shared in joy; the rides we took to ease the sadness of my heart when I was Lady de Ferrers, these loving moments, my memories of you. I shall always keep you here in my heart, most close to me. I thank you for your kindness and this most thoughtful and generous gift." The children clamored around their grandmother as she had little gifts for them all.

"Now for you Lord Douglas, my William, son I shall always love; I give you these to wear in health." Helisant brought out four beautiful buttons of ornate silver with gold workings of an old design and a beautiful matching brooch for his cloak or supertunic. "They were my father's, I his only heir and daughter yet residing. You have won my trust dear Gilley." She reached up and kissed him on the cheek as he bent down to her. "You are too kind Lady Helisant, dear mother of my sweet wife and only love. When I wear these next it will be for the coronation of Scotland's good Queen and it is you and your own dear father that I shall recall with love and fair admiration. I thank you so." Gilley reached into the pouch at his waist and brought out a small package. "These good herbs of healing should bring you some relief of headache. Use them at night, before you fall to slumber in your bed chamber." Helisant nodded with a peaceful smile. "I know my daughter is in the best of hands. A fair truth now known by one Lovaine of Little Easton; you are a true healer and loving knight, proud father and faithful husband. Thank you for your kindness to this grandmother," she said, proudly speaking her new title.

Douglasdale Late July 1290

The Douglas household returned to Scotland and Douglasdale in time to hear the first news of the summer missed during their many days of travel. King Edward had taken back the Isle of Mann into his custody as lord on June 4, just as they began their journey homeward from Essex; but they heard nothing of this news as they traveled through the marches, Scotland's borders. It was only when they arrived at Douglas Castle that Sir Andrew informed them of the sad tidings of Mann; after reporting the normal news of Douglasdale to his laird. William bid his seneschal good night, thanking him for his good work during their absence. He joined his wife and children in the withdrawing room. Gilley told her about the events of Edward and Mann. "I fear him Ellie. That greed within Lord Edward's soul burns slow for more that he would conquer. Perhaps this marriage now arranged of Queen Margaret and Prince Edward will temper his foul humor. I do pray so, but worry all the more of Scotland's fate." Ellie was doing some fine embroidery for one of her new cotes. "Your words and humor are most unsettling to me; you think his plans include now Scotland as his kingdome?" Gilley furled his brow and sat to reflect further on her last question of concern. "I know not his motives nor understand the grandness of his strategy. But fear him now I do; not as lord in council for a license of our marriage, but for the ambition of his sorry self that may include our Scotland." They bid the children a good night as their nurses now appeared.

Figure LXVII-Part Two; Stebbing Park gates; an ancient motte and partial moat still define the landscape; the farm lands that once comprised the manor held by Eleanora Douglas are owned and worked today by the Lanyon family of Stebbing

"A game of Merels my dear, perhaps too some more wine?" he asked her. Ellie looked up to him in the warm light of torches spent and a small fire to deter the dampness of the days of rain that filled the mid summer days. "A warm tasine of pear now to my liking I should think." Gilley called to the kitchen to thus prepare it and returned to find his wife with tears falling down her cheeks. "I worry so about my mother now," she whispered. He came and kneeled in front of her, taking her hands in his in a prayer position, "We can only ask of God and dear St. Bride to thus watch over her; her fate to rest with them dear lass." He told her that a game of Merels could wait, for he had other plans. He rose now to his feet and picked her up in his arms, "You are growing great with child, or this knight grows old past time for tournament I fear," he teased her for the weight as he carried her to their chamber. She counted the steps, six, then five, the second landing, then seven more, "A husband with a smile and gleam of eyes as I would see some months ago, I know your thoughts this night," she teased him.

August 13th

Ellie was in the withdrawing room with some of her lady friends working on the heavy intricate embroidery for a large wall hanging for the great hall. Large with child much too soon for an October birth, she mused; then suddenly a feeling of great urgency to find the latrine closet, "Call my Ana, my child does come the noo!" she cried to Lady Amy. The ladies led by Lady Amy went to find Ana and see about the midwives. Gilley was in the great hall and spied their urgency. "Thank you dear ladies, I will see to Lady Eleanora. Do find her good Ana for the lay-in now." Lady Amy was confused. "Should we not call the midwives then?" Ana entered the chamber, "Sir William is the midwife for my girl, it is his way," she told them; then to Gilley, "The lay-in was readied most last week Sir William." From the garderobe came Ellie's call, "Dear Ana, come to me please!"

Figure LXVIII-Part Two; Parkhall as it is today in Douglas, Lanarkshire

Lady Amy Fleming interpreted the look from William as his words for her to gather the others of their group and take their leave. "I will have our squires bring about the horses Sir William," she said. "A son I pray for you that all the ladies here will be outnumbered!' she said happily, leading the embroiderers to the front courtyard of Douglas Castle to await their mounts for their return to their homes; or for Lady Alice a short walk about. The ladies were all giggling as they passed through the large carved oak doors that lead from the great hall to the open air. "Imagine to have husband in the lay-in, then to deliver too the child!" said Lady Helen, a friend of Lady Amy's. Lady Amy replied quietly, "A curious knight and laird this Sir William; but one I admire all the more from today his words: *I will see to Eleanora*. A kind and generous man Lord Douglas; I will stop to pray at the Douglas kirk for safety and a son in this birthing, before I leave for home of Parkhall." Lady Alice and Lady Helen both decided to join her at the kirk, "I am not returning to my manor this day for I am staying in the family tower, the rear one overlooking Douglas Water," said Alice. You must not know then that Sir William was married to my sister and delivered as the midwife the wee lad James, named for my good brother." The two friends were surprised to hear the laird of Douglasdale a healer and midwife of experience; and begged to know more about his Celtic ways. Chattering all the while; these three gentle ladies made their way along the path and up the wee hill to the family kirk; fast friends to share their evening meal at Parkhall.

A long night grew into morning as Ellie struggled with the birth of her third child. "Lord Will, this child is taking long in coming, is there such a problem that you have not shared?" she asked him wearily. "No sweet lass, a wee laddie on the way I know now from the way he wants to stay with his dear mother." Almost immediately the tempo of the birthing began to increase, and within the hour Gilley cried out, "A son, finally we do have a laddie to name for our friend Wishart." He christened the child John, holding his left hand, the unblessed one; Gilley spoke in both Latin and Lallans and then handed John to the midwife just arrived from Douglas Village to be bathed in the fine oils and salve he gave her. Ellie was flushed and awake, but not for long. When the midwife returned Ana was giving her girl some tasine with ginger and lavender in pear with honey. Gilley gently took his new son and held him. John was a wee laddie, smaller than his sisters or brother James. He had fire red hair that was streaked with darker hues almost raven colored; the wild tuffs of full hair protruded in every direction from his head. Ellie held him for but a moment then fell off to sleep.

Gilley sat down in the great hall to write his friend Baron Wishart, addressing the letter to his estate at Pittarrow, he wrote of their son just born. The christening was set for 25th September so that Ellie could attend; a mother was not allowed for forty days in a kirk once giving birth. Sir John would be the God parent that they chose that spring two years ago, he reflected. "And good we settled the matter with Lord Edward to appear St. Hilary's term the next," he said out loud to himself. Ana came down the stairs with the Deerhound at her side. "The wee hound was scratching at the door; Sir Shamus to lie next to Ellie in the bed I fear," chuckled Ana. The children trailed behind her, coming down the stairs with their nurses. "John is born!" cried the laddie, "James and Muriel and Martha have a new brother with red hair!" William's exhaustion for the night long hours of his work with Ellie left him for that moment; four wee ones do we now have; all heirs for Douglasdale he beamed with pride. "Come here to sit with your dear father and rejoice at the arrival of young John of Douglas!"

Early October

Gilley and Sir John Wishart were just returning from three days in Ayrshire on a hunting trip of some twenty men at arms from both their households. They entered the great hall and found Ellie and Sir Andrew discussing something in hushed tones. "Oh Gilley, a terrible tragedy for our Scotland; the Maid of Norway is now with God since late September in the Orkneys did she make her passing." William lost the ebullience of their hunting trip's success and turned now to his friend Wishart, "I fear trouble now about to strike; from which direction, south is what I know but how far south only time can tell us, aye." The Baron from the Mearns added his own concerns, "From the north as well we will reel from ambition the next few months; as you well said, only time can tell us true."

William's squire Patric came in excitedly; a messenger with a second rider now approached. The messenger was immediately recognized when he entered the hali as a servant of the Lovaine family from Little Easton Manor; a look of fear crossed Ellie's face. "Come here good Walter. Pray tell me now, my mother…" her words trailed off as the look on his face turned to tears; he loved M' lady Helisant he told Ellie, "And now she is with God." Gilley went to Ellie's side and held her hand, stroking her shoulders with the other. "Such sad news for us this day," said Ellie as the tears streamed her face, sobbing now into Gilley's side. Walter handed Gilley the parchment message, "There is more Sir William," he said with dread. Gilley read the word of Father Paul, noting the message was not from Lord Lovaine.

Dear Lady Eleanora With your sweet mother yet just laid to rest; your father thus has chosen to remarry. I pray you will understand my reluctance in sending you this letter sooner. But I could not believe a father's callous actions; to not inform a daughter of her dear mother's passing one long month ago. I gained great courage to write you upon hearing that Lady Maud Poyntz would be the lady of the manor within the week in Bildeston. With heavy heart I take your leave and pray for all involved in this sad matter.

with God's true blessing, Father Paul

"Maud Poyntz is but my age," cried Ellie, "and he now fifty-three. My sweet mother, his faithful wife of twenty years and more, yet weeks just laid to rest. Is there no end to his cold ways and cruel actions!" she said, sputtering now in Latin. Baron Wishart decided he would speak, "More heirs for his estates; ambition for this Lord living now in Essex. My dear friend and mother of my God son waste not your tears nor anger on this foolish man," Gilley interjected, "I informed old Wishart that our troubles with good Edward thus to escalate with your father's lies and pompous fury." Ellie held her hands to her head, shaking it back and forth, "How can such a man exist in God's own world of his creation; to hurt the ones who love him most; though not the more, I swear!" Gilley noticed the nurse bringing in baby John, "That is enough swearing for this fair day, good wife, here comes the namesake of one old baron of the Mearns. For thanks we give to God and the Good St. Bride for His gift of one named John."

Ellie began to smile a little, apologizing for her fit of pique, she got up and poured some wine to cheer them; offering some smoked salmon and porridge, with cakes and custard just prepared. Ana had been listening from the kitchen stairs now entered in the hall.

"There lamb, should there be a time you need your Ana, I will be in chamber," and she turned to leave. "Dear Ana, would you show our Walter here the way to some food and sleep, and yes, good Johannis here as well." Ana took them down to the kitchen and Ellie regained some of her composure. "Most happy am I to see you two this morning now," she told them. "Were I alone, much grief of self would I thus feel. Thank you both for your true words, my kind husband and my dear friend, Sir John."

Early December 1290

After evening prayer Ellie planned to go looking for her husband; saying goodnight to all four children in her chamber. "Ana," she said, "Give me my chamber cloak, the fine green one with the fur and brocade trim; I am off to find my William on the parapet I feel." Ana sighed softly, "You look so lovely my dear girl; go find your knight while I have a scented bath brought up to cheer him, he worries so now of his Scotland." Ellie went up the turnpike stairs that led to the parapet of the keep and there she saw her knight in his special place of privacy on the wall-walk. He smiled quietly when he saw her coming towards him and rose to put his arms about her. "I can fit my arms around my sweet wife entirely with some length to spare," he teased her. She giggled; happy he noticed and pleased with the warmer turn of weather. "It feels more like Michaelmas than Christmas come upon us, my husband," she cooed, smiling softly in the moon bright night.

Coyly Ellie spoke to him now, looking up at the stars twinkling down at the lovers. "Tha i breagha a – nochd, nach eil?" Responding to her words in Scottish Gaelic that asked him, it is lovely the night isn't it, he agreed "Tha – i ciuin," it is calm. Then realizing what just transpired, "My ears do hear the truth, my sweet Essex lass speaks the Gaelic of our Scotland, our highland cousins in the north to speak?" asked Gilley in astonished tones. Ellie giggled, "Not the noo, but more soon I do hope. When you take leave of me for council of King Edward, I should thus be fluent in the highland tongue upon return; ready to visit your kin in Morayshire, beautiful Kinloss or on the Black Isle with dear Andrew and his new bride Eugenia." And motioning him to the stairway, "Another surprise do I have for you my husband; the tub of hot scented waters where I shall bathe you." The worries he had for his country with the mysterious death of the Maid of Norway some months ago preyed on him still. But those concerns of state would have to wait Gilley resolved. His bride has set a trap for romance, he beamed happily to himself. "This humble knight so fortunate to have one as you for his sweet wife." And he picked her up and in his teasing way threw her over his shoulder and carried her fast to the laird's chamber for their playful frolic of their love.

Another week went by and his time to depart for England drew near. Gilley entered the cozy withdrawing room from his place in the great hall. The little girls Muriel and Martha were sitting and playing near their mother on the small carpet on the floor next to Ellie. Wee John was asleep in a new cradle with rockers. William had instructed his farrier turned wood carver on how to cut the wood and then assemble the pieces into a wee cradle for his son. The small wooden bed had rockers that Ellie could move with her foot as she sat nearby. The wee lad looked up and smiled as she rocked him; in the tradition of the old ways he was laying still, tightly bundled in swaddling bands to keep him safe. Gilley got down on the floor now with the wee lasses and one by one he picked them up sitting them on his shoulders. He stood up, holding his girls in place; his two daughters giggling and laughing with their father all in unison. Lord Douglas turned around with his back to his dear wife; in preparation for this game. Then slowly, ominously he turned round to face her. Transformed by magic the three now became one. Ellie squealed in concert to their game as she beheld not her husband and daughters, but a vicious, growling monster! The burly creature moved menacingly towards Ellie. The wee ones made their monster paws and growled their monster tongue, just as their father showed them, while they sat high on his shoulders. Fiercely now, ruthlessness pretended, Lord Douglas and his wee daughters became the terrifying **Three Headed Monster** as they crept around the small chamber of the withdrawing room snarling in three voices; clawing at imaginary villains. Ellie feigned fright and screamed again. This ingenious game was invented by Lord Douglas and his wee lasses when they were in Essex and had now become their evening ritual, their entertainment for the winter nights in Scotland.

The terrifying menace made his tour again, the little girls growled with their small voices, gnarled the air with their monster paws; looking for their unsuspecting victims. "Grrrowl!" roared the three headed monster. "Oh please Sir Monster of Essex's marshes, now of Scotland's braes, with those fearful sounds do spare me so I pray you. I am a mother yet with child," pleaded Ellie as she put down her embroidery to participate even more. All the while a quiet James was standing to her right, near the fireplace. Slowly, carefully James moved in stealth like steps, grabbing a poker from near the fire box. Suddenly he stood directly in front of Ellie, as if protecting her; he raised the poker with all his might and pointed it at the treacherous beast, this Three Headed Monster. "Back monster, I command you now as I am James of Douglas do you know." The monster growled and snarled in three voices, waving six fierce paws of fearful prowess. "Men at arms I command your attention here, the noo! Monster, one more the time I give you, kneel and pledge fealty to your laird, or pay for your sorry deeds." William was suppressing his laughter, trying to growl he sputtered some guttural noises.

Douglas men at arms entered the chamber, hearing young James' commands; amused but circumspect in their demeanor. Ellie was sitting in stunned amazement, watching her young son. "Monster, I, James of Douglas do banish you from Douglasdale. Good men at arms, take him now this dreaded beast." The men at arms moved in as Gilley began to speak as the father now, "Very good young James, our game now over; our son the champion of the contest; your mother's gallant knight and protective warrior victorious this day."

Gilley set the little girls down and got out a board for Merels to play with Ellie; it was now the children's bedtime and their nurses were coming in to get them. "Dear laddie, where ever did you think to do this; what fright you gave the monster as you were defending me!" exclaimed Ellie, complimenting her young son on his strategy and brave actions; hugging him to her. James' nurse came to bring him to his chamber and he told her he was not going to bed at this time. "I am James of Douglas and I will retire when ready." Gilley stood up, "And I am Lord Douglas, your lord paramount and father of one James of Douglas. You will retire the noo!" Off went the reluctant warrior to his bed; his father breaking out in peels of laughter. "Pledge fealty monster....I am James of Douglas. The words of one so young; he does amuse me so!" Ellie was chuckling too. "I but noted his presence ever so quiet in the corner there; he watched your moves to study all so cleverly. What strategy he has so natural thus within him; wish I had such for me to play this game of Merels now with you!" she replied, laughing all the more.

Then suddenly Gilley recalled her words, "Dear wife, were you true in what was said, you are again with child?" he asked in disbelief. Ellie shook her head yes, "I have reason now to remain in Scotland while you visit with dear Edward; fortunate for me!" she declared. "Fortunate aye, that is true; for us and Douglasdale our family growing all the more!" Gilley boasted in loud praise of their good fortune. "Another heir, wee lass or laddie to share our dear lives; blessed by God and the Good St. Bride are we my wife." John's nurse came in to bring the baby to his nursery. The pause gave Gilley time to pack up the board and game pieces, "There no will be a contest of Merels this night again dear wife, for I have something on my mind, sure aye!" Before Ellie knew his intentions he had swept her up in his strong arms, pulling her feet up so she could see them, "Take a look dear lass, soon they will vanish from your view! With child is how I love to see you, aye that is true!" He carried her up the stairs and closed the door behind them in their chamber. There was a knock at the door, "Come in," said Ellie to his mocked disdain and complete surprise. There at the door were a number of Douglas servants bringing in the large bathing tub followed by containers of scented, steaming water; and carafes of wine and little cakes, a favorite of their laird. "It is with such surprise I planned to tell you so this night. Then hence forgot when young James' courageous valor fought against the monster foe and blurted out my news of child." Gilley pulled her close to him, "Lady El, will you love me tomorrow as you love me today," beginning the rituals of their love.

Christmas passed and the feast of St. Stephen would see Gilley leave reluctantly for England and the council of King Edward. "My dear wife, our first time to lang be apart; and the celebration of Hogmanay left to your own ambitions." Ellie smiled at him from the large chair in the withdrawing room. "Lady Amy and Sir Andrew will help with gifts and feasting for our good families of Douglasdale," she told him reassuringly. "And upon return, we will thus exchange our presents and celebrate the more! But first this gift have I been keeping for you now; since Hertford to surprise you," she told him as she brought out the lovely ermine mantel she bought with Alice shopping that day so many months ago. Gilley's eyes were wide with amazement. "That I didn't see you pack this gift when we left Essex; oh Ellie this mantel perfect for this laird your husband. He leaned down and kissed her deeply, passionately.

Ellie smiled up at her husband and said quietly to him, "Thank you Lord Will for meeting with King Edward not in company of this lady much relieved." Gilley looked into his wife's eyes; kneeling down in front of her, he took her hand in his. "So long ago you twice refused me privilege of marriage; your fears of a king's reprisal. I pray dear wife, have you once reconsidered the boldness in our deeds of matrimony?' he asked her. Ellie giggled, "You mean have I thought to see my feet to walk the aisles of kirks from county to county, shire to shire with anyone but you Lord Douglas?" She reached for him to bring him all the closer, "Lord Will, no man has ever loved me, nor have I loved another the way I love le Hardi, sure aye," mimicking his words when he was certain. He kissed her hand, his eyes welled with tears of happiness. She continued her words, with their private ritual, "And you my husband, would you love me tomorrow," she paused again as he kissed her deeply; giving his answer to her question.

England 27 January 1291

William de Douglas, miles and Ellie's two procurators, le Porter and Giffard, were called before the council and King Edward. William did not contest the charges but submitted to the will of the king in the matter of the license. Edward then inquired of Lady Eleanora; her required presence to answer for her contempt; her broken vows to her liege lord. But before the solicitors could reply on her behalf, William interjected with some hint of boast that his wife was yet again with child having three already to her measure; was thus unable to make the journey to his court and council. The king exchanged looks with the Scottish knight; having many children of his own to bespeak of his prowess, he understood the meaning of le Hardi's words. But he barely smiled; Lord Edward was still annoyed with this Douglas knight.

The king granted the license and made arrangements for William to set up four payments in settlement of fine to secure the income of the estates. The financial offering of £100 would be settled in four collections, increments of £25 to commence the first on 16 May 1291 with the second to be paid on Ellie's 23rd birthday this same year. The last two installments would be paid on the same two dates for 1292, the year next. Then the dreaded hearing was over. William thanked the solicitors and made haste with his men at arms to return first to Fawdon, then home to Douglasdale. Sadly William was home few days when Ellie lost the baby she was carrying. There was something wrong with the wee one growing then within her; the sickness of child not to come as others before was her clue she told him.

William was surprised at her great calm; to lose a child is a mother's greatest fear he knew. But she told him the cause was not her fear of Edward's charge for license; the infant did not thrive but for some other reason she did know. "It is God's will that this one has come to pass so quickly from us," she told him quietly. "We have been so blessed that I do understand some; wee ones called to His Heaven sooner than we want. But this mother still does mourn her child," she said, the sorrow in her voice now more apparent. "Ellie my girl," he spoke to her calmly. "We are Douglases that mourn for all we lose from this life. But know in our Celtic tradition that we are never far from the eternal. Our young one is going home to be without pain or sadness now; I truly know." They held each other close; he picked her up and carried her to pray with him in private chapel. When they returned to the laird's chamber Gilley administered some pennyroyal to bring her through the loss, that she would clear her body of the poisons from one that passed to the Otherworld yet still within her womb.

May 1291

On the unauthorized invitation of William Fraser, Bishop of St. Andrews and long time ally to Lord Edward, the king of England boldly rode into Norham, then invaded Scotland, to claim his Lordship over the kingdome. Edward summoned his military vassals in the north, and the nobles of Scotland along with Scottish clergy. On the 10th of May the Adjudication began. The noblemen present included many barons of the realm and clergy as well including one outspoken bishop: Robert Wishart. In response to the Edward's announcements, in his attempt to overawe the Scotts, some of Scotland's magnates were unimpressed. The English king's feeble explanation for his presence there and his self proclaimed status as Lord Paramount irked many in the kingdome including the Bishop of Glasgow who boldly moved to action.

Robert Wishart stood proudly and spoke the noble words of his country's sovereign independence; the same words that would reverberate in passion some twenty-nine years later at the Abbey in Arbroath: "The Kingdom of Scots was once noble, strong, and powerful among the other kingdoms of the earth. After repelling the Britons, Norwegians, Picts, and Danes, the Scots nobly upheld their rights." These brave words Edward passed over with a deaf ear as he continued his theft of Scotsman's rights. His intention was to put down any errant thoughts entertained by nobles on the control of Scotland. In his mind neither a Robert Brus the senior nor a Josh de Hastings, nor any other kin to Alexander should fancy himself a potential heir to the throne of Scotland without his consent and approval. This invasion was pure folly and falsely staged the Scots insisted.

But Edward deemed his military move was justified; he was coming to the aid of Scottish nobles he claimed fraudulently. He held up a letter written in October 1290 to prove his case. Bishop Fraser had written the king in earnest Edward told the magnates; decrying the tenuous state of the kingdome, calling for the English king to intercede. Edward claimed that this letter validated his presence; he was needed in Scotland to stave up the divided kingdome, rocked by the many competitors for the Scotland's crown. The Regents were not amused; William Fraser had sent this communication without the consent or knowledge of the magnates of the realm; they were not even consulted on such a letter to the king. But this fact was a small inconvenience to the English lord and would not deter him from

MY TRUTH LIES IN THE RUINS

his mission. Secretly to himself Edward vowed that one day he would bring Scotland to her knees; this my first act to that end he mused.

On 2nd June in Norham, the Regents of Scotland reluctantly acknowledged Edward Plantagenet as Lord Paramount of Scotland; oaths of homage from the Scottish nobles were to follow in the months ahead they promised. This decision on the part of the Regents did not come with favor but with grave discussion and deep concerns in the matter. These Guardians had little choice they believed than to acquiesce; competitors for Scotland's crown were dividing the country haplessly with strained allegiances and Edward threatened war if they did not accept his terms. So the magnates capitulated; swearing allegiance to the English king. William Douglas was in his Douglasdale when the word came by messenger; his presence was required to do homage to Lord Edward, on the orders of the Regents of the Kingdome of Scotland. He was to appear before the Lord Paramount and his witnesses at the manor of Thurstanson owned by Walter de Lindsay, kin of Sir Alex; here William would pledge his fealty; swear of his allegiance to Edward Plantagenet.

Another storm appeared on the horizon, threatening the peace for the laird of Douglas. Beginning in the early spring of 1291 a lawsuit was making its way through the king's council regarding the Douglas manor of Fawdon. A man named Geoffrey de Lucy claimed that William Douglas dispossessed him of two hundred acres of pasture land in Fawdon. On 8th June Edward issued a writ from Norham first compelling twelve men of the neighborhood to view the lands and pastures in question; summoning the same good men to New Castle on Tyne for a judgment by jury on 2nd July to settle the suit brought by de Lucy against William Douglas. The laird of Douglas was also ordered to attend the examinations of the suit in July or his bailiff should come if he is not available to the court.

As William was reading the second summons from Edward in less than a week, he became very agitated. Their manor of Fawdon was once more the matter for some magistrate to settle for their ownership or seising. De Lucy was the kin of de Umfraville's wife, the laird who held of the barony of Alnwick that included Fawdon. Geoffrey was also heir of the de Lucy's tangled estates; the grandfather having mortgaged many of his lands to pay sponsors for the Crusades; taking liens against his estates to raise the coinage for a knight's fife, then forgetting the reason of the lien to contest it. William studied the details of the outrageous charges that de Lucy had contrived; claiming that he held ownership to the land with his freehold in Aungerham. "This humble knight will fight this suit of infamy to the last breath of my being," he declared defiantly; subconsciously rubbing the facial scars from his first time encounter with the reprobates, defending Fawdon Manor from the thieving escapades of de Umfraville.

"Ellie, again to Fawdon must we go to settle this suit of nuisance from de Lucy and his kin de Umfraville," William said reviewing the two writs he recently received. They were sitting together in the great hall of Douglas Castle as he related the entangled web of de Lucy's deceit. "We will go first to Newcastle then to Thurston," he told her, speaking in a clipped fashion that revealed his impatience for both appearances. "That we could have some time to spend in Fawdon," she replied thoughtfully, "the children would enjoy the journey too. Let us make a time of it to thus be all together, have some adventure and fun in our need to be there." Gilley reread the notice requiring his homage to Lord Edward. "On the 5th July we should return that we must be in Thurston in East Lothiane," he added in a half distracted manner. "We will take our place at Thurstanson, the manor there of Sir Walter de Lindsay, kin of our dear Alex; that I will make my pledge to dear Edward, Lord Paramount," speaking sarcastically, Gilley was not relishing the unpleasant deeds at hand.

Fawdon 25th June 1291

The Douglases arrived at Fawdon with pack animals and horses, children and nurses, Sir David and some squires, and Sir Shamus with days to spare before the hearing in Newcastle. Gilley and Ellie had plenty of time to enjoy their manor; taking their children to visit some ruins near their lands; to hunt for ancient treasure, in the higher reaches of the River Breamish. Muriel happened upon an ancient coin while James found a piece of iron that William told him came much from a blade that a warrior from long ago might carry. "These were remains of hillforts," Gilley said, "from centuries gone past." The family journeyed onward, through the village of Alnhamsheles and home to Fawdon. The children carried home their treasures proudly; the day of adventure proved very exciting with their valuable finds.

Another day's exploring took the family west again, stopping this time at Cobden; a site of some amazing waterfalls. They rode just east of the Cobden Burn where it meets the Breamish to find many of these beautiful gifts from nature, created by the wild rushing waters cascading down through the splendor of the Cheviot Hills. Along the way were more fascinating settlements of the ancient ones. Gilley reminded James of the times they went searching for standing stones and stone circles on Mann and in Wigtonshire.

MY TRUTH LIES IN THE RUINS

Figure LXIX-Part Two; the Breamish River near Ingram, Northumbria

 These same Celts in Scotland and Northumbria lived hundreds of years before. They had built such stone circles and covered them with timber, sod and grasses, housing several families under one roof he explained in detail as was his way. "Learn from the old ones that have gone before us," said Gilley to his young children, "They hold the secrets we have yet forgotten." He showed James how to ford a stream; how to set temporary bridges across the bogs for safe passage made from plaiting the boughs of young trees. It was on the Cobden that Gilley gave his son and daughters their first fishing lessons. He also spoke of hunting to his children; preying on game with bow and arrow, to learn the ways of the ancient ones, without the aid of hawk or hound. "We will be privileged to retain our lands, to defend our home when others come to take it from us if we hold true to the knowledge of those who have gone before us," Gilley patiently said, "The lessons of our Celtic forefathers that your father shares with you now are to be remembered; hold them here in your heart and they will serve you well."

 In Newcastle on Tyne on the 2nd July the jury found in favor of Lord Douglas; his Fawdon was restored as his in freehold. The day next the family began their journey northward, feeling the triumphant confidence from prevailing in court; repelling once again the attempt of de Umfraville to steal their Fawdon manor. Their entire household rode eagerly northward; leaving Fawdon behind, they loaded up their pack horses for the journey north through Scotland as a crazy Deerhound ran along side Gilley and Ellie, playfully enjoying his day. The family was happy and relieved in their victory. For the moment the laird of Douglas was basking in his success and victory in Newcastle's courts. Douglas banners blazoned proudly as they made their way towards Berwick; the warm sun seemed to shine all around them as the bright July day sheltered them in a clear blue sky of dry summer weather.

Outside of the royal burgh the Douglases headed northwest, making their way towards the parish of Thurston, arriving with time to spare at their destination. But Ellie was anxious to move on. She decided that she would travel further west to their manor at Glencorse; to await William's arrival when his business with Edward was complete. "That Lord Edward would prefer to see you I do know it," said Ellie teasing her husband and his need to attend. "It is Lady Douglas he would feign to see," chided William, "to discuss the more her marriage to Lord Douglas!" Ellie insisted that she was not to see Edward on this journey; she preferred the serenity of Glencorse and would travel there with their children. "It is done!" she told him.

William rode on alone to the de Lindsay manor of Thurstanson. He met with other nobles and Lord Edward as they proceeded to the lovely old family chapel of the de Lindsay manor. There before Alan, Bishop of Caithness and Anthony, Bishop of Durham, William swore his oath and pledged his fealty with other Scotts of his station, kissing the gospels and saying his words. He appended his seal to the document, making his mark in the warm wax dangling from the silk ribbons. As he was about to take his leave, the king's vassal beckoned him to come speak directly with the Lord Edward. Edward had a legendary memory for names and faces, especially of the nobles in his kingdome, and now in Scotland as well. He knew well the name of William Douglas; not just from his Crusading days in Acre or from the Lovaine de Ferrers' marriage debacle, but also from more recent occurrences at Berwick. The King had heard two complaints of major proportions that he addressed immediately; issuing not one but two writs of great importance to this nobleman, Lord Douglas. "Again we meet Sir William," said Edward wryly. "Are you yet informed of my interest in one man yet detained in your donjon prison in Lanarkshire?" he asked le Hardi. William explained that he had yet been on some business in Newcastle; a matter just resolved in the courts there. He had not recently been in Douglasdale, but would be there soon he allowed.

Edward smiled in his sarcastic manner and happily elaborated on one of his latest writs. "While the Douglas family was entertaining themselves in Northumbria," Edward began, "this king was finding pleasure in his work at Berwick on Tweed, hearing complaints and issuing writs to pass the days there as Lord Paramount to Scotland's nobles," he told William with a hint of derision in his manner. "Specifically," he allowed, "on the 28th of June a royal mandate was contrived by me; addressed to Alan, Bishop of Caithness and Chancellor of Scotland; the very bishop standing there," he said pointing to one of prelates witnessing the roll of pledging, the document where le Hardi just affixed his seal. "This writ is for one William Douglas on behalf of the Comyn; that the husband of his sister should be released from Douglas Castle, the donjon prison there; the prisoner known as Hugh de Abernathy." William uncharacteristically held his tongue before responding. Walter de Lindsay, kin of Sir Alex, listened from across the chamber to le Hardi's response. "My lord, that I might review the writ you issued; upon doing so to respond immediately would be my intention. That perhaps we could chance to so discuss the circumstances of this incarceration and the murder of my wife's own kin, young Lord de Ferrers' half brother, the good Earl Duncan, late of Fife." But Edward was hearing none of it; he would allow Douglas to have his words in Council yet another day he said dismissively. "But first to release your prisoner to my men at arms; de Abernathy to remain in my prisons until then," ordered the king. Le Hardi bowed graciously and told him that he would be in Douglasdale two days hence to address the matter.

William took his leave hastily. It was not his intention to release Abernathy to anyone; especially an English king who was unlawfully imposing his will upon the Scottish kingdome, he mused. When the laird of Douglas finally arrived back at Douglas Castle, he found the royal writ regarding de Abernathy awaiting his reply. William's choice was to ignore it; his brother in law was to die in Douglasdale he vowed. Abernathy's confinement ended within the year; when he passed to the Otherworld some few months later, he was yet a prisoner of Lord Douglas, a guest in the donjon prison of Douglas Castle. Edward did not forget this transgression. But to William le Hardi Douglas the de Abernathy matter was just one more in a growing list of disagreements between an English king and a Scottish nobleman. Adhering to one's truth was not without a price; this le Hardi knew would cost him one day.

Unfortunately, this initial writ was just the first of two such mandates from King Edward. To William's great dismay, a second royal order from Plantagenet awaited his attention. Surprisingly it was issued from Berwick on 3rd July, just two days before Gilley made his appearance at Thurstanson for his pledging to the English king. This mandate was astonishingly not even mentioned to him at the de Lindsay manor; likely for good reason William surmised. "That our English lord was most busy in his days in Berwick on Tweed; to find displeasure with his faithful laird of Douglasdale," he scoffed indignantly. Edward's second writ was issued in response to a complaint by the abbot of Melrose Abbey. William was ordered to answer for the injustices alleged by the Abbot and Convent of Melrose; the order commanded his compearance for the 2nd of August. Lord Douglas flung both documents aside with great disdain; they sailed across the great hall of Douglas Castle in a flutter of fury. Ellie was just coming into the hall when she caught site of his outburst of temper. She immediately became alarmed. "What is it my husband that distresses you so this day?" she asked him. Sir Andrew their steward joined them in the hall as well; having just heard the enraged words of his laird. The steward was working on the estate accounts in the withdrawing room; but wondered aloud what he might do to help. The laird of Douglas answered both their inquiries with rippled anger in his words. "The mischief making monks of Melrose are directing their complaints to Edward Plantagenet; not to Scotland's Guardians," growled le Hardi, his brow furled in deep anger for the arrogance of the Abbot circumventing the governing rulers of Scotland.

Figure LXX-Part Two; Mauchline Tower in Ayrshire was built by the Abbot of Melrose to manage the Abbey's lands in that shire

The history between the abbot and le Hardi was troubled. Even before he became Lord Douglas succeeding his brother Hugh, William was being plagued by some annoying occurrences extending from Mauchline. For some years these white monks played their game; obstructing the waters flowing to the Lugar where it meets the Ayr near his Douglas lands in Kyle Stewart. This ploy deprived Douglas tenants of valuable water for their crops; farmers who paid their rents in grains they grew for their laird had their lands and crops dry up in drought from the dammed river beds. Now too these churchmen were flaunting their power in Douglasdale; crossing the park lands, Douglas lands on their way to Mauchline without the laird's permission. "That it is the wizard Scott I fear! These thieving monks took

MY TRUTH LIES IN THE RUINS

back his soul from God's own Heavens for their devil's work; to divert the waters for their use, stealing from Lord Douglas!" scowled Gilley, now speaking directly to his wife and Sir Andrew. "What is this poor knight to do; no complaints will Edward hear of William, damaged so is Lord Douglas of these Melrose monks. That they cross the park of Douglasdale in their journey now to their Mauchline; no justice for this sorry knight I fear!" he yelled the louder.

Figure LXXI-Part Two; Melrose Abbey; the monks would make their trek from this abbey to Mauchline by traveling through the Park of Douglas

The Melrose monks had been accustomed to traveling west on a road through the Douglas valley from the marches as they journeyed first to the kirk in Douglas. They complained that when they used this road now, passing in front of Douglas Castle, that the baron of Douglas frightened them; spooking their horses. But in truth the laird of Douglas had tried in vain to approach the abbacy on the water rights while the arrogant abbot ignored Gilley's water claims and dismissed his attempted reconciliations with the monks. Le Hardi decided that another approach was required; one that would get their attention more quickly. He would inhibit their travels through Douglasdale; make them as uncomfortable as possible as they rode near his estates. After nearly a week of reflection on the complaint form the Melrose churchmen, William chose to ignore the summons to Berwick all together. "That this laird does most prefer to wait; the selection of a Scottish king to resolve this injustice," he told Ellie and Sir Andrew just a few days later. Instead he would send two solicitors to plead his case and bide him time he explained. These good attorneys did as they were directed; but Lord Edward denied them Douglas' justice. Edward chose to set aside William's complaint for water rights in Ayrshire; he would deal with Douglas soon enough he mused. King Edward preferred instead to wait the outcome of his request for the release of de Abernathy before he would entertain any relief from the abbot's complaint for Lord Douglas.

The summer in 1291, filled with the indecisions of leadership and the lack of a true king lingered like a grey cloud of confusion over Scotland. The competitors filed their claims with Lord Edward; each making their case that he should be the next King of Scots. English knights and vassals to King Edward became custodians of Scottish castles that Edward deemed strategic to his control of the kingdome; to keep the peace he snickered in deceit. The English in effect occupied Scotland or at least part of the kingdome. In July Nicky de Segrave resigned his ward of young William de Ferrers; Ellie's step was son now of age to manage his own estates. Sir Nicholas de Segrave became a custodian for Ayr Castle in Scotland; in service to Lord Edward. About the same time a wee laddie was born to Maud Poyntz and Lord Lovaine; young Thomas de Lovaine was now the heir of his father's estates; while there was a new brother for Lady Douglas. Lord Lovaine was ebullient; a new heir and a male meant that the Scotsman would have no claim to his land; his daughter Eleanora would be left out of his will, he vowed!

Mid-Summer 1291

William took his time this morning, lingering in the great hall; Ellie sensed he had something important on his mind. "What thoughts are you yet keeping from your wife?" she asked him quietly. He was waiting for the right moment to blurt out his intentions; but now Ellie gave him the perfect opportunity, and he could take his time telling her of his exciting plans. He began by suggesting a trip to visit the de Morays, his kin in the Highlands; to clear their minds and hearts he told his bride. They would begin their travels north immediately he proclaimed; before the cooler months of late September. Gilley laid out his maps and charts as he began telling her of his ideas. He opened the one of the northern frontier of Scotland to show her the Highlands; here they would visit Ormond Castle he told her excitedly. "To stay here, on the Black Isle with Sir Andrew de Moray, the justiciar of north of the Firth," he boldly gestured to the parchment drawings that he made. "That we can enjoy good Highland hospitality; visit with many more of the clan de Moray is my plan," he said, looking over eagerly at Ellie, to see how his bride responded.

Gilley didn't have to wait long for her answer; her eyes were alive with excitement. To see Sir Andrew again and meet his new wife Eugenia and their children thrilled her she squealed; her usual animated fashion relieved the laird completely of any concerns that she might not want to leave

Douglasdale just now. "Your good cousin Andrew; he boasted so highly of his homeland and of Moraydale, most as you my husband to speak so of our Douglasdale," she sighed, delighted at the prospect of leaving their troubles in Lanarkshire behind for adventure and a journey to the Highlands.

Gilley told her that he planned to take them eastward as well; to the other side of the Moray Firth where they would meet more of his kin from the Highlands. "Then to see the face of my sweet lass as you behold the many fine fortresses constructed by my ancestors," he said beaming with pride, his eyes dancing excitedly as he spoke. "Strongholds of uncompromised strength, some built of walls eight feet wide and more!" he said enthusiastically. Ellie giggled with anticipation; she loved Gilley's family spirit and was eager to hear more about the Flemish and Celtic people that called the Highlands home. She was also anxious to practice the Gaelic language she was learning, almost religiously in anticipation of this very visit to the kingdome in the north.

William was in his glory; he was eager to teach them all about the Douglas family history. He could also share many exciting tales; stories for his bride and children about the brave knights, soldiers of fortune that forged his family's heritage in the wilds of the Highlands. "We will begin our journey north staying first at our manor in Livingston; then to continue on to Stirling where one of Scotland's most powerful castles stands impenetrable on an edifice of sheer rock; nearby to Cambuskenneth Abbey. We might yet stay the night there at the abbey," suggested Gilley. "Our next day's journey then to Scone will be," he said brimming with pride. Young James had just joined them in the great hall, sitting down beside his mother his eyes were wide with excitement as he listened attentively to his father. "The history of Scottish kings resides there; that they were all thus crowned as they sat on the Coronation Stone to give their oath to Scotland's nobles," he explained. "Have you seen a king so crowned there?" asked young James. Gilley told him no. "Alexander became the king before my birth; and as he was in minority they did not use the Coronation Stone just then," he said "When Scotland's next king is chosen, we will venture there, to witness history and his good ceremony!" he promised the lad.

Gilley's plans were very detailed and well thought out; obvious to Ellie that he had been hard at work on this idea for some time. "That you so managed all this, without my knowledge," she laughed, amazed with his ingenious proposal. He showed her where they would stop at Conveth and stay with the Wisharts and their family. From there the Douglases could travel northwest to Newtonmore. "Our first destination of importance will be the Black Isle and Ormond Castle held by our dear kin Sir Andrew. Though not an isle in reality, the de Moray fortress overlooks a true land of enchantment," he said hinting at excitement. He and Ellie reviewed the remainder of his plans. The rest of the journey was designed to take them to Kinloss, then further east to the imposing fortress at Duffus; from there to venture out to Spynie Loch, traveling to see the majestic Spynie Palace. "Duffus Castle was the first of many my ancestors built in Moravia. This structure my father most preferred of all such designs," Gilley explained.

Ellie interrupted, "This lass so thought that Freskin was the Fleming of West Lothianes; building such a fortress in Strabock, was he not the same knight in Moravia?" she asked trying to get her facts straight. "Aye, the very one; using a smaller structure but with the same intent; he was indeed our dear Hugo de Freskin. Later he was induced to move north, given these lands by the king some one hundred-forty years ago," Gilley told her. "He then began the building of the classic motte and bailey Norman structure you might so recognize from your English castles. It is impervious to attackers; a series of wet ditches and palisades devised to obstruct invading forces. King David was once to stay there while they built the Abbey at Kinloss," Gilley continued; pleased that his storytelling and sharing of Douglas history was still holding the attention of his wife and young son.

"Though Duffus castle no longer bears the de Moray name, their descendants on the female line the de Cheynes are kin and hold of that castle," Gilley said, giving far more information than Ellie knew she could ever remember. "When first you see that majestic fortress, rising like a mountain made of stone and earth high above the moors, you will never forget the site, a fearful statement to any foe; do not attempt to come here without good invitation that otherwise grave peril should become of you, sure aye!" The family would not stay at Duffus Castle however as it was currently being reinforced; new buildings were being built while massive stone structuring was being added to the hall on the motte. Gilley planned to stay instead at nearby Spynie.

Ever ebullient with his plans, he was still not through describing the adventures he anticipated as he continued speaking to James and Ellie, "Then to Spynie Loch and the palace there of the same name built by my Great Uncle Brice." This former residence of the good St. Brice when he was the Bishop of Moray was where the Douglases would stay while they explored this side of the firth. The palace had served for many years as the center of the church in Moraydale. "Many Douglas uncles served as canons of the cathedral near there," he told his wife and son. He went on to list the Douglas names one by one who served the kirk: Freskin Dean of Moray, Henry Canon of Spynie, and Alexander Canon of Spynie, but also Sheriff of Elgin. "Why is it the de Morays have names the same as our Douglases?" interjected James quizzically. "They do some aye," smiled Gilley, "but not the name of James as that is a Stewart name," he chuckled. "That our families are descended from the same brave Flemish knight; the soldier of fortune who journeyed from Flanders lang years ago; one named Hugo de Freskin as I have said. Our good family takes great pride in our names of heritage, that we so use them now that we may honor our brave warriors of the past."

Figure LXXII-Part Two; ruins of Duffus Castle, once the stronghold of Freskin the Fleming later Freskin de Moravia or de Moray, kin to the Douglases

Gilley went on to explain that the bishopric later moved as the see of Moray changed locations. "The glorious cathedral at Elgin was so built to replace the one at Spynie; built by Bishop Andrew of Moray. We will have the privilege to visit personally this new cathedral, the guest of Bishop Archibald of Moray," he said triumphantly. "But a tragic fire of momentous proportions just some twenty years ago destroyed this magnificent structure; alas they are still rebuilding it," he sighed. "Our final visit of importance will be to Gauldwell Castle; an immense fortress, towering above the Fiddich on a bluff overlooking the majestic glen that bears the river's name. This castle was first built with an impressive courtyard; the envy of many; built as well by our Freskin, the knight of Moravia," Gilley said, finalizing their destinations. James asked how big the castle was; if it was bigger than Douglas Castle. "My father, your own grandfather, when he was laird of Douglasdale coveted such a stronghold for himself," Gilley chuckled. "This large hall castle was nearly forty-three ells in length, with a massive curtain wall for protection built around it," he said indicating that their own fortress dwarfed in comparison to the structure Freskin built near Dufftown. Looking at Ellie and James, Gilley finally took a breath; he paused should

DEBORAH RICHMOND FOULKES

they have more questions. Ellie was overwhelmed with all the information; James was excited for the adventure as any five year old would be. Their stunned yet happy faces prompted Gilley to conclude in his characteristic manner, "It is done!"

Figure LXXIII-Part Two; remains of Spynie Palace where a portcullis once secured the fortress on Spynie Loch

Finally the day arrived; their journey was about to begin and everyone felt the excitement in the air. Gilley was still lingering at his special place on the parapet, taking in one last look of his Douglasdale before he started the great trip north. Ellie was coming up to join him; her eyes smiled brightly in her child like exhilaration as she spotted him at the wall-walk. Gilley turned as he heard her final steps on the turnpike stairs; beckoning her to him, he wrapped his arms around his bride as she snuggled into his chest. "Lord Will, that I knew you were most here," she giggled. He sighed aloud; then whispered in her ear, "That I most had to take just one more look at my Douglasdale," he chuckled knowing she would understand. His eyes met the hills in the distance that were beginning to turn a light shade of purple; the Tinto about to bloom in heather in short weeks he mused. "Ellie, my dear sweet Lady El," he said softly, "this humble knight is most pleased that you are here." Ellie leaned into him, burrowing herself between his powerful and muscular arms. "Often have I dreamed to take such a journey with my family; to teach the wee ones of our past ways; to show our children from where we came; these wild lands tamed some now by other Douglases, brave Celtic and Flemish warriors gone before us." Ellie turned to look deeply into his eyes. "Lord Will, it is my fantasy come true to join you in this dream; to be part of this adventure with my knight and husband for all the ages is my happiness, healing my very soul from any sadness come before." They kissed each other deeply and passionately and held themselves in a long enduring hug before they made their way down to the turnpike stairs to begin their journey.

The gonfalon of Willelmi de Duglas had been removed; the laird of Douglas was not to be at Douglas Castle for many weeks. The journey planned was very well thought out; a Douglas trait Ellie had noted from her first meeting three years ago with Lord Hugh. The children were chattering away with their nurses, except for James who rode with Lord Douglas. The convoy of pack animals and palfreys and men at arms proceeded north; leaving their wee manor of Livingston behind them, they now headed north to the Highlands. As promised their first scheduled visit was with the Wisharts at their manor near Conveth. Both Sir John and his wife Lady Johanna were delighted to see the Douglases at their estate. Lady Wishart was especially pleased to meet Lady Douglas. The raid of the heart that took place at Fawside Castle had been the topic of many conversations for the Wisharts over the years. Their lands in Tynedale and other parts of Northumbria were seized than later restored for Sir John's role as Gilley's accomplice in the abduction of his bride. "Lady Eleanora, so many children of your household; the raid most worth the trouble I do see now!" she said laughing as she counted the three wee Douglases since then. "And this is John, God son of my husband?" she asked looking at the laddie with the beautiful golden red locks of hair surrounding his fair face. Even Sir Shamus received his recognition. "This is the hound that won the day; finding a bride for my dear friend William," chuckled the Baron of the Mearns.

Looking now to Gilley, "You have been to see Lord Edward; swear your fealty to this English king; greedy for Scotland's kingdome as his own I fear?" he asked his friend. Gilley told him that he was just in New Castle on Tyne fight the false suit of de Lucy, "Kin of our lord paramount de Umfraville who holds of our lands in Alnwick from the earl," he reminded Wishart "his wife's own family that they would try again to steal our Fawdon from Lord Douglas; an annual event I fear." Then le Hardi told his long time friend reassuringly, "This William did his pledging and kissing of the gospels in de Lindsay's chapel in the Lothianes; unhappy is the knight to do so I can say." The Baron of the Mearns shook his head ruefully. "The Wisharts are most concerned as well; to have Lord Edward here, his vassals as custodians of our strategic castles of defense that should be held of Scots! This nonsense makes my blood to boil; his trickery so hostile to our ways. What hear you of the competitors?" he grumbled. William told him that if Lord Edward has his way the kin of one de Umfraville, John Balliol would be his choice. "That we are next to travel to Avoch, to visit with my kin Sir Andrew de Moray," he allowed; then adding, "As you most know he holds for Balliol his kin; that he is also an auditor for this competitor. As de Moray is my kin that makes this Balliol Douglas kin as well," he sighed contemptuously. William was adamant that he held for no one; disliking of all the competitors. "But this John Balliol I question most as he holds little stomach for a fight; to become the vassal of Edward Plantagenet would be most natural to him I fear," said Gilley with disdain.

"That my uncle the good bishop holds as auditor for," reminded Sir John. "This elder Brus; a man with many lands in England, our Northumbria, then Cumbria too as well your Essex, does this one have some strength to be for Scots not of Edward?" Gilley was not sure. "This Lowland baron trusts few men. The father no, I do not trust him, though I feel his claim is stronger than the others," he allowed. Gilley also told Wishart that this Robert's eldest son, also Robert, was of Carrick blood, distant kin of his own; the lad held promise he allowed. "Kin to my mother's family, spending time in Scotland, he favors in his heart the Celtic ways" said le Hardi. "As for Edward, he is busying himself with writs against one William of Douglas. This Lord Paramount listening all the while to Melrose monks about the frightful laird of Douglas; scaring their horses, prohibiting their use of Douglas park for their travels. And this poor knight, his land less useful in Kyle Stewart; without water as they block the waterways for their use," William scowled as he spoke the words again; complaining of his problems with the king and the Melrose Abbot.

Late August 1291

The Douglases arrived on the Black Isle; happily anticipating some time to spend in one place that they might rest awhile. As they made their way north in the Highlands Ellie was overwhelmed by the great beauty; the lush lavenders from the willow herb that flooded the vales she had never before seen. The mountains were also turning in their color; hues the shade of rich violet rolled through the Ross-shire hills as the heather was beginning to bloom. But nothing could prepare her for the great splendor of the Moray

MY TRUTH LIES IN THE RUINS

Firth; now before her, overwhelming in its powerful beauty; it barely took her breath away as she beheld the mighty river for the first time. It flowed as far and wide as she could see, following below the hills of the Black Isle. Now as she rode with William toward Avoch, seeing Ormond Hill off in the distance, she knew at once that it was their destination. The de Moray stronghold was a formidable castle of enclosure with four square towers two of which looked eastward with breathtaking views across the firth, then south to Munlochy Bay. The other towers perched high above the lands reveled in expansive views of the valley and village of Avoch, and the western Highlands beyond.

Figure LXXIV-Part Two; Avoch village viewed from the ruins of Ormond Castle once the stronghold of Sir Andrew de Moray, Lord Petty

Sir Andrew and his wife Eugenia were pleased to greet their kin; offering them of the legendary Highland hospitality. It is well known in these parts of the Scotland that should a traveler in need knock at their door to bide a wee, the lady of the house regardless of her station would give of her own dinner as so required to feed a weary guest who happened upon their home in need of sustenance. Sir Andrew was very happy to see William; they had not set eyes upon each in the two years since the baronial court was held at Douglas Castle and Lord Douglas handed down the doom to the de Percy knight and the de Abernathys. William told his cousin about the writ Lord Edward issued in June from his idleness at Berwick. "To hand over the Abernathy laird at once to Edward's care," Gilley told him with disdain. "The words of Sir Hugh's wife and her good kin Scotland's regent to address Lord Edward; he to overturn the laws of Scotland in such matters, freeing the murderer of Earl Duncan is his plan."

Sir Andrew was concerned for the ever expanding powers of 'Lord Paramount' as he sarcastically referred to the English king; that in few short months this *invader* from England had usurped much authority from the Scottish nobles. "This baseless claim; that Scotland is a not a kingdome; that he is Lord Paramount; what a travesty this interference of dear Edward," he bemoaned. They discussed the competitors, Brus, Baliol and Ellie's kin Josh de Hastings: Brus was designated by Alexander II, then king of Scotland to be his heir; de Hastings' position for his claim found for lands, though not a country, that the 'estate' should be divide between the three heirs; and Balliol the closest in lineage though through another female line, seemed too tractable for these knights of renown. These redoubtable lairds and cousins found themselves in grave agreement; Scotland was in trouble. The nobles would quarrel and make forced agreements with the king of England they feared and this would be their folly in the future. "This good knight to worry where our foolish pride and crossed allegiances will thus lead us; I fear this Edward," said de Moray with premonitions of future strife upon his tongue.

Five year old James held fast the hand of his wee sister Muriel, as they ran into the great hall. Muriel was turning a spry three in a few weeks; keeping up with James was her passion. The two wee ones were returning from their tour of Ormond Castle with de Moray's oldest son, also Andrew, barely a page himself for his eight years. Following these exuberant children was Sir Shamus and de Moray's own 'family' Deerhound, Genny, named for Lady Eugenia; a gift on her recent wedding day she told the Douglases. "That we have something in common," she told Ellie with a grin. "Our Deerhound tales that brought us to our lairds; that I met my Andrew at the hunt of my uncle; with him a hound of great distinction this lass was told; the father of this sweet lass, this bitch," she said chuckling as she smoothed the hair of Genny, cleaning her eyes with her fingers. "When dear Andrew came to rescue me from a dreary widowhood like your own, he brought with him a wee pup of his prized greyhound; this lovely bitch the pride of our kennel here at Ormond. That our Genny has brought us many good litters since," she boasted of the Deerhound.

James told his father that Andrew was tending the hounds in the kennels. "Every morning he must clean the kennels out; to change their bedding with clean straw every other day," James said excitedly, impressed by the responsibilities held by his cousin. The elder Andrew chuckled and told le Hardi that his son favored tending the hounds and was now old enough to learn such skills. "That these were different times would I send my son to you dear William; a good training would he have there at Douglas Castle." William told him that he would be proud to have young Andrew as his page; and he would certainly be pleased to train a squire from the house of Moray. "When you think it wise do send him; Douglasdale is always welcome to de Morays; our dear kin, trustworthy men of good intentions," said Gilley. The Douglases and de Morays enjoyed much feasting and good wine that evening and the next. The parting came too soon for everyone, even the children and the hounds hoped for longer visits in the future. On the morrow next they would journey to Kinloss. The de Morays promised to visit Douglasdale in the spring. "Good friends and kin should thus see more of one another, sure aye," said Gilley as he bid farewell to Andrew, "We expect to see your good self in Douglasdale May after the spring settles in the Lowlands!"

Figure LXXV-Part Two; Kinloss Abbey where William 5th Lord Douglas signed family charters in 1249

Their travels continued: from Kinloss' picturesque bay, they spent a day of traveling to see Spynie, taking another occasion to journey to Elgin; taking some time as well to spend at Duffus the original seat of Freskin the Fleming, Gilley's ancestor; followed by a day at Dufftown and a final trip to see a mysterious monument in Forres. All of these wonderful villages and manors were places of adventure to both Ellie and the children; exciting and of course, educational. James learned more about fishing with his father; in Avoch the de Morays had taken the lad and his father on their fishing vessel into the Moray Firth. James was instructed by his cousin Andrew on how to set traps and clean fish. Returning from the trip James regaled his sister and mother with stories of dolphins and seals. He explained excitedly, "The dolphins were ancient sea creatures that jumped through the air; they escorted our boat for safety as they once did for their Celtic ancestors our father told me; taking us to the secret waters of good fishing," he said with the awe of young lad on his first expedition. Gilley then explained that the seals were there as well; they loved to bask in the warm sun on the rocks of the shoreline.

This time in Kinloss Ellie and Ana, Muriel and the wee Martha, all went fishing with Gilley and James while baby John stayed on the shore with his nurse. But they did not see any dolphins this day; disappointing Ellie and the wee lasses tremendously. "Not to trouble yourself lassies," Gillie soothed his wife and daughters, "this journey will not be our last to Moraydale," he promised them. As the family met others of their clan the children found cousins to amuse them; young Muriel enjoyed her new friend and playmate at Dufftown, speaking Gaelic with her as wee ones do, learning a new language quickly. William shared stories with his family on the history; telling them all about Spiney Palace and the Cathedral where his uncles served as canons in the church. Yet William did not take them into the Abbey of Kinloss, though the lovely structure resided in the heart of the family seat and was on the way to Elgin, their next destination. Kinloss was affiliated with Melrose Abbey and he decided to avoid a confrontation with those same Cistercian monks with whom he shared a divisive relationship over their grange lands in Ayrshire.

Riding their horses through the Highlands in the summer was a soul's journey to the very wealth that nature had to offer, William boasted. Ellie smiled broadly as his words found her ears. She too felt the joyous essence of the country of his ancestors. Her eyes absorbed every color, each precious gift of nature's bounty. She spoke softly as she beheld the lush contours of the foliage, changing hues from yellow to purple then exquisite multi shades of greens; wafting to and fro in the gentle breezes. "That I must always see the subtle grace of these brilliant colors; the beauty of these Highlands forever in my mind for all eternity," she cooed. The fragrant sea air, the pungent, brine filled smells of the bustling fishing villages were as delightful an experience as the scenery to these Lowland visitors; the fresh salt air intoxicating the riders as they made their way to the next destination.

The weather stayed sunny most every day, with the occasional cool breezes winding through the cart paths to keep them comfortable on their journey. At the majestic Elgin Cathedral they met with Bishop Archibald of Moray who took them on a tour of the vast reconstruction project, still taking place. Ellie marveled at the expansive processional doorway that was the new entrance to the lovely cathedral. "The most ambitious of so

MY TRUTH LIES IN THE RUINS

undertaken of its kind in all of Scotland," boasted the bishop. On their return home that evening to the lodgings of their kin, the Douglases rode discretely passed the ancient Abbey of Kinloss. As it was the site where his father witnessed many important charters in Moraydale and one specifically for the family in 1249, one year before his own birth, Gilley decided to at least allow his children a look at the outside of the stately structure built by King David I.

Figure LXXVI-Part Two; ruins of the 13th century structure at Spynie built by Bishop Brice of Douglas

As his luck would have it, while the wee merry Douglas household rode by the abbot's farms the commotion of such a large party caused a bit of a stir; exactly what Gilley tried to avoid. Their many horses and riders, children singing in their new language of Gaelic and a silly Deerhound running circles around them as he barked happily in unison with their chanting; disturbed the abbot's sheep in the pastures. With these travelers so arousing his flock, the farmer came running to warn them off. "This is the Abbot's land," he scoffed. Gilley doffed his hat politely as he made his amends and led their contingency homeward, far from the lands of the abbot. "That this knight can never be without some incident with these monks," he sighed. Little Martha just two years now was talking more the Gaelic than the Lallans of Douglasdale from these travels; this ancient language of their Celtic forefathers was spoken everywhere in the Highlands; it was also the language used by some of the Douglas servants at the castle and many others too in Douglasdale.

DEBORAH RICHMOND FOULKES

Figure LXXVII-Part Two; the stone figure remains of a bishop and a torso of a knight once stood proudly, high up on the central tower built at Elgin Cathedral in the early 1400's

Martha was chattering away with Muriel, each riding horses with their nurses side by side; speaking the language of Moraydale. Ellie chuckled; she too was learning more Gaelic every day and enjoyed how it rolled lightly off her tongue. She also thrived with the adventures of their journey to the north; thrilled with all the many wonderful ladies that she met; inviting them all to Douglas Castle for a Ceilidh in the spring. But too soon it seemed it was time to return south and home to Lanarkshire. With their adventures almost behind them now, the entire Douglas household unanimously agreed that they must return to this fair country again!

On one of their last days in the shire William led his family on a ride to Forres to see a great and ancient monument in stone. He told them that once there was a serious battle fought almost three hundred years ago in 966. Scotland's king was Dubh; a terrible ruler who met his fate with the men of Moray when he was killed. The body of King Dubh was left under the bridge at Kinloss, some short distance away. Gilley pointed to the carvings on the huge stone, some six ells high. The huge arch at the bottom of the battle scene depicted the bridge he told the children. "The head so framed alone is that of the king who was decapitated in the fray," Gilley said. James was very interested in the stone carvings. "Were there no other records in this times?" he as his father. Gilley told them that writings and language

MY TRUTH LIES IN THE RUINS

were different then; pictures took the place of words. The visit to the Forres stone was a wonderful way to end this trip of exploration and new adventures. The story of a fallen king depicted in pictures by the ancient men of Moray captivated the attention of all the Douglases this day.

Figure LXXVIII-Part Two; standing stone in Forres

Douglasdale November 1291

The cooler months brought a strange illness to Douglasdale; it came only to the infants feeding on the milk of breast. Milk fever was the name thus given it. The lovely laddie with the golden red hair ceased to thrive; writhing in the pain of fevers, unable to retain the milk he fed upon; that sent him to his God so suddenly. This loss of her wee son kept Ellie to her chamber most alone for many days. William would try to console her grief; his own so badly shaken from the tragedy. A tiny coffin was brought into the great hall. The children, James and Muriel with little Martha gathered round with Gilley as he said his prayers to send the wee lad to the Otherworld of his Celtic faith. He would join with Ellie in the chapel where she spent her days when out of chamber; consoling her grievous sorrow now with prayer.

Then one day seemingly without reason she returned to her former self. Despite the great losses that a mother fears most, the passing of her children, Ellie seemed resolved to accept the tragedies and go on with her life. She joined her husband in the great hall. William rose to greet her, thrilled that she smiled some as she descended down the stairs. "Dear Ellie, thank you for coming here to be with us this day. We have missed most the warm smile and tenderness you give us," he said happily to her. Ellie pulled out a small parchment that she had written words upon; and a small carved chest with a lid painted all in cherubs. "Most grieving have I been to lose these babies; first a child in womb then another, our dear son John. I have put these words out to him, but mostly have I painted now his face, see here, inside this sweet coffer to hold his wee things." She showed Gilley an exquisite painting of the laddie's face inside the lid of the wooden box. "That I could not see his face again nor remember what he looked like, held me in our chamber for so long. Now that I see his loving eyes and sweet mouth, his hair so beautiful to touch; could I paint his face never to forget again my wee son John," she said wistfully but with some strength that only just returned. Gilley held his wife close to him; feeling her again, so alone these many weeks she had kept herself in sorrow. "Sweet lass; this humble knight so happy to have you back to share his life," he said softly, cherishing her; healing his own heart that was bearing the scars of a father who lost two children this year as well.

The snows fell on Lanarkshire early in December; followed quickly it seemed by the calendar events of Christmas then Hogmanay. While the Douglases spent their days together in Douglasdale, celebrating their joys and healing from their sorrows, in Northumbria not far from Fawdon, an English sheriff passed to the Otherworld; Lady Knut was now a widow. The good sheriff who escorted Lord Douglas with his wife and children to Knaresburgh just two years ago was now with God. Lady Eva Bolteby, relic of Knut, accounted for the financial year and the first quarter of the next, as she had done when Sir Richard was on business of the king. Now Lady Knut and the Douglases both shared something in common this year; the sorrow of a loss words fail to describe, a dear husband and sweet children departed from the loving arms of their families for the Otherworld. Their leaving was more difficult for those they left behind for the grief of such magnitude was impossible to understand. Only through prayer and the guidance of Spirit can we began to understand; to accept in the knowledge that we will survive the change called death, Gilley would tell his bride. To the Celts death was the middle to a long life. And with the Celtic way as well, with a death comes a birth; Ellie was again with child to lay-in by the solstice she predicted.

Douglasdale January 1292

On 20th January 1292 Edward Plantagenet remembered Baron Douglas' absence from the August hearing; brazenly sending solicitors in his place. His memory was jarred by the appearance of the Comyn, bringing to his council another request for the release of Hugh de Abernathy from the Douglasdale. Edward was indignant; face to face with William's blatant refusal to release Hugh de Abernathy to his lord paramount he was spurred to action. He seized the Douglas kirk worth 200 marks annually to the laird of Douglas to give it to one Eustace de Bilkerton, a loyal subject of the king. Edward Plantagenet would remind this knight who was king and who was vassal in his realm he vowed! As the patronage for the family kirk fell under the Bishop of Glasgow, a letter of this action was sent to Robert Wishart; notifying him that William Douglas had forfeited his lands in Lanarkshire and the Douglas kirk as well for his transgressions against the monks and his failure to release his prisoner to the king. The good Bishop wrote to Gilley and offered help to mitigate the actions as Guardian. But for that moment these lands in Lanarkshire were forfeit to Lord Edward; at least on the face of writs this day.

Later in the spring Gilley resolved to take some action concerning Edward's latest writs. He knew he would pay a price for his truth; yet he was taken aback by the actions of the *Lord Paramount*, he scoffed. So the baron of Douglasdale began in earnest to set up a meeting with the good Bishop of Glasgow and the Steward to join him in negotiation with the abbot and monks of Melrose Abbey, to mitigate the problems that he faced with the churchmen. As to the other issue, Edward's demand for the release of Sir Hugh de Abernathy, that situation resolved itself. Sir Hugh met his God in some short months; his wife then a widow remarried Malis Earl of Strathern and his remaining son yet in minority was deemed his rightful heir.

Douglasdale June 1292

The Douglases had held their Ceilidh in the spring as planned. Many kin from Avoch, Kinloss and Duffus came to join them. The Scots celebrated and danced and discussed the politics that ruled their lives these days. All agreed that much change was coming to their Scotland. The competitors were notified that the challenge to succession was now limited to John Balliol and Robert Brus; by November they would have a new King of Scots. And by that same month one Robert Brus resigned as Earl of Carrick in favor of his son, also called Robert, not yet of majority. It was still June in Douglasdale when a competition of their own enveloped Douglas men; archery practice was being held in the courtyard. A raven haired laddie growing taller than his six years was taking up archery using a wee bow fashioned by the farrier now wood-master of the castle. "Father come look," called James to the laird of Douglas, "the target that I hit, on center twice!" William had been working with Fortis, training him with the farrier for riding, using a special saddle for his son. He came running with great excitement, a proud exuberant father, "Two bull's-eyes for you James; one feat I could not so accomplish till older now than you!" he said chuckling. "Here stay you now; I will call your mother to come look."

Gilley ran into the tower keep, looking for his wife; finding her in the withdrawing room with her friends he burst in upon them. William spoke excitedly, "Come quickly Lady El, our son to make a statement with his bow!" Ellie looked up from her embroidery and told him she would be there quickly, when she could. To the laird of Douglas such delay was not to his liking. He walked calmly to her, asked her one more time to join him in the courtyard; again she delayed him with her words. "Recall now wife the third time Lord Douglas does not ask; he takes his bride thus so!" he exclaimed as he picked her up, holding her in one arm, passing her embroidery to a giggling Lady Amy. "Lord Will be careful with this lass; or our child won't wait for lay-in now to join us!" she chided him good naturedly. All the ladies were smiling and laughing at her husband. Ellie was beginning her well known verbiage, references to Sholto and Scottish larceny of person; le Hardi was not hearing any words of protest: his son had put two arrows on the target center, one then two! "A mother most to come and see, sure aye!" he told her loudly.

James was grinning ear to ear with pride for his prowess at archery; so much so that Ellie was grateful that Gilley insisted she come. She praised her son profusely; took the two arrows to keep them as a remembrance of this special day. Then suddenly those old familiar feelings wrested in her belly. She looked at William; grabbing his arm to keep from collapsing. "Dear Ellie, is it now our child to come?" With a spirited look of 'I told you so...' she answered him "Le Hardi, take me to the lay-in chamber quickly that we should have our child born inside the walls of Douglas Castle!" He scooped her up into his arms while she laughed at him; sending James to go find Ana and Muriel to help. Shamus woke up from his snoozing in the courtyard; his place was by his lady's side he decided, following her to the lay-in. He ran large circles wildly around William as he carried Ellie inside. All the while Shamus never stopped his barking. "What are you doing silly hound?" asked Gilley at his antics. "He plans to guard the room; he did so last time, you must now recall," she told him. "At least he knows his place is on the floor not there beside me in the bed during lay-in!" she chuckled.

The gloaming blanketed Douglasdale; the gleaming twilight danced through the arrow slits of the donjon tower that held the lay-in chamber while Gilley and Ellie welcomed yet another member of the Douglas clan to the world of the living. "Another girl for Lord Douglas and his lady," cried William as little Amy arrived; named for Ellie's grandmother and her mother Helisant too, using her middle name. Gilley looked at the lovely lass; the very image of her precious mother, he so said to himself. The wee one had the Douglas thick raven hair but the light olive skin of Eleanora he reflected. To the chapel he went; christening his Amy; whisking her back to Ana and the midwives. "A perfect lass and beautiful is she, the face of my dear wife when she was but just born I know it!" he exclaimed proudly. Ellie was thrilled; with all the sorrow of last year she was afraid that it might continue. The wee one growing within her she feared might be affected by the sadness of the recent days. Now they had another lovely daughter; pretty and perfect to enjoy! "God and St. Bride have truly blessed us my husband," she told him smiling that contented way he knew so well and loved to see. "Wee Amy; your father loves the joy that you have brought us, and happy so that you are here," he sighed.

The summer days continued joyously in Douglasdale. Ellie and Gilley took long rides together; to their favorite place by the Corra Linn Falls. This day they offered to take both Muriel and James along; Muriel rode with her mother and James rode on his young palfrey Fortis. The wee saddle James used was fashioned well for riding; an ambler was this horse, nobly bred and highly trained was Fortis. But James wanted to ride a destrier like his father's war-horse in the stable. "My son, a war-horse is not for hunting or traveling on journey; a war-horse never trots but runs," Gilley explained. "Your Fortis is an ambler; determined by his gait and good breeding. This ambler too of goodly disposition; calm in his demeanor, a fine example of his noble blood."

William had spent many months training James on horses; specifically this palfrey. When first they began their work he told James step by step how each piece of equipment was used and why they chose certain ones, not others for their mounts. "We take this double pair of reins; the broad one to thus fasten here directly to the snaffle bit; the narrow ones the same below it." Gilley also explained how the many saddle types were constructed; the different needs of stirrups on a horse. "A knight in tournament must ride high, using his stirrups that he does but stand in the joust," he told the lad. "The horse must too have nerves so steady and heart so strong to accept the battle training. For you these next few years to ride an ambler like your Fortis. Once of age to be a squire will I begin your training on a destrier," Gilley told him bluntly. But James was ready to perform some feats he was trying when his father was absent from the stables; to jump an ambler was not allowed he was told; but jump this palfrey he would try. "Look father," he called out as he led his horse ahead of the others in their group. Ellie looked on in horror as the six year old lad was thrown from his horse while attempting to rear him up.

James got up slowly not wanting to look upon the face of his father, but knowing he must in his disgrace. Rushing to his side was Lord Douglas more with fear than anger for this lad. Leaping from his palfrey William grabbed his son; checking his legs and arms, to determine the extent of his injuries. James' face was covered with blood; his lips were cut by a jagged front tooth and chipped eye tooth as well, a bloody nose completed the gory visage. The main of his injuries were not serious William surmised. But when the wee lad began to speak, apologizing for his foolishness, his words came with a slight lisp from the accident. Ellie grieved his injuries profusely. "Oh James, the perfect speech and diction you did have; we worked so long and hard to teach you languages, words properly pronounced now gone!" she cried.

With the depth of understanding of one only six but three times his age in knowledge, her son responded thusly to his fate: "The lesson of my imprudence; to make me humble before my God, that now I lisp in words I speak." He shook his head, now looking at his father, disgusted with his impetuous behavior. William hugged his son to him. "We each to learn our own way young James; better to do what others more experienced in such matters advise in training for your knighthood," said William calmly. "That you are most in one piece is a pleasure to this knight your father. Let us continue on our journey once you clean your face of battle in the burn ahead there." William then went to Ellie. "Dear wife, not all knights are so fortunate in their first encounter. To break a tooth or two and not a leg or arm; take heart in this relief of injury," he told her, holding her hand in his to comfort her. "All our work," she sighed. "Lessons come at a price; lucky for us the cost is small but everyday to remind him, pay attention to Lord Douglas, your father," Gilley reassured her.

Berwick Castle November 17 1292

In the Great Hall of Berwick Castle John Balliol was selected to become the King of Scots before Lord Edward, twenty four of the king's auditors and eighty Scottish nobles. Robert Brus had abruptly changed his tactics; presenting the same position Johannis de Hastings and his solicitors had given the auditors. He likened Scotland to an earldom that should be divided between the remaining contenders. This change in stance brought about quick decisions; the staunch supporters of Scotland as an independent realm, the Bishop of Glasgow, Robert Wishart, joined with James the High Steward and immediately responded with muffled outrage. The two powerful men were previously ensconced in the camp of Brus until this new tactic was revealed; now they called for a vote, changing their support to Balliol. It was done; John Balliol was selected the next King of Scots. Lord Douglas was in his Douglasdale with his family; preferring neither Brus nor Balliol, not taking sides with either of the competitors he wanted only for peace in Scotland.

He had promised his son a coronation; and to his wife he promised the celebrations of the parties to be held in Scone when John Balliol would speak the words sitting over the Coronation Stone. The spectacular events, the feasting and the dancing, the entertainment all; an amazing extravagance of splendor this coronation would be he told his family. But when the time came for Balliol to repeat the blessed words in Scottish Gaelic, "Benach de Re Albanne," the looks exchanged between the laird of Douglas and Bishop Wishart spoke volumes of their concerns for King John and their fears for Scotland's future with this choice for king.

Ellie looked magnificent in her new brocade surcote of green and violet with gold velvet trimmings hemmed with ermine. Lord Douglas appeared in the same glory in his surcote of white brocade with black and purple trim and a cloak of gold velvet accentuated with more ermine and red velvet. His hat of black with gold velvet trim against the ermine was the perfect touch. Young James wore a new black velvet surcote trimmed in gold brocade with a white cote underneath in silk. His hat was decorated in exquisite embroidery of his mother; no fur was there to see however, not yet his father told him. This day Ellie would remember her mother by wearing her gift; the de Hastings family brooch of pearls and rubies in gold; a perfect accent for her lovely surcote. Gilley wore the lovely buttons on his surcote once belonging to Ellie's grandfather; with the brooch as well from Lady Helisant fastened to his mantel. Ellie and Gilley stayed only short hours at these great parties; James' presence was not their reason for their quick escape. They planned to travel south before the full onset of the winter; to be in Essex for late December, celebrating Christmas and Hogmanay at Ellie's manors in England. The pack animals and hand carried litters were filled and the children were readied for the journey when the laird and his lady with young James returned to Douglas Castle. These mild days of early December were misleading for this winter. By February the harsh snows and winds that continued almost steadily since the feast of St. Stephen brought much sadness to the regions of Essex northward through the lowlands of Scotland. The violent winter storms uprooted trees, ripped up roofs from homes and killed many animals and people in its wake.

It happened that on 10th February 1293 when William was to be at the first Parliament of King John he was happily detained in Essex by the perils of inclement weather; the harsh winter of 1293 was the excuse he gave the new king. He offered further proof of his inability to return to Scotland: that he was kept from a court session in Northumbria, his bailiff for Fawdon Manor appearing in his place. Early in 1293 the ever persistent Gilbert de Umfraville devised another plan to rid his barony of Douglases. He called upon William Batayle, the son of the same William Batayle who originally sold the first portion of Fawdon manor to Gilley's father, sometime before 1227. This vassal of the lord of Redesdale concocted a story that his father was insane at the time he sold his lands to Douglas and the deed should be cancelled. A court session was held and a jury of peers from residents of the parish of Ingram in Coquetdale was selected. With little time spent on the frivolous case they came to a unanimous conclusion: resize Fawdon to Lord Douglas! The inopportune halt to the Douglases travels spared Gilley some distress; he found out about the court case when they traveled north staying in Fawdon on their home to Douglasdale.

But his absence from the feudal duties for King of Scotland was another matter. Others who defied the call to Parliament were young Robert, Earl of Carrick, John, Earl of Caithness, and Angus, son of Donald of the Isles. The Council decided to compel their submission and called them to come on 6th April, the second Monday after Easter to perform homage and receive sentence for their absences in February. When the Douglas household returned in mid April William had already missed the summons date for this Council; he sent a messenger to the king, explaining once again the reason for his absence that he was on feudal business in Essex. A curt reply returned with the Douglas messenger: report to Parliament and a hearing August next, one day past from Lammas to answer charges for grave conduct that occurred before the coronation of King John. The old business from four years ago, the sentencing of the murderers of young Duncan, was still causing William trouble. The baronial court, the de Abernathys and de Percy knights, the passing of the doom; the scandal of the realm as Balliol would deem it, was now before King John and his Council.

Since Lord Douglas was defaulted from King John's first Parliament, he was compelled to attend the second one in August; but this meant displeasure to King Edward: failure thereat to attend some feudal duties then in Essex was the charge made against him in England. "Ellie, we must discuss the retention of your lands in Essex for this Lord. The difficulty now

MY TRUTH LIES IN THE RUINS

that I might miss dear Edward's Council for Essex duties whilst I go to King John's in Scotland: two masters too much trouble for this business to continue," he told her. Ellie agreed; she was not pleased with the annual travel down to Essex that was required of them. "Perhaps a meeting with young de Ferrers now in majority; we can settle matters in my dower limiting the lands to Scotland for our income," she suggested.

More writs followed; new problems for Lord Douglas arrived in the form of court orders to Douglasdale. Ellie and William were reviewing the rents due next month at Whitsun when their squire announced that three riders were approaching. Sir Andrew had just returned to Douglasdale as well and had seated himself next to his laird to review their accounts. The riders were officers of the court from Lanark; on the business of Lady Constancia; her dower lands in Lanark, her income having been effected by the seizure from Lord Edward last January was not at all to her liking. "140 merks of damages we must collect and will!" these officers told Lord Douglas sternly, demanding payment before they would leave they insisted. William was trying to compose his anger; his father's second wife was becoming troublesome in her requests for more income. He also believed that the escheators had levied Edward's seizing on the wrong lands in Lanark, causing him much damage from this fine. "The sum you must collect too dear a portion that we have not here on hand to give," he told these royal officers trying to beg time for further investigation. These bailies for Lanarkshire were quite insistent; threatening greater action should they not relieve him of the fine for damages and sasine for Constancia. The writ they provided called for levy of 140 merks; most true and just they told him, issued by the Justiciar in Lanark.

William asked them again for delay, "That it is almost Whitsun the quarter day; our rents now due and payments to collect," he told them. "Pray that you would give this lord some days for payment of so large a sum." When they refused Lord Douglas said some time would he allow them for more prudent thought; into the tower prison of Douglas Castle they would go; to stay for one day and night. When the next morning they agreed to go without the levy paid William let them depart peacefully. Ellie was concerned that Constancia would pursue the matter further. "Lord Will, whatever must have happened that they took Constancia's dower for your own lands in Lanarkshire?" William was not sure how it happened; he simple knew he would not pay his stepmother for an escheator's poor records and mistakes. Sir Andrew offered to investigate. "Your words of concern and offer to reveal the theft of dower from Constancia is most appreciated," William told his steward. "Most weekly so it seems another writ; more accusations that this humble knight denies rights to everyone. Taking dower lands; denying Monks their passage; holding murderers against their will in Douglas' donjon prison. What a brigand this laird of Douglas is!" he exclaimed sarcastically.

Stirling August 1293

Just before William was departing for Parliament he received a messenger from his cousin in Linlithgow. A son had finally been born to this William, the eldest son of Andrew Douglas, and his wife; would the laird of Douglas be the God father; a lad so named in honor of William le Hardi's own son and heir, James Douglas? "The happiest of news for this knight and father; a God father to be!" he boasted proudly. With little time for matters of other family members in the many shires around the kingdome, William was thrilled for this opportunity to see his cousin. He sent back the messenger that he would be pleased for the honors. "To go alone it saddens me," he sighed to Ellie. "That this business with our king has caused to keep us from a Douglas celebration in this christening event. But this laird shall represent our family to take his leave most quickly for the king's business in Stirling."

William Douglas left his family behind in Douglasdale to attend first the ceremony in Linlithgow, then Balliol's Parliament; taking with him Sir Andrew the steward and his men at arms. The Douglases were to leave for Essex quickly after the king's Council they decided; but King John had other plans for this baron. When he arrived in Stirling William discovered that there were two charges being levied against him. First there was the imprisonment of King John's bailies at issue and the dower of his stepmother that the laird of Douglas obstructed. The second and more serious indiscretion alleged by the new king of Scots was the baronial decision some four years ago in passing the doom on Justiciar de Moray's prisoners. William made defense for the imprisonment of the king's men seeking Constancia's award of court; they had threatened him with violence, disallowing time for proper collection of the levy he claimed. He told the Council that he was deceived by the king's men where more investigation was required. He was denied his justice; placed in ward to wait the sentence of King John.

The second complaint was brought directly from Balliol. He charged him with taking three men during this time before he was king. That they were imprisoned in Douglas Castle against surety and pledge read the charges; one was beheaded, another escaped the third to die in the donjon prison of Lord Douglas. William did not attempt a denial but placed himself at the mercy of the king. King John fined Sir William £1000 holding him in ward; too late now for Lord Edward's feudal business he mused. Before he retired to his new chambers, a reluctant guest of the king, William made arrangements with his steward to acquire pledges for his surety and the first partial payment of his fine for damage to the king. "That this knight has vast experience at fines and prisons to his lord; that I know most of what to do," he told Sir Andrew ruefully. "Prey to tell Lady Douglas: to Essex we will go but not the noo!" As he waited for his release he mulled over the huge court levy against him; the king must need of coinage for his coffers he mused.

Sir Andrew made arrangement with the solicitors in Stirling and the Council of the king. Once arrangements were made for twelve payments over six years and lands were pledged of two barons named de Moray, one in Ros-shire the other in Roxburgh; Douglas was set free before September. Ellie was teaching languages and dancing at the castle when Lord Douglas returned home. Muriel and Martha ran to greet him; eager to end their instructions for the day. "Dear Ellie, we must leave for Essex on the morrow next. One day will this weary knight take now for his rest; then off to Fawdon traveling then to England," he sighed haplessly. "This Essex lord must beg for Edward's clemency on his feudal business that we missed."

The next morning Ana ordered about the others; preparing for the journey south to England. She came upon three giggling children in the chapel all gathered at the door now closed that lead to the laird's chamber of their parents. "What is this about; you three not in prayers from your faces most surprised to see your Ana!" she scolded them. "Off to break your fast all of you! Your mother will hear of this," Ana promised James and his sisters Muriel and Martha. As she proceeded to the main door of their chamber she heard much laughter coming from within; preferring not yet to knock but wait for word from M' Lady, she mused. My dear girl and her knight now three weeks separated by his imprisonment at Stirling; there is much to celebrate she chuckled to herself.

The Douglas household stayed at Fawdon two nights. William enjoyed this time though shortened by his incarceration, to be with his family. He took his son fishing, foraged for ancient relics with his daughters in the nearby Roman sites; and went riding for short distances, taking in the beauty of the countryside and splendor of the Cheviots, alone with his bride. He shared with her the quiet words that a loving knight shares with his favorite lady. "That I had much time for thought and writing, this I have for you Lady El from your poet knight," he declared proudly. He read her three poems that he wrote and finished with these sweet lines for their ride today:

A fine day to look about
To see the sky unfold in colors

Hearing birds and smelling roses
Our God's sweet blessing is this life

And my own sweet blessings, you my wife

Ellie leaned into his broad frame. "When you are not with me Gilley I am most sad, no one to share my joys or woes; but more than that do I miss the comfort of your warmth next to me in our bed," she told him sweetly. "The Shamus tried his might to replace you though," she giggled as the Deerhound now approached them returning from his own adventure and exploring.

That evening Ellie and Gilley stayed up later in the great hall of their messuage at Fawdon. They played a game of Merels; Gilley wanted to let her win but she was obstinate. "You will not feign loss and give me false victory," she chided him. Finally she grew tired and they agreed to call it a draw. Gilley was in a teasing mood; he picked her up and held her high above his head. "This laird to get his due this night; his wife his prize in chamber do I claim!" Ellie shook her head; this is not your Douglasdale, more lands do I have here in England; were I the man, Lady Douglas would be your lord superior," she said with a twinkle in her eye. "That you are not a man my happiness; this knight to have his pleasure this night, sure aye," he said boastfully as he carried her off to their chamber. Ellie looked around for the Deerhound that was not in his familiar place upon the bed. They had sent their servants off to sleep; preferring to attend themselves as they did some nights at Fawdon, this simpler life.

Then suddenly the whimpering of Shamus was heard in their chamber; trapped was he in the garderobe from the sounds they heard. William went to investigate and found three children most asleep and one Shamus happy for his release. Gilley cleared his throat loudly and James bolted up from his slumber; the girls responded in a groggy fashion awaking now as well. "Whatever were you doing there?" asked Ellie of her children. James was sheepishly looking at his sisters to see if they would reveal their tale of intrigue in their parents' chamber. Gilley suddenly realized what this hiding was about, remembering Ana's strange words from the other day when she found the children in the chapel at Douglas Castle listening at the door of the laird's chamber. "Spies are hanged from trees or battlements; no trial or pleas accepted!" said Lord Douglas in his booming voice. "Who is the one that planned this unsavory venture?" he asked his children. James looked at his sisters; they would not tell he knew. "Father, it is I, James who thought of this foolish strategy."

MY TRUTH LIES IN THE RUINS

Figure LXXIX-Part Two; smaller latrine closet in donjon prison at Tantallon Castle

William looked at Martha then at Muriel; then to James he said, "Never again will you press to make your siege upon your parent's chamber and their privacy," he told them, kneeling so he could look directly in their eyes. "Next time there will be no clemency for spying; to bed with you!" he bellowed. The three children ran off to their chambers. Ellie was laughing now. "That his younger sisters would not tell on him I am most proud," she said to Gilley. "Our children have their loyalties and honor I can see!" Gilley added, "At least with one another they hold their integrity; with their parents is another story!" he said in mocked disdain. "Sir Shamus must have found them; that they took him captive to keep him quiet I should guess," Ellie giggled at their cleverness. Gilley said that to have such enterprising children was a blessing; but he must teach them enemy from friend, whom to spy on and what boundaries to respect. "What will this boy think of next to plague his father?" he asked his wife. "Children are always curious William," Ellie said. "My sister and I once hid as well from Lord Lovaine, but we were found by Lady Helisant before the game was played. Safe from the ire of Sir Matthew!" she told him, "never to spy on them again!"

Stebbinge Park October 1293

William made his appearance before King Edward on 3rd October; explaining why he obviated his feudal duties in Essex, held in Stirling prison by Balliol. Lord Edward saw this a perfect time to denigrate King John again by the words he commanded written for the clemency of Lord Douglas: "Whereas our beloved and faithful William of Douglas was in our prison by our instructions...." the King said, relieving him of the £20 fine that was imposed. While Lord Douglas was given clemency in this month of October, King John was being summoned to London. Lord Edward accused this Balliol of contumacy for his willful disobedience of dear Edward's orders that were given. This further embarrassment of Scotland's king was just another step, an indication of Edward's true ambition: to make the king his vassal and Scotland his own kingdome.

William was the feudal lord of Stebbinge Park and made the required baronial decisions; hearing the pleas and requests of his tenants. He was approached this day by one John de Dalham; a Stebbing tenant, a farmer who held of six bovates near the water mill. "Would my lord so approve this humble villien to care for the mill by the lower pasture waters; the ford so requiring a daily presence there," he told Lord Douglas. William inquired of his steward Foster. "The mill provides an annual rent of 20s. yet the costs are rising most above that fee," he explained. Lord Douglas told the tenant de Dalham that he would grant the request; the rent of 20s. would be transferred to him by the quarter day next. The grateful villien took his sasine with cheerful spirit. "Thanks will be most given at our Stebbing church this day; in praise of the lord of Douglas for his fair generosity," he exclaimed happily. Ellie was pleased; her husband was a respected lord, unlike the late de Ferrers who would ring the very last of coinage from his tenants and request of more.

On their journey home to Scotland from Stebbing the Douglas household stopped in Ware to visit young de Ferrers who was visiting at the manor there outside of Hertford that he held in chief. Young William was occupying the fortified house of the sub manor; the principal manor being held by his great uncle's family as a gift from his grandfather, a complicated charter to be sure. "Dear mother and Lord Douglas," said this William chiding Ellie good naturedly, "most pleased that you have come." Ellie accepted his teasing as his way. "Dear son, that you are here for your mother now appeals to me as well," she said, beginning with her tale of woe with Essex lands. Ellie related the difficulty with the travels required for feudal business, and how extremely taxing it was on their household. "Would you most consider changing my dower lands?" she asked him. He told her that he was reviewing the estates and would make such plans with his solicitors. "To sell some manors I must do to pay off debts of others on the de Ferrers estates;" he told her. "my solicitors to find a buyer for these lands and I will gladly do it." Gilley and Ellie were both relieved to hear his intentions. Ellie even offered to take further control of the remaining de Ferrers lands in the

Scottish counties of Ayrshire, Dumfries, Wigton, Berwickshire, and Fife, to join with her lands already held there; disposing of the Essex manors from her dower was now the whole of her ambition and focus.

The Douglas household made their way north now, stopping at various de Ferrers manors along the way until they reached Fawdon. There were no more latrine incidents; the culprits having learned their lessons that spies were hanged! But there was some teasing on the journey west once they reached Selkirk. Ellie was forever getting the Tweed River mixed up with other bodies of water, landmarks they used when they rode these cart paths in the Borders. This time they did not turn north to Traquair; desiring to travel to their manor near the Yarrow and Douglas Burn. From Dryburgh west she would ask at every turn, when they came upon some burn or loch, "Is this the Tweed then?" Gilley would answer politely no each time until they approached the Ettrick Water when James spoke up. "Mother I believe that is the Tweed," he said teasingly. She was not sure if he was saying that in jest and Gilley was further up ahead talking to his wee daughter Martha riding with her father.

The Douglases journeyed some miles further when another large appearing body of water came into view. They had just crossed the Yarrow ford; but Ellie was confused and nervous that it might be the Tweed knowing that the river and the Yarrow join together near the ford. She feared that they were lost; that William was distracted up ahead. James teased her all the more, "Dear mother that is of course the Tweed then, I am sure." Now she knew he was spouting foolishness and rode quickly to his side. "James Douglas," she spoke her words of fury, "that water not the Tweed now I do know it! Quickly, save yourself and tell me now in true words, the name of that good water. The noo!" she exclaimed. He grinned from ear to ear at his folly, "Hangingshaw Burn it is my mother; we are not lost," he told her happily. She started to laugh at him and his pranks, shaking her head, "What ever will I do with you?" she asked him smiling now herself at his silliness and the folly of her own fears.

By now the Douglas household was riding north through Cowans Knowe and into the wild and sheltered glen where the Douglas Burn meets the Yarrow; home at Blackhouse Tower. They were happy to arrive at this hidden stronghold; a fine comforting shelter, only a days journey from their Douglasdale, if the good weather held. Gilley decided to take a couple of days rest here and enjoy the time with his family; exploring trips were planned for the children and James was allowed on the morning hunt, his first such privilege. Young James was becoming very accurate with his bow; bringing home several rabbits for the evening meal with great excitement. Ellie fussed over his new found abilities; providing food for the household in these times was a requirement, not a passing fancy for a lad. Hunting and

DEBORAH RICHMOND FOULKES

fishing together became favorite pastimes for both James and his father. Nothing pleased the laird of Douglas more than a son who cherished his every word and learned each lesson well; this perfect son the epitome of one name James.

Figure LXXX-Part Two; St. Mary's Loch near Craig Douglas, Gaelic for the rock of Douglas

On their second day at this stronghold near Craig Douglas, Gilley and Ellie took James, Martha, and the wee Amy with them to discover the "Douglas Stones," a circle of standing stones near the tower house. The silly Deerhound played for their attention along the way. He ran ahead and then back again, repeating his antics several times; leaping and bounding with glee as he led the way for them to follow. Amy was giggling at his performance, "Father, Shamus is funny!" she cried aloud, animated and laughing. Gilley had to chuckle at her happiness with their boisterous hound. Amy went ahead to run with the Deerhound, making her way to the upper part of the hill of a craigy slope; she slipped and fell into the green growth growing around the rocky terrain. The wee lass screamed in pain holding up the palms of her hands that braced her fall. "Father, Amy hurt," she cried. Gilley was at her side quickly as he picked up his daughter. "There my girl, your father is most here to sooth your injury," he said so gently.

Figure LXXXI-Part Two; the remains of Dryhope Tower near Craig Douglas and Blackhouse Tower receive some repairs

There were not any visible bruises on her hands as he examined them. It must be the nettles he knew at once! Ellie arrived by Amy's side and tried to calm her wailing in pain. "James, find the dockins plant, there near the nettles as I showed you," motioned William, pointing to the foliage on the sloping brae. The nettles is a low growing plant that when touched feels like the pain of little needles on the skin; a dockins plant often grows nearby, and is an antidote to subdue the pain. Ellie had never heard of such plants, common in the lowlands, her husband told her. The dockins plant removed the pain and Amy ran off to play about with Shamus as if nothing happened to disturb her day; her father healed her was all she knew. When they arrived at the Douglas Stones, William spoke of the sacred site.

"Our Celtic storytellers speak of such ceremonies of importance from these circles, some many hundreds of years now gone," he explained. James reminded his father of the standing stones they found in Wigton so many years before. "These are most the same though more complete in their arrangement, said the father to his son. Ellie was speaking to Muriel, "You were only a wee lass then, but your father told us all about the stones and you just smiled and ran about, in and out and through the circle openings of that sacred site," smiled Ellie recalling those days visiting Scotland's southern shores. Gilley continued with his teaching. His way was that of the storytellers: repeating the words, the knowledge committed to memory for his children, that they would pass their wisdom on to their own sons and daughters. "Others even speak of the Druids that may have held their rituals within these stones of deep symbolism," he told Muriel. "James you recall now the wand used in the Baronial Court, a Scottish ell in length?" he asked his son.

DEBORAH RICHMOND FOULKES

Figure LXXXII-Part Two; stone circles and standing stones are common throughout Scotland; these stones are in a pasture in Moy

    The young lad remembered well the wand used by the magistrate and the stories told so many times of that first court, the fateful day when Lord Douglas imprisoned Sir Hugh de Abernathy; to die in their donjon. James spoke up proudly, "Most often do I think of the baronial courts held at Douglas Castle, especially of that wand Sir Andrew used to mark the boundaries for those sessions held then out of doors the spring, one year past." Gilley explained that the wand of the court held its history from these ancient Celts and their traditions. Amy was by now drawn to his words as well, to learn more of this magic rod; she came to stand next to him and watch. "This instrument so used now to designate God's blessing; granting God's own power to the magistrate as once it did for the tribal chief or priest of these ancient ones," he said quietly, when words of importance were said. The wee lasses were impressed by this sacred site; very eager to hear more of this "magic Celtic wand." "Why are they called the Douglas Stones?" asked Muriel. "As they are on Douglas lands so should they be named," said William. Their father continued to explain that just as the Celts would hold their ceremonies of sacred worship in the openness of the fields, so would their good descendants the Douglas barons and others in Scotland hold their baronial courts out of doors, open to all and under the watchful eyes of their God.

    Gilley showed his children that there were the normal completeness of twelve stones standing; eleven the same size and shape, the twelfth of a

MY TRUTH LIES IN THE RUINS

different stature. He also pointed out two outside stones nearby; most often to find four such stones standing beside the Celtic circles he told them. Ellie marveled at her husband; his inherent need to instruct all his children of the ways of their ancestors: the Celtic ways of the ancient ones whose wisdom came from the lands. "Our people came to love and worship the lands in groves; those who most valued its great gifts received the largest benefits from its majesty of protection. For these lands will provide us safe hiding when the invaders come; food for our bellies when we are hungry; and peace to our lives when we are weary from the strife of the world that has become the royal burghs of great business and trade." Muriel was still curious about the mysterious rod. "Father, tell us more of the magic that comes from the white wand," she said with eyes wide, the excitement in her voice making it tremble some. Gilley told her that magic came from the powers of the Otherworld; the protection from Spirit through the work of saints or gods and goddesses. "We become what we believe we are," he told her, "and our work in this world is what we are to be in the next life."

Lanark 1294

Another Parliament of King John was called for February 1294; this time in Lanark. The winter of 1293 had passed quickly from Christmas through Candlemas, February 2nd; it was even warming some now. For this special event William brought not only his son James but his daughters as well to view the proceedings; held so close to Douglasdale, it was not far for them to travel. James was a page now, in training to become a squire first, then a knight; an early gift for his birthday yet to come was a hat with some fur upon it, his mother's surprise for him this day. Ellie called to him as he was bringing Fortis around from the stables. "Come James," she said beckoning him to take a small parcel tied in silk; Gilley stood behind her, "your father and dear mother here have an early birthday gift to start your day!" Gilley was excited too, "A special one my son; for Parliament!" he chuckled as he said it.

James was smiling curiously, not daring to guess what was held in the small package. He was dressed in a new surcote of blue like his father's only lighter; without fur trim. But when he unwrapped the gift his face smiled ear to ear. "Lo these many years have I been waiting on this fine hat with fur; for Parliament, sure aye!" he exclaimed imitating Gilley's own exuberating words. His three sisters were watching him open up his gift; standing around him they looked closely. The girls were dressed in various surcotes of white and gold with some green about them; all different, but all alike in fashion.

DEBORAH RICHMOND FOULKES

Elegantly attired themselves, the Douglas lasses were surprisingly impressed; they ooh'd and ahh'd over James' new addition to his attire. Muriel was the first to come to James; she praised his outfit in glowing terms, running her hands over the soft fur. "What loveliness to have such a hat to wear my brother; you look most like father now in that new chapeau so fine!" she cooed. Their younger sister Martha who turned five this year came next; she smiled and flattered her older brother as well; her loving eyes widened by excitement and sheer happiness as she looked over the fur adornments. James was suddenly sensitive about his fur hat. He acted overwhelmed by the words of praise words coming from his sisters; stunned that his long time playmates were now admiring him for his appearance and attire.

Figure LXXXIII-Part Two; view from the Blackhouse Tower on the Douglas Burn near where it meets the Yarrow

Ellie caught a glimpse of James' embarrassment, and quietly said to William, "Our son most shy from the attention of his sisters," she whispered. Gilley told her that at his wee age he too was at a loss for words when with a lass; even with his sister Willelma when she had her friends about. "Even before the scars that came from Fawdon, this knight so painfully shy a lad was he," Gilley told her privately. That was his first reference in many years now married made to the scars on his face; making him self conscious before women. "I have told you most before Lord Will, those scars were for a purpose; to save you from the others, keeping you for this lass alone to find you for her very own!" she said lovingly. "So proud that you are mine, my dear one," he told her as he held her close to him. "Will you love me tomorrow," he began their words they shared in ritual together.

At Lanark Gilley paraded his children around to see where they would meet in Parliament. The good Bishop of Glasgow was there to greet the Douglas family. "A fair sight," said the bishop, "these fair Douglas lasses with their handsome brother. Hello young James, a page now you must be and, yes, I see you are dressed for Parliament this day," he chuckled when he eyed the fur hat. James doffed his hat, bowing for the Bishop out of respect, exhibiting his newly acquired skills in salutation. Turning to William, Wishart asked, "Have you seen the Steward yet?" Gilley responded quickly, yet quietly, reading the concern in Robert Wishart's tone. "No; is there a reason for your query?" Gilley asked. "Word came to me that after this Parliament the Abbot of Melrose to come to visit with the king; a certain baron once creating trouble for these monks; most again to bring them fear, these monks will claim," said Bishop Wishart.

Gilley told him that the Abbot had built another obstruction near the Lugar; keeping water from his lands and those belonging to the villeins there. "Perhaps the river is where you should fight your battles dear William," suggested the Bishop. "With Edward's backing these monks are sure to get the ear of our weakened king. He to do most anything to please that English lord I fear." William acknowledged that Wishart's words were valid, "Perhaps to settle this in Mauchline near the waters there. In the spring will I thus send Douglas men to resolve our dispute; no laird or king to listen to my pleas for service in this quarrel now, I do know it," he said, resigned to his powerless position with this king and vassal to Lord Edward.

"This baron took no preference, Balliol or Brus no difference; both suspect in their motives and their ways I knew," said Gilley to Bishop Wishart. "Where this course to lead us I do not know," he sighed unhappily. Robert Wishart shook his head he too was concerned for Scotland's future. "Balliol so chosen king now bows before King Edward to do homage. The pitiful charades is not acceptable to this prelate. Not my desire for this kingdome's future," he scowled in quiet tones so only William heard him. Gilley quite agreed with the bishop. "There are others here among us with these same views," speaking in low tones as well, "Look, here comes the Steward to grace our presence here!" Young James was the first to greet his uncle; his sisters giggling behind him as he bowed, with fur hat in hand, repeating his poised ritual. "The Douglases increasing still in number, lasses of great beauty like their mother; and dear James, are you now eight years grown?" the Steward asked his nephew. "I will thus be eight in April next some six weeks and more," he told them. As the children made their way to other chambers the Steward took the opportunity to also warn William of the Abbot's complaints. "Were your Douglas Kirk most free of Glasgow they would set upon that sanctuary most to seize it for their own I fear," Sir James said. Gilley discussed his plans to resolve the issues at the site of the water diversion; on the Lugar, with no further actions to be taken at the park in Douglas.

April in Douglasdale

It was a special birthday for a lad turning eight; the parents of young James decided that he should now retain his own lodging, a private chamber with his own bed. Ellie and Ana had been working quietly for weeks on their surprise: new bed drapes that would fit on William's former bed, used before he was Lord Douglas. A tester bed of distinction with drapes that would serve for warmth as well as beauty; when he marries he can take the bed to his new manor with his bride Ellie thought out loud. "But a wedding for our James is long away; for now he will have the chamber we first used when here at Douglas Castle, with his new bed!" she said proudly. Ana was pleased with the results of their handiwork; even the lasses, his sweet sisters did their share of embroidery with not a word of it to James. "After the feasting then will I bring his sisters up to this chamber?" asked Ana. Ellie nodded yes, "And then Gilley and I will bring him here to see our fair surprise!" exclaimed Ellie, happy and excited with her plan to surprise their new page.

That evening after feasting, Ana quietly removed the lasses from the great hall; stealth like they all went to the new chamber that would belong to James. Here they all hid quietly, waiting to surprise him. Ellie and Gilley began to speak of his new charges, his daily assignments as he officially became a page. "With each new step that one does take of responsibility, there must come some fair reward for elevated stature," began the father. "Lady El and I have decided to secure our good son a new place that he might reside." James was stunned; was his father planning to send him to another manor that he would learn his skills as page in another household, he wondered; this was the way with other noblemen he knew. Ellie further confused the lad, as was their intention, "Please follow your good father and dear mother as we will help you; tend to your requirements for the relocation." James followed, not knowing what to say or think; something must be wrong here. Then the ever observant lad looked at the faces of his parents; mischief was about, their eyes were twinkling, secret looks exchanged between them. Relieved some by what he saw James called to Shamus to follow as they all went to the third floor and the family chambers.

James went quietly behind them as Ellie and his father walked passed the chamber he shared with the others, down the corridor to his father's former room. Shamus began barking furiously as William opened the great oak door to the lovely chamber. The wee lasses screamed words of birthday cheer as James saw the grandness of his father's old bed now reworked with purple and red velvet drapes and fine gold embroidery. "Your mother's doing; her idea to give life to this old bed as well," he told the lad, "once Lord Douglas had resigned to keep her in his chamber, there was one to spare!" Gilley teased his bride. Ellie beamed as James' young face made plain his true feelings, "Mother, this is my dream to be in this chamber; and this lovely work, so fine these drapes and linens for this bed," said the shy lad, as he went and hugged and kissed her. "Lady El, dear mother, six years ago when you did come to Douglasdale this lad most told you, and the same is true to day: I love you, James wants you to stay!" he proclaimed. As Muriel and Martha were teasing him and begging him to let them share his new prized bed as children do, William came behind his wife, wrapping his long arms around her he whispered in her ear, "I love you too, and this humble knights wants to you never leave. Will you love me tomorrow," he began his words to her as they walked slowly off to the laird's chamber, arm and arm, smiling at each other, happy in their love.

The night turned into day and the Douglases were celebrating their sixth anniversary of their sacrament of marriage. Before Ellie woke from her slumber Gilley had slipped something into her hand: a small velvet pouch filled with a small brooch of gold and silver. He lay down again next to his bride, watching her as she slept; waiting for her to wake from her dreams, so peaceful from the calm smile upon her face he reflected. Then as her breathing became more animated she woke, smiling as she opened her eyes to see him watching her. Then she suddenly realized she was holding something in her hand, and giggled knowing it was Gilley's sweet way to surprise her on this special day. "So here now, what is this that I do find in my hand; did a faerie bring this lovely soft purse of velvet in the night, I do wonder?" she joked with him. Then as she opened the pouch her eyes widened with awe. "Oh my dear husband, this brooch is most lovely!" she exclaimed. As she was admiring the exquisite workmanship Gilley began to explain the sentiment of his extravagance. "The simple circle represents the continuity of life. That there are six of these fair flowers of the primrose; of significance to the Celts for the Queen of Elfhame is most the one to use the primrose in her work," he began. "The number of the flowers is most six; our years thus far together in this life. And the primrose to further tell you of my work that so intrigues your knight: his Alchemy." Ellie wanted to know more about Elfhame. "Our Celtic queen is the goddess to so stand for life in the Otherworld, for the promise of reincarnation as our beliefs do hold." Elfhame was the home of the faeries or our Heaven he explained.

Ellie always marveled at his understanding of these intricate concepts of the ancient Celts and the mysteries that he seemed to accept as true. "So my husband, that I wear this brooch, will I so see the faeries of the Otherworld?" she asked him coyly. Gilley chuckled. "Would that it was most easy," he said "but this knight does humbly ask what life next would you so choose for us to share?" Ellie wrinkled her brow feigning great thought. "A life with you in the Highlands, living in a cave!" William le Hardi was dumfounded, surprised by her wild answer; he had often felt that he was once a painted warrior of the Celts, doing battle in the hills with spear and shield, naked but for the paint that covered his body in patterns of the ancient ones. "That you would so join me, painting on your fair self, running through the glens with spear and dagger, side by side two warriors defending their cave," he teased her. "It is done!" she told him as he roared in laughter at her contrivance. Or was it, he wondered; had this life she feigned to plan been one they shared together centuries before?

Roxburgh

The Abbot finally met with Balliol in Roxburgh and the king issued a letter to Geoffrey de Moubray the Justiciar of the Lothiane. He narrated the circumstances and ordered sasine be given of the disputed road to the Abbot and the convent of Melrose. A further order was given: seize all who disturb their travels on that road; bring those before this King and Council who disturb these holy men in their rights now given. This order was signed on 13 April 1294; William's forty-fourth birthday; a copy of the writ and order was delivered two days later to Douglas Castle.

An angry Lord Douglas was wont to rip the notice to shreds; instead he commenced a sign post to be erected with words that read most opposite the true direction. This legend written mocked the holy men in their travels; making them fearful the Baron of Douglas was ever watching. Ellie found her husband with the farrier who was carving the signs, "Whatever are you doing Lord Will?" she asked fearful of reprisals for the writ he just received. Gilley told her solemnly, "No justice for your husband with the malicious monks and Abbot; that he should have some fun with it his right!" Ellie shook her head now laughing at his folly, "Ah, my William is forever William," she said now playfully, finding his plan most humorous as well.

With the summer came the training that would begin for James; to become a knight required skills that would be developed both with use of sword and with his chores now required. He worked first with the farrier. A page must learn to take care of a knight's horse; mucking out the stables was required his father announced plainly. James was also working daily with Sir David. He was taught how to care for a knight's armor. The leather hauberks had to be oiled and cared for on a regular basis. The fine mail that Gilley wore under his tabard required weekly cleaning. "That you must put the mail in this wooden barrel with some salt and vinegar; to dislodge the rust that may be resting so, you shake and roll it thusly," Sir David explained. James was also trained in keeping a knight's knives; cleaning them and storing them in the fat of geese to keep them clear of the destructive red rust.

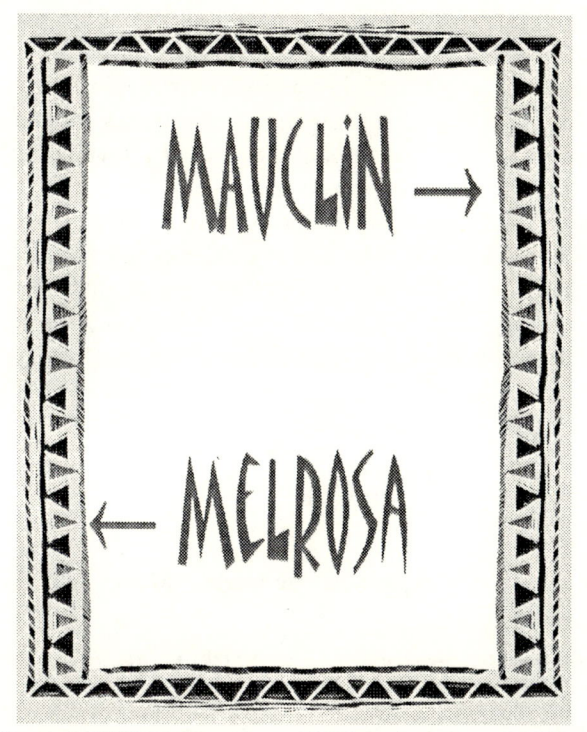

Figure LXXXIV-Part Two; William is forever William

Ellie was called upon to do her part; to train their page in the amenities. Even though most step mothers were not required to fulfill this deed, she deemed it her pleasure to be part of the process to train James for knighthood. As with any page in service to his nobleman, James was taught his way about the feasting table. Ellie first began his tutelage by instructing him on how to pour wine properly. In addition to the service skills at feasting time in the great hall, a page must also learn to dance; to read and write as well in Latin and in Norman French. James found himself very busy with his training. In the courtyard in the early morning he trained with sword under the careful watch of Sir David, a proven warrior with excellent skills and good demeanor, William had entrusted the English knight with the training of the Douglas page in armaments. Sir David required James to hold the sword straight out, most even with the ground; to not flinch or lower it was the objective the knight explained. The pain and quivering of young muscles strange to this position, holding the sword so awkwardly was a grueling battle for young lads; but James held the sword fiercely till he could hold it no more. In stead of braces from the backhand of his knight James won praise for his first day's training.

William was watching from afar; not wanting to interfere with Sir David and his work. This English knight approached the skills most differently than the father of Lord Douglas who would apply the swiftness of his sword, when as a page young William dropped his arm while training. Sir David told Gilley's son that the sword must become his arm's extension; his friend to serve him most properly in combat. "A knight's loyal companion is this fine weapon; treat it with respect and it will serve you well young James," he said. James respected his sword and learned to take good care of it. As Gilley came about to inquire of his day the lad explained what he was doing. "To clean and preserve this fine blade, the knife to smear with grease of goose to keep it right, no rust to fall upon it," he said proudly as Gilley smiled approvingly of his work. That evening the father presented his son with his own part of the initial training for knighthood: his guide for being a chivalric knight; the objectives in the course of learning.

The Art of Chivalric Warfare

1. All Knights are subject to the codes of conduct in battle and tournaments
2. Utmost and careful presumption of battle to attain the highest order, highest good
3. To best the opponent in skills of combat not in the demise of trickery or chicanery
4. To be the best one can be in the common transcendence evident of their skills
5. To conduct ones activities with honor at all times
6. To abide by ones sworn oaths and allegiances to God, Lord, and Self
7. To adjust to the confines of a certain battle but only in the type of combat as a horseman, schiltron, foot soldier, or other combatant as directed by the Lieutenant of the Lord or leader that one follows

8. *To outwit, out flank, out play your opponent in skill and physical prowess*

9. *To protect and defend the lives of your fellow Knights*

10. *To protect and defend the lives of women, children, elders, and the infirm*

11. *To be respectful of ones opponent and allow for fair combat that would not forego the allowance of the opponent to cross a bridge or other wise prepare for the combat event, on fair, equal footing*

12. *After the conclusion of battle, take prisoners as possible and allow for the sworn allegiances of former foes, the dignity of combat to decide their demise or survival of those formerly in opposing battle placements; this allows for sworn surrender or retreat with dignity and the protection to do same from the battlefield*

13. *Chivalric dignity at all times is expected and demanded*

14. *Victory comes from cool heads in battle with courage brought from experience and readiness in training. Always be ready to fight and fight bravely*

15. *Always go into battle with the blessing of God; Prayer is as important as the armaments and protection you wear*

"These are my own words young James," said William. "They have served me well lo these many years as Knight in service to his king. Some others might amend my code, changing the sentiment; but it is my truth thus said, regard it as your own and it will guide you well my son." James was pleased; he reveled in the sentiment, the parchment written by his father for the occasion of his training as a page. "I will treasure your words dear father," he told him proudly, "and commend them to my heart and memory. To serve my God and Scotland as well as you, Lord Douglas, my dear father; is my desire." Gilley added one last thought to his sentiments on knighthood, "Know well your opponent; if he is not to follow rules of chivalric codes in battle, you must adjust your plans to overcome his foul advantage. But never deviate from the core values that you hold my son."

No summer approached for the Douglases without plans for a trip to Essex; feudal business was calling them south again. Ellie was with child; the lay-in after Michaelmas she predicted. It had been two years since Amy joined them that she feared there would be no others in their family. The sickness with child came most quickly this time and left as fast as it arrived. They were traveling through England when Ana became more concerned that Ellie's estimate was wrong; how large she had become these few weeks gone by. "My girl, these long days of riding show deeply in your face," she told her, "the fatigue is growing more that we should travel less between our stops." Gilley heard Ana's words and came up to his lady's side, "Our dear Ana's words are true," he said most concerned as well. "We will stop to rest more frequently; the laddie that you carry should make no haste to join us that you are weary from this journey. It is done!" he said.

Ellie didn't argue with her husband; she was exhausted and the traveling not half the way to go yet. And the wee one was kicking harder every day that she was riding side saddle now. Then as she reflected on her husband's words she wondered how he knew it was a boy that she was carrying. "Because we have so many daughters; more sons for Lord Douglas should now follow, thus I know it!" he smiled broadly at her with his well known bravado that she started laughing at his silly self. "Lord Douglas does proclaim it; a son to have!' she shouted for all the household now to hear, imitating his voice when he bellowed his proclamations, following with his familiar, "sure aye!" William looked at her and feigned his attack, she countered with her well known response, "savage Sholto beast!" Everyone in their party was laughing as they rode further south into the East Riding, Yorkshire.

Woodham Ferrers Late July

The days seemed warm this year in Essex; the three lasses spent much time in the courtyard of the manor playing. James and his father practiced their archery; and Sir David held his training of the laddie with the sword holding it for lang times of endurance. James exceeded their expectations; his enthusiasm for the chores in the stables too amazed them all; he loved tending to the palfreys' needs. No matter what was asked of him he did it; most graciously, except for learning Latin. "Father how much of Latin can you write and read?" James asked him. William told him plainly that he was fully fluent in the language; his work in Alchemy did require that knowledge as well; and the Douglas charters, that his son must read, they too were written in Latin. "My son, Latin is the language that is used most often by the laird of Douglas; study it you must to fair efficiency," he told him, "Languages open doors where many can not follow; your noble birth allows these benefits of life. Take advantage of these offerings to the fullest and you will not regret one day of it, I swear to that!"

The days were passing in a pleasing manner; the girls learned their needlework and their languages including Norman French. Martha was so silly with her work, giggling all the while she stitched; but she had such a fair hand no matter how she toyed with her handiwork the result was beautiful and perfect. Muriel would work so diligently but hers was never as perfect as her little sister Martha's hand. Their mother had them learning how to paint as well; cherubs were their favorite adornments to create and now appeared most everywhere as decorations on the walls and capitals. Again little Martha had such an artist's touch that Muriel would choose to paint most anything but cherubs; hers were so inept she brooded. Ellie tried to cheer her older lass, "My faces too so clumsy when first I tried to paint; keep trying Mura, you will do well with practice I am sure. Sometimes we don't have gifts given to us right away, we must earn them by our persistence," she told her daughter.

Ellie was also busy teaching all her children to dance. By nightfall she was exhausted. Her size was so huge she really wondered if she had made a mistake in knowing when her lay-in was. Or perhaps this child most large, she chuckled at herself. The next morning began quietly; Ellie and Gilley were teasing each other in the privacy of their morning in their chamber, giggling in bed as the sun rose on their Essex manor. Then a loud rapping came upon their door, all the children with their nurses and Ana not far behind them had entered their chamber. But where was little Martha, Ellie wondered? Just five and full of life, she was always the shadow of her sister Muriel. Ana spoke up first. "We can not find our Martha; she was missing from her bed this morning." Ellie panicked and William rose from the bed immediately. They both knew the little girl loved to explore things on her own, her curiosity was profound. They always tried to caution her but she was full of life; being careful was not her way no matter how closely her parents and her nurse would watch her.

William gave some orders: bring in the squires and the others to the great hall; Lord Douglas will be there directly. "Ana help Ellie here to get dressed; Amy and Mura go you to the nursery with your nurses; wait for us to call you there," he said curtly, "James, you wait for me in the hall; tell the others that we need to find our Martha, she has been missing from her bed. Then too they should bring the horses; three will do, she must not have walked too far." Ellie was barely able to move about on her own; Ana saw her face and knew she shared her fears. The little girl had quietly gone out before at Douglasdale; falling in the shallow of Douglas Water outside the postern by the rear tower where she wandered. But here at Woodham Ferrers the moat feeding from the nearby springs was the only body of water in short distance. And it was very deep with a slippery edge.

When Ellie and Ana joined the others in the great hall she noticed at once the secret door to the passage that led to the old priory was slightly ajar. "Oh no, dear Blessed Virgin, spare my Martha," Ellie cried out. William was already down the stairs with James; just then he was returning, the lifeless body of his wee Martha held in his arms. "She must have fallen, sliding fast into the deepest part of the moat where we saw her face down,"

William said quietly, "Perhaps to be lost in the darkness, taking the wrong turn you warned them so about," said the father sadly now. He brought his child to his wife; they both held her; then together they went to the small withdrawing room alone with their sweet Martha now with God. There was not a dry eye in Woodham Ferrers manor that day; the little lass with so much joy was gone from them forever. Her nurse was struck through her heart by this tragedy; screaming her sorrow, blaming herself. Ana was consoling her when William returned to the hall.

Figure LXXXV-Part Two; site of the moat at Woodham Ferrers Hall, once the manor of Eleanora Douglas

"Sir David will you take young James and ask for Father John from St. Mary's to join us here; a funeral must we plan," he said grimly. "Ana, my Ellie needs you so now." William called his steward Matthew Foster, the brother in law of le Parker to come and assist with his immediate plans. "We will block this evil passageway forever; such use of wicked intrigue that I knew, I should have sealed the entrance then and then!" he shouted in his anger, the loss of his wee Martha was pressing on his heart that it would break he knew it. William drew plans for a wall to cover up the door completely; no sign of the trap that led his daughter to her death this morning would be visible again for the Douglases to see. "We will leave the morrow next after the funeral. No longer can we stay here in Essex with our loss so great this day," he told his seneschal. To the others of the household he instructed to begin their packing for their journey home to Scotland.

Ware, Hertfordshire 8th August 1294

The Douglases were returning homeward, riding north; their days in Essex were ending, their work completed for another year. Only they traveled with heavy hearts; their sister and good daughter was just laid to rest in Woodham Ferrers. Ellie could not bear to bring Martha home with the family as she was in too much in pain; another tragic loss for this young mother. Her mind was so confused; so strangely she responded when Gilley talked to his wife that he wondered aloud to Ana, "Will our girl ever be the same again? So tormented is she by our Martha's passing," he spoke his words mournfully and Ana had all she could do to restrain her own tears. "Give her time Sir William; a mother holds a child she nurtured in her womb most differently than the father," said Ana. Gilley looked up, his eyes filled with tears, "But this father grieves most painfully as well."

Ellie would only consent to have her daughter's coffin buried at Woodham Ferrers. William was tormented by the decision; he wanted his daughter buried in Scotland, the place of her birth, to rest with the bones of her ancestors in her peace. But his wife was so much withdrawn; too saddened to look upon the coffin that held their child so full of life just three short days ago that William consented to her plans for the funeral. He also worried for his bride and the child she yet carried within her. The wee Martha was put to rest in the orchard at Woodham Ferrers Hall; a temporary bidding he told Father John. Gilley quietly sent for a cart from Stebbinge Park with some Douglas men at arms. When Ellie was more herself he would tell her: Martha was coming home to Douglasdale, traveling some few days behind their household. It is done, he said to himself.

As they journeyed home to Douglasdale Ellie spoke little; she felt as if she was riding in a fog of sadness. The hurt was too devastating; like a hollow feeling it filled her once loving heart with chilling guilt. She kept thinking she would hear Martha's voice riding up behind her on the horse with her nurse most anytime now. Why was God so hurtful to us, she wondered to herself. Her depression made her all the more weary. No longer shy about asking for some needed rest; they stopped at the de Ferrers' manor in Ware just outside of Hertford. Barely did the family arrive that Ellie felt some pains and knew the lay-in was now upon her. The nearest one to her was Muriel. "Mura, quick get Ana, and your father, my time is now!" she exclaimed. William bolted from his palfrey and swept her up in his arms, carrying her into the manor house. "Where to?" he asked her and she directed him to the small room by the laird's chamber. Ana knew her way about the manor and the lodging provided at the priory as well; for many days they spent their time in Ware when Lord de Ferrers was alive. She directed the children on what to do; no other midwife was there to be found so fast the baby comes now.

Figure LXXXVI-Part Two; Ware, Hertfordshire; Alien (French) Benedictine Priory is seen in the background of the Ware church; used by the de Ferrers and their kin when they stayed in the Ware manor

In two short hours young Hugh was born; named for William's oldest brother as they had agreed. The wee laddie was long and thin like his brother James; not at all appearing as if he were arriving ahead of time. "Dear Ellie, the date you had for our son's arrival to appear most wrong; his size too large for such an early date. It is no wonder to this knight and husband you were so tired and in pain from the journey," he consoled her. "To ride a horse so close to the lay-in most dangerous to you as well; this midwife to check you next time making sure of the date!" he teased her. Then he left her side with young Hugh; to baptize him in the small chapel of the Benedictine Priory that was part of the Ware Manor, as his practice gone before. Ellie looked upon her son when Gilley brought him to her side. "An English born Douglas; the weight of that to bear for life," she sighed. William told her that he was a Douglas and a Celt. "No soil from England to change that!" he proclaimed proudly. "And another August child," he beamed making reference to the old Celtic belief that a child born in that month held special abilities and talents.

Ellie looked sadly at her husband. "Our God does take from us a daughter to give us a son; why can it not be that he gives us both our Martha and our Hugh?" she cried out to Gilley. He sat down next to her on the bed,

pulling her to him, holding her gently in his strong arms. "My girl, my dear wife I have no words to say; too soon our Martha's left us now, then God gives us this healthy lad," he shook his head sadly. Then trying to cheer her, "Young Hugh most like our James, so long and thin is he; another Douglas lad to train in knighthood. Perhaps with our next sons to come we will have Lord Douglas to train many knights for Scotland, sure aye!" he exclaimed. Ellie started to grin a little now, "More knights, more sons; this lass needs time to rest, perhaps alone that I should sleep..." her teasing words stopped as Gilley interrupted. "We have some years of children now to have that we should have our twenty," he sparred with her, his eyes sparkling as he reminded Ellie of his plans when they first married. She looked deeply into his gaze, realizing now that she had been no comfort to her husband these last days. "Lord Will, I am here to comfort you as a wife should, so sorry is this lass." William drew her close and kissed her softly, "That you are back with me is all that matters now," he told her truthfully, "This humble knight most worried, now rejoices in your fair return."

Arran May 1295

In early spring a messenger from the Steward arrived at Douglas Castle with an invitation for the entire Douglas family to join him and his family on the Isle of Arran located in the Firth of Clyde just off the coast of Ayrshire. The Stewards held this isle and the castles there, using the location for hunting parties. King Alexander was said to have enjoyed hunting on Arran, staying at Lochranza tower on the north end of the isle where the Douglas household was to stay. The normal procession of Douglas men at arms, children, nurses and the laird and his lady were joined this time by the master of the hounds, leashing yet half of his hart hounds for the trip, and the falconer who brought several hawks for hunting with the hounds.

Gilley was very excited to return to Arran; he had not been there since he visited with his first wife Elizabeth, the birth mother of young James. She used to enjoy riding her palfrey throughout the isle and the lands of her ancestors; Gilley would relish telling her stories about the Celts and the symbolism of the standing stones and chambered cairns they found scattered throughout Arran. Now he would be able to teach James the same way; show him the caves near Machrie Moor and the standing stone on the shoreline near Machrie Water, explaining more of the ways of their Celtic ancestors.

The hunt was exciting to watch as well as participate in; the ladies and younger children remained at the tower, watching the procession as the hunting party made its way through the carefully choreographed paths of the chase. Laying out the day was the mental challenge; not unlike formulating

DEBORAH RICHMOND FOULKES

a battle plan, Gilley approached the task like a general drawing up his attack. At the sounding of the hunting horns the hounds were unleashed and the party raced forward in search of the hart. It was often said that Arran was unlike anywhere in Scotland for hunting; this day would give certain proof of that. James accompanied his father; the hunt was warfare in peace time Gilley told his son, an important aspect of a pages training to be a knight was going to the hunt.

Figure LXXXVII-Part Two; ruins of Lochranza Castle on the north side of the Isle of Arran

Gilley was forever telling James the reason for his decision; the necessity for things to be a certain way. Today was no different. He told the lad of how he drew up the chase; taking into account the cover given to the hunters, the direction of the wind, and contour of the battle lines. "One must be well armed and well horsed," Gilley said, "To consider the prey our enemy, most like in war. And to always fight into the wind, hunt to that aim as well," he concluded. James asked why would one move into the wind in battle. "That the breathing for a warrior is good to move in that direction," he carefully explained.

Horses were saddled, hounds were leashed, supplies readied, nets, arrowheads and hawk-bells were assembled. The hunt today was known as a park hunt; within the park of the castle lands that the ladies could watch from the wall-walk of the tower. There would also be displays of falconry; the single combat in full view was thrilling and heralded the beginning of the true battle or chase in pursuit of the hart. Ellie was thrilled to watch from

MY TRUTH LIES IN THE RUINS

the castle; the dazzling events of the hunt were exciting and the other ladies loved to ooh and ah at the knights and squires as they rode to the hunt. The Steward had mounted falconers as well; a practice left over from more prosperous times in Scotland when Alexander was their king. The ladies marveled at the showmanship, including Mura and Amy who were allowed to watch their father and brother in the chase. An older knight who had recently broken his arm did not ride to the hunt but joined the ladies on the wall-walk. "Ah, the greyhound," he sighed, "with the muzzle of a wolf, the haunch of a lion," he said in awe of the great animal. Mura turned to add, "And the sense of fool," she laughed, "except when the quarry was near." Ellie was surprised that her daughter had retained what Gilley told her about the hounds; this was in deed a fine day, she chuckled to herself at Mura's revelation. The old knight continued. "A fine thing it is to see a beast taken by the craft of man and hounds," he marveled wistfully as he watched the hunt continue through the park.

James was led through the chase by his father. The experienced hunter and warrior told his son how from the age of a varlet, the huntsmen learn to track their quarry and identify it by the droppings. "The best time to hunt of hart is in July," Gilley offered. "That we are here in May is not of sorrow though," he joked with the lad. "Anytime was good for the hunt if man knows how to look for tracks and droppings from the animals they stalk," he allowed. James was eager to learn all aspects of hunting. He questioned everything; he wanted to know the patterns and meanings of the soundings from the huntsmen's horns. Gilley explained that each sound or group of tones had a meaning. "You just so heard two long sounds followed by five of the shorter moot or notes; the meaning is most clear, the beast has left its territory," he said. James was impressed with the planning and training that was required to facilitate a proper hunt; he relished to learn more.

While the days were filled with the chase, the nights were taken up with feasting, much wine and wild stories of the great hunt. Ellie and her daughters were laughing most of the night as Gilley led the group with tales of great capture and remarkable success in taking down their prey. The Steward was prone to hyperbole Gilley later confided to his wife; some of their success was luck or tired prey, giving up the chase in the end. But the men were often boastful of their recounting of the hunts, "to tell the tale, impress a lass, to feast on the spoils of hunt; this is what a warrior so lives for," he chuckled. Ellie enjoyed their days on Arran; she loved seeing her husband enjoy himself, while teaching James the skills a man should have to become a knight of prowess.

DEBORAH RICHMOND FOULKES

Figure LXXXVIII-Part Two; wall-walk on the parapet of Rushen Castle, Isle of Mann provides an excellent example of the expansive views offered through the crenelles of a tower, between the merlons.

Before the Douglases returned home to Lanarkshire, Gilley took them all riding to the western side of the isle. He showed them the standing stones in Machrie; the chambered cairns or burial places of the ancient ones. He was forever telling his children the stories of the Celts and the Vikings, fierce invaders to their homelands. Everywhere they went he could show them history he told his children; they must learn from the past and retain the stories to teach their own wee ones some day he said quietly. Even Mura was enjoying the day of exploration. "Arran is most grand," she allowed, to Gilley's own amusement. As they rode further down the coast towards Whiting Bay Ellie noticed the caves along the shoreline; hidden from view but easy to access. The children decided it was time to explore the caves; Deerhound in tow, Mura, Amy and James went in search of adventure with Gilley as Ellie and Ana walked the shoreline.

"A glorious time this was for us to have," sighed Ellie. Ana knew it was important for her lass to enjoy these days on Arran. The politics of a nation nearing wartime loomed before these peace loving Scots. The climate was right; their weakened leader appeared for the taking and the opportunistic Edward was champing at the bit to fell his prey. The clash of wills was eminent and would change their lives forever they knew. But for now, there was fun and pleasure; time for a family to enjoy their Scotland, their warriors would practice their peacetime skills in hunting and their children could all learn their history from their father.

Figure LXXXIX-Part Two; a standing stone near Machrie Moor, Isle of Arran

Douglasdale June 1295

Almost one year had passed since their last trip to Essex. Now Ellie and Gilley sat with their seneschal Sir Andrew to discuss the coming days. Balliol was falling fast away; becoming more the vassal of Lord Edward then a king for Scotland. "That I will be leaving for a Parliament in one short week, there is much that we must do before we make our journey to Essex," he told them ominously. "You fear then that it might be your last such trip to that country for sometime then?" asked the steward. Ellie shook her head gravely, "Yes, and we must travel there as well that I may retrieve our belongings left at my manors there; whatever that we have to fit in our returning coffers and wooden chests or leave at Ware with young de Ferrers. Much room to find there for our things of value," she sighed.

Gilley told her that he felt young William was trustworthy; she could safely store Lady Helisant's gifts of furniture and tapestries that she could not bring back to Douglasdale this time in the de Ferrers manor house. "The unrest with Edward does so scare me; what are his true motives with our Scotland?" Ellie asked her husband. William knew that the noblemen were ready to form a council; a group of twelve good men of Scotland, four bishops, four earls, and four barons, to rule their kingdome and control the titular king. "The ruthless strategy of one named Edward can only be surmised," he said gravely. "We will leave for Essex when I return from Stirling in some four weeks," he responded sternly; then adding "We must be in Scotland before your birthday sweet lass; more for the business of the kingdome I do fear than for the celebration of your good day."

Scotland's nobles were feeling uncertain these days; their king was weak and vacillating. Just four months ago in February, King John called another Parliament. He had just taken fast leave of London, fleeing England, out of Edward's grasp. He summoned the leaders of both his clergy and his people; put forth the injustices, slights, insults and ill treatment he had thus far endured at the hands of Edward Plantagenet. A plan was devised by the council that King John would revoke the homage and fealty he offered to Edward on the basis that it was given under much duress. The King of Scots would include as well the great fear of force that might have followed had he not sworn his allegiance then to this Lord Paramount. There was also the matter of a marriage proposed between the daughter of Lord Charles, brother of the King of France and Edward de Balliol, son of the King of Scotland. The nobles believed that this marriage would solidify the two countries in their allegiance to each other; they also hoped this alliance would deter the English king from further aggression against their nations; that their firm opposition to him might temper his future plans. The discussions for renewing the Auld Alliance between France and Scotland continued as well. At the conclusion to this winter convention the king set the next date for Parliament in July, 1295 to be held in Stirling.

The July convention began with the establishment of the Council of Twelve. The Scots drew up a Treaty with France that was later signed by King Philip on October 23rd. Edward bristled in fury when he was told of the treaty between Scotland and France; a grave act of defiance, he scoffed; one that required harsh and severe punishment he determined. The signing of this treaty in 1295 eventually proved the demise of Scotland's independence and her prosperity for twenty years to come. But Scotland's nobles felt they had no choice; they could no longer accept Edward's trickery and debasing of their king. Sadly their strategy was based on false hopes. Scotland's successful rebuke of Edward as Lord Paramount relied upon the French to live up to the agreement; to supply military and other support when needed. The Scots agreed to raid the north of England in 1295 as Edward planned his invasion of French soil; a military strategy to convince Edward of his folly to try to conquer either nation as he would face both these nations at once. The French proved poor allies for the noble and brave Scots; they capitulated to Edward; leaving the Scots to their own devices, with an angry Edward seeking revenge for the burning and pillaging of northern England.

Back in Stirling, after many meetings, the final adjournment of Parliament was called; and the long day of 5th July was finally coming to a close. William le Hardi made his way from the council chambers to gather with several of his friends, other nobles and clergy, in private. Ale and wine flowed freely; platters of fine food filled the tables while peels of boisterous laughter could be heard through the thick oak doors that led to a private withdrawing room of the old inn. Le Hardi was joining with but a few nobles, to sit in this sequestered room with only those that could be trusted. Here they began to contrive another plot of their own. "If Edward takes us at our word on this Alliance with King Philip," said Bishop Wishart, "would he not come to fight us now in Scotland?" he asked them all.

Sitting at this table were some of the bravest men of Scotland, knights of the realm; there was the Seneschal James and his brother John, with Alex de Lindsay, Andrew de Moray from the north, who brought with him some men of Perthshire that William did not know. Sir Andrew immediately introduced them all to le Hardi; making special mention of one good man named Whiteby. William knew his cousin Andrew would not bring spies to their meeting so he continued on the bishop's thought. "Edward will come," boomed le Hardi's deep voice as he took his seat next to de Moray. "We must be so prepared for his attack I fear." James the Steward spoke, "So taxed are his nobles now from his wars with France and Wales. How can he afford it?" William told them all plainly, "Lord Edward cares little for his nobles and their loss of wealth to fight for him; only his greed does this lord follow. He will come and if we do not fight him he will steal from us our freedom if he can. He will also take with him the symbols of our independence were he able," warned le Hardi. Bishop Wishart stood up to draw the nobles' attention to his words. "That he will rob our Scotland of our wealth; crush our kingdome with his might is his intention. He will come to steal our very souls if we allow it; to tamper with our kingdome, the fair traditions of our people and our history. I promise you that he will do it!" proclaimed the Bishop, exhibiting his wrath for Plantagenet. He continued speaking with the passion of a great statesman as Bishop Wishart told them all of his greatest fear: that Edward would come and take the Stone of Destiny, abscond with the Honors of Scotland. Having their attention now, the noble patriot and prelate began to reveal his plan to circumvent that evil plot. "That we must not allow this madman to have the Stone; no King of England will usurp our power that we must steal it ourselves!"

Le Hardi looked over to Robert Wishart, finally realizing why the Bishop had called them there to meet. He wanted them to come to this conclusion about the English king; that they would be so moved to steal the Coronation Stone, Scotland's Stone of Destiny to keep it from Lord Edward's greedy hands! Robert Wishart told the others why he asked de Moray to fetch these good men of Perth. The bishop explained that they had contrived a stone from quarries on their lands. "We can thus replace it now in Edinburgh; taking the real Stone to hide first in Cambuskenneth Abbey here in Stirling. We can move it later to a better place; unless our theft and false replacement are discovered early, then we must return it," said the Bishop. Le Hardi championed the idea readily; he did not require carafes of wine to come to such bold conclusion as it was his way to do such things. Alex de Lindsay was in agreement with the plan as was the younger Stewart brother; but James was more wary. "This baron can not see his way to commit this crime, for that is what you ask of us; the stone is not for us to take, it belongs to Scotland and her people," said the hesitant Steward. "More wine for this seneschal," le Hardi called to the sommelier. "Better the stone in our hands than in Edward's, would you not agree dear brother of my sweet bride?" asked de Lindsay. After much wine and little food it was finally agreed that in one week they all would meet in Edinburgh to replace the ancient Coronation Stone with the new stone quarried near Whiteby lands in Perth. The raid was most successful; these men were Scotland's trusted nobles, given access quickly to the Stone of Destiny.

They made their false replacement look the same; the real Stone they quietly removed to the hidden cellar tunnels at the abbey near Stirling Castle. In late December before the Abbot returned these little known but trusted men of Perth would come back to Cambuskenneth Abbey. They returned home taking with them the Coronation Stone; to hide it in a newly constructed stronghold on their lands. This small cellar dwelling was near a wee burn; with narrow steps down some seven thus in total to a door that barely showed to anyone. Inside this small chamber a sword was left with a wee stool and one famous Stone of Scotland. The grasses grew high in this pasture land; covering the oak door to the secret chamber. Whiteby and his good friends of Perth and true patriots of Scotland were to keep the location secret until Scotland had a King to crown again. Some of these patriots were still alive to sign the Ragman Roll the year next. But by the time the Bishop of Glasgow looked for them to return the Stone to crown their king some ten years later, these brave men of Perth had perished; all dead from Scotland's fight for independence. The real Stone quite lost from them.

Stebbinge Park Late September 1295

Ellie was busy packing things with Ana to take to Ware; their carts were very full from things they brought from their hastened stop at Woodham Ferrers. No one wanted to linger there; the memories of little Martha and the moat haunted them. When they arrived at Stebbinge Park little Hugh, Ellie's precious Hubicus suddenly became ill. His nurse was coming to advise his mother of his current condition; sadly Ellie's youngest son was still quite ill. "My William will see to him now Maudie," she said. "Oh Ana, he must help our wee lad; another child I can not bear to lose!" Ana tried to calm her fears; she too was worried about the fevers that he had with fits of crying and unrest. As Hubicus was just a baby of fifteen months, the illness seemed too similar to the one that took their wee John near that age. Ellie went to find her William. Gilley was working in the kitchen cellars on some treatment for the laddie. "My husband, our Hubicus is not improved. I fear we should leave him here with Maudie; the steward le Parker will we send to bring him home to Scotland when he is better." He agreed, "But before we decide that drastic action," he said hopefully, "allow your husband and healer with his Alchemy one more try to end his fevers. With the rumblings of war and Edward's penchant for thus seizing our good lands to his; this knight would feel most better with our Hugh to travel home with us the noo!" Ellie was terrified to leave her son; she wanted to stay, fearful that he might pass to the Otherworld all alone in Essex with his family back in Scotland.

"Eleanora, you must come home to Scotland; you are married to a nobleman who has taken sides against Lord Edward. Young Hugh's English birth a blessing in this inconvenience to thus leave him; if we must. Pray this works dear wife!" he said and off he went to administer his cure to Hugh. The wee laddie was just coming through another bout of sickness; he smiled up at William, just learning to say "Fad' er," the same way James once said it. Hugh was smart and his words were many; but he seemed to stutter some. "You must take this tasine Hugh; it will make you strong and feel much better," Gilley told him. This wee lad loved his father; so attached in his very shy way, Gilley almost missed the sentiment until Maudie told him that in his fevers he kept calling for Sir William. "So young a son; good Hugh, your father will bring you home to Douglasdale when you are healthy; you have my word I promise you!" he told him.

Maudie told Lord Douglas that if they stay she will tell him all about his father everyday; that he won't forget the laird, his family or their Scotland. "We must leave the morrow next; this recent fever has compromised his stamina, that he will likely stay in Essex for the winter. I will leave with you some herbs and more instructions for their use," he said, giving her a number of the ingredients including pennyroyal, cayenne, thyme and ginger mixed with honey. "The winter months he can not travel; as soon as spring is here, come north. I will send le Parker for you both when time draws close to travel," he told the nurse. "Good lad, sleep now. Your father and your mother love you so," he smiled at the laddie who smiled back so happily. Ellie came in now as well and kneeled by her son's bed. "Dear Hugh, I love you so much; please be brave. Be a good laddie for your mother to your nurse," she said as she held him to her, kissing him on the head.

Douglasdale Late October 1295

Ellie was distraught the entire journey home to Scotland, she worried about her wee Hugh too ill to make the journey with his family. Even home in Douglas Castle all she thought about was Hugh alone in England. "He is in the best of hands; our Maudie knows what to do for him," Gilley told her reassuringly; though he worried more himself about his son. A messenger that day brought news from England. William was reading the letter to his wife; when he stopped. Ellie looked up, "Tell me the now! What of Hugh?" she demanded, frightened that her husband paused so in his reading to spare her some ill tiding. Gilley told her calmly that Hugh was well, having no fevers for some lang time he explained. "But dear Edward has seized chattels and stock from Stebbinge Park and Woodham Ferrers for the fine unpaid; £14 in all were taken from the receipts given to our steward there," he said sputtering at himself.

Ellie said again more pointedly, the strain of the times prevailing in her words to her husband; "And what of Hugh; is he safe to live there? Should we send him now to Ware with young de Ferrers?" she asked him, not concerned at all about the seizing of their goods; she feared only for her Hubicus! Gilley said that Foster had assured them that no harm would come to the laddie there. "Maudie is doing well to care for our son our steward tells us; following perfectly in his treatments he is improving in his stamina each day." Ellie was extremely worried about her son far away in Edward's England. But there were even more frightening challenges coming her way. William had just received the orders from King John to become the Governor of Berwick Castle. The battle lines were being drawn; the men of Fife were called to muster in Berwick and Lord Douglas would be the garrison commander. Ellie excused herself to pray in the chapel and William followed her, joined in the praying, as both gave thanks for the improving health of their wee Hugh and asked God to protect their Scotland. When finished they held each other for some time; their family, their home, their very lives may be at risk they feared. Only God's love and their strong faith could keep them calm; the love they shared became the basis of their strength and moral courage.

The New Governor of Berwick: 1296

In early February of 1296 King John was summoned by Lord Edward to answer for more charges of contumacy; violation of his pledge of fealty to his Lord Paramount. Balliol refused Edward's ruse; he declined his invitation to visit England. Surprisingly King John was committing yet

MY TRUTH LIES IN THE RUINS

another act of disobedience against Edward; the pagan despot king would not mince his words when he heard of these unconscionable deeds; he vowed to rid himself of the turd, speaking crudely. On the 23rd of February King John signed the Act of Ratification at Dunfermline, Scotland's treaty with France; the Auld Alliance was officially renewed. The Douglases with pack animals, litters, men at arms in full armaments, children riding double with their nurses and the family Deerhound were beginning their journey east to Scotland's coast. William le Hardi Douglas was taking his family with him to Berwick Castle to become the garrison commander; to defend Scotland's most prosperous royal burgh and port, Berwick on Tweed, from the expected invasion and attack of King Edward and his army from the south. The Douglases journeyed first to Blackhouse Tower where they stayed two nights before continuing on to Berwick.

There was an odd feeling permeating their glen much like the dampness of a winter's chill, piercing the walls of their fortified tower house; a sharp, gnawing anxiousness that prevailed during their stay in Craig Douglas. One tangible difference was in the attire of their lord. William rode his palfrey for the morning hunt wearing a gambeson and mail hauberk; his sword belt with dagger to accompany his quiver and bow for hunting game. This second morning of their short stay Gilley was being aided by his squire Patric, who was strapping on the padded elbow guards that fastened by two leather straps to provide more protection to the knight. James had never seen his father wear such armaments before. He was just about to inquire of his father when three men at arms carrying de Moray banners and pennons approached the glen from the highpoint of the cart path that wound its way down to Douglas Burn.

Riding hard on their palfreys gaited for comfort and long distance these men of Moray came to join the Douglases as they broke their fast. Staying last night in their stronghold in Philipbaugh just some miles away a knight and his son, both Andrew, were traveling light with another knight from Petty; on their way north and home, then to a muster in Ros-shire. William cheerfully greeted his kin, turning now to James to allow the lasses their escape and freedom to run about on the banks of the burn that bore their name. Ellie was pleased to have some company; she longed for times when they could journey to Kinloss and the Black Isle again in peace and safety. "Good Andrew and your wee son so tall is this squire now!" she praised the lad and his father. Andrew told his cousin the reason for their stop this early in the day; sure was he that English soldiers were about. "In the forest we could sense the eyes of others; the game we tracked for some distance moved about as if provoked, the owls too, alerting of some invaders, unknown to the good Forest of the Borders," spoke Sir Andrew of his suspicions.

DEBORAH RICHMOND FOULKES

Figure XC-Part Two; the existing Smailholm Tower ruins are part of a later structure built in the parish of Smailholm, the Borders, Scotland; at one time the manor was held by the de Morays

Gilley spoke to his cousin in hushed tones to not alarm his children; he too felt that others were about. There was a different smell to the air he knew, aye. "Come good Andrew let us talk more of this, over some porridge and fresh ale," said Gilley as the travelers followed him into the keep. As if reading his mind James rounded up his sisters; bringing them inside as well with the Deerhound close behind. Ellie was not frightened. But the concern expressed by her husband for the presence of English spies made her most attentive to their words. James asked his father about the English intruders sent to the marches by their king. "These are men at arms to scout Scotland's army; locate its whereabouts, perhaps our Edward to engage our kingdome for some future battle," he spoke frankly as was his custom.

Sir Andrew told them that he and his squire young Andrew were recently visiting William de Moray at the Manor of Smailholm in the fortified tower that was his home just outside of Kelso. Gilley acknowledged he knew well the manor as Andrew continued talking. "From the summit of Smailholm crags one can see into the Cheviots, some fair distance clearly seen on the horizon. When we distinctly saw some several fires newly there; campsites in that region not yet existing some months ago," remarked this Scottish knight, a good soldier knowing well the lands of his ancestors and the secrets they can yield with careful study. James made conscious note of all Sir Andrew told them; these English were most careless with their travels, their actions to be tracked so easily if one learns how, this thoughtful page said to himself. Gilley was pleased later when his

MY TRUTH LIES IN THE RUINS

son would comment on Sir Andrew's sightings; learning fast was this lad the value of the Celtic lands, insights of the ancient ones to guide him.

The Douglas household continued on their journey to Berwick Castle the next day as planned. When they arrived Gilley became immediately amerced in military planning; surveying the defenses of the burgh and castle. The garrison was comprised of two hundred good noblemen of Fife all waiting patiently for their Governor. Everyone in the garrison knew of the garrison commander. He was William le Hardi Douglas, the redoubtable Lord Douglas and renowned Crusader to these brave men. The fortress was a Royal Castle for the King's business in the burgh; many towers and many rooms were available for Douglas children to explore. The great hall of this impressive castle was used for ceremonies of much elegance; once used for the grand announcement in 1292, awarding the competitor John Balliol a crown and kingdome to rule.

Now it was the military governor's command post for the war he much expected with the English king. William le Hardi was concerned; word had come to him of the English muster called for Newcastle some weeks before. On Monday in this Passion week the Comyn had taken the Scottish army south to lay waste the lands in northern England. Lord Douglas was not yet informed that Edward's army had also moved, that they had marched north from Newcastle, and were camped in nearby Wark, just on the English side of the Tweed. But the old warrior, the knight who once fought on the side of Prince Edward at Acre, felt something was terribly wrong. Le Hardi's last messengers had not returned from their scouting in Northumbria. Taking too long William feared they might have encountered an overwhelming force: an English army on its way to Scotland.

Many Scots with land in England had been choosing sides; Robert Brus, Lord of Annandale, father of the Earl of Carrick, was called upon by Edward to write letters to his friends and kin. Both father and son had forfeited their lands in Scotland last October when they did not attend the earlier Parliament. This elder Brus wrote to other nobles, asking them to not take up arms with other Scots against King Edward. In Wark as the thousands of English armed horse and foot filled the fields with campsites, the Bruses, both father and son pledged their fealty to King Edward. Another Scottish Earl was present there as well; the Earl of Dunbar. He was also pledged; loyal to the English lord. Three days later on Wednesday in this Easter week, the 28th of March word by messenger finally came to Lord Douglas: Lord Edward had moved north with many armed horse and foot soldiers, so encamped were they at Wark. William sent out word to the commander of the Scots; make haste Lord Edward has marched north towards Berwick. But this message never made it to the Comyn until the siege of Berwick had taken its sad course.

Edward crossed the Tweed at the normal ford at Coldstream; bringing his huge army with all their camp workers and followers, cooks, grooms, farriers, armourers, and sundry others to camp at the priory that day. With the army of the Bishop who just crossed at Norham lower down the river, their combined contingent was now 5000 horse and 30,000 footmen. As Edward approached Berwick he sent word to the townsmen, demanding their surrender. After waiting one full day for their fair reply, this invading king received a strong refusal: there would be no surrender for these good men of Berwick! He thus withdrew his army, moving them towards Hutton, just four miles from Berwick's gates where he finally set up his camp.

Lord Douglas called a meeting of some citizens and leaders of the royal burgh to the Great Hall at Berwick Castle. As he looked out across the seas the site of English provision ships and possibly some warships could be seen on the horizon; just sitting there quietly. These vessels were waiting the command from their king; some to move in with their stores to supply the army; others to join in the military attack of the royal burgh. Berwick's good leaders presented Sir William with the letter from King Edward; his demand for the surrender of Berwick on Tweed, that was pointedly refused. "But happily he has withdrawn his army, moved his camps from Berwick's border," said the Fleming from Red Hall. "Standing firm to his requests has sent this English king retreating, to re-think his fight with Berwick's good citizens," he boasted to Lord Douglas. But William was not as confident. With no word from the Comyn of reinforcements he felt they were sitting prey to this invading king. "That we have sent word of Edward's marching to the Comyn," said the castle governor, "with no word in return does worry this old warrior. We must be patient and sure with the battles that we pick with such a large contingency, if the word of our own messengers is to be believed." The Fleming was stunned. "What size of force are you expecting Lord Douglas?" he asked. William told him that in addition to the fleet of English ships yet visible to the eye, there were some 30,000 or more in the English army. "We had better pray that relief of Scotland's good army to enjoy this burgh and soon!" Lord Douglas said, expressing his concern for the safety of Berwick's citizens and burgh.

Friday 30th March 1296

It was a long night for William; he did not sleep, Ellie was restless too with nightmares that woke her just past midnight into Friday morning the third of the kalends of April, five days after Easter. They had shared their love together in the wee hours before dawn; warming their hearts and bodies. Lord Douglas hoped to calm his wife with words of comfort; to hold her close and let her know he would protect her and the children. They spoke together quietly for some time; as she leaned into the strength of his broad chest she told him of her fears. "Something is so wrong here; I can feel a raw chill about my sorry self," she told him. William could sense it too; an eerie calm seemed to surround them even as the sun rose on Berwick harbor this 30th day of March. "My Ellie, your husband knows your sentiments; our castle stands so mighty but impersonates its strength I fear." She knew he was suspect of the fortress and its defenses. Gilley feared too that the royal burgh was too difficult to defend adequately; the only barriers to invading armies were the high embankments that surrounded the royal burgh, interspersed with a simple wooden palisade and deteriorating stone walls.

Then suddenly their quiet intimacy was abruptly shattered; Gilley's squire Patric entered their chamber barely waiting time from the first knock. "English war ships approach, they have moved into the harbor of the Tweed!" he exclaimed. Ellie's heart was pounding; Ana appeared just behind the squire, running to her side to help dress her lady. William was already changing to his silk cote; he donned a quilted surcote as he barked some orders; "Bring forth my mail hauberk and a coif as well!" he commanded to his squire. The English were attacking; they were at war! "Ana, we must get to the children and their nurses!" cried Ellie. James arrived now in their chamber, "Mother, I have sent the others with their nurses to wait in the withdrawing room as was your plan for emergencies. I chanced a look into the harbor; a wee cog is stuck in the silt of the shoreline," he told them. "Are the English ships going to attack us?" he asked. "James, your father orders you to stay with your mother and good sisters, with Ana and the others of our household here; protect them with your awareness and good sense," said William as he buckled on his sword belt. "I will send word if you should move our family to another location for safety; you are assigned with their protection!" declared Lord Douglas to his page and son now ten. James was deeply disappointed but knew obeying his father showed more sense then questioning his words as the tumult of battle approached.

William was in full armaments as he left their chamber; moving swiftly to muster the garrison and devise his plan to defeat the English ships in the harbor. Then as fast as he departed he abruptly re-appeared. He rummaged through his war-chest and pulled out an ornate trumpet, "My oliphant," he declared with prideful ceremony, taking with him now the ivory horn made from the tusks of the great beast of the same name. Le Hardi had brought the elegant trumpet with its fine carvings and peculiar sounds all the way back from the Crusades; using it successfully in every campaign since he boasted. "We will be led in charge by this fair horn; like our Celtic ancestors, our war-cry sounds in victory when this trumpet signals Douglas men to battle with its deep and frightening roar!" he bellowed heartily. Then turning to James he said he changed his mind, "Follow your father now my son to hear the strategy of the battle plan; then to report back at once to secure the family in the withdrawing room of the castle," he told the lad respectfully. James' eyes lit up and he quickly made his way to the great hall in close step with the garrison commander.

Lord Douglas was speaking with two of his sergeants; quickly he told of his intentions. The plan he put before them: assemble eight knights with their squires, making thirty-two armed horse; twenty bowmen would be called out as well with another twenty six armed foot. "With some of Berwick's good citizens we should be a force of one hundred growing," growled le Hardi, "leaving more than half the garrison behind to defend the castle or provide us reinforcements should the need of it come." The strategy for the assault on the English fleet was simple: draw in the other ships at sea to engage the Scots already in assault of their stricken shipmates; staggered in the Tweed, they could not all land at once. It would take time to pull anchor and row towards shore once the decision to attack the Scots was made; if it is made at all.

The garrison would first focus on the doomed vessel lying in the silt of the Tweed he told the sergeants. The bowmen would move unseen behind the stricken ship to engage Edward's archers on the cog. The armed horse would make their charge to draw out the knights and horse from the deck of this first ship; the onfoot would await his command laying low behind the boats, hiding in the wee hills of the shoreline on the inlet of the harbor. The armed foot of the cog were few in number he speculated. These small ships could hold sixty or more good men; but each of the ten or so horses took the space of twice that number of men, limiting their force considerably. And some of these vessels were used mainly for provisions; lightly guarded with fewer armed horse as well.

In minutes the squires had brought about the war-horses; destriers who could maneuver in small quarters, rear up to avoid another horse or the clash of an opponent's war-sword. The lookout from the tower guard position came running with his information for the garrison commander; the four ships anchored nearer to the shore were war ships of similar size, bringing close the same number of men at arms he told Lord Douglas. "Each cog is to carry no more than four knights by their armor; to carry their horses too, where you see them there!' he pointed down to the deck of the beleaguered ship James had seen permanently anchored in Berwick silt where the English were bringing destriers up from the hold. Le Hardi was pleased; the lookout had confirmed his expectations on the English forces of the fleet. "Remind all the armed horse what this knight learned in the Crusades," he began to instruct his sergeants, "after a lang sea voyage the destriers need

MY TRUTH LIES IN THE RUINS

time to acclimate themselves on shore. Take full advantage of their weakened state and attack quickly; force them to strong maneuvers to further tire the beasts."

The old knight vaulted to his horse as if to signal his own prowess; there was still a lot of fight left in the redoubtable Lord Douglas and the English were invading his burgh. The crest of Douglas shown brightly on his helmet; the three salamanders painted red around the shield reminded his opponent that he had walked through fire and lived to tell the tale. The garrison force was confident in their leader; a Crusader, then a knight under the banners of King Alexander III; this bold warrior would lead them to victory they resolved. The knights of Fife mounted their destriers; their squires handed them their helmets and war-swords, battle axes and shields or targes. Some of the armed foot carried a mace or spiked club while others carried pole-arms, shortened spears with cutting and thrusting blades; some held swords and shields for combat. The portcullis rumbled loudly as it withdrew, moving slowly upward with the monotonous turn by turn of the ropes on the huge shaft. Le Hardi grew impatient and furiously rode under the iron gate only partially withdrawn; he and his horse ducking in unison to miss the sharp edges of the formidable barrier. The drawbridge lowered with a thud as he moved forward, his supertunic flying perilously behind him; William le Hardi was on a mission.

Clamoring hooves met the wooden planks of the bridge; the running gaits of the great war-horses of the commander and his armed warriors set a maddening pace in a frightening din of momentum. Lord Douglas led his men in a furious ride down the treacherous hills from Berwick Castle and into the cart paths of the royal burgh. The garrison followed him; armed foot rode double with squires and pages to move out more quickly. Then through the main gates of the wooden palisade rode le Hardi, leading his men at a fevered pace towards the banks of the harbor on the Tweed to do battle with the enemy. The cog that ran aground was a private sailing ship from Rye, one of the Cinque Ports commandeered by Edward for his invasion of Scotland. The English knights on the Rye ship saw the approaching force of the Scots; they mounted their own war-horses preparing to do battle. Shouts from the lookouts told of the impending fray. Commands barked by knights to their squires filled the crisp March air with a furious bluster. From the outer vessels came frantic calls for assistance and bellowed impatience. A controlled pandemonium ruled the decks of the English war ships; knights readied for combat while captains mulled over a decision to land and attack or hold their position in the Tweed.

The open area for battle in the harbor was long and thin; unlike the wider lists of tournaments there was little room to maneuver. Forty armed horse would fight in these tight quarters. Each combatant had to be aware of the close proximity of the other knights and squires doing battle; taking care not to over run his own series of combats. Standards blazoned; pennons flew as the Scots moved closer to shores where the cog lay helplessly in the silt. Some of the Scottish armed foot took their leave of the horses now; joined by town's people, men wearing gambesons and leather hauberks, carrying axes, swords and daggers they made their way to their positions out of site of the harbor. Le Hardi surmised correctly; his number now was at least a hundred men at arms with the influx of Berwick's good citizens. The four knights from the unlucky cog rode bravely forward with their squires; swords held outward in the attack position. Destriers ran full tilt as trained, faster and faster they moved towards their opponent; these fearless war-horses of renown. Le Hardi was correct to urge his men to attack quickly; to the trained eye, the English war-horses exhibited signs of weakness from their confinement.

The Battle Cry was sounded, "A Douglas! A Douglas!" reverberated on the beaches. Patric blew the ivory oliphant; the horrible noise signaling the formidable power unleashed to repel the invaders. The battle was on! Le Hardi carried in ready his war-sword. His great strength gave him advantage in battle; complimented by a longer reach to keep the combat further from him and his horse. His sword held in his left hand, the strong hands of a seasoned warrior allowed for a loose grip to release tension in his strikes. He was in the lead as was his fashion and the first to engage in combat with an English knight. Le Hardi rode tall; finding his center of gravity easily, never off balance. Ambidextrous as were many knights, he always carried a smaller weapon behind his shield that he could wield with equal agility. His true advantage was his confidence; perfectly conditioned he was equally strong in both the right and left arms, able to fend off attackers from every stance. The clash of metal on metal came quickly; sparks flew in the air. Le Hardi's longer sword engaged his opponent. The short cross guard allowed him added alacrity as he extended his long range even further, slipping his hand down lower on the oval flat grip. He struck first, his sword hitting the shield of his opponent; his hand saved from the smashing impact by the guard as it hit the flat surface. The English knight made a counter strike that was easily repelled. The combatants withdrew briefly to begin again.

The soft, slow, sinking terrain of the shoreline made even short runs at high speed or tilting albeit impossible. Le Hardi would have to rely on the horse's agility to move quickly in tight combat. The English knight reared his destrier and made a pivot turn as le Hardi brought his war-horse Pageant round for the counter blow. He held his fast shield low, a smaller shield he preferred in battle that gave him more maneuverability. While gripping the reins in the same hand that held his war-sword, almost standing in his stirrups, the high back saddle supported his body like a knight in the joust;

he appeared braced for the blow. Then just as the English knight turned to attack, le Hardi reeled Pageant left, deftly switching the reins to his right hand, he lunged forward to bring the war-sword flush in the side of his opponent, piercing the gambeson, severely injuring and unhorsing the knight simultaneously. William's squire Patric came like a ghost through the fog, out from nowhere he seemed to appear; to grab the reins of the Englishman's horse and withdraw the animal from the field.

Le Hardi and his squires were a perfectly trained unit; four armed horse to handle four directions of attack at once. Other knights disagreed with the rigid formation; but Lord Douglas found this style worked best in small areas, especially with the obstructed view from the hovering mist. Riders floated through the heavy sea air appearing and disappearing into the fog of the shoreline. It was a dangerous field of battle for every reason. As the fog was lifting, Le Hardi turned to see one of the garrison's armed foot dealing a fatal blow to a squire caught in the fray of armed horse and a determined Fife freeholder carrying only his pole axe. In the melee of combat he was unsure if the onfoot had responded to his signal for them to join the battle; happily they were already engaged. Then he returned his eyes to the unhorsed knight lying motionless since he hit the ground. There would be no counter attack there he surmised.

The commander moved above the fray momentarily to survey the battlefield. The bowmen were attacking from the inlet sandbar; preying on the unprotected side of the cog that lay in the waters of the Tweed. When first the English armed horse had raced from the decks of this vessel to the forward shoreline, the Scottish archers in perfect unison moved stealth-like to close in on the defenseless cog; the plan of the commander was being flawlessly enacted. These Scottish archers were followed into battle by armed foot coming from the other direction; the simple strategy prevailed. The Scots set the boat ablaze hurling liquid fire: oil soaked bundles of cloth stuffed with dried grasses and weighted with stones onto the decks. The garrison was winning the battle easily, but had not yet won the day, the old commander mused. Then abruptly he swung Pageant around; little time for reflection le Hardi chided himself. He had quickly perceived reinforcements from another cog that had just landed, eager to do battle with Scots! For this encounter it was the English knight who struck first. The commander parried with his fast shield as the English battle-axe made a huge thud; the impact of the axe on the flat of the shield deadened his right hand and arm up to the elbow. "Old age," he muttered sarcastically to himself.

He reeled Pageant to the right; the war-horse flowed perfectly in motion to his commands. The Douglas destrier seemed to take on the persona of le Hardi as he snorted defiantly; his hot breath spewing smoke from his nostrils into the raw chill of the March air. Lord Douglas held his small shield in the ready, pulled his head right as if to attack straight forward; then as if by some secret pact between them, Pageant lowered his head and swung left, then reared up and pushed forward right, bringing Lord Douglas to wield his war-sword swiftly in a left to left diagonal motion, cutting across the torso and into the exposed leg of the English knight. The leg injury meant that his opponent could be unhorsed more easily, unable to sustain another blow from his weakened state. As Lord Douglas brought Pageant full circle to meet the knight once more he gathered his thoughts; studied the knight, a young man with great strength but flawed in his skills of combat. Once more the old warrior motioned Pageant forward, faster and faster towards the English knight. He held his shield low then parried the opponent's axe with its edge; holding his war-sword in the high on guard position, le Hardi's strong knees and sturdy thighs held his stance. His body flowed easily in rhythm; the hilt was aimed directly as his opponent. Then he delivered a quick, punishing blow that unhorsed the knight; the battle-axe flew from the hands of the unseasoned warrior as he fell helplessly to the ground. Coming to his commander's aid, the Fife freeholder ended the young knight's battle days with one swift thrust of his pole axe.

By now the remaining seaworthy English ships were fleeing the harbor, one almost totally engulfed in flames; the result of the steadfast assault of Scottish bowmen and armed foot when first this vessel tried to land on Berwick's shores. Le Hardi and two knights from Fife went to board the English war vessel that ran aground, now under the Scots' control. They grabbed the captain of the cog and interrogated him about the rest of the fleet. Several minutes of questioning took place before William's squire Patric let out a blood curdling scream, "Look out Lord Douglas," as a smoldering timber from the mainsail came crashing to the deck, glancing off the shoulder of the garrison commander. Le Hardi was knocked to his knees and his shoulder was split open nearly to the bone from a jagged piece of metal that once held the sheets or ropes guiding the sail. He sputtered some words in Latin, his disdain for the injury was obvious; but he would not surrender to the pain.

Lord Douglas continued his words with the English sea captain until he was finished. Before he rode out of Berwick harbor, he had boarded three more vessels and personally interrogated the few survivors. Most of the English invaders were slaughtered by the good men of Fife with some help from the brave citizens of Berwick he observed with pride. Thankfully, few of the garrison would succumb to their injuries; of those harmed in combat, the armed foot held for minor gashes and one knight sustained a deep wound on his thigh. Only the garrison commander was more seriously injured though he was wont to admit it.

MY TRUTH LIES IN THE RUINS

As the English fled by sea, the fires blazing on the deck of the last vessel made an impressive site for le Hardi; a satisfying rebuff of Edward's naval contingency he mused. Of the few cogs that could not withdraw all were finally sank in the harbor of the Tweed. Le Hardi rode back to the Berwick castle, the ache in his shoulder overshadowed by his thoughts: what next? If only some word would come from the Comyn, the Scottish army to relieve them soon, he sighed to himself. With Edward's ships now in distress how quickly will he send his army here and how many in that muster from Newcastle, then too in Durham, wondered the garrison commander; was it really 5000 horse and 30,000 foot as his observers' messengers had so reported? So much to ponder.

Safely tucked away in the withdrawing room, Ellie brought Amy and Muriel painting and embroidery to do, while she and James played a game of Merels to pass the time. But Sir Shamus was strangely uneasy with the family; pacing in front of the closed door to the great hall from this chamber relentlessly until some hours later when the door opened to Patric. Ellie looked up at the squire from her Book of Hours; she had been passing the final moments of the battle unaware, reading prayers. Your husband requires your good assistance in the care of his men she was informed. Then Patric told her quietly, "Sir William took a falling timber on his shoulder; he needs some tending to as well I fear." Ellie sent him for the healing box and ran quickly to her husband's side; bringing James to assist her. Ana was with her lady, setting up tables for the injured; getting other healers to attend to members of the garrison. Ellie wouldn't listen to her husband's words when he told her to first see to the wounds of others. "Lord Douglas, you are most long in tooth to these young knights and others in this fine garrison," she told him with a smirk, not intending to leave his side no matter what he told her, until she was finished with his treatment. "I will stitch this shoulder closed once I have used these herbs here to cleanse the wound and subdue the pain," she told him. James was ministering to her surgery on the shoulder; the throbbing subsided quickly from Ellie's compress and good care. "James, come here and hold this while I sew well this wound to shut,' she told him.

"Father," said the lad quietly, "Mother allowed me to visit the guard tower and view some of the combat," he spoke more excitedly as he realized his father was being receptive to his words. "You noticed the good and steady movements of our Pageant this day then," William said to his son. "As often I have told you, only through continued practice can the perfectly trained bodies of the knight and his horse learn to work in tandem. And only by this means can a warrior hope to prevail in such close combat. A perfect example today for you James; while the clash of swords and battle axe, shields in parry, appear from a distance as simple maneuvers, the impact alone requires great strength and endurance not only for the rider but for his war-horse as well." Lord Douglas continued his teaching of the young squire, his oldest son. "And it is wise to train two war-horses at once that their movements mirror the other. Should your horse fall in battle, another is ready to take his place. In longer sieges one must change horses during combat; a weary mount can get a warrior killed as fast as any strike from an opponent," he told James.

Another knight unknown to Ellie came to the side of his commander who was sitting while she stitched closed the injury to her knight. Then she applied more compresses and a dressing and some bandages. "Lord Douglas, our messengers to the Comyn have sent back one of their member," he told him gravely, "Edward has moved his army back to Hutton, marching east toward this burgh!" William was being helped by Patric into his gambeson and hauberk, "And what of the Comyn; how many days away is he?" asked Sir William. The knight told him that with good luck perhaps some few days the Scottish army could arrive; he was not sure of this however. "Call the other sergeants here; we must determine a plan to secure the castle and protect the burgh as much as possible," he told this chevalier. Turning to his wife and son, "More than ever does this knight need your help," he told them quickly. "Look after the others of the injured; we will need them all to fight this invader to our kingdome!" he said. Then to Ellie he gave a hug and kiss. "Thank you both for your bravery this day; more to come of this I fear unless the Comyn returns to aid our cause," he said, concerned now with the advancing army just short miles west of Berwick Castle.

The garrison was preparing for the attack of English soldiers when a strange occurrence was viewed from the parapet of their castle. The defense commanders of the town were opening the gates of the burgh; an army under Scottish banners entered through the high embankments and small palisade of timber that defended Berwick. It was then the garrison guard noticed the pennons; these men at arms carried the armorial achievements of Dunbar. "But the Earl of Dunbar has pledged to Edward!" yelled the sergeant of the garrison, "Quick with you; inform Lord Douglas of this distressing news!" William was incredulous; the gates were opened to the English on the ruse of a traitorous Scot with banners blazoned of the Scottish army; the town's good citizens mistaken, that the enemy's men at arms were welcomed inside the burgh defenses. The slaughter of Berwick began. In some short hours as the garrison watched in helpless horror many good citizens were slaughtered. A banner of the king was sent to the castle; would a truce of surrender to save the town be of interest to the Governor of the castle, the king's vassal proposed.

MY TRUTH LIES IN THE RUINS

After some few hours of negotiations a surrender was agreed upon between Lord Douglas for the Scots and King Edward for the English; Berwick had thus fallen in one day so quickly to the pagan despot king, the ruthless invader of Scotland. Edward guaranteed William that should he surrender the castle and give himself as hostage, the killing of the town's citizens would end immediately and Ellie and the children could leave with the garrison in safe conduct. With the Scottish army occupied to the south and west, and no relief in sight, there was no choice. Edward and his vassals were allowed into Berwick castle where King Edward and his household lay that night, remaining there a month. Lord Douglas was detained, held in ward by Edward in Hog's Tower; Ellie attending to his wounds once more before she left with the children, Deerhound, and the rest of the Douglas household in the company and escort of the good men of Fife on Saturday, the last of March. Her Douglas men at arms would lead them out of Berwick and southeast, first to Kelso, then onto to Craig Douglas, to arrive finally at the castle of the Bishop of Glasgow in Carstairs as was their plan. Their Douglas lands and castles in Douglasdale were unsafe; seized by the English for Lord Douglas's part at Berwick in rebellion to his Lord Paramount King Edward.

As Lady Douglas left the royal burgh the next morning she noticed the occupation of the southern gate by knights with pennons of the blue lion on a field of gold; Lord Lovaine her own father was serving Edward in the war with Scotland. The brave men of Essex that she knew; good men all, now were part of this tragedy, under the banners of Matthew Lovaine as vassal of the King. The shivers of sadness, the fear of uncontrolled peril ran through her very soul. Her heart but broke as she looked about at the slaughter and the carnage; riding by the shops of merchants that she knew, most everyone was dead or dying in the wake of the English invaders. Merchants in their day's chores cut down like vermin; sitting at their slanted writing desks, nodding on their stools or benches strangely peaceful. Not many yards beyond the path that led to castle she had to stop; her stomach was about to relieve its contents. Ellie dismounted quickly, then looking down she realized that she was standing in pools of blood; human blood from the good people of Berwick mercilessly struck down by the Edward's army.

Her stomach was in spasm; she wrenched the muscles in her chest in dry heaving that followed, unable to stop her body's reaction to the vile nature of the murder of innocent women and children with their brave men of Berwick. James was watching every move of the English soldiers from his palfrey; then he rode up quickly to his mother's side. "Something is very wrong here," he said, motioning her in the direction of the paths along the banks of the river Tweed, near the castle where they once were. "Father said that Edward promised to relent on the killings should he surrender the castle to the king; conditions of their agreement to spare the citizens of the burgh," James cried out to her, incredulous of the slaughter he was seeing: was the King of England recanting on his word he wondered aloud?

Ellie mounted her horse and looked in the direction of the royal fortress; not believing an English king would break a treaty with the governor of the castle as her son inferred. James saw her disbelief of his discernment, so he continued, "Why then has he rounded up the men but for the hanging? Look there!" he said sternly but quietly now, trying not to alarm his sisters riding up in front of them. Ellie watched, tears were falling fast, overflowing her eyes as English knights supervised a mass hanging of Berwick's men; so many at a time! She then looked up at the castle tower right above, overlooking the grizzly hangings, the tower where Lord Douglas was imprisoned; Hog's Tower where he watched helplessly as Edward Plantagenet carried out the genocide of the Scots.

Ellie could hear her daughters crying; she ran her jennet ahead to comfort them. "James, please come quickly!" she called to him. Amy was crying uncontrollably. One of the noblemen's daughters, a friend who had visited at the castle was one of the wee lasses in the heap of bodies lying near the gate at the embankment that once protected the burgh. "We must get out of here, ride faster!" she commanded to the nurses carrying her daughters. Suddenly they were beyond the site of Berwick on Tweed; the castle faded in the background of a sea of bodies and blood. The smell of carnage was beginning to overcome Ana by now; she dismounted and headed for some underbrush off the cart path to relieve herself. Ellie went to Amy and pulled her down to sit awhile. James had asked the escorts to wait until the family had composed the wee lasses.

One of the Douglas knights came and asked if he might help. Amy went to him and sat quietly; he was of great size, with long black hair like her father and she felt comforted by him. Muriel then walked over to her mother and clung hard to the skirts of Ellie's cloak and surcote, sobbing hard, crying as if she would never stop. James stood away from all of them, vowing never to forget one person; one child or woman that he saw there cruelly slaughtered by King Edward and his men. What does a mother tell her children about the cruelties of war asked Ellie to herself; then shaking her head she realized this was not war, this was blatant murder by the pagan despot Edward as her William called the English king. Treating Scots as vermin was but sport, their slaughter but a game to this unholy ruler. No true English man of God would permit such relentless carnage, a crime against humanity she knew.

The Douglas household would take their leave of Berwick on Tweed this day, but the memories were forever etched in their minds; the scenes of the innocent laying in blood soaked paths; the stench in their nostrils from the perished not yet buried; these memories returned whenever their thoughts wandered to that place. The wailing sounds of the dying visited Amy in her dreams; waking the wee lass most every night it seemed for some many months to come. The king spared no citizen, regardless of their sex or age or country of their origin. Foreign merchants died as well. Forty Flemings perished in Red Hall; fighting valiantly against the invader, they were trapped inside by the English army, the building set on fire burning all inside to death. After the second day the clergy came to plead with King Edward; stop this carnage, and he did. The mill wheels were made to turn an eerie red as the blood flowed into the water supplies. The first known genocide on record: Berwick on the Tweed, then in Scotland now of England; eight thousand or more perished that day in the sea of human blood; a anguishing slaughter of innocents led by the good and just Edward Plantagenet.

William watched with disbelief and horror; each death he felt as if it was his own to do. No greater punishment for this sorry knight to watch, thought Lord Douglas, "than to behold such massacre before me, from my sad surrender to this devil of a king!" William roared in painful words out loud. As the night settled on the second day the hangings stopped; there were no more male citizens left to execute he mused. His squire came to his chamber in the tower to change his dressing on the wound. "We have heard the good men of the church have interceded with the king; the slaughter has ceased, mercifully so." Patric then handed his knight a parchment note, "from the English knight we met in Knaresburgh," he told his laird. Gilley read the message sent from Johannis de Hastings. He said that when Ellie came upon him guarding the city for the English, well beyond the burgh's outer gates and the defensive embankment, she asked if he might get word to her husband, held in Hog's Tower. Josh agreed and had his messenger deliver this letter to inform the governor that his cousin, William's wife, and their three children with their Douglas household had made it safely out of Berwick; heading for Kelso Abbey by her words, wrote the English knight. His promise to Eleanora was thus fulfilled with the delivery of the message to Lord Douglas, he concluded graciously. My only consolation thought Gilley; my family most safe from this dreadful horror.

Part III

Stebbinge Park April 1296

Young Hugh de Douglas was still recuperating from his grave illness at Stebbinge Park when Ellie's steward John le Parker arrived there in late April. Sir John planned to return the lad to Scotland when he was able to travel. He was also there as seneschal to evaluate the remaining stock and chattels at the manor; to assess the results of last October's seizure by the Essex sheriff of values taken for payment against their fine for the trespass of their marriage. Faraway in Berwick Lord Edward was holding William Douglas the father as his prisoner in Hog's Tower. On the 27th of April just as the king was leaving Berwick for Dunbar he signed new royal orders against the Scots. These writs would dramatically affect young Hugh's status in England: ***All Scots residing on the lands of Scotsmen in England would be removed immediately.***

Figure XCI-Part Three; Stebbing church as it appears today; the lovely old screen dates back to the 1300's; parishioners of this village have thoughtfully preserved the church; once held by the de Ferrers family it is situated within the old manor, part of the dower lands of Eleanora Douglas

The sheriff of Essex and Hertford arrived this day at Stebbinge Park manor to enforce these new writs of the king. To his surprise he found a two year old English-born boy named Hugh, son of William Douglas, a Scottish nobleman; the little boy was in the company of John le Parker who was also residing at the manor, he recorded in the Essex pipe rolls. The sheriff arrested the wee Hugh and confined him to Edward's prison in Hertford; the father and son were now both held in ward, committed to imprisonment by Lord Edward Plantagenet.

In Berwick, William's shoulder was healing quickly; but his heart was slow to mend from the grueling sights he saw during his incarceration in Hog's Tower. He was held in ward some four weeks already, when Edward took his leave for Dunbar. On this sad occasion, Edward was beginning his march of victory throughout Scotland, in pursuit of King John; while also seeking the Regalia of Scotland. Lord Douglas was left behind with Edward's household at Berwick Castle; released some days later, near the Ides of May. Ellie and their family had soldiered on to Carstairs and the castle of the Bishop of Glasgow as they planned. She was there about month when William was granted his freedom.

Around this same time, on the 10[th of] May, Edward issued yet another writ from his court now held at Roxburgh Castle. To further alienate the Scots, to awe them with his power, the king commanded his sheriffs to seize unto the king all lands in Northumbria owned by Scotsmen. The manors taken unto Edward included William's Fawdon and Baron Wishart's Tynedale manor of Monilawes. Everything that Edward did seemed to invite further rebellion. Uprisings continued to erupt in the north of Scotland though many Scottish prisoners were being captured daily. Edward moved north, dispatching his vassals to suppress the unrelenting Scots. He commanded his loyal knight Hugh de Saint John to move some eleven prisoners from Aberdeen to the confines of Berwick Castle prison. Among these Scottish patriots was Sir Thomas de Morham who would remain at Berwick's prison for some time. More rebels seemed to lurk about that Edward sent others of his trusted adherents, including Josh de Hastings, Ellie's kin to suppress the rebels and capture recalcitrant Scots. De Hastings accompanied other English knights into the Highlands; rightly ordered by his king to secure more districts for Edward as they scoured for the enemy. Telling friend from foe, patriot from enemy was more challenging with each passing day of occupation as Scottish patriots were on the run from the invading English forces.

A small group of riders with Douglas banners blazoned approached the castle in Carstairs; the gonfalon of Lord Douglas furled in the wind as the armed men rode into the courtyard of Bishop Wishart's castle. Muriel was the first to recognize her father riding his palfrey, Pageant trailing behind with Patric. Le Hardi was leading his squires and man-servants newly freed from Berwick to join his family and bring them home to Douglasdale. "Mother, come quick!" she screamed. "Father is here to save us from this dreadful wait." Ellie was engaged in another game of Merels with her son. "Game over!" said Ellie triumphantly. James was happy to forfeit the victory he was about to turn; his father's homecoming was upon them! Ellie ran through the doors to the courtyard, into the open arms of the laird of Douglas. "My dear lass, that you are safely held by this knight the answer to my prayers; the many weeks as Edward's guest now over!" he said happily. James and Muriel were unable to greet their father until the wee Amy had her turn. "Papa!" she exclaimed, running past her older siblings to her father; she tugged at his supertunic that he might see her first. "Come here my Amy, your father is most happy to see you too!"

William told them all to start their packing; on the morrow they would leave for home and Douglas Castle: his lands would be restored. "The word will thus be sent to Scotland's sheriffs, now English knights, vassals of Lord Edward: repledge the lands to Lord Douglas! And in June this baron to make his haste to Edinburgh and that king, treated of peace in the Holyrood Abbey there with Durham's good Bishop once again; for this knight to do his pledging, to offer fealty to Lord Edward," Gilley explained with more than a hint of sarcasm in his voice. He also told Ellie that in August he must return to Berwick for a Parliament and once again pay homage to Edward a second time with the other landholders of the realm. Muriel asked her father what he meant by pledging and offering fealty to Lord Edward. "Our King of Scotland is no more; King Edward is our sovereign; lord paramount of Scotland's noblemen. To give fealty requires much in ceremony; we touch and kiss the gospels," Gilley explained patiently. "As tenant in chief to retain our lands I must renounce the treaty with France; and swear that Lord Douglas has thus come voluntarily, uncompelled by fear or force. Then my seal will this baron thus append letters-patent as required by this lord."

He turned to Ellie with a smile of relief. "For now its Douglasdale and family for this humble knight, to celebrate his freedom from Edward's ward!" Gilley said. He reached for Ellie, picked her up high over his head; laughing all the while. "Unhand me Lord Douglas," she teased him, much as he expected. "Beast, Sholto beast, release this lady, the noo!" she ordered to no avail. "Put me down le Hardi!" she chided all the more. Chuckling with his capture William shouted out to Ana, "Which way the lady's chamber that her husband would take his prize?" he asked her. Ana was beaming; happy for his safe return and thrilled to hear the laughter in their household once again. "Up those stairs Sir Gilley; the first chamber on the right will be M' Lady's," she told him.

Figure XCII-Part Three; remains of Douglas Castle, Douglasdale

Douglasdale Summer 1296

Douglasdale was just as they had left it some five months ago. A joyous homecoming awaited these doughty Douglases; cooks, maid servants, villeins, steward, men at arms, all were present to greet their laird's return raising the gonfalon of Willelmi de Duglas to let all know: Lord Douglas was home again in Douglas Castle. But with their Scotland, everything had changed; their kingdome was extinguished from existence, now just an English domain. The sheriffs residing in the shires were indeed English vassals of Lord Edward, just as William predicted; the escheators and the treasurer too were of English birth. "Many courtesies to grant these English, our lives we must adjust to their ways I fear," sighed William as he sat in the great hall. But an even bigger reunion was yet to come: Little Hugh unannounced and unexpected arrived with Sir John this day. "Fad' er!" screamed the excited laddie as he was carried in by his nurse. He wiggled free from Maudie and ran to William's open arms. "Hugh miss you!" he said quietly as William held him tightly in his arms; hugging and laughing together the son and the father rejoiced. Ellie ran to her son's side and he leaped into her arms as well. William was surprised the wee lad remembered them, so young a son to leave behind in England. "Oh my Hubicus, so happy is your mother to hold her dear one in her arms again!" cried Ellie, barely able to hold back her tears of joy. "Maudie what good work to bring our son to his health again!" she told the nurse. Now everyone gathered around young Hugh to welcome him home at last. Smiling ear to ear,

Hugh's grin was warming their hearts, helping them all forget for the moment the dark days of Berwick.

Sir John explained that the wee lad had been arrested at Stebbinge Park, held in ward of the King. Le Parker had to ride to Hertford to retrieve him. "Your solicitors still residing there were most helpful," he explained. "Young de Ferrers was in nearby Ware and the one to post his bail." The news of Hugh's confinement was a surprise to everyone. "No messengers would proceed without escort and great expense for their trouble since Edward's invasion began in March," he sighed, apologizing for not informing the Douglases of Hugh's arrest. "Two Douglas men held in Edward's prisons," said William sarcastically. "Hubicus, wee lad, you were very brave, a true Douglas and Scottish patriot held in the king's ward; sure aye!" he said approvingly to his son. "Your father so glad is he to have you back in Douglasdale!" roared the laird of Douglas. Hugh smiled, beamed in all his joy to be home at last. The shy laddie finally decided it was his turn to speak. He very slowly and deliberately began, quietly and carefully he uttered his words that his stuttering was not noticeable to anyone. "This Hugh most grateful to be again in Scotland," he told them.

Le Parker explained that he had planned to leave the next day when the sheriff arrived and seized the boy. "What mad men this Essex sheriff; to arrest a wee laddie of barely two!" he said with some consternation. James spoke up, "We Douglas men to give them worry now; when we are grown we'll drive them out or perish I do promise!" he told them with a cold resolute voice that startled Ellie. Gilley was looking away from them now; on his mind were the many brave Scots who died at the hands of Edward. "That he broke his word to this knight will never I forget," said William ruefully. "That the pagan despot king butchered our friends and neighbors after giving his promise to set them free; I vow to return the same fair fight to you King Edward!" his voice growing more stern, louder with ever word. Ellie watched him as he spoke; noticing a look on her husband's face that she feared for what might happen next. His face was contorted in anger and remorse; a strange grimace of guilt and sadness to do vengeance against a king with no core values. William would become a rebel; she knew it in her heart, while trying to deny the course before her.

"In one week with few days will I go to Edinburgh and make my pledge to that pretender to the crown," he scoffed. "Our lands will be repledged to us; our chattels thus restored. But there will be no mending of the sorry heart, for Lord Douglas has seen death that was his doing; not in brave battle fought and lost, but in weak surrender given to Lord Edward." Ellie put her arms around her husband. "Lord Will, your word you gave; to not raise sword that we should leave unharmed with the garrison's good escort. To know that a king would break his word of safety for the burgh was not possible," she calmly told him, trying to reassure him with her supportive words. "The Comyn lead Scotland's army in the south; not near us, they were unable to come to our good rescue," she said trying to bolster his morale. But these words fell on deaf ears. William blamed himself for the butchery of some eight thousand Scots as if he raised the sword to murder them himself. The man that returned from Berwick was not the same warrior chief that led his family from Douglasdale earlier in the year to command the garrison of Berwick Castle. A raw, icy chill permeated his very being every time he thought of Berwick on Tweed the last of March, 1296.

William went to Edinburgh and Holyrood Abbey in early June as promised; accompanied by his wife they stayed at their Douglas manor in nearby Glencorse. The laird and his lady spent some days together while the children remained in Douglasdale with their nurses and servants. Ellie and Ana were seeing to the unpacking of her trunk; choosing her surcotes for visiting the royal burgh. A grimace came across her face, "Oh Ana, the sickness with child this must be!" running for the latrine. "With all these children thus about would that this sickness thus avoid me?" she asked poignantly. "Ana will find your knight; the healing will he do for you my lamb." She went about and retrieved Gilley; "A lad or lass to come, your wife with child; the usual manor of her sickness is about I fear," she told him. Gilley was surprised; he had no thought of another heir for Douglasdale. "Ellie, dear lass; when did you know?" he asked her as he brought in his healing box to help her. She just shook her head weakly; "As we rode out of Berwick did I know," she said sadly. "A child to come when so many others were lost that dreadful day." He shook his head knowing the Celtic way so true; the sadness of death too hard to bear that God does give us cheer with others to be born.

William was thrilled by Ellie's news and made some plans to honor the fine tidings in Edinburgh with his bride. He decided that they would stay at the de Ferrers manor in the Royal Burgh for the night to take in some feasting and entertainment. "The mournful pledge that I must make will take few hours," he told her, "But followed now some pleasure from this journey; your good words of family now to celebrate, sure aye!" He and several other noblemen would swear their fealty on this 10th of June; before the Bishop they promised to serve Edward against his enemies, upon pain of lands or person. First to come and sign in Holyrood Abbey was William de Douglas, miles (knight); then Waltier Logan conte de Lanark; another Robert Muschance; all to put their seals as pledge in fealty to their new sovereign; that they should retain their lands. Lord Douglas did not linger from the ceremony that he so loathed; but hurried on to meet his wife, and remove the foul taste of contempt he held for Edward and the words he was forced to say. When a man is made to pledge with threats so prevalent;

MY TRUTH LIES IN THE RUINS

neither my God nor Justiciar would thus enforce the false word that was given, William reflected to himself as he made his way out of the abbey. Finished with the distasteful business Gilley had better things on his mind: to meet his bride; to share in merriment her joyous news of another Douglas heir.

Figure XCIII-Part Three; page 32 of the Ragman Roll of 1296; signed by seal, entered as William de Douglas, chevalier in Edinburgh 10 June, noted on the second line form the bottom of this image; document used by permission, National Archives, Kew, Surrey England

Douglasdale August 1296

William spent the summer days with his family. He taught James some tricks at archery; taking him hunting almost every morning to try his skill. Muriel would have lessons from her father in horsemanship. He bought a small mare for her to learn to ride using James' old saddle; she was not to learn side saddle until she mastered what William deemed proper horsemanship for a Douglas lass. For the other children, Amy and little Hugh, he took them walking in the park of Douglas Castle with his wife; accompanied by their silly Deerhound running all about. With Ellie at his side William rode for hours; at the Falls on the Clyde one day they had a picnic with good wine and much food; he told her stories from Celtic lore; read poetry to his bride. He was Gilley; trying hard to regain his love of life, and bury those memories of Berwick with the bodies of the dead. "Ellie, the Celts do know of time and happiness; when there is joy in the life we share each day, time flies. These last three months have passed most quickly; so pleasing to this knight, returning home to Douglasdale has been such paradise." Ellie snuggled into him as they sat by the falls, listening to rush of the deep waters as they cascaded over the rocks beneath the surface. As the Clyde wound her way down and around the crag, the peaceful sounds of the constant showering engulfed them in soft harmony with their surroundings. "Lord Will," she smiled, "Your wife is most content to live here in our Scotland; not to return to Essex in this life; this is my own paradise this day," she cooed.

Gilley understood her words; they were true enough but Ellie was trying to let him know that if they lost their lands in England for his rebellious course, it was not a tragedy to her. He responded to her unsaid words; reassuring her about their lands and income in Essex and Northumbria. "Your husband will be granted his request; our lands to be repledged, seized to us again. On the morrow must I leave for Berwick. What do you think of our James to accompany his father to this Parliament?" he asked her. Ellie giggled, "Another fur hat to spare for him do you have; he has grown so since the first one that we gave him?" she asked in jest remembering his penchant for the attire of his father. "Ellie, another fur hat shall he have!" He helped his wife mount her jennet and just held her hand like those first days of their courting. "Ellie, the passing of each day does this knight know how fortunate a man he was to marry one as fair and brave as you my lass." Ellie leaned down from her horse to kiss him, speaking to him quietly, "Lord Will no man could I love more. Will you love me tomorrow as you love me today?"

Berwick 28th August 1296

Lord Douglas and his son left for Berwick in late August while Lady Douglas remained behind. William only went as was required; to pledge his fealty to King Edward, a ruse to regain his lands and income. As Willelmi, dominus de Duglas, he put his seal to the Ragman Roll. As the wax hardened he looked up to see the two English knights who stood witness to the grave event and this ultimate humiliation of Scottish lairds. One of these witnesses was Ellie's kin and William's benefactor at Knaresburgh, Johannis de Hastings; Gilley acknowledged him with a brief yet courteous exchange. The other witness was an old nemesis and adversary, Gilbert, Earl of Angus and Lord of Redesdale. William's furled brow and icy stare said what words could not. As he stood before de Umfraville, William looked right through the smaller man; as if piercing his armor with the stone cold glare a patriot gives a traitor to his homeland.

On August 30th their lands in Scotland were restored by a writ issued in Berwick. At home in Douglasdale Ellie waited nervously for the return of her husband and James; even the formalities of Scotland's implied surrender were unsettling to her. More frightening than the unconscionable ceremony were the memories of her last days in Berwick. Ellie besieged St. Bride with daily prayers that she would never again return to the site of the massacre of Scots; it was too much for her to bear. Her decision not travel with William was not because she was with child. Ellie confessed her true reason to

MY TRUTH LIES IN THE RUINS

William. She happily chose the comfort of Douglas Castle; disdaining a revisit to the macabre site of the Royal Burgh. Ellie held an unparalleled sadness within her; a personal guilt for the slaughter at Berwick that chilled her very soul. When ever she recalled the events of March 30th, and that was often now, the images brought her nightmares of Lovaine banners and pennons waving proudly while the murder of innocent men, women and children continued long into the night. The paralyzing site of her family's armorial achievements, raised proudly by her father's men at arms, woke her frequently from an already fitful sleep.

Figure XCIV-Part Three; three Douglas seals from the Ragman Roll, August 1296 Berwick on Tweed; from left to right, Willelmi dominus de Duglas (Sir William le Hardi), William son of Andrew de Duglas and Freskin de Douglas of Linlithgow. Images of Seals from the National Archives, Kew, Surrey, England.

Each day now when Ellie walked about Douglas Castle, she thought she perceived that odd asphyxiating smell; that acrid stench that lingers in a person's memory when they first smell death. She could not shake the visual reminders either; the scenes were perfectly etched in mind and did not relent. She discarded her blood stained shoes by burning them in a sort of strange ritual. She tried every thing to avoid thinking about that Saturday morning, the last of March. But all she saw when she closed her eyes were the cart paths she was forced to walk through; strewn with bodies, piled high of mangled limbs and other carnage draining into gory pools of human blood. Each day as she put on her new shoes she remembered why she had to burn the old ones. No matter what she did to avert the painful memories, the functions of daily life reminded her. The irony of citizens at work, doing their daily chores; then savagely struck down as they performed their normal, every day activities confused and devastated her. Just today as she reviewed the orders with the cellarer at Douglas Castle the image of the old ale merchant in Berwick, sitting on a hogshead outside the doors of his shop came to her mind. He just sat there most dead but with a strange and peaceful grimace on his countenance she recalled. Everything she did to forget the massacre only seemed to remind her of Berwick.

The Douglas children were also tragically effected by those scenes of devastation. James and Muriel remembered every detail too they told her while little Amy yet cried out in the night from wicked dreams as she revisited the horrors of Berwick. The Douglases were days west of the royal burgh and the castle; but they brought with them to their Douglasdale the carnage that yet lingered in their dreams and daily thoughts. Ellie acknowledged that the tragedy greatly affected her. She also understood the devastating impact the massacre had on her children. But what of Gilley she wondered? Her husband was strangely quiet; his memories of Berwick he held back, deep within him. When Ellie told him of her feelings, why she would not accompany him to the royal burgh, he turned away from her; shielding his thoughts from her. His silence, his private world of self loathing, was building barriers to their love and lives.

Edward was returning home to England; he made his plans for his new kingdome, leaving English lords in place of Scottish nobles where ever he could place them. He had publicly humiliated John Balliol and removed this sorry king to the custody of the Tower of London. With him went the Regalia of Scotland, all but the scepter of the king which was symbolically broken; destroyed for all to see. But Edward Plantagenet did not get the Stone of Destiny; thanks to the bold plan of Bishop Wishart and the brave work of some of Scotland's nobles, great patriots all. The Coronation Stone King Edward captured and removed to England as his own was an imposter; as much a fake as the benevolent king who took it from the Scots.

September 1296

William and James finally rode the length of the drawbridge and under the portcullis, into Douglas Castle with only their men at arms in their company. Gilley remained longer in Berwick than originally intended, waiting for their English lands to be repledged. By early September he successfully received fair writs in decision; restoration of his charters in Northumbria and Ellie's two manors in Essex and dower lands in Hereford as well, from his king; No! not *my* king he fumed as he reflected on his achievements. He found his wife in the great hall alone with Ana; the other children were in their chambers fast asleep. "So late my William, is everything what you had hoped for our good justice?" He shook his head yes, but ruefully. "Ellie, the lands are thus restored; few Scots with lands in England can so state." The knight with heavy heart sat down next to her. "To pledge again my fealty, to appear once more in council with that madman brings my blood to boil; my truth thus compromised with every word I speak." He told her that again they must report for Parliament in St. Edmonds on All Saints, "the day of our Muriel's good birth, November 1st. Were it not for our son James and his good council I would have left without the seizing of our lands to us; that I know."

Ellie's grief for her husband brought tears to her eyes; nothing she could do or say would cheer him. The horror from the brokered truce at Berwick castle that Edward cast aside for grotesque slaughter; Edward's vile ambition and broken promises lo six months ago, caused guilt in William that would destroy his very soul she feared. Over and over she pondered the gravities of that brutal day. William poured himself and James some wine and offered some to his wife; then to Ana sitting there as well. The ladies both accepted what was poured; fearing to upset him if they refused. "There are some of your favorite cakes I had most ordered for your return to Douglasdale," Ellie told him, offering to have them brought from the kitchen. "No food for this knight, wine is mine to have and plenty of it!" William's anger was startling to them; he had left in such good cheer. James as if reading their thoughts began to tell them why. "When first that we arrived outside of Berwick we found the crowds gathering near the gates; stone walls to begin construction by Edward beside the embankments where small lengths of wooden palisade once stood. Inside the gates the carnage of the slaughter still remained out in the open! The bodies of our friends left to rot and feed as fodder to the vermin," he said in grieving tones. William spoke his venom that increased with every syllable. With tears in his eyes the proud warrior spewed his mangled words of torment. "The disdain for the lives of these good citizens; their bodies not yet interred though five lang months have come and gone since they most passed to the Otherworld. Dear Edward thinks of Scots as animals in squalor."

Ellie was stunned; how could they not have buried the dead she wondered in horror. James spoke as his father fell silent. "The sight of these proud patriots not laid to rest made all the worse with stench and filth that comes when bodies are left so unattended. The many men to scurry now about to put them to their gory rest; it was defaming to us all, I was so angry," young James said with unbridled scorn. The silence that filled the room now moved Ellie to excuse herself, to retire to their chamber. Ana joined Ellie as they went up the stairs to prepare her for the slumber of her night. Then a knock at the chamber door: a scented bath was being brought by the servants, surprising Ellie that William would have ordered it for their pleasure. The ebb and flow, the highs and lows of his humor told of a tortuous state of mind, she mused.

Figure XCV-Part Three; a castle would employ a pulley system to distribute water in large quantities to upper levels of the tower; an example on exhibit at Castle Rushen, Isle of Mann

Ana finished combing her lamb's hair as Lord Douglas entered the chamber followed by the kitchen servants with carafes of wine and platters of food and the cinnamon cakes that Ellie planned for his arrival. "Goodnight dear Ana," he said as she walked past him through the door. She nodded and smiled; pleased that he decided to join food and pleasure with the wine he was consuming. The couple was alone and Ellie told him that she would help with his undressing; dismissing his valet so they could have their privacy this night. She began to remove first his coif then the fermail, his mail hauberk that he wore over a gambeson. As if reading her mind, "These are unsettled times; full armaments must we wear when not on Douglas Castle's lands," he said respectfully and then bellowed, "Another gift of dear Edward's peace."

He brought them each another glass of wine; encouraging her to join him which she did. "Ellie, your kind patience with this laird is never mentioned by my sorry self," he said to her as she continued to remove his sword belt and then his surcote. With only his thin silk cote yet covering his body he turned round to face her. He removed her robe of chamber; suggesting that they both share the scented bath. In the soft light of the fireplace Gilley could see the curved softness of her body and the child she carried. "The only joy from that fateful Berwick morning six months ago just after Easter last," he said softly, "our sweet child that braves this world to join us by Christmas I would guess; but so large are you this day!" She told him that she is sure her time for lay-in late December; but she was surprised by her great size as well. "A large laddie by his sturdy size within me; and more the way he kicks to let me know he's there. I am sure this child another son to come, one Archibald," she told him confidently, using the name they had chosen in honor of his grandfather and dear brother lost at so young an age.

Lord Douglas and Lady Douglas felt the months of sadness lift some as they sat in the large steaming tub; even their conversation seemed more like their own than it had been since last March. They sparred a bit as well. Then Gilley spoke words she had not heard for some weeks perhaps or longer. "My Lady El, what can I say to you that has not been said afore, in love with you I am so still." He moved closer to her, "Your eyes warm my soul with their infinite love and your mouth welcomes me with the open arms of a lover's kiss, your hands to touch me as no other dares; and when I am with you there is nothing else I do desire." He kissed her and held her to him. "Such kind thoughts have I so missed these many days and more, Lord Will; I love you so much, that my soul has ached to hear your words so spoken this night." Ellie talked on about the family and their son yet to come. Then feeling the time was right she said, "Gilley, come the spring would I enjoy again a journey to our Morayshire; Kinloss's fair beauty or the charm of the Black Isle to cheer our family from these months of sad treachery. Gilley got up to dry himself and handed Ellie her velvet chamber robe. "The sad news I must share; our kin Sir Andrew de Moray and his brave son and squire also Andrew were captured at Dunbar. Sir Andrew is now held in the Edward's Tower of London with our former king; his son they tell me held in ward as well, I know not where of certain, perhaps in Chester Castle," he told his wife. Ellie started to cry; so much had changed, so many families destroyed by Edward, she could not find the words to express her sentiments. Gilley began to speak again but of another matter that was more pressing to him. "I have some words to share with you; perhaps it is the wine that I do this now, the timing not of order."

He brought her to sit by him on their bed, so he could look into her eyes by glow of candle light. "Ellie, I have never told you how proud I was, your bravery six lang months ago; to bring our family west while I in ward in

Hogs Tower, a guest of our new king, dear Edward." She cuddled into his shoulder, resting her head on his chest. "Lord Will it was you so brave to stay alone, giving yourself as surety for our flight with the proud men of the garrison," she told him. "No other action could you take but the one you chose; Scotland's army plundering in northern England; no help to Berwick's citizens or the governor of Berwick's castle," she said slowly, quietly to reinforce the truth of her words.

Gilley poured them more wine; showing signs of the vast quantity he consumed with little food. Then he brought his sword newly made, stored in his war-chest; to lay it on the bed behind them. Ellie was confused by his last move, but waited for his words to explain the action. "Lady El, some foolish men thus told me an English lass can not be the lady of our Douglasdale," his continued, his words taking on a more serious tone, "You must be told by this humble knight: you have earned well to be a Douglas and true Scot; such bravery and great courage that kept our family safe from Edward's violence and wrath. There is an old Celtic ritual I would share with you to make it right and true." He was sitting on her left side and brought round the sword, holding her left hand in his right. "Lord Will, I do not doubt your fine words, but the wine has clouded your thinking; what ever would you do with that war-sword?" Gilley looked at the sword in his left hand and put it back on the bed. "Perhaps this dagger you had given me my birthday when in Knaresburgh, 40 years and 40 more, would work the better for ceremony thus intended."

He told her that she would be a true Douglas, that they would mix their blood. "A cross of St. Andrew do I put on the thumb of my bride to touch my right thumb, now with the same sweet cross of Scotland's saint." He put their thumbs together, left on right that joined their blood as one. "There, a true Douglas you are now, my dear wife and love for all eternity. "Lord Will, to see my own sad father bring Lovaine horsemen and foot soldiers to do harm of slaughter into Berwick; I decided then and then, a Scottish lass was I to my last breath. I love you with all my soul and Douglasdale is my true home, my dear husband and sweet knight."

Douglasdale, December 27th 1296

The November Parliament in St. Edmonds came and went; Sir William of Douglas retained all his lands and possessions by so attending. Now it was late December and William and James were sitting at the games table near the fire in the withdrawing room hovered over a board of Merels. It was snowing heavily in Douglasdale and the winds were blowing hard sending a strange howl through the chimney of the fireplace behind them. In the stone walls of a castle the temperature stays the same most every day; little change

MY TRUTH LIES IN THE RUINS

comes within the walls. Tonight a fire burned of wood and peat to break the dampened chill of the windy evening. Ellie had just finished mending a tapestry; she began applying the arms of the chief on another smaller one that would hang in the nursery for the child still growing within her. Young Hugh was playing quietly with the old blocks that a younger James once had to occupy his time eight years ago; Shamus cuddled into him on the floor. An eight year old beauty, young Muriel was applying fine embroidery to her new cloak received last week from the tailor in Edinburgh. "Papa," said little Amy coming up to her father; she held onto his knee as she peered at the board game they were playing. "May Amy come sit?" Gilley opened his arms to welcome his wee daughter to his lap. "You may watch sweet lass, but to yet learn this game in years to come, not the noo." William loved his children, as much as he loved his wife, almost as he loved himself. These days not much would cheer him for any length of time; the shadows of Berwick still provoked a loss of sleep and isolated him from those he loved.

"Tomorrow will I ride with Thomas Dickson to Carstairs Castle Torres to meet with men you would know by name," he said to his wife. James was still seated at the games table; the other children having said good night were most asleep in chamber. "With my lay-in so close, you would take your leave my husband?" Ellie asked him. Gilley rose and closed the heavy oak doors of the withdrawing room.

Figure XCVI-Part Three; Carstairs Parish Church stands in the middle of the village common near the site of the 13th century Castle Torres once held by the Bishop of Glasgow. The stones from the old castle were said to be used in the construction of this old kirk.

"Eleanora, this meeting is of secret work before us; to meet in days so near our Christmas and Hogmanay not to raise suspicion in our deeds. I must go to speak with these good barons, men of thoughts reflective of my own; I am not one to be idle in our cause for Scotland." Gilley turned to his son, just four years to come and he would be a squire he reflected. "James, your mother will rely on your good sense; should Archibald decide his time to come into our troubled world you must ride my smaller palfrey to the castle of Bishop Wishart where we meet. Travel only with my steward Sir Andrew and his squire; one knight this Andrew you may always trust in word and action, sure aye." James told them both he would be most proud to be of help to his dear mother. "I know the ride from having stayed there on our journey west from Berwick Castle. I can find it in my sleep should need arise," he said with confidence. "It is done," said Gilley.

Ellie's dreadful look betrayed her thoughts; their lives were changed, a rebel would her husband be against the king. "My dear wife, these many months since I was governor to surrender Berwick have I struggled with my pride and painful guilt of that decision." He continued speaking, with James listening closely to his words as well. "Restoring lands, castles, messuages and rents to our dear family would have kept this knight's pledge of fealty true; had but Edward let the good citizens of Berwick live, not slaughtered in their beds as he would do." Pouring himself another glass of wine and filling her glass, he poured one for his son as well; continuing his words to them. "These good barons and brave bishop with others of their knights that owe allegiance have plans that once commenced might relieve Lord Douglas of his painful memories."

Gilley's words trailed off, as the sad grimace on his face revealed a mournful heart. Ellie rose to put her arms around her husband. "Lord Will, the plans you make will I support as wife of the laird of Douglas, witness to that barbarous attack on friends and kin; citizens of that fine burgh. We must discuss your thoughts when you return." Then looking at James, "James and Lady Douglas will stand bravely for their laird. And God willing, young Archibald will but patiently await your good return," she said softly. He kissed her on the head. "Lady El, I made the best choice for a wife a husband could thus make when I chose you for my bride, mother of our children." And looking over to James, he opened his arms, motioning his son closer to them. "Dear lad, you make your father proud this day as well," Gilley told him, hugging both his wife and son; a fortunate man to have such loving family he said to himself.

Gilley rode off to Carstairs with just his vassal Thomas Dickson as he planned not to raise alarm of his intentions. Ellie remained in chamber with Sir Shamus warming William's side of the bed till his return. I do hope he comes home the morrow early, she sighed. There was a light knock on her chamber door; it was James and she invited him to enter. "Mother, just how are you feeling this day?" he asked her. She motioned for him to draw the chair and sit next to the bed. "Dear James, I fear so for your father as he meets with others that plan treason," she said to him. "Your brave self I need to get me through this day." James began to speak in low tones to her, "Mother, word has come in the village of young Andrew de Moray, son of the Justiciar captured with his father at Dunbar. He has made escape from Chester Castle; and may join with others in the north calling for rebellion." Ellie looked at the ten year old lad; a young squire he was fast approaching though his age did not reflect his maturity and brave spirit. "The winds of war are coming with the spring; many will consider; more will take up arms against the king," she predicted with misgivings.

Figure XCVII-Part Three; the North Rising led by the squire Andrew de Moray is commemorated the last Saturday in May at this memorial site on the motte of Ormond Castle, Avoch

"I have a story to share with your wee self my son; of first I met your father; what makes me worry so the now." Ellie began by telling him of Lord de Ferrers, the English baron twenty-eight years her senior, of fierce temperament and little time for his young wife. Then when he died, the lands, manors and castles were so divided for her dower that she would go to Scotland to claim her rents. "The manors in Essex and Hereford that you know from our journeys there; the castle in Leuchars and a manor house in Berwick, with the other smaller manors in Ayrshire, Wigtonshire, and Kirkcudbrightshire where we stayed are the Scottish estates of my dower,"

Ellie said, continuing, "We arrived at Fawside Castle safely; filled with wonderment and expectations. Elena de la Zouche kin of the de Ferrers set upon us a speywife from Winton." James listened intently as his mother explained how this woman described her grievous marriage to de Ferrers and then warned her not again to marry; telling her that her husband would be murdered by a king with the name of Edward. "So my son, this worrisome news so many years ago your father told me not to tarry for there was not King Edward then of Scotland; that fair sentiment has changed with Edward's campaign in Scotland. Now you know my fears dear James; that old woman's words haunt me so."

James told her that the memories of Berwick have changed his father. "He is not the man that led the garrison to sink English ships in the Tweed that fateful day. Now a shadow of himself; he seeks redemption of some kind I fear." Ellie looked at the young man, imparting wisdom far beyond his years. "Your words are true; we share the thoughts the same I know now. We can only pray to our God and dear St. Bride to watch over our sweet knight your father and my husband." James came closer and hugged his mother. "Thank you for your honestly of words; your faith in me your son will most be honored, and not a word of this to anyone will I speak.

Ellie woke in the early hours the next day, William's side of the bed still occupied by Sir Shamus. These pains first telling of my son to come she sighed to herself. "Ana, are you so close that you might hear my words," she called loudly. Ana opened the door, having slept outside her girl's chamber through the night. "No word of Sir William yet M' Lady, would you to go to lay-in now my love?" asked Ana. James entered the chamber, with Muriel beside him. "Mother, I have my Fortis ready for the ride to Carstairs, faster than our father's palfrey; Sir Andrew is most here already to ride with me and his squire too now comes here." Ellie was calm but knew there was not lang time to wait. "Go the noo, my James; Ana and Muriel to attend with the good midwives of Douglasdale should your father be detained the more." James kissed her on the cheek, "Lady El, dear mother, I command young Archibald to wait," he said with a big grin, "until you see five Douglas horsemen with Douglas banners blazoned can he come into this world!"

Muriel went directly to the lay-in room to ready it for her mother; then she and Ana assisted Ellie into the room beside the laird's chamber, in the donjon tower that adjoined the keep. This is where young Archibald would be born Ellie said to herself as she lay down on the bed. "Mother, shall I at once inform the midwives your time is here?" asked Muriel. Ellie was feeling great pains; remembering now this the first birth to be without her husband; midwife to his girl the six before. Ana motioned to Muriel to find the midwives from the village, "There now my girl, your husband has thus left your Ana with some herbs to relieve those discomforts from your lay-in." Ellie smiled, shaking her head in her resolve, "Dear Ana, this large laddie wants to come the noo I fear; I do pray my William soon to be here!" Ana wiped her brow already wet with struggle of the child that wants to join the world this day. Shamus was heard barking; coming up the stairs with Muriel and a Celtic midwife from the village, a speywife William knew and trusted. "Good you came so speedily my dear Isabel; my husband off on morning hunt this day," she told the midwife, concealing her husband's absence for his clandestine work in Carstairs.

Ana and Isabel reviewed the preparations of the lay-in. Muriel went to the kitchen to inquire about the wine for the others and a tasine for the mother. It was only two hours passed that James now left us she mused. Then suddenly a sound of a lowering of the drawbridge, "Pray that is father with our James," Muriel said out loud. Gilley was riding his palfrey hard; his supertunic flowing wildly behind him in the wind, while his noble horse sped on to Douglasdale. The doors to the great hall opened; the men at arms announced the arrival of Lord Douglas. Muriel peered out into the courtyard to see her father leading the charging horsemen, horse's hooves pounded on the wooden bridge, Douglas banners furled proudly onward, his son and vassals were but a short distance now behind him. At full gallop, under the portcullis he flew. A sight to see was this knight and father; in more the hurry than his young son to come he prayed! Gilley barely leapt from his horse as he threw off his sword belt and riding cloak to his greeting squire. "Muriel, come with me the noo!" he bellowed at his daughter. "Our James thus met us on the road from Carstairs; riding hard we arrived the sooner!" Muriel quickly told him that Archibald had yet not yet come. Three strides, six stairs and he was on the landing, two more, then three and he was near the family chambers, running fast to his wife's side. Gilley swung open the door of the lay-in, rushed in with bold intent; still wearing his mail, the coif and hauberk of a knight in armor, the father to be presented a stirring image as came to her bedside. Ellie started laughing; shaking her head as she looked him up and down. "Was le Hardi or young Archibald, a contest who arrives the sooner; Lord Douglas wins the first of such encounters with little time to spare I fear!" said Ellie, forgetting the armor he wore; happy and relieved to have Gilley at her side.

Ana told him how soon the pains were advancing; then she too started to laugh at his appearance. "Perhaps time it is to remove armaments Sir William; the laddie coming might decide the better to wait seeing one so fierce a knight as you!" Gilley looked down in startled amazement and laughed when he saw he was still wearing mail armor. "Good Ana, you remind me of my foolish self. It is time that I must wash and pray before this matter of a birth to do. Thank you for your good counseling," he said, leaving the lay-in for a few minutes to prepare himself for the work at hand.

Ellie told Ana how relieved she was; and pleased that he would welcome his son into the world himself. James and Muriel came to her side. "We can bring in Hugh and Amy to keep you company as well dear mother should the need to be more crowded," teased Muriel, the three of them laughing; calmed by their father's arrival. Gilley returned to the lay-in, "Lord Douglas will thus preside; all others but our Ana, take your leave, the noo!" Ellie chuckled, "William is William;" and happily, "my husband now is back in Douglasdale, praise be to St. Bride for that!"

Gilley was home but one hour when young Archibald came into the world. "As large a lad or lass just born as we have ever seen, my wife; soon I will return," he exclaimed, taking the wee laddie to the chapel next to the laird's chamber. "I baptize thee in the name of the Father, the Son, and the Holy Ghost, dear Archibald," first in Latin, then in Lallans, holding separate the left hand of his son, the unblessed one for a knight to do his work, Gilley mused; repeating the ritual he used for all his sons before this wee lad. "What fateful time of Scotland's sad events have you chosen to begin your sweet life. These matters of grave treachery with ambitious English lords who would steal our freedom; a brave laddie you must be," said Gilley. Then he looked over this giant of a son with the red and black streaked hair and eyes already darkening to a shade of brown. "You uncle Hugh would hold you now to say, your father is the one you most have likeness," chucking as he realized the laddie looked just like his own image when he was born, if his mother's stories were true.

Gilley returned to the lay-in to give his wee son to the midwife for the bathing. "Ellie, I must take more stitching now I fear; the laddie did some hurt to your fair self when thus he made his sweet appearance." Ellie was looking up at him, glowing with the knowledge of another son; not listening to her husband's words. "Our son, the dark red hair; and so large a lad as he!" she marveled. Gilley looked up from his healing work, "He is the very likeness of his father; the size and hair all true in image to one name William!" he chuckled. The happiness they shared with the arrival of their new son seemed to renew their spirit; rekindle their love. "Lord Will, to see you coming through the door short time ago; it was a blessed sight for me!" she giggled as he sat down next to her on the bed. Gilley smoothed her hair from her face. He held her hands in his and kissed her on the mouth. "I love you Lady El with all my heart for the ages; all my intellect of time, I am humbled by your love, my one and only," he paused as she interrupted his words. Ellie told him quietly. "I thought I had lost your love these last long months since Berwick; yet this day's good cheer renews our vows of sacrament so long ago. I love you too with all my heart and soul for God's eternity, humbly grateful for your love Lord Will."

1297 February 14th

With the cruel year of 1296 behind them, Archibald was christened in January 1297; Alexander de Lindsay was chosen as the laddie's God father and was happy to attend the ceremony. Hogmanay had come and gone though it was not as opulent as years before. But the good men of Douglasdale, their families too, were most aware of the reason; Edward Plantagenet had usurped Scotland's throne and kingship, stealing freedom and prosperity from its proud citizens. With February half over and the lean times of winter still upon them, Ellie was surprised to hear Gilley announce this morning that he and James were traveling to Edinburgh for shopping. "That we will take our leave the week next for some necessity of purchase," he said. Ellie guessed at once he meant their anniversary; they would be nine years married in early April. But why would he leave so early for his shopping she wondered.

Gilley read her face to know her thoughts, saying quietly, "Another matter to discuss in Carstairs on our journey's way to Edinburgh will I stop the night." Ellie sighed deeply, knowing the spring would bring more of such trips or worse a battle with the English; her own countrymen. "Lord Will, can these men be trusted for their honesty, their words of secrecy?" she asked him. Gilley came closer to her, barely whispering he said, "We have formed a band, a secret agreement of support against Lord Edward. But as for their oaths, I can only say my truth; even the most accurate of words are lies, they but point to the reality. I would not know nor can predict their allegiance under fire and sword of one Edward." He reached down and brought her up in his arms, they stood together and held each other very tightly. "My dear husband, I am much worried for our future; the months ahead I dread." Gilley removed her veil, letting down her plaited hair, "Shhh now my dear bride; the future is yet to be, the now is what we make it." He began to play with her brooch closure on surcote, she wiggled from his grasp. He smiled at her playfulness; her seduction by refusal, the game they played.

"I have surprised you then this day, for St. Valentine's good cheer do I now give you," she said reflecting his apparent change in mood, bringing out a small painted parchment of cupids and cherubs, reds and whites with gold lettering of simple words, I love you; all hand painted by his bride. Gilley chuckled as he read it. "You thought I might forget this day, a celebration of our love?" Then he brought out a small scroll and presented it gallantly on bended knee, "From your poet knight Lady El," he said, as he began to read out loud his words of verse.

DEBORAH RICHMOND FOULKES

A partnership of love supreme
Has carried me this day

To find you sitting comfortably
That sets our mirth this way

I find the words for you so dear
Then I can truly play

My thoughts of all the days we've known
The first so far away

For so many days have given us
Bold courage now to say

We are truly two in one
The presence of our stay

Then rising to his feet he reached for his girl and lifted her up high above his shoulders, both lovers giggling and laughing all the while, at play. "Put me down Sholto beast!" She teased him. He ignored her words of protest and threw her happily over his shoulder, carrying her up to their chamber to celebrate their love in private.

This same day Edward Plantagenet sent Euphemia, Countess de Ros a valentine; her husband the Earl yet a guest in Edward's Tower of London for his treason at Dunbar. The countess would justify her unseemly actions with the king; her choice to make, to save her dear family and estates at any cost to her good name. England and Scotland once two countries with common borders, became now one with common enemies; each other of their kin and friends to choose allegiance in the fight; which lands to fight for, which to forfeit in the end. Young de Ferrers would fight the family of his kin in Scotland to lose his lands and castles there, the largest landowner to thus forfeit; his English lands with liens and highly mortgaged, sold post mortem to pay his debts of war. Nicky de Segrave would twice switch sides, English then to Scots, later to capitulate to Edward, to compromise his life's years and health of body for service to his king. And Josh de Hastings would recall one wee Scottish laddie, his slight lisp and pleasant manner that he met at Knaresburgh some years ago; to abscond with supplies intended for de Hastings and Brodick Castle and compromise his safety in the end as well to die too early from this life. All adversities could have been averted; the sad tragedy from greed and blind ambition of one pagan despot king, Lord Edward Plantagenet.

Edinburgh

Leaving Carstairs in the wee morning hours, the riders fought a bitter cold wind and light snow. James asked him if they should turn back to Douglasdale to go another day to Edinburgh. "No my son, it is the now we must go; for later times there will be other tasks before us." James thought for some time before asking William about the clandestine events at Carstairs. "Father, the men attending; they are all united in their actions now to take?" he asked. William rode in silence for some time before he offered his son a reply. "James, when one's own way of life and lands are at risk, some find it difficult to part their ways with income and the comforts of their homes. For my truth there is no other way; a stand must now be taken. The when and where to draw our line remains the only question for your father," said William. He went on to explain that even the most pious of men can be manipulated when one puts lands and coinage above one's principles and honor. "Without core values, my own humble life would not be worth the living; without God's good grace I would feel a hollow to my soul," he told his son.

William brought James into the currier's shop. "You are fast approaching such a time when a sword belt you must learn to wear. As you have done so well with the squires' work of strengthening; holding your sword straight and true for hours in your training; a reward so due to one named James," said Gilley, pointing to a fine selection for his son to choose, "A good sword belt with some length to grow, sure aye!" said Gilley. James' eyes grew large, "I can choose from one of these fine belts, dear father?" he asked surprised at the reason for their stopping at this merchant's shop. His father looked with pride as James selected the very belt his father wanted for his son. "A good preference do you have; we will take this for your birthday." James carried his treasured belt himself; not wanting to let go of it. Father and son continued on their journey to purchase Ellie's gift celebrating their marriage. The merchant's shop of tapestries drew Gilley's attention. He and James went through many piles and looked at many colors until one in green and blue with gold caught their eye. "This one father, of the castle on the loch, with the birds in flight," said James excitedly. Gilley knew his son was true in his words; Ellie would delight in this fine tapestry. "It is done," said Gilley. "Come now, let us feast and make our rest tonight in Livingston, at our wee manor there. It is most important James that you recall our lands and their location; without charters, committing them to memory. Three days the week you must sit with our good steward and your mother; review the lists; know the boundaries of every carucate and messuage," said Gilley. "On the morrow we will ride to see my dear sister and her daughters; staying there the night."

    The next day Gilley, James, and Sir Andrew were all feasting with Willelma at her manor of Dalserf. "So long ago it seems that we last celebrated at our Douglasdale," she said to her younger brother. "What think you James of a Ceilidh for our Douglas Clan to hold around your birthday?" asked Gilley of his oldest son. James told him that all would welcome a time for feasting and celebration to blur the grimness of the English occupation. "It is done," he said, "Lord Douglas will arrange with our good Sir Andrew here a Ceilidh now to come. We will send out messengers to invite our many guests and family the week next!" he said in mocking tones of his baronial decision. "Willa, you and your sweet daughters too must join us." His sister was thrilled with the prospect of some fun, Douglas style at Douglas Castle. "That my dear William were still alive; would he love to come, I miss him so these days."

Figure XCVIII-Part Three; Dalserf Kirk is still an active parish church near the surviving mains or demesne buildings of Dalserf Manor

James and his father departed with their men at arms and arrived at Douglas Castle in a few short hours. "Mother, a Ceilidh is now planned!" said James enthusiastically as he entered the great hall with his father. Shamus was rolling about the floor with Amy and Hugh until he spotted James; then galloped for his favorite lad. "Good hound, Sir Shamus; a fair celebration now is coming. Great feasting for our family and friends," said James gleefully, dancing with the Deerhound as he stood on hind legs, they bounded about the great hall gleefully. "Oh mother, is it true?" asked Muriel. "Are we to have a Ceilidh? Ellie was smiling broadly, happy with the thought of dancing and feasting; to fill their home with family and friends. "If Lord Douglas wants a celebration, a Ceilidh shall we have." "It is done," said Ana, coming down the stairs from the family chambers. Gilley burst out in laughter hearing Ana's uncharacteristic words that mocked his own. Soon everyone was caught up in the exciting prospect of some happy times.

Three days of celebration; two birthdays and an anniversary of their vows some nine years ago at Kelso Abbey happily took place as planned. Many guests from Douglasdale and the surrounding countryside arrived as did the de Lindsays, the Stewarts, and the ladies of Dalserf. Sir Andrew and his Lady Amy joined them as well. The only ones so missing from their happy crowd were the Andrew de Morays: the knight was still held in Edward's tower while his brave son and squire organized rebellion in the north. There was music and dancing and feasting. And for three days there was no talk of Edward; there was no mention of Berwick. The minstrels in the gallery played the small pipes with fiddles and a dulcimer as well. Platters of roasted capons and eels with sticky sauce graced the tables; wild boar filled the bellies of their guests. Hog-heads full of fine wines were emptied as magic acts were performed between each course. For the three days of celebrations the guests and the entire Douglas household consumed two boars, four carcasses of beef, four does, six pigs and seventy fowl of capons and some hens. Nine geese were also added to the tables and platters of fish of many types including salmon and much eel; with many breads and cheeses to enjoy. Ale too was served with more than forty gallons of red wine and some small quantity of white. The Scots celebrated and rejoiced; the Douglas family was at peace in their beloved Douglasdale.

Ellie was thrilled with the lovely tapestry Gilley gave her for their anniversary and had it mounted on the wall of the laird's chamber near her bed the day next. "James, your father says that it was your keen sight that found this lovely gift for me; I do love it so!" Then she brought out James' gift to accompany the one his father bought him in Edinburgh. "A sword for you, your very own that was your grandfather's, kept at Fawdon. The blade reformed for your size to use now in your leather sword belt." Muriel had a gift for him as well. "Dear James, a piece of fine embroidery for you to keep wrapped about one thusly," she said, showing him how to wear it. Now it was William's turn to receive his gifts. Little scrolls came from James and Muriel; promises to yet collect some fine deed from his dear children, showing off their prowess with their writing now in French, the language of the court. Ellie feigned disinterest as if she had no gift. Then in came Ana with this large leather sheath, carved and painted, decorated with intricate silver that would hold his new war-sword. "Your artist's hand a true source of joy for me dear wife; one design as only you could do. Your husband is most pleased," he told her, kissing her in view of all the children. "Lord Will, you are most bold to show affection so!" she chided him that he did it once again. "Lady El, your children must all know that we are lovers true; if just from all their number in years so few!" he said, with a broad smile that broke into hearty laughter, joined now by all about him in their laughter.

Early May 1297

Lord Edward was preparing a letter that would direct from Portsmouth fifty Scottish magnates principally in the south of the Forth to summon for a muster. The barons were to meet the King in London and accompany him to Flanders on 7th July. On this list the names all too familiar: William de Douglas and John Wishart; and another name surprising in its mention, one William de Ferrers holding lands in tenement in Scotland. The 24th of May these letters would go out to the good Scots south of the Forth. William le Hardi was not at Douglasdale when his letter arrived from England. He chose to be in Sanquhar in May, routing the English from their stronghold there. Having recently enlisted in rebellion with William Wallace, William le Hardi, Lord Douglas was the first nobleman to join the brave patriot in the fight for Scotland's War for National Independence.

Le Hardi did not conspire with Wallace lightly; he did so after receiving some intriguing news. Word reached the village of Douglas that Sheriff Livingstone, de Hesilrig, with some English soldiers garrisoned at Lanark Castle had been killed by some Scottish rebels. A man named William Wallace holding lands in Ayrshire was the brave Scot who won the day. Lord Douglas dispatched a messenger, a trusted vassal familiar to Wallace. The man at arms was sent in secret from Douglas Castle to find this Lanark rebel and bring him to the laird of Douglas; delivering an invitation to discuss like deeds, not yet done. I wonder now if this man William is the kin of Malcolm Wallace, our good neighbor in Kyle Stewart, thought Gilley to himself. The nights were bright in Lanarkshire so late now, and under cover of darkness must the outlaw Wallace travel; that finally late when most were yet asleep did he arrive at Douglasdale. He brought with him another man from Ayrshire, a knight, Sir David of Pinwherry. These brave Scots came quietly on horseback, first to greet Lord Douglas and his Lady Eleanora in the great hall of Douglas Castle for much needed food and wine.

Figure XCIX-Part Three; a haunting view of the ruined tower of Castle Dangerous, Douglas, Lanarkshire

Gilley asked his guest if he was kin to Malcolm, a tenant of the Guardian and Seneschal of Scotland. Wallace's face brightened now with recognition, "You must be le Hardi who married the Steward's sister, gaining charters to the lands in Kyle Stewart adjacent to our own." Gilley told Wallace that his lands and small manor in Auchinleck were in deed part of the same barony and the source of grave irritation; the mischief making monks of Melrose shutting off the water flowing to his lands. "From dear Edward came this mandate for Lord Douglas: leave the Melrose monks alone. All the while they block the flow of the waters to my lands from where Ayr River joins the Lugar, with no satisfaction for this humble knight!" said Gilley. "Then as if to say Douglas has no rights; they travel from Melrose Abbey to their lands in Mauchline using the park of Douglas Castle as their private way for passage!" Ellie added, "We had to have our dear James, the Steward, and the good Bishop Wishart intercede on our behalf; to settle on the Abbot an agreement for our lands."

Wallace's eyes opened wide at the last name he heard. "You are friends with Bishop Wishart then I see?" he asked them. Gilley was careful to not reveal the nature of his last meeting with the Bishop. "A good friend dear Robert, his castle in Carstairs makes him a frequent visitor to Douglas Castle." Ellie added that he allowed the family to stay in Castle Torres there while Lord Douglas was held prisoner in Berwick Castle. Wallace looked at his companion as if to say they guessed correctly; coming to Douglasdale and meeting with this laird would yield a good alliance for their cause of rebellion against the English king. Gilley then adjourned their meeting to the earth and timber hall in the middle of the castle courtyard; bidding good night to Lady Douglas, they would discuss their plans for rebellion in the privacy of that old baronial hall.

Ellie watched with grave misgivings as the two men left with her husband; joined as well by Thomas Dickson. Wallace was a plain man of pure deeds and actions she could see. He struck a large appearance, one as tall as Lord Douglas and most the same as broad as he though half his age, she mused. Ellie had withdrawn to the laird's chamber when she heard a light rapping at her door. "Come in, the door not bolted to your entry," she said. It was James. "Mother, is that man William Wallace, the one who killed the English sheriff on Lanark's Castle Hill, that meets with father now?" he asked. Ellie nodded sadly, "The son of Malcolm whose lands adjoin with ours in Kyle Steward; and the knight that does come with him Sir David of Pinwherry, one of Carrick . The rebellion has come to Douglasdale as we have feared," she told him. "And too Wallace came to tell us that young Andrew de Moray, son of the justiciar now in the Tower of London, has moved from Inverness to Urguhart; the rebellion in the north he leads," said Ellie in low tones. "Mother, do you imagine that our father would thus engage the English and join in the rebellion?" asked James. Ellie begged him to come closer now, "Your father joined the rebellion while Edward held him in Hogs Tower; forcing him to watch helplessly when our friends and kin were slaughtered. That he will take action I know it now; but fear it most I do!"

William led the men to sit at the large table in the old hall. He introduced his good and loyal vassal Thomas Dickson of Douglasdale as one with plans to capture Sanquhar Castle; killing its English garrison, to open Galloway's district to Wallace and the Scots now in rebellion to Edward's tyranny. Dickson laid out the details; a ruse would gain them access to the castle. As the laird of Douglas had been a guest in that great castle, he knew the layout well and would lead the way. "And it is agreed that we should spare of no one of the garrison; all must perish to keep our identity a secret for the raid," said the Douglas vassal. Wallace liked the plan and promised his assistance from his location the morrow next south of Dumfries should the need arise. Gilley was pleased with Wallace and his loyal lieutenant Sir David.

He told them of the treachery at Berwick followed by his imprisonment by King Edward. "My own dear wife of gentle English birth yet so tortured. To know Lord Lovaine her father sent men from Little Easton where she was born, friends and family of her childhood, to slaughter Berwick's citizens. She wakes from nightmares still." Wallace told Gilley of his own losses, so devastating that he can only think to murder every English knight and sheriff; any soldier in service of King Edward cherished victims of his sword. "Your agony at Edward's treachery I share," said Gilley, realizing his pain was not his own alone; others too, so tortured now to take up arms in the rebellion. "And you can call on Lord Douglas to thus assist in raising armed horse and foot. Let us meet again the week next after victory is ours at Sanquhar." Wallace and Sir David left through the great hall under the watchful eye of James of Douglas; not yet old enough to squire for his knight and father.

Figure C-Part Three; ruins of Sanquhar Castle

William said goodnight to Dickson; the raid was planned for the morrow next. He slowly made his way up the stairs to the family level and found James with Shamus in the shadows near the chapel door that adjoined the laird's chamber. A weary father embraced his son, "Dear James the more will your father thus rely on your young years to stretch the further. You will be needed to defend our castle with your mother in the absence of Lord Douglas; now a rebel to the King," he said softly. "And you too Sir Shamus; in service to your laird defending Douglas Castle!" James was surprised by his father's candor. "You have agreed to take up arms; aligned you are with Wallace?" he asked. Motioning the lad into the laird's chamber, "James, I will share the truth of my endeavors with both you and my dear wife your mother, to save this old knight the requirement of words repeated." Gilley told them both about the raid they had devised on Sanquhar Castle. "And Wallace just the south below us to come to aid should trouble we run into. Thirty men of Douglasdale shall gather on the morrow next and raise fire and sword to Edward's treachery; his occupation of our Scotland."

"Lord Will, your wife and son will remain so here to defend our castle. Are there other preparations we should make; rebels have few rights, fewer still with Lord Edward, twice forgiven in his mind?" asked Ellie. Gilley told his wife and James that he wanted them to take the coinage from the coffers of Douglasdale now hidden in the secret passage from the rear tower leading to Douglas Water. "Sew as much as nimble fingers can to all your cloaks and surcotes; the children's cotes as well. Ask Ana for her help; but not a word to the others of our household. More who know are more that we endanger with our deeds," he told them. "Take some gold and silver treasures that you favor and secure them in the vaults of our great cellars hidden well to others; behind stone and mortar cleverly disguised." He told his son that should there be a seizure of the castle, his job would be to secure of the charters. "Give them to your mother, hiding them she will within her cotes and surcotes that she wears; a sewn closure should you fashion for that purpose Ellie. I will assign to Ana the nurses and their wards to bring about." Ellie's tears betrayed her fears, "Lord Will, I am so scared." Gilley motioned James to take his leave, "More will we discuss when morning breaks; James is set now to retire, your William here to comfort you in your worries." Gilley held his wife as she sobbed uncontrollably into his chest; unable to see alternatives to his rebellion, he must prepare his family for the worst, he sighed.

Sanquhar Castle

Lord Douglas set out with thirty men at arms; four knights, their squires, armed foot and four bowmen, all from Douglasdale as they headed south for Dumfrieshire and Sanquhar Castle. Traveling the day into the night the Scots made camp at the ravine near Craw Burn, unnoticed by the English garrisoned at the nearby fortress. Thomas Dickson's strategy was to gain entrance to the castle by a ruse; a daring plan that if successful would provide a stronghold for the rebels in the shire. The Douglas vassal had a compatriot named John Anderson who brought firewood to Sanquhar; this brave Scot would leave a pole-axe hidden inside the gates for Dickson to use once freed from his hiding place in the wood cart. Dickson was successful; he escaped the cart and slew the watchman at the gate. He signaled Lord Douglas; the raid began.

Quietly, the brave men of Douglasdale followed their laird through Sanquhar Castle gates and into the courtyard there; they had secreted their horses from view, hidden near a cleugh of the Euchan Water. The Lord of

MY TRUTH LIES IN THE RUINS

Douglas took the lead; revenge for Berwick's citizens was on his mind. Up the turnpike stairs of the four story keep of rubble and stone went the old Crusader; his old standard held in his left hand, his small shield in the right, in the middle guard position he moved, ready to strike instantly. Le Hardi would say after the fight that he was lucky as he climbed the steep winding steps that everyone was fast asleep. Without a sound he crept towards the laird's chamber. Knowing the layout of the keep made the entry simpler in the waning darkness of the spring morning. He found the Captain of the garrison and ran him threw at once; a man groggy from sleep, without so much as a gambeson to protect him was no match for the end of his sword.

By now the other Douglas knights and squires had found their way to other levels of the tower; some of the forty men garrisoned at Sanquhar were clamoring from their beds to meet swords and pole-axes. Sixteen lay dead or dying in the first hour; but there was much more work to do. A young knight was astute enough to don his gambeson and hauberk quickly when he heard the mayhem in the chambers below. A fair man with a sword he made his way down the turnpike stairs, sword and shield in the low guard position, as he approached the third level of the keep where Lord Douglas had just permanently subdued another of the English garrison. Le Hardi was leaning over the dying man, removing his dagger from the opponent's abdomen. Breathing hard from the treacherous combat just completed he rose to find himself face to face with a young and eager English knight, ready for battle!

Grabbing his shield le Hardi moved sideways to broaden his stance and bring his sword back to the middle guard position; a stance he preferred in close combat, allowing himself the option to thrust or just tangle up his opponent. The young knight committed early and moved forward to strike; Lord Douglas parried with his shield, moved round, transitioning his movement in one fluid motion to the back guard where he delivered a hard cut to the opponents right knee. The young knight had recovered soon enough to ward off the full brunt of the blow; or his lower leg would have been useless. The knight's blood covered William's sword; and now rushed profusely down the leg of the young warrior, oozing quickly from a small opening from behind the knee. Le Hardi realized at once that he had hit a major blood line and would just need to bide his time in the combat to win the bout. He used his footwork to feint another strike then he pulled back to invite another attack of the young knight that he would deftly counter. The blood was flowing faster and faster now, making the flooring slick; Le Hardi used his precision footwork to move forward, appear to commit and then move to the side. The English knight was loosing consciousness as he made one last lunge his last living act.

Four men were dead by le Hardi's sword this morning few hours old; four more Englishmen, one for each thousand of Berwick's good citizens was his desire this day. He proceeded cautiously down the turnpike stairs. In the dimly lit great hall of the second level he counted seven bodies, all men at arms from the English garrison. Then from the floor above he heard some stirring. He crept up the stairs slowly; cursing himself for not checking the floor thoroughly enough before proceeding downward. Le Hardi knew better; Ellie must be right; this knight is growing too long in the tooth to hold in combat with men at arms half his age, he mused. As he reached the top level of the stairs he was met by a smaller opponent, a squire from his dress; swinging a mace wildly in the direction of le Hardi he almost surprised him successfully. William fell backward but caught himself before losing his balance. The old warrior's instincts took over; in one swift, smooth movement he lifted his small shield perfectly to ward off the strike of the gruesome mace and made a strong forward strike, to run the lad through. It sickened William to realize the age of the young squire; he was perhaps only a few years older than James. But they had decided before the raid that prisoners were not an option; the entire English garrison had to be destroyed.

Lord Douglas looked around and thoroughly checked each chamber before descending again to the great hall, then to the vaulted cellars below. Bodies were lying everywhere; dark circles of blood oozed from beneath some of the stricken garrison. Douglas men at arms were outside in the courtyard as le Hardi made his way up the stone steps that led from the keep. Dickson came to his laird to report his count; two men had ridden out on horses, one was felled by the bowmen while the other apparently got away riding towards Durisdeer. "How many have we here," asked William of his vassal. "Forty three are dead, two more are dying by our count," said Dickson. Le Hardi furled his brow; they had a few more than forty in the garrison then he surmised. "Five more on the upper floors of the keep then are mine," he told him.

"How large is the garrison at Durisdeer?" asked another knight. Le Hardi looked over to Dickson, "You had better ride to where Wallace is and tell him our troubles; we can not move north to Douglas until we settle now with the garrison further south. We will follow to Carronglen and meet you there," he said knowing they might be facing forces of one hundred or more; le Hardi was not taking any chances, he would call on Wallace for reinforcements. Always honest with his men le Hardi told them the numbers they may be facing further to the south. "At least a hundred armed foot, perhaps another fifty armed horse; and that can only be the least of it," he groused, angry at their loss for the one member of the garrison that got away. But there was time for recriminations later; now they must take their leave and quickly into the hills that would give them a temporary hiding place to wait for Wallace. Before departing Sanquhar the men of

Douglasdale gathered supplies from the larder. They might need to keep safe in the hills for several days before Wallace's men at arms could reach them.

Figure CI-Part Three; Village of Durisdeer; the motte of Durisdeer Castle is all that remains of the old Borders fortress and lies below the village in the middle of cattle grazing lands.

Days later le Hardi and his band of rebels cheered as Wallace entered their sheltered camp near Carronglen. He wasted no time in chasing down the garrisons of Durisdeer and others in pursuit. When the battles were over, the English were withdrawing from Dumfries and the south of Scotland was rallying to the rebel's call. These armed horse of the English garrisons in pursuit of Douglas were overtaken at nearby Dalswinton by the Lanark Rebel and his armed foot; most were put to the sword, few escaped. Two men of Douglas were injured while fighting the English and several too of William Wallace. But for each Scot that fell at Sanquhar or took injury at Durisdeer, nearly fifty English men at arms were slain. Sadly the English warrior that escaped their grasp at Sanquhar had alarmed the garrison commander at Lochmaben; he not only told him of the raid in great detail, but also spoke of the identity of the Scottish rebels. "Lord Douglas was in command; William Wallace was fighting with him in Dumfries." For his mettle William was made warden from Drumlanrig to Ayr. Edward's wrath was to reach a frenzied pitch; but not before another Douglas deed came to his notice and council.

DEBORAH RICHMOND FOULKES

William rode into Douglasdale bringing with him the injured men. He led the armed horse around to the rear of the great hall to the old family residence behind it. Barking orders, he sent his newly knighted Sir Patric of Douglas to wake Lady Eleanora; the good healer was now needed in the service of her laird. William Wallace carried in one of his foot soldiers; a lang gash across the shoulder with much loss of blood. Seeing the injured man, Lady Eleanora motioned Wallace to carry him to some bedding she was setting upon the large table of the old hall. "This will require the work of Lord Douglas to sew now up his wound; but first to treat it with his herbs. Sir Patric take now your son young Patric, our new squire and find Lord Douglas with his healing box, the noo!" Gilley came up behind her putting his arm around her shoulder, "Lord Douglas is here dear wife. I see as well I had expected; that you have this healing chamber now in your good stead. Your husband will tend to this brave warrior; take your leave to treat the others as you can." Wallace and Sir David of Pinwherry were impressed by the tandem work of these two healers; Lady Douglas and her husband treating the wounded with precision and compassion, strangely as if they were experienced at this work; it all seemed came naturally to the couple.

Figure CII-Part Three; view from the grounds of Scone Palace; the old chapel of Scone lies near the Palace and is all that remains of the old village that moved to another location.

James entered the old hall and Eleanora put him fast to work; but not before she introduced him to the Lanark Rebel as she called William Wallace. "My son, the nephew of the Steward; William Wallace, from Kyle in Ayrshire good men and tenants of Steward lands, dear James," said Ellie.

MY TRUTH LIES IN THE RUINS

Wallace's concern for his men mirrored that of his father's noted James. Gilley always told his son treat your men well; good care brings fair reward; true compassion yields true loyalty for life. Before the sun began to rise on Douglas Water, all three injured men were on their way homeward to recover. Wallace agreed to meet with Gilley three days hence to discuss another plan; this one of Wallace's own ambition and design. The sacking of Scone and the ousting of the English justiciar Ormsby would bring much booty Wallace thought; worth their while he boasted to his new accomplice and friend. "You are the first noblemen to join with us in rebellion Lord Douglas. Welcome to the fight Sir William!" Gilley was pleased with William Wallace; a simple man with core values, one that he could trust.

William Wallace and William Douglas rode out to Scone with two dozen armed horse from Lanarkshire and Ayrshire both and most the same in armed foot. Upon hearing word of their approach the English justiciar hastily departed; abandoning his post to make fast his escape to Edinburgh. Ormsby was no fool to arms; better to take leave and live to tell dear Edward of his prudent bravery of caution. Before fleeing from his duties at Scone, Ormsby sought in haste the identities of these marauders; William Wallace and Lord Douglas do lead the horsemen in rebellion he was told. "Good Edward shall hear of this false deed and their fool heartedness, these vile felons!" vowed the justiciar, "To meet with the king's wrath I swear so, as much booty did they lift from Edward's coffers."

Having another successful raid of Edward's strongholds under their belts, Wallace and Lord Douglas led their armed horse and foot south; stopping to make camp near Stirling. There the rebel leaders counted their coinage and divided the rest of the spoils with their men. Most of the coinage went to Wallace this day; to fill the treasury of the rebel forces that he led. Their men at arms were allowed to pilferage and loot at Scone before they took their leave. The rebels wisely took swords and armaments for their trouble; some horses and saddles were acquired; several bucklers and many bows with arrows stacked in great piles were found; all the booty was brought to the Stirling campsite to divide among them. Lord Douglas took his share of coinage; allowing Douglas men their fair portion of the remaining spoils.

In less than three months time, very near the spot where these brave Scots now stood, Wallace would pick his fight with the English. He would align himself with the brave young squire Andrew de Moray and they would hold Stirling; defeat the Earl of Surrey, using the spoils of Edward's own coffers from Scone to arm and feed their men. Wallace and Douglas parted good friends today, happy in their success, pleased with their rebellion they agreed to meet again in two weeks hence. This time they were going to Irvine where a growing list of nobles planned to meet with men at arms and horse; angry with Edward's call to muster to fight in Flanders, these Scots considered their course. They took courage in the rebellion of William Wallace and young de Moray and agreed to a muster of their own at Irvine. Wallace reflected on le Hardi as he took his leave; he trusted the laird of Douglas. He wondered about the other nobleman; these Scots now gathering in Ayrshire in large numbers. Could they be trusted as well; he hoped so. The Lanark Rebel had ridden in raids with Alexander de Lindsay before; he held lands of the Steward; and the Bishop of Glasgow, Robert Wishart, was his benefactor before; these men he could follow he decided. If the bishop organizes more nobles at Knadgerhill like these good men then perhaps the time is right that we can rid our lands of the English, Wallace mused as he rode on to Ayrshire.

Douglasdale Early June 1297

Ellie was teaching some of the older children in the withdrawing room. Today's lessons were again in Norman French. Muriel, James, young Patric their new squire, and little Beatrice de Lindsay were there to learn to speak and write this day. Beatrice was visiting for the week; her father dropped her off on his way to his manor Barnweill in Ayrshire he told her. Lady Alice would be along shortly with her escort to return to Ayrshire with her children, coming from a few days in Edinburgh. The children were of ages eleven down to five, all at different levels of learning. Speaking languages was the easiest to learn, Ellie mused, so she would try that method first. Gilley interrupted his wife; he asked a favor that she dismiss the class and continue it another day. The children were ecstatic; a beautiful day it was to be outside! Shamus ran behind them; he loved to play in the courtyard of Douglas Castle with the children. "Sweet wife I pray you help your husband here; please sit," said Gilley, pointing to her chair at the table in the great hall. He was showing Ellie some lists of goods that he needed for the muster set for Irvine. "How strange Lord Will that you would go there; to fight a major battle with the English, with such numbers not to fail," she sighed. "What irony that we did start our life together from that port; to leave for Ireland and Mann."

Gilley shook his head sadly; he wished for better days. But fighting the English on Scottish soil was all he could focus on now. He told her where he would camp; set up the tents and sites for his men from Douglasdale. "That we should most be near the gailes," he explained carefully. "So much has changed for us dear Ellie; our dreams and plans to rest un-wakened for our future I do fear. This knight reluctant in his fighting; your loving husband and poet knight preferring Douglasdale to stay," he said ruefully. She rose to go to him and put her arms around him. "Lord Will, my heart breaks to see your sad self plagued by Edward's crimes upon our Scotland. Fight you will and bravely; your wife and family to wait your safe return, dear St. Bride I do pray so!" Then tears fell from her eyes uncontrollably; she tried to catch these telling signs of sorrow but was too late as he grabbed her hand; bringing her round to face him. He helped her up to sit upon his lap. Wiping her face of tears with those large hands, he held her fast and rocked her for some time. "I will be brave for you my husband, do continue now," she said as her composure returned and she dried her eyes.

"Lady El, I need you now to sit and read our Douglas charters once again. And then to fairly calculate our coinage here; safely setting some aside for haste in travel to some other place. Will you do that for your laird and husband?" he asked her quietly. Throughout the remainder of the day Ellie and Gilley counted and talked and planned. "Ellie, we must make sure our thoughts; where to flee that there would be a problem. Our small manor now at Stewartoun, a safe stronghold for you to go." "Lord Will, it is one too close to Irvine for this lass to feel safe. Your wife and children would pray to stay at Auchinleck; a manor better hidden and larger for our household." Gilley smiled, "I could find that manor without much delay should there be the need. Auchinleck our choice; it is done." He hugged his wife for some time, clinging to their love of nine lang years; hoping it would be enough to keep their family safe and free from Edward's grasp.

The grim realities of being brandished a traitor, the punishment they might face for their rebellion were all unknowns in the early days of June. The Douglases braced for the retaliation from the king and did not have to wait very long. Word of Douglas' deeds in Sanquhar, joining in rebellion with William Wallace had finally reached the king. On the 7th of June 1297 Edward began making his own plans to deal with these traitors; first he issued mandates for the seizure of the Douglas lands in Essex and Northumbria. Five days later on the 12th a second mandate was signed by Edward Plantagenet. He had just received a letter from William Ormsby his justiciar in the north of Scotland. The letter was in his own hand: to inform my lord the king of my unfortunate displacement to Edinburgh; that the King's coffers in Scone were contemptuously emptied by Lord Douglas with his accomplice William Wallace. This debasing act most damaging to the king must be avenged he declared!

Edward did not need to read Ormsby's last request to act; his fury at le Hardi was seething, he was livid at the impetuous Douglas. These foolish Scots have spent their last days in their Douglasdale vowed Edward. He ordered all the lands in Scotland of William Douglas and Eleanora Douglas seized at once. His anger was still not satisfied that he ordered the capture and abduction of Lady Douglas and her children from Douglas Castle. He commanded that they be held at Lochmaben; in the good company of other rebel families that he imprisoned there. "The young Earl of Carrick will I send; this deed to test his true allegiance for his king!" Edward declared to his council.

Douglasdale, Late June

Gilley was awake most of the night; his head ached from the injuries of Fawdon that still plagued him. But neck pains were not the reason for his sleepless night; his fears for his family and his wife preyed heavily on his mind. Ellie began to stir and reached instinctively for him in their bed. She cuddled into his large frame as she spoke. "Lord Will this fateful day has come that you must leave for Irvine; I do worry so," she sighed softly. His large hands wrapped around her body, he felt tears welling in his own eyes. "Will you love me tomorrow as you love me today, Lady El?" he asked her, beginning the rituals of their love enduring now a decade. She answered Gilley as she always had and would forever; then asked him the same question. He began to untie the neck closure on her bed cote; ever so shyly a ritual that never changed. "May I?" he asked her. They remained in their private solitude, the curtains of their tester bed were drawn closed on this summer morning; making a safe sanctuary for their exchange of love.

Ellie and James stood staunchly together in the front courtyard of the castle, behind them stood Ana and the other children. Muriel held Amy's wee hand in hers; Hugh stood over by Sir Shamus away from the others. The wee lad Archie as Ellie called him was held by Ana now, his nurse taking leave, finished with his feeding of the morning. "Papa," screamed Amy, "Papa, Amy wants to ride with you!" Lord Douglas was riding his palfrey, leading his war horse beside him, as he gave Pageant's reins to his squire. William was in full armaments coming from behind the keep, following under the archway beside the stable entrance. James brought his young sister to sit for a few moments with her father in his saddle; the wee lass, his youngest daughter was very special to her father; he always favored her requests. "My dear Amy, you must stay here with your sister and good brothers, taking care of your sweet mother in your father's absence," he said, kissing her goodbye. "Lord Douglas will return unharmed with the blessings of St. Bride!" he vowed, turning now to leave. Then he stopped seeing the wee Hugh waving to him, quietly standing there with Shamus. James turned to see the laddie smiling sadly and brought him to his father who waited to say goodbye to his shy son.

Hugh extended his hand to shake it so politely. "Young Hugh, both warriors are we, once prisoners of this pagan king," said Gilley, "Be brave for your dear mother while your father fight's for Scotland's freedom from this despot," he told him heartily; grabbing his son he kissed him and hugged him hard. Ellie ran to William unable to control her feelings any longer, "Lord Will, a word with you my husband," she called to him. Whispering now she said, "I love you with all my heart and soul for all eternity; you must promise me you will return, that I will hold you to your word!" Gilley leaned down to her and held her face close to his, kissing her deeply and passionately. "If our God is in his Heaven then I will!" He turned his palfrey sharply round, to cross the drawbridge to the good men of Douglasdale called to muster in the Park. With banners flying and Douglas standards waving proudly, the hundred horsemen with two hundred foot soldiers, spearmen, squires, and their pages walking pack animals carrying supplies of armaments, food and wine; other men at arms leading extra horses or working in tandem transporting war-chests; the Douglas retinue proceeded west to Irvine following their brave and noble leader the laird of Douglas to fight the English.

Knadgerhill, Irvine

Lord Douglas greeted these barons of the lowlands gathering with others of like minds, to stake their lives and lands against the English tyrant and drive his vassals south where they belonged. Alexander de Lindsay was in the tent of the Steward, talking with William Wallace, when William le Hardi arrived. "All here I see but the good bishop, where might he be now?" asked le Hardi. "Here behind you Douglas!" came the loud voice of Bishop Wishart. "Good company I see from all the faces; much work that we can do here with God's good blessing, I do pray." Wallace spoke now, "Young Andrew de Moray soon to follow from the north will he come to join us. Much trouble to have caused the English vassals doing Edward's shameful bidding."

These brave Scottish magnates and the prelate joined with William Wallace without worry to his station; his deeds of valor were more important to them than how much land he held in freehold. Wishart spoke heartily to his friend Wallace, "The booty that you pried from shaking hands of one named Ormsby; the legend now the talk of Glasgow's merchants, smiling all the while at his near captivity!" Wallace was laughing that deep laugh of a great warrior celebrating the few times when battles go so perfectly. "And Lord Douglas here feigned to chase him; Ormsby fleeing fast, pleading all the way to spare his life. The sword of Douglas nearly touching the justiciar as he departed Scone!" The Steward rose to speak, "I am weary of the war and battle not yet started; let us enjoy good food and drink much wine at the Steward's table. You too Douglas; though much feasting do I see on your fair self since last I saw you in Douglasdale," he chuckled, pointing good naturedly to the broadened girth of William's stature.

William le Hardi was quick to respond to his brother in law; "Fast must a father eat with all the wee mouths to feed at table there about; with another sure to come this year I do profess!" he boasted. Alexander de Lindsay was chuckling; "That these brave warriors believe Lady Douglas is kept locked in chamber, here de Lindsay stands to speak the truth. Le Hardi's wife to roam the castle freely; when last I left our sweet Beatrice for the language teaching Eleanora does so well." William le Hardi smiled broadly, "Your fair bride Alice there last morning to bring young Beatrice to Barnweill. By her looks your family too increasing," chided William. Alex admitted proudly that he would be a father again this year as well. Le Hardi turned to his brother in the law the Steward. "Our good James here will soon discover since he now claimed a bride; the wee ones come most quickly to the feasting and eat most heartily for their size!" he teased as Wallace and the bishop roared in laughter. The Steward bellowed loudly; he was through with talk. "Time for feasting, the noo!" he announced.

Figure CIII-Part Three; Irvine Gailes; campsite for William le Hardi Douglas and his men

Douglasdale

Ellie was not sleeping well these nights; as she reached over to William's side of the bed, the furry Deerhound greeted her in the early morning light. He suddenly began barking; jumped from the bed, running to the guard the door. Could that be our William now returning, the noise to rile our Shamus so, she wondered aloud. Her excitement at the prospect was tempered quickly when Ana entered the chamber. "M' Lady, riders do approach, many horsemen in full armaments, with banners known to us from Essex; the Earl of Carrick." Ellie rose quickly to dress. "Wake the children, call their nurses, something is not right with this encounter I do fear." Just then James entered the chamber. "Mother, Sir David and others of our men of Douglasdale are on the morning hunt; we are but alone to defend the castle!" said her son. Defend the castle! Wild thoughts raced through Ellie's mind; we are under attack, alone now in our charge to protect ourselves from these intruders! "Dear blessed Virgin, give me strength, I am so scared," she cried out loud. "James, you know what you must do; bring me now the charters. Ana, find the children's nurses, dress them in the robes with coinage hidden; we may take haste to leave our home."

Figure CIV-Part Three; the portcullis required a sturdy mechanism to operate the heavy iron fortification; this example is on display at the Tower of London

The drawbridge was securely drawn and the portcullis defiantly lowered; but with so many armed horse brandishing fire and sword the Douglases would be unable to defend the castle for very long with William on campaign and their remaining men at arms on the morning hunt. James brought the charter chest and the coffer with the coinage Ellie hid on her person. Ana came running hard, "The children are most ready. But with heaviness of heart I must report three fires set and catching fast; the rear courtyard and the palisade are on fire though valiantly cook and the others try to extinguish the flames." Ellie looked at James, "We have no choice but to surrender to this foe; God protect us now, our only hope." James was about to offer another plan when several armed men in full armaments mounted the stairs and entered the laird's chamber.

Loud shrieks could be heard down the corridor from the chambers of the wee ones as nurses cried out in peril for the safety of their children while fearful screams emanated from the wee frightened lads and lasses. With swords drawn these foolish and outrageous men at arms were rounding up the wee ones from their chamber. Horses' hooves could be heard running fast ominously pounding the planks of the drawbridge now lowered by the invaders as the rest of the Carrick entourage entered Douglas Castle. Little resistance could be given now. There was no time for escape through the secret tunnel from the donjon tower by the postern. Lady Douglas and her children were prisoners of the Earl of Carrick in their home; Douglas Castle had surrendered.

Figure CV-Part Three; Portcullis, the iron-gate entrance to a castle; this example is from the Tower of London.

The men at arms escorted Lady Douglas to the great hall; James stayed close to her side. Earl Robert was there directing his men, all loyal to Lord Edward and his father. They would be allowed to plunder Douglas Castle in

MY TRUTH LIES IN THE RUINS

payment for their service in this raid the Earl told them; but not until he gave the word. "Lady Douglas, your lands and castles have been seized by King Edward for the treason of Lord Douglas. These orders you can read," he said, giving her the writs ordering their forfeiture of lands and chattels in England and in Scotland. "As the king's vassal this Earl has been sent to bring your good self and children to Lochmaben. In ward now of the king you must reside there." Ellie's resolve and James' steady arm kept her standing as she spoke, "Earl Robert, we must have some time to load our pack horses with coffers and other chests; five children and their Deerhound with nurses and my servants, and a litter for the wee ones all to go. But pray you now reconsider; Lochmaben's hospitality must we avoid." She motioned to James, "Please take leave my son and help our Ana put aside our belongings to take along our journey. I will speak alone with the Earl of Carrick."

Ellie sat down at the table in the great hall of Douglas Castle; her head confused by all that happened, to choose her words now carefully. "Earl Robert please sit here that I may have private council with you." Lady Douglas was determined to persuade this young earl to take the Douglas household to her manor in Ayrshire, adjacent to his own in Turnberry; if only he would listen to her story, she prayed. "Lady Douglas I have no quarrel with you or your family; my own loyalties are questioned. Lochmaben and King Edward thus await your good arrival." Ellie bit hard on her lower lip to keep from crying. "Dear Earl Robert, I can not go before Lord Edward. When first I was widowed from my English husband did I make pledge not to marry without Edward's license; the same pledge made by the Countess of Carrick, your mother I do recall. King Alexander fumed when your sweet mother broke her vow and married your dear father Robert Brus."

She reminded the earl that the embarrassed King of Scots seized Turnberry, only to relent to true love's covenant, "approving their license for marriage then and there for your own dear mother and faithful father both," Lady Douglas told the earl. "King Edward is of different temperament; Lord Lovaine my father to ire him the more with words of falsehood of my lover and good husband Lord Douglas. I beg you to consider now my request," she said almost breaking down in tears. "I am Essex born as you, from Little Easton, not far your family's manor of Montpelier in Writtle I do know."

The young earl looked at this sad lady pleading with her eyes to change his plans. "I must secure this castle and remove one Lady Douglas and her children to journey south to Annandale. From there I will address the justiciar in the king's absence from Lochmaben on your behalf. That you are English and have no quarrel with the King I will address him; to another

313

manor I could take you and shall request of him permission. Should he accept my offer; I will bring your household to stay in Turnberry for some days. Ellie glanced up at young Robert Brus, a look of relief coming to her face. "My late husband's lands in chief reside near Maybole; our good household would find ourselves quite happy to be there. I thank you Earl Robert."

James had started down the stairs, but stopped to hear the words being spoken between the earl and his mother. Lady El has such courage; to speak so calmly now, our lives in such peril of existence, he thought to himself. "Mother, the others but await your word. Shall I get the horses for our travels?" The young earl beckoned his squires to attend young James should he chance escape. "Bring the two litters and six pack horses for our journey," said Ellie, calmer now, but apprehensive for her husband's fate that this should happen. Ellie excused herself to join Ana in the laird's chamber as she was packing Ellie's cotes and surcotes, cloaks and veils for their leave of Douglasdale. "Let us put the mantels and some good cotes, surcotes and the cloaks of my William in the chest to take there too; and be sure to bring his hats."

Ana had thought her girl was acting calmly and thinking clearly until she heard Ellie's concern for William's hats. She shook her head ruefully; my lamb is sure to break under this great sadness. Then thinking of this Robert Brus; his raid for Edward's pleasure, what kind of Essex man is this young earl to do this to my lady, she asked herself. Is he an English nobleman or a Scottish earl she wondered for his loyalties? These fair noblemen of Scotland seemed confused thought Ana. "If these Scottish knights united they could drive out Lord Edward so; his vassals damaged, their estates well mortgaged for his wars of personal ambition. My thinking is more a Scot than Norman now I fear," said Ana, chuckling at her words. Both ladies laughed and cried; "Scared I am Ana, but sadder still to leave our Douglasdale the last time for some many years I fear. We will return I promise you!" This Lady of Douglas is as true a Scot as any born in Scotland, Ellie said to herself defiantly. One day this lass shall return to her homeland she vowed.

Ellie looked around the laird's chamber; their private sleeping chamber, where they shared they shared their love together; trying to commit every last detail to memory. Then she looked to the side of the tester bed where her beautiful tapestry once hung; the lovely green and blue wall hanging in the design of a castle on a loch with birds in flight. "Ana, these thieves made fast with my fair tapestry!" she said in despair. Ana looked up surprised; she had not noticed that anyone had come into the chamber to do their looting. "Oh my Ana, there is no justice in our Scotland now," she said sadly, "to steal from a lady in her home; our own countrymen thus set upon us," she moaned as tears welled in her eyes and flowed down her cheeks.

Ana went to her side to comfort her; held her and rocked her as Gilley would do. "There my girl; your Ana has most taken all the others of your prized gifts from your sweet knight," she said comforting her lady. Then she pulled her surcote aside to show her girl how she was deceiving the Carrick men at arms; hiding jewelry, including the de Hastings brooch Ellie received from Helisant, in her own draw string purse secreted under her surcote. Ellie smiled; she kissed Ana on the cheek and thanked her profusely for her quick thinking that saved her memories from the looters. Some of the Douglas servants came to the door of the chamber and offered to help take their things to the pack horses waiting in the courtyard of the castle. Ellie and Ana got up; ready to take their leave now.

Figure CVI-Part Three; ruins of Lochmaben Castle constructed by Edward I in 1297; Annandale

In the great hall they were stopped by the Carrick men at arms demanding to search the wooden chests. Ellie's heart pounded; would they search her husband's clothing she wondered as they grabbed the first chest, where she hid some of his jewelry. Just then Earl Robert re-entered the great hall and told them to allow the lady her privacy. "Take your belongings Lady Douglas," he said quietly. Ellie breathed a sigh of relief; some of the Douglas charters were hidden in with her own surcotes; the remaining ones she concealed under her supertunic.

The journey down to Annandale was somber and slow going. James and Muriel kept the younger children occupied with tales of travel and adventure. Ellie held tightly to her wee son Archibald, trying to hold herself together and remain composed. It was early night time and they had made camp several hours travel outside of Lochmaben the earl informed her. The rains burst through the evening clouds; the heavy air was damp and chilled her to the very bone. She was sitting alone under the thin cover of a small tent with her wee son, preparing to feed him at her breast. The other children were staying in other tents provided by Earl Robert.

An overwhelming fear engulfed her, the sound of the heavy rain pelting down upon the thin covering, soaking and dripping through in some places demoralized her resolve; Ellie started to cry uncontrollably, shuddering in the raw cold of the night. What sorry deeds have been cast upon us dear Archie; your mother most the cause of it I fear, to have married after warning of that woman long ago at Fawside....Her thoughts were interrupted by Ana bringing her a dry cloak and warm tasine to cheer her. "Oh Ana, why does God hate me; what have I done to displease him so?" she asked. "God has taken me from my home and loving husband; while he gives King Edward all that he desires. That Winton speywife's words so true I fear."

Earl Robert of Carrick rode out early the next morning with some of his men at arms to meet with Edward's vassals in Lochmaben. True in his word, the young earl made the plea for Lady Douglas; to return her with her children to a residence in Ayrshire at a manor of de Ferrers, another loyal English knight in service to his king. The request for leniency was approved for Lady Douglas by the Governor of Lochmaben Castle. The fortress in Annandale was overflowing with Scots; not yet completely built the castle was filling fast with families of Scottish lairds in disfavor with their king. Robert Brus returned to tell the captives they were free to go with him to Carrick, South Ayrshire to the de Ferrers manor there near Maybole. Another small victory said Ellie to herself; I must get word to William when we arrive near Pennyglen. How strange this life has been that I should be returning to Ayrshire; the very manor where I stayed when first I met my dear husband. And how much my life has changed she sighed.

When the heavily loaded pack animals and palfreys arrived at the small manor, the Douglases were surprised to find young Patric and Sir David there to greet them. "How is it you knew to come here?" asked Ellie. "Sir David, dear Patric this lass is most pleased to see you!" The English knight chuckled. "James left me word with the farrier of your intent to not travel to Lochmaben, coming yet to Pennyglen," said the de Ferrers family knight. "I put on my full armor with my English tabard and rode hard to your assistance with our squire Patric at my attendance." Ellie laughed heartily.

"Dear Sir David, there will be no more early morning hunts for you! Each time you leave my castle unattended I find my good self abducted by some men at arms from my very bed!" teased Ellie, very relieved to see her knight and friend. Ana rejoiced to see her lady laughing in the face of such sad circumstances and went off humming happily as she made her way into the manor house to assist the others.

Seeing the resolve of these hearty Douglases brought reflection to the young earl. He turned his horse to leave when Ellie stopped him. "I know not what your heart speaks now to you; but for this Essex lass who witnessed Berwick's slaughter, it is Scotland now that holds my love and loyalty," she said in low tones that only he could hear. "This lady thanks you for your escort to our manor here; good day Earl Robert." The Earl of Carrick rode off with his men at arms; fewer now than those that stormed and sacked Douglas Castle two lang days ago. Upon reaching Turnberry Robert Brus had come to a tentative decision; he would go to Irvine where rumors held of other Scottish nobles gathering there. These magnates were going to take a defiant stand against Edward; they opposed his order to muster for battle in Gascony and decided it was time to unite and rid the English from their homelands.

Ellie led her family into the great hall of the wee manor house and ordered wine and food be brought to them. "Lady Eleanora, your good spirit does amaze this old knight," said Sir David. "Your castle and lands all seized, this is true then?" he asked her. Yes she nodded, "This time though different from afore. Edward sees again Lord Douglas for rebellion, surely no forgiveness in his heart I fear," she said. James came back to the hall, having settled in the rest of the children with their nurses in their crowded chamber. Relieved and happy he came to greet Sir David and young Patric. "Good that you did heed my words!" James said and then turning to his mother, "I spoke to our farrier in the Gaelic; that he would send Sir David to our rescue. Fortunate too these Carrick men at arms were from an English garrison; knowing not the language of our Celtic people." Ellie told James how proud she was of his quick action. "Your prudent words have helped me most today that I not worry so. Sir David and Patric here have calmed my fears."

"We must get word to Sir Gilley the noo," she said aloud, back in control of the household. "This humble knight would tell you this Lady Eleanora," said Sir David. "When first I returned from hunt we found the others putting out the fires at the Castle; damage to the earth and timber buildings there was some. Then the farrier told us of the sacking by the Earl of Carrick with a message from young James to come to Ayrshire. Before departing I sent word to Sir Andrew; he would ride to Irvine and advise Lord Douglas of this mischief." Ellie wrinkled her brow, "That Sir Andrew and Lady Amy will have to leave Parkhall saddens me as well; so many thus affected by this war." James spoke up; distressed by her words. "Does that mean that all our lands are seized and others will be living in Douglas Castle, holding Douglas lands?" he asked, expecting that her answer would confirm his fears. "Not just others James," responded Ellie, "but loyal vassals of Lord Edward; English barons to enforce his rule. Unless the battle forming in the north is thus successful, returning Scotland's freedom and self rule; we will be as rebels with no home."

Ellie told them all of her ideas; to rest the night and then to journey to their lands in Auchinleck. "Lord Douglas agreed that we should go north to our manor near Lugar Water. He will send us word there that I know." Ana asked her if she might enjoy more rest than just the night. "Ana, we must travel from this manor on the morrow. Others loyal to the king might use their knowledge of location; making hostages to compromise Lord Douglas, to take us all in ward." Sir David agreed that it was better to remain only the night. "We shall travel first to Trabboch; a Douglas messuage to keep us safe the night, half the journey to the manor for our hiding in Auchinleck. Do you recall the way to get there James?" she asked her son. "Mother, I am sure the path to take once we reach Martnaham Loch," he said confidently. "The last we went on hunt, with father do you recall Sir David?" The English knight remembered now where Trabboch was, "Only some few hours from Lugar Water; the shorter journey for this tired household will please our Ana too." Ana agreed whole heartedly, nodding her head. "Then the morrow next we will arrive in Auchinleck; a good arrangement for our part!" Ana said she was very relieved to travel less each day. "It is done, as my dear husband would now say!" said Ellie proud of their consent to her proper plan.

Knadgerhill

The Scottish nobles and their men at arms were encamped near Knadgerhill in Irvine. The many horsemen and the infantry assembled would more than double the English army's foot soldiers in number as they approached from the south towards Kilmarnock. Lord Edward's army was under the command of Henry of Percy, nephew of the Guardian of Scotland, the Earl of Surrey, Johannis de Warenne. The Scots were united in their task as ever they had been; Wallace was among them in his power; he brought with him most the infantry in their muster. Two Douglas horsemen were approaching the camp; a knight with his squire went to the tent camp of Lord Douglas. "Good steward, what cause to bring you from our Douglasdale," William started to ask him, but the look on Sir Andrew's face revealed his tragic news before his words, "The Earl of Carrick on the mandates of Lord Edward seized Lady Eleanora and your children; sacked Douglas Castle, carrying off much booty and your family too." Fear and terror swept through the knight's body. "Pray tell me, did he take them to Lochmaben?" asked William le Hardi knowing it was this castle in Annandale where Edward held in ward some families of his barons in rebellion.

"No Sir William; Lady Douglas convinced Earl Robert to take them to the manor of de Ferrers near Maybole," he said gasping for breath, having ridden hard to get there. "We came quickly here to tell you my laird." William sighed with great relief. The Scots had just the night before attacked Lochmaben; burning many huts where the English were encamped, near the castle being constructed on the loch. "You are sure it was the Earl of Carrick?" he asked Sir Andrew. The steward nodded yes, pulling out a pennon of that house that was left behind. William le Hardi grabbed the evidence from his loyal knight. "The young earl has much to answer for to Lord Douglas; the others shall hear of this at once!" Ordering his own squire to ready his palfrey he offered Sir Andrew and his squire some food and ale that was waiting on the table in his tent.

"You have le Hardi's thanks for all your troubles. And remove what stock you can from castle grounds; divide it among our good men of Douglasdale, some palfreys for yourself as well but do it fast. And of Lady Amy, is she safe?" The steward told his laird that his family moved back to Glenbuck until the Douglas lands were restored, "And Scotland rid of these invaders to our peace," he added. William le Hardi took his leave of them; riding to the camps of de Lindsay; then the Steward. Sir Alex was greatly harmed by the word that Lord Robert had sacked the castle and made off with William's family. "Just for one day my daughter Beatrice would too have been abducted with your wife and family. We must alert the Steward; word was the Earl might join our army thus assembled."

Anger marked the brow of one named William; for a Scot to abduct another's family from their home and safety while the laird was mustering for war was outrage to this baron! On their walk to the Steward's tents these lowland barons encountered William Wallace and young Andrew de Moray, son of the justiciar and Douglas kin. "What troubles you le Hardi; your face has anger that could kill I fear," said the Lanark Rebel. "The mischief of the Earl of Carrick on the writs of this despot king, Lord Edward; with fire and sword he abducted Lady Douglas and our wee children, sacking the castle of Lord Douglas too!" Wallace turned to the young de Moray squire; they exchanged looks of grave concern. They both realized at once that the blatant act of treachery by Earl Robert, his kidnapping of the Douglases and sacking of the laird's home, was bringing trouble and change to the Scot's camp at Knadgerhill.

These brave patriots of Scotland joined together and boldly stormed the Steward's tents to find him not alone. Robert Wishart the good Bishop of Glasgow was there, in quiet conference with Sir James. "Greetings to you," said the bishop, "What brings you all about so early in the day?" William le Hardi threw the pennon of the house of Carrick to the bishop. "The evidence of Carrick treachery, Earl Robert; left at Douglas Castle that he sacked some few days ago. He has brought great shame to that noble house; Earl Neil his grandfather my dear mother's own kin." Bishop Wishart and the Steward exchanged fearful looks. "What about your family, were they not at Douglasdale?" William le Hardi's furor was sputtering in his words. "Lady Douglas, with your good nephew James and the others of our children were abducted. The persuasive words of Eleanora bringing him to his senses some, he left his Douglas captives at her manor near Maybole; is what I hear."

Le Hardi went on to explain that Lord Edward issued writs to seize all his lands and castles both in England and in Scotland. Then looking at Wallace, "My steward brought me these mandates that followed our good raid on Scone," he said to his accomplice on that raid. "The words from Edward's justiciar the reason for his actions," said le Hardi. De Lindsay looked at the writs and was himself concerned. Pointing to Wallace he said, "This brave Scot and I have formed some Lanark mischief of our own; should Edward seize my lands as well?" The bishop shook his head gravely now. "We have another come to join us; bringing some horsemen and few foot soldiers to our company," said Robert Wishart in tones of great dismay. "Here Douglas; read and tell us what you think." William read the parchment message; the Earl of Carrick was bringing men at arms to join them now in Knadgerhill. "What strange loyalties does this man call his own I do wonder?" asked William ruefully. "We will hear him out; first thought for this knight would be to slay him here and now I know!" Wallace and de Lindsay showed their concern as well; but agreed to hold their judgment of this earl.

When Earl Robert arrived at Irvine he went first to the camp of James the Steward. He guessed the former Guardian of Scotland was there on convictions of the Bishop and brave examples of these knights that had married his sisters, Alexander de Lindsay and William le Hardi Douglas. "Greetings dear seneschal; I have come to join the fight for Scotland; in rebellion is this Earl of Carrick now," said Robert. James allowed the young earl to continue. Robert told him about the unhappy raid upon Douglas Castle and the abduction at the request of the king. "My loyalties were questioned and I was thus selected for this sorry deed. I made it right by freeing Lady Douglas and her children from their report to ward; making fair excuse their absence to Lord Edward's vassal at Lochmaben. Now comes Robert to join his countrymen in their good fight." The Steward advised the earl to make his peace with Lord Douglas, camped near the gailes.

Robert was surprised the word had come so quickly to the Douglas laird; but decided he must make amends and now. He rode over to the tents and camp of Douglas men, with several of his Carrick men at arms following behind him. William le Hardi invited the young earl to come join him; to discuss in private his intentions and his sorrow for his wrongful deeds. Robert came alone so le Hardi dismissed his squire from the tent. Earl Robert did much talking; le Hardi listened with furled brow of painful grimace, his anger simmering beneath his calm demeanor. He studied the young man; he had great heart this younger Brus, but lacking in core values has made him vulnerable to other's whims, thought William to himself.

"Lady Douglas prevailed in her good wisdom that I should leave them safely there near Maybole at the manor of de Ferrers. Much circumstance and many words did I give to Lochmaben's Governor to avert their coming to Annandale thus in ward. I put my deeds before you Douglas," he said in all sincerity. "I have come to fight for the nation of my mother; never again to raise a sword to my own people. This I pledge to my God as true." William waited for some time before he answered. "As men we are called upon to act by lairds holding their supremacy; as knights we are pledged to act with honor first to God, then to men. I have fought in many battles, serving Scotland's kings. My decisions are my own; my truth. It is you Earl Robert who must align yourself with core values, to thus build on strong convictions of your own. Your truth is God's truth and lies within you. I thank you for your brave words to me this day. And too your faithful promise fulfilled to Lady Douglas; to carry our family to Ayrshire's safe protection. William le Hardi stood up, towering as he did over most men; he ushered the young earl out to take his leave.

William Wallace with young de Moray came to see Lord Douglas not long after the visit of Earl Robert. Wallace found his friend le Hardi in sad humor. "Come in Wallace, you too young Andrew. Your word good Wallace I trust above all others here, including nobles that are my kin. My wife and children are in peril; no home or lands to call their home. They are hiding well in Kyle Steward; but Lord Douglas is pressed to take his leave and join them." Wallace spoke quietly; only Douglas' vassal Thomas Dickson and Andrew de Moray were with them in the tent. From months before at Douglasdale, Wallace knew this vassal could be trusted. "These words I have to share might make such decision the easier. Earl Robert has come to lead us, not to join us. He seeks to rule Scotland; not fight for King John as is my loyalty," said Wallace. Young Andrew spoke as well. "Sir William that my father most respected your words dear kin; with that brave knight yet held in Edward's prison I seek your good council," he told le Hardi. "As you know Lord Petty held for Balliol, our kin. The good men of Moray trust my word; to lead them into battle but not for benefit of Earl Robert," he said quietly. Le Hardi shook his head with grave premonitions. "I suspected he might be here for that matter. He would be one to unite our Scotland if he could be trusted. But his motives do confuse me some I fear," confided William le Hardi.

Wallace spoke directly as was his manner; telling le Hardi about the grumbling around the camp; some nobles were no longer in agreement on which laird to follow. "If this temperament continues, Wallace and his men at arms must take their leave for better battles in the east or north," he said, indicating sadly that his decision was already made. Young Andrew agreed. "Sir William my father said you could be trusted. He spoke of your word and honor as he would his own; advising me so at Avoch when you last visited the Black Isle; then most again when we journeyed to see you at Blackhouse Tower. My dear father said your were of all men most like him," the young squire paused his words, then added, "I fear that Scotland's magnates now lose their will to fight this battle; to the north towards Moray will I take my men." Lord Douglas looked off in the distance, he was not really present with the others in his tent; his mind on his family and their troubles. When his thoughts returned him to the place of Knadgerhill he had these words for Wallace and young de Moray. "You know in your heart what must be done. Dear Andrew, your father the Justiciar proud he would be to know his son's true bravery, a great patriot whose fight continues. Your valiant raids of mischief in the north to drive out Edward's vassals from our Scotland would draw most certain praise!"

Then turning to the Lanark Rebel William shared more words; coming from his heart, he spoke his truth to him. "Good Wallace without your following, your men at arms this group of nobles has no chance to hold the field against the army of Lord Percy. We do better battle among ourselves I fear." With heavy heart William le Hardi knew what he too must do. "If Wallace and de Moray leave than I will seek the Steward to propose a peace to the commander of the English army. I must remove my family from Scotland to safety of another place; to fight another day." Wallace knew le Hardi hated giving up the fight without a battle; the pain of Berwick still darkened the visage of this brave laird and knight. "Le Hardi, your words are true. Would my own wife and family be alive and in the peril you thus face must Wallace too decide to seek the peace; for now. Soon again to raise my sword against the English; with you brave Douglas once more, God grant me that I pray!" William Wallace, young Andrew de Moray and William Douglas patriots and friends departed their own ways; their hearts heavy with their love for Scotland, under the hammer of a king named Edward.

The next morning the Steward rode into the Douglas camp. "Wallace with de Moray and their men rode out by dawn; the Steward here is seeking your wise council," said Sir James. William told him of their discussion the day before. "The Earl of Carrick causing rift with other nobles now is he?" asked William. Sir James said that last night Earl Robert made if clear he would not follow Wallace on the field; nor would he fight for one King John. "Do you think that Edward has thus sent him to disrupt us here?" asked the Steward. Le Hardi shook his head no, "I fear that this young man has many faults but coming here to break our unity was not his intent. He has no truth to follow; he has ambition though I know. His Celtic blood does flow; but his father's words are what he hears for now. Recall you now his father the first out in rebellion; to seize the crown when good King Alexander was thus killed ten years ago."

Then William told his brother in law that he wanted to seek the peace with Percy. The Steward seemed relieved at last and quickly agreed. "We should meet with the others and de Lindsay, should he come with us to present this peace?" he asked. Le Hardi nodded that he agreed. "Your brother John must also come to join us," he said, his overwhelming sorrow now telling in his voice. Le Hardi continued in grave tones, "I came here to right the wrong of Berwick. To remove my guilt that all those died and I was spared to remember every face that trusted in my protection. The anger that I feel for broken promises of Lord Edward to diminish with mace and sword of battle here in Ayrshire; now another such surrender for this sorry knight," he said then to himself, my agony my own in silence and despair.

On 7th July 1297 a covenant by Henry de Percy and Robert de Clifford, on the part of the English command to the Scottish party, was sent to the Scottish nobles agreeing to the peace proposed by Robert Brus, the Steward, de Lindsay, John brother of the Steward, and William Douglas. On behalf of Sir Edward, King of England these commanders to avoid greater peril and make some appeasement, covenanted that these Scots leaders and those of their parties would not be imprisoned for any trespass and would be assured safety of limbs, lives, lands, tenements, goods and chattels. Two days later a letter of response, a confession to their deeds of treason was drawn up by Bishop Wishart.

Seagate Castle 9 July 1297

The Earl of Carrick, James the Seneschal, John his brother, Alexander de Lindsay and William Douglas signed a submission to Henry de Percy and Robert de Clifford in Irvine at Seagate Castle. The document was written in

DEBORAH RICHMOND FOULKES

Norman French by the bishop; a confession of their rebellion against the king. The instrument of their capitulation read as follows:

To all those who see or hear this writing: Robert de Brus, Count of Carrick; James, Steward of Scotland; Alexander de Lindsay; John brother of the Steward, and William of Douglas, greeting in Jesus Christ. Be it known to all men: Whereas it is a thing known to you all that we, with the "Commune" of our lands, did rise in arms against our lord Sir Edward, by the grace of God, King of England, Lord of Ireland, and Duke of Guienne, and against his peace within his lordship in the land of Scotland and Galloway, have committed arsons, homicides and various robberies.... we, on our own behalf and on that of those of the said "Commune" who were our adherents, make submission to the will of our lord the King aforesaid, to make whatsoever amends as may be his pleasure for the said homicides, arsons, and robberies. Saving always the points reserved in writing which we hold from Sir Henry de Percy and Sir Robert de Clifford, commanders of the host of the noble King of England in Scotland. In witness whereof we have placed our seals on this writing. Written at Irewin, the ninth day of July, in the twenty-fifth year of King Edward's reign.

They each affixed their seals in red at the bottom of the document. It is done, mused a saddened William by this unfortunate deed.

Thus they admitted to atrocities of arson and murder and robberies, committing their men to do the same; treason to the king. A second agreement was signed on this 9th July where the Bishop, the Steward, and de Lindsay all agreed as surety of their lands and persons for the surrender of Earl Carrick; his young daughter Marjorie to become the ward of Edward's

324

MY TRUTH LIES IN THE RUINS

vassal to insure the peace pledged to his king. The bishop was permitted release, but not as the others to cross to France in service to his king; he left Knadgerhill for Glasgow immediately to report for his parole in late July in Berwick so he agreed. William Douglas having stayed the night in the de Ferrers manor of Dreghorn had readied to depart Irvine. Le Hardi and some several Douglas men at arms were riding to his stronghold in Auchinleck, to join his wife and family, before his seal was set and hardened on the lamented document. The others remained at Seagate Castle to quibble more about the terms and dates of their parole at Berwick; to serve or not in Gascony.

Figure CVII-Part III; the Capitulation of Irvine; used with permission of the National Archives, Kew, Surrey, England

The next days brought word of more unrest in the north; Wallace and de Moray drew swords with many in their following and chased more English south to Edinburgh's protection. At Seagate Castle other issues and agendas ruled the day; though hardly any knew yet of their significance. The de Percys have long memories it has been said. Sir Henry de Percy recalled indignantly of Walter once of Yorkshire; himself beheaded without allowance for surety, the custom of the realm. This treachery upon his kin; to disallow such pledge, the doom passed by orders of Baron Douglas and Andrew de Moray the Scottish justiciar recalled Sir Henry angrily. This same Douglas recently submitting to the pleasure of his king, he smiled in contemplation. And that Justiciar de Moray held now in the Tower of

DEBORAH RICHMOND FOULKES

London at Edward's pleasure; father of the esquire in league with William Wallace in the north. Perhaps there is more justice that can be done here, Sir Henry said to himself. William le Hardi would come to know this truth: the Percys are a rotten bunch, sure aye!

    Lord Percy reflected on his chance meeting not long ago with his kin in Yorkshire, Lord Matthew Lovaine. This Lovaine held lands from his grandfather Godfrey, while Sir Henry's lands came from the kin of Lord Godfrey, known as Joscelin Lovaine. Their family lands adjoined, but were a nuisance to Lord Matthew; growing older, having lands and tenements in Essex, Suffolk, and Gloucestershire for his income; his Yorkshire lands he could remove from his estates in chief, for a price. For Sir Henry, these Lovaine estates if acquired would be a prize to measure out his tenements; increasing his vast holdings of Yorkshire lands, hoping as he would to become an earl. This day Lovaine spent as he had the last, much lamented and enraged at one Scot named Douglas. His complaint the same; the savage Douglas kidnapped his daughter; holding then his only heir captive to steal her inheritance from Lord Lovaine. The Steward of Eye was much damaged; enraged the more to find this Douglas governor of Berwick Castle in rebellion to Lord Edward.

Figure CVIII-Part Three; Seagate Castle in Irvine; the ruins of the original castle were moved to this site to preserve it from the rising water levels near the old port city; photo courtesy of Hugh Robertson

MY TRUTH LIES IN THE RUINS

Now the time has come to get my justice and secure some lands of favor in the process conspired young Henry; so he took advantage of the moment and entered into a gentlemen's agreement with Lord Lovaine. The plan was formed; to find Douglas and set the trap; to yield him to some final English prison. When he accomplished this task, the Yorkshire lands would become de Percy lands. The revenge for his kin Walter would be obtained. And Lord Lovaine, the grieving father, would be satisfied to see Lord Douglas no longer at liberty.

Sir Henry returned to Seagate Castle and called back the remaining nobles to his court at Irvine: the Earl of Carrick, the Steward, and de Lindsay all politely reported. Earl Robert was pressed to swear that he had no knowledge of a new uprising with William Wallace, but since Douglas and Wishart were no longer present, "Could thus these two noblemen now missing be involved?" asked Percy in his convincing manner. Fearing grave reprisals, no defense was given for Wishart or for Douglas; the nobles present allowed de Percy his contrived words, to accuse Lord Douglas and Bishop Wishart of breaking their agreement; joining again in rebellion against King Edward. De Percy told the Scots that he needed to speak with Douglas and Wishart face to face; he ordered de Lindsay and the Steward to find the baron and the prelate and ask them to report to him in Edinburgh. He did not divulge his true plan: he was going to charge them with breaking their agreements when they reported to his court. His plan of brilliance as he characterized the ruse was set into action. And when they finally reported, he would arrest them; imprison them for treason.

Percy dispatched the Steward to find Wishart in Glasgow; to beckon the good bishop to Edinburgh to answer the charges of his compliance with the rebels in the north. "I will be in Edinburgh in one week with four days," Henry de Percy told the noblemen. Then turning to de Lindsay he instructed him to report the same day as surety for the Earl of Carrick until the young Marjorie was surrender to his ward. Before reporting he also told de Lindsay to search out William Douglas and have him come to Edinburgh in person. "For Douglas to attend and answer with impunity; defend himself of alliance in the rebellion of the north with Wallace," he allowed. Having set his trap for Douglas, Percy left for Edinburgh where he would be surrounded with English men at arms and have a sound donjon prison to hold these rebels of his king.

Auchinleck

Ellie was in the laird's chamber, doing embroidery with Muriel to pass the time. "Mother, I am so scared that we might leave our Scotland; where might we go to flee from Edward's wrath?" she asked. Ana brought them in some watered wine and small bannocks to ease their hunger. "When your father joins us we will make our plans. Perhaps to go to Brabant and stay with my family; that would be a place fine young ladies would enjoy!" smiled Ellie. Muriel sighed and wrinkled her nose, pouting at her fate. "You are always so hopeful; for this lass to worry more and sleep less these days I do, fearful to leave our Scotland." Ellie told her that she always hoped for some travels and new places to explore. "That is how Ana and I came to Scotland; to take our leave of Essex for adventure," she told her daughter. Ana added that they found much more than they expected; true love and courting from a handsome knight, "Your father and Sir Shamus to come upon this lass in the forests of Ayr, writing poetry and charming your dear mother all the while!" Ellie smiled warmly, while fondly remembering those days.

Figure CIX-Part Three; remains of Auchinleck Tower in Ayrshire; the Douglases held a manor house near this site in the 13th century. The ruined tower was built on a motte.

Patric de Douglas rushed in, announcing with great excitement the arrival of Lord Douglas! James was in the great hall of the Auchinleck manor and came running to the laird's chamber, "Father has returned!" Little Amy was playing on the floor with the Deerhound. "Papa," she squealed, running to her father as he entered the chamber. Ellie beamed and she too rose to embrace her husband. "Lord Will, so relieved of heart I am to see you," she said so poignantly that William felt his own heart shiver. "Lady El, what sorry fate have I brought to you and our dear children; to be abducted in the wee hours of the day from our home in Douglasdale!" Ellie and Gilley held each other tightly for some time, only to be interrupted by the wee tugging hand of Amy, "Papa, Amy missed you so." William knelt down to his wee lass, the very picture of her dear mother at that age he thought. "Your father is here to protect you all; never to leave your side again, that God does will it so I pray!" Then to his surprise the shy laddie Hugh came to put his arms around his father. "Hugh wants his fad' er home!" he said quietly. Sir Shamus was reserved in his exhilaration as he greeted Gilley; quietly wagging his tail he came to lick his master's face as he held Hugh. The homecoming felt warm and comforting to William; I need my family more than ever in my life, he sighed to himself.

Ellie told him of how the Earl of Carrick came with fire and sword, setting fires and plundering the castle; paying his men with Douglas booty. "We had the coffers emptied as you told us; the coinage sewn so neatly in our surcotes. The charter-chest James brought to me; and neatly did I place the deeds and documents safely here," she boasted, showing Gilley how well they followed the plans he made should mischief come to Douglasdale. "And our James when readying our horses spoke the Gaelic to the farrier to send Sir David and Patric to our rescue; to Pennyglen." The old warrior smiled broadly "The Doughty Douglases, my good wife and children; fearless in their tasks. That you escaped from Edward's ward by cleverness and great resolve, does cheer me still!" Gilley said proudly, then praising Ellie and James and the rest of the Douglas household for their bravery all the more. "When Sir Andrew came into my camp he brought with him evidence of Carrick treachery," said William showing them the pennon that was left by Earl Robert's men at arms at Douglas Castle. James took the Carrick silk from his father to keep it as his own.

"When first I went to tell the Steward the fate of my lands and family, he informed me that one Robert comes to join us now." Ellie gasped, "Earl Robert met with you and others now in rebellion?" she asked Gilley. He nodded yes and continued with his story. "Riding confidently into Irvine, through the camps of Scots there he came to stop at Neadgweres, overlooking Scots Loch; swearing allegiance to our cause. My first thought to run him through for his grievous act upon our household," said William showing his disappointment in the young earl.

He then explained that after speaking further with the Steward, he decided first to hear Robert's tale to tell; then to use the sword upon him. "Tempered by the forces of the Percy and the Clifford now advancing to the south side of the river at Tarryholm near Warrix, Lord Douglas sought a temporary peace with one Robert Brus the younger," he concluded. "When the Earl of Carrick told you of his deeds, what then was your response?" asked James. Gilley told his son the exact words he shared with the young earl. "My dear James, more than once before I told you; core values must one have to avert strong influence of another that would compromise your truth. That Robert has a good heart can well be seen; but he has yet to learn the meaning of his truth within him; God's own truth to speak his heart not yet I fear."

"And the others there; did Wallace come, de Moray too?" he asked his father. William told them that they were all at Knadgerhill, Scots united in their cause; until the arrival of one Robert Brus, when discontent and arguments prevailed in camp. "Some nobles would follow only Balliol; others inspired by the arrival of Earl Robert to follow him. Lord Douglas was there to fight the English and rid himself of Berwick's shadows still upon him," said William shaking his head in sorrow for the nobles now fighting among themselves. "And when Robert Brus swore for himself Wallace and de Moray thus took their leave with many of their followers. Too few Scots remaining to fight the mighty numbers of Lord Edward." Then a curious look crossed William's face. "Ellie, the shield of Sir Henry de Percy was the lion rampant dexter, azure; the blue lion, arms of Lovaine at Douglas Castle. Why would de Percy raise this banner?" he asked .

Ellie told him that long ago one Joscelin Lovaine married Agnes de Percy, but they deferred to use the Percy family name for their issue. "The rampant lion azure the arms of my grandfather Godfrey Lovaine, so used by his grandson Matthew now in England. Curious this de Percy would use it on his shields," she reflected. "My first thought the presence of your father now in Scotland," joked William.

"No safe surrender for Lord Douglas should he be there; to Edward's prison would I be before the wax had hardened for my seal!" William said, laughing at his words of humor. Ellie had a grave look on her face. "Is this de Percy that commanded Edward's army a knight about the age of Earl Robert?" she asked him. He nodded yes, then more curious, "What troubles you my sweet lass? Ellie thought for some time. "I am frightened by his association with my father" said Ellie, "to use a shield with my father's armorial achievements are new to this de Percy knight." She told William very clearly that a fearful alliance of Lovaine and de Percy could only bode trouble for the Douglases. He tried to calm her with his assuring words, "Your William is here now, not to meet for his parole in Berwick until three weeks or more." James spoke very slowly, with concern as well. "Father, you made your peace but then you must report for your parole? Are you going to prison?" he asked. "It is mere formality to surrender then to muster in Gascony with dear Edward; later will we speak of this and the plans for our good future."

Gilley sat at the table with his family and realized they were in shortage for some fish and meat of game upon their platters. "On the morrow we will go on morning hunt James with good Patric here to replenish now our larder. As for Sir David; he must not venture out until Lady Douglas feels more secure now in her manor; that I heard from our Sir Andrew of that fateful morning!" said the contented laird amused by his own jokes. "Lady Douglas has thus told me; no more hunts, that she might be abducted from her castle!" said Sir David. They were all laughing at their strained circumstances but pleased to be together in this Douglas stronghold. Muriel was the first to speak directly about their plans for the future. "Father, pray where we live now that our lands are seized. Mother said that our cattle, sheep and crops growing are also to be sold."

Ellie interjected words of calm to the discussion. "Your father will arrange for our safety; when once decided where to go, we will announce it to the Douglas household. More than our children will thus be affected by our choice." "Though I would want to stay in Scotland, living in Paris would be my second preference for a home!" said James, always happy for adventure in his plans. William rose to from the table for their feasting. "Lady El," he said, holding out his arm in escort to her now, "your husband would enjoy your good company in chamber to express his sentiments in private for her bravery of countenance these days." Ellie's smile was growing to a grin as she felt her cheeks flush; feeling most like that day she first met him in Ayr's forests. "Lord Will, my pleasure it would be to join you."

They entered the small laird's chamber; surprised to smell the lovely scents of rosemary and lavender. Ana was supervising the pouring of a bath; readied now for Lord Douglas and the Lady of his heart. "Dear Ana, this old knight is pleased by your good thoughts!" said William. She smiled and told him she was sorry for the trouble in his Scotland; but she would be pleased wherever they would choose to move their household. "Ana will go and happily; so long as you and my girl want me, Ana will be there. "Hush now. You will never leave us; I could not live without your great help and good words. No more of these silly thoughts!" said Ellie, hugging her dear Ana, more friend and family than maid-servant of all these years. Ana excused herself, chuckling that the scented bath was so well received.

The steaming hot water ran down the body of the grateful knight; his wife washed his back and massaged his neck stiff with pain from the dampness of tents and war camps. "Sit here with me dear Ellie," he motioned for her to join him in the tub. "I need your good counsel for our plans to make." The softness of her body cuddled in against him relaxed him so; he but forgot the sad surrender signed this day and his parole in three short weeks. "Lord Will," she said to him softly. "Pray where shall we go?" Gilley sighed heavily, "Lady El, that decision this laird has yet to make." Ellie asked him if he would prefer Lovaine in Brabant or Paris, the Isle de la Cité. "The one or the other makes me no difference; I only want to be here, to live in Scotland," he said mournfully. "Douglasdale is my paradise Ellie; to live elsewhere is not to live at all I fear." Ellie's eyes welled with tears; her husband's sad demeanor overwhelmed her now. "Lord Will," she sobbed, "Your wife needs her husband to lead us and protect us from Lord Edward." The strain of the events these last weeks crushed her from within; though he held her tightly she was crying uncontrollably. "William Douglas!" she shouted to him now, "Eleanora needs you; your children demand your help. Lead us from this nightmare that we have known these fifteen months since Berwick!" she pleaded with him. Pounding her fist into his large chest, she sobbed and sobbed. 'I need my husband, Lord Will!"

William's words would not come; his devastation silenced him. A warrior must fight he said to himself; even that was stolen from this humble knight he mused. He stroked her hair and softly said to her, "Lady El, I will entertain your thoughts; to take our household where ever you would go." Strangely he was not sure what he meant by his words; never before was he so uncertain. What should he do he wondered to himself. His love for his wife and children seemed separated from him, in a fog lost now to his heart; he felt isolated. So many were dependent on his words of counsel but he could offer nothing; their lands for income gone, the table barren of food, his coffers dwindling and soon there would be no Douglas stronghold to secure for shelter of a home. He held his wife and began to weep himself; the depression of his circumstance was too difficult to bear alone.

"Dear Ellie, it is your husband who needs you and your healing ways. Everything I risked now lost; yet no battle came of it, to cure this wounded knight of his great sorrow." For some lang time they held each other; realizing the gravity of their situation they turned to prayer. Each one rose silently from the tub and dressed. Kneeling together in the small alcove used as a chapel, they sought the guidance of God and St. Bride. Ellie and Gillie had always been faithful in their religion; devout in their ways. Dear God and Blessed Virgin keep our family together, safe in your arms she prayed; Gilley shared words and sentiments much the same, asking for the healing also of St. Bride. Silently they got up from the supplication and fell gratefully into each other's arms to sleep in comfort for some time. When Ellie finally woke she rolled over to cuddle into him. "Lady El," he said quietly kissing her on her head, "If Brabant is where you want to go; it is done." Ellie looked up into his eyes now dry from tears spent. "Gilley, my dear one, I only spoke of Lovaine in Brabant as I have family there; Paris is too a place where I could so remain. Scotland is my home but not safe for us to stay here. Lord Edward seized our lands for greater purpose I do fear." William agreed that the writs thus issued were ominous. "We must make our plans; to remove ourselves from Scotland," he told her. "Perhaps to leave from Irvine in two weeks. Our coinage will take our household to Brabant;

we will need more funds when we arrive though. There are others here in Scotland who might help us; ease the burden of our expenses some," he said to her.

The early morning hunt gave time for father and son to sort out the sadness of events, making plans to restore some stability to their lives. "James, your father will most depend on your good assistance lo these few months. We travel now to Flanders then to Lovaine lands and your mother's family; in exile will we live until others rally to our cause," he said with some semblance of hope in his words. "Father, someday I pray to return to Scotland and make Douglasdale our home again. That wish has become my daily prayer to St.Bride as she watches over us," the lad said to his father. James also added with dispassion, "Douglas Castle once our home, now better razed to the very ground than to house the English garrison of Lord Edward." William looked over at his son riding Fortis proudly; a grown man in thought he had become these last months his father knew now.

Figure CX-Part Three; Auchinleck churchyard with motte in the background; situated in Kyle Stewart

The small band of Douglas hunters and hounds cast shortened shadows on the glen as they rode down to the banks of the wee burn where they would set up camp; tie up their horses while they took their bows with them on foot with some of their hounds leashed in service, in search of game. William stopped his horse briefly before descending the brae with the others; to take in the scenery of his Scotland. If Brabant is to be our home and Scotland but a memory; this old laird must get his fill of Celtic beauty this day, he mused sadly. He ran his eyes between the groves of forest hills and over pheasant woods. The lush of summer's green foliage and purple willow herb blowing in the light whispering breeze spoke a language of gentle memories to this old knight; of happier times in his Scotland. William loved the early light of dawn; marveled as the rays of sunlight danced over the mid summer broom going to its hairy seed. I will miss most the lands of my ancestors; the friends will come about, but the lands cannot, he sighed. As the sun rose on the moorish lands, the old warrior's eyes teared some; he blamed it on the wind, but knew it was not so. He watched wistfully now, noticing the remaining sea mist rise up from her bed, making her escape to the sky, a grey filmy mass streaked with bright diagonals of golden light. William spurred his palfrey on now, carefully and slowly down into the glen where he joined the others.

The lands of Celts seemed to know that this was William's last hunt in his homeland. And they offered up a bounty that most bowman hunters could only dream about. With so much hare and doe and the grouse to grace their table after such short time at hunt, the Douglas party decided to take their rest near a small spring that fed into Lugar Water down below, running south of them. James and Patric made a small fire to cook their bannocks on a griddle. The dry branches of ash crackled in the small flames; the smoke waffled in the air, curling straight up to the bright blue sky of an unusually clear day in Ayrshire woods. The weary knight took his rest to sit some small distance from them with Sir Shamus by the spring's small pool. "Father," said James, "would I be some bother to offer you a share of bannock now; you look so lost in thought?" William looked up and motioned his son to sit by him on the boulders circling the spring. "Our Celtic wisdom always tells us to seek the magic power of the water for reflection; revelations from the Otherworld to help us here in this one. The water thus a symbol of the truth that lies beneath the surface; that I could see it now would please me so."

Sitting beside him the lad asked thoughtfully, "You are not yet convinced of going into exile, leaving Scotland?" Sadly William shook his head; "A poet knight am I by preference; a warrior was I bred to be. It is my truth to never leave the battle field without a fight; twice now have I compromised my values, far to the east in Berwick, the same distance west to Irvine," he told his son with some foreboding. "No, I want to remain in Scotland, but must take leave to protect my family." William sighed deeply, wanting his son to know him truly. "Three most important duties of Lord Douglas are to be Clan Chief; Lord and Chief Magistrate for his lands and adherents; and husband and father to his family," he said, adding that only his family mattered now. "This warrior's heart to tell most soon no other place but Scotland would I be; a knight-errant with no loyalties or obligations, to fight alone against Edward's tyranny. But I found true love

MY TRUTH LIES IN THE RUINS

with Eleanora; and my children I love most as I love my self, you so included there my dear James. No father could have a better son than you." William rose to leave. James got up and put his arms around his father, hugging him tightly for some while. "Thank you for the honesty of your thoughts. You have never spared me the truth and I hold that as a gift close to my soul dear father," said the young man with heavy heart for his family, himself, his country and the patriot Lord Douglas.

William and James with Patric returned to the manor house with much meat for the larder. The cook was one of the tenants in Auchinleck, not having much experience preparing meals for such a large household every day. Ana, Muriel and Ellie were throwing in their hands to help when Lord Douglas brought in the rewards of their hunt that morning. "There will be some good feasting for this evening," said William. Everyone was in a jovial mood with the thought of full bellies of meat. "Look what cook brought from Mauchline," said Ellie, showing William a half hog's head of good wine. "We will enjoy much wine with that feasting; some music too if we can persuade Lord Douglas to play the small pipes!" Ellie was laughing now; holding up the bagpipes that she found packed away at the manor house. Gilley's eyes lit up when he saw her find, "I do recall now that my father had them put away so many years ago that was!" he said happily. "James, your father William will show you how to play the small pipes on the morrow." A silly smirk crossed the face of his oldest son. "Rather would I learn more to play the dulcimer," teased James, "Mother, you did not find such instrument yet hidden now away?" he asked her, feigning interest to secure one. Muriel teased her brother, "No we did not find one, but now that we know your good intentions we will secure one for you on Hogmanay!" laughing heartily as she joked good naturedly with her brother.

William seemed to come alive again with his family's determination and their resolve to make do with their meager station. He beckoned Ellie outside the kitchen to the hall; but she was resisting, pretending to be too involved to stop her work. Then suddenly the knight returned to the kitchen and swooped her up in his arms, holding her high up over his head, "So you prefer the work of a kitchen lass to joining your good husband when he calls you. Your William will now instruct his wife on the proper way to greet her laird!" he threw her boldly over his shoulder and carried her out of the kitchen laughing like "the savage beast Sholto," as Ellie called him now. "Put me down, the noo!" she cried out as he carried off to the laird's chamber. The kitchen staff, young Douglases and Ana all were laughing, Sir David sitting in the great hall just looked up to nod in his amusement; everyone was happy that Lord Douglas' good humor had returned, if only it would last.

Figure CXI-Part Three; Barnweill Manor was held by Alexander de Lindsay and was near Craigie Castle in Ayrshire held by his kin Walter de Lindsay

Three days later William and his small hunting party were returning from their second morning hunt. As they arrived William recognized the horses and men at arms of de Lindsay near the stables in the rear of the small courtyard. Few men knew the location of this messuage; fewer still knew the Douglases would be there. Trouble has come to Auchinleck feared William and I but here four days, he mused. In the great hall sat a grim knight talking quietly with Lady Douglas. "Dear Alex, what brings you here? Is there trouble at Barnweill, your manor there I know," asked Gilley. Alexander de Lindsay's face was clouded by worry and fear that William had never seen. Alex rose to greet his friend and kin, hugging him, though not his fashion in the past, he asked William to sit down. "Sir Henry received the word of de Moray's rebellion in the north accompanied by William Wallace," he told them. "The English commander called the nobles yet remaining at Knadgerhill, all to speak about Wallace and young Andrew; did we believe that the others now so missing were responsible for the mischief in the Highlands?" Alex described the rigorous questioning of Sir Henry and the Clifford. He felt that they were contriving mischief of their own, for one bishop known as Wishart and a baron named le Hardi. "What trouble do you have with this young knight de Percy?" asked de Lindsay. "He speaks your name with such disdain I fear."

Ellie looked on sadly; their lives were so peaceful these last four days, yet now ugliness rose before them. "Gilley, something seems so wrong here. This de Percy is known to us as kin to one named Walter; the very one to whom you handed down the doom, that was beheaded. And thus recently he holds this strange alliance with my father that his banners carry the Lovaine blue lion," she said ominously to her husband." Gilley showed concern to her last remarks but it was Sir Alex who responded out loud. "Dear Eleanora; this Walter, kin of Henry, that this knight knows him most as well. He trespassed on the king's rights; married the widow of my dear kin Walter de Lindsay, to steal the dower lands of Lady Christina of Craigie without license; though this was many years ago. A villain was he; not to be so trusted." Ellie continued to elaborate; telling them both that the de Percy's were obsessed with their name and more so with their lands and holdings; scoundrels all. "There were problems of clear title for Lovaine lands held in Yorkshire for this de Percy. The manors of my father adjoined these messuages and carucates that passed down to Sir Henry from his father. Perhaps that he has ambitions for my father's lands;" she conjectured. "To have changed the de Percy armorial achievements, to use now the Lovaine Or, Rampant Lion Azure; indicates a fearful alliance with my father; to flatter him for gain, I know it!"

Alex de Lindsay was terribly confused so William explained the strange interactions and relationships between the de Percys and Lovaines; that might include some grave contrivance and false accusation against le Hardi. "Here is what I question: Would Sir Henry desire satisfaction for the doom passed on his kin Walter; thus detain this Douglas for false crimes against the king? And would his accomplice be Matthew Lovaine, Ellie's father; seeking vengeance for this Scotsman's marriage to his daughter?" William paused himself to contemplate the frightful thoughts. "And are some Lovaine lands in Yorkshire once of Matthew now pledged to Henry as payment for this deed I wonder?" he asked. "Strange that you would say that," said Alex. "The Steward inquired of de Percy lands in Yorkshire when Sir Henry was describing his good interests in Scotland and Northumbria to come." Gilley shook his head and threw Ellie an ominous look; thus could it be true, are Ellie's fears valid? He pondered the possibility with raw fear. If de Percy's intentions were to falsely accuse new rebellion of this humble knight, an ambitious knight and an angry father could easily have this Scot imprisoned or worse, William reflected gravely to himself. "This intrigue is compelling and frightening to me," says Ellie. "With this Henry and my father there is de-mischef here about, I know it now!"

Alex was greatly unsettled by this news; he continued with the rest of the message from Edward's vassal, to see if it might reveal their motives more clearly. "Dear William you are asked to report to Edinburgh, as soon as I do find you; to make explanation of your impunity in the rebellion with de Moray now and Wallace. My own report of person now required there in Edinburgh most as well, as surety for Earl Robert to bring his daughter to their ward. What should I tell Sir Henry on your behalf?" he asked Gilley. "Surety for Brus?" gasped Ellie. "What of your surety for parole, dear William? Do you have hostages to surrender to Edward's ward?" she asked, her fears greatly aroused. "My surrender of parole in Berwick to fight in Gascony with Edward; no surety required as I was to muster with the king," le Hardi assured his wife.

Alex told them that the Steward was going to Bishop Wishart with the same message from the Percy; come to Edinburgh Castle to give evidence with impunity for the rebellion after the covenants received at Irvine's Seagate Castle. "Only three short days from the time we set our seals to that dreaded document do we now have a change to terms from one Sir Henry; another broken promise of Lord Edward do I fear," said Gilley. Alex was not sure if this was a broken agreement; but he was sure that de Percy had extorted an accusation from Earl Robert that the only nobles involved with Wallace and de Moray must be Wishart and Douglas for their absence here. "Dear William, I would speak on your behalf that you have been here with Lady Douglas and your family since when you left from Irvine; to help you clear your name and reputation as rebel to the king," said de Lindsay. "I still hold my lands and titles; my word should count some for merit I do feel."

Figure CXII-Part Three; Dreghorn manor in Ayrshire was held by William de Ferrers; the old village kirk that lies within the manor was being dismantled this day

"Your good words and kind support most welcome dear Alex. I will report some five days hence to Edinburgh Castle to clear my good name. I need some time; our plans to make from Irvine's port by cog we go to Flanders," said Gilley quietly. Alexander was stunned by his words. Le Hardi answered his shocked grimace. "The Douglases to go into exile; with no lands or income we must chance to live with Ellie's kin away from

Scotland's shores. It is done." Alex sat in silence for some time. "For your journey, I have some coinage in my war-chest that I will bring to you the morrow; no need for armaments and men at arms to pay for Irvine's muster gives me bounty to my coffers." The grim words of their discussion were being happily interrupted by the arrival of young Archibald and two year old Hugh with their nurses. "My dear God son he has grown so!" said Alex of young Archibald. "And Hugh, so pleased I am to see you as well." The wee lad was so shy and stammered as he spoke; yet he was always smiling and content in his demeanor. "Hugh is happy to see Uncle Alex," as the Douglas children called de Lindsay. The lasses and their brother James with Shamus were returning as well, eager to feast on the morning's hunt. "Will you and your men at arms now join us at our table; cook has some fine surprises thus prepared," said Ellie, relieved by Alex's generosity of coinage and Gilley's openness about their plans to sail for Flanders and Lovaine lands. Muriel and James assisted cook with the platters for the meal and Patric poured the wine. Some semblance of normalcy always seemed to come around the good bounty of our table thought Ellie.

After Sir Alex left for his manor at Barnweill, Gilley called his son James and Sir David to join them in the small withdrawing room where they would make their plans. "Now that Edward's commanders have journeyed on to Edinburgh we will leave for Stewartoun on the morrow. When we reach Kilmarnock, the most of our household will continue to that manor; the turn to Irvine will I take to secure our ship; sailing now to Brabant to serve our plans for exile. Again I can secure the hospitality of the de Ferrers manor in Dreghorn." He told Sir David that he would need his help in getting the horses and pack animals to Fawdon, then transfer the goods to carts to continue south through England. He also explained that the family was taking few belongings when they sailed; a few trunks and Lord Douglas' war-chest was all they he planned to bring with them on the cog.

"Sir William I am pleased to be of assistance; wearing the tabard of de Ferrers and carrying the banners of that family will bring good cover to escape with your horses and belongings," said the English knight. "I will travel with our squires undetected in our true course, staying on in Fairstead near the de Ferrers' manor where I hold my lands. You can send me word there when it is safe to travel on to Brabant." Ellie was pleased with Gilley's plans and the help offered by Sir David to their household. "I was not aware you held your lands in Fairstead; I was first given that manor but then accepted Woodham Ferrers in stead." Gilley continued with his words, their deeds to thus accomplish these next few days. "James are you sure of the location for our manor there in Stewarton?" he asked the lad. "Once leaving Kilmaurs, following the cart path there we ride along the Annick to find our manor house short miles from our uncles' hunting lodge." Gilley was pleased that his son was so accurate with his directions and locations of these smaller Douglas manors. "You have been studying the charters well, your mother's influence I feel, sure aye!"

Figure CXIII-Part Three; Medieval paintings of the Passion of Christ were discovered during restoration work at the Fairstead church located in what was an original de Ferrers manor in Essex

Gilley told them that once he secured the passage for the household setting the date of their departure he would join them in Stewartoun. "The morning next we will depart for Dalserf to tell my sister of our decisions here." Sadly he added, "Her own husband now with God I her only kin to yet remain here." They would travel quickly to Livingston he explained, to the manor house that was well hidden there; unknown to the escheators for the confusion in the charters. "Then I will leave for Edinburgh only some few hours ride to meet there with de Percy; restore my good name, this knight's last possession thus allowed from dear Edward's wrath and vengeance now upon us." Ana and the other Douglas household members were invited in now and told briefly of their plans. "Your choice to leave with us and sail to Brabant or return to Douglasdale," he said, offering guarded escort to Lanarkshire if they desired to return to their former homes. "Good Ana, you will go to Brabant; Lord Douglas does so will it!" he teased her, knowing her decision was to remain with Ellie and the children where ever they would be.

MY TRUTH LIES IN THE RUINS

Lugdon

Fawdon

Figure CXIV-Part Three; an attempt at uniformity in writing was taught to priests and others who recorded charters and rolls of the pipes in the 13th century; but letters and spelling varied greatly; here Lugdon or Lugton and Fawdon are compared in the handwriting from medieval records may explain why Chalmers once wrote that Elizabeth Stewart married the laird of Lugdon, a title that was used much later with respect to a Lothian(e) manor, and not William le Hardi Douglas, Lord of Fawdon. Spellings of Douglas differed as well: Dvglas; Duvglase; Duugelass were recorded in some records.

Livingston 18th July 1297

Ellie woke screaming in the middle of the night, it was barely past midnight when a nightmare scared her from her sleep. In a cold sweat she was crying from the ordeal so vivid to her that she told William he must not go to meet de Percy. "Dear husband this dream so real I could feel your hands when I reached for yours, so cold from the rain, sitting on your palfrey, held prisoner!" The night was an uneasy one for William as well. He wondered if the meeting called for him and Wishart was a ploy to capture them and revoke their parole. "Ellie, dear lass," he said as he rocked her in his arms, "Come let me make you forget your fears." He rubbed her back and soothed her with his words and touching ways. "Will you love me tomorrow as you love me today?" he smiled at her, beginning the rituals of their love.

He held her tightly to him, but her calmness left her as quickly as it arrived when he first began their love making; she was truly scared now, worse than when she first woke up from that dream; he sighed so to himself as she continued her warnings. "William, I fear that if you go that I would lose you now; please reconsider from this premonition of my dream," she pleaded with him. William rose from the bed, to dress himself for his journey; no valet to be had this morning. "Eleanora, I must go; I have told you this before; your husband must defend the one possession he retains, his good name and honor." Ellie was not hearing his words; she was angry. "My dreams so real, are for good reason; the Percy wants you in his prison. I do know it now! William! YOU MUST NOT GO!" she screamed at him. William had never fought with his wife; his words to her were always calming; but he could give no words of comfort to her now. I must defend my honor; no sword have I raised in rebellion since I put my seal to that document of shame. "Eleanora!" he shouted back at her "I will go. It is done!"

Ellie was crying; shocked at the anger in his words and arguments, fighting that the couple had never before experienced. She ran to him with anger in her eyes, desperation in her voice, "You can not go; I forbid it!" she yelled grabbing him with her hands. He pushed her aside with cold rebuff, as strongly as he could without hurting her. His face was contorted with words he would not say. Dressed now, downing his gambeson and coif, grabbing his mail hauberk, he turned and left her standing there in abject pain; no sweet goodbye or kiss was forthcoming from Lord Douglas for his bride. He was leaving; he slammed the great oak door to their chamber. Why could she not understand, a man must have his honor and his name, he cried out to himself!

Figure CXV-Part Three; Livingston Village from the church yard; the Earl of Fife deeded the manors of Livingston and Hermanston to Archibald Douglas, grandfather of William le Hardi

He shouted to his squire to bring his palfrey for their leaving now! Ellie was with Ana who came in when she heard Gilley leave. "Ana, he hates me. I told him not to go; a nightmare did I have where he was a prisoner, the de Percy laughing all the while." Ana held her and rocked her back and forth. "There child, your husband does not hate you. He has lost everything, his lands, his titles, his Douglasdale. Now go, run to him; tell you are sorry and you love him so." Ellie wiped her face and ran to the great hall where he was breaking fast with porridge and some ale. "Lord Will," she cried and ran to his open arms as he stood up. "I am so sorry my sweet lass," he said with tears streaming down his face. "No Gilley, it is I who must apologize for my angry words. I love you with all my heart and soul for all eternity." He brought her to sit in his lap. "Your William will return to you and we will go to Brabant; I promise my dear wife." "Will you come with me to pray for safe return?" she asked him. He nodded and picked her up, taking her to the small chapel in the tower, a wee corner barely room for two to pray at once. They returned to the great hall when de Lindsay's arrival was announced.

"Lord Will, here I sit in robes of chamber with no veil for my hair or covering on my feet; I must go and get myself dressed before you leave." She barely ran by de Lindsay. "Good morning Sir Alex," she said with an embarrassed smile, her long dark hair flowing down her back. He sat down with William. "We have never had such angry words in nine years more now married," said Gilley. "A nightmare Ellie had that I would be taken in ward, never to see her again." Alex looked at his friend and kin and quietly told him that his wife Alice too was fearful of their reporting to de Percy. James came from his chamber that he shared with Hugh and baby Archibald. He was looking sheepishly at his father having heard the disturbance coming from the laird's chamber early on. "Come here to sit my son. Your mother will require your good humor this day while I travel to Edinburgh to return tonight or early morning." James told him that he was worried for his father and wanted to join him on the ride. "No James, but thank you for the offer of your good company. Your father needs your presence at the manor with our family.

William had sent word for Thomas Dickson to join them at their manor house in Livingston. They would ride out together joined by Alex de Lindsay and his squires and men at arms, to meet at Edinburgh Castle with Sir Henry de Percy. Ellie joined everyone now in the great hall, looking radiant in a lovely surcote of bright blue, hardly worn before. She knew that Gilley would like the way she appeared; she smiled when he saw her. His eyes radiated his delight and he rose, ready to leave, but first he went to Ellie and held her, kissing her in front of their guests and James. "Your husband appreciates your bravery; by St. Bride will I be home the morning, or the sooner, sure aye!" he told her with his well know bravado. Out the front doors of the tower he went with Sir Alex; he vaulted to his horse, showing off his physical prowess to his Lady Eleanora. Gilley was gone, into the morning sun, on to Edinburgh.

The small group of riders appeared on the great hill of the castle to be received with courtesy as they entered the great hall where de Percy was holding council with his own vassals. His men at arms were stationed around the great chamber as if he was expecting trouble from outside attack. "Greetings Sir Alex, and Sir William; good that you could come this day.

The good bishop arrives on the morrow; delayed some now in Glasgow." De Percy wasted no time in getting to the issue most strongly on his mind. "Sir William, your presence in the north with Wallace concerns this vassal of the king, commander of the army of Lord Edward." William started to repudiate the charges, but was silenced by de Percy's words, his English men at arms now moving to Douglas' side. Thomas Dickson was taken out of the great hall. William's heart began to pound, chilling silence filled the hall; was Ellie right, this a trap set by Percy and Lovaine, to drum up charges of rebellion, false treason added to his list of transgressions he asked himself. Sir Alex spoke up, "Sir William was all the while at his manor near my Barnweill, in Ayrshire with his wife and children recently abducted by the Earl of Carrick."

William spoke as well now, "If it pleases you Lord Percy, I am a knight of this good kingdome, holding lands in Northumbria as well. I fought with Lord Edward in the Crusades, following the banner of Earl Adam to Acre as a squire. My seal upon that document is my word and bond; making peace with King Edward my ambition. I seek only to be with my dear wife and family…" William's words trailed off again, this time a sword placed on his person. He had disarmed before entering the chamber; his vassal Dickson held his sword belt and sword, most other of his armaments as well, before they were escorted to the great hall. Sir Henry of Percy would hear no more from these Scots. "Take these men to the prison cells below; when Wishart arrives he will meet the same fate," he ordered. Then we will take these rebels east to Earl Warenne that he will dispense his justice!" gloated this knight named Henry.

William was overwhelmed with fierce anger; he tried to free himself from the three men that held him fast. He used every physical response he could to obtain release from his captors; cursing and gauging at their eyes, he called out to Percy. "What greed or false profit inspires you to commit such treachery on this humble knight; coming here to you in all truth and honor; you defame your family and your own kin, my dear wife," said William, as he spit in the faces of the men at arms taking him to his cell; struggling to free himself from their grasp, a wild animal snarling to protest his captivity in every way he could. His displeasure was apparent; to detain him forcefully and steal his dignity, Lord Douglas was held in chains and fetters. The English guards taunted him; boasting that he would be leaving on the morrow for Berwick Castle and Douglas Tower, renamed for its famous prisoner, the garrison commander in defeat.

Bishop Wishart arrived late that afternoon, earlier than expected. Before his words of protest could be said he was too taken to the donjon prison of the castle; passing the cell of le Hardi, one angry and dejected knight. "We leave on the morrow Bishop," said de Lindsay from the smaller cell across form William Douglas. The heavy doors that closed their cells had one small aperture; they could hear the others but not see them. Le Hardi sat dejected now; unable to believe how foolish he had been to trust the scoundrel de Percy. And what about my Ellie and the children; our plans to leave for Brabant now forfeited by my actions of false pride. She will despise me for my selfishness he berated himself over and over in his head. At that moment his trusted vassal was making his way fast to the Douglas stronghold at Livingston. He must get word to Lady Douglas so she can intercept her husband; making plans for his release. I pray she is able to secure Sir William's freedom, he said pleading to his God.

When late that evening a strange occurrence; only the de Lindsay squires returned with Thomas Dickson. He arrived now on a palfrey, leading William's Pageant; as he rode into the manor. Ellie was sitting in the great hall with the others, Sir David, Ana, Muriel and James. She shrieked in terror when Dickson told of her husband's fate. "They have tricked my William; he will lose his life I fear now! What ever shall we do?" she asked of William's vassal. He told her that they were riding out the next day to Roxburgh then to Berwick where Sir William was returning to Douglas Tower, the prison at the castle held now by the Guardian, Earl Warenne. Ellie devised a plan quickly; James and Sir David with his squire would leave early in the morning escorting Ellie to Edinburgh Castle. There they could encounter Percy with his prisoners; a chance to see William and tell him they would follow. Thomas Dickson planned to stay at the manor until their return, with Ana and the rest of the Douglas household.

Riding hard, her heart pounding and thoughts rushing, Ellie was totally consumed by fear; racing to some unknown outcome as the sun rose on the morning, clouds portending rain shadowed the day. Nothing she had ever known could prepare her for this moment; her husband was a prisoner for treason to the king. Once forgiven when at Berwick, then again at peace for a covenant at Knadgerhill; her William thus accused now for a third time to take up sword against Lord Edward. James was barely keeping up with her great speed as she rode William's palfrey, the jennet or smaller horse she normally rode was not fast enough today. Sir David was the first to recognize the caravan of Lord Percy. The commander of Edward's army and his men at arms with the Lovaine blue lion brandished on their banners was coming down the cart path leaving Edinburgh. The site was so formidable that this de Ferrers knight was visibly shaken when he first saw Lord Douglas in the middle of the procession; a deathlike stare across his face, devastated by his captivity; held in fetters and chains as he rode his horse.

Ellie was unable to speak. Seeing her William in chains, the look of hopeless despair upon his face; she sat frozen in her silence. Sir David first approached Lord Percy on her behalf. The banners that they carried were of

Douglas; the English knight that led them of de Ferrers and Lovaine, his tabard and pennons thus revealed. De Percy received Sir David and listened to his words as he looked upon Lady Eleanora and the young page thus beside her, possibly her son. James was indignant as he dismounted Fortis; Ellie cautioned him to remain aloof. "Anger shown will only thwart our work here James," she whispered to him, encouraging some restraint to his words. "Come, Sir David is returning," she said to her son. Ellie and James rode towards her escort. "Lord Percy has allowed that you may speak with your husband some short time; they are taking him to Berwick as we were told," he told her. "He asks only that you dismount before you approach." Ellie and James got down from their palfreys and walked slowly to William. The rain began to fall again upon them; as it fell intermittently, now and then as nuisance.

Her lips quivered as she tried to speak; all she could do was hold his hand in hers. The damp coldness she felt was exactly as she remembered from that awful dream that was now reality; Lord Douglas was a prisoner of the king. William closed his eyes to keep the tears from streaming down his cheeks. "Eleanora, what misery have I thus brought to you and James for my stubborn self," he said in whispered words barely audible to her. She was squeezing his hand hard, as if for strength to tell him, "Lord Will I love you so," she said, then in Gaelic she continued "We must be careful in what is said. I will move us to Berwick, the de Ferrers manor of my dower lands; then to see Earl Warenne in this matter." James spoke to his father also in the tongue of their Highland cousins. "We will not fail you father; do not give up on us. We love you, believing in your truth that others mock with their foolishness of ignorance." Ellie leaned up to William to embrace him; he leaned down to her for a kiss so dear to him now. Ellie and James turned to leave; their time allowed with William had expired.

The rain was hitting hard upon their faces that they could barely see Lord Douglas as the procession of Lord Percy continued east toward Roxburgh. At Roxburgh Castle Sir Henry remanded the prisoners to the constable of the castle while he rode with some number of men at arms on to Alnwick; here he would meet "my lord the earl" as he called Earl Warenne. The old castle prison was the very one where Richard Knut sheriff of Northumbria once resided in the custody of the Guardians of Scotland; one of them was Robert Wishart. Bishop Wishart would remain in the care of the constable of Roxburgh Castle prison for some time himself; but for Douglas and de Lindsay, Lord Percy had other plans. The return of the Percy men at arms signaled the departure for these two knights; heading further east for Berwick Castle.

MY TRUTH LIES IN THE RUINS

Figure CXVI-Part Three; ruins of Roxburgh Castle on the Tweed; Bishop Wishart was held by constable of the castle in 1297 following his arrest by de Percy

Berwick Castle 24 July 1297

Lord Douglas was again the king's guest in the tower renamed for its famous guest in Berwick Castle; while Alexander de Lindsay resided in another tower for safe keeping, he too was held in ward. The constable at Berwick Castle wrote to his king and lord about his new prisoner; yet indignant at his confinement:

"Because Sir William Douglas has not kept the covenants which he made with Sir Henry Percy, he is in your castle of Berwick in my keeping, and he is still very savage and very abusive, but I shall keep him such wise that, if it please God, he shall not escape."

The letter concluded with a hint that since the church of Douglas was now vacant and worth two hundred marks that it might be given to his majesty's treasurer of Scotland de Cressingham.

For their grave concern of interference in these deeds of treachery, the captain of the castle wrote another letter asking the king not to liberate Sir William for any profit or influence until he heard the true words of the charges brought against him. The many friends Lord Douglas had at court, his personal influence in Scotland, and the great influence of his wife exhibited before when aided by de Hastings and de Segrave now serving Edward with distinction in his wars were all of major concern to these pretenders to the truth. Their fears of discovery was marked; the true nature of their false charges, contrived rebellion following the Irvine covenant were reflected in the haste of these two letters dispatched to their king. But Edward was not amused with Douglas. He chose to ignore any motives behind his captivity or the pretense of the accusations that was likely unfounded in fact.

Fawside Castle

Lady Douglas had dispatched a messenger to Fawside Castle announcing her arrival with the Douglas household. Her lands and manors had also been confiscated and her income seized. Ellie was making some disciplined decisions on where they would travel before reaching the Berwick manor near Ayton she held with her stepson William de Ferrers. She would take no chances; staying only at manors and estates she owned with others. If she needed sustenance she took it to worry the return another time, she said to herself; this was a family fighting for survival. When they arrived at Fawside only the remaining de la Zouche servants were present at the castle. Elena de la Zouche had died right after the siege at Berwick; her estate with the escheator; the Inquisition Post Mortem was given the year before, on the 20th of August 1296. Now Elena's son Alan and his wife Eleanor de Segrave, Nicky's sister, held the manor and they were safe in England; leaving Ellie to have the castle to herself and family. "Ana, you know well this castle," she said as she dismounted her horse, "will you show the others and the nurses where to go?" Ana nodded, "My girl, let Ana help you too; too much work have you taken on yourself these days," she said worried for her lamb.

"Sir David, you shall have one of the family rooms, near my chamber; and no morning hunt!" she chided him. "The steward of this castle to do the hunting for our family's table, this I promise." James was so quiet it was frightful to her. "My son," said Ellie, "we will go the morrow next to Ayton. Once settled at our manor there will I travel to see your father held in ward in Berwick on Tweed some few miles away. Will you accompany your mother to the castle?" The lad could not speak his heart was so heavy; he was only able to nod in agreement to her suggestion. Muriel was taking Amy to her new chamber and a nursery playroom that their nurses were preparing; the wee lass only knew her father was away on the business of Lord Douglas. Ellie was exhausted but only felt it now when she sat down at the large table in the great hall. Archibald's wet nurse was ill from the rainy weather that prevailed this long day of their travels. "Ana will you see about a tasine of William's herbs for Maudie; Archie's nurse so sick this day."

So much to do; and all I want is to wake from this nightmare, and see my William walking through the door now, she sighed softly to herself. Muriel came to her side and sat in the chair next to her mother. Her eyes were sad as she held her mother's hand. "Mummy, are we to roam from manor to manor without a home forever?" she asked. James slowly came to join them and sat on Ellie's other side at the table. "Mura, mother's heart is breaking can't you see; try to be brave and help us now," said James. Reluctantly asserting himself, he added, "Please take Amy and Hugh and bring them to the courtyard with Sir Shamus to play; the rains have stopped." Ellie smiled a grateful look at James as Ana came in with some wine, followed by the kitchen servants carrying platters. "Good food to feed our bellies; and this fine wine," gasped Ellie, "I had forgotten how nice it was to stay at Fawside Castle with its fine larder that could be replenished daily."

Everyone took heart in the fine food put before them; the largesse of the de la Zouches was comforting. When Muriel and the other children finished she happily took them outside. "Much better do I feel now that I have eaten," she told her mother, "Come here Hugh and Amy, let us go and find the silly Deerhound to chase and play with us!" James and Ellie glanced up at Sir David as he returned himself to feast and drink some wine. "Not quite ten years and this is where we started; to end our days in Scotland at Fawside not the dream I had for us," sighed Ellie. Ana told her that she may have to nurse young Archibald herself if Maudie is not better by the morrow. "Then two sons might I take to Berwick's tower to visit our good knight and father. The constable sure not to refuse this wife with so many lads that come with her; the sad request for access to my dear husband he will acquiesce," she said, seeing a benefit to every inconvenience this day.

Sir David cautioned her, "Since Sir William is in ward for treason, the reluctance of the captain of the castle may arise to let you in there. Would you want to see him thus held fast in disgrace of fetters and chains, M' Lady?" he asked her. Ellie looked at her de Ferrers knight and knew he was trying to prepare her for this dreadful time to come; to see her William in such bondage. "This lass appreciates your kind concerns my dear Sir David,

To see my William under any circumstance is better than to see him not at all I fear. I will go; and Lady Douglas will gain permission to meet with her dear husband, with her sons as well I know it so!" she said with her growing resolve. James realized that every day he watched his mother, the more she was challenged the more relentless she became in her cause. "Mother, you are a doughty Douglas in every way; father was so true in his words," said the lad. "He gave me his thoughts of you as well that last morning we were on the hunt, *'I found true love with Eleanora',* he hath said to me. I thought those words some comfort to you now." Ellie held his hand and thanked him for the sentiments. "Your kind remembrance from your father I hold so dear; the words feed courage into this shattered heart," she said thanking James with a hug.

Berwick Castle 1st August

The Earl of Surrey wrote a letter to the king; he had finally returned to Scotland and its foul weather there as well. Earl Johannis told his lord that he was expecting the arrival in three days to complete the covenants agreed with Henry de Percy, three Scots: Earl Robert of Carrick, James the Steward and one Bishop Wishart of Glasgow. Earl Johannis' expectation from this writing was the appearance of Robert Wishart to report in Berwick; a situation that was most intriguing. Had not his nephew told him? Henry de Percy had remanded this good bishop to the constable of Roxburgh Castle and the prison there just one short week ago. The earl also informed dear Edward that William Douglas was being held in Berwick's tower prison most securely now in irons; having not produced some hostages to Sir Henry as was his agreement. The uncle had not been correctly informed by his nephew Henry; a lie had been presented to him; the true charges and reason for the imprisonment of Sir William were yet unknown to him. Two stories were being told; misinformation was being given, a conspiracy was clearly afoot at Berwick Castle. The goal of the de Percy scheme of duplicity was clear: to imprison William le Hardi Douglas and end his life.

Ayton near Berwick on Tweed

The Douglases reached the manor house near Ayton just north of Berwick on Tweed in fine fashion; the sun seemed to peek in and out of the cloud cover all day; but no rain fell upon this group of travelers who were long weary from their days of wandering about with no home of permanence. It was very late when they arrived and everyone happily fell into their chambers for a good rest. Ellie felt safe this night; knowing they would be here for some days to stay; no need to move from place to place in fear of capture. Perhaps that God will send fast a miracle to free my William; then we will be happily making our escape to Lovaine lands in Flanders and leave this manor, she thought gleefully. Ana was helping her prepare for slumber, "How is our Maudie?" she asked of Archie's nurse. "Her milk is less this day; you must consider taking your wee laddie with you and James when you visit with your husband," advised Ana. Ellie shook her head, "At least I can see my feet these days; no child to grow within me now. Perhaps too for William to see his son; many months has he spent thus away to not see the changes in this wee one, the mirror image of his father."

The next day Sir David escorted her with Archie, Maudie, and James to Berwick Castle with his squires. "We have not been here since that fateful day; but the feeling now I get, the smells seem much the same from that awful carnage," she moaned. Ellie was ill; her stomach felt as if it would expel its contents. "I fear now I must stop," she said, getting off her horse, she relieved her stomach, standing off the cart path in short distance from the others where she ran. Returning to the party, she excused her absence for her sickness, "The blood on my shoes I see it still," she said gravely. "The 30th de Mars a day of horror for us all." They rode down the path to the castle gates they knew too well. Some time was spent waiting for permission to meet with the constable. Ellie did not prepare well for their arrival to the castle. She had neglected to have her solicitors arrange for their visit with Lord Douglas. "That I had not the mind to wait for attorneys to make requests on our behalf was foolish," she chided herself aloud. Then she was invited to the council of the Earl of Surrey; bravely forward she went, followed by James and Sir David, his squire, and Maudie with the wee Archie. All I need is Sir Shamus to make this group complete she chuckled to herself trying to keep her spirits up.

Earl Johannis was gracious; he told her that she might find her husband's confinement frightening. "Lord Warenne, this Lady does assure you no better privilege could be granted to this wife and her sons; that we would meet with my dear husband and their father." Her request for access to Douglas Tower and Lord Douglas was granted. Sir David and Maudie waited outside the great hall as the Douglases made their way with the earl's men at arms escorting them to the guarded tower of the dejected knight. Ellie was permitted to stay in the lower chamber of this great tower. Sir William was released to come down the lang stone steps, though he still had fetters on his arms held at the wrist. The sallowness of his face with several day's growth of scraggily beard upon it revealed his demoralized self; the dark circles under his eyes told her he was not sleeping much as well. James went to greet his father first and just hugged him hard. "Your father is most thankful that you came today my son," said William quietly. James was looking at the open sores on William's arms from the shackles that held him in custody.

Ellie beckoned James to come take Archie as she reached under her surcote and brought out William's healing box. "I will send young Patric to be with you on the morrow; Earl Johannis has approved your attendants and one man-servant to come. Word too will I send for Gillerothe of Douglas that he should join his laird here," she said offering words of comfort to her husband. William came slowly to her, no longer fearing recriminations from her. "Your husband so sorry," he began apologizing that she interrupted with her words. "Your son dear William; he has come to speak with his father," Ellie said, taking the wee lad from James. Archie made a sound, a mimicking of James who called out Fad' er when he saw Lord Douglas. William held his youngest son and smiled broadly as he spoke to the laddie. "What troubled times have you chosen to come into this world, as once said afore to ye laddie; a brave one you must be young Douglas!"

William spoke to James and Ellie quietly now. He told her she was correct; de Percy had set a trap. "Dear Alex spoke in my defense to say we were in Auchinleck; far away from the rebellion in the north. This shameful lord dismissed our words, ordering my arrest and imprisonment for crimes of treason." Ellie came around him as he sat on the bench; she put her hands on his neck to relieve the pain as she had done so often for him. "Lord Will," she said, "tomorrow I will seek out my solicitors on your behalf. My only fear is that these false charges will carry merit with Lord Edward; the collusion of de Percy and my father well concealed." James asked his father if others were taken with him from the west. "Just de Lindsay and Bishop Wishart; Uncle Alex is here in Berwick; Robert enjoys his days to spend at Roxburgh," William told them. "Perhaps with improved behavior these fetters to remove," he sighed.

Given a glance from his father he knew so well, James moved to give them privacy; taking the wee Archibald and hold him awhile, sitting on the opposite side of the small hall in Douglas Tower. William beckoned to his wife, come around him he motioned. Though encumbered by the fetters he would not concede to hold her close to him. "Dear Lady El," he whispered in her ear, "your body here against my own to favor this good knight with your embrace so healing. I do thank you for the forgiveness of your heart." She gently took his scruffy face unshaven and unkempt; holding it with her long fingers and strong palms. "My dear husband; we must have said those vows of sacrament some dozen times or more. Those words of faith I do recall quite well; there is no relief to quit a marriage over stubbornness for one's own truth of purpose, honor and good name." She smiled into his eyes, looking for some glimmer of hope to emanate from his.

The guards appeared in the doorway of the hall; sent by the constable to return the knight to his tower cell. Ellie and James prepared to say their goodbyes. "On the morrow I will visit first at the offices in Berwick that I told you; then to come and see the progress on your good face, removing that loathsome beard!" she teased him, turning to take Archie from her son. James went to speak to his father as the guards still waited by the door. "The laughter and the taunting for Lord Douglas' fate we both heard; the misfortune of your truth berated by pretenders," the young man told his father. "The Celtic wisdom you once taught me dear father comes to mind, the kinds of men in threes: There are men of God who return good for evil; there are the brave and righteous men of our world who give good for good, evil for evil; and the last are men of the Devil that reward good with evil. Your son to be a man much like his father now I swear;" James said, his impediment of speech growing more apparent with his anger. "I will remember those who mocked the truth with lies and laughter, rewarding evil for their evil," he cried out in hushed tones.

The slight lisp reminded William of the lad's resolve. When this speech impediment first revealed itself from his riding accident those years ago, James told them confidently that it was meant to happen, to keep him humble always before God. William hugged his son hard; James bravely fought back his tears and said "I love you father." Gilley held his son away from him some and looked deeply into his dark eyes, "James, I will always love and respect you; your father's son, sure aye." The guards approached William now and he began to climb the lang stairs back to his confinement.

Berwick on Tweed August 1st

Ellie's meeting with her de Ferrers solicitors that once settled her estates in Scotland for her dower income were eager to assist in getting some relief for her husband. She spoke to them with grave concern for the motives of de Percy. "That he would falsely accuse my husband of rebellion when others told him true; Lord Douglas was with his wife recently abducted from their home; to calm her and the others of their family," she told them. "Lady Eleanora our friendship with the Earl of Surrey is well known," they said. "We will approach him on your behalf; to seek the truth for Lord Douglas' detention, held in his ward. Perhaps some financial offering would soothe the king's demeanor; being damaged by this sad occurrence. We will see you the week next or earlier if Lord Warenne has time to hear our pleas." Ellie was relieved that these good attorneys showed slight concern in the matter. But then she realized that Lord Surrey was the uncle of de Percy; would he see the ruse or fall captive to the prevarication of his nephew.

James stayed behind today with the other Douglas children; the sight of his father being so ignominiously detained was overwhelming to the lad. Ellie had some letters from her solicitors; she could go directly to the constable for entrance to the castle and its tower prison. Sir David and his squires escorted Lady Douglas. To her delight, four other men at arms from Douglasdale now arrived to stay in Ayton; she had a full party to journey from the manor without fear of vulnerable attack. When William joined her in the hall he appeared more like himself; clean shaven and of a lighter step she noticed. The clothes she brought him yesterday he wore happily. His face lit up when she came to greet him and she embraced him laughing and joking at his appearance the day before. "When first I saw your scraggily face I most wanted to instruct the guards: return this pretender; he's not my husband with that beard!" she chided him. William's scar from Fawdon kept a beard from growing on one side; he always kept his face clean shaven to avoid the hideous look of a half bearded man as he described himself in mocking terms.

"Eleanora," he said to her an indication of his serious concern, "what was the response of your de Ferrers attorneys? Do they offer some promise for solution?" he asked her. She described their demeanor as hopeful and mentioned their good standing with de Warenne.

"I pray only that a fine and your report to muster with the King in Gascony would resolve this matter of incarceration here in Berwick," Ellie said, "They are sending letters to Nicky and Josh for their support and others in good stead with Lord Edward here in Scotland; good men that know your actions after leaving Irvine Water." William was pleased with her findings. "You have not berated me for my foolish actions," he said to her. "Your husband expected many words of anger from his wife; that he did deserve it too I must admit." Ellie shook her head woefully. "No William; I blame myself for the words of that old woman; to bring a curse upon you known to us as Edward. No escape from that prediction so long ago I do fear," she sighed.

He started to refute her silly notion, then stopped when he saw a twinkle in her eye; what next he wondered? "Then of course there is the truth of this situation; William is William!" she blurted out. "Stubborn Lord Douglas," she teased him. "Uncore mout sauvage e mout araillez; abusive and savage from the laments of the English garrison, like Sholto." Ellie looked at her knight and wished she had not said those last words. "I am sorry Ellie. I was so angry; the outrage so consumed my soul it struck out at all around me in grave violence. My indignation ruled my decency; my horror recalled your words that morning now fulfilled. Lord Douglas was more a captive animal than a knight following God's will; so helpless did I feel at my grave situation; trapped, imprisoned for a deed I did not do," the drawn look

MY TRUTH LIES IN THE RUINS

returned to his face as he continued. "Your husband failed to consider your wise counsel; and now the weight of selfish deeds falls to his wife to find solution; freedom from this maze of intrigue."

The visit was drawing to a close; the guards returned to take the knight, still in fetters at the wrist; to the tower where he must reside. Ellie looked at William with true remorse and said, "Forgive my tongue; the words I meant in jest were poorly chosen. I meant only teasing; not to hurt you. What's done is done. We will prevail here that God is in his Heaven, I do pray so," she promised him firmly. They shared a fast embrace and then he was gone up those lang stone steps. Ellie and her escorts returned to her manor; to await the word of her solicitors. Her children were more calm in their surroundings and Ana could see an improvement in her girl's demeanor. I only pray she does succeed so this time, said Ana to herself. If she should lose this fight it might be her sweet knight's death at Edward's hand I fear.

Days turned into weeks and still no word came from her solicitors. Ellie visited her husband as she was allowed; twice the week and Sunday she was permitted to see him. Finally she relented and went to the offices of her attorneys. "Earl Johannis was called to business in other parts of the realm; an uprising in the north that draws him with his army now to Stirling do we hear," they told her, explaining the reason for the delay in their request for William's release. "The letters were received both from Sir Nicholas de Segrave and Sir Johannis de Hastings; supporting release of Lord Douglas." They handed her a personal letter addressed directly to her from Nicky. He told her that he suspected mischief as the source of William's incarceration. Try to get him out of Berwick quickly, he cautioned her. Ellie was nervous with the warning of Nicky. Outspoken in his frankness; loyal to his kin, he wanted her to know to wait the longer might result in tragic endings for her knight. What ever could he mean by that she wondered as she rode back to her manor?

11 September 1297

The Earl of Surrey with his army met William Wallace and his retinue of brave rebels at Stirling Bridge; this fierce Scot led his men with young de Moray; they battled hard and with some luck of circumstance they were victorious. The English army with their fine equipment numbered 60,000 men at arms. The Scots were well out numbered six to one; mostly common men with little armaments they fought with hearts so brave they won the day. Chasing de Warenne and his army East, routing the English as they came across them in their path; Wallace moved on towards Berwick. The Lanark Rebel made his way alone with this band of Scots; de Moray took a mortal wounding somewhere after Stirling's valiant fight. The English made haste their retreat many by land through Northumbria; some by ship, sailing off to London without notice of their leaving. The victory of Wallace put such fear into the Earl of Surrey's men that they deserted Berwick Castle quickly; taking with them prisoners from Berwick's royal prisons. Little did Ellie know that the small ships she watched sailing out of Berwick harbor that wee hour of the morning under the king's banners hosted a cargo of Scottish prisoners in the hold.

Lady Douglas was on her way to visit her solicitors in the burgh, then to see her William. She rode into Berwick with Sir David and his squire; hoping to meet with these attorneys early and have the rest of the day to spend with her husband. As she sat waiting to be seen by her solicitors, strange actions were going on about her; all the associates were speaking in whispers with grave looks of consternation. One brave attendant came to see her; to reveal the devastating news. The council meeting with the Earl Warenne was cancelled, she was told. But more sadly, the English garrison at Berwick Castle sailed for England, the ships lo still in view. To Ellie's grave horror, Lord Douglas had sailed with them she was told!

These Berwick prisoners on the orders of Earl of Surrey were being taken to London for confinement in the Tower of London; to await the sentence of their king. William le Hardi Douglas was never to see his Scotland again in this life; he and Thomas de Morham a prisoner since Dunbar's battle, along with their man-servants and attendants reached the Tower of London on 11th of October. They were brought through Traitor's Gate; forced to walk in fetters and chains up the stone steps to await the official processing of prisoners. On 12th October 1297, Edward Prince of Wales signed the documents ordering the constable of the Tower of London Ralph de Sandwich to receive the Scottish prisoners of Earl Warenne. William Douglas, John de Fortone, and Thomas de Morham were admitted to the Tower fortress to be kept safely there until otherwise informed.

Ellie was stunned and sat oddly in grave quiet, as if she left the present and living world. Entreaties from the solicitors' assistants did not break her silence. Sir David returned to find her sitting with a blank expression looking towards the windows and the views of the harbor on the Tweed. "Lady Douglas, Eleanora," he said to her. "in the tailors shop we heard the devastating news of the English sailing with their prisoners. By your look I do determine Lord Douglas was among them I fear?" Sir David asked her quietly. Ellie barely moved her head to tell him yes. "My life is over here; no tears do I have left to shed," she replied in a low voice almost inaudible. And with those words she collapsed, caught by Sir David before she hit the floor. He told the attorneys to set a chamber for some privacy at once. "How can you tell this lady such tidings in the openness of this front chamber with no comforts for herself or friends around to help her through this tragic news? Can you not know she is with child?" he shouted at them. Seeing the de Ferrers arms on the tabard of this knight, the solicitors and their associates ran about making amends and bringing a tasine to revive the lady.

Many apologies came from her attorneys; could they assist her in obtaining sustenance from Edward in England to be near her husband, they asked of Lady Douglas. Ellie felt weak and feeble as she became more aware of her surroundings; anguished in her soul, her heart was broken. And the sickness of child was overwhelming; what more will my God ask of me to bear she moaned to herself. Sir David told them to start about the business to regain her dower rights that she might return to England to be near her husband. Ellie was in confusion, a mist of overwhelming sorrow; the hollow sounds around her were strange and disconcerting, ringing sounds in her ears in stead of words. Her beloved William so wrongly taken from her; lies from her father and her kin that accused him falsely. "Please, I pray you, do what you can to beg us sustenance from Edward. I must have a place to live with my children and be near my William. And I will need documents of safe conduct for my stepson James; the other children are mine by womb, English in their birth rights," she said to them as if in a trance, so painful a life to live now without her one and only love.

In mid October Ellie's solicitors told her that Edward had approved her request; Woodham Ferrers would be restored to her. Documents for travel were received; allowing her to bring her household; all her children including James, some servants, and her men at arms, into England. The de Ferrers servants and knights and squires were free to travel with her as before; English by their birth. Before Edward and his council issued the official writs for partial dower rights restored, Lady Douglas began the long journey south to Essex with her household. They stopped first at Fawdon for shelter; the larder was bare of grain and other stores. For the plunder of the Scots or the English it mattered not; nothing greeted them in the kitchen or cellars for their eating. Ana spoke first upon their sad discovery of the theft. "Good that we brought with us all the cellared grains and salted fish from Ayton," she said reassuringly to Ellie. James and Sir David offered to hunt game the next morning. Ellie was hearing none of their supportive words; carrying William's child, the burden of a family to support on her own, a husband held in Edward's Tower awaiting sentence of a despot king; all weighed heavily upon her soul. She found the laird's chamber and closed the door on the world and her family, only Shamus joined her there.

DEBORAH RICHMOND FOULKES

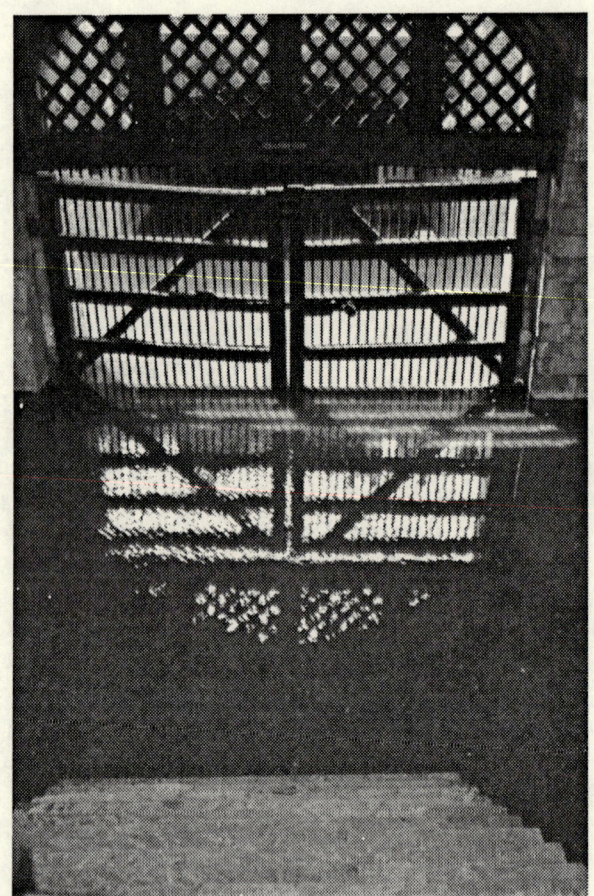

Figure CXVII-Part Three; steps from Traitors Gate where prisoners were made to walk up to their confinement from the barges off the Thames; William Douglas was forced to enter the Tower of London through this entrance in 1297.

On 23rd October 1297 an official writ was signed re-granting Woodham Ferrers to Lady Eleanora Douglas for her sustenance. Valued at £16 2sh. and 6d annually, she was required to pay the King's exchequer £6 annually. A letter was sent by her solicitors to William le Hardi of Douglas, in ward, the Tower of London to inform him that Lady Douglas would be returned to this de Ferrers manor; safe conducts for their children, James and others of the their household had been received. Gilley read with little comfort that she was returning to Essex; numerous sad memories awaited her there he sighed sadly. He wrote a response to the attorneys' letter and addressed it to Lady Eleanora Douglas, Woodham Ferrers. He wrote her with a heavy heart, begging her to please come see him. That next day a letter from his wife arrived. He read painfully of these first days of their journey; the empty larder at Fawdon and the child she carried now within her. This news of another Douglas child; more a burden than a joy to her do I fear, he sighed to himself. Then out loud he cried in abject sorrow, "A wee one I may never see or hold in love. What agony to bear our God has so given us? Is this sorry knight the cause of this despair and anguish to his family? I do fear so," William said gravely, talking to himself in the lonely confine of the prison cell at the White Tower.

The Douglas family made their way further south into England staying in Yorkshire in Fryton, a Lovaine manor held by her father. Ana was surprised by Ellie's insistence on staying there. They left with many supplies for their larder in Essex; and a cart with horses to transport their booty. "Let him deny his daughter and grand children," she vowed bitterly to anyone who would listen. "Send the sheriff after me for my oversight; the taking of Lovaine goods without consent a grievous matter to contend, I fear you not!" she spoke in vengeance to her father Lord Lovaine. Another day's travel and then on to Sutton at this second Lovaine manor, further south in Yorkshire they would stop. This time servants of her family fully sympathizing with her plight further filled their cart and packed their beasts of burden with corn and peas, and luxuries of honey and cinnamon; offering to hunt for game with Sir David and James to feed their bellies. The stay was jubilant for all but Ellie; unfeeling in the love that was offered, fearing emotions that might pierce her heart the more, Lady Douglas was cold in her demeanor.

Ellie would not stop for more than one night as she was very sick with child; something was wrong she knew it. And Amy too was not fairing very well on the long journey south. The wee lass missed her father so; despondent at his long absence, without her mother's love to comfort her as well, she cried herself to sleep each night. Ellie was absent from her family; riding everyday together, sharing food at the same table, she appeared in person, but only her body was there, an empty sham. Eleanora was fierce in her anger; in her heart she held no love for anyone these days. Why should I ever love again, she laughed sarcastically. So many have I loved that God sees fit to take from me; to punish this sorry lass. That any might refute these words my grave sorrow, she sighed to herself. And no one, not even Ana or James could shake her morbid convictions; Ellie's despair was so great it hollowed out her soul.

Woodham Ferrers, reflected Ellie as they rode into the village; we have not been here but one night to remove our belongings since the loss of our wee Martha in that dreadful moat, she moaned in silence. She was greeted by Father John from St. Mary's as they entered the gates to the manor. "Lady Eleanora, a letter has arrived by messenger," he smiled, handing her the sealed parchment as she dismounted from her horse. She recognized at once the writing was her William's and something seemed to sparkle now within her; a smile came to her weary face. "Oh, my Gilley, you are yet alive!" she squealed. It was then that James and Ana knew the dread that was in her heart; she feared that William was already dead at the hands of the king. "Thank you Father; you have saved me so this day!"

She was reading quickly and started to exclaim loudly, "He wonders that I might come see him! Foolish husband; that I would be there sooner is my wish; one day's rest and I will be in London with my knight!" she exclaimed, kissing all her wee ones, then Muriel, her Ana and James, Sir David, anyone who stood still long enough, followed by the wee hound as well. Lady Douglas was wildly jubilant and very much alive. To James it seemed as if she had been sleep walking since leaving Berwick. Now their mother had returned, her happiness rekindled from the words of her dear husband and our sweet father, reflected James, yet so relieved. "Ana, a feast we shall have tonight in Woodham Ferrers!" she exclaimed. "You will join us Father in our celebration; my dear husband is alive and wants to see us; truly God is answering my prayers this day I know."

London November 1297

On 6th November the Sheriffs of London were commanded to pay William Earl of Ros, Andrew de Moray, John de Moubray, Nickolas Randolf, William Duglas, John de Fortone, and Thomas de Morham, Knights and Scottish prisoners in the Tower for their sustenance since Michaelmas, as may be required, the earl 6d and the others 4d a day and their three warders each allowed 3d per day. The escheators were so notified from the king's treasury. This measure to relieve the burden on their families; coinage due for their needs of stay drawn from their estates now seized. One day later Wallace and his loyal Scots plundered lands and villages, moving south to Tynedale. He passed over Fawdon in the north already looted; he took the priory at Hexam yet giving letter of protection to the monks. And Eleanora Douglas with her men at arms and son James arrived on the Thames; at the Tower of London to visit Lord Douglas.

William looked up from his reading as he heard the draw bar slide back and door creak open, to see his son and wife appear at the entrance of his cell. He smiled with joy and held the smile deliberately to hide his shock at Ellie's drawn appearance. She looked so thin; too frail to carry the child growing now within her he feared. "Sit down lass; James, help me here my son," said William. Ellie fell into his arms and sobbed deeply. "Lord Will, that you are alive that I can see you," she cried in halted words of deep emotions; her worry hopefully resolved. "There dear girl; of course your

William is alive. He has done nothing wrong to be otherwise," he says motioning for James to sit beside him on the bench that fills the cell.

Figure CXVIII-Part Three; ancient entrance to the Beauchamp Tower as it is now called where many Scottish prisoners were held; across the courtyard is the White Tower where Lord Douglas was held

James was pleased to see the wounds on his father's wrists had healed; the fetters no longer used to secure the knight to his confinement. "Father, your healing box have I here; what would you need from it?" he asked. William looked through the box and told James what must be replenished. "Then for your mother you must mix these herbs of ginger, lavender, and rosemary with some lemon, thyme and good honey; thus prepare a tasine for her," he instructed. "Ellie, you must not stay long this day; rest is what you most require," he cautioned her. "I would not have written that you come had I known now your condition." Ellie looked happily into his face, her eyes were shining with her love for him, "Lord Will, that I am here with you; my hope for life's continuance. On our journey here from Woodham Ferrers I took each day more pleasant than the last. Without you this sorry lass an angry woman who feared to be a widow; journeying from Berwick south to Essex, oblivious to her family and their needs," she admitted sadly to him.

Figure CXIX-Part Three; the Tower of London on the Thames; the White Tower looms large over the defensive walls, upper left corner of the photo; location of the prison cell occupied by William le Hardi

William held his wife in his arms; rocking her as he had often done when she was frightened or sad. "There sweet wife, your husband is here to love and comfort you. Your son stands near as well to hold your hand for reassurance of resolve," Gilley said as he looked approvingly to his son. James face was frozen in expression. He was masking his discomfort in the cell; hiding the fear he felt for his father in confinement; and concealing well the loathing and contempt he held for de Percy and the others who falsely condemned his father to this prison. William sensed the silence from the lad; poignant in his quiet observations. "Dear James, pray tell me of the others; Mura, my Amy, Hugh and the wee Archie, have they made well the journey to our home in Essex?" he asked.

James related their stay at Fawdon, not knowing of his mother's letter to her husband. He described the cellars once so full of yield from their many crops that were now barren, empty in their stores. He noted how shocked they all were to see their manor so destroyed by looters. James also told how Muriel helped with Amy and young Hugh. "Sir Shamus has sensed our stressful times; his antics are the more amusing than before, hiding half himself to feign his cleverness," he laughed describing the Deerhounds entertaining ways. "But of all the children it is young Hugh who speaks of you the most; some nights he calls out for you, waking from some fearful dream." Ellie was surprised to hear this about her shy son's yearning for his

MY TRUTH LIES IN THE RUINS

father. "Dear Lord Will, you see now so sorrowful a mother your wife, consumed by my self pity; I did not know of this sad story of our Hubicus," she said, beginning to cry all the more. William wiped her tears from her face, "Lady El you are so brave; so much have you thus gone through," he told her quietly. "Be gentle with my girl and that child that grows within your sweet self."

Ellie told him of the day he sailed. "I saw your ship leaving Berwick's harbor and did not know to look for you," she told him wistfully. "Only later did I come to know your fate," she said. "Lady El, remember that I told you of others' plans made for escape from Berwick prison?" he asked his wife. "Now the details will I share with you. Thomas de Morham had his squire tell young Patric of the offer; refused by Lord Douglas for any merit. I said no, the words of Lady Douglas warning her husband, de mischef in this deed." Ellie told him how sad she was in refusing him their last coinage to bribe the gaolers; accomplices in this secret plan for his escape with his fellow knight and friend. William continued his tale. "Once on board King Edward's sailing prison who should I see but one de Morham; Sir Thomas tells me the plan was false, a contrivance to steal our coinage. Lady El, our coffers would now be empty but for your wise counsel to your husband." Ellie shook her head. "I felt such guilt that I did refuse you. Then to have you stolen in the night; taken in that vessel, no goodbye to say. My heart but broke in two that sad day," she sighed softly.

James now realized the whole of the burden she had carried these last weeks: not only did she fear for his life in the Tower; but also she held tremendous guilt, having refused William their last coinage to risk a plot for his escape from Berwick Castle. Ellie had said no; the plan appeared false, the idea suspect. She told William honestly as was their way; the family needed what little they had, to survive without a home or husband to provide for them, she made the agonizing choice. "Mother, why didn't you tell me of the plan and your decision?" James asked her. "When you share such burdens they become half the weight; our father has thus told us. Please allow this faithful son to help his mother," said James. "Lady El," William interrupted, "Your son's words are correct. Your fears unfounded. Your decision in Berwick was most true; declining the offer of such intrigue a wise choice, sure aye." William held her and looked sternly into her eyes, as he did when he had something serious to say. "Lady Douglas, never again carry such burdens by yourself; promise now that you will seek the help of James while your husband is so detained here. Others of our family depending on their mother; your good son would want to help I know," he said. Ellie shook her head yes, "I promise Lord Will," she told him, and turning now to James, "My dear son, your kindness and good character console me so this day. I thank you." The Douglases held each other in steadfast embrace; knowing their strength was their profound love for one another, their truth.

Woodham Ferrers late November 1297

Ellie has been in great pain all throughout the night. Ana brought her a tasine that James has prepared from William's instructions. "My girl, your head is burning with a fever; we must send for a healer from the village to assist us," said Ana with profound alarm. Ellie slipped off into three days of twilight sleep; the nightmares only woke her to true consciousness now and then. She wanted to die the pains were so treacherous; she lost her baby to God on the second day; though she was not aware. Eleanora was perilously ill from the toxins of her fevers; the fitful sleep brought her such little rest that she wanted to quit her life. By the third day James was sitting with his mother, holding her hand; pleading with her not to die. In a fog, between two worlds she lingered. "Dear mother," cried the lad, "we have most lost our father to us; please don't die! You must not give up mother, James needs you so," he sobbed into her writhing body. "Dear St. Bride, heal my mother; bring her back to us this day," he pleaded, his face covered in tears of abject fear and total sadness. Then a miracle occurred; Ellie's fever left her, a cooling perspiration enveloped her body. As she lifted her head to look around her, her hands found the lad sobbing at her breast. She held him fast, "Shhh now my love; my dear son. Your mother will not leave you; by St. Bride I will recover from this gravity of my condition," she vowed.

Ana took heart with Ellie's improved condition. But she agonized over another tragedy; beyond a saddened state, she was deeply consumed by yet one more devastating event the just occurred in the nursery chamber. Young Amy, the wee lass so favored by her father lingered at the gates of Heaven; then was gone to be with God, her older sister Martha, and the baby Douglas that was alive in Ellie's womb but yesterday. Two deaths for us, the Celtic ways say three to be this year; at least my girl will stay with us for now, this brave mother is so needed by her children, sighed Ana. The illness Amy took on during their journey south began in Yorkshire and continued to worsen a little more each day as they traveled towards Essex. The Douglases even stayed on one extra day in Fairstead manor some miles north of Woodham Ferrers that she might improve some. But Amy's illness was not just from the rain and cold that seeped into her wee body; it was from missing her father. That devastating loss tugged at her heart. She seemed to slip from life just a little more each day; now she too was gone. When my girl is the stronger will I tell her, mused Ana in the silence of her sorrow.

The poisons, her ill humors seemed to gradually leave Ellie; each day she showed marked improvement. When finally she was able to sit up some and even take a few steps, Ana and James decided it would be today they would tell her the tragic news: first of Baby Douglas, then of Amy. Ellie was horrified within herself, torn apart by the loss of not one but two lovely children. A strange awareness seemed to move over her, to envelope her very being within a cloud of distance to the words they spoke. Eerily calm was how they saw her; but they knew she was in shock. "What ever are we to tell my William; his Amy now with God, the baby he could not bring into this world there beside her there?" asked Ellie, suppressing the tears unsuccessfully they over flowed from her eyes. James had to look away, the sorrow that he felt was overwhelming. When would these tragedies subside; will there ever be peace and happiness again in their lives he wondered with bewilderment?

Ana knew that Ellie was hiding her true feelings from James; perhaps herself as well. To lose a child was terrifying to a mother; that excruciating feeling; numbness with no words of consolation as to why. But Ellie lost two children in one day; how was she to hold herself together for her family she wondered to herself. These two babies; one lass half grown to maidenhood, our wee Amy with such joy and happiness to give; and then a child to come to birth too soon, that leaves us; no words can mirror the emotions of a mother with such losses, cried Ellie to herself. There is no consolation that will come to cheer us this sad day Ana knew. Dear God and blessed Virgin; please watch over Eleanora, prayed a fearful Ana. The room was silent; their breathing almost audible from the desperation of their sorrow; the deep agony complete in its control.

Early 1298

The year of 1297 closed quietly in Woodham Ferrers. The little household held together by love and respect; survived on the strength of faith. Word on Scotland came in small pieces here and there. Young de Moray passed late December from his wounds; his young son was born some short time later. The news from London's Tower was not forthcoming; only word from the attorneys that she was yet refused another visit to the Tower. Lady Douglas contacted these Lovaine solicitors again requesting time for visits to see her husband. She was told there would be some delay. She also had no word from William in some weeks and she was growing worried; a visit to the Tower was necessary and immediate she determined. Ellie kept herself busy reviewing her estate's finances; waiting for the reply on her intended visit. She developed a plan to request relief from Edward's escheators; increasing her sustenance by more than half. She had her solicitors draw up a complaint. In May she was granted her request; the manor of Woodham Ferrers was hers free of yearly payments to the escheators and dear Edward.

Woodham Ferrers, 13 October 1298.

Ellie was sitting in her room doing some fine embroidery on a robe of William's that she shortened and was going to give to James for Hogmanay. She hoped it would cheer him, but knew in her heart only having his father home again would make that happen. There was a light rapping on her chamber door, and she recognized the knock to be that of young James. She folded the garment and put it in William's war chest, "Come in," she said. He entered with a solemn face that broke into a broad smile, "Mother, we respectfully request your presence in the great hall, for festivities that reflect the celebration of your birthday." Ellie stood and smiled up at her son, and he put out his arm, "Lady El," he said with that slight lisp that she found so beguiling, "may I escort you?" Lady El she mused, how many times had his father called her that, and looking at James she realized how grown up he had become, though not yet thirteen. He was just three inches from being six feet tall or about 17 hh as his father would say; with a strong, yet slender frame. He had been such support to her these last fifteen months she knew she would have been hard pressed to go on without his cheerful resolve.

As they entered the great hall, Ellie noticed all the household staff, those she was still able to retain; her beautiful daughter Muriel, and the two younger boys, Hugh and Archie all seated at the large table in front of the fireplace, that now kept the Deerhound warm on these chilly days. "Oh you shouldn't have done this for me," she exclaimed, "And cinnamon cakes, where did you find such quantities of spice? And all that honey, why it must be a month's supply." Ana, now both her housekeeper and maid in wait, said "M' lady, don't go worrying yourself now, asking foolish questions that we can not answer truthfully. A lady should have a celebration for her birthday, especially a landmark one, and that's that." A landmark one, yes, I am thirty now, she thought. James made a bow as he pulled the chair at the head of the table out for her. "Thank you all, this is so wonderful," she said. "I truly was surprised. Oh, look, presents too?" Muriel had made a small box of wood that she painted with a clever design. "This is beautiful Mura," said Ellie, "You have acquired a talented hand at painting cherubs I see here." A small scroll of parchment, tied in a piece of silk and a lovely handkerchief, with embroidery she recognized at once was Ana's. "Oh Ana, it is so lovely," she said, rising to give her a kiss on the cheek.

As Ellie untied the little scroll, she began to read aloud, the beautiful Latin prose in the hand of her son:

To our dearest mother on the occasion of her thirtieth birthday, we wish to thank you for the support you have given us all in these tragic days following father's unfortunate incarceration at the hands of that murdering pagan tyrant.

Ellie was reading in Latin, and looked over to James with a knowing grimace as she continued to read, replacing *murdering pagan tyrant* with 'Edward.'

We pray for the quick return of our dear father, our precious father to complete our family and restore us to the prosperity of the past when we were but simple subjects living under God's grace and guidance, serving our God with utmost humility, at home in our beloved Scotland. This I remain, you loving son, James.

And at the bottom of the scroll in Lallans, he wrote: I grant you the following gifts on the occasion of your birthday: three requests of assistance that I will perform with immediate response, one man I will spot you at our next match of Merels, and a day's study of Latin without protest, all to be claimed prior to the feast of St. Stephen, 1298, so that I may renew same.

"Your studies with our priest our showing you good stead with Latin," she said, "and will help you when we can send you to Brabant to complete your education. Now, let's enjoy these wonderful delicacies. Oh Ana, you did yourself proud on this caper. And to all of you, thank you for your love and support of me and the children, these have been such trying times for us all. Please, take some everybody there is plenty to share for us all." But a brief moment in these many months that his mother smiled; pleasure enough to enjoy this day, sighed James

London

A gaoler came to William's small prison cell in the White Tower. One small torch lit the cell, and he peered over his spectacles, to see what the interruption was. "Sir William, I have been directed to bring you and the others here to the constable's Hearing Room. We will have to put these on you there," he said, as another man came and placed fetters on William's wrists.

DEBORAH RICHMOND FOULKES

It was late October; William had tried to send Ellie another letter as it was her thirtieth birthday. But it had just been returned, unopened. Why would she still not take my letters he sighed, as he was reread his words, the love he poured out to her and the children, the loneliness he felt for her, and the despair for knowing it was his own doing? So now some event was about to happen that would alter his life again, he thought. He feared the worst as word had come down in August to inmates at the Tower that Edward's armies had slaughtered the Scots at Falkirk in July, and Wallace was on the run. Now William Douglas had become redundant, a living thorn in Edward's side that should be removed, permanently. After the Scots overwhelming victory at Stirling the year before, under the leadership of young Andrew de Moray and William Wallace, Edward had seen that the Scottish nobility under ward in the Tower were well treated, in case he would need to exchange them for hostages later or coerce them into joining his war with the French. Now as William and the two other knights in this small, highly guarded procession made their way down the dark, damp corridors of the White Tower to a lighted hearing room, things were about to abruptly change, forever, for Scotland, for Edward, and for the redoubtable Lord Douglas.

The three knights sat on small benches to the left, in front of the magistrate. William's name was called first and he was asked to rise. The charges of treason, murder, and plunder against the King were read. William de Douglas, Knight acknowledged his own name and seal to the document signed during the capitulation of Irvine some fifteen months ago. And then the words of one de Percy and de Clifford both; the false charges of his rebellion after the covenanted peace of Knadgerhill were read. It was like a long tunnel of sound, so far away, floating around him, so surreal, as the clerk read the next words: Sir William Douglas, you are hereby sentenced to death, by hanging and by the rack as befits your crimes of rebellion against the king; to be hanged cruelly. What say you to this sentence? William stood in stunned silence for a brief time and composed himself. "I would my last request as is my right as a Knight, and one who fought with Lord Edward's Crusade, that I be allowed first to make my peace with my God, and church, and then with my wife, Lady Eleanora Douglas, now of Woodham Ferrers," the old warrior said quietly. The Magistrate, having expected more from this stalwart knight and lord, granted the request immediately, and set the execution date for 6th November. "Return with him to bring his things to his new quarters in the upper chambers of the White Tower gaoler," spoke the magistrate. And that was it, in just three minutes he went from long term political ward to a man convicted of treason against the king, and with less than two weeks of life remaining. As he made the return to his old cell, he could only think of one thing, his family. I must get to see Ellie again, and I

MY TRUTH LIES IN THE RUINS

will tell her how sorry I am for all the pain I have caused. And I will have word of James and of our other children; he said softly to himself as he helped Gillerothe pack the few possessions he retained, carefully putting his new spectacles in the small box he carried himself.

Woodham Ferrers

Two weeks had gone by and there was still no word from William. This would be her first birthday with no remembrance from him to enjoy. She looked down at Shamus, "Come here my wee hound," petting his ears and smoothing his brow, "I need your comforting ways. I wonder why our Gilley has forsaken us, old friend." They were both sitting in her room by the fire, when she heard a commotion outside that the hound could barely hear now. She looked out to see some riders, accompanied by Father John from St. Mary's church, approach the front entrance to the manor. Ellie went down to see what was going on, and was greeted by a messenger from London. He spoke briefly and said he was instructed to wait her reply. Father John took her aside and asked the others to leave them. He said, "We have some bad news." A look of terror swept across her face, and she began to shake, "Not my William?" she cried. Ana, drew close, and knew at once that is was indeed about William. Barely composing herself Ellie asked all the others to leave except Ana. James was still out at the stables putting away his mount from his ride that afternoon.

Figure CXX-Part Three; ruins of the Woodham Ferrers Priory now called Bicknacre Priory; a tunnel from Eleanora's manor house Woodham Ferrers Hall led to this old priory.

DEBORAH RICHMOND FOULKES

She opened the letter, and read that she was being requested to come at once to London, and certainly by 5 November, for the final request made of her husband, William Douglas, Knight and Crusader, on the event of his execution; the last words trailed off in her mind, somewhere she found herself, somehow she could, and the tingling, the lightness, and Ellie slumped to the floor. As she awoke, Ana was wiping her brow. "Oh my God, Ana, is it so, are they taking my William from me forever?" and to her priest she turned, "Father John, I must go immediately, its almost two days ride to the Tower of London from here." James appeared in the hall, and he took the letter from Ana, reading it his face grew dark in rage, with an anger welling in him that she had never seen even during the days following their abduction from Douglasdale, and the sacking of their castle by the Earl of Carrick, before Brus reversed his course. He crumpled it in disgust and turned, swiftly leaving the hall for the solitude of his own chamber.

Barking out orders, directing others, writing to her family priest in Little Easton, Ellie made quick plans to leave at day break on the morrow. She then went to knock softly on James' door, "may I come in son?" He opened the door and she could see the tears as he was wiping his face and just grabbed and held him, "Will you come with me James?" she asked. He pulled back from her and turned away; the lad was so angry, so despondent. Ellie had never seen him this way. "I have written this for you to take to father, and I have sealed it with my new seal I have made for my use," he said stiffly. But his pain betrayed his voice as he spoke the next words, shaking, and filled with emotion of a son who loved his father, no worshiped his father, "I want him to know that I love him, that I will never, ever forget, I shall always keep him with me in my heart, my father, and I will not play for a tie with honor." Ellie looked at him, and the tears filled their eyes again, "I will never, ever forget him too you know, and we must keep him alive in our souls for the sake of your younger brothers, Hugh and Archie, who will never know his love or warmth, or the virtue of his truths. It is our charge to keep." Ellie knew not to ask him again. James was slow, careful, and thoughtful before he made a decision, and would never vacillate once it was made. "I will go to the stables to prepare my Fortis for you to take; you should take my palfrey for this trip, as I know you will ride hard to get there mother," said James, clearly taking on his new role in the family. "Thank you James, I shall also take father's horse, not Pageant, but St. Andrew because he is older now, and a little smaller than Pageant." They left his room, a sense of lamented purpose at hand, resigned to their sad fates.

Ellie, Ana, Sir David and other men at arms from Douglasdale and Essex, father John, and her steward le Parker, rode out the next morning with some extra horses and pack animals, one carrying a small trunk of Williams's clothes. James led Fortis around from the stables, followed by

Shamus. "Oh there you are my wee hound. I missed you in my bed this morning," Ellie said, trying to make light of the departure. "I will see to the other details as the situation requires mother," James spoke so low she could barely hear him, "And I will be in Little Easton when you return." She hugged him hard, unable to really catch his eyes; they were both tearing up as she mounted his horse. Two other men at arms brought a large cart with three horses from around the grooms' quarters. They would travel behind carrying the wooden coffin Father John obtained on her behalf. The plain wooden box contained the black pall and a large shroud that would be sewn around the knight's body. Ellie didn't look at the coffin or its contents. She was focused on the living. It seemed so ironic to bring new clothes, but he would be pleased that she had remembered his deference to fine attire, always striking a handsome figure; or would he? I wonder if he has aged, all these thoughts were racing through her head, as they rode west to London.

She had not seen him in over a year. And he had refused to allow her to visit him at the Tower, or so she was told by her father's solicitors. She hated using those solicitors, but she didn't know whom to trust to assist her in regaining more of her dowered income and lands; she had no funds of her own to pay them. Both her de Ferrer's attorneys from ten years ago were now deceased. What truly worried her was when William began returning all her letters in July, coincidently right after Falkirk. William had always said there were no coincidences, so there must be a reason. Was the reason her prophecy of long ago, that she doomed their fate with the words "you must never remarry or your husband will suffer the fate of death at king's hands"? The old guilt began to well inside her as she rode harder still. The additional riders with the cart were holding them back Ellie believed and she was becoming anxious. "Don't trouble yourself," Father John told her, "we are making good time. I will let the cart riders know where to meet us, and we will go on ahead. Save your worrying, you'll need your strength for the next days Lady Eleanora."

They stayed overnight at a de la Zouche manor, a little more than a days ride from the city and arrived late day on the 2nd November, with plenty of time to set things up for her daily visits on the 3rd, 4th, and 5th. She thought little of what was to happen after the 5th, and rode with the constant pain, that sense of what must I have done to God to anger him so much, that he steals away the lives of those I love and cherish on this earth. The children she had lost, John, little Martha, and Amy, and baby Douglas that came too early last year; and her beloved grandmother Muriel so long ago now; then her dear mother. And now God was taking her William, her loving knight and husband. Oh what must she have done to anger God so?

They arrived in London, staying at young William de Ferrers' manor house there. They were met by one her father's solicitors, reviewing any charges that had to be settled for William's final care in ward and that of his servants and vassal. The cart with the casket arrived that evening and was sent on to the Tower with Father John while Ellie kept William's trunk of clothes to deliver the next day. She was so numb, nothing seemed real, like sleep walking through a dream, only she was awake and the one feeling she had was that constant pain of being so unworthy of God's love that he would take the very person she loved most, sometimes more than herself, or her children. The fear of a year ago was gone, the dread of now hung over her like the stench of death at Berwick, over two long years ago, but still so clear in her mind.

It was that Friday, the 30 March in 1296 she began to hate her English heritage and Edward, that pagan despot, that murderer of her friends and their families; treasonous thoughts she knew only for her private counsel. As she reflected on the massacre she realized it was then their lives were changed forever, their love, their marriage began to quiver and crumble under the strain. William blamed himself so for not seeing through Edward's offer of truce, and not anticipating the devastation that began within hours of the surrender. The treachery, the false truce and the brutal slaughter that followed for days, he set upon himself for blame. No matter what Ellie said though, William would not forgive himself. He fully expected Edward's wrath to end his days in Hogs Tower at Berwick Castle; but then he was set free and his lands restored. His grief permeated his very being as he returned to his Douglasdale that June 1296.

How happy Ellie had been when he was released and home. But the man who returned to Douglasdale was a different man. He was moody and pensive and spent nights of sleeplessness, with the agony of those headaches that began at Fawdon, returning stronger than before. He didn't have nightmares he said, but she did. She could hear the screams, smell the stench, and see the tides of blood that ran down the streets and soaked her shoes as she dismounted her horse once while negotiating the cart trails cluttered with human carnage, making her way out of town. Over and over these nightmares persisted. Now everything was so final, she moaned to herself. Why couldn't Edward change his mind, why must it end this way, why, what did I do? She lay awake in her bed most of the night, catching only a few hours of sleep. Morning came and she looked at herself in the little compact mirror William gave her for her birthday so long ago. Oh how tired I look, an old crone of a wife for you Gilley, she moaned.

Ana knocked on her door and came in with some porridge. She got up and Ana helped her get in her fine surcote of gold and green brocade. She would at least present him with her best appearance she mused. Ana said the others had prepared the horses, and taken the trunk of clothes. Just then the two looked at each other, as Ellie began to cry, then to deeply sob, burying

MY TRUTH LIES IN THE RUINS

her head in Ana's shoulder. "Oh Ana, I could never have made it this far without your strength." "M' lady, no one has more courage than you, no woman has been asked to do more for her family in these sad times than you. I just stand back and admire my lamb," whispered Ana softly as she dried Ellie's face, smoothed her veil and fillet, "Good as new my dear, now go on with you, I will wait here love."

Figure CXXI-Part Three; a guest in Edward's Tower for over one year and estranged from his Ellie, William le Hardi Douglas could not hide his aged visage of despair; shown here in November 1298 just before his execution.

Ellie arrived a few minutes before eight in the morning when they were permitted entry. Every minute's wait now was agony. Then she and Father John were escorted up a small staircase of stone steps, then turning to the right at the landing she saw him. He was squinting, peering over his spectacles, a much larger, stouter man than a year ago. The strain of incarceration was fixed upon his face. The Tower's priest met Father John to go over the next several days, so Ellie and William were left alone. Careful to smile and breathing in calm, Ellie managed to say, "I am happy you received the spectacles you asked for." And then he spoke.

"Eleanora, come here, let me see you," he said, "These months of dear Edward's hospitality have dimmed my sight." His face was much rounder, his eyes surrounded by deep circles. She came close to him and he carefully reached for her fillet with those big hands, removed her veil, and ever so slowly, loosened her hair to fall softly on her shoulders. William just gazed at her, taking in her beauty as if he had never seen her before, touching her hair and absorbing her with his penetratingly beautiful eyes, now shadowed in concern and sadness. She couldn't keep quiet any longer. "Why did you return my letters William," she blurted out, "why would you refuse me a visit, then send for me now?" He pulled back and with a quick stern look, "Refused your visits, never! *You stopped* writing, didn't you?" Ellie could barely speak, "I never stopped writing you," and she pulled a carefully wrapped bundle of letters, tied neatly in silk ribbons from under her surcote.

Figure CXXII-Part Three; William le Hardi, Lord Douglas was admitted into the Tower of London 12 October 1297 and remained there until his death 6 November 1298; an unwilling guest in the White Tower he might have looked directly across the interior courtyard to this view of what is now called the Beauchamp Tower

Tears of anger flooded his eyes, and for a moment the old rage furled his brow. "Edward's wrath or the collusion of de Percy and Lord Lovaine, Ellie" he sputtered. Ellie fell back to the bench in this bleak cell and tears ran rivers down her cheeks, her body trembled, shook in sobs that reached her soul. "I believed you must have hated me for your peril, blamed me for your fate, for that prophecy from long ago," she said between halted breaths from her crying. William moved over to sit next to her, and put his arms around her small frame. "Oh Ellie, treachery has stolen our last year form us," he said as he combed her hair with his fingers. "Were they not satisfied when they destroyed our lives, pilfered our homes, and absconded with our lands?" He moved to kneel in front of her and held her hands inside his in that prayerful hold as he did when they would comfort each other, linked in prayer so long ago.

They sat together then, side by side, on that little bench, as old lovers would; the months of anger, despair, and betrayal washing down their faces as the truth of the intrigue against them renewed their love. "There is barely room for us both on this bench Ellie, let us move over to this large chair." "Oh Gilley, I have grown larger too, but not with child, she laughed. "Aye, with child, the way I love to see you lass," he chuckled. "How does it feel to have an old crone for a wife, now that I am thirty," she asked playfully. "Oh, woeful at times, but I make due," he feigned a grimace. The old smugness, the quick retort were a comfort to her. "I see you have done well yourself on 4d a day, with some 3d each for your attendants," poking him lovingly in his now round belly. He scowled, "4 d a day, they take 4d a day for my sustenance alone? The larceny of that pagan never ceases to amaze."

Figure CXXIII-Part Three; view through the small arrow slit of a prison cell window in the Tower of London, the Beauchamp Tower

DEBORAH RICHMOND FOULKES

"I have a letter from James for you" she said reaching for a small scroll. He put on his spectacles, "Thank you for these," he said, holding up the spectacles, "the many months with little light have taken my sight." He read the letter, in Lallans, "but Father John is teaching him Latin, as you can see at the end," she interrupted. Deeply moved by his son's words, he laughed out loud at the last ones in Latin. "He is under your influence now I see, one who would not utter a swear word except in Latin," he shook his head and smiled, recalling the words: don't allow those inferior souls to break your spirit, in Latin yet. His eyes begin to twinkle as he looked at her. He turned back to small window that looked upon the outer wall and continued to read the rest of James' words: Father, I love you and I will never forget, ever, and I will not accept a tie with honor." The words were foreboding; William knew his son was planning, plotting to even the score on his father's behalf even now, at his young age. Where will it all end he mused?

He moved back towards Ellie, and opened his arms in a playful pose she fully remembered. "Oh no you don't now William, stop it, have you no shame," as he continued to move towards her, closer still, he quickly wrapped his big arms around her and lifted her high, up over his shoulders. She was laughing and giggling as he brought her down, "Come here my little one, sit on an old man's lap." He held her like a father holds a child, "How are the others, Muriel, is she happy to begin her schooling; and my little Amy," his words trailed off as he saw her face cloud. "In my early letters, many before these that were returned, did you not receive them as well?" He shook his head in disbelief, no. "Our Amy took ill when she came south with us, that began in Yorkshire; her body withering away from this life each day. And your wife returning from our visit here last November took ill as well. During my fitful sleep and fevers, baby Douglas came too soon; he was then with God leaving the same day as our wee Amy, breathing her last breath in the nursery chamber next door to me." Ellie told him with heavy heart; the emotions she felt were yet too raw to accept or understand. Upon hearing her sad words William froze in abject despair, appearing emotionless; stunned.

She continued her story as she began to sob again, reliving the torment of those days. "Your wife then recovering from her condition of this illness, only to be told our youngest daughter was most gone; our child that came to birth too soon to thrive had passed as well." She looked at Gilley, he had been so strong, but now his tears fell slowly down his face, "My precious girl so much her sweet mother in her ways, like our Martha, with so much joy to share now gone." Ellie spoke softer still and held his hands for strength. "William, my letters only started to return in July, those written of our Amy were so sent in January." William put his lips to her mouth and kissed her deeply, a comforting solid kiss. "Quiet now, my girl, you have had the world crumble about you, and I have been no help." He rocked her slowly, quieting her fears. She cuddled into his chest; as the time she spent in the comfort of his arms began to cheer her she whispered to him more hopefully, trying to be more cheerful for him. "Hugh is getting taller, as he is almost five now. And Archie is a terror, like our James he is so curious, mischief is his middle name. He sees my brother Tom frequently when I visit there at Little Easton; on the way to see my friend Alice in Hertford or Ellen, young William's wife who comes to stay in Ware. Tom lives alone in Estaines Manor, training as a page to the knight and vassal residing there, of Lord Lovaine. His father, mother Maud and his sister are always at Bildeston or his Sezincote in Gloucestershire."

He asked her why she thought she could not come to see him and she relayed the messages that were sent; Lord Douglas was refusing all visitors, she was told. William shook his head sadly at their fate; I must calm my anger to enjoy our time now left he said to himself. Ellie quieted down instinctively as well, listening to the comfort of his heart beating next to her body. They locked their gazes and he asked with a shy nod, may I? They touched carefully at first; then she slipped into a familiar pose as they both forget the times and where they were.

William ran his hand over her face, the last painful months had disappeared and they were lost in each others love; only then to be jolted into reality, interrupted by the afternoon meal delivered this day by a Douglas family servant, one of two, along with his valet Henry that served him in the White Tower. She looked at Gillerothe of Duglas, like an old friend, "It is good that you are here for my dear husband, Gillerothe." Then another thought clouded her face. "You may stay until after prayers this evening" William said, as if reading her thoughts. "Here, sit down Lady El," as he pulled out her chair, "let us relish the repast of our own reluctant largesse." Ellie shook her head approvingly, "Thank you Lord Will," as they both used their private names for each other. "There is no limit to their greed at our expense I fear," she added. The normalness of their meal, the camaraderie they shared was startling to anyone who might have passed by the cell that was their private home for now. The lovers were oblivious to the outside world.

"The sun is fading from the sky," Ellie pouted, "it will soon be time for prayers then I must leave you. Will you love me tomorrow as you love me today?" William wrapped his arms around her from behind, to answer that old question, the ritual of their love, "No, but I will love you all the more." He turned her around to face him, "I have always loved you Ellie. Only true lovers can feel the way we feel, overcoming the treachery of those who have tried to keep us apart. I knew that you had loved me. And I knew, even when I allowed myself to be trapped by de Percy; carried off to Berwick's

Tower then in chains; that you loved me and I loved you. Only I just did not love you enough then; my selfish pride to clear my name and reputation my undoing," Gilley told her, shaking his head in self rebuke. "I love you now the more, enough that I do so admit freely my false pride to cause our sadness here." He held her close and kissed her on the head, saying softly, "Berwick destroyed my spirit. I felt such compelling guilt for all those who lost their lives, while I lived. I could not stand by without a fight. I was bred a warrior, my sweet girl. But that was no excuse to indulge my self loathing with recklessness that cost us everything we owned, and almost nearly, even our love for each other. For it is only love that survives us and now, thank God, we have rekindled that love again.

It was time for evening prayer and Father John joined them. The day had passed so quickly and they would have two more such days, beginning tomorrow. Only then to have but three hours left to share on Thursday, November 6th that would be their last. Both lovers were reluctant to part, a marked change from the couple that met earlier that day, on guard to the other's every move or sigh. Now they were one again and it was a difficult goodbye. "Here Ellie, this is for you, I wrote you this for your birthday" he said, giving her the last letter that had just returned to him. I will find the others for you too. Yes, here they are. You may keep these now, they are yours," he sighed as he gave her the rest of the letters he had written that she never received. "And I will read these over the next three nights," gesturing to the neat stack of her letters to him that she put on the table some ten hours ago. "At least we found out now before," her words trailed off. She looked up into his eyes and said as she had so many years before, "Oh to be so loved, my dear Gilley."

Ana greeted her when she returned to the manor of her step son. The look on Ellie's face was aglow with love, a look she had not had for so long. "He loves me still Ana, there was mischief afoot to keep us apart and one of my father's solicitors is involved. I will deal with him in time." Ana asked looking at the pile of letters from William, "Oh lamb, you mean they intercepted your letters?" Ellie shook her head angrily. "Worse than that, I could have come to him, and been with him, who knows, I may have been able to change the course of this tragedy." She looked at Ana, and continued, "I will sleep well tonight, I am so tired. He still loves me Ana, he does not blame me." She fell off to sleep before Ana left the room.

Ellie woke with a start, did I over sleep? No, Ana was just coming in with my tray she gasped, catching her breath. She dressed quickly, in a quiet blue surcote, an older surcote she had dressed up with some new embroidery. At least I have two more days, two more days to be with my William she whispered to herself. "I would trade a lifetime of new cotes for one week more with my husband," she sighed. "Ana, I feel so helpless

MY TRUTH LIES IN THE RUINS

seeing him there, but I can't let him know that." "There my love, you just go in and smile at him, like you did those days so long ago in Ayrshire, and he will be happy. That is all he wants, just to see you smile, and send love with your eyes, like I see you do so now." Smoothing her veil she went down to meet the others who would accompany her to the Tower.

Figure CXXIV-Part Three; turnpike stairs at Spynie Palace; an excellent example of the stone steps leading to other levels within a tower

Ellie made her way up those tedious, small stone steps that led to the cell holding her husband. It was so dream like, to walk these drab corridors, to open the heavy door of his cell, and enter a dark chamber, that filled with a glow of love the moment she entered, and for an instant, that seemed to her as if she was going back in time. "Lord Will, the guard tells me there are many Scottish nobles here, did you know of them?" William nodded. "Yes, my Ellie, there were enough nobles here year last that we could call a Parliament," he remarked facetiously, "Yet some have fallen in to fight with Edward in Gascony or our Scotland for their freedom and lands returned. The latter choice I could never so make," he growled defiantly. Then he resumed more calmly, "I often receive visits from de Moray, and others taken from Dunbar two years ago. Then too Thomas de Morham, the one with foiled plans of escape from Berwick, you recall? He has come to see me as well. Some of the other prisoners have more rights than I and can come about," he paused; "then there is our good King John," William sputtered, his tone turned scalding, "a fool so given hunting privileges, bringing with him countless servants, squires, priests, clerks, two tailors, a pack of hunting dogs, and many horses for his pleasure. He can go on hunt within a radius of twenty-one miles of the Tower, for they fear not that he would leave; that would require courage, intestinal fortitude that he has not," his words trailed off. The mocked praise lifted to an angry sentiment; "Toom tabard!" he reflected out loud. Ellie looked at him, trying to make sense of why he must endure this cruel imprisonment; this indignity for such a noble man, a true and honest knight, her redoubtable Lord Douglas. Again Gilley changed his tone to speak more softly. "These letters whet my appetite for more of the same, come tell me in detail of your days in Essex, since we left our beloved Scotland behind," William told her gently, smiling warmly with his eyes.

Ellie described the lean winter in 1297 living in Woodham Ferrers, how they had meager stores in their cellars; the cache she secreted from Fryton mostly used. She told him how much help James was to her and how happy she was in securing him safe conduct, entering England as her ward. And of the Hogmanay they spent; everyone making wee gifts for one and all to share their love as a family. "Mura tried so hard to find a dulcimer for James. Recall when you were going to teach him how to play the small pipes?" she asked him. Gilley laughed and smiled, "The small pipes, my legacy for our son, sure aye!" She told them of young Hugh being helped to ride a horse by James, using an old child's saddle at Woodham Ferrers. "And our Muriel so lovely; her embroidery so light and perfect, more so than her mother's heavy handed," she chuckled at herself. And she told him that young Archie was told stories everyday about his father, by James as he played with the wee lad to keep him entertained. "Though mostly spending time with his brother to escape his Latin lessons some I do fear," she said with mocked disdain.

Ellie continued telling him of her travails, of her times without him. She admitted how bitterly she felt towards God after losing the baby she carried since their last nights in Ayrshire one year ago. Lady El shared her sorrows about her losses; her fears and the anger she held in details of emotion that only her husband could comprehend. And she acknowledged how remiss she had been in thinking only of her self and her sad circumstances. "It was like looking through a mist one night, I didn't know where I was so sick in fever-bed was this lass. I could not recognize my Ana as she sat next to me, but I knew the touch of young James, as he held my hand fast and cried, tears streaming his face, his words included these: *Mother, please don't leave us, we have lost our precious father, we must not lose you as well, God could not be so cruel to us to take our loving mother too, please live, for us Mother, try hard, please,*" it was then that I came to more consciousness, and the bed soaked with a fever broken, I placed my hand on his head and held him hard against me. I would live; I had to go on for the sake of these sweet children, who remind me so of their brave father," Ellie went on, "Lord Will, I was giving in to my own self pity, the fate of my life

I decried to my God and I could not see this precious boy so sad. He gave me back my life; William, he gave me the courage to go on when I had none of my own."

William looked at his wife, she had grown up so in these ten years, the weight of the world on her shoulders and she had stood so tall. "Young James is a credit to his race and to you who have been his mother and raised him so well. Were Elizabeth here herself she would tell you what a great mother you have been to the boy." His heart was heavy and he wanted to tell her more, "Lady El, would you favor this old man with your presence, here" he motioned for her to come and sit on his lap. She moved gracefully to the familiar place, how many times he had held her when she was troubled, when they were happy and celebrating the joys of their life; what strength he emanated when he cradled her in his arms. "Lord Will, do we send young James to Scotland now?" she asked. "No Ellie, he will want to stay with you and the boys. You should be able to retain your dowry once I am gone," She clapped her hand to his mouth. "Shhh, now my husband, let us not speak of these things," she whispered.

"Eleanora, I need to speak of these things, we must decide for our children the best course," he said in that tone she recognized, forceful, yet not angry. "James must go to Flanders, the country of his Flemish ancestors, Freskin the Fleming. There he must so stay to complete his education, to find himself, to learn the arms of that country and the customs of its cities. If Scotland is not home to him, Flanders, your Brabant, shall so be. You will be able to afford that for him in a couple years of careful management of coinage." Then Ellie sat up, "Oh you would be proud of me as I fight for what is mine. I was finally able to retain all of my income from Woodham Ferrers, when this May I went before Edward's court and pleaded for his relief from the escheator on my only manor of sustenance. I was granted all, but not before that lord took some £6 more this term."

William beheld this woman, his wife, the one who feared Edward so, was now fighting him in his court for her rights and income. "How brave you are my Lady El. Would you be so strong to send your James to Brabant then?" he asked. "I will do that William. I have already told him that he must go; it will not continue to be safe for him even in the remote countryside of Essex under my protection. I am glad you said Flanders; I believe he should have such an education. I must regain Fawdon to pay off our debts, some £81 remains on fine, by the escheators' accounts. But I must look into this further as I believe we have been twice charged in fine for our trespass of marriage." He looked away from her, why was I so stubborn about paying that fine, it is such a burden to her now. But how astute of her to catch the escheator's error of fine twice recorded. "You have such a good mind for the finances, would that you had been my steward, that fine would have been long paid," he smiled into her eyes, amazed still by the beauty that concealed an intelligence held by few men, let alone the women he had known. "And now, we must discuss what you should do for the others of our children."

"Hugh has a sweet and careful nature that may change, but should he continue his shy ways, a life in the church as that of my uncles before, like the good St. Brice and his brothers; that would be a favor to Bishop Wishart in Glasgow. You can endow the church and send him to a priory, perhaps to the Augustinians as would be my choice when you are able. Young Archibald, should he continue like his brother James, he can learn the work of a page with the household of his God parents, in Ayrshire or in their estates in Crawford or Lothianes, whenever and wherever dear Edward sees fit they would repledge the lands to them. Being near to our Douglasdale in Ayrshire would be my choice. It will be difficult for you to let him go, but for some short time you must; allow him time in Scotland to find his way among his people. His future is in his homeland, but his heart will be with his mother in Essex. You must be firm. And after his return, at a squire's age you can let him choose, perhaps the house of Moray for his training; our kin and a good highland clan of core values and true courage." Ellie was shaking now; the tears she unsuccessfully fought back fell from the tip of her nose, down on his hands. "I will miss your counsel, you wise words, and the comfort of your voice. But most of all, I will miss the warmth of your body as you hold me close. Forgive my tears, but I am lonely for you already Lord Will." He held her hard and fast, as his own eyes filled with the tears of a life time gone, a life they planned so long ago in the forests of Ayrshire. "Lady El, you are the bravest warrior I have ever known."

The afternoon meal had arrived, and Ellie looked up to recognize one of William's valets from Douglasdale, "Welcome M' Lady," said Henry. She smiled at his words and thanked him. The lovers enjoyed their meal, a fun feast to them, as before, sparring and joking at the cost and the quality. When they had finished, she returned to sit in that familiar pose, and he took her hand and drew it close, "May I, my wife?" Shyly, like lovers lost and now found, they began the rituals of their love. When the sun had long settled for the day, Father John returned for evening prayer to find them asleep in each others arms. "I am sorry to wake you both, but we must adjourn for prayer, and then our stay is over for this day M' lady." A sleepy eyed Ellie peered into the darkness, as Father John lit a small candle on the table in the center of the prison chamber. "Oh Father, I am so sorry to have kept you, were you waiting long?" William had awakened before her, but did not move, he just wanted the moment to last for as long as it could; how very right this time together felt, how intolerable the reality that it must end so soon. "No, I have not waited long. Shall we begin?"

MY TRUTH LIES IN THE RUINS

Ellie made her way down those long stairs, out into the darkness of the night, to the horses and her knight and squires escorting her back to the manor house of de Ferrers. One more day, one more day to last a life time, it is so unfair she kept repeating to herself. Ana was waiting up for her, and saw her face lined with tears that had dried into dark stains on her cheeks. "Is everything all right, you have been crying my dear lass?" Ellie shook her head, yes. "Ana, he insisted on making plans for the children; that finality too much for this lass to bear without tears. I felt so helpless, and he was being so brave." Ana moved to change the subject, "I have ordered a scented bath for you. It is something nice, to treat yourself, and your husband." Ellie looked up at her, "You know? You realized that we have shared our love in the White Tower?" she asked. Ana put her arm around her shoulder, "M' lady, you and your knight have had a special love for all these years; one that few have ever known. I would be ashamed if you had denied him and very much surprised! Now, get along with you, you need your rest for tomorrow."

Figure CXXV-Part Three; ruins of a Roman wall adjacent to the White Tower; sometimes erroneously called Caesar's Tower due to the age of the building

The third day she woke at a normal hour, hearing the light rap of Ana's hand on her door. The sun was shining for the first time since they arrived in London. Ellie knew she could be better company today; sleeping well calmed her nerves. "Here's your lovely green surcote, one of the laird's old favorites I recall." "Oh, I didn't see you pack that one! What a nice surprise. I wonder if he will recall when I last wore this for our anniversary and his 47th birthday, and our James' birthday as well when we held our last Ceilidh at Douglasdale." Chuckling as she put it on; he'll remember I know he will, she said to herself, now almost giggling in anticipation. She turned to Ana and said, "I recall most that time in Pennyglen, when you gave me that bright green cote to wear, giving up my mourning for Lord de Ferrers, and riding out to meet him that first day. I was so headstrong then." Ana was shaking her head, "You have not changed one bit my lamb, and good that you haven't. To endure the pain of your fate, to hold your family together as you have, no one would know your strength from looking at you; but what courage you have my love." Ellie sighed deeply. "He told me I was the bravest warrior he had ever known," she confided to Ana quietly, "and I feel so weak inside, like a little bird with wings of spun gold, too frail to fly. I don't know what he sees in me."

The daily ride over to the Tower was the same, except the warmth of the sun comforted her now, a change from the dampness and cold of a November day in London. The cell where her laird slept had only a small fire; there was no tester bed with curtains for his warmth, she mused. She noticed the guard as he turned the key in the heavy door, holding his head down, as he began to speak, "Your husband has been most generous to me, and he tells me it is you I must thank for the coinage that he gave me. My words of appreciation to you then, Lady Douglas, I thank you." He stepped aside, and locked the cell door behind her. William was seated at the table, with his spectacles on as he read from some of her letters. "Ah, there you are, my lovely wife, I am almost finished these. A nice hand you still have, were I to read them again and again, I would not read them better." He was smiling broadly, and when she drew near, he said "What wonderful memories you have awakened in this old body," as he noticed the surcote at once. Rising from his chair, he started in that playful way, to chase her, and she responded in kind, feigning fright and indignation. "Oh no you don't, there will be none of that now, behave yourself. I command you at once, unhand me Sholto beast!" With those words, he lifted her up, turned her about, then danced around with her before he drew her back down; bringing her close for a kiss. She was giggling by then, "Lord Will, you are the strangest of men that I would ever know." Gilley just beamed, laughing with amusement at his captive bride.

William would not allow Ellie to pout; he would raise her spirits with his silly antics when she began to look sad, or look off in brooding thought. "Here now, I am one to be cheering you," she finally said. "Would you like to play Merels with me? I warn you though, I have been playing often with young James, and he has taught me strategy." He chuckled, "You, you have learned some strategy? Yes, we must play then." She had brought the board game with some things Ana had sent for William. "What else do you have in your creel, sweet lass?" "Oh, just some of those cinnamon cakes you have a fondness for, my laird of Douglas," she said with a smug smile that caused him to laugh the harder. The hours flew by, the afternoon meal came too suddenly she mused. And afterward, they sat together, and he motioned to her, even now, in that shy way that was always his "May I?"

As the sun began to sink on the horizon, Ellie walked softly to the small window. "Lord Will, the day sets now upon our lives forever. What are your thoughts for us, your words have always been so well spoken, most comforting to me." William came up behind her, and slipped his arms around her waist. Whispering in her ear he said, "My dear wife, your love for me, this old warrior is love divine. I had never beheld such beauty till I found you that day, brushing the dust of Ayrshire's forest floor from your surcote, chiding our beloved Shamus for his silly ways. If we could have stayed in that moment for ever then we would be there still: in love, in the comfort of each others' arms in the joys of our love, a spiritual love for the ages. Let us go there now in our minds and spend the rest of lives in that peace, never to return to the angry reality of the injustice done to us; this living world of sorrow; that we are victims to the desperate greed and infamous folly of Edward's demonic oppression. Hold fast to me Lady El and fear not, for we will be rejoined in God's Heaven. I love you, my wife," and he turned her around once more to face him. She looked into those deep, loving eyes and knew that his words were true. She only hoped that it was not a curse that came upon this wonderful knight; that it was not God's wrath against her that caused his horrible fate. "Oh my William, Gilley, I love you as I have never loved another. I will always feel responsible for your grim punishment at the hands of Edward. If I could go in your place I would."

"Silly girl, you are not the cause of my pain, but the reason for the very joy in this warrior's humble life. Please do not ever allow yourself to believe that speywife's unkind words, they were not words of second sight. Those words were messages of fear given from an old angry crone, jealous of a young woman's beauty and loving heart. Remember my words Ellie, for this is important: William caused his own fate. I alone brought this end upon us. You are only a victim in this tragedy, certainly not the instrument of its inception." She looked up at him, and wanted to believe him, but her heart was not to be changed. "I will try Lord Will; I will try to believe you." They both turned to look at the cell door, as the key turned in its lock, and Father John came in for evening prayers. When it was time to leave, Ellie felt the first tension of fear for the events on the morrow, and she felt her head get cloudy, as the room began to spin. She awoke with William holding her and Father John wiping her brow. "Oh forgive me I am such a little fool to trouble you both." William sighed softly. "Allow yourself to breathe little one, then you may go. And don't fret, the burdens upon you are many, for it is you who must remain, here in the sorrow of our parting. There now, walk carefully. Father, will you take her hand down the lang stairs to the courtyard? I will see you both in the morning." They kissed good night and she was too soon in the evening air, feeling the loneliness as it welled within her: she would be a widow taking her husband home at this time tomorrow. The tears weren't there, she had cried enough for these last days, she would not cry again in London she vowed.

It was Thursday, and Ellie woke at three in the morning, unable to sleep. The dreadful day she so feared had finally arrived, and it was raining hard. She was trying to eat something to break her fast when Father John knocked at the door. "I will go ahead Lady Eleanora, and meet you there. I want to see Sir William first alone." Ellie turned away her eyes, "Thank you Father John, you always know what is appropriate," she replied; only then realizing how truly numb she was to the reality of the day. "I will meet you there at eight." Ana would meet them both at the Tower at eleven; they would all be leaving London today. She met the guard and Father John at the gate. They went up the same small steps, as they had done the three days before, only today the priest from the Tower joined them in the prison chamber. This priest gave William the last rites, the sacraments, taking confession from the Crusader knight for the final time. Then Father John performed a quiet blessing with Eleanora and William, renewing their vows of marriage. Father John left to return later, when it was time for Ellie to leave.

William returned her letters, all tied neatly in the ribbons. "I read them all, over and over again, to cheer me through these last nights. They truly helped me pass the hours so," he spoke softly now, "This is for you Ellie, and I would like to read it to you:

For Ellie- Remember me Lady El, keep me alive in you always, as I will wait for your return home to God's Heaven. I will be there to hold and caress you, to walk in Paradise with you until the ends of time and existence, for I am yours and only God in his infinite wisdom loves you more."

MY TRUTH LIES IN THE RUINS

He motioned for her to come and sit in his lap, and he continued telling her so many things that were on his mind, "I always thought Edward could be thus be contented and leave us to our lives; for I knew that I led a good life and faithful life and I loved my time with you and the children in our Douglasdale. Then Edward entered Scotland with his army and our fair existence forever changed. I underestimated Edward's anger and capacity for cruelty; the carnage at Berwick too great a shock to comprehend. And when I surrendered at Irvine, I knew it was the last time I could surrender without a battle first to fight. Then to come to this: I blame myself each day for dismissing your good counsel; I should not have trusted de Percy with our lives and fate. My foolishness to thus believe my honest words would clear my name; free me from their false accusations," he sighed. Ellie just looked at him and allowed his words to flow, sensing he had more to share with her; she felt mesmerized by his impassioned voice. Gilley continued, "Finding myself again a prisoner at Edinburgh, then onto Berwick I thus reacted savagely to my imprisonment. The collusion of your father and de Percy only amplified the desperate deeds of one Edward. And then this king, a man given so much by God; that he wasted so on personal greed was his eventual dishonor. This English lord so damaged by his selfish glory that he allowed his vassals to falsify my honor for their vengeance. So troubling to me," he paused for a breath then continued. On and on he went, recounting things to Ellie, scanning his life, trying to make things right in her mind and in his. His words filled the hours that remained theirs, and she listened to every syllable. Ellie loved this man with all her heart, deep within her soul. She knew now, this was her husband, the one man she would love for all times.

Too soon Father John came in and the others followed. One more embrace and he would leave, taken from her again. His last act was to hand her the small box with his spectacles, and a tiny parchment scroll. "Read this later Ellie," he said. Then he was gone down the long corridor to his fate. Father John led her to a small room on the other side of the White Tower where she noticed the coffin for the first time, then William's small trunk, containing the rest of his clothes and small possessions he had kept in the tower cell. She sat and untied the little scroll, this last verse written in Lallans:

To know you is to adore you
To Worship at your feet

To kneel in quiet supplication
In the knowledge of your love

And I will wait at Heaven's gate
For the sound of your voice

To comfort me again
Goodbye for now my love

Ellie bowed her head in prayer. She knew he would be hanged, "Hanged Cruelly" but not allowed to die, before he was racked, and then they would use an ugly tool of torture, sharply curved with a jagged end, to add to his agony, cutting open his chest. When he was brought to her side she was not sure he was yet alive, but slowly he was opening his eyes when he must have felt her cool hand on his face. She could see the salt, poured into the open cut down his chest. He was dying in enough pain she moaned silently; they had to pour salt to torment him more. She brushed it out with her fingers, ever so lightly, placing some cooling herbs she took from under her surcote to remove the pain from his wounds. He could not speak, but he moved his lips to say "I love you." She barely held him in her arms for some few minutes when suddenly she felt this great surge of energy from his body; a powerful jolting within, followed by a sense of swooping upward. She looked down at his massive body but he was still lying in her lap. It was then she noticed he seemed different, as if William was no longer in that body and it was but a vacant shell.

She reached again under her surcote, this time for the beautiful compact mirror he had given her so long ago. Putting it to his mouth, as he showed her once when treating the wounded returning from battle, she realized there was no breath, Lord Douglas was gone: that great chest no longer moving in the rhythm of his breath, those great hands no longer able to hold her or pick her up. She pressed his palms together in prayer, between hers. And she closed his eyes. Those beautiful eyes that pierced her to the depths of her soul could no longer see her. She stood up and called for Ana. They began the process of cleaning the body, to prepare him for burial and to dress him in his finery that she brought with them in the small chest. Then they began to wrap him in the shroud. "Don't sew it closed, not yet," she said. "We will carry him in the open coffin to the funeral cart, covering the top with the pall, but we will not shut the lid, not until I say. I want the sun to shine on his face this last time." Just like that, they were done, and she was walking beside a coffin carrying the body of her husband. They were all going home, at last.

Ellie sat beside him in the cart, the traveling was slow and cumbersome. Ana rode St. Andrew, pacing herself with the movement of the cart so she could monitor her girl. But Ellie just sat there, with her hand touching

MY TRUTH LIES IN THE RUINS

William's, for the three days it took them to get to Little Easton. The cold, damp air was the not the cause of the chill that greeted her when they arrived at the home of her childhood, Little Easton Manor. Her exhausted state was met with more bad news. "I am unable to allow you to bury Sir William here in Little Easton. Lord Lovaine forbids it. I did not find out until I received his letter this day, my apologies Lady Eleanora," the old priest said. Even in his death they still try to hurt him she sobbed inside. "Where shall I go Father?" He spoke to her quietly, "I have made provisions for you to hold the burial at the priory at Little Dunmow near the tomb of your dear grandmother and kin there. Ellie bowed her head to hide her tears, "Thank you, Father John will take care of the service then." Then in a flash of rage, she turned back to the priest, "And you may tell my father that I shall never forget his callousness, and pray he meets the same fate for his folly, answering to God for his hatred. I have no father now!"

Figure CXXVI-Part Three; a young James looking more a monk than the twelve year old squire at the funeral of his father in 1298

It was then that she noticed that William's horse Pageant was outside the stable of her family's manor that adjoined the church. Ana tugged at her arm, "Young James was to meet us here as you know; but he brought with him others from Woodham Ferrers who will help with the funeral procession. I arranged it for you with James and the steward at Woodham Ferrers. Let me go and get him now." James came out directly with Ana, a stern look was upon his face. He showed Ellie the funeral hatchment for his father that had her armorial bearings of Lovaine upon it as well as the

Douglas three stars on a chief, azure. "I had this completed for today," he said. He rode with Ellie in the cart, Pageant tied behind it. The shroud was now sewn shut, the knight lying on a bed of charcoal that lined the wooden coffin. James looked down upon his father's body, that large form forever silent. There were no more tears to shed, he thought.

Figure CXXVII-Part Three; Little Dunmow Priory; only the church of St. Mary's remains standing and in use from the buildings of the original structure

Then he noticed his father's hands. "Mother, look here, you have forgotten father's ring." And so they opened the shroud to take off his seal ring: **SGILL. WILLELMI * DNI* DE DVGLAS.** "Good that you have put his hands thusly mother as we would never have gotten off the ring without much trouble here," said James as he handed it to her. Ellie just looked down at the ring and tears flowed from her eyes. "I can't believe I had forgotten it. Where is my mind this day?" James reached over and hugged her to him. "Mother, you are so difficult on yourself. And you have held us together so well this day of infamous tidings." She leaned on his shoulder and was glad for this young lad who had become a man today. Then after sometime she reached down for the small trunk and pulled out the coffer holding the seal William used on charters and other documents. "I want you to take this James. I will be most happy to wear his ring, but this should be yours. One day you will be Lord Douglas."

With one more stop, they ended their long journey at the priory. It was evening when they walked in small procession to the cemetery in Little Dunmow adjacent to chapel of the priory. A light rain was falling, and the cloak of darkness barely shielded their grief as James lit the wax torches, insisting to do this himself. There at the priory was a large stone coffin near where they would lay Lord Douglas to rest. The priest at Little Easton had it moved there; a special carved coffin for a de Hastings Crusader knight he told her; but a tomb was then erected by the widow and the coffin never used. The men from Woodham Ferrers helped young James roll the stone encasement to the site. The lad went to the cart to retrieve the package he had brought: fresh charcoal with some thyme, rosemary, and lavender to spread about the bottom of this carved stone housing. Then these men lowered the body of the knight into his final resting place.

Figure CXXVIII-Part Three; a lid of a stone coffin displayed at Fairstead church, once part of the de Ferrers manor; another such lid was found at Little Dunmow Priory from the medieval stone coffin of an unknown Crusader Knight. It can be seen lying near a back wall at St. Mary's church in Little Dunmow.

James looked like a ghostly apparition as he approached the stone coffin that held his father; wearing a long belted surcote and hood he resembled a monk not a twelve year old lad. He had taken one of his father's shorter, standard swords and would now perform the ceremony his father told him of so many years ago: Celtic warriors who fought God's battles were sent to Heaven with this ritual of sword: "From earth to the Heavens I send you now with sword in hand." Then he tapped the knight gently on both shoulders as he removed the sword from the coffin to present it to the widow. How ironic on this 9th November in 1298, that Lord Douglas was laid to rest in Essex, England. Someday he would bring his father home to Douglasdale, to rest in the Douglas Kirk, to bring him home to Scotland, "This is my promise to you, dear father," James said quietly, careful not to reveal the smoldering rage within him, as they began the ride back to Woodham Ferrers.

With a great solemnity the small group traveled back to Little Easton where they stayed the night. Leaving early the next morning the riders returned to Woodham Ferrers with an emptiness that only the living know when one so dear, so loved is gone from the physical realm into the Otherworld of their Celtic ancestors. On 24th November 1298 Edward signed a grant at Newcastle on Tyne to Gilbert de Umfraville for the Manor of Fawdon that he held from the lordship of Alnwick; Lord Douglas' lands would now be levied to pay his fines and costs for his imprisonment; the overlord would hold the lands for feudal business. Ellie kept her promise to her husband; she had her new solicitors file for dower rights for his lands and those she held from Lord de Ferrers. The time she spent on financial business of her lost estates filled her days; giving little time for self pity, the thoughtful design from one named William. His influence upon her would be felt for years to come, she mused. While Ellie busied herself with solicitors and matters of her dower, an incident of great malice and revenge occurred in London. Some days before the end of this sad year another knight of Scotland held in Edward's Tower would meet his end. Andrew de Moray, kin of William le Hardi, father of the squire who fought bravely with Wallace and the Justiciar who captured the murderer Walter de Percy was fast asleep in his cell in the White Tower. In the middle of the night as he slept some felons in the service of Sir Henry de Percy ran this brave patriot through to kill him; then slit his throat to make the deed his death certain. Revenge was most complete; Lord Douglas and Lord Petty were now with God, by the very will and deeds now done of one de Percy knight and one Lovaine lord with the blessing of an ignominious king.

Part IV and Epilogue

January 1299

Hogmanay was celebrated solemnly at Woodham Ferrers. "Despite our mourning," vowed a determined Lady Douglas. She insisted that everything should continue as before; but nothing felt right. It was as if a foul humor settled over the manor; cloaking them in despair. Eleanora decided as the head of the family, it was her responsibility to lead her Douglas household through this tragedy. She organized the festivities for Hogmany; arranged for gifts for the family, the household servants, men at arms and the others including Ana and Sir David. But Ellie felt neither joy nor sorrow in her work, only a chilling numbness; keeping busy seemed to be her only solace. This year was their second New Years celebration without their father; but now there was no hope for his return.

Lord Douglas always presided on Hogmanay with grand flourish; making speeches, reviewing the year's achievements and presenting each with a special gift. Eleanora took his place as most she could these days, but was unable to summon the courage to make any proclamations or great gestures as Gilley might have done. She finally assembled the entire household in the great hall to parcel out the gifts, calling each recipient one by one as was her husband's wont. First came James as she beckoned him forward. He received a beautiful surcote with intricate embroidery; pieced together from one of William's with new braid and brocade trimmings. As he opened the cloth bundle he smiled broadly; then quickly feigned a grimace, "No sweet dulcimer for this sorry page again; when will I thus learn to play that instrument?" he teased his mother. It was Muriel's turn to surprise him; she excused herself to retrieve a strange package from her chamber. Ellie and Ana were laughing so hard that tears streamed down their faces; in their silliness they could barely speak. James looked about the hall, even Hugh was laughing, covering his mouth to hide his knowledge of a ruse That must be what this is all about thought James; something must be afoot here, to play some sort of silly trick on this brother, he surmised. Even the wee Archie was chuckling as the rest of the household was laughing openly, no longer trying to suppress their enjoyment of the subterfuge. The youngest son had escaped from his nurse and ran to James's side so he could watch the opening of the mysterious package that Mura was handing to her brother. Cautiously James took the gift; with deliberate motion he opened his prize: the small pipes of his father from their manor in Auchinleck.

Tears filled the lad's eyes. "My dear father's fair lowland pipes!" he said incredulously; how did his mother accomplish this feat and without his knowledge he wondered. Ellie volunteered the priceless story of her deception, "Sir David when he left us for some time the solstice last; returned to Ayrshire for us and found the wee pipes as once we stored them, hidden at the manor," his mother explained. She was very excited that she had pleased him. James was overwhelmed and speechless for some time. Slowly his words came to him. "I will honor the memory of our dear father and sweet husband; I will learn to play these pipes, sure aye!" the lad told them proudly, imitating his father's favorite exclamation as he assured them of his plan. "I thank you Sir David for your trouble." Ellie told him that Gillerothe would soon return from Douglasdale to teach him how to play. The long time attendant of Lord Douglas left the White Tower last November when his services were no longer needed there. His remaining family still resided in Lanarkshire; he wanted to return to celebrate Hogmanay with them. He would return after New Years and bring with him Patric and Henry; two others that were in William's service in the White Tower. Gillerothe, Patric and Henry were grateful for Ellie's offer of employment; they would join the Douglases in Woodham Ferrers by the Ides of January 1299 they promised.

Ellie distributed the presents for the others of their family, their wee clan in Essex as she called them. Many of these gifts were made from trinkets found in the war-chests of Douglas chiefs: Sir Hugh the brother and Sir William the father of her late husband. To Sir David came a sword belt of fine leather with a silver buckle, once of Hugh. "This knight most indebted to you Lady Eleanora; but such a noble belt as this, I must not accept," he protested. James interrupted him, "My good uncle would have wanted you to have it; my dear father as well for all you have done to secure our family here," spoke the lad compassionately. Sir David accepted his leather belt; he was pleased and touched by their kindnesses. For Ana there was a bronze ring that once was worn by William's mother Martha. "My first such finery to wear M' lady; I do thank you so," cooed Ana, surprised at her gift as well. Muriel was presented her very own supertunic that Ellie fashioned of velvet from her older surcote and some of William's mantel for the trim. "To cut and fit these garments all in the secrecy of my chamber caused dear Ana and your mother much distress!" Ellie chuckled. "Children running in and out that might stumble on my surprise for my daughter. Alas, we were successful in our efforts to conceal our work!" boasted Ellie triumphantly. Both she and Ana were pleased in their successful charade, hiding their handwork as they made her daughter's tunic.

Muriel was truly taken aback; she had not expected anything as grand as this. With so many to provide for and the small count of coinage that remained in their coffers, Mura had not gotten her hopes up for any gift this Hogmanay. "Mother, I am so pleased with your fine embroidery here, yours too dear Ana for I know your handwork on this supertunic here as well," she praised them, saying she was truly satisfied and very grateful to them both. Watching the others open their fine packages young Hugh stood next to a sleeping Shamus, back away from the table that filled the great hall at Woodham Ferrers. The laddie was mesmerized by all the finery and the wee pipes as well; what would be his gift he wondered with eyes now wide as saucers as he was next. "Come here my Hubicus," beckoned Ellie. The wee lad was grinning ear to ear though he had not seen the gift his mother had for him; he was so happy just to be part of this excitement. James was bringing a small wooden coffer that he opened for his brother to see.

Inside of the box was a silver and leather double pair of reins that once were the prized possession of Sir William his grandfather. Hugh's face lit up with sheer joy, "Thank you mother," he said softly, believing that the reins were the total of his gift. He turned to leave them, but Ellie stopped him, cheerfully tugging on his surcote. "Where are you to go my son?" asked Ellie with a wink to James. This gentle soul turned round with a quizzical look upon his face. "More?" he asked them. Everyone gathered round the little laddie, then behind him moved Sir David to open the doors of the manor to the courtyard. James took his brother's hand and led him to his prize: a horse for his very own. Ellie had exchanged three cart horses for one young palfrey from her friends the Maysons. This family lived on a hill above the village; holding a sub manor of Woodham Ferrers in freehold for a fee, they were known for their breeding of fine palfreys. One day Ellie was out for a ride to clear her thoughts; she happened upon one of their horses grazing in the fields, so she inquired and was rewarded with a successful acquisition for her middle son. Hugh went to the horse so gingerly, gently patting the noble head of the fine beast not fully grown. "Does he have a name?" asked Hugh.

James told his brother that when he was given Fortis, the palfrey was his to name. "This young one once had a name, but you should give him one of your very own," said James, kneeling next to his little brother so he could look straight into his eyes just like Lord Douglas would have done when words of importance were said to the wee ones. Without one moment of hesitation the shy boy blurted out, "I name him Sir William." Ellie bit her lip hard to keep from crying; the tears overflowed her eyes and ran down her cheeks quickly. The son who was so attached to his father knew immediately how he would honor Lord Douglas in his passing. He would name his noble palfrey William. James was wiping his own tears from his face; hoping Hugh would not see him cry. "It is wrong?" asked Hugh when he saw his older brother's tears. James shook his head and smiled, he was so touched and impressed by the lad's thoughtfulness; he had not devised such a tribute to his father, "No dear Hugh; it is very right to do this."

Ellie ran to the boy and hugged him tightly to her. "So proud of you this mother, to name your horse after our dear father. I love you so my Hubicus," she said through her own tears of joy. The others were crying as well; sentiment was overflowing until the wee Archibald was free of his nurse and ran to Hugh and his palfrey. "Archie wants up!' he told his brothers, pointing to the horse in solemn indignation; he was going to ride the palfrey and the noo! By this impetuous outburst the Douglases found their laughter returning. This Hogmanay was one they would recall for many years to come, bittersweet in their loss of their dear William; memorable for the love they shared and the will they summoned together to survive their tragedy.

Later that same month the hard work of Lady Eleanora, widow of William Douglas, miles, would bring her household the relief in revenues that were so badly needed. The loyal servants would finally be paid and the manor's larder would return to proper levels.

On the 20th of January 1299, King Edward commended a writ;

To his chancellor John de Langeton:

As Eleanora, widow of Sir William de Douglas "who is with God" as so she states in her petition, has begged the King for her dower lands from William de Ferrers which were seized with the said William de Douglas' other lands for his rebellion, the King commands the said dower be restored to her.

As there were still the arrears of £81 for the fine of the marriage so pledged and the allowances for Sir William's sustenance while yet a prisoner of the King, the lands of Fawdon in Northumbria will be levied until so satisfied.

A second order was thus sent by King Edward to the Chancellor of Scotland:

For the dower sought by Eleanora widow of Sir William de Douglas for lands in Scotland, to assign her reasonable dower from lands in Scotland of the second husband William de Douglas. To restore to her as well all her lands of dower from William de Ferrers the first husband. For the lands of William de Douglas, the lordship of

𝔇𝔬𝔲𝔤𝔩𝔞𝔰𝔡𝔞𝔩𝔢 𝔰𝔥𝔞𝔩𝔩 𝔫𝔬𝔱 𝔟𝔢 𝔰𝔬 𝔦𝔫𝔠𝔩𝔲𝔡𝔢𝔡 𝔞𝔰 𝔱𝔥𝔬𝔰𝔢 𝔩𝔞𝔫𝔡𝔰 𝔥𝔞𝔳𝔢 𝔟𝔢𝔢𝔫 𝔤𝔦𝔳𝔢𝔫 𝔱𝔬 𝔱𝔥𝔢 𝔎𝔦𝔫𝔤'𝔰 𝔪𝔬𝔰𝔱 𝔩𝔬𝔶𝔞𝔩 𝔳𝔞𝔰𝔰𝔞𝔩 𝔎𝔬𝔟𝔢𝔯𝔱 𝔡𝔢 ℭ𝔩𝔦𝔣𝔣𝔬𝔯𝔡.

On the 24th of January in a writ issued to Walter de Gloucester 'escheator this side of the Trent' the king ordered that the lands of dower from William de Ferrers should be delivered to Eleanora Douglas. Stebbinge Park was valued at almost four times that of their small manor of Woodham Ferrers. For Ellie though, the income was of little comfort. It was the time she spent to regain her dower that filled her days. To the widow her trials with escheators and solicitors just postponed her sorrow; Eleanora was now left to grieve the loss of her dear William. Ellie would stay alone in her chamber with Sir Shamus for hours on end; causing much worry to her Ana and her children by her absence. When Ana would enter M' Lady's chamber she noticed Ellie had barely moved; she was just sitting in the same place twisting William's large ring that she wore; the seal ring she had taken from William's hand the day they laid him to rest at Little Dunmow Priory. Ellie's mourning was a private matter she believed. Her pain was hers alone she told herself; just as before when her wee son John had passed to God she could not see William's face. To lose him was excruciating of its own merit; but now Ellie was totally depressed; she could no longer recall her William's loving countenance. What devil took her memory of those handsome eyes so loving; that looked so fair upon her with that knowing gaze, wondered Ellie. She tried each day to draw his face; but nothing came of it. Today she was jolted from her solitude when she heard a soft knock on her door; Muriel asked if she might enter.

The haggard face of the grief-struck widow peered around the door, opening it but some few inches. Her daughter begged to show her a simple drawing she had just completed. "This I have fancied looks most like our father," stated the wee lass shyly. Ellie gazed down at the picture, then gleefully held it to her breast, closing her eyes she could see him most again! "My dear daughter, how pleased you have made your mother this day," she cried aloud. "That I was so troubled not seeing my dear William, your sweet father in my mind. Thinking it was the devil's work, you mother was so sad; driven most to madness by his absence from me," she told her daughter, thanking her and praising the lass for her thoughtful drawing. "Your good portrait has restored my humble self to happiness. That I will seek the light of day again," said Ellie joyously, hugging and kissing Muriel as she spoke her words of gratitude. "Come here and sit with me as I will paint this drawing in some colors that would bring him more to life," she motioned to her daughter. Ana came in too, happy and relieved to see her lamb smiling once again. Muriel told her mother that it was Ana and James who suggested that she try to draw her father's face. "And that this would make you happy," said Ana, coming to Eleanora's side. "So she drew most carefully this expression we all knew so well, our Sir Gilley with his teasing smirk."

Oh William, don't you ever leave me again Ellie said to herself; you must assist your wife, to remember you sweet face that I can always see it, she cried silently. "I am so relieved this day," said Ellie. "I have struggled so to draw his eyes," her words were now interrupted by her three sons coming to greet their mother. Hugh leaned into her to look at the colors Ellie was applying to this sister's drawing. "Fad' er," said Hugh when he saw the drawing. "Hugh sees his Fad' er most every night; we talk," said the wee lad. Ellie and James looked at each other; Hugh's animated discussions in his room each night were widely known in the manor. The laddie turned to Ana and told her more about his visits from William. "Archie sees him too; Hugh told him not to be afraid that it was Lord Douglas and his Fad' er." Ellie held the wee lad to her, smiling at his simple ways, his true faith in God's own goodness. "When you speak to him again your father, you tell him to come see your mother," she advised her son, meaning every word of it!

Figure CXXIX-Part Four; interior of St. Mary's church in Little Dunmow at the priory ruins site

Stebbinge Park

MY TRUTH LIES IN THE RUINS

Spring was fast arriving this year and the Douglases were spending happy times together at Stebbinge Park. Ellie was thrilled to leave Woodham Ferrers; too many sad memories were held in that manor. And this larger estate was closer to Hertford where her friend Alice lived and Ware, the sometimes home of the de Ferrers and their cousins. And most importantly, Stebbinge Park was but a mile away from Little Dunmow Priory; the adjoining graveyard there the final resting place of their noble knight and father Lord Douglas. Most Sundays they would ride first to the priory, stopping to say prayers for their father's soul; then they rode to Little Easton to attend her family church. Ellie's brother Thomas was living at the manor of her mother; generally alone, he was training as a page. Muriel told her younger brothers that this was where their mother and father celebrated their vows with Lady Helisant their grandmother, some eight years ago. James made certain his brothers knew about the tiny Lovaine knight and told the story often of his questions for his mother and their father's teasing reply: "Yes dear wife how does he ride his horse?" Where ever the family traveled James, Muriel and Ellie would relate the stories of one named William; to keep his presence with them and to bring him alive to the wee lads Hugh and Archie who barely knew their father.

Even Ana would recall the stories of Sir Gilley. "When first our Muriel was being born he surprised the midwives of the village there in Douglas on the Isle of Mann; that he would deliver now his daughter!" she told them. "And with those big hands he brought the wee lass to the chapel to christen her himself; there was nothing your dear father would not do for his family," she sighed, admiring Sir Gilley for uniqueness all his own. Ellie told them all of how young James would ride with his father on his palfrey when they were staying at Stebbinge Park. And how one day the son bested the father: James wants a fur hat he told Lord Douglas. "And our father asked, 'where ever did you get those ideas my son' only to have our James point directly to the fur and velvet chapeau that graced so our beloved William; elegantly carried on that noble head," said Ellie cheerfully; she was happy to talk about her Gilley with her family.

When they returned from Little Easton this day she received a messenger to the manor; a servant from the de Ferrers household, William and his bride Ellen de Segrave. Would the Douglases enjoy some company? A quick reply of welcome was Ellie's message; having friends and family to entertain will ease my pain of loneliness thought the widow. When the de Ferrers household arrived there was much feasting; fine wine was served, poured by a page who would soon become their squire: one James of Douglas. After much gossip and good cheer young William had a question for the lady of the manor. "Dear mother," began de Ferrers, "how good to see you back on this fine estate. My Ellen has never seen these lovely lands.

DEBORAH RICHMOND FOULKES

Would you join us in a ride and show her most the manor?" he asked her. Lady Douglas quite agreed to show them all about.

As Eleanora and the de Ferrers headed for the stables they were joined by Muriel and James, riding their horses with their escort, they decided to join this group to tour Stebbinge Park. "Eleanora," spoke young William, now using a quieter tone, "As most I wrote to you last month, much sorrow does this knight feel for your loss of dear Lord Douglas." Ellie nodded her head, finding it difficult to discuss his passing with others, friends or family. Lady Ellen walked to her side, just before Ellie mounted her jennet, "Lady Eleanora, our prayers for you and your sweet husband since his passing in that awful Tower. We wrote my Uncle Nicky of your dreadful news; he has been in Scotland; a knight in service of Lord Edward; to return by summer we do hope." Ellie was surprised to hear that her favorite cousin Nicholas was a knight under Edward's banner, putting down the rebellion of the Scots. "That he was the lieutenant for the Earl of Hereford, residing in that shire was my last word of him," said Ellie. "He was summoned for campaign; his knowledge of the lands and people that he knew when de Segraves served as castellan of Dumbarton castle and of Ayr as well," said Ellen.

Lady Douglas was depressed by the discovery that others of her kin were now being sent to do battle in Scotland; the country she loved so much. She sadly mounted her horse and rode on ahead with her children. Sir Shamus joined them on the ride as well; though he only walked beside them now, no longer foraging ahead as he once did when he was a rambunctious pup. Young William took note of Ellie's reticent demeanor and realized the need to change the conversation to another topic. "Eleanora I have come here to ask if you would like to join us in Newmarket for a Tournament just some few months hence," he said most proudly, "Would you do us the honor of your good company; perhaps too your James would join our merry group?" Then motioning to her knight following up behind them he added, "Sir David has agreed to join us." Ellie turned to give a look of surprise to her de Ferrers knight; a member of her household. Sir David rode up quickly and begged a word with Lady Douglas. "Young de Ferrers and Sir John de Segrave, son of Sir Nicholas, are going to be in Tournament in Newmarket. This knight would like to take his leave to accompany them," said Sir David adding quickly, "Too old to now participate, but I would surely like to go." Ellie nodded yes, knowing the Suffolk village very well as it resided west of her father's manor in Bildeston. But before she could utter another word James interjected, "Mother, as I am most the age of a squire would I like to so attend as well. May this lad accompany Sir David and *your other son Sir William* at this good Tournament?" adding his last words with his teasing smirk.

MY TRUTH LIES IN THE RUINS

"This lady knows when she is bested in a match," said Ellie. "Set the day and we will journey with you for this fine event; a tournament *à plaisance*, I have yet to see!" Muriel decided she too wanted to attend the event in Newmarket, and asked to be allowed to go. "This fair lass would love to watch these noble knights in combat. May I join you all as well my dear mother?" Ellie smiled a response of "yes" to her daughter; not able to deny her children anything these days, she also hoped that this event might cheer their sadness some; she prayed it would. William de Ferrers had heard of James' good progress as a page; soon to be a squire. He was learning his way quickly at blows and thrusts with a pell, the wooden post set in the courtyard of the manor for daily exercise with sword. Sir David told de Ferrers not long ago that James would become a knight of renown one day; his best student in many years of teaching squires. As this William rode along side Ellie, he told her circumspectly that the de Segrave knight was in need of a squire; to give him three esquires attending him at tournament. "Perhaps your James would be the one that our dear John now seeks," said de Ferrers. "That this knight should add, the tournament is more a pageant; drawn along the lines of dear Edward's tournament in 1278 where no armor of metal was allowed or required."

Figure CXXX-Part Four; Knights of Royal England a premier medieval jousting reenactment group; shown here at Linlithgow Palace at an event performed for Historic Scotland

Ellie abruptly stopped, pulling up her jennet. James was reaching that age in deed she mused as she watched him up ahead. He soon would take his leave of her and Essex for Brabant to finish his schooling in the arms of that province; to learn of his Flemish heritage. She sighed heavily; with so many things to decide these days, where will I begin, she pondered. "For that decision I will need the night to think on it," she told her stepson. Then remembering what she had heard some weeks ago that Edward had outlawed tournaments, she asked de Ferrers about it. In his usual bravado he told Ellie that it was not a major tournament; reminding her again that it was a pageant for friends to thus enjoy. Ellie knew this lad well and found him loose often with the truth, a trait that followed the father as well as the son. She would speak with Sir David; he would know if the event would be safe for all to attend. After all, James was not an English squire; he was James of Douglas, son of the noblemen and rebel to Lord Edward; only allowed in Essex for safe conduct issued from the king.

That night Ellie discussed de Ferrers' proposal with Sir David before retiring to her chamber. He told Lady Douglas that few tournaments are known to the king though many come about in fields of villages in every shire; but this one in Newmarket was different. "There are only five such lists so authorized for tournament; all located as this Newmarket, south of the Trent," said her knight. Sir David was the epitome of fair honesty her late husband had told her; he could be trusted. The knight continued to tell Lady Douglas that if they attended and James became the squire for Sir John, he would guarantee the good safety of James, Muriel, Ellie and her Ana, should there be trouble. "Lady Eleanora, your son is growing fast; so hard now is he working at his skills to be a squire, then a knight. Each day with perfect footwork, practicing most diligently his walking and the stepping for his development of great balance; to compliment his dedicated work with sword so early for a page not yet a squire."

Ellie was feeling the guilt of a mother unable to teach her son like the father, a great warrior and knight of renown. And as James' mother and the widow of William she understood well the heavy hearted loss this boy felt; the deep sorrow he held for the passing of his father. "I trust your good judgment Sir David; we will attend the tourney in Newmarket. It is done," she said quietly. On her way to her chamber she knocked on the door next to her own, "James, your mother and Sir David have decided. You will squire for my kin and friend, Sir John de Segrave at this tourney. If there should be de mischef then about, Sir David has assured me for our safety to withdraw us quickly." James rose and went to Ellie to hug her hard. "Mother, this lad, your humble squire, thanks you for your trust and faith. I only wish as you, our father could so attend. This is my promise to you: to do honor to that faithful knight our father for his chivalric training, as the tournier's esquire in Newmarket."

1299 Autumnal Equinox Newmarket

Figure CXXXI-Part Four; medieval weaponry on display in Stansted, Essex

The young squire was circumspect as he assisted the English knight. In the lists he assisted de Segrave, holding his bascinet and lance while the nobleman mounted his destrier. James followed all the commands of the tournier perfectly. He tended to the horse of his knight as well; adjusted the silks that adorned the noble beast and corrected the armor used for the animal's protection. A squire would assist the knight in every way but one: should he become unhorsed the varlet would attend the tournier to help him on again. This squire performed his tasks perfectly; the training of his youth so vivid in his mind, he knew without a doubt his father approved of his work at tournament today. His knight the son of Ellie's cousin Nicky, the nobleman they met at Groby manor, was an English knight that he respected. Nicky attended the tournament as well; but he would not participate, too old for the joust he claimed now at forty-two. But Ellie knew there was at least one other reason; he had sustained an injury in Scotland by his gait.

Nicky came to visit with his kin; he wanted to speak with her quietly in the gallery before the competitions began in the list. "Dear Ellie, so sorry and so angry both to hear of your great loss. When we can sit in private at your manor I would share more words with you. Perhaps another day will I come to see you at Woodham Ferrers." She told her cousin that since her dower lands were restored some months ago the Douglases had moved to Stebbinge Park. "Too much sadness for us at the Woodham manor," Ellie said quietly, "and too far was it from Little Dunmow Priory where we laid my sweet William to his rest." Nicky moved even closer still and whispered his words so only Ellie would hear him. "Long these years have I meant to ask of you, in Berwick when Lord Douglas thus surrendered, was there covenant from the king to stop the slaughter?" he asked. Ellie nodded yes, "And that my William offered himself as hostage for the burgh's good citizens; held there in Hogs Tower while this lass and children left in the safety of the garrison," she told him, then curiously, "Did Johannis tell you then?," she asked, adding, "At the gates of that royal burgh when we departed, we saw that sorry knight; he to give a message to Lord Douglas that we were safe, departed from that burgh of devastation."

Nicky told his cousin sadly, he too was there in Berwick in the service of the king; to see first hand the butchery that followed the surrender. "Our dear kin, that de Hastings knight so well known to us, told me he suspected foul play, that there was stipulation, the surrender of castle by the governor so done if the killing stopped." Nicky was studying his cousin, realizing that he had never seen her so frail and thin, even when she was the frightened wife of the other William, Lord de Ferrers. "The pain of these long months without that Scotsman shows mightily on your sweet self. The true sentiment you shared together was one I envy for myself that I might find such love," he told her softly, wistfully as he looked away, so sadly this knight grieved for his cousin and her loss, her beloved Gilley. Nicky had warned her as best he could in 1297; but too late for Ellie to gain release for Lord Douglas that he perished. The passing of that honest was unjust; a profound tragedy in truth he told his cousin quietly. The grievous treachery and collusion of her own father and that scurrilous de Percy are most distasteful to this humble knight, he sputtered to himself. Ellie bowed her head in sorrow; those painful memories of Berwick, would they ever end, she wondered?

Ellie, Muriel and Ellen de Ferrers along with Ana sat together to watch the events from the gallery. Lady Ellen de Ferrers was very worried; her husband was less restrained than the de Segrave men; he might run afoul of the Marshals she feared. Ellie told her not to fret so; in all tournaments the primary concerns were Chivalry and safety. First, the Chivalric virtues: that all combatants must behave in a Knightly and Chivalrous manner. And the second of importance, safety: that the intent of the tourney was a mutual test of skill, not to injure an opponent. "The last such tourney I did know was in Dufftown, in the Highlands of our Scotland some nine years ago. But I did

MY TRUTH LIES IN THE RUINS

not attend so then. Many men of Douglas went there; returning with great tales of virtuous knights, most skilled as well," she told her cousin. "Was your William in tournament?" asked Ellen. Ellie told her William did indeed participate in 1278 at Windsor Park as many others did that were on Crusade with Lord Edward. "At this fine tournament the swords were so provided, made of whalebone and of parchment," Lady Douglas told her kin, "the armor was of leather gilt; their arm-defenses were of buckram. Though not as dangerous as weapons so rebated as here today where knights are wearing leather in place of mail with gambesons thickly padded; the combat rough enough to be exciting was I told," said Ellie.

Figure CXXXII-Part Four; onfoot combat before and during a jousting tournament was common in the 13th century; shown above, Hugh Robertson of Fire and Sword in reenactments for Historic Scotland as James, the Black Douglas, son of William le Hardi

The conclusion of the event came much earlier than expected; there would be no dance and banquet to follow the tournament or presentations of prizes by the ladies in the gallery. The Marshals came to say that the word of their convening was now out and the sheriff had been sent to find them at their play; the tourney was finis! Knights were scurrying, pages and squires working feverishly to disband the tournament. Sir David came quickly to young James; bringing with him Fortis saddled and ready for their ride home to Essex. Ellie, Muriel and Ana made their haste as well; their horses were prepared for their departure, they all took leave without delay, barely having time for words goodbye to kin and friends. For Scots to be found at tournament in England might mean confiscation of their lands or worse, imprisonment. The Douglases stayed overnight in Suffolk at a smaller manor of the Lovaines near to Bildeston; leaving early the next morning. They arrived home at Stebbinge Park feeling great relief for their escape. Ellie said teasingly, "Sir David, you will be the death of this lady yet! If that sheriff had but found us; a prize of Scots in Suffolk, at a tournament would have made his mark in service of dear Edward."

Figure CXXXIII-Part Four; the Lady's Parlour in old Hastings was the first designated tournament site in England after the arrival of William the Conqueror in 1066

Hugh and Archie came in the great hall with their nurses and their aging Deerhound Sir Shamus. "Mother," cried Hugh, "you are home!" He ran to Ellie; and hugged her hard. "Tell us of the tournament and knights in armor," he said, stuttering in his excitement. Archie climbed up in Ellie's lap, "Archie miss you," he said smiling with his eyes, cuddling into his mother; he had the charming way of his father with his smirk. "This mother should never leave her sons again for tournament!" she told them. Then James began talking about the event, telling his wee brothers in great detail of their experience. "The Marshals announced the tournament, trumpets played to introduce each competitor as he entered the lists followed by his esquires; each event was finely structured, the pageantry was majestic, splendid for all to see" he said. James told them too of the music played at intervals to honor feats of gallantry and enliven the gallery for the excitement of the combat. "Safety for the tourniers and those in attendance was the watch of the Marshals; their charge to keep. They commanded the standards for the armor and the arms, crying out 'Halt!' or 'Hold!' as it was required during the fight."

Hugh was sitting on the bench at the table in the great hall, next to James, listening with enthusiasm and full attention. His older brother was certainly his idol. "James, you were wearing this?" he questioned, motioning to the leather hauberk on the squire. Ellie told them that it was one of their father's first hauberks; his newer ones were made of mail. "But since our James was not a combatant and this event was more a pageant than true tournament, the leather one would do most fine for attending my cousin's son," she told her wee lads. "Our James had this leather armor so reworked to fit him with new buckles; your father was years older than our squire and much taller and some fair rounder than our James when last he wore it," said Ellie, chuckling to recall that vision of Gilley in that leather armor. This squire left for his chamber to return with the scroll that William gave him some years ago: **The Art of Chivalric Warfare**, William le Hardi Douglas. The lad read from the scroll the fifteen principles for a knight in tournament, battle and in life. Archie left his mother's lap and stood beside his brother as James spoke. Sir David was listening as well. "Most like the **Book of the Order of Knighthood and Chivalry** from Ramon Lull some many years ago; but different. How like your father to write his own truth; the code of virtues of Sir William, Lord Douglas, a knight of renown," said Sir David thoughtfully. He stood looking over the shoulder of James reading the words from the scroll himself while the lad recited aloud to his brothers.

Ellie turned to exchange a look with Ana; even in death her Gilley was teaching her lads of manhood; training them in chivalry to become knights of good character. "I had most forgotten that dear scroll," she said softly. "That you should copy it with your good hand and give it to your brothers would be of great comfort for your mother." James told her that he would present each lad a scroll by their birthday next. Then Ellie realized she held writings of William too. She knew at once what she do for James before he left for Flanders: give him a copy of *My Truth*. Ah, Gilley's core values she reflected, those lovely thoughts her knight had shared with her in Ayrshire's forest some dozen years ago; she would copy the scroll for each one of her sons she decided. Hugh was learning to read and these parchments could benefit him greatly with his written languages; comfort him as well to know his father yet watches over him with the legacy of his own words, she mused.

James continued his enthusiastic description of the tourney, setting the scene from start to finish. "First came the jesters and the Marshalls; the gonfalon of the lord presiding carried by a rider on a noble palfrey, pennons flying, the kingdome standards carried by another rider in attendance; ah, these flowing silks of many colors," he described to his brothers, conveying the awe he felt as the procession marched past him. "It was my joy to serve this noble knight; one of renown, not vainglory. As esquire, this lad so pressed to yield the basinet and then the weapon most efficiently to his tournier. Not a common helmet for this knight, one with flourish and much style; the lance and shield of wood and leather, fashionably decorated as well!" James explained; adding that he was most hurried to clean their knives and blades of all their weapons for each good fight; taking care to exclude the ones of normal service that were sharp and true. "The tournier's weapons were thus so rebated," said the squire, demonstrating how the points were rounded and the blades forced thick on either side of the swords or other weaponry, "and it is the esquire who must make certain of the instrument so taken for his knight. An error in selection, this tournier would unknowingly imperil his opponent with a true blade." Hugh asked James if the English knights were as well trained as Scottish knights. "Of training most I see is very good; but nothing does compare to our good father's work, his precision and perfection were most impressive; his skills the best yet seen by this humble squire," he allowed. Turning to his instructor, James teased the old warrior, "Sir David is most like a Scot in his good training than an English knight."

Ellie explained how they would call the scoring of the attacks. "A knight must so perform that he does win the field in competition," she said. "And the ladies of the gallery were all of true virtue; oh, to be so honored, worthy of a knight's chivalric defense!" she sighed and gushed both at once, feeling the excitement all over again. Ellie continued to describe events of combat. "In the joust the horses must be as brave as their knights, running at full speed these destriers in the tilting as they so call it," she said excitedly; her eyes were aglow in wonder as she told them more. "There were foot encounters, à outrance, with battle axe and sword rebated, and a combat of quarter staves to so display a knight's prowess with his weapons." Then James told them all about the ceremony that concluded with the tournament, "We had to flee from the Suffolk sheriff that he would find us there," chuckled James, "Or we would have seen the knight with fewest points of recognition in a ceremony of true humiliation, that they had planned for this good tournament. This lowly warrior, much maligned now is his skill in combat that he is so disgraced, to make his apologies to the ladies of the gallery, to take of their ridicule to his poorly showing, then to ride his horse most backwards from the lists to take his leave." Hugh was most upset that they would have such ceremony of embarrassment to the knight with fewest points but James was careful to explain that events of competition followed years of training prepared one for such a day. "If as a page, then squire, to become a knight one does the daily training the best he can, in such tourneys will he flourish; practice and more practice is what our father told me would secure good place in tournament," said the young squire to his brothers. Ellie told them all as well that in times of tournaments and much knight-errantry the losing combatants would give up their horses and armor to the victor. "In this day's ceremony of contrivance for a knight's poor showing the embarrassed warrior would yet retain the armaments and destrier," she explained.

Sir David added that he was making plans to construct posts in the courtyard for training; James and the wee ones when they learned to ride their horses could use the ring posts to practice their skills Sir David explained. He also described games to tilt or run the rings that would help them attain good aim while remaining steady in the saddle. "We would allow each one to practice with the sword and lance, baston and battle axe; without the risk of personal danger or the possible injury that could occur in combat of a tourney." James was excited to begin training; to participate in the joust was very intriguing to the young squire. "This knight to set a shield; to hang it from the post that we build for training," Sir David enthusiastically continued, "More ideas will I include; teaching fair abilities with horse and lance are never lost on a good squire." Ellie was pleased with all the plans for training her sons; it was very important as she had promised Gilley their skills as knights would be developed properly to follow in the footsteps of one named William.

In the spring of 1300, the 28th year of the reign of Edward I, the king sent about his sheriffs, one in Leicester and one in Warwick to find young William de Ferrers and a younger John de Segrave, knights that they should both be brought to him and his council to answer to a charge for a participation in a tournament in Newmarket, now in Suffolk long prohibited by writ of the English king. These two knights came reluctantly and with their solicitors as well; making financial offerings to the king for their transgressions of participating in a tourney forbidden since the wars with Scotland began. They would be forgiven as Edward needed knights, many more than he had at present; and coinage too was lacking in his treasury that he welcomed their payments to the treasury.

1301 April 13th

Figure CXXXIV-Part Four; village of Little Dunmow is just one mile from the Stebbing manor of Eleanora Douglas; the location of the priory of the same name that sheltered the gravesite of Lord Douglas

Ellie had ridden out alone this day as was her habit long ago in Stebbing when she was the wife of Lord de Ferrers. Only this time in stead of going to Little Easton she went to Little Dunmow and the priory for a talk with Lord Douglas. "Today would mark the 51st year of your life and our thirteenth anniversary of our sacred vows just two days passed. Our James now fifteen, so tall a lad is he," she sighed heavily, breathing deeply to hold back her tears. "Wishing so this lady that you were here with me Lord Will." She quietly spoke her words to her Gilley as she knelt at his grave. She talked of Muriel turning thirteen soon; the time nearing for her betrothal. "A proposal now of marriage for our sweet daughter do I have; so arranged with my kin and friend Lady Isabel of Leicester, cousin to the late Hugh Lovel of Castle Cary; father to this Richard now Lord of Cary. Our Muriel has met this knight and found him most a gentleman and kind," Ellie spoke aloud to her husband as if he stood before her.

The lonely widow started to cry, tears engulfed her, sobs shook her body. "Lord Will I need an answer; your good counsel for this lass is most required! The lord is of English birth and not a Scot, what shall I do?" she said, starting to cry again; the lady was so sad, longing for her knight. Sitting there by the grave of William she suddenly noticed little flowers growing all around behind the stone markers, beautiful Bluebells! She remembered the time when she and Lord Douglas were riding to Park

MY TRUTH LIES IN THE RUINS

Castle, near Parkhall where their steward lived in Douglasdale. Seeing a wee fell or hill near Park Burn all blazoned in azure hues, Gilley stopped and picked some of the lovely flowers to adorn her veil and fillet. Recalling his fair words to her, "Remember me Ellie when you see the Bluebells, your William will always be with you, held here in your heart." Ellie knew at once she had her answer. "Lord Will, thank you for your good counsel most again," she whispered. "And I will love you even more tomorrow my Gilley." Feeling the comfort of her husband's memory around her Ellie brought about her jennet to ready herself for the journey home to Stebbinge Park.

Ana had been worried to have her girl ride out alone as unrest pervaded Essex making it unsafe to travel alone even for short distances. English nobles were rebelling against their king; the taxes were high and crops growing scarce, a situation ripe for strife due to Edward's wars with Scotland. Ana sent James to follow her some time later; being sure that Ellie went to Little Dunmow Priory on Gilley's birthday. Ellie looked about and saw her son coming towards her on Fortis. "Are you here of Ana's bidding?" asked his mother. James rode over to her and dismounted. He shook his head yes then quietly went to speak some words to William and pray to his God; as any pious lad would do. And James was devout to his church and God.

Figure CXXXV-Part Four; old gravesite adjacent to the ruins of Little Dunmow Priory

DEBORAH RICHMOND FOULKES

"Mother, riding alone is unsafe; promise me that when you need the counsel of Lord Douglas you will ask your son for escort, for even this wee journey now is dangerous alone." Ellie bit her lip, but the tears came none the less. "I was unable to agree for betrothing our dear Muriel without Lord Will's wise words; and thus he spoke to me, see here!" she said excitedly and smiling through her tears she went to show him the Bluebells. "The secret of our love was in sharing simple things. These sweet flowers; to find them here most comforting to me that I would know his answer would be yes on this marriage for your sister." Then she told her son the story of the Bluebells at Park Burn. James hugged his mother hard. "Lady El, I miss him so our father. This lad to come here often for his words as well," said the squire, a Scot in exile from his country, living in Essex.

Figure CXXXVI-Part Four; Bluebells near Park Burn, between Park Castle ruins and Parkhall

Mother and son mounted their horses to return to Stebbinge Park. "I wish that our William would speak his words aloud to me as he does for the wee ones, Archie and our Hugh," said Ellie with a smirk. James spoke quietly, in very low tones, "I have seen him our good father; in the stables late one night the week last at Stebbinge Park." Ellie stopped her horse to listen carefully. He told her he had heard a noise about; and he went out to check. "Then as I approached the stables I heard my Fortis stirring. As this lad went to his palfrey, there in the dark of the stall I saw our father standing as if most alive, but I knew he was not there to stay," said James deeply serious. "He told me to return to Scotland with our family. I made the pledge to him that very night that I would do this." Ellie realized that her

412

son's words were true; his father would want them back in Scotland. "Dear James, let us sit down this night and make those plans together," she said solemnly yet relieved that such decisions she could share with her oldest son.

After the evening feast and good wine, Ellie moved into the small withdrawing room and was joined by James and Muriel. "We must address our days to come; to return to Scotland and our Douglasdale is my desire; but not so quickly as I would hope," she said to her children. Muriel objected "That we are here in England, not to move again!" she protested indignantly. Ellie calmed her daughter's fears, "Mura, we know your worries and concerns; that is why we sit here now," she told her calmly. "First, there is the betrothal to Richard Lovel. I have thought this day to write young de Ferrers that he might help me with my dower lands for your dowry in marriage." Ellie carefully explained, "I was thinking most of seising Woodham Ferrers to young William for these lands for Muriel." James said that all the manor lands should not be taken from Ellie's dower there; "Two carucates should be sufficient," he told his mother, "perhaps to use some of your dower lands in Hereford for this purpose.

"Your strategy is well conceived; I will so request that from him," she said confidently. "Dear James, we must devise a plan, a means for ends we so desire; to achieve an agreement with young de Ferrers that provides us coinage we sorely need just now." James suggested that she would have success appealing to the young lord's well known shortcomings. He reminded his mother of young William's need of coinage to become a banneret and his reluctance to venture to Scotland, the travel there was too dangerous to go himself. "From the list of that good tourney would he talk of need for rents to most collect; to pay for knights' fifes and armed foot," he told his mother. "Perhaps your skills as steward will be sufficient to persuade him; he would sponsor a journey to collect his much needed coinage, paying us a fee for our trouble as well," proposed James with his usual cleverness. He told his mother to suggest a trip on his behalf to collect his rents; de Ferrers would pay expenses for her wend to that achievement he assured her. "A scheme of excellence; to appeal to his greed and his fear to travel into Scotland on that business; this lass to write most immediately of that good plan," she said pleased with her son's strategy.

"Then when we return from Scotland, we will have a fine wedding with many friends and family at Little Dunmow Priory." Muriel again was in disagreement, "Mother, why not Little Easton Church?" Ellie told her that Lord Lovaine would certainly arrive and spoil their ceremony, "We will make our plans for Little Dunmow; your father would so want to be with us this special day. This decision is now mine and made," Eleanora spoke firmly, "June the year next; we will set the date certain by the day of Holy

Rood, the 14th of September, with Lord Lovel." The widow continued to tell them how she would collect her own dower rents in Scotland, "We must travel to my manors there in Fife, the shires of Dumfries, Wigton, Berwick, and Ayr; traveling with Sir John our seneschal for the Scottish manors and Sir David with our Douglas men at arms as well, to bring back to Essex much needed coinage for our coffers; trading the yield of crops wherever we can for coin of the realm." James inquired very quietly if his mother intended another stop. "Will we not travel to Douglasdale or Lanarkshire dear mother?" he asked shyly. Ellie shook her head. "I can not bear to see that awful Clifford, vassal of de Percy, in our home; no Douglasdale for this lass until the lands repledged to Lord Douglas, our James!" she vowed, her voice shaking with emotion. The thought of going "home to Scotland" without her William was suddenly upon her. Tears flooded her eyes; the reality, the ordeal of some two years and few months since the execution of her beloved husband was deeply felt within her, cutting to her very soul. Eleanora Douglas was alone, the widow of Lord Douglas.

Ellie sat quietly trying to compose herself; she expected her feelings to remain in check; dissolving into tears was not acceptable she scoffed. When she felt she could contain her emotions and not cry she continued. "We will leave in some few weeks," Lady Douglas told her children solemnly, trying to exhibit some constraint; to mask her anger and despair. James spoke up at once. "I most agree with your ideas and good decisions dear mother," he said cheerfully, "One day when I return from Flanders I will request a word in council with dear Edward to repledge our lands to Douglas lairds, I promise this to you!" Ellie smiled quietly. "It was your father's most fervent plan for you to travel to that land of your heritage and learn the arms of that country." Ellie went on talking about Gilley and the pride he held for his kin. How often he would speak of Freskin the Fleming; the brave soldier of fortune with great courage and strong heart he begot the powerful de Moray clan of the Highlands; his sister marrying into the Douglas Clan to unite these powerful families. "I will write our Uncle Alex and ask of his advice for that end." Ellie knew that her family in Lovaine, the duchy of Brabant would be suitable for training a Scottish knight to be; she told James that his father had approved of this those last days in the White Tower. "And our dear Archie in three short years or less to begin his training as a page in the de Lindsay barony; at Barnweill or at Luffness if dear Alex is so reseised there or wherever he may be our wee son will serve the lordship of this God father and dear uncle," she continued. "This I promised as well to Lord Douglas that Archie should be educated in the country of his birth."

And what of Hugh asked Muriel? Ellie told them that she would write the Bishop of Glasgow, "Your father had so told me that I must contact our old friend Robert Wishart; endow the see of Glasgow, send our Hubicus to to study with the Augustinians in Scotland when we are able so he might train for the church." Muriel sighed aloud, "Hugh to live near Castlecary now in Scotland so fortunate a lad is he. Ah, Castlecary, a special place; one good reason to love my Richard, for the Lovel home. My good fate to find another place so named, Castle Cary in Somersetshire, for another so missed of Lanarkshire near our Douglasdale." James shook his head. "Mura, first you pine for Scotland; then you protest to leave this Essex, just this day! Now you choose a husband for the village name of his good birth, Castle Cary?" asked an exasperated older brother, completely perplexed by his sister's words. "Mother, are all lasses so confusing in their ways?" Ellie just chuckled. "That your sister is most happy to arrange for this good wedding pleases me!" she said relieved to have her concerns resolved. James was laughing by now and began to talk about his brother Hugh. Smiling softly, he spoke out loud to them, "One lad so strong a man to be, yet so gentle in his thoughts. A good sword he would learn to wield so expertly but to prefer the chant and words of God's good praise to that of armaments, I know!"

"I would most agree. But for two years to come and more he will learn his Latin with his mother and Father Paul in the village church. The good bishop and church of Glasgow to wait some for my Hubicus," Ellie replied, knowing well her heart; that it would break without a son or daughter to live with her just now; she was so lonely without her Gilley. Ellie told them she would write de Ferrers that very night of the good proffer James devised. "The proposal should be accepted by this lord," she told her children. "That I am successful; and an agreement is so met with young William, the dower lands for Muriel will be secured. Then too the expenses for our travels now to Scotland most devised to us," said Ellie proudly, "We will then visit Hertford's fine shops to see about some silks; colorful brocades and velvets for this wonderful wedding now at hand. We will embrace the new styles for a lady of your station dear Mura." Muriel's face was all aglow; new surcotes, silk finery, velvet cloaks, "All for this lass, just as before when father was alive and with us," she sighed happily.

Then James revealed his plans for his sister's wedding. "And I will be most practiced on the wee pipes to play them for your ceremony of sacred vows with Lord Lovel," spouted the jovial squire boasting of his new found talents, "That you will know of one such tune by then will surprise this lass!" said Mura teasingly. "It is my plan to learn some six tunes or more; that when our father hears me he will find his way back to this life, I know it!" he told his sister, his face glowing with the sentimental thought of seeing his father appear. Ellie sighed quietly to herself, were it only so that you could thus return my Gilley, reflecting on the sweet memory of one named William.

DEBORAH RICHMOND FOULKES

May 16th 1301 Hertford

Ellie, John le Parker and young de Ferrers were meeting in the office of this lord's solicitors, reviewing documents and deeds. An agreement had been made between the parties that she would travel to Scotland on his behalf as tenant in chief and for her own dower interests there as well, to evaluate the state of their fees; rents now due from Scottish lands but uncollected for some time. "Dear Eleanora, seneschal of vast experience, do you intend to capture much coinage in your travels?" he asked her with an amused grin. "That these escheators for Lord Edward have so collected revenues for the king while holding none for us is my certainty. Yes, that is my plan indeed and Lady Douglas will insist on payments most immediately." Then she paused in her words, "I so pray that this widow can recover her dower payments. Much expense with this wedding must I plan when Muriel weds Lord Lovel," sighing softly to herself. "Are you not concerned that Edward plans a muster in just eight weeks?" asked one of the solicitors. Ellie was not aware of any muster. Young de Ferrers interrupted; with a grin he told her that the king was planning one for 12 July in Berwick on Tweed.

It occurred to Ellie that young William knew the king's army was moving into Scotland even as she first wrote her letter to this lord. "Perhaps that Edward would remove himself from Scotland our rents could be collected for our use!" she retorted indignantly. "This lass not to quiver from the marching of his army; we will go to Scotland, it is done," she told her step son adamantly. Turning to the solicitors, "Will the bovates and the carucates that I hold in dower now in Hereford be sufficient to impart two carucates in freehold for my daughter and her betrothed Richard Lovel? That this widow will retain some income for my own sustenance?" she asked them. "Sir William has so provided in this agreement Lady Douglas," said the attorney, "with small value to effect now of your income from that shire."

Ellie read through the document in Norman French twice before she placed her seal in agreement to the terms; hoping not to miss a word that might be trouble for her later. Young de Ferrers was often shrewd to his own gain and these were his solicitors. "And this one Lady Douglas," said the attorney, "does compel Lord de Ferrers to so pay for your expenses of the journey now to Scotland with this advance for all your troubles," he continued. "And that he will set aside one in every ten coins that you collect on his behalf for your good use." Ellie was pleased with the agreement. She could travel with her children and the entire Douglas household at de Ferrers' expense; no financial risk was extended by the widow for their return to Scotland. Eleanora could only benefit by the coinage she might collect from her rents held by Edward's escheators. The strategy of her son James had brought them success; their plans were now in place to return home.

"Dear William, should we stand here until Scotland comes to peace with Edward, then tarry there? That we might collect our fees is my desire; or perish in this Essex for our hunger in the wait," she said pointedly. "Some many weeks ago dear Edward issued more writs for purveyance; his demands on shires here and in the north prohibitive as you know. For our Essex the king was forced to reduce his requirements; the scarcity of oats and malt in this fair district was the reason," she told them. "We will find our way and will not perish in the journey," she continued. "Your fair mother to return to Essex by Assumption Day, I do promise it," she vowed confidently. The solicitors shook their heads; this Essex widow was too head-strong for her own safety. The armies were marching from the north of England, soldiers coming too from Wales and Ireland to muster soon in Berwick; the Douglases were traveling to their Scotland at the same time. The solicitors feared this lady might not return alive. Young de Ferrers was indifferent and said not a word. "Bon chance Lady Douglas," the attorneys mumbled solemnly.

Ellie spoke politely with her stepson and cousin, "This lady thanks you young William." He smiled in his circumspect way. "Eleanora, if such rents can be collected it would be you *dear mother* that would accomplish that fair task. I salute your perseverance in the matter." Ellie handed her duplicates of the documents and deeds to Sir John. As her steward reviewed the records Ellie chatted more calmly, happy to have the negotiating behind her. "Tell me about the Wigton manor on the sea," she began to query him. "And the fortified house in Dumfries, what have you heard of the condition of these manors?" she asked. De Ferrers told her that he had little news of the Wigton manor, "But in Dumfries, the Senwick Grange boasts a fine manor house still undisturbed with the de la Zouches fair tower residence of Balmangan but one mile from there, still standing yet most empty save for servants since the submission began some five years now."

Submission in deed; *the invasion* is what this lass calls that usurping of our kingdome sputtered Ellie angrily under her breath! "When Lady Douglas so returns to England it will be with coinage for your trouble," she said albeit boastfully; turning now to take her leave of them. Then something strange happened; she heard a voice, a deep male's voice coming from behind her, with a very familiar tone, "It is done!" were the words so said. Ellie's heart was beating fast, she moved back around to see de Ferrers and his solicitors engaged in quiet words, "Did you say something gentlemen?" she asked hesitantly. No they all answered, "Good day then," said Ellie.

Figure CXXXVII-Part Four; Balmangan Tower remains near Senwick Grange

She sighed gratefully to herself; that you have been most with me this day and I have beheld your own sweet voice Lord Douglas! Most like you speak with our dear Hugh, God's sweet gift of courage to me now, she chuckled to herself, knowing she had heard the words of one named William! The Celts with second sight that they must hear as well she marveled; recalling Gilley's ceremony with the dagger, mixing her blood with his. She was in deed a true Douglas and a Celt, she knew it now. Another gift from the Otherworld and her William; did he so plan his ways to help us from beyond Ellie wondered? I do pray so!

Ellie and John le Parker left together quickly. Ellie was meeting her children with Alice to take them shopping for the wedding and their journey across Scotland. The advance of coinage from young de Ferrers made her days easier to manage. But the light heartedness was not from fees or rents to come it was from hearing the words of her lost love. Le Parker escorted Lady Douglas to her rendezvous and then departed for his kin in Bennington. "Lady Eleanora that was a great achievement with much merit; the agreement to your advantage I would say," said her steward, seldom so effusive in his words. "That we will arrive to leave that country before the conflagration I do hope," he said quietly. Ellie was beaming but barely listening to his words. "Thank you Sir John. We will see you three days hence to take our leave again of England. Let us pray for much success in our endeavors," she said almost blissfully. Ellie now ran to her son standing outside the tailor's shop by the cart filled to the top with many boxes. "Dear mother, most in time you are to stop this lass; not one more package to so fit here," James exclaimed as he laugh heartily at Mura's expense with the rest of the men, Sir David and the other squires traveling with the Douglases.

"James, I heard his voice," she said excitedly. "Where, what do you mean?" he asked. "Your father's voice, 'it is done' said he and I heard it so plainly just behind me, with the solicitors and de Ferrers there in chamber. As I turned to leave, the documents most signed, I heard those dear sweet words from Gilley I do know it!" she squealed. "A true gift from God this day; our William is so pleased for us, to leave for Scotland now he came to tell us so!" Ellie proclaimed. James smiled at his mother then laughed heartily as he knew exactly how she felt. "Hearing our father's voice in the stables that night strengthened this lad's resolve, sure aye!" he confessed adamantly. Mother and son were exchanging silly looks; laughing at the significance of his words: le Hardi would get his message through! The lad became more serious as he commiserated with her about the meeting with the solicitors. "How did you settle with de Ferrers?" he asked of the business transactions. "Le Parker feels we bested him; your strategy most worked my dear son," she said congratulating him on his plan. "Oh to think of you in Brabant far from this lass; a most disagreeable circumstance I fear! What will I do without your plans to guide me in my dealings with that young lord of fair greed?" she asked him. Ellie continued speaking of young de Ferrers with disdain for his attempt to cheat the widow of his father; explaining that he was unsuccessful because of James' boldly conceived ideas. "Those games of Merels we played for good reason," she teased him.

"And now your cleverness takes us home to Scotland," she exclaimed. "And more triumphs will we have when you collect the rents most due," James praised his mother. "We are a strong match to such chicanery of a greedy lord, aye!" he said proudly. James looked down at this little lady, his sweet mother and thought about the great strength she showed. "Our dear father was most fortunate to marry one named Eleanora; so stalwart in your courage and love for your family. I truly love you too, my mother," he told her quietly. Ellie beamed as she returned his smile and praises. "There is no truer son than had you come from my own body. Most indebted is this lass to your mother sweet Elizabeth," she told him quite honestly.

"Come let us find our Muriel before we most own all the goods in Hertford's fair shops. She is her father's daughter; taking great pleasure in filling up our carts!" chuckled Ellie as she grabbed hold of her son's out stretched arm, an escort offered from her squire. Ellie grew excited again upon seeing Ana there with some Douglas men at arms; another one with whom to share her good news. Aye, hearing William's words is great comfort to this lass she mused. "Ana, come quick, some words of joy to share with you this day!" cried Ellie excitedly. Ana was taken aback to see her lady so ebullient with a twinkle in her eye. Through tears of true joy Eleanora began reciting the strange tale and the words she heard from her dear Gilley. "It is done," said Ana shaking her head, "how many times that he did use those very words." "Lady El," said James with his gallant smirk, "It is done, in deed!"

Ana led them all into the shop where Muriel and Ellie's friend Alice were purchasing their fine silks and velvet from the tailor. He would have their new surcotes, brocade cotes and fine cloaks for travel in time for Muriel's departure for Castle Cary he told them. Muriel would not tarry to her Scotland; staying first with Lady Alice then to visit Lady Isabel and her betrothed while her brothers were in Scotland with her mother. The day next Ellie returned to Hertford's tailor, this time she brought a squire, a page, and her Archie not yet five. These three sons would have new clothes as well for their return she decided. "That my lads are growing fast, will you arrange to make the cotes and surcotes larger, longer than they need now?" she asked the tailor. He chuckled, thinking of his own sons adding inches to their size most every day, sharing the same ages as these Douglas boys. The old merchant assured Eleanora that he would make cotes the size to fit her boys to wear in some few months. "When you return in August Lady Douglas will all these cotes and surcotes be so ready for your boys," said the tailor. If she was successful in collecting her rents some three years owing now, she would return again to order surcotes for herself and more for James.

But Ellie held some grave concerns about her income from Scotland. Her dower lands of de Ferrers were damaged by the English; armed foot marching through the shires, occupying villages and towns. Little income was possible if the tenants were gone and many Scots had fled the lands for safety or never returned from the battlefields fighting Edward's army. From reports from the de Lindsays the Douglas dower lands in the Borders were fairing poorly; few crops growing and little coinage for the "harvest" of her income. Everyone's lands in England and in Scotland were effected by the wars. In the Rolls of the Pipe, the entries from Northumbria recorded their Fawdon as *'**nichil by waste**'* not one penny or crop growing because of the destruction of the lands from the war. Were all her lands so affected? Was not all of Scotland submitting to Edward? Were some shires yet free from his control, she wondered? Perhaps the problem with my rents to be with Scots not loyal to the king, she postulated. This lass will appeal to their good cause; if they have fees for Lady Douglas they will give them up for the sons of our true patriot and hero, so they can return to Scotland schooled in languages; trained in knighthood; ready to defend their country! It then occurred to the widow that she was in deed raising future leaders and brave warriors for that kingdome; perhaps to drive out Edward and send him back to England she reflected proudly. As for herself, traveling through Scotland

MY TRUTH LIES IN THE RUINS

took on a further meaning: she was visiting places with fond memories of the life she shared there with Gilley.

Ellie finally received fair responses from her letters to the de Lindsays and Bishop Wishart just before departing for Scotland. Both extended invitations for the Douglases to partake of their good hospitality. But the Bishop was concerned for the timing of her travels; foul rumors of one Edward to return in campaign. The burgh of his fair cathedral was under Edward's rule; but Ayrshire was still three years now in rebellion he told Lady Douglas. The road from Glasgow to Ayr was controlled by the Scots, wrote the Bishop. Ellie realized that her suspicions were true as she continued to read Robert Wishart's words. Her rents from dower lands in the west and south of Scotland were likely withheld; or taken by the escheators of that kingdome. Dumfries too, that county of independent folk, was in the control of Scotland's government not Edward's, the letter read. That she should stay away from Ayrshire and her manors there was the advice of Bishop Wishart. He provided letters for her journey in any case knowing this Douglas widow would likely ignore his good advice. Should this household so traveling come upon some rebels to the king, such a document would provide some safety he conceded.

Sir Alex responded to her letter to say that he was pleased to hear his young God son Archie would be entrusted to his care; to be fostered for his training in the de Lindsay household. He wrote that this knight would be most pleased to provide this favor for the widow of his friend and kin, William le Hardi. De Lindsay also expressed his concern for the timing of their journey; the campaign of Edward was known to Scots loyal to the English king. Sir Alex was awarded lands of James the Steward and the castle of Dundonald for his service to Lord Edward; but those lands in Ayrshire were held by Scots to disrupt the trade in Scotland. Sir Alex too had rents that were seized for his loyalty to England. Strangely though for a baron pledged to Edward this knight advised the widow of an opportunity to meet with William Lamberton. Bishop Lamberton of St. Andrews was kin of the de Lindsays; his lands were near to those of Lady Douglas both in Ayton and in Leuchars. Ellie was reading Uncle Alex's words to James, "That this good bishop has the words to speak and be heard by King Edward without malice; a skill of courtly cunning your good husband and this humble knight seldom could thus muster," he wrote with honest humor.

"Perhaps we can enlist the help of this good bishop; his propensity for speech so well received by Lord Edward," Ellie speculated. James agreed that the suggestion from his uncle held for further study of the matter. "Mother, lang times as you know have I thought at the age close of majority, to request from that pagan despot, feigning graciousness of forced demeanor; a ruse to thus secure our Douglasdale to Douglas lairds," he said expressing his true ambition. "This further introduction to this bishop might well assist us in that end," James told her. Ellie nodded in agreement. "My desire too my son to thus return to Scotland. No longer am I happy to live here in Essex; feeling closer to my William and your dear father in our Scotland; perhaps again in our sweet home, our Douglasdale with all those fond memories to surround me in his love," she sighed recalling happier times when they lived in peace before the war.

June 1301 Fawdon

Figure CXXXVIII-Part Four; the old nemesis Gilbert de Umfraville in effigy with his wife at Hexam Abbey

Fawdon lands were held for the king by Gilbert de Umfraville; the rents were levied to Edward's treasury for the balance owing on their fine of marriage. But the manor house was part of the widow's dower to use on their way to Scotland as it was restored in 1299 to Lady Douglas. This messuage was a mere shadow of its former self. Only the Cheviot Hills retained their former beauty; the lands sustained their grace and dignity despite the war. The Douglas household was traveling with several pack horses and two carts to hold some furniture and stores of grain and smoked fish; expecting the pillage of their manors to greet them. Fawdon was barren in the larder but for their trouble there were some chambers complete of furniture, enough for their use. As Ellie and James took the lead in riding up the wee hill to their manor house, they were dismayed to see not one ewe about; crops growing not in much measure as well. "An ill feeling to these lands do I find," said James as he looked at Ellie. His mother was not deterred; this was Fawdon and their home, a manor that she shared with William. "James, your sweet father almost lost his very life here defending this manor; then a lad of seventeen when de Umfraville's men so attacked him and your grandfather here. He would want that we rebuild what has been lost," said Ellie. We will do this Gilley; it is done she vowed.

Hugh rode up on his palfrey Sir William. "Mother, this is our manor?" asked the laddie now seven. "I most recall a bigger place than this when last we came here." Ana had arrived by now and was feeling Ellie's joyousness. She chuckled at his comments. "Dear laddie, that you are bigger too does change your view of things!" she told him. Archie had ridden in with Sir David. He headed directly for his mother when the knight set him down from the palfrey. "This fair manor of my father would this lad so cherish as his own," he proclaimed solemnly. Ellie was surprised by her youngest son's quiet sentiment. She kneeled down to be at the laddie's height, the Douglas custom; told him of the invasion by the men at arms from Harbottle Castle sent to oust the Douglases from their Fawdon manor on that fateful eve, 19th July 1267. "Then your father felled the third of three who thus attacked him; he ran the felon of de Umfraville most through." James continued to elaborate, to share the lesson from his father; how Lord Douglas reminded him to always wear his armaments, to put on his gambeson and hauberk as the battle waits for the warrior. Hugh listened intently as well; he heard every word they spoke; his eyes wide with wonder as his father became a giant among men in size and valor right before his eyes. The brave and noble laird, the knight of renown was alive to him this day as the storytellers wove their tales.

Hugh asked them about his father's recovery. "How did he regain his health, his head mostly so cut off?" James told his brother of the Celtic healing that William studied while convalescing; then later as a Crusader he learned of Alchemy Healing. "That study would this lad pursue, in my father's honor will I thus become a healer of renown to take care of brave warriors like my father and now older brother James," said Hubicus. Ellie looked at James, then Ana. "That we are here at Fawdon some few moments and already do we feel the presence of our father here in the words of your fair self my precious Hugh," she smiled broadly. "I have decided well to come here now I know it! Dear son, that you would be a healer true; this would please your mother so." James thanked his brother for his sentiment. "Someday I plan thus to return as laird of this fine manor; and our Douglasdale. I pledge this true," affirmed James to his brothers and Ellie. "How many battles must we entertain to reach this end I do not know; but to have a healer in the family like our father would be a gift from God for this knight and warrior to be."

Figure CXXXIX-Part Four; another view of Fawdon Manor in the Cheviot Hills of Northumbria

Archie was chattering away with Ana and then with his mother. "Muriel has chosen wrong I fear," said the five year old. "Whatever do you mean my son?" interrupted Ellie. He told them that it was her mistake not to return to Scotland with the family. His mother explained that Muriel had deep feelings for this home but missed her father; the memories were too painful for her to bear to come to Fawdon and Scotland. "Mura is a lass; strange feelings does she have that we as men can not explain," James said with a wink at Sir David. "She loves her Scotland but will not come to see it; preferring an English place with a Scottish name, Castle Cary," he scoffed, rolling his eyes for emphasis. The youngest son looked at James most quizzically. "Our mother is a lass and she loves to be here at our manor and travel to our Scotland. How is this so my brother?" asked Archie. Ellie was chuckling now, "Yes James, how is it that this lass does love her Fawdon?" she begged him to explain, throwing him a teasing smirk. "You are indeed your mother's son," said James to his wee brother; throwing up his hands in defeat, as he feigned his great dismay.

The Douglases stayed in Northumbria for two days; stocking the larder of the manor for their return when they would be traveling south again to Essex. James took his brothers with him to look for ancient forts and stone circles; he was Lord Douglas for these days to his wee siblings. Ellie and Ana were in the manor house with the aging Shamus, a Deerhound now fifteen, he rode in the cart for journeys and slept in Ellie's bed for warmth and comfort; in Scotland they would fashion him a litter for his travels. "My dear silly hound," she said to him, "how many times have we romped and played in the Cheviot with our dear William; he and so many of our children now together most again with God," she sighed, fondly remembering their pleasant times here. "Our glorious Fawdon, these variegated hills of Northumbria; I have missed this land so." Ana and Ellie were enjoying their day. "That we are here now my lass is tribute to your hard work. To have some dower lands of Sir William directed to you and the de Ferrers dower lands restored as well was your relentless will; I know it," she praised her girl. "It is only for our James and your good care that I chose life not death lo those many years ago in Essex when first we fled our Scotland, so ill was this lass to lose a child as well," Ellie said wistfully. "My courage comes from love that I receive each day from you and Muriel and my sons, each so unique but of strong character. And the love of William that yet endures here in my humble self, that I continue this fight to regain what was stolen from us by the despot pagan!"

Figure CXL-Part Four; Roman fort site and ruins in the beautiful Borders region of Scotland; forts and settlements can be found throughout Northumbria and Scotland

The day next three visitors came to Fawdon manor: Thomas Chaunceler arrived with his valet and his son. This knight had been in service to his laird, William Douglas, in 1297 at Irvine when William made his peace with Edward. Thomas had heard Fawdon was now occupied with Douglases in household. His lands in freehold of Lord Douglas he came to hear of Sir William and his family. "Greetings," said the rider as he dismounted near the manor house. "Your banners bear the arms of Englishmen; but are you then Douglases?" he questioned them. Before Sir David could speak on her behalf Ellie joined them. She seemed to recall the knight staying with her husband. "You are Sir Thomas?" she questioned as she walked through the courtyard of the manor. "Lady Douglas, how good it is to see your fair face and so many years since last we spoke" said this happy tenant of their Douglas lands. Ellie bid the three to come inside for feasting and some wine. James was eager to speak with a knight who rode with his father; his brothers too were happy to greet the gallant warrior.

"We are traveling under the banners of de Ferrers but carry Douglas pennons most as well. Lord de Ferrers was my first husband, before I married dear Lord Douglas who is now with God," she told him plainly. The knight heard that Sir William was taken to be held in the Tower of London. When? asked this vassal as he expressed concern for the noble Douglas laird; the martyred knight as he now called Sir William. "Lord Douglas was executed for treason by the king most unjustly; on the false word of Sir Henry de Percy and Lord Lovaine. The fateful Thursday, 6th November, 1298. Some weeks later our Fawdon granted to de Umfraville the laird we held our manor from, for collection of our fees and rents," Lady Douglas said sadly. "Fawdon revenues so levied by Lord Edward; the manor house restored in dower to this widow." Sir Thomas extended his deep sorrow for the loss of the doughty Douglas laird.

"That I have shared a similar fate of imprisonment that November 1297 for one lang month and days in Durham castle, staying with William Douglas the king's enemy the charge. My horses and armor were falsely confiscated; this knight detained until he found his surety. Admitting truth that I was in service of Lord Douglas, then at peace since July that very year with the king. But the sheriff would not listen to my pleas, arresting this knight in Tynemouth then in flight," said Sir Thomas Chaunceler. Ellie and James were saddened by this news; it seemed that many others yet unknown to them suffered for the lies of de Percy and Ellie's father. It was shocking that William's unjust imprisonment for false treason harmed Douglas men in service to their laird; all were victims of de Percy's ruse and just as anguished as the Douglas family. They had not thought about the fate of others; their plight for their adherence to Lord Douglas. "So sorry this Douglas son and squire is to hear of your troubles good knight and vassal of our dear father," said James.

Sir Thomas began to speak of my lord the baron as he called Gilley; how revered he was by his men for his honesty; his truth. Hugh and Archie listened with deep interest as this good knight told of William's valor; martyred for his rebellion: his beloved Douglasdale in the hands of de Clifford. Stories were shared of Gilley's courage; his fair ability with sword and other weapons. He was respected by many men far and wide all throughout Scotland and Northumbria, Sir Thomas informed the Douglas lads. Ellie's eyes teared to hear these dear words; others speaking praise of her dear husband. James was finding it difficult as well to keep from crying. The two wee Douglas lads had many questions for this knight; both were thrilled to hear from others of their father that only Hugh could truly hold in memory. The afternoon passed quickly; many honest tales were told and would be remembered for some years to come by the children of this laird and martyred patriot William le Hardi Douglas.

Sir Thomas offered to escort them through Scotland. "That there is much unrest about; and this knight knows well the lands and manors of your late husband," he said. "A good hunter with his bow is my young son also called Thomas, to provide food for your table as we journey." Ellie and Sir David agreed that having the assistance of her husband's vassal would be of great benefit. The impending muster in Berwick made traveling more dangerous and in Ayrshire where the Scots held most of the roads, another Douglas knight would be welcome to their party.

Ayton Manor

The Douglases stopped near Ayton, at their de Ferrers manor in Berwickshire, north of Berwick on Tweed, before traveling on to the Lothianes to visit the de Lindsays. Sadly Sir Alex and his family had yet to return to their lovely estate of Luffness; they were staying at nearby Byres manor as well as Garleton Castle, another de Lindsay tower less than a mile away; splitting their extensive household between the two estates. The castle was a fortified keep securely hidden behind the Garleton Mountains. The old tower in Athelstaneford was smaller; less grand than Luffness and about the same size as their manor house at Byres. Both manors afforded Sir Alex a fortified residence near their remaining lands in the shire, including those of Ormiston. Their former and more elegant stronghold was situated majestically on the Aberlady. A Carmelite friary was newly built nearby in honor of the family ancestors who went to the Crusades. Currently Sir Alex was again held in favor by Edward; yet the Lord of Luffness remained Edward's English vassal, Sir Henry de Pinkney. Even an insurrection of the tenants of the barony against the English laird the year before did not persuade Edward to reseise the castle to Sir Alex; feeling it was too important to surrender the fortress to his sometimes loyal vassal, the knight he personally dubbed some fifteen years ago.

The Douglases would stay in the Lothianes at a messuage, once a dower house of Garleton; giving them some privacy and space for their growing household of travelers. The time they spent in Athelstaneford also permitted Ellie's steward le Parker time to determine the reason for the slowness of her dower fees to come to her coffers. He traveled first to the royal burgh of

Berwick to begin his enquiry; the tenants of the manor had told him that fees and rents were paid by Scottish Quarter Day. When Sir John returned to Lady Douglas, he had some words to cheer her. "The fees were being held; the escheators had so ordered, not having proper word from the Chamberlain of Scotland on the rightful dower thus restored," he told her. "Your solicitors will follow now to file a complaint on your behalf." Ellie was thrilled at first. She had feared that her income was not forthcoming because of the devastation of the war; but this discovery was heartwarming; the king's writs were missing and causing her rents to be delayed in coming to her. She would seek again in England through the king's council for the required orders to restore her dower; to sue the seneschal of the king to release the needed income for her family.

Then Eleanora realized with frustration that she was once more forced to fight for rents that already belonged to her. "More writs, new filings, begging of the king to thus obtain what is mine thus now!" she scoffed. "That this will never end and I will always be the prey of dishonest escheators or careless chamberlains in their orders from the king. The battle for this widow just for sustenance, most trying to this lass." Ana attempted to soothe her with her words, but it was James who won the day. "Dear mother, that we shall one day battle the same king is my fair wish: you with words and numbers, this lad with sword and armaments should he not grant our request for seising to our lands. Pray think of this as war against dear Edward," he told her, "that each time you are successful in recovering your fees and rents, you reinforce the martyred laird our father's good work, to undermine this sorry king's foul deeds against us." Ellie realized his words were true. The more she was victorious, the less successful was the English treasurer in stealing her fair coinage for the king's own use to war against her Scotland. "Thank you James," she told him. "Your words I value so; our father's life most given for our freedom here this day. I will continue to do the fighting that he can no longer do here." Sir David did not lend a word; he worried now that the squire he trained would take up arms one day against the English king. That Sir William was a noble knight he knew; how long would this battle rage between the Scots and this English lord he pondered; how many more will die for the greed of his English king.

East Lothianes Garleton Castle

The beauty of the Scottish coastline on the Firth of Forth was breathtaking on this clear day. The Douglas household had stopped at the little friary near Luffness Castle, with its compelling views of Aberlady Bay. Ellie decided their course of travel and stopped to give thanks for the safety of their journey at the wee chapel there that she and Gilley visited ten years

MY TRUTH LIES IN THE RUINS

before. Following the cart paths south towards Haddington brought them to the lands of the de Lindsays at Athelstaneford. "Sir Alex, dear Alice how pleased we are to be here in your lovely tower house; and what a moat to so protect this wee castle," gushed Ellie, "so safe does this lass feel to be here in the Lothianes with kin." "Dear Eleanora, how good to have your precious family here with us in Scotland," said Lady Lindsay. Uncle Alex was busy with his God son, "Last I saw this laddie he was just an infant, then in Ayrshire," he said. Ellie chided him now, "The baron of Ayrshire; holder of the Steward's lands I hear," she chuckled. Alex shook his head sadly. "Trusted once again by Edward; yet suspected for his oath that he so taunts us with our Luffness, the bait for future biddings of the king," he said sarcastically. Then he added wearily, "That our dear Seneschal of Scotland held his own lands and our William was again in Douglasdale the wish of this humble knight so sad for his Scotland now." Ellie looked away trying to compose herself; she was finding it difficult to speak of her Gilley with others that knew him, though it was nearly three years since his passing.

Figure CXLI-Part Four; the gates of Luffness Manor once the stronghold of Alexander de Lindsay

Young Beatrice joined them in the great hall. "A true beauty you have grown to be," said Lady Eleanora. The young lass thanked Ellie shyly for her kind words. Then Beatrice took her mother's nod and led both Hugh and Archie to the courtyard with Sir Shamus that they could enjoy the warmth of this summer day in Scotland. The old Deerhound found a shady spot to snooze; he too seemed to relish their return to Scotland. James poured their wine and then joined in the conversation. "Dear Uncle Alex that we could use your good guidance here this day," he began in earnest. "In three short years will this squire return to our homeland; to seek the barony of Douglasdale for our family to return and live there," said James. Ellie explained as she had told the de Lindsays in her letters that it was the wish of Gilley to have his son train in armaments in Flanders, then perhaps to go as well to Paris if he so desired.

Sir Alex reminded them of his letter and his plan: to introduce them to his kin, William Lamberton. "This good bishop with his manors near your dower lands both in Fife and Berwickshire," said Uncle Alex, "the brilliant and trusted man of both the Scots and the English king; to have the ear of true patriots of Scotland and the English spoilers to our kingdome, true agility of tongue. Some days this humble knight is most unsure which side he's truly on," he chuckled. Ellie was not surprised to hear the sincere tone of Sir Alex; a knight trusted by the king yet holding rebellion in his heart. She appreciated the opportunity to meet with the de Lindsay kin, the house of Lamberton from Berwickshire. "That he is most now in Fife is what he told us," said Lady de Lindsay. "That is fine news; our Douglas household to travel next to Leuchars there in Fife," Ellie told them happily. "Would the de Lindsays join us at our fine castle there; much room for family to so join us as young de Ferrers is home in England, with only our servants residing there at the manor that we share." The de Lindsays were in deed ready to journey north to Fife; they could leave on the morrow next if that pleased Ellie. "It is done," said James, delighted with the prospect of meeting Bishop Lamberton; one step closer to regaining the lordship of his father he believed; to reside in peace again in Scotland was his prayer and dream.

Ellie allowed for John le Parker to take his leave with an escort; to give him time to ascertain the problems with their rents and fees from Fife. "Dear Alex, that we are having much difficulty with the sheriffs in these counties here in Scotland," she told him of her problems with her dower rents. Alex told the widow that the English escheators were most corrupt; each one satisfying his own greed and gain in the shire, to line their pockets at the expense of others' losses. "Your rents the victim of their faulty records, would be my conjecture for this folly," he said sadly. "One day soon will we be driven to take the field against this despot king." Lady de Lindsay was terrified by the words of rebellion from her husband; his English lands were taken from them for his role in Irvine and many of his manors in Scotland too were forfeited. "Our castle in Crawford overrun with English; retaken then by Wallace, no peace for this family in our Lanarkshire as well," she moaned. "Dear wife," said the disgusted knight, "these English sheriffs and escheators will be the end to any peace. Much talk in every shire for rebellion to their grievous actions so contemptible to Scottish land holders."

Ellie asked him quietly, "Does this mean that once again dear Alex," then whispering almost inaudibly, "will you and others lead the way for

Scottish barons to defy the English king?" de Lindsay shook his head in response; yes, he told her, a revolt was coming to retake the lands under English control. "That Edward comes again to put down the Scots in the south and west is my conjecture for his armies set to muster in our country," he told her ominously. Ellie said that she had not been aware of the king's plans to return with armed horse and foot soldiers when first she wrote of their plans to journey through their Scotland. "It was only when I signed the agreement with de Ferrers that he told me of the muster; that he *feared for my dear safety!*" she said indignantly. "But this lass does not shudder from an army coming; that we should finish most our work here to return before the king arrives is my fair plan," she told him, seemingly unconcerned for the impending battle.

Sir Alex spoke freely now; the trust he showed for Lady Douglas was evident as he told her more of Scotland's rebels. "Should they have a Scottish king to lead them a major war would start today!" pronounced the noble knight, once fighting side by side with Wallace in the west in Scotland's lowlands. "That a de Lindsay heiress could claim the throne of Scotland," said Alice to the others, "we are under careful watch by the English spies around us," she said most fearfully. "But good rumors come to us that King John in France to leave his papal custody and return to his Ballieul." Ellie was very saddened by the news; how many years would this continue, she mused; Balliol, toom tabard as Gilley called him, his perceived weakness the reason behind the invasion some five years ago. What good use is this foolish King of Scots, she scoffed. Ellie believed that only a new king, a true leader of men could unite the nobles; to send Lord Edward home again to Westminster.

Ellie held other concerns; if the war escalated again her Archie would be in the thick of it; soon to be a member of this household in service to be a page, then a squire for his training to become a knight. She tried unsuccessfully to talk of other things; but James continued to speak of the rebellion. He was interested in learning more about these brave patriots; who was taking charge he wondered; were yet unknown to Edward or his spies? Then from the corner of his eye James saw his mother becoming eerily aloof and quiet; he decided at once to quit this topic of discussion. With so many worries for this lady, James changed the subject to another cause he relished: tournament. "Uncle Alex that I have squired in Newmarket for a knight in tourney for the joust, Sir John de Segrave," said the lad. Alex looked over to the tall youth; thin but of large frame still growing. "You were in the list in our Suffolk?" asked Sir Alex.

Ellie's eyes returned to sparkle with the talk of her son attending the knight. "Oh the thrill of tournament; and James most there with young de Ferrers; attending my cousin Nicky's son as squire" she told them all so proudly. By now they were joined by the wee ones; running to them when they heard the tales of their brother attending the tournier last year in Newmarket. "Our brother with the knights; holding their swords and weapons for their combat," said an excited Archie. "Our James the esquire to teach this lad to ride a horse in Ayrshire when we get there," he told his God father, his eyes wide with excitement for that thought. Hugh told them all proudly of the fifteen rules his father wrote for knighthood. "Our dear brother to so copy for this humble lad and Archie too, a clear hand in lettering, the scroll of these fine words of Sir William le Hardi, our dear father," said Hugh. That the children spoke so freely of Lord Douglas made it easier for others to acknowledge that he was now with God. The tension of their visit was broken; laughter and chatter prevailed in the great hall of Garleton. The talk of rebels to the king abated; Lady Alice was smiling now as well, though ever fearful for her family as was she living in Scotland under the hammer of the Scots.

Later when they were alone in the dower house of Garleton James speculated that Bishop Wishart was most in the thick of the rebellion. Ellie looked at her son soberly, "Bishop Lamberton the same, though he is more secretive about it," she told him in confidence. "Lady Alice has so told me privately of his plans to wait and see; taking sides with Scottish nobles when a king so comes to lead them against Edward," she paused as she thought she heard a noise outside her chamber; that it was the wind she mused, continuing her discussion with James. "His cleverness at diplomacy; his wits to use in France that there might be another alliance, but Edward will try his ways with the French as well. If Edward keeps his promises to the nobility of France an alliance with our Scotland will be more difficult," she told him quietly. "But mother, that Lord Edward lies we know it; Berwick's butchery the example, promises so made but seldom kept," said James reflecting on her words. "Perhaps this alliance, the diplomacy of Lamberton will open doors for other knights to lead us in our cause," then he paused, to reflect on his own future.

Ellie was staring at her son; his handsome face framed by lovely raven tresses falling to his shoulder, the picture of his father when she first met him years ago. "That you will be a 'knight-errant' is my fear," she told him, her eyes clear but thoughtful and quite sad, "most like your dear father, my sweet William. Had our knight not found this lass in Ayrshire forests might he yet live to fight for Scotland's freedom? I do think so," she said so poignantly. "Dear mother, you knew that father wanted most to be a knight to wander in the cause of liberty for our kingdom?" asked James, surprised in her words. "My son," said Ellie with a broad smile, "the secret to our love affair was true honesty. My Gilley told me from his heart so plainly; that he loved his children and this lady deeply," she continued, "but he loved his

Douglasdale and Scotland most greatly there as well." Beaming with love she recalled his words so clearly: 'My Lady El that you have let your laird to ramble with his thoughts. Know this: your love for this humble knight the very reason for his happiness in this good life, that sweet love for all eternity we celebrate most daily in our children.'

Ellie continued telling her son another reason for this journey; to be in Scotland again with James and the wee ones as she called Archie and Hugh. "That this mother will not see you most again when you return from Brabant; fearing you will be a knight-errant, a rebel to the king." James held his mother to him and kissed her on the head. "Lady El, I will always find a way to see you. We will be repledged to Douglasdale and live again in the kingdome of the Celts and the brave Sholto," he said with his smirk like Gilley's. She started to laugh, chuckling at his wit to end this serious pledge with the well known Douglas humor, "Sholto beast, just like your father, knight-errant most to be!" she teased him. Then he told her again, "This lad to find his mother wherever she may be; to help his brothers live their lives as well, we are all true Douglases and family," he said firmly. The years in Essex had blunted their will to fight, to battle Edward for their lands and rights in Scotland. But James and Ellie were feeling patriotic surges rise within them; remembering their outrage for their father and dear husband murdered by this grievous king, the invader to their homeland.

"Why did Edward ever come to this kingdome," wondered Lady de Lindsay out loud, while breaking fast with her Douglas guests the morning next. Ellie told her what her father had often said: English wars for English rights at sea. "The grievances of our good captains in the channel; the activities of the Cinque Ports of fishing, trade, piracy and war were so entwined to not differentiate between them," she said thoughtfully. And James shared his understanding of the war, ideas he grasped from discussions with his father. "The port activity in Berwick most one forth of all of England's commerce in its day before the butcher of Berwick so invaded that royal burgh," said the lad. He paused to drink some ale and then continued, "Our father told us that the king who rules the seas controls the world. That Edward feared the French and Scots renewing the Auld Alliance; to be so detrimental to his shipping interests and good trade," said this squire.

"Quarrels between sea captains the reason for the invasion of our Scotland?" asked young Beatrice now ten. "Not as simply said as that," James told her, "but fair enough in sentiment to be so regarded; a catalyst it seems for the slaughter of our good citizens at Berwick that spring day." Ellie told them that King Edward made the Cinque Ports his main matter for concern. "But the sea controls the land he soon found out. In 1287 the very year this lass set out for Scotland as that widow of de Ferrers, a terrifying storm eroded so the coastline, taking with it many towns and villages including Edward's pride and joy the vast port of Winchelsea," she said ironically. Lady Alice was stunned; the seas and ship captains the cause for wars that killed their friends and kin, destroyed their homes and took their freedom. How confusing the world really was she mused.

Leuchars, Fife

Figure CXLII-Part Four; farm lands at Leuchars Castle farm in Fife; a manor and castle once held by the de Quincy family, then the de Ferrers; part of the dower lands of Eleanora Douglas

The good bishop of St. Andrews was arriving today at the castle in Leuchars. William Lamberton's family and kin the de Lindsays had invited him to join them at the castle. The bishop and his trusted entourage arrived at this vast estate overlooking the River Eden by the early afternoon. The old keep sat upon a grassy knoll near the beautiful Norman church of St. Athernase as it shared a vantage point of the surrounding village. What a peaceful setting the bishop said as he was greeted by a smiling Lady Eleanora Douglas. He had heard of this Essex widow; how she had bravely taken her family alone, back to England in poverty having been stripped of all her dower lands as well as those of her rebel husband Lord Douglas. Bishop Lamberton was very gracious. But it was only after feasting and good wine that he finally began to relax and speak more freely of his sentiments for a Scotland without Edward. "That we continue to make our case diplomatically; to draw this war out while English barons take their paths to revolt of Edward's taxing of his subjects," said the Bishop, "most our only hope to be rid of this invader," he sighed. He went on to explain that many of the Scottish nobles were coming to the conclusion that Balliol was no longer considered their king; to fight for such a king was foolish they concluded, that many came to submit to regain their lands.

Ellie told him that James was to go to Flanders. "After the wedding of our Muriel will we travel first to Paris, then to Brabant; even though the Count and many of my kin and family are now allied with Edward," she explained. "My father had so requested that this son travel to Flanders the home of our Douglas ancestors, and to live in Brabant for some time; learning the arms of that fair region was his plan," James elaborated. Lamberton smiled and allowed as he too was a descendant of those brave folk. "That I am of Flemish stock," he boasted, approving the squire's venue for his training. Sir Alex then told his cousin that young James would be approaching his age of majority; in few years he would be ready to return to claim the barony of Douglas and bring his family back home in the king's peace. The bishop reflected on their strategy. "This is most possible to accomplish. More Scots to pledge their fealty for that very purpose; two countries so damaged from the wars of Edward," said Lamberton. He offered to present the lad to the English king when James returned to Scotland; unless there is another king for Scots to call their own he sighed to himself.

Ellie thanked the bishop for his offer. She brought out the letter from the "evil bishop" as King Edward referred to Robert Wishart of the Church of Glasgow; introducing her and the Douglases under his protection. Lamberton knew this Wishart well. He was himself Chancellor for that very church, with that same bishop just a few years ago. "That good Bishop of Glasgow did shelter us after Berwick's slaughter, hiding us at Carstairs when we fled that royal burgh. Our dear William was then held prisoner in Berwick's Douglas Tower," said Ellie. "When Scotland was at peace, before the invasion, we often entertained the bishop during his visits with us in Douglasdale." James too spoke highly of Robert Wishart; recalling those weeks they stayed in the safety in Castle Torres. "My brother Hugh a bright and pious lad with great reverence to do God's service; to take up with the church of Glasgow, in the footsteps of our dear uncle the Good St. Brice," James proudly informed them. Uncle Alex and William Lamberton were impressed by these doughty Douglases; their losses in the war were both heavy and tragic, but not enough to break their spirits and their love for Scotland it seemed. Bishop Lamberton would meet this lad again and remember his promise to both mother and son: to present James before the king. But Lord Edward had a long memory as well; William le Hardi

Douglas was his enemy, breaking his pledge of fealty some few days after he put his seal to that document in Irvine, as de Percy had so told his lord the king. The lad would meet Edward Plantagenet with Bishop Lamberton in some short years; the outcome from that rencontre to forever change the future of Scotland.

Livingston

The Douglases upon leaving Leuchars brought with them a harried seneschal; le Parker was troubled. When rents were collected they were taken by the sheriff of the shire; if the lands lay waste and few tenants remained, the fees and rents were nowhere to be found. Their income was less than a third of what it was from only five short years ago, he concluded sadly. "Lady Eleanora, the wee coinage and some grain that we have found is painful reminder of a country now in ruins from the wars. We have notified the chancellor of our findings but will require more time to collect the little left for us, small payments to find I fear," said Sir John. Ellie was concerned as well. Her income once £170 or more a year, coming mostly from Scotland was vanished. The hard work Gilley did to increase her estates' fees and yields was rendered useless now. Ellie reflected sadly on his tenure as lord of these manors; in just a few years he more than doubled their share of income. Now their lands were all in shambles, their income had disappeared. What would they discover in the other counties of her dower lands she wondered to herself? "Perhaps in Ayrshire or in Wigtonshire we will be more fortunate," she reassured him.

As Ellie rode through Fife she was struck by the beauty of the countryside; the lush hues of fragrant flowers. The beautiful lavender stalks of the willow herb seem to wave softly, beckoning her back home to Scotland. Eleanora had forgotten how truly lovely all the shires in this kingdome were; each with their own distinctive characteristics, but all were her precious Scotland, the land she shared lovingly with her William. The Douglas household had been traveling two days since leaving Leuchars. They arrived at the Abbey in Dunfermline where they stayed overnight. The next day they would ford the Firth of Forth by ferry. The small ferry of eight oars took six trips in all for this family now grown in number to some thirty-five with eleven pack animals, a wee litter for Ellie's furnishings and aging Deerhound followed by many palfreys for the riders. When finally all had been collected in Queensferry they rode to their manor house in Livingston. From their short stay there they continued on to Lanarkshire and Dalserf, the manor held by Willelma, William's sister; a widow herself with four daughters.

Ellie and Willa greeted one another quietly; smiling through their tears, with little left to say about the loss of both their husbands. "Pray who are these wee ones now so grown?" asked Willa of Lady Douglas. James introduced his brothers. "This is Hugh, named for your dear brother; and this of nonsense is our Archibald, God son of Sir Alex de Lindsay, soon to be a page in that good household in the Lothianes and Ayrshire," announced the handsome squire. "The image most of his sweet father at that age," said Willa of her nephew James. Lady Douglas grinned in her response, "And most the teasing way of that dear knight, I swear it!" Ellie was pleased to be among close family, relaxing in the great hall of sister in law's manor. And they were not just anywhere in Scotland, but home in Lanarkshire, just few miles from Douglasdale.

Lady de Galbrathe told them of the recent troubles in the shire. "Two sheriffs, one of Scotland, the other of dear Edward for the English; both are here to collect fees for the treasury. Too many so to rule us, confusing in the payments of our taxes," she expressed her dismay to them, "my sadness is so deep with the futility of situation, our Lanarkshire and dear Scotland so destroyed." Ellie told her about rents from her dower; the fees that were missing from her manors wherever they would travel. "Lord de Ferrers the younger has sent us on this journey to collect of his income as well. Three men at arms is he to thus supply for lands held in Scotland as tenant in chief to garrison the castles here for Edward," she told Lady Willelma, "and not one shilling for us to find for him so far to thus take back!" Archie was a bored five year old as he came romping in to interrupt the feasting and the wine enjoyed by these ladies and his brother sitting until then, peacefully in the great hall. "Mother, a horse must this lad have of his very own to ride," he told her. Ellie's laughter came most quickly.

Willelma spoke before the lad's mother could utter a word. "When once we told your father at this very age of five: when you can ride a palfrey and not fall off, will you thus have one for your very own!" she told her nephew. Archie looked first to James then to his mother; not seeing much support for his request he changed the subject. "That you are named for my dear father William?" he asked his aunt. "No, that he is named for me!" she said laughing now as well, "Your dear father the young William most my wee brother, younger than this lass was he. Our dear father also known as William thought that he would never have another son, so named me Willelma after his good name," she said with the Douglas smirk. The wee lad turned to take his leave of them then stopped. "On Hogmanay the next this Archibald to thus receive his palfrey for his service to his mother!" he declared and left. "Are all your sons most like my good brother in temperament? By their looks, they are of le Hardi's own volition," she said to Ellie in amusement. "If this be so than you have my prayers to so go with you," said Willelma, chuckling at her sister in law's dilemma. James told her that their Hugh was pious and remote, "Most unlike us so shy is he, a gentle soul, happy to pray for us as well. That we will need his prayers I know it!" declared the squire.

Lady de Galbrathe inquired of their plans to travel further. Ellie explained that she was warned to stay little time in Dumfries; that they would travel south through Ayrshire and then to Wigtonshire. The great hall doors opened to three knights in Ellie's service: Sir David, Sir Thomas and Sir John. Eleanora started to make the introductions, but Willa said she knew most of these men already. The three knights joined them at the table. Sir David expressed their unanimous concern for further travel; too risky for their household. "Spies from either side are lurking Lady Eleanora," he said most worried for their safety. "Wearing tabards of English households, carrying Scottish banners, or the reverse of that; so many rebels and English soldiers we could be in the thick of battle, or wee skirmish," he warned her. But Ellie was resolute. "We will be safe in Ayrshire and Wigtonshire," she proclaimed. "The letters that we carry from de Ferrers and the Scottish letters from our dear friend Wishart, and then too de Lindsay and Bishop Lamberton; who would stop this widow of de Ferrers and Douglas both?" she asked her knight. Sir David knew his lady was most head strong from those long years ago when he first brought her to Scotland.

Sir Thomas spoke again trying to caution the determined widow. "We have done some scouting in this shire; to discover that the English and the Scots are planning to attack in small numbers," he warned Lady Douglas. "Perhaps this Douglas knight would escort le Parker here to Ayr; to speak with the escheators for the Scottish government still in existence there. And then Sir David with five men at arms to stay with you in Stewarton or Trabboch while we seek rents on your behalf," he suggested. Ellie asked Sir John if that plan was to his liking. "Would you so speak to them as well of fees and rents from Dreghorn for Lord de Ferrers?" she asked him. The steward said he would and that he liked the strategy they spoke of; feeling safe to travel with this Douglas knight in the shire controlled by Scots.

"That Lord Hugh most brought me to this Douglas household some thirteen years ago," said the steward, "And in this knight of de Ferrers and this vassal of Lord Douglas both do I so trust. The word of these good men of your household will I follow, to heed their advice as truth. I will go to Ayr to seek your payments now most due to you Lady Eleanora." "It is done," said James, relieved to have his mother listen to their good counsel. "It is done, sure aye!" said Lady Douglas. They all laughed at once; chuckling that their words were still influenced by the one they called le Hardi, Lord Douglas to them all.

MY TRUTH LIES IN THE RUINS

Trabboch

James and Sir David were returning from the morning hunt with Henry and the son and squire of Sir Thomas. Ellie had persuaded the other knights to wait for their return. "Now that you have rejoined this household and the search for game is over; Sir David," she said turning to her knight, "I am still here at my manor, not kidnapped by English or Scots, that you may now take your leave" said Eleanora teasingly, reminding them of other times when this knight would go on hunt and disaster would strike. "The most of what I see here, a great feast this family is to have this night!" she declared, thrilled with the success of their search for meat for the larder. Hugh was old enough to go on hunt but preferred to stay and study Latin with his mother. Archie was "five and ready," but his mother made him stay with her as well. "Look Ana, we have game for our table this day and for several days more from what I see her," she told her joyously. Ana told James and Sir David that cook waited for them in the kitchen building behind the manor house. "M' lady, so happy is this lass to see you smiling again," giggled Ana. "Scotland is your home even in its devastation, so barren from the wars with England; its fair beauty brightens your dear face, more so than we have seen in some years."

Figure CXLIII-Part Four; Wigtown Harbor near the site of the castle and moat that once served the manor

DEBORAH RICHMOND FOULKES

James gave the squires all the meat they acquired; instructing them to take it to the cook. Returning to the great hall he was delighted to see a noticeable difference in his mother's demeanor; she appeared calm and cheerful. "That we are in the middle of great conflict, yet my dear mother you are so pleased to be here," said the squire. Ellie beamed with her thoughts, "This lass feels closer to her William here; your father's paradise the kingdome and now ours to share with him in pleasant memory," she sighed wistfully.

July 1301 Wigtonshire

Figure CXLIV-Part Four; Balgonie Castle in Fife; a good example of a Tower; the castle dating from the 13th century has a lovely restored chapel that is used for public weddings and the laird's private chapel

The Douglas household arrived at the de Ferrers manor in Wigton. Ellie was relieved to find her dower lands with tenants and crops growing. These hardy citizens remembered Lord Douglas; ten years ago it was that he came to Wigtownshire. They would pay what fees and rents they had to give her. "The legacy of my husband is his fair treatment of Douglas villeins," said Ellie, "That when most this family needs their income it is here for us to have," she told him. Le Parker knew that had de Ferrers been more like Lord Douglas, his lands in Dreghorn would have yielded more rents and fees due him now; but this younger laird was like his predecessor and father, in his views of others. The legacy of the father on the son; that William le Hardi

MY TRUTH LIES IN THE RUINS

Douglas was a good man and true was his gift in life as in death the same whole benefit to them. A man takes nothing with him but his name and reputation when he passes to the Otherworld; to his sons he leaves the legacy of noble character; his philosophy in life Gilley shared often with his children. James reflected on his father's teachings this day; he heard Lord Douglas' words resound. De Ferrers the elder was a cruel and selfish man; the inheritance for his son was lean. James thought of the young knight and son of this lord; choosing vainglory for renown in Newmarket's tournament year last. My father's words most true he mused.

Figure CXLV-Part Four; Whithorn Priory; an unusual safe still survives in the ruined walls

Before departing for their home in England, Eleanora Douglas insisted that her family take a day to ride to Whithorn. They stopped first at the lovely church in the center of the village erected in honor of St. Ninian. "Candida Casa means Whitehouse," she told the Douglas lads, "and is over eight hundred years old." James joined in the storytelling. "Whithorn is the Cradle of Christianity, our faith, for Scotland," he told them as they rode under the archway and up the hill to the wee chapel of the beloved saint. The children toured the priory as well. The unusual safe caught the eye of Hugh. Ellie recalled the stories told to her by Gilley when they first came to Wigtownshire ten years earlier. He spoke of the stone wall compartment where pilgrims on their way to the shrine of St. Ninian brought gifts to put inside. Following the Celtic tradition, they gave offerings for protection of their souls in safety when they crossed to the Otherworld. "All Celtic circles have an opening, with one side incomplete like the box of a safe. This signifies the entrance of the soul to the Otherworld," Ellie told her sons, remembering clearly the words of her Gilley, handing down another of the storyteller's tales to her children.

They rode their palfreys south towards the shrine of Ninian, the small cave of Scotland's brave saint. "Our James was just your age when last we came to this fair shire," said Ellie to her wee Archie. His older brother had been training him to ride a horse using an old saddle that they found at their manor at Trabboch two days ago. It was once used by Gilley as a lad. The saddle was the perfect fit for Archie as he rode the jennet of his mother. "That this lad will have a palfrey for his riding soon," said Archie. "Perhaps this visit to the shrine of our beloved Ninian is well timed," teased Hugh, riding his own palfrey proudly. "Would a prayer said to that saint bring Archibald a horse?" asked the younger brother. "That a sinner's prayer is answered first," chided his mother, "yours will be the sooner granted." Ana was chuckling, remembering the quarrel with the wee one just that morning. Archie was insisting to ride alone so he could earn his horse for Hogmanay. So he disobeyed his mother, secretly escaped from the manor house and ordered the farrier to saddle a horse for him to ride. Ellie was furious to find young Archie attempting to take a horse, to journey on his own; she decided not to take him to the shrine. Then Ana interceded; convinced her on the merit for this journey, reminding the mother of impulsive and strong willed behavior of her own that begot some poor decisions when she was younger.

Figure CXLVI-Part Four; St, Ninian's Cave; somewhat collapsed from the 13th century when the Douglases would have visited

Ellie sighed as they rode down Physgill Glen to the cave; the glen was still adorned in the beauty of wild Bluebells; of course Gilley was with them this day she smiled to herself, it is his way. They finally came upon the rocky beach of Burrow Head on the Solway Firth. The crystal clear waters with the imposing rock cliffs gave Ellie and Ana more reasons to ooh and ah at the beauty of Southern Scotland's shores. A short turn to the right and the wee clan of Essex arrived near the mouth of the cave. They each took their turn in private at the shrine; went one by one to pray in the cave. Ellie told them all of St. Ninian just as William would have done; to educate them on their history, the story of Scotland's fair saint who brought the message of the Gospels to their kingdome when the Celts were most a pagan lot. "He is the first Apostle of the Picts and Britons," said Lady Douglas to her sons; born in Galloway and educated in Rome, she told them. "He even stayed with the Roman soldiers nearby in their camp," Ellie continued.

Figure CXLVII-Part Four; the pathway into the beach and shrine of St. Ninian

Hugh was fascinated by the holy cave; the seven crosses carved into stone inside interested him no end. "What was the purpose for such place of isolation?" he asked his mother. She told him that he would retire here when he needed peace to meditate and pray. James was in the cave for some time; praying first for their safe return to England; then for the soul of his dear father. Hugh was next to pray at the shrine; he too said some words for Sir William and asked that he might be worthy for his intended study in the church and of the Celtic ways of healing as well. But Archie surprised them all when he told them of his prayers to St. Ninian. "Archibald so asked that he be granted wisdom and humility, the traits of his dear father now with God," said the lad quietly. Ellie's eyes watered, she bit down on her lip to keep herself composed. The overwhelming sense of God now filled her; she knew the influence of the shrine of Scotland's Ninian was upon her. The answer to my prayers she sighed; my wee son to seek the wisdom of my William, to seek his truth, God's own truth for his own.

Blackhouse Tower July 5

Figure CXLVIII-Part Four; Blackhouse Tower where the Douglas Burn meets the Yarrow; a Douglas stronghold

James was with the laddies, his wee brothers as they were returning from their ride to the Douglas stones. The tradition of their family was to continue the ways of William and re-tell the stories of the ancient Celts; no one did this better than James. Ellie and Ana were supervising the packing for their return to Fawdon, then on to Essex. "Mother, there are many camp fires burning in the hills to the south and east," he told her. Ellie was nervous about the remainder of their journey; she hoped to leave Scotland before the English muster in Berwick. She knew from Gilley's teachings what James was telling her. "On the morrow will we take our leave; one day earlier than planned," she told him. "I have told Sir David and Sir Thomas that we must travel quickly; from the telling signs of camp fires in the hills, the decision is most prudent." Ana knew that Ellie had an unsettling dream the night last; her prophecies of dreams were to haunt her in the days to come. This nightmare spoke of armies that would conquer many Scottish castles; her beloved Bothwell would be destroyed, the walls disintegrating from some mighty power was what she saw. Now fearing Edward's wrath they must depart, the noo!

When they reached Fawdon they were pleased to find Sir Thomas' good cooks and other servants busy at work; the manor felt like home again to these Douglases. "Someday when we return we will explore the forts and ancient stone circles just like your father showed us long ago," she promised Archie and Hugh. Sir Thomas agreed to look after Fawdon. "That we will return to live in Northumbria, spending time most here and to journey to the Douglas Burn and our other Douglas strongholds in the marches of our Scotland," she told them happily. "To see these lovely Chevoit hills that we enjoyed so with our William has brought me much happiness; a fine gift to this widow that had not been expected." Ana was quite relieved to be returning to the safety of Essex. But the journey throughout Scotland was necessary she concluded; rejoining England was a very different Lady Douglas. Her true beauty radiated as if reborn; a joy inside rekindled that Ana had not seen since that sad day when they left the Tower with the body of her knight. The love of the land these Douglases shared was the eternal flame that burned within them to this day. Eleanora and her William still in love; yet together in the Sprit of the lands they cherished most: Scotland and Northumbria.

Ellie's dreams of prophecy were sadly accurate. Many castles were captured by the English in this campaign. Edward brought a trebuchet to bear on Bothwell Castle; a strange siege engine that impaled the thick walls with large cylindrical balls of stone; destroying the grand structure. Young Andrew de Moray the heir of this fine estate was but three, living far away in Petty, hidden from dear Edward; not present for the siege. This infant was born after the death of his brave father: the hero with Wallace at Stirling. The wee knave was also the grandson of Sir Andrew de Moray, the Justiciar north of the Firth; the same knight who died of vexation, de mischief in the Tower of London, meeting his fate with his compatriot and co-conspirator William, Lord Douglas; martyred patriots, victims of Henry de Percy and his lord the king. The young nave would live to fight another day.

Edward brought his army west desiring to camp there for the winter, while an event of huge proportions simultaneously took place in Berwick. This odd occurrence foreshadowed the beginning of the end of English occupation and successful campaigns in Scotland. The unrelenting strain on English nobles to pay the fees and taxes after many years of war became too overwhelming; no coinage arrived to pay the men at arms. At the very center of the English administration in Scotland the threat of mutiny was heard; leading to a riot in late August of 1301. The foot crossbowmen and archers in the garrison at Berwick were joined by other men at arms; mutineers demanding pay owed to them, with a month or more now in arrears. Edward's garrisons were so wanting of provisions and money that stabilizing the English control throughout the kingdome would have to wait. The Scots were making inroads by their raids on supplies to castles garrisoned by the English; this practice would become the successful staple of warfare for the Scots in the years to follow during the Wars for National Independence.

Early spring 1302 Essex

The year began quietly; contentedly. This was only late March but sunny days arrived to portend a spring of hopefulness and rebirth. Ellie, Ana and Muriel were organizing her daughter's wedding for early June at Little Dunmow Priory. It was Ellie who requested this summer date specifically for the celebration of Muriel's and Richard's vows of sacrament and happily Lord Lovel agreed. Mura was finally marrying Lord Lovel of Castle Cary, the cousin of the de Ferrers, kin to the de la Zouches; but this baron of Cary lived in Somersetshire in England, not in Lanarkshire in Scotland. When she was born fourteen years ago on Scotland's Isle of Mann, no one would have believed she would become a lady to an English lord. She was the daughter of Scottish noblemen, who later became Lord Douglas, an influential baron of the Lowlands. Dame Muriel Douglas would marry a Scot; that was her destiny. But many things had changed since 1288.

In two short months they were to host that wedding and there was much planning left to do; Ellie reflected this day. Then the most startling of messages arrived: Lord Lovaine had taken ill and died in Bildeston. The funeral at Little Easton church had been arranged wrote Father Paul; would Lady Douglas the lord's eldest daughter pay respects he asked the widow of William le Hardi? No was her stern reply; his passing brings this lass only fair relief that he is gone, she told her family priest. The funeral was attended by his widow Lady Maud, grand daughter of the de la Zouches, with her son Thomas and her daughter Alice; but few others came to pay homage to this man, late the Steward of Eye, the reluctant grandfather of Mura, Hugh and Archie. Eleanora Lovaine Douglas went to Little Dunmow Priory this day instead; feeling no forgiveness in her heart for her father. A heart yet filled with sorrow for the loss of her beloved knight at the hands of Lord Lovaine and his kin, that sinister accomplice, Sir Henry de Percy.

On May 24 the Inquisitions Post Mortem revealed that only the Lovaine manors of Fryton and Sutton remained in chief from Mathew Lovaine's many Yorkshire holdings, while the other Lovaine manors in Gloucestershire, Suffolk and Essex were exactly as Eleanora had remembered them, all accounted for by the escheators in those shires. Curiously some carucates and a messuage of Lady Helisant left by deed to her daughter Eleanora suddenly appeared; arrearages of rents some twelve years gathered were presented to Lady Douglas. Dear mother thought Ellie to herself, this coinage to arrive well timed that I might journey with our sons to take my James to Paris then to Brabant she sighed happily to herself. Ana joined her in the great hall of the Stebbing manor, "My dear lass, so happy is your Ana to see you smiling so!" she exclaimed. "Oh Ana, my prayers have been answered most again," said Ellie, reading her the letter from her father's solicitors in Suffolk, "that I should have these rents now paid to me; our James to now complete his training in the arms of Flanders as I promised my dear Gilley four years ago. Our sweet William, must be so pleased with this glorious event of good fortune, I am sure of it!" Ana hugged her brave girl tightly to her. "You have done so well by all your children. That each will have their lives now apart from dear their mother is most difficult for you to do. Your love for them, to send them on their journeys; this mother's courage you have is most impressive to your Ana."

Later that night in the darkness of her chamber Lady Douglas thought she heard a familiar sound, a deep male voice; the comforting words of her dear William as he spoke to her "You are a true Douglas Lady El, sure aye." The sleepy Deerhound raised his head to look about as well. "Even you heard our Gilley," she said quietly, stroking Sir Shamus behind the ears. "It is not my dreaming then that brings his words to me." In the far corner of the room, by the heavy oak door and entrance to the chamber she saw an image of a tall and handsome knight; standing there so clearly Ellie recognized at once that young nobleman from Ayrshire's forests, fourteen lang years now gone since then. He was smiling that smirk she knew so well. "My dear Gilley that you have come tells me so completely: I can now leave this Essex and that priory that holds your shroud and bones. That you will be here with me where ever that I go, with your good counsel when I need it, I do believe it now," she told him gratefully. She recalled his last words to her in the White Tower, words she committed to memory so lang ago it seemed:

"Remember me Ellie; keep me alive in you always, as I will wait for your return home to God's Heaven. I will be there to hold and caress you, to walk in Paradise with you until the ends of time and existence, for I am yours and only God in his infinite wisdom loves you more."

The image of her husband faded and she was alone again. When a knight and his lady share a special love there is a bond that only God can sever; this Gilley had told his lass in Douglasdale lo many years ago. That he would come again she knew, forever now in her heart she held him true, deep within her soul for all eternity.

Final words; My Truth Lies in the Ruins

GLOSSARY

armed foot	soldiers on foot
armed horse	cavalry
battlemented	readied for warfare with crenelles, merlons and other devices
Book of Hours	medieval prayer book
brae	hillside
bovate	eight acres or what one bovine can plow in a year
carucate	parcel of land 100-120 acres
cellarers	servants in castle cellars taking care of food provisions, wine, ale or other storage areas
chamberlain	eight acres or what one bovine can plow in a year
charter-chest	small wooden chest securing charters or medieval deeds
cleugh	ravine
coffin	coffer or small box used to store items including coinage (paper money was not used)
coinage	money, coins; silver penny was the common coin
craig; craigy	a crag or a rocky place; rocky
crenelles	a notch in a parapet, allowing defenders to look through to the area below the tower
d	2d: fourpence; serf earned 1-2 d weekly; 4d a day was a large sum.
destrier	war horse
donjon	an angle tower
escheators	exchequers or financial records keepers and tax collectors
freeholder	holding land that may be passed down to heirs, usually for a fee
gambeson	a quilted surcote used under other armorial equipment such as leather or mail
gonfalon	Banner of armorial bearings hung from crossbar; indicating the laird in residence
goshawks	kitchen hawks used for hunting for the larder
hh	hands high; hand is four inches
hauberk	worn as armor over gambesons usually of mail or leather
Hobini	fast and sturdy horses indigenous to Ireland
keep	dunjon or tower house; traditionally of four stories in Scotland
knight	dubbed in ceremony by another knight, ranking nobleman, land holder usually age 21
laird	Scots word for lord
lang	Scots word for long
larder	kitchen stores
latrine closet	indoor plumbing with a bottomless drop to the ground below; garderobe
lay-in	birthing room or birthing time
leirwite	laying with; a laird could fine tenants for unwed intercourse
Lothianes	Lothians was a district, the older spelling was used
mail	small iron rings strung together in sheets; armor for protection
Mann	Isle of Man using the old spelling
Merels	a cloister board game
merks	marks, two-thirds of a £; 150 merks in 1296; modern value over $100,000
merlon	the solid part of the parapet between two crenelles
miles	Knight
moat	body of water usually man devised that surrounded a castle or castle motte

motte	large hill or mound upon which castles and tower houses were built
nettles and dockins	common to Scotland nettles produce a nerve tingling sting; dockins a numbing remedy
old standard	a sword that could be wielded in one hand
page	generally an eight year old in training for knighthood
palfrey	a noble horse known for his comfortable gait
parapet	a wall or wall-head for defensive position; usually battlemented, it protects the wall-walk
pennon	small flag with a swallow like tail or single pointed end
pit	the lowest part of a tower or donjon, with one entrance; barbaric form of prison
portcullis	large iron protective gate, raised and lowered at the opening to a castle gate or walls
sasine	seising; proof of ownership; an owner is seized or pledged to their lands
scale-and-platt	traditional wooden stair case not often found in medieval towers or keeps
Scots ell in length	about a yard
seneschal	steward or financial manager
squire	usually a lad of fourteen or more in training to become a knight
surcote	outer garment, coat
tasine	fermented concoction of fruit and water
tofts, messuages	lands with buildings and dwellings upon them
varlet	valet
villein	manorial tenant in bondage to the laird or exchanged for a place to live and work.
wall walk	the walk way on the upper level or parapet of a tower
war-chest	larger wooden chest used a piece of furniture holding armor and warriors' clothing
willow herb	a purple flowering long stemmed plant; grows early summer, before the heather blooms

WHO'S WHO
HISTORICAL FIGURES AND WHO THEY WERE

Alexander de Lindsay	Knight, patriot; kin to William le Hardi, the Steward; of Byres, Luffness, Barnweill, Crawford
Alexander III	King of Scots during the Golden Age of Scotland; died mysteriously in 1286
Alice de Lindsay	Wife of Alexander de Lindsay; a Stewart
Amy Douglas	A daughter of William le Hardi and Eleanora
Andrew de Moray Knight	Justiciar North of the Forth; murdered in the Tower of London where he was held after Dunbar
Andrew de Moray Squire	Son of Sir Andrew, Lord Petty; responsible for the North Rising, rebellion in the Highlands
Anne de Spencer	Granddaughter of Hawise Lovaine; widow of Earl Colban 1270, remarried William de Ferrers;
Archibald Douglas	Youngest son of William le Hardi and Eleanora; Regent of Scotland; knight
Colban Earl of Fife	Crusader in 1270; father of young Duncan, he died in Acre
Duncan Earl of Fife	Son of Earl Colban; murdered by de Percy and de Abernathy; mother Anne, kin of Eleanora
Edward Plantagenet	Ruthless sovereign of England; Edward I, responsible for the genocide of Berwick 1296
Eleanora de Lovaine	Second wife of William le Hardi Douglas, 7th Lord Douglas
Elena de la Zouche	Sister to Eleanora's mother in law and co heir to some de Quincy estates
Elizabeth Stewart	First wife of William le Hardi; mother of the Good Sir James, named for her brother James
Eva Bolteby	Wife of Sheriff Knut
Father Archibald	Archibald was a son of Andrew de Douglas; pastor of the Kirk of Douglas
Freskin the Fleming	Douglas and de Moray Clans' ancestor Hugo de Freskin, Soldier of Fortune from Flanders
Helisant Lovaine	Mother of Eleanora and wife of Lord Lovaine, Steward of Eye
Henry de Percy	Edward I's vassal; grandson of Jocelin Lovaine an illegitimate son of the Duke of Brabant
Henry III	Father of Edward Plantagenet
Hubicus Douglas	Surviving son of William le Hardi and Eleanora; Canonic see of Glasgow; 10th Lord Douglas
Hugh 6th Lord Douglas	Older brother of William le Hardi; husband of Marjory de Abernathy
Hugh de Abernathy	Convicted of the murder of young Duncan Earl of Fife; died in Douglas Castle prison
James Douglas	Son of William le Hardi; known to the English as the Black Douglas; Good Sir James to Scots
James the Steward	High Steward of Scotland; Guardian; brother in law of William le Hardi, Uncle of James
Joanna de Fawdon	Ward for William le Hardi in his minority when he was given Northumbrian land by his father
Johannis de Hastings	Powerful English nobleman; kin to Eleanora de Lovaine; stood surety for le Hardi
Johannis de Warenne	Earl of Surrey; governor of Scotland under the occupation of the English from 1296 forward

John Balliol	Contender awarded crown 1292 as King of Scots; toom tabard, stripped of his crown 1296
John de Haulton	Ward for William le Hardi in his minority; the minor held land in Northumbria from his father
John Douglas	First son of William le Hardi and Eleanora
John le Parker	Hugh Douglas was in his ward, Stebbinge Park, Essex; held position of steward
John Steward	Brother of James the Steward; uncle of the Good Sir James
John Wishart	Nephew of the Bishop; Baron of the Mearns; joined le Hardi in the raid of the heart, Fawside
Margaret de Quincy	Heiress of Roger de Quincy; late mother in law of Eleanora, relic of de Ferrers
Marjory Abernathy	Wife of Lord Hugh of Douglas; contract marriage 1259; her brother Sir Hugh de Abernathy
Martha Douglas	Daughter of William le Hardi and Eleanora; drowned in a moat at Woodham Ferrers Hall
Matthew Lovaine	Father of Eleanora de Lovaine; grandson of Godfrey, brother of the bearded Duke of Brabant
Maud Poyntz	Second wife of Matthew Lovaine; kin of Elena de la Zouche
Muriel Douglas	Oldest daughter of William le Hardi and Eleanora who later married Richard Lovel
Nicholas de Segrave	Second son of Nicholas the elder; powerful English nobleman, kin to Eleanora
Patric de Douglas	Douglas household member since before 1267; here he is a squire to Lord Douglas
Richard Knut	Sheriff of Northumbria
Robert Barduff	English knight, nobleman of Staffordshire, kin of Eleanora pledged surety for William le Hardi
Robert Brus	Earl of Carrick; kidnapped Lady Douglas and her family 1297; born in Writtle, Essex
Robert Wishart	Bishop of Glasgow; the patriotic prelate who supported William Wallace; defied Edward I
Sholto Du-glash	Brave warrior; Douglas ancestor rewarded for service with land in Lanarkshire by the king
Thomas Chauncelor	Knight in service to Lord Douglas who was captured and imprisoned in Northumbria
Walter de Lindsay	Cousin of Alexander; owned Thurstanson Manor and many other castles
Walter de Percy	Kin of Sir Henry de Percy; beheaded at Douglas Castle for the murder of Earl Duncan
Walter the Rich	Walter de Moray married an heiress of the Olifard family; started building Bothwell
Willelma de Galbrathe	Older sister of William le Hardi Douglas; her daughter married Bernard de Keith
William de Duglas	William le Hardi; Crusader, Poet Knight, Willelmi, dominus de Duglas; Guillame de Duglas
William de Ferrers	First husband of Eleanora de Lovaine; also the name of his son
William de Galbrathe	Brother in law of William le Hardi Douglas
William de Rye	English knight and nobleman of East Sussex who pledged his surety for William le Hardi
William Lamberton	Bishop of St. Andrews; kin of the de Lindsay family
William de Moray	Uncle of Andrew de Moray the squire who fought with William Wallace
William Wallace	Patriot; valiant warrior loved Scotland more than life itself; executed cruelly by Edward I

Author's Notes

Lewis Carroll, Through the Looking Glass: "Well, now that we have seen each other," said the Unicorn, "if you believe in me, I'll believe in you. Is that a bargain?"

I found the lovely quote again about a year after I began this journey and felt it appropriate to share; this trust and faith has been earned through long hours of deliberation and investigation. I am profoundly grateful for these gifts from Spirit.

William le Hardi first identified himself as William Douglas, coming from a place in Scotland called Moray. Later he began giving explicit information of his passing; elaborated on his time held in ward of the king at the Tower of London and showed details of his execution providing a date of 6 November 1298. Most historians disagreed with this information; only William Fraser who wrote the Douglas Books held for some of these facts. Finding original documents on file at the National Archives in England and translated records from the Rolls of the Pipe in the National Library of Scotland and libraries at Harvard University proved to me that the information disseminated from Spirit was valid. So began the journey in writing My Truth; many more pieces of the puzzle were subsequently provided; tracked down and validated through primary sources, that now comprise the story of this martyred patriot and redoubtable laird, William le Hardi Douglas; my guide in this lifetime.

From Robert Brown, author of We Are Eternal:

"All good books are controversial. (I think) You're opening the door in a new way to show we are eternal." (Westbury Long Island sitting)

From Rita Berkowitz, author of the complete idiot's guide to Communicating with Spirits: Deborah Foulkes has done exciting and extensive research to prove her connection with her spirit guide over the centuries. The way he touched her heart and lives is an amazing story.